Object Lessons
One True Thing
Black and Blue

Object Lessons
One True Thing
Black and Blue

by Anna Quindlen

With a New Introduction by the Author

Book-of-the-Month Club
New York

INTRODUCTION

I HAD TO LAUGH last year when my eldest child told me, in his no-nononsense fashion, how he intended to begin his career as a writer when he graduated from college. "I figure I'll write a thinly veiled semiautobiographical novel," he said. And in a fine display of literary sibling rivalry, his younger brother has already produced a 130-page manuscript and given it to an editor. "I have to admit, it's mostly me," he says succinctly.

Why should these two be different in their starting points from almost every other writer extant, from D. H. Lawrence, Louisa May Alcott, Ernest Hemingway, or Charles Dickens? I'm certain readers thought the story of my life was what I had produced with the publication of my first novel, *Object Lessons*, in 1990, the first fictional foray in a fifteen-year career as a newspaper reporter and columnist. Maggie Scanlan, the young protagonist, was the product of what passed for a mixed marriage decades ago, between the son of upwardly mobile Irish-Americans and the daughter of working class Italian immigrants. So, some readers knew from my more personal columns, was I. The airless hush of the suburbs, the seductive lure of the city, the rending of old mores, even the mother who could not drive: I knew them all from personal experience.

But what makes the writing of fiction more than simply a memoir with the names changed is intent, and my intent in *Object Lessons* was what eventually pulled me loose from the moorings of autobiography. I wanted to answer that existential question that trumps all others: Who are we? What in our past and in our backgrounds makes us that way? How can we change? Why is change so often doomed to failure? A daughter of the great wave of feminism that swept over America in the second half of the twentieth century, my obsession was inevitably changing identity, what we are by birth and inclination, and what we can become through transformation, accident, and risk. The search for identity would be my lodestar, whether it lead me to the journalistic examination of my own experiences or into an informed invention that could more surely illuminate.

What I could not know at the time, of course, was that this was the issue that would inform all my later novels as well. That is not to say that they were all the same; in fact by design each was quite different from the one before. *One True Thing* was the story of the eternal Oedipal triangle connecting parents and child, and how the strengths and weaknesses of that relationship would be writ large in a time of turmoil, specifically the terminal illness of one parent and the terminal inability to deal with emotional tumult on the part of the other. *Black and Blue*, by contrast, was set in a very different milieu with very different concerns, the story of a mother fleeing with her young son to escape the abuse of her police officer husband.

With each I drew farther away from the realm of the personal and more surely into the land of the largely fictional. Because my own mother had died of cancer when I was a teenager, there was always about *One True Thing* the whiff of autobiography, but with Maggie Scanlan's family as their template readers who had read both books were more willing to accept Ellen and her parents as invention, as indeed they were. *Black and Blue* was another matter entirely. There are a thousand ways to ask a woman whether her husband beats her up, and I've heard them all. ("Oh, no," my husband said when he first read the manuscript.) But as I was denying that I had either lived or researched the vagaries of domestic violence, I also added over and over that I did not think the abuse Fran Flynn suffered was the point of the novel. I believed that I was limning the understanding, common among women, that we become merely the sum total of the expectations, obligations, even tyranny of those we love, and that I had set out to describe one valiant woman trying to overcome that.

As in *Object Lessons*, both stories had as their underlying theme the question of identity in the lives of modern women, and of how much we can afford to define ourselves in terms of the beloved others that surround us. Ellen Gulden, the protagonist of *One True Thing*, is not only caught between the intellectual life of her college professor father and the emotional pull of her uber-housewife mother, she is also playing out the great dialectic of the women's movement, in which an entire generation moved from rejecting the life of the home and the heart to trying to incorporate it into a framework of ambition and achievement. Fran Flynn, who begins *Black and Blue* before the bathroom mirror transforming her ordinary appearance into a kind of disguise, is terrified, not only by her husband, but by the notion of a life without the bulwark of family and friends that has become the biggest, perhaps best part of who she is.

Some readers might be befuddled by these descriptions of these two novels. *One True Thing* is known through plot shorthand mainly as a book about terminal cancer and assisted suicide. *Black and Blue*, as the title telegraphs, is often thought of as a novel about domestic violence, the reasons women stay and how they finally find the strength to leave. Yet this was so far from the forefront of my consciousness as I wrote that it was my editor who had to inform me that the second book was suspenseful and sometimes terrifying. My focus was on the transformation of Fran, not on the pursuit by her husband Bobby. Naturally I wanted to render Ellen's caregiving and Fran's flight as realistically as possible, and it was enormously satisfying when readers who had known the situations intimately told me I'd done so. But in my mind, these were not themes but background. The theme in each case was the becoming—becoming more, becoming different.

At the end of each book, I understood a bit more about what makes us behave as we do. I suppose I ought to say that I am pleased to do that because I wish to enlarge human understanding, that it is a gift to you, dear reader, a shared notion of what it means to live, to struggle, to prevail, and to grow. But that would be a lie, and a lie is different than fiction, which always must have its own inner invented truth. I write about my life in columns, and the lives of others like and unlike my own in fiction, to understand myself. To find fellow travelers when the work goes out into the world is an enormous bonus. "Writing a novel is like driving a car at night," E. L. Doctorow once wrote. "You can only see as far as your headlights, but you can make the whole trip that way." I am always traveling, traveling down different roads, all toward the same place. Toward the characters, the ending, and toward myself. And, I hope, toward you as well.

—Anna Quindlen
January 2003
New York, New York

Object Lessons

For my mother and my father

VER AFTER, WHENEVER SHE SMELLED the peculiar odor of new construction, of pine planking and plastic plumbing pipes, she would think of that summer, think of it as the time of changes. She would never be an imprecise thinker, Maggie Scanlan; she would always see the trees as well as the forest. It would have been most like her to think of that summer as the summer her grandfather had the stroke, or the summer her mother learned to drive, or the summer Helen moved away, or the summer she and Debbie and Bruce and Richard became so beguiled by danger in the broad fields behind Maggie's down-at-heel old house, or the summer she and Debbie stopped being friends.

All those things would be in her mind when she remembered that time later on. But they always came together, making her think of that summer as a time apart, a time which could never be forgotten but was terrible to remember: the time when her whole life changed, and when she changed, too. When she thought of herself and of her family, and of the town in which they lived, she thought of them torn in two—as they were before and as they were afterward, as though there had been a great rift in the earth of their existence, separating one piece of ground from the other. Her grandfather Scanlan always referred to life on earth and the life to come as *here* and *hereafter:* "You've got your here, and you've got your hereafter, little girl," he had said to her more than once. "Take care of the first, and the second will take care of itself." Sometimes Maggie remembered those words when she remembered that summer. Afterward, all the rest of her life would seem to her a hereafter. Here and hereafter, and in between was that summer, the time of changes.

Perhaps she saw it all whole because of so many years of listening to her grandfather create labels, calling everything from bare legs in church to the Mass performed in English "the Vatican follies," lumping all the bullets and the bombs and the bloodshed in his native Ireland under the heading of "the Troubles." Or perhaps it was because Maggie needed to find a common thread in the things that happened, all the things that turned that summer into the moat which separated her childhood from what came after, and which began to turn her into the person she would eventually become. "Change comes slowly," Sister Anastasia, her history teacher, had written on the blackboard when Maggie was in seventh grade. But after that summer, the summer she turned thirteen, Maggie knew that, like so much else the nuns had taught her, this was untrue.

Sometimes change came all at once, with a sound like a fire taking hold of dry wood and paper, with a roar that rose around you so you couldn't hear yourself think. And then, when the roar died down, even when the fires were damped, everything was different. People came to realize, when they talked about those years, that they were years which set one sort of America apart from another. Twenty years later they would speak of that time as beginning with the war, or the sexual revolution, or Woodstock. But Maggie knew it right away; she believed it began with the sound of a bulldozer moving dirt in her own backyard.

For that was the summer they began building the development behind the Scanlan house. That was the beginning.

On a June morning, a week after school let out, Maggie came down to breakfast and found her father standing at the window over the sink with a cup of coffee in his hand, watching an earth mover the color of a pumpkin heave great scoops of dirt crowned with reeds and grass into the air and onto a pile just beyond the creek. Maggie stood beside him and pushed up on her skinny forearms to look outside, but all she could see was the shovel when it reached its highest point and changed gears with a powerful grinding that seemed to make her bones go cold.

"Son of a bitch," Tommy Scanlan said with an air of wonder.

"Tom," said Maggie's mother, just "Tom," but what it meant was, don't swear in front of the children. Maggie's father didn't turn around or even seem to hear his wife. He just drank his coffee, making a little sibilant sound, and watched the earth mover lumber back and forth, back and forth, its shovel going up and down and over and up and down and over again.

A sign announcing the development had stood in the fields behind the house for four years, since before the fourth Scanlan baby had been born. It started out white with green letters. "On this site," the sign read: COMING SOON. TENNYSON PARK. A COMMUNITY OF HOMES FROM $39,500. "Ha," said Maggie's grandfather Scanlan, who knew the price of everything.

Two men with a post digger had come and put the sign up at the end of the cul-de-sac behind Park Street. After the sign went up, the older children in the neighborhood waited for something to happen, but it never did. For years it seemed to stand as a testimonial to the fact that everything was fine just the way it was, that everyone in Kenwood knew one another and was happy in the knowledge that all their neighbors were people like themselves: Irish, Catholic, well enough off not to be anxious about much except the slow, inexorable encroachment of those who were not their kind. The sign got older and the paint got duller and someone carved a cross into the back of it with a knife and all the excitement about new construction and new people died down. One Halloween the sign got pelted with eggs, and the eggs just stayed there through that winter, yellow rivulets that froze on the white and green.

Mrs. Kelly, who lived in the house at the end of the cul-de-sac and whose driveway was nearest the sign, was by turns enraged and terrified at the prospect of the development. She said that they had built a development near her sister in New Jersey, split-levels and ranch houses, and the next thing they knew there had to be a traffic light at the end of the street because of all the cars. But Mrs. Kelly's husband died of emphysema three years after the sign went up, and Mrs. Kelly went to live with her sister in New Jersey, and there was still no development, just the sign.

Maggie sprang up onto the kitchen counter and sat there, swinging her legs. "Get down," Connie Scanlan said, feeding Joseph scrambled eggs, although Joseph was really old enough to feed himself. Maggie stayed put, knowing her mother couldn't concentrate on more than one child at a time, and Connie went back to pushing the eggs into Joseph's mouth and wiping his little red chin with a napkin after each spoonful, the bowl of egg balanced in her lap. "You heard your mother," Tommy Scanlan added, but he continued to look out the window.

"Is that it?"

"What?"

"Tennyson Park," Maggie said.

Her father looked over at her and put down his cup. "Get down," he said, and turning to his wife, his hands in the pockets of his pants, he said, "That's the best-kept secret in construction. They're digging foundations, you've gotta figure cement within the month, you've gotta figure actual construction in two. My father hasn't said anything, my brothers haven't said anything, and I haven't heard a word from any of the union guys. But they're out there today with an earth mover, they'll have cement trucks by next week."

Without looking up, Connie Scanlan said, "Your father doesn't know everything, Tom."

"You're right my father doesn't know everything, but he happens to know what's going on in construction," Tommy said. "And this is the kind of thing he usually hears about. And being in the cement business you'd think I'd have heard about it, and I haven't."

"Maggie usually hears because she listens to everything," Damien said in his squeaky cartoon voice.

Tommy looked down at the second of his three sons, a skinny little boy as angular and jumpy as a grasshopper. Suddenly Tommy grinned, the easy grin that lit his face every once in a while and made him look half his thirty-three years.

"We'll keep that in mind, Dame," Tommy said, as Maggie glared at her brother across the kitchen table, and then he looked out the window again. "Jesus, am I going to catch hell," he said, and the grin faded to a grim line. "The old man will be on me about this for six months."

"I don't know why everybody calls Grandpop that," said Maggie. "He's not that old. Sixty-five's old, but not that old." She hopped down from the counter. "Daddy, will you drive me to Debbie's?" she said, as her father took his white shirt off a hanger bent to hang on top of the kitchen door.

"What happened to the president's physical fitness program?" Tommy asked. "She lives just up the street, for Christ's sake."

"Tom," said his wife, as the baby grabbed at the last spoonful of eggs.

"The president died," said Maggie. "There's no more fitness program. It's really hot, and Debbie's mother always drives me places."

"You'll walk," said her father, knotting a brown tie. "I'm late." He went into the hallway and took his jacket from over the banister.

" 'Bye," Connie said, but the click of the door sounded over her voice.

" 'Bye," Maggie said.

The Scanlans had lived in Kenwood, a small town on the Westchester border of the Bronx, since Maggie was a year old. It was not really a town, just one in a string of suburbs which had grown up around the city like a too-tight collar. The houses had been built right after the First World War, adequate houses, not grand ones, with a few flourishes—a stained-glass window on a landing here, a fanlight there. There were some center-hall Colonials, some mock Tudors, and a few boxy Cape Cods. Kenwood was no more than a dozen streets surrounding a spurious downtown: a dry cleaner; a drugstore with an attached medical-supply business with bedpans and laced corsets in the window; a real estate office with photographs of houses pinned to a cork bulletin board just inside the door; a hobby shop; and a stop on the railroad line into New York City.

Maggie's father helped run a cement company in the Bronx. His office was underneath an elevated subway line and next to the big wholesale vegetable depot. Unlike most of the fathers, who could be found at 7:00 A.M. reading the newspaper at the train station, Tom Scanlan drove into the city every day.

The pitch of their driveway was too steep, ever since a friend of Tommy's from high school had done an asphalt job on it, and whenever Tom backed out, his rear bumper bounced up off the street. As Maggie left the house that morning her father was just pulling out of the driveway, and she could see his mouth form the words "son of a bitch" as the back of his car hit the road and then bounced up level again.

It was hot in the June sun, and bright as a bare light bulb, but Maggie felt cool beneath the maple trees that lined the street, their leaves so green they looked almost black. Their branches hung over all but the center line of the street; in springtime the whirligigs that held their seeds floated down in tiny spirals, and they fell so thickly that the sidewalks were sticky with them, and the lawns grew untidy with seedlings. The trees were so large now, and cast such an indelible shade, that shrubs only grew in the backyards of the houses in Kenwood, except for the leggy rhododendrons that were planted on either side of the front doors of almost every home. Occasionally there would be talk about cutting down some trees to give the azaleas or forsythia a fighting chance, but most of the adults in the neighborhood had been city kids, and they found themselves incapable of cutting down trees. They tended their lawns with reverence, buying rotating sprinklers and hoses with holes along their lengths so that the water made little arcs of diamonds in the sunshine.

Maggie felt at peace here, on these quiet streets. She did not think of loving Kenwood, just as it did not occur to her to think about loving her parents, or her brothers Terence and Damien and little Joseph. It was simply her place, the place where she did not have to think twice about how to get where she was going and what to do when she got there. She remembered vaguely that when she was little her house had been that sort of place, too, but it seemed a long time ago. Now her house felt too crowded, too public. Once Maggie had heard her mother say that it was impossible for two women to share the same kitchen. Connie Scanlan had been talking about living in a beach house for a month with her sister-in-law, but the words had stayed with Maggie because she thought they applied to her and her mother as well. The house belonged to Connie. Kenwood, with its scuffed baseball field and its narrow creek and its ring of tousled fields, was Maggie's home. As she listened to the sound of the earth movers grinding away behind her, a faint shudder shook her shoulders, the feeling her aunt Celeste once told her signified someone walking over your grave.

She glanced back at her own house, but it looked empty and still, the two white pillars on either side of the doorway grubby with fingerprints. When they had first moved to Kenwood from a two-family house in the northeast Bronx that belonged to Connie's aunt and uncle, Tommy Scanlan had repainted the pillars every six months or so. But he was tired when he got home from work these days; he worked most Saturdays during good weather, and keeping up with the dirt the children left behind now seemed futile. He was the only one of his friends who had lived in the suburbs before he was married; his parents still lived there, in a big fieldstone house with a gazebo and a fountain in the backyard, in a section of Westchester County a little north of Kenwood, where the houses were so far apart that the neighbors' windows were only an occasional glint of sunlight through the trees. Tommy had lived there from the time he was fifteen until he got married at the age of twenty. Aunt Celeste had once told Maggie's mother, when the two of them were drinking beer on the front steps one night, that she suspected the pillars made Tommy feel he had come down in the world.

"Paint 'em black," John Scanlan said with a great guffaw on one of the rare visits he and his wife, Mary Frances, had made to the home of their middle son. Maggie noticed sometimes that when her father passed the columns a little white scar above his eyebrow jumped and writhed like one of the tiny white worms that sucked the life from her grandfather Mazza's tomato plants, and she supposed he was remembering John Scanlan's words.

That was what impressed Maggie most about her grandfather Scanlan: not that he dispensed down payments, tuition money, doctor's fees, with nothing in return except everyone knowing that he'd bought and paid for your house, your children's school, your wife's single room on the maternity floor. It was that he could, almost magically, make his children bob and move and sway like marionettes. Tommy's scar was the least of his accomplishments. His other four sons could be made to nod, pale, blush, shift in their chairs, pace on his Oriental rugs, simply by the words and looks John Scanlan could turn upon them. Maggie's grandmother sometimes seemed seized with St. Vitus's dance when her husband was angry. Only Sister John of the Cross, Maggie's aunt Margaret, John Scanlan's only living daughter, could sit motionless, expressionless, in her father's presence. Maggie sometimes thought her grandfather would have stuck a pin in Margaret if he could have been assured it would make her jump. She had paid a heavy price for her composure. "Hiding behind the skirts of Jesus, Sister?" John Scanlan would sometimes say, and then Margaret would smile slowly, without mirth, and so would John, because they both knew he had put his finger on it.

Maggie's mother managed to remain calm when she was around her father-in-law, too, although John Scanlan would have been delighted to hear how Connie railed against his machinations in the privacy of her own small kitchen. Sometimes Maggie felt that no one ever talked about what was really going on in her father's family, although everyone seemed to talk all the time. But she had heard enough from her aunt Celeste and her cousin Monica, and even occasionally—when Maggie was eavesdropping—from her own mother, to know that her mother's place amidst the Scanlans was not a comfortable one.

And she had only to look at the family gathered around John Scanlan's mahogany dining table at any holiday dinner to know which of his grandchildren were different from the rest. All of Maggie's many cousins looked a good deal alike—fair, even colorless, with placid faces. The children of Tommy Scanlan did not conform. Maggie herself was olive-skinned, with thick, heavy hair and curiously opaque green eyes, catlike and surprising. She had realized some time ago that no one would ever call her cute. She was thin—not slim and graceful but lanky on its way to being something else, caught in that uncomfortable place between childhood and maturity. Sometimes she felt as if her whole family was caught in some middle ground, too. If she heard that she was her mother's daughter one more time, she was sure she would start to scream.

Three blocks from her own house, over the railroad tracks, Maggie's closest friend, Debbie Malone, lived with her seven brothers and sisters in a large center-hall Colonial. Mrs. Malone was pregnant again, her muscular little legs sticking out of brown maternity shorts beneath the great cantilevered thrust of her belly. In the afternoons she lay on a yellow chaise longue made of strips of rubber that was set out beneath a maple tree in the Malones' backyard. Her calves and arms stuck to the rubber in the heat, and as the children eddied around her, demanding money for ice cream, complaining about one another, asking permission to do things they had never been permitted to do and would not be permitted to do now, she lay perspiring in the shade, staring up at the motionless leaves. Mrs. Malone was a good-humored woman who liked sports, but the heat got her down. One of her favorite activities had always been shoveling the snow off the long cement walk that led up to her front door. Her children slipped out of her as easily as if she were a water slide into the crowded pool of their household.

Maggie never knocked when she went to the Malones; she just walked around back and let herself into the kitchen through the screen door. Mrs. Malone treated her as if she were a member of the family, which was strange considering that she had more than enough family to go round. But Maggie loved the easy feeling, and responded by being more solicitous and communicative than the Malone children, who, with the exception of Helen, the eldest, were simple machines. Mrs. Malone, Maggie supposed, was a simple machine, too. She seemed to like her family, her husband, and her house with a kind of straightforward good humor. Maggie threw herself right into this; she was constantly struck by what a welcome change it was from her own family, in which she felt as if she were moving through a carnival fun house, waiting for a skeleton to leap out from behind a closed door. Mr. and Mrs. Malone had met in the fifth grade at St. Cyril's School in an Irish section of Manhattan, and when they were together they seemed more like brother and sister than husband and wife, at least from Maggie's experience of married people.

"Doesn't all that hair make you hot, Pee Wee?" Mrs. Malone said, as she turned from the sink and looked Maggie up and down. "Nope," said Maggie, the way she always did when she was asked that question, and she threw her hair over her shoulder, pushed her damp bangs back with the flat of her hand and sat down at the redwood picnic table in the kitchen.

"Can we go swimming?" she asked.

"Did you bring your suit?"

"I left it here the last time."

"Is that red one yours?" Mrs. Malone said, rinsing some forks. "I was wondering where that came from. I asked Aggie and she said it wasn't hers, but I put it in her underwear drawer anyway. Go up and get it and get your partner in crime and we'll all go."

"Are you going swimming too?"

"No I am not," said Mrs. Malone, wiping her hands on a dirty dishtowel. "I'll sit by the pool and put my feet in and wish it was a month from now and I was twenty pounds lighter."

The pool was in the next town, at what was called the Kenwoodie Club. It was really nothing more than a swimming pool and a nine-hole golf course surrounded by a chain-link fence, with an entrance gate where a guard checked laminated membership cards. Nearly all the people Maggie went to school with spent the day there, doing cannonballs off the diving board or spitting in the baby pool.

Helen Malone had become famous at the Kenwoodie Club after a trip to California the summer before, when she had emerged from the locker room one day in the closest thing the club had ever seen to a bikini. It was an abbreviated two-piece with push-up cups, and a bottom half that rode a full two inches below her navel. Mrs. Malone had been asked to see that the suit stayed at home next time. "If they think I can control Helen Malone," she had muttered in the car on the way home that day, "they've got another think coming."

Even her own mother talked about Helen Malone in the third person, as though she were someone none of them knew. Maggie thought that the only person who truly acted as if she knew Helen Malone was Helen herself. Her legend was considerable. At Sacred Heart Academy all anyone needed to do was mention Helen Malone's name and the girls became stern and watchful. She was known to be terribly sophisticated, and perhaps even something more than that. But what really riveted all of them, all the freckled, pleasant, ordinary girls with whom Helen shared study hall and Bible history and glee club, were two things. The first was that Helen was beautiful. This was never agreed upon, of course; there were girls who said she was odd-looking, that her nose was thin and pointed. But they never said this in front of the boys they knew. Helen's eyes were a clear blue, and her nose straight and small, but her lips were full, as though they'd been inflated, and her hair was full, too, full and glossy. Mrs. Malone sometimes said that at the hospital they'd given her Liz Taylor's baby by mistake.

But, more important, her beauty seemed to stand for something inside her, a kind of apartness, and a feeling that she knew exactly where she was going and how she was going to get there, and that she would go, happily, alone. She rarely spoke, never gossiped, was never silly, and had never seemed young. She was grown up, and had been for as long as anyone could remember. Perhaps this was what obsessed Maggie and Debbie about her most. They rifled through her drawers constantly, trying on her old prom dresses and tossing her underwear back and forth as though they were playing hot potato, embarrassed by their curiosity but compelled by it, too. There were always letters from boys they had never heard of, and some of them wrote poems. "I long to peel you like a ripe peach," someone named Edward with an address at Cornell University had written, and Debbie had read it over and over. "What does that mean?" she said, her freckled cheeks scarlet.

"You don't even peel peaches," Maggie said, and Debbie looked at her pityingly. "What do you want him to say, that he wants to peel her like an orange?" Maggie stared at the envelope. "The stamp is upside down for love," she said.

Last year, Maggie remembered, Sister Regina Marie had asked them to write down, without thinking, the answer to the question: Who are you? It was the only time in her school career Maggie could remember not knowing an answer. It had been a kind of psychological trick, really; Sister didn't even ask them to hand the papers in, just told them to put the answers in their pockets and think about what they had found to say about themselves.

"What did you write, Mag?" Debbie had asked on the playground, blinking her blue eyes, like Helen's but paler, smoothing back her black hair, like Helen's but kinky. In fact Debbie looked like a blurred version of Helen, angles blunted, colors muted. "I put that I am still becoming who I am," Maggie said. "God," Debbie sighed. "That's why you get As and I get stupid Cs." And she took a piece of paper out of her pocket and handed it to Maggie. In Debbie's rounded writing, with the circles dotting the i's, was written, "I am Helen Malone's sister."

Afterward, when she was in her own room, Maggie had taken her own paper from her blazer pocket, unfolded it and put it on her bureau. It was blank.

Helen was the only Malone child with a room of her own. On its door was a small blackboard for messages. It was always full. Maggie passed it now on her way to Debbie's room, up beneath the slanting roof of the third floor. "In by 11!" Mrs. Malone had written at the top in capital letters, and below "John Kelly called—will call again" and "Can I wear your white eyelet blouse tonight? Aggie (I'll wash it)." Underneath the second was written neatly in blue chalk "NO." Her neat penmanship on the blackboard and a glass in the sink were often the only signs of Helen in the Malone house for days at a time.

Debbie was lying on her bed staring at the ceiling, still wearing her nightgown. "Summer's just started and I'm bored already," she said as Maggie came in.

Maggie sat on the edge of the bed, silent. Debbie shut her eyes. Her nose was sunburned. "Today she got a dozen red roses," she said finally.

"Really?" said Maggie. "From who?"

"Who knows?" Debbie said. "Some guy. She stuck the card down the front of her shirt."

"Can we see?"

"They're in the living room. She said she'd put them where the whole family could enjoy them. I think that means they're from somebody she doesn't like that much."

Maggie sighed. "Amazing." The two girls stared into space. Maggie bit a cuticle. "Your mother said she'll drive us to the club," she said.

"Same old thing," said Debbie. "Boring, boring, boring." But she got up and started to put on her clothes just the same. "I'd better get boobs soon," she said, her voice muffled as she dressed beneath the tent of her nightgown, but Maggie just said "Shut up" and started to look through Aggie's underwear drawer for her old red bathing suit.

"Sometimes you're such a baby, Mag," said Debbie listlessly.

"Shut up," Maggie said again, taking her suit and heading downstairs.

IN LATE AFTERNOON, WHEN THE HUmidity had begun to ebb somewhat and the sheen of perspiration on all the children to fade, Connie Scanlan sat down crosslegged on the floor of her dining room to look at her good dishes. She always waited until she was alone to do this, for she thought that if anyone saw her they would surely say to themselves, "Well, she's finally lost her mind."

Her pale knees glimmered amid the china spread out in front of her, as though they, too, were porcelain. Twelve dinner plates, twelve saucers, twelve cups, twelve dessert plates, a tureen, three serving dishes, a coffee pot, a creamer, and a sugar bowl. They were all a pale, pale cream color, with purple and red flowers painted around the edge and a gilded rim, and each dish, each cup, came with its own gray chamois bag, as though they were pieces of jewelry. The china seemed to Connie the only vestige of some foolish feeling she had once had about what her adult life would be like. Day after day she washed the plastic bowls in the sink, and now and then she thought of these others, shining beneath their little shrouds, too good for everyday, for meatloaf and macaroni and cheese.

It had turned out that her life was an everyday sort of thing, too. She did not know why she had expected something different. Perhaps it was that her own family life had been so dark and peculiar, her elderly parents rarely exchanging a word, herself the only child, that she had easily fallen prey to the images of bright domesticity conjured up by popular songs and movies. Perhaps it was that, daring as the union between Connie Mazza and Tommy Scanlan had been, flying in the face of John Scanlan and his family, it had started off as the stuff of grand opera, and she had expected it to go on being so. The bitter taste in Connie's mouth was the residue of disillusionment.

Her marriage was to have been her entry to a normal life, the life she imagined everyone else lived when she looked at the world from within the gates of Calvary Cemetery. She had supposed that a husband and children would teach her to be one of the group, but instead she felt more and more alone among more and more people, a woman whose universe was contained beneath her own sternum. Sometimes she wondered if the cemetery gates had grown inside her as well, closing her off from a world naturally communal and gregarious.

Her aunt Rose had always told her that children would be the joy of her life, and even though Connie felt she had been the bane of her own mother's existence, she had believed what Rose said. And sometimes, when the children were small, still attached to their mother by the umbilical cord of weakness and primitive need, she felt that this was true, that with a baby on her hip she was not alone. Looking at each one in the bassinet, the little fingers splayed like small pink starfish on the crib sheets, she imagined what they would become, to the world and to her. In this, too, she sometimes felt that being an only child served her poorly, and that her imaginings came from books and women's magazine articles and movies. The eldest boy would be her helpmate and protector. The youngest would be slightly sentimental, a little mischievous, always allied with his mother. Perhaps the picture in her mind had been most vivid for the first daughter. "Now you will have someone to do things with," everyone told her after Maggie was born, and that was what she had thought she had given birth to: her closest friend, her soulmate. Her imaginings had turned out to be as useless as her wedding china. Connie's need and her children's maturity combined to cause bitter disappointment, for as the children grew and moved away, from her and her dreams of them, they seemed to her strangers, Scanlans.

She remembered the day her father-in-law had first met Maggie. He had found her playing on his lawn with her aunt Margaret four years after Connie and Tommy's wedding. Connie had thought that the child was at the convent until she saw the little hand, still dimpled at the knuckle, clutching a hundred-dollar bill.

"I'm sorry, Con," Margaret had said. "They took to each other like fish to water." Connie's narrow chest had gone cold. A year later her daughter was in private school, her tuition paid for by her grandfather. Connie had never felt the same about her since.

After that she had waited for the vultures to circle her marriage, but with the exception of a few obligatory holiday dinners and the occasional party, she and Tommy had somehow managed to stay outside her father-in-law's grip. She supposed that, with the exception of Maggie, he found them all beneath his notice.

John Scanlan had gotten his son James named chief of his department at Christ Hospital by giving them new X-ray equipment, and he had chosen a house for Mark and Gail, not far from his own. His younger sons had come to work for him and without a whimper had become completely dependent on their father's industry, and his whims.

Only Margaret had escaped for a time, sent to study philosophy at Tulane while living in a New Orleans convent covered with wisteria and wrought iron. She had written home about a doctoral degree and the fiery food, and had bloomed in the heat.

And then John Scanlan had taken the Mother Superior to lunch in a steak house, given her a check for ten thousand dollars for a new chapel for the order's retreat house, and Margaret had been reassigned to a school not five miles from the house she had left for the convent. She taught first grade and read Kierkegaard on the sly. Sometimes Connie looked at all of them, gathered around the big table in John and Mary Frances Scanlan's dining room, and thought they all were covered with blood except for her.

Slowly she stacked the plates and placed them on the bottom shelves of the breakfront. From outside she could hear a peculiar noise, and looked out the dining-room window to watch Maggie come up the street, moving toward home, flat-footed and slow. It struck her again that Maggie walked a little like Connie's own mother had, head down, shoulders thrust forward. "The weight of the world on her shoulders," someone had once said to Connie of her mother, and it was true of her daughter, too. Otherwise, she knew, the two couldn't have been more different.

Anna Mazza had been built like a cardboard box, and Connie had often thought she had all the sensitivity of one. Maggie was always thinking, thinking, thinking, keeping silent only so she could figure out what made the world work. Connie didn't feel qualified to tell her; she was still trying to figure it out herself. And so the two of them had sunk into silence just around the time that both had noticed that Maggie would soon be taller than Connie.

Her cousin Celeste had assured Connie that this was the way it was with girls, that they should be put in the deep freeze until they were twenty-one, that every mother was made to feel she was a palpable insult by a daughter of a certain age. But all Connie could remember was how much she had loved Maggie as a baby, how the nurses would hold her up at the nursery window and perfect strangers on the other side would say "oh" with such conviction that small spots of fog would appear on the glass.

Maggie had had a great furry head of black hair, navy eyes that seemed bottomless, a moon face, and two small violet bruises where the forceps had reached in and pulled her out. She had weighed an even ten pounds, and Connie, small and wan in her satin bed jacket, had felt that Maggie was her great accomplishment, the finest thing she had ever done. But the connection between herself and her daughter had slowly disappeared, until there were only memories of warm curves, of a little pink mouth working against her skin. When Connie had asked the last week of school whether she should order next year's uniform blouses with darts in them, Maggie had seethed for three days, leaving the house for hours on end, discernible when she was around by the way she made the closing of a door or the placing of a glass on a table sound like something between profanity and physical violence. "You know why they call them growing pains?" Connie had said to Celeste, who sometimes seemed to be the only person she could talk to. "It's because I'm going to kill her."

From the window Connie could see the length of the street, could see Maggie coming slowly toward the house and realized that the noise she had heard was the slapping of Maggie's rubber flip-flops hitting the pavement. From this distance Connie was struck anew by the way in which Maggie favored Tommy, who was skinny, with one of those bony Irish-boy bodies that hang from the shoulders as though their shirts were still on hangers. Maggie was thin and bony, too, the moon face of babyhood now squared off at the jaw. She insisted on wearing last year's bathing suit, even though it was too short for her lengthening torso and she spent all her time yanking it down to cover her butt. Connie thought of Joseph up in his crib, pink and wet in the heat, his mouth open, silver slug trails of saliva on the sheets. An hour ago she had stood over him and thought that the rift would come soon. Now he was her little love, warm and sweet, always ready to wrap his arms around her middle and lay his head on the pillow of her breastbone. Soon he would change, develop edges to his character that would come to cut the connection between them. It had happened with each of his brothers. She supposed the boys were down at the ball field, Damien trailing after Terence forlornly, although Damien hated athletics nearly as much as Connie did. The odd couple, their mother had thought as she watched them go, the elder boy dark, stolid, and so attached to his baseball mitt that he cradled it in bed at night, the younger as high-strung and uncoordinated as a colt.

Connie put her hand up to touch her hair. She realized that she had gone all day without once looking into a mirror, and she wondered if there would be no reflection in the glass, as if she were a vampire. In the house in which Connie had grown up, there had been only one mirror, over the sink, and its silver was scarred and grubby. In her own house there were many more mirrors, but somewhere along the line she had stopped looking into them. The silence pressed in upon her like a damp hand.

Connie Scanlan had been raised in the Bronx, and had never been able to adjust to what she considered the sneaky sounds of the suburbs, the hissing of the sprinklers, the hum of the occasional car, the children's voices calling to one another, carrying so clearly that they had learned to whisper anything important. The city sounds had a primary color: horns, screams, the solid *thwack* of a broomstick connecting with a hard ball, the *clunk* of the ball coming down into the leather glove. The section of the Bronx where her family lived was considered a kind of suburb by them all, not like the Lower East Side or Little Italy. But it still smelled and sounded of the city. In Kenwood sometimes, particularly on summer afternoons, the street would be so still that she would be tempted to put *South Pacific* or some Sinatra album on the stereo and turn it up loud enough to drown the quiet out. But she was always afraid someone would hear; she didn't want to give them one more reason to talk about her behind her back.

She was sure they did already, in this homogenous place where the second generation Dohertys and O'Briens and Kellys lived after they married one another's sisters, cousins, friends, and left the city behind. Only a few had muddied the blood lines with outsiders, and often those brave or foolish ones had done it to spit in the face of their families. Connie had not believed this was the case when Tommy had proposed to her, even when Celeste, big and bold as a helium balloon in bridesmaids' blue taffeta, had said at the wedding, "This is a pretty elaborate way to make sure your old man never talks to you again. You sure you want to play Cinderella the rest of your life, kid?" Instead of fading with time, experience had intensified those words in Connie's memory.

The back door slammed as Maggie came in and dumped her damp towel on the counter. Her wet hair had made a big spot on the back of her blouse, and for some reason this made Connie angry.

"Don't they make you wear a bathing cap at that pool?"

"Yeah, but it doesn't work with my hair," Maggie said, drinking water at the sink. "It's hard for me to get it all inside the cap."

"So it gets wet anyway."

"No it doesn't. I wear the cap and then I take it off when we're ready to go, and I go under to get my hair wet."

"Let me get this straight," Connie said. "You wear the cap to keep your hair dry and then at the end you take the cap off and get your hair wet? Does that make sense?"

"You don't understand because you don't know how to swim," said Maggie. "Everybody does it."

"If everybody jumped off the Brooklyn Bridge, would you do that too?" Connie said, without even thinking.

"You always say that."

"Hang this on the line before you leave," Connie said, unrolling the towel with a snap. The red suit fell on the floor, and with it a flutter of damp dirty paper. Connie stooped down. It was a twenty-dollar bill. She picked it up between two fingers as though it was a bug. "How is your grandfather Scanlan?" Connie said.

Maggie took the money and her wet things and turned away. "He said we're all going to the house on Sunday. How come?"

"On Sunday I am cleaning the linen closet," Connie said, turning toward the sink. "Go hang up your suit."

From the window she watched her daughter fumble with the clothes-pins and slip the money into her pocket. It enraged her that even without being present John Scanlan could ruin her day. "Don't you wake your brother up," Connie hissed, as her daughter came back through the kitchen on her way upstairs.

She looked at the sink filled with cereal bowls, coffee cups, Mickey Mouse glasses with low tidelines of orange pulp. Upstairs she could hear Joseph humming to himself. "Damn it," she said, spraying detergent onto a sponge.

A thousand times Tommy had told her she was doing it wrong, that you were supposed to fill the sink with water and let the dishes soak. A thousand times she had shut her mouth and done it her way. She'd been doing dishes since she was seven years old, standing on the red leatherette seat of a stepstool, when there had been only her own plate and glass to wash. She'd washed her own cereal bowl before school and her own plates after dinner, while her father and her mother worked. Nobody was going to tell her how to do a dish.

Suddenly there was a stultifying silence, oppressive as the heat, as the last earth mover working in the fields behind the house quieted, rumbled once like a death rattle and was still.

Connie was a short woman, low to the ground, and even if she stood on tiptoe, she could not quite make out how much work had been done, except that there seemed to be great gashes in the reedlike weeds, and here and there a massive pile of fresh brown earth. A half dozen of the big machines stood at rest. For the first time Connie noticed that someone had placed two portable toilets at the far end of the field. The man who had been driving the last earth mover was almost at the back door before she realized he was coming to her house. Connie noticed that his gray undershirt was stained black beneath the arms with huge half-moons of perspiration. He peered through the screen at her, blinded by the dim indoors after the glare of the day.

"Hello?" he said.

"Yes?" Connie's voice was cold.

"Could I trouble you to use the phone?" he asked, still peering through the screen.

Connie opened the door a bit. The man had glossy hair, like an animal's pelt, and eyebrows so thick that they looked like an amateur theatrical effect. He looked at Connie and Connie looked at him; for a moment they just gaped at one another, and then both started to laugh.

"Connie Mazza," he said, smoothing back his hair.

"Oh," she said, snapping her fingers. "Don't tell me, I'll get it. Don't tell me."

He laughed again. "Martinelli," he said.

"I knew *that* part."

"Joe," he added.

"Joey. Joey Martinelli. I would have had it in a minute. Come in. Use the phone. Do you want a beer?" She started to laugh again. "It's nice to see a familiar face."

"I knew you lived in the neighborhood," he said, "but I swear to God I didn't know this was your house."

"You're working on this project?"

"I'm the foreman. But we're in such a big hurry that I'm driving the backhoe part time. We did six foundations today. I swear I thought somebody was going to have a stroke in this heat."

"You dug foundations for six houses today?"

He nodded. "And we're supposed to do six tomorrow. The people are in some kind of a rush."

"I don't know why," said Connie. "They've been planning this for years." She pointed to the phone. "Go ahead."

She watched him as he dialed. He had the sort of muscles men developed from heavy lifting, and he stood awkwardly when he stood still. She remembered that he had been one of the good athletes when she was a girl, one of the nice boys in the neighborhood who always held the door if you left the drugstore when they did. She hadn't known him well, although she had gone out with his younger brother a few times.

She heard him talking on the phone about dinner. "Your wife?" she said after he hung up.

"My mother," he said ruefully.

"How 'bout a beer?" she said, even though it felt strange to be alone in the house with a man. A noise from above made her start; she hadn't counted the children, or even remembered them for a moment.

"Thanks, but I gotta finish up and get home. We're supposed to be done here by the end of the year. Nice houses, too. Laundry chutes. Disposals. Carpet. Not like these old ones, but nice houses."

"An old house is a lot of work," Connie said.

"Yeah." He looked down at his shoes and at the grime he was leaving on the speckled linoleum. "Oh, boy, I'm sorry. My mother would kill me if she could see this."

"You're right," said Connie, and they both laughed again. As she watched him cross the fields she remembered that his father had died in the excavation of a subway tunnel somewhere deep beneath the surface of the borough of Queens. Perhaps that was why she was surprised to find him in this line of work. Or perhaps it was that she vaguely remembered he had been smarter than that, one of the boys likely to break free of the Italian immigrant tradition of dirt beneath the fingernails. His brother had worn aftershave that smelled like peppermint. And Joey had delivered papers to earn pocket money; he had brought the *News* to her father every morning. It was odd what you remembered, like her remembering those bruises on Maggie's head after all these years. It was interesting to find that one short conversation with an almost-stranger had improved her mood immeasurably.

Hot as it was, she stretched up to get the big bowl from the top shelf of the kitchen cabinets, and humming to herself, began to make a cake.

3

OMMY SCANLAN STARED OUT THE WIN-
dow of his office in the gray-green cin-
derblock building that was the home
of First Concrete. Below him was the
lot where he and the other men parked
their cars, and behind the chain-link fence was another, larger lot
where they kept the cement mixers, great clanking beasts incongruously
painted in red-and-white candy-cane stripes. At the moment there was
a single cement mixer there, its hood up, its enormous greasy motor
exposed like the entrails of a big animal, and next to the cement mixer
was a black Lincoln Continental with a high-gloss shine.

"Ah, shit," Tommy said aloud, looking down at the big car. There
was a faint tapping at his office door, and Tommy switched off the radio
atop his filing cabinet. "Ah, shit," he said again, going to open it.

One of the mechanics, a squat, swarthy man named Gino, whose
wavy hair looked like the ocean on a rough day, stood at the door in
his red-and-white striped First Concrete shirt. All the men hated the
shirts, but Gino was the shop steward and he never showed up at First
Concrete out of uniform.

"The old man is downstairs," Gino said. The men never used a
salutation when they addressed Tommy in the office; they weren't sure
whether to call him Mr. Scanlan or not.

Tommy had failed to notice this particular semantic dilemma, but he appreciated the fact that they always said "the old man" and not "your old man." It made Tom feel small to be reminded of his father's power.

"Did you tell him I was here?" Tommy asked, looking out the window.

"Downstairs they told him they weren't sure where you were," Gino said. "I don't think he's coming up. He's got us changing the oil in his car. Your brother's with him."

Tommy could see his father standing in one of his gray suits, in the maintenance lot, looking at the disabled cement mixer. The old man turned and said something to the mechanic working on his car, and the man handed him a rag. John Scanlan wiped the striped side of the cement mixer, then shook his head. "Oh, hell," Tommy muttered, lighting a cigarette.

The stripes on the trucks had been Tommy's father's idea of free advertising; no one, John Scanlan had reasoned, would ever be able to mistake a First Concrete cement mixer for the cement mixers of Reliable, or Gatto Brothers, or Bronx River Cement. On the other hand, no one ever made fun of those other cement mixers, either. Sometimes, when Tommy handed his card to a developer, or a factory owner, or someone from the city who was looking for a couple hundred dollars in exchange for a contract to lay some sidewalks or pour the foundation for a school gymnasium, he would see a look of discovery pass over the guy's face. No matter how often it happened, Tommy's chest would tighten at that moment. "The ones with the stripes, right?" the customer would say. "The red-and-white stripes?" And the look of discovery would be replaced by a big grin. "Can't miss those babies."

Tommy was in charge of keeping the trucks looking good, but he hated the stripes so much that he would let them go until they'd faded to pale pink and dirty gray. It wasn't the ridicule; it was the reminder. "Look at me!" the stripes seemed to shout, just as John Scanlan always did. If Tommy had had his way, the trucks would have been gray. They would have looked like what they were: trucks that carried cement, not big pieces of peppermint candy on wheels. But Tommy never had his way. Sooner or later his father would see one of the trucks, on one of his trips around the city to have lunch in some parish rectory or another—"good booze at Queen of Peace," he might say to Tom the next time he saw him, or "one more plate of corned beef and cabbage and I'm not going back to St. Teresa's"—and the old man would be on the phone complaining that the trucks needed a fresh coat of paint.

He never called Tommy directly. Buddy Phelan, who was the president of First Concrete and, not coincidentally, the godson of the monsignor who handled purchasing for the biggest suburban diocese in the metropolitan area, would come into Tommy's office with a bemused grin on his face, and say, "Hey, Tom. Time to give the trucks a going over, whattaya say?" And Tommy would know that his father had called that morning to suggest that the man who owned one hundred percent of First Concrete, and who had the right to hire and fire those who worked there, did not like his clever subliminal advertising gimmick compromised by a failure of upkeep and a heavy layer of city grime.

Buddy Phelan always assumed that Tommy hated him, but this was not true. In his heart of hearts Tommy hated no one, except occasionally himself, and he was pleased to be vice president of operations at First Concrete, a big title for a mundane job. If he had been the "big boss," as the men who drove the trucks called Buddy, he would not have been able to chat with the workers so effortlessly when they came in at the end of the day, smelly and glad to talk without the roar of the mixer or the road in their ears. He would have felt constrained from going into Sal's at lunchtime and sitting at the bar with a sandwich and a draft beer, putting in his two cents about the Yankees, the weather, or the coloreds. It would have been impossible for him to join the pick-up basketball games that took place across the street most afternoons, when he felt free and young and extraordinarily competent: dribble downcourt, push off from the knees, send the orange ball sailing with a motion of his wrist that had become second nature in Catholic school gyms, watch it sink with only that slight lisp of a sound that had given the shot the name "swish." Basketball made him feel simultaneously like a man and a boy. Everyone nodded to Buddy Phelan when he left for the night, climbing into his Olds 98, but no one ever asked him to join them for a beer, except Tommy, when he had nothing better to do. He felt sorry for the guy.

When he turned from the window, Gino was gone and his brother Mark was just coming up the stairs. Mark was flushed bright pink in the heat, but his tie was still tied tight, while Tommy's was at half-mast. They looked like brothers, both mostly beige: beige hair, faded from the tow they'd had as boys, beige freckles, darker beige eyes. But where Tommy was long and rangy, Mark was solid and short. It was only after Mark had married that he had been able to convince his family to stop calling him "Squirt," although John Scanlan, who was an even six feet tall, still felt compelled to make comments about his son's height from time to time.

"We're going to have to paint the trucks next week," Tommy said.

"I don't know why you fight him on that," Mark said. "You know who wins."

The two stood silent, sweating. Tommy took a great deal of satis-faction out of the fact that he didn't work directly for his father, and Mark resented him for it, thinking that depending on John Scanlan's largesse once removed was worse than simply facing facts and going to work for Scanlan & Co. "We're all in the family business," their sister Margaret always said with a grin. Mark could not understand how this could apply to obstetrics or a religious vocation, but Margaret said that was simply because he was always too literal.

In fact Tommy would have preferred not to work for any Scanlan enterprise. When he and Connie had first married they had talked of moving to California, of living where it was always warm and no one had ever heard of John Scanlan, where they didn't care if you were Italian as long as you weren't Mexican. But their own fecundity had laid waste to that dream. During the first five years of their marriage, when they had heard not a word from Tommy's parents, they had learned how difficult it was to pay the bills on a working man's salary. Then John Scanlan had taken an interest in Maggie, and Tommy had been hired, after a perfunctory interview, as a vice president at First

Concrete. His wife had barely spoken to him for nearly two months after he took the job. The words she had used to break the silence were "I'm pregnant again."

There were only two reasons why Tommy preferred being an executive to being one of the men carrying and shoveling cement. The first was that he needed the money. He and Connie had practiced rhythm since Maggie was born, and they had three sons to show for it, and a suspicion of another on the way. Saddle shoes alone ran him two hundred dollars a year. The other thing he loved about his job was his office. As offices went, it was on the small side, with a window that looked over the parking lot to the basketball court and playground across the street, and the red-brick public school building beyond that. When two trains passed going in opposite directions on the elevated line, his office shivered like a child with a high fever. Sometimes in the summer the Sanitation Department would not be quick enough about picking up the garbage, and the wholesale fruit market across the road would give off an overripe sweet smell. But Tommy had a gray desk, a gray file cabinet, a gray table that held an adding machine and stood beneath a wall displaying a full-color map of the city of New York, with pins in it for job locations, which made Tommy feel a little like a general. He kept his framed Fordham diploma, the result of two years of full-time studies and four years of nights after Maggie and Terence were born, in the big bottom drawer of his desk, along with a bottle of Four Roses and a sweatshirt to change into for basketball games. He also had a studio photograph of Connie on her wedding day, her eyes so big and black amid the whites and grays of the picture that it looked as if they'd been made with the end of a lighted cigarette. When certain clients, mainly the big boys, came to see him, he put the picture on the filing cabinet, but most of the time he kept it in the drawer. His brother Mark had noticed this once, and had gone home to report to his wife that things in Tom and Connie's marriage were even worse than they'd imagined. In truth the picture had been put away for exactly the opposite reason; while most men considered it simply part of their office equipment, like a stapler or a striped tie, Tommy Scanlan believed that the photograph would tell the world a private thing: that he was crazy about his wife.

Like so many of their friends, Connie Mazza and Tommy Scanlan had gotten married because they were expecting a baby. It had come as a great surprise to both of them. Connie's sole exposure to sex education had been the day before her twelfth birthday, when her aunt Rose had given her a box of sanitary napkins almost a year too late. Tommy found out afterward that it had never occurred to Connie that the surge of heat and compulsion and the aftermath of embarrassment she had felt on weekend nights in his car could result in the conception of a child.

Tommy had known better, but he had been similarly dim in not realizing that it was impossible that the answer to "Is this a safe time?" could be "Yes" every Friday and Saturday night. It was not until after they were married that he discovered that Connie had supposed he was asking only about the chances of someone catching him under her long skirts and net petticoats. Maggie had been born six months after their wedding, and Tommy's explanation of her prematurity was for many years a great joke among his brothers, given the fact that the infant was the biggest baby in the nursery. Connie said nothing. By the time she had her baby, she did not care what anyone thought.

Even all these years later, when Tommy Scanlan looked across the kitchen table after a couple of beers and wondered who the hell this woman was, he knew that if they had not gotten caught he would have married her just the same. When they met at the YMCA jitterbug contest he had been going with someone else, a lively girl named Mary Roe, who had freckles and wild auburn curls and was a friend of his sister. He had danced with Connie only because the two winning couples in the contest had been asked to switch partners after the trophies had been given out. Connie was so small she had come only to his shoulder, her back as narrow as a child's. She had black hair waved off her face, and black eyes so big and blank that he almost felt he could see inside her head. Her skin was white and her lipstick a pure clear red. She looked like a painting to him. She spoke not one word during the entire dance—the song had been "Moonlight Serenade," and he thought he could very faintly hear, or perhaps feel, her humming—but as the music stopped she said "Thank you" and did not step away. He felt as though he'd been punched in the chest.

When the music started again, he simply held on to her and began to dance some more. That was the way it was for the rest of the night, as Mary Roe watched from the sidelines and finally went out to a car with Mark Scanlan and let him do everything she had never let a boy do to her before.

Connie went home that night with Jimmy Martinelli, the boy who had brought her to the dance in the first place. He drove her in silence to the cemetery where the Mazzas lived, leaned across her to open the door from inside, said "Good luck" and drove away.

Most people assumed that Tommy had fallen in love with Connie because of the way she looked. The fashion of their adolescence had been for pink-skinned blondes with small noses and soft mouths, and so Connie had never believed anyone, including Tommy, when they said that she was beautiful. Tommy remembered their first Christmas, when she had brought home two boxes of cards to send to their friends and families, the message "Blessed Christmas" inside on cream-colored paper and a Renaissance painting of the Virgin Mary on the front. Connie had picked the cards because she thought they would go over well with various Scanlans, but when Tommy had seen the painting he had burst out laughing. "I've heard of people who send out pictures of themselves on their cards, but nobody who sends out paintings," he said. And in truth the serenely beautiful Madonna, with her slightly sallow skin, dark hair, prominent nose and full lips looked very much like Connie. Tommy had turned over the card and read the fine print. "Giotto," he said. "Did you pose for this?"

"For your information, we invented the Renaissance," Connie had said in a huff, going up to their room until he came and kissed the frown from between her eyebrows.

But it was not her looks that had so compelled him. Tommy had never been able to put it into words, but it was the blankness of her he was so mesmerized by, the feeling of an empty bottle waiting to be filled, and filled by him. He had been waiting for so long for someone to take him seriously, to listen to him. Looking at her great bottomless eyes he got the feeling that that was what she was doing, although as the years went by he would sometimes wonder if it was simply that nobody was home in there. He could never get a word in edgewise with his family, and he was a little afraid of both his parents, his mother with her patently false patina of elegance and control, his father with his seemingly effortless ability to rise in the world and his disdain for those who did not. It had not escaped Tommy's notice that Connie Mazza would rise in the world simply by moving to a place where people lived, instead of one where they were buried. He was also sexually enthralled by her. When she would lean forward to tune the car radio and he would get a whiff of her, his blood felt as if it would burst from his body.

He had suspected that there would be trouble when, after a highly public breakdown by Mary Roe in the ladies' room at Sacred Heart Academy, his sister Margaret had come home and asked him, meaning no harm, whether he was really going with a Puerto Rican girl from Spanish Harlem. But there was little talk of the affair until, six weeks after they had begun dating, and five weeks after Tommy decided he meant to marry Connie, he had brought her home for Sunday dinner.

Connie had shopped for a week and had spent all the money she had saved from her secretarial job on a red satin dress with a sweetheart neckline and a tiny tight waist from which her bust loomed like a stretch of cream crepe de Chine. As they drove up the long driveway to the Scanlan house and saw Tommy's sister and one of her friends sitting on the steps in navy-blue skirts and pale-blue sweater sets, Connie had known she had made a dreadful mistake.

At dinner no one spoke to her except Mary Frances, who handed dishes across the table and said "Peas?" and "Potatoes?" as though she and Connie were characters in *The Philadelphia Story*. After Tommy had driven Connie home, he had come back to find his father sitting in the living room in the dark, his cigar burned to the nub at one end and chewed to the nub at the other. "If you think I busted my ass so you could marry some goddamn guinea from the Bronx, you've got another think coming," said Mr. Scanlan, who was quite drunk. Tommy went upstairs while his father continued to talk; the only other word Tommy caught was "wop." The following Friday Connie told him that her period was late.

And that had been that. They had gotten caught, and Tommy had felt that the ties had tightened with each of the babies, each of them unplanned, each of them making the ties more fast, each of them keeping them from—what? He did not know. His feeling about what their lives might have been were as vague as his feelings about Connie, formed of odd, intense, momentary yearnings. He sometimes wondered what they would have been like as a couple, what life would have been like had they not instantly become a family, had not his empty vessel been filled year after year with the babies she loved so much and watched grow so sadly. Sometimes he would wake in the morning, the sky blue-gray as a dolphin's back, and for just a few moments he would wonder who this was in bed beside him, and whether he was going to be late for his nine o'clock class. It would come to him slowly that the house was filled with people, created by him, connected to him for life, and he would be weak with incredulity and fear. He knew what it meant to be a father; it meant being sure, outspoken, critical, bold, controlled. It meant being John Scanlan. This life of his was a masquerade.

Then he would roll over, embrace his wife, lift her frilled nightgown and straddle her narrow body, as he had this morning. And he would be all right again, throwing off the sheets afterward, pulling on his shorts, going to the bathroom, thinking only for a moment of another baby next year, wondering if it was a safe time, putting on his T-shirt and his suit pants and going down to breakfast.

"So I hear you and your boss drove a half hour out of your way to get his oil changed," Tommy said to Mark, running his hand along his damp forehead. "What did I screw up now?"

"Is it a possibility that the owner of this company just might want to stop in occasionally and see how things are going?" said Mark, who had flushed at the words "your boss."

"Is it a possibility that he wanted to see how things are going? No," said Tommy. "Is it a possibility that he wants to give me a hard time about something? You know it. What'd I do this time, except let the goddamned candy canes get dirty?"

"He says you and Connie and the kids should come to the house

Sunday," Mark said, running his finger around the inside of his collar.

"Why?"

"Would he tell me?" said Mark. "I'm just carrying the message. He was smiling when he said it."

"That's the worst news I've heard all day," Tommy said. "That means something's up. Maybe he finally got my marriage annulled."

Looking out the window again, his back to his brother, Tommy watched his father climb into the cab of the cement mixer. There was a low rumble as the engine turned over, and then John Scanlan began to drive the thing around the lot in circles, like a child with a new bicycle.

Tommy began to examine his conscience. Before confession you were supposed to consider your sins; as a boy, Tommy had tried to do this, and come back time and time again to petty theft, disobedience, and self-abuse. But when he had to face his father there always seemed to be an infinite number of sins to consider, although lately he had felt as if he might be in a state of grace. First Concrete was not losing money. Maggie had justified John Scanlan's investment in her school tuition by getting the highest average in her class. Connie had actually agreed to attend a card party with the other Scanlan wives. He was trying to figure out why his father wanted to see all of them at once when Mark added, "He said something about some new construction behind your house. I think he's pissed we didn't get any of the contracts. Particularly cement."

"I didn't know a thing about it until all hell broke loose this morning," said Tommy. "The company's in the Bronx. Who says we have to get work in Westchester? We're plenty busy with city work."

"Come to the house on Sunday," said Mark. "What's the harm? The kids can play outside. Maybe he's just trying to be sociable."

"Get real."

"We don't see you enough, anyhow. Gail never sees Connie. She asked her over for bridge last Thursday but she said she couldn't come."

"Connie's not feeling too well."

Mark's mouth narrowed into a bitter line, making him look as if he was trying to hold his teeth in. "What, again?" he finally said.

"Maybe, maybe not. It's too soon to tell."

Below them the cement mixer was still circling the lot. John Scanlan narrowly missed taking the passenger side off his own freshly waxed car as a mechanic backed the Lincoln out of one of the bays. The old man laid on the horn, which gave off a deep throaty honk, like some big water bird.

"I have to go," Mark said. "I'll see you Sunday."

Tommy did not reply. He watched his father climb down from the cement mixer. The old man stopped to talk for a moment to the mechanic, and Tommy saw the man begin to grin and bob his head.

So many people were drawn to John Scanlan—drawn by his power, and by his personality, too; by the big voice, the vigor, the gift he had for colorful language, the sheer force of the man. On the wall behind his desk at Scanlan & Co., he had hung a framed copy of a quotation about Teddy Roosevelt: "The baby at every christening, the bride at every wedding, the corpse at every funeral." No one who knew John Scanlan had to ask what it meant. Anyone who had ever been to a christening, a wedding, a funeral he attended knew he outshone the baby, the bride, the corpse. He could inspire love in an instant from anyone who happened to be in his good graces. It was just that so few people ever were.

Tommy could not remember a time when he had ever been in his father's good graces. As he watched, Mark loped across the parking lot and got into his father's car.

Tommy turned the radio back on. Sinatra was singing "A Foggy Day in London Town," Tommy's favorite song. He closed his office door and sat down at his desk. From his file drawer he took out the photograph of his wife and placed it on one corner of the desk. Another baby. More saddle shoes. Another place at the table to be filled. His stomach had turned sour and his head hurt.

In a half hour, he would go over to Sal's for lunch. He could think things over. Not whether he would go to his father's or not; he'd be there, and he'd have Connie with him, even if it meant another argument. It was a question of what he'd do when he got there. He looked at the photograph, at those beautiful eyes. Another baby. He could only push his father so far. The last time he'd taken him on had been the now unimaginable night when he'd won his wife. Tommy would always think of that as his greatest triumph.

"Shit, what can it be now?" he said, as the strings swelled and Sinatra finished singing.

4

AME THE SEVEN DEADLY SINS," JOHN Scanlan said absently as he stood in the kitchen of his house mixing martinis.

"Sloth," Maggie said. "Gluttony, envy." She stuck her finger into a jar of olives, trying to coax out the three remaining in the bottom. "Avarice," she added. "Lust."

"The twelve apostles."

"John," Maggie began, as she always did.

Her grandfather had something on his mind. She had known it as soon as she'd seen him that morning, his blue eyes dim, as though turned within. For just a moment, when he saw Connie and Tommy enter the house together, Maggie's father's hand held protectively at the small of Connie's back, John's eyes had brightened, blazed, danced. Now he seemed preoccupied.

Maggie had been able to recite the deadly sins since first grade. The apostles were a throwaway question. Most recently her grandfather had asked her to recite from memory the Passion According to St. Mark, and Maggie had been amazed when she had learned it successfully. She was even more amazed to be corrected by her grandfather on two small phrases. When she got home and looked at the New Testament, she had seen that he had been right. She wondered who had made him memorize the Passion; she couldn't imagine anyone making her grandfather do anything.

John filled the glasses from a silver shaker with his initials on it which his wife had purchased because she thought it might make a good heirloom someday. He picked up the matching silver tray and turned to Maggie. "Come into the living room for the entertainment," he said, and his eyes glistened, his wide mouth creased into a humorless tight-lipped grin.

"What entertainment?" Maggie was still going after the olives.

"Ha!" her grandfather said, pushing through the swinging door.

Maggie heard a little stage cough behind her and knew that her cousin Monica had entered the room. She was wearing the moiré taffeta dress with the high waist and enormous puffed sleeves she had worn the week before for her high school graduation. In it she looked beautiful and virginal, her honey-colored hair flipping up on her shoulders, her nails polished the same color as the add-a-pearl necklace her parents had completed as a graduation gift. When Maggie had stopped after the commencement ceremony to congratulate Helen Malone, who had been in the same graduating class as Monica, Helen had smiled slowly and said, "Your cousin wins the award for best disguise." Looking over her shoulder at Monica now, Maggie thought she knew exactly what Helen meant. With her pretty face and her curved smile, Monica looked kind and sweet. She stared at Maggie with the cool, direct look she did so well. Then she looked pointedly at Maggie's fingers in the olive jar. "How attractive," she said, and Maggie withdrew her hand so quickly that the jar toppled over onto the counter, and brine splattered onto her flowered skirt and the linoleum floor. "Most attractive," Monica said, leaving Maggie to clean up the mess and wish she was back home in her shorts.

On Sundays, when Maggie went to her grandparents' house, it was usually with her father. Her mother stayed home with the younger children. Maggie had known everything she needed to know about her mother and her father's family when she had started to page through Tommy and Connie's big white leatherette wedding album when she was four years old. She could never understand what had moved the

photographer to go up into the choir loft, look down, and take a picture
of the congregation, which showed a great massing of relations on the
bride's side of the church and no one behind the groom except his
brothers, the ushers, who had appeared in their cutaways in defiance
of their father's wishes. She could never understand why her mother
chose to put that picture in the album. "It's a sad picture, Mommy,"
Maggie had said once when she was young, before she had begun
quietly to take sides.

"It shows something," her mother had said, her lips closing like a
red metal zipper. Maggie supposed that whatever the something was,
it was long-lived, for her mother came to her in-laws' home only when
a special invitation was issued.

Maggie was there often. She liked the order, the cleanliness and
the smell of polish, smells that were absent from her everyday life. In
her grandmother's living room there was a baby grand piano, a painting
of flowers over the fireplace, a corner cabinet filled with china statues
of characters from Shakespeare, and enormous quantities of brocade
in a color her grandmother called mauve. There was a big kitchen
with geraniums on the wallpaper, and curtains that matched, and a
pantry with glass-fronted cabinets. All the food behind the glass was
arranged in alphabetical order; the family joke was that Mary Frances
Scanlan never served mixed vegetables, because she wouldn't know
whether to file the cans under M or V.

It was the house of people who had money. "Mag, are you rich?"
Debbie had asked her once when they had ridden up the long driveway
on their bicycles, the lawn stretching away on either side. Maggie had
answered, honest as always, "They are. We aren't."

Now the brocade furniture in the living room was full of people.
Her mother was sitting in the corner of the couch, Joseph slumped
against her, his eyes half closed as he sucked his middle fingers. Next
to her mother was her aunt Cass, Monica's mother. Uncle James was
sitting next to his wife.

"Delivered twins last night, Concetta," James said with a grin.

"Oh, God," Connie said, her stomach fighting the martini her
father-in-law had pressed upon her. "That poor woman."

"No, no," said James, waving his left hand, his wedding band sunk a little into the flesh of his finger, "Very easy delivery. Just popped right out, one after another."

"For God's sake," said Mary Frances Scanlan, putting her drink down on a coaster on the coffee table. "It's bad enough, shop talk, but your shop talk is the worst, Jimmy."

"Sorry," said James pleasantly. "All part of life, Mother. No sense denying it."

"No sense discussing it," said Mary Frances as Maggie came in with another tray of drinks. "Maggie, here's your cherry. Come quick or I'll give it to one of your brothers."

Her grandmother held a maraschino cherry by the stem, dangling it, dripping, over her whiskey sour. Maggie always ate the cherry from her grandmother's drink, trying not to feel the bite of the liquor before she got to the syrupy taste of the fruit. Like so many other customs in her family, it had continued long past the time that those involved enjoyed it. In fact, Maggie could not remember that she had ever enjoyed it; it had simply become tradition and could not be tampered with. By the time she had eaten the thing, the back of her tongue was usually numb. For a moment she thought of refusing, but instead she took the cherry and held it over her cupped hand, hoping for a chance to throw it away. She looked across the room and saw Monica smiling at her, and she opened her mouth and popped the whole thing in, stem and all. When she wiped her hands on her skirt, Monica laughed.

"Well, gentlemen," said her grandfather, coming up behind Maggie and lifting his Scotch from amid the martinis on the tray, "The Roman Catholic church is going to hell in a handbasket." John Scanlan had a tendency to choose phrases and stick with them. "Hell in a hand-basket" was one of his favorites.

"Shop talk," said Mary Frances, crossing her legs and pulling at a stray thread on the brocade chair with her index finger and thumb.

"It's shop talk that pays for this house," her husband said. "It's shop talk that pays for that Lincoln Continental and the private schools for all these children."

Maggie heard a sigh from the hallway. Monica had moved back into the shadows.

"And for your orthodontia, miss," John Scanlan said without turning around to look at Monica, whose teeth as a child, before she became perfect, had been as crooked as the tombstones in an old cemetery.

John Scanlan said it nice and evenly, the way he said almost everything else. The oldtimers at the factory always said that it took a man a couple of hours after he'd been fired to take it all in, because John Scanlan said "You're fired" in the afternoon in exactly the voice in which he said "Good morning" each morning. Maggie had noticed lately that it was a good bit like the voice in which she answered catechism questions: Why did God make me? God made me to know Him, to love Him, and to serve Him in this world and to be happy with Him forever in the next.

"Today in church I see four women without hats," he continued. "Without anything on their heads. Never mind those flimsy little black veils that all you girls are wearing"—her grandfather looked over at Maggie, whose rayon mantilla was sitting on top of her little patent handbag on the hall telephone table—"now we've got women bareheaded. Bareheaded! As though they were going to Coney Island instead of the House of the Lord of Hosts.

"This is all because of that woman," he added, meaning the president's widow, who had begun wearing the mantilla to Mass on summer Sundays several years before, "who has probably never given a thought to the millinery industry in her life.

"Similarly, Johnnie, who runs the hat shop on Main Street, tells me that business is bad. Men are not wearing hats anymore, he tells me. Now whose fault is that?"

They all knew the answer. Mary Frances, who was her husband's straight man as well as his wife, sipped her drink, put it down, folded her hands in her lap, and said obediently, "The president."

"Exactly!" John Scanlan slammed his broad flat hand down on the table next to him.

From behind her Maggie could hear Monica sigh again. She looked over at her mother, whose eyes were shiny from alcohol. Connie looked as though she had left her consciousness at home in Kenwood and sent her body on to the Scanlans without her. Maggie realized that that was how her mother always looked when she was around Tommy's family. She also realized that her parents never sat together when they were at John and Mary Frances's house. Maggie's father was sitting on the piano bench across the room.

Variations of this conversation took place every Sunday at the Scanlan house. John hated the Kennedys, whom he saw as a bunch of second-rate Scanlans with too much hair. And he hated what was happening to the Catholic church because of Pope John XXIII, not because, like his contemporaries, he thought the changes were blasphemous, but because he thought they were bad for business. "The two Johns," he called the men he thought responsible for unnecessary change in America, although both were now dead: the boy president and the populist pope.

While all around him in Our Lady of Lourdes people slowly, pain fully adapted themselves to the Mass in English, John Scanlan whispered the Latin. It was disconcerting to share a pew with him. The priest would intone "The Lord be with you," and from John's seat would come a sound, like a snake exhaling, the carrying sibilants of "Dominus vobiscum." Occasionally when they were together her grandfather, a tall handsome man with yellowing white hair, would turn to Maggie and inquire, "Confiteor deo?" and Maggie would be expected to answer "omnipotenti," or, on occasion, to finish the entire prayer. "A plus," Monica sometimes called her, and, like everything else Monica said, the tone was pleasant, the smile ubiquitous, and the meaning mean as hell.

John Scanlan had started manufacturing communion hosts when he was twenty-one, a newlywed with two years of college, eleven younger siblings, and a mother dying of the same lung cancer that had killed her husband ten years before. For a week after he quit school John had thought about growth industries and then he had rented a pressing machine and space in a garage on a back street in the South Bronx and begun to stamp out little wafers of unleavened bread. The Jews who rented him the place thought he was crazy. Two years later he had his own factory and twenty-two employees.

He began to make holy cards, vestments, and assorted communion veils and confirmation robes, and the three sons who worked in the business knew how to market them all: buy from a Catholic. It was as simple as that. John Scanlan's only real competitor had been a company in Illinois owned by a Methodist; the year Maggie was born it had gone out of business, only six months after its founder had gotten drunk at a convention and made a joke about Scanlan & Co., the Irish, and booze.

John Scanlan now had a plant in Manila doing machine embroidery on vestments and altar cloths, a plant in White Plains that employed 160 people, and a not-so-hidden interest in three construction companies, two garment factories, and the cement company for which Tommy worked. He was very, very rich.

He was rich enough to retire and be rich for the rest of his life, but he had no wish to. All he wanted to do was to manage the lives of his children, and to be left alone so he could become richer still. Already there were a few parishes in progressive suburbs which were simplifying their altars and the rites that took place upon them. John Scanlan predicted that by the year 2000 priests would be saying Mass in Bermuda shorts, handing out kaiser rolls at communion, and Scanlan & Co. would be bankrupt.

"Now he'll say 'Then, good-by easy street,' " Maggie thought, looking down at her skirt.

"Then, good-by easy street," said John Scanlan, picking up his drink.

"Pop," said Mark, "we can diversify. We can modify. If the Church decides to simplify the vestments, change the altar cloths, it would take us three days to change the machines over from the old lamb motif to a simple plain cross. The church changes, we change with it."

"We are not talking about embroidery. We are talking about disaster."

"Jesus, why do I bother?" Uncle Mark said, refilling his glass from the cocktail shaker.

"I often wonder the same thing," his father said flatly.

Maggie's father pumped the piano pedals and stayed out of the way. His glass was empty but he made no move to refill it. Connie's glass was still half full. She had a sheen of sweat on her upper lip, which even for early July seemed a bit extravagant.

"Concetta?" said Mary Frances, leaning forward with a pleasant smile, like a woman in a magazine. "Another?"

"No. Thank you. Really," said Maggie's mother, who had never been able to think of a term of address for her mother-in-law and so for thirteen years had called her nothing at all.

"Well, let's talk about Tom here," Mr. Scanlan said, without looking at his middle son. "They're ripping Tom's backyard up. Making a shantytown. I have knowledge of this only secondhand, because no one saw fit to give us any of the contracts for this development. Be that as it may, it will be all over in that part of the world by next year."

"They dug six foundations in one day," Maggie said.

"Good girl," said her grandfather. "Six foundations. Soon it'll be thirty-six. They're planning seventy-two houses for that site, and not houses I'd want to live in. That plasterboard stuff you can put your elbow right through. Maybe even septic tanks. Cheap kitchens. You know the idea: Come live where the other half lives."

"Maybe the development will bring property values up," Tommy said. "Nice new development behind the old houses. Lots of people think those houses are better than the old ones."

"I think they'll be beautiful," said Connie. "I heard they're going to have laundry chutes and garbage disposals in the kitchens. And sunken living rooms and patios."

There was a long silence. Maggie picked at a cuticle and avoided looking at her mother. It was a canon of the Scanlan household that old things were better than new ones. It was not to be argued with, like eating the cherry. Maggie chewed her little finger.

"The first thing a man looks at is your hands," Mary Frances said softly to Maggie, pulling at her granddaughter's fingers, frowning at the dried blood in the corner of each bitten nail.

"I heard they're very nice houses," Connie added, and Maggie could hear the anger in her voice.

"No such thing, little girl. When you see them you'll tell me different. Half basements. Wall-to-wall on slab. Property values over there will land in the toilet. Sheenies to the right of you. Sheenies to the left of you." John took a big sip of his martini and smiled, a smile Maggie noticed was oddly like Monica's. Maggie thought her grand-father's eyes looked like the sapphires in her grandmother's big sapphire-and-diamond earrings. She remembered when she was a little girl thinking that she could see through the blue of her grandfather's eyes into his head, see wheels and cogs and clicking things, like the inside of a watch. She could almost hear the clicking now.

"But you two won't have to worry about all that," John said, pulling something from his pants pocket, tossing it with a grin into Connie's lap, where it made a little metallic sound as it hit her engagement and wedding rings. Maggie turned to her father, but he was looking down at the piano keys. The room was very still.

"Congratulations," Mary Frances said brightly, but still Connie had not lifted her hands from her lap. Joseph murmured softly in his sleep and turned to tuck his head into his mother's side. Finally James said, "Those look like keys to me."

"Oh, brilliant," John said under his breath, and aloud he said, "And the door they open is oak, four inches thick with a mullioned window in it, and the rooms inside, none of them are smaller than twenty by fifteen, not even the kitchen. Six bedrooms, four baths, a fireplace you could stand in in the living room. The prettiest azaleas on the block."

"Remember the Ryans, Tom?" Mary Frances said brightly. "They've moved to Florida. Only three houses down from us. Maggie could walk up the hill to have Saturday lunch with your father."

"We could never afford that house, Mother," Tommy said quietly, and Maggie looked down at her patent-leather shoes, luminous in the half light.

"Bought and paid for," John Scanlan said. "Bought and paid for." Connie raised her head, and Maggie thought her mother's hair looked like patent leather, too, and Connie's voice sounded soft and warm.

"What took you so long?" she said, and she stared right into John Scanlan's eyes, and the room was quiet. Maggie saw her grandfather look right back at Connie, as though there were only the two of them in the room, as though he loved her. "Ah, little girl," he said, "I have the gift of perfect timing."

"We're not moving, Pop," Tommy said, but his father did not look at him.

"We'll discuss it another time," John said, but he still looked deep into Connie's eyes, and he still smiled.

"No," she said, but no one seemed to hear her. Suddenly, as though of one accord, the various Scanlans by birth and by marriage rose and began to gather up their handbags and call to their children. It was as though they had come for something and now it was accomplished. Only Connie remained sitting, staring over at her husband on the piano stool.

"Tom, bring the glasses into the kitchen," Mary Frances said as she walked into the hallway, and Tommy stood up and lifted the tray, his wife watching him silently.

Maggie could hear the sounds of departure and cleaning up as she went upstairs to the bathroom. She heard the front door slam and knew her parents would be waiting for her out in the car, not speaking, the boys bouncing in the back seat.

Monica was in the bedroom at the top of the stairs, looking carefully at her face in one of the mirrors. The room had two single beds with pink spreads, two dressing tables with pink-and-white ruffled skirts, two bureaus, two bride dolls. It was always called the girls' room, but only Maggie's aunt Margaret had ever used it. The other girl was Elizabeth Ann, the Scanlan baby who had died at birth. Sometimes Mary Frances would come up to this room and sit on the bed that was never used, the better one, the one by the window, and she would stare out over the big lawn and the shrubbery like a person struck blind, holding a pillow to her chest. And if Maggie came upon her on those occasions she would beckon her to the bed, and stroke her hair until Maggie's head started to feel numb and her shoulders to cramp. All the time Mary Frances looked far, far away, staring without seeing a thing.

It was just like Monica, Maggie thought, to seat herself carelessly on that bed now, pulling the carefully arranged spread a little awry.

On those few nights when Maggie had slept in this room, she had always been careful not to sleep in, even to sit on, Elizabeth Ann's bed.

"So you're moving," Monica said.

"You heard my mother," Maggie said.

"I heard your mother, and I heard our grandfather. 'Oil and water,' my mother once called them. The oil part was absolutely right for your mother, but I'm not sure about water for Grandpop. I guess your parents are oil and water, too. I guess that's what happens when you meet, get engaged, and get married all in a couple of weeks. Oil and water."

"Shut up, Monica," Maggie said.

Monica turned back to the mirror. "Just think," she said, studying her face. "We'll have a whole week to catch up on things when we go to the beach with Grandmom. My last year going, too, now that I'm out of school." She locked eyes with Maggie in the mirror. "I have so much to tell you. Just the other day, Richard Joseph's older sister was telling me how her brother and all his friends call you a carpenter's dream—flat as a board. I didn't know he was your boyfriend."

Maggie looked down at her skirt. On one side was an olive juice stain, on the other a wet mark made by gin. She sniffed and realized that she smelled strange. Then her head snapped back. She did not want Monica to think she was crying. She started downstairs.

"I can't wait to see your new bathing suit," Monica called after her in her pleasantest voice. "Or your new house."

When Maggie got to the bottom of the stairs, her grandfather was standing in the doorway, looking out upon the great sweep of his lawn, and at the station wagon in the driveway. Maggie stood next to him for a moment, trying to see it as he did. She hoped her mother couldn't see her.

"Your grandmother's right, for once," John Scanlan said, putting his big hand atop her head. "You and I can have lunch together. You've got a lot to learn, little girl. This whole kit and caboodle is going to be what they call an object lesson for you. For some other people, too."

"I don't really want to move, Grandpop," Maggie said.

"Not a question of want, miss. We're talking about a question of need." He put his hand into his pants pocket and took out the keys he had thrown into Connie's lap. "Your mother left these on the couch," he said with a grin. "Give 'em to her."

"I'll give them to my dad."

"Your mother," John Scanlan said. "You heard me. Go on."

5

HE NEXT MORNING MAGGIE WENT TO the Bronx to see her grandfather—her grandfather Mazza, not her grandfather Scanlan. Her grandfather Scanlan tried to stay as far away as possible from New York City, although he had grown up there; he had moved his business to White Plains when he bought the big house in Westchester County, and he always referred to the Bronx as "the godforsaken Bronx." (Brooklyn was "the slum," and Manhattan "that hellhole." Queens, for some odd reason, was "the home of mental midgets." John Scanlan never spoke of Staten Island.) Maggie's grandfather Mazza, on the other hand, had not been out of the Bronx for almost ten years.

Maggie was supposed to take the train to his house, but she usually rode her bicycle, getting off to run beside it as she sprinted across the highways that took people from New York City to New England. She brought her grandfather groceries, and put the brown paper bag, still warm from the sun and the metal mesh of her bicycle basket, on the red table in the middle of the kitchen. Then she put all the groceries away, except for the tomatoes, which she left on the kitchen counter. Once she had forgotten to put the groceries away, and when she came back a week later they were still there, the meat and vegetables giving off a sweet dead smell, the milk and butter high as Gorgonzola cheese. It seemed safer and more proper to dump all the stuff in the can at the end of the drive than to ask her grandfather for an explanation. She knew of no monosyllabic explanation for such a thing, and was sure no polysyllabic explanation would be forthcoming. Her grandfather Mazza preferred contemplation to conversation.

In fact her two grandfathers would have been a perfect match—one a talker, the other a listener—except that they would have had complete disdain for each other's background, work, family and character. No one seemed to find it odd that they had never met.

Angelo Mazza was a small man, very elegant, who always wore a white shirt buttoned to the top button and a pair of beige or pale gray pants tailored by his brother-in-law, a pants maker. When he had arrived from Italy after the First World War, one of his cousins, who had come over earlier, had found him a position as the caretaker of Calvary Cemetery, a Catholic cemetery nearly on the border of Westchester County and the Bronx. Angelo had taken the job until something better came along, but nothing ever did. The job paid a very small salary, and provided him with a tiny stone cottage just within the cemetery gates: a living room, a small dining room, a kitchen, one bedroom downstairs and a very small one upstairs under the eaves. To make ends meet, his wife had taken the subway to the city, as they called Manhattan, to the garment district, where she had been a finisher for ladies' lingerie.

There were some in his family who had thought Angelo would stay single all his life. He was a very private man, the eldest of five, all the other children girls; he had always had his own room, and his mother, who had been a widow almost as long as he could remember, treated him like a prince. But as soon as he had been old enough to grow a mustache his female relatives had been on him constantly, bringing this girl and that girl to the house, the poor young women turning red as they listened to the phony excuses about why they had shown up at this or that particular time. He was forty years old when he finally married. At a party at his sister Rose's he had sat next to a young woman with fat black plaits crossed over her head and a face and shape both bovine. She spoke no English and knew no one at the party; she was a niece visiting a woman down the street, who had been invited merely from politeness because she was a young widow whose husband and two children had died in a flu epidemic in the countryside outside Milan. Angelo had been so moved by the widow's discomfort and fear that he had sat beside her, not talking much, all afternoon, and had gone to her aunt's to have coffee the next day. Three months later they were married.

His only child had once turned to him, after yet another quarrel with her mother about her clothes, her manner, her schoolwork, herself, and asked tearfully, "Why did you marry her?" Angelo had turned away, begun wiping the kitchen counter, then suddenly had turned back and, lifting his silvery head, said in Italian, "Because she needed someone." "Why you?" Connie had screamed back, weeping, the tears falling onto the hands she held against her cheeks. "She needed someone like me," said Angelo, and went outside to his rose-bushes while his daughter sat at the head of the kitchen table and sobbed.

Maggie usually found her grandfather by the rosebushes, kneeling on a square of cotton fabric he kept in his tool closet especially for that purpose. He believed those who tried to tend plants standing up were doomed to failure. He would cultivate carefully around the roots, mix a handful of peat moss in the black topsoil, and occasionally allow his only granddaughter to help him. It saddened him that Maggie's brothers did not seem interested, but secretly he thought of them as Irish children, children with no ties to the earth at all. Maggie he thought of as one of his people.

He never called her Maggie, always Maria Goretti, which was her full name, after the young Italian girl who had been canonized because she fought off a rapist and died rather than capitulate and live. Angelo had always thought Concetta's decision to name the first child so flagrantly was a rebellion against her husband's enormous, ebullient family, but if it had been, then the nickname given her by her grandmother Scanlan had effectively muted the protest. Not even the nuns at school called Maggie by her given name, except when they called her up to get her report card.

"Hi, Grandpop," she said, as she sat on the ground next to him.

"You catch cold," he said.

"Grandpop, it's July. It's too hot to catch cold. The ground is dry. Can I work?"

"You get your tools."

When she came back from the supply closet she went for a moment inside the house to go to the bathroom. As always she opened the door of the medicine cabinet and peered inside, at the small cake of black mascara and the disc of rouge left behind by her mother. In the small bedroom, its ceiling sloped with the roof line, there was also her mother's high school yearbook and a closet full of old clothes: a black suit, a red satin dress with a low neck, a checked dirndl, a peasant blouse. It was stifling on the top floor, and Maggie did not stop to look again at the yearbook picture. She knew it by heart: Concetta Anna Mazza, Chorus, 2, 3, 4; Dance Club 4. And beneath that, in italics, the quotation: "She walks in beauty, like the night."

Outside, over the low stone wall just behind the rose garden, was the neighborhood—blocks of clapboard row houses shining clean and quiet in the sun, like so many others in the North Bronx, the backyards filled with tomato plants and the ornamental urns filled with hydrangeas. No one had ever suggested, however, that there was another cemetery like her grandfather's anywhere else. When Angelo Mazza had taken over the place it had seemed half empty, tombstones only on one side, although a good many of the other plots had been purchased by families moving into the area around it. It had looked a little like a golf course, satisfyingly green and yet a bit austere, with its great metal gates crowned with one enormous cross flanked by two smaller ones. Angelo had gone to work.

On either side of the gates he had planted pink azaleas, and along the fence that separated the cemetery from a back alley and a block of backyards he had put a wisteria, a stick of a thing with three skinny tendrils. Along the fieldstone wall he had planted orange lilies he had found beside a creek one day in Westchester Country, growing wild in mats of green foliage. He put violets around his own front door, which duplicated themselves as fast as field mice, and around back he put the rose garden and a vegetable garden and herb patch. When

Concetta was a little girl he had sometimes taken her upstate for picnics on Sundays, when there were few funerals and her mother liked to rest, and he would dig up wildflowers and roll them in damp sheets of newspaper and plant them when they arrived back home. Angelo had been doing this for nearly forty years, and the result was that in Calvary Cemetery in July there were flowers everywhere. People said it was more wonderful than the Botanical Garden, and once, before Maggie was born, the curator there had even come to talk to him. Her grandfather always told Maggie that the man actually knew surprisingly little about the proper care of plants.

When Maggie knelt down next to him he was working coffee grounds into the soil with his hands. Beside him was a bowl with soap, water, and a sponge, to clean the aphids from the rose bushes. The roses he liked best were white with an edging of bright pink along the petals. There were three bushes behind the house and two on either side of Maggie's grandmother's grave, grown so thick in the three years since the headstone had been put in and the bushes had been planted that only MAZZA in capital letters was visible, the "Anna 1890–1963" and "Angelo 1880–" hidden beneath the leaves of the plants. The grave was in the back, near the wall, and today there was a tan canvas tent not far from it. Paul Fogarty and his mongoloid brother, Leonard, had just finished digging and were standing, sweating, leaning on shovels.

"Who's getting buried?" Maggie said.

"Mrs. Romano," her grandfather said. "She died in her sleep."

"Her daughter was a friend of Mommy's."

"Her niece," Angelo Mazza said, running the sponge down one long green stem, the paler green bugs leaping before him. "This one, only boys."

They worked together under the hot sun for half an hour, but Maggie was restless and her hair kept falling into her eyes. She went inside to wash her hands and pull her hair back from her face with a rubber band, but instead of returning to the plants she began to wander around the cemetery grounds. The older graves were in the back, the pale gray headstones blackening where the letters were cut and the roses were sculpted in the granite. Maggie's landmark had always been an angel on a pedestal, blank-eyed as a blind man, a spray of flowers slanting over one arm as if the angel was a beauty queen, to mark the grave of a woman who had died forty years before. Her grandfather had planted azaleas around its base, but they lasted only through the beginning of May; their white flowers turned mocha-colored, then curled and dropped to the ground. The green leaves of the plants looked as though they were perspiring in the July heat. A man squatted by a monument against the back wall.

"Hello, sweetheart," said Mr. Gennaro, who carved the inscriptions in the stones. "You're getting big. Bigger than your mama, I bet, by now."

"Two inches," said Maggie. "She says I'm a Scanlan."

"Never mind that crap," the old man said, unstrapping his leather tool belt and placing it at the foot of a square pink marble stone with nothing on it but the name JESSUP in capital letters. Maggie remembered that when she was first learning to spell she thought this was the place where Jesus was buried, and she was punished in school for insisting that the Holy Sepulchre was in the Bronx and wasn't half as big as Joe the greengrocer's mausoleum.

"Who's Jessup?" she said.

"Old guy lived a couple blocks up the avenue, over his office. A lawyer. Nice man, no family, did house closings and things during the day, upstairs in three rooms at night. About ten years back the doctor told him he was sick and he came here and picked out a plot. Your grandpop found the guy a nice space. The stone went up about five years ago. I'm doing name, date of birth."

"He's not dead yet?"

"Nah. You know doctors. He wasn't really that sick."

Mr. Gennaro squatted down and began to measure the stone. He pulled a wax pencil from behind one ear, hairy as a coconut, and made a mark here and there. Maggie jiggled her legs.

"You look more like a Mazza than a Scanlan to me," he said after a while, outlining letters with his pencil. "You look a lot like your mama did when she was your age. She was smaller than you are and she didn't have so much hair. But your faces look alike."

"You've been around here a long time," said Maggie, squinting in a shaft of sun that had suddenly cut through the trees, trying to think about a girl her age, looking like her, hanging around the cemetery, jiggling her legs in the light.

"God, yeah," Mr. Gennaro said. "I know your grandfather almost my whole life. Your grandmother, too, may she rest in peace. She was a tough cookie. And your mother. I remember the day she was married. There was a funeral coming in and your mama coming out of the house in her dress, some shiny stuff with all kinds of lace, and she almost got in the wrong limo. You think they look at you funny, a kid in the cemetery, you should have seen the people in that limo when they saw your mother all dressed up like that. Ten o'clock in the morning and they thought they were seeing ghosts. Jesus, she looked beautiful, but so little, like some little bird. I told your grandfather, never mind that the boy's not Italian, that he's an American boy, he's a nice boy, he'll be good to her."

"What did Grandpop say?"

"Jesus," said Mr. Gennaro, letting his rear fall back on his heels, wiping sweat from his forehead with his arm. "I don't remember. Nothing, probably. Your father was a nice boy. I remember one day he was out back with the old man, trying to help with the tomatoes, but your grandpop didn't want nothing to do with him. So your father was talking to me. God, that boy got red in the sun. I thought he was going to have a stroke. And all of a sudden he says to me, 'Mr. Gennaro, I love her with all my heart.' Well, what the hell could you say. It was beautiful. So what if he was an American boy? All you see are Italian names here," he added, his eyes searching the cemetery for an exception and finally coming back to JESSUP. "But you have a lot of Italian boys here married to American girls."

"We're all American," said Maggie a little primly.

"Yeah, well, that's one way of looking at it," said Mr. Gennaro, digging into the marble with his chisel. "Anyway, your parents were a match. Look at all you kids. How's your dad, anyway?"

"Fine, I think," Maggie said. "I think we're moving."

"How come?"

"How come I think it or how come we're doing it?"

"Jesus," said Mr. Gennaro with a grin, "you are some philosopher. Answer both and let's see what happens."

"I think it because my grandfather said we were, and we're doing it because he wants us to."

Mr. Gennaro's smile faded. "Your other grandfather." Maggie nodded. "People aren't always right, and people don't always get their way," he said, looking off into the distance.

"He's not people," Maggie said, but Mr. Gennaro didn't reply.

Maggie watched him work for a minute more and then wandered down Consolation Way, her hands behind her back. It had never occurred to her to think of her parents as human beings before, and particularly as human beings with some secret and tenuous connection to one another. When they danced together, as they had last night, or when occasionally they touched, she had always felt that she was watching something artificial and far away, as though they were in a movie, acting the parts of husband and wife. Until now she had always thought of them in much the same way she thought of the house, as something that allowed her to live.

The night before, she and her brothers had wandered through the field after dinner, counting the holes the construction crew had made, looking into them with a flashlight. Tommy and Connie were sitting on lawn chairs on the patio, and looking back in the darkness Maggie could see them, and see deep into the lighted kitchen of the house, could even see the little trivet over the stove from the Pennsylvania Dutch country that said: No matter where I feed my guests, it seems they like my kitchen best. The bulk of the house was a gray-black shadow, the yellow rectangles of windows floating within its vague borders. Maggie could see twin specks of red near the ground, the tips of her parents' cigarettes, and occasionally the soft murmur of their voices would stop and her father would say loudly, "Be careful out there. I don't want to drive to the emergency room tonight."

Damien had the flashlight, although both Terence and Maggie tried to take it from him; crickets leapt up from beneath his sneakers, and his thin legs flashed in the beam, as though disembodied. "Here's another one," he said, as he came to the edge of another hole; as his

brother and sister edged nearer, afraid of falling in, he let the light
rove around the sides.

"They're not that big," said Maggie. "I thought they'd be a lot bigger
than this."

"Grandpop said they're only half basements and the rest is on slab,"
said Terence.

"They're still not that big," Maggie said.

"There are five of them," Damien said.

"The man in the kitchen said six."

"There was a man in the kitchen?" said Terence.

"Talking to Mom."

"Are you sure?" Terence said. "A man we don't know?"

"I saw him, stupid," said Maggie, running away without thinking
of the holes pocking the fields.

From the back of the street at nighttime you could see into all the
houses, see the blue light of the television and the heads of the people
as they moved about inside. Maggie roamed the perimeter slowly, the
reeds stabbing at her legs, not as a Peeping Tom might, but like
someone looking at pictures in a museum. Other summers, at this
time of day, she would have been cooling off after a game of Kick the
Can or Monkey in the Middle on the street, or catching lightning
bugs in an old mayonnaise jar, or sleeping over at Debbie's house in
Mr. Malone's army issue pup tent pitched in the backyard. All of these
things suddenly seemed dull, but she did not know what else to do
with herself. She sometimes went to the day camp at the park, weaving
key rings out of strips of plastic and making mosaic ashtrays, but after
five years of day camp she was sick to death of key rings and ash trays.
At night she had taken to wandering in the fields, seeing an argument
here, a kiss there. She liked the way the houses looked from the outside
staring in. The air was fresher at night, even though the heat did not
let up much; it felt as though the day was shaking itself out after the
still stuffiness of the afternoon.

Through a side window of her own house she could see that her
parents had moved into the living room. They were standing face to
face, and as she drew nearer she could hear music playing. She rec-

ognized the song and the singer: Frank Sinatra, "Here's that Rainy Day." Tommy Scanlan loved music, and Maggie got a quarter from her father every time she could identify a song after only the opening notes, before anyone sang a word. "Here's that Rainy Day" was her father's second favorite song, after "A Foggy Day in London Town."

Maggie realized her parents were dancing. Their heads turned slowly, and she could see their shoulders swaying in time to the music. Sometimes her father would pull Maggie off the floor to dance with him, but she would stumble and step on his feet and he would become impatient after only a few turns. "You're leading," he would say, and Maggie would say "Who cares?" and leave the room. But Tommy and Connie had met at a dance contest, and they were perfectly partnered. He led effortlessly, and she followed easily. It seemed hard to imagine that the man and woman gliding around the living room were the same two people who often stepped sullenly around each other in the kitchen, bickering over who had forgotten to buy breakfast cereal and whether the screens needed to be washed. Maggie wondered if everyone was really more than one person, like Jekyll and Hyde or the woman in *The Three Faces of Eve*, who changed from one personality into another. She thought that perhaps there was more to the Malones than met the eye, and to her aunt Margaret, and certainly to her cousin Monica, whose manners were flawless as long as anyone over the age of thirty was around. The only people she was sure were exactly what they seemed were her aunt Celeste and Helen Malone. She had often suspected that her parents were not entirely what she saw at the dinner table, particularly since she had learned what it had required for them to conceive four children. Two very different people from the ones she knew would have had to be involved in that. She watched carefully as they spun silently to the music. She suspected she was watching those two people now, and the blood rose up into her sweaty face, heat upon heat.

Behind her Damien and Terence were approaching, making much too much noise. "Shut up," she whispered, all consonants, and they did, peering over her shoulder. "I think Mom is prettier than aunt Celeste," said Damien, who still sometimes liked to climb into Connie's lap and wordlessly touch her hair and face. "I do, too," said Maggie, and the boys looked surprised, for Maggie was critical of everyone, particularly those she knew best.

"They're kissing," said Terence softly, his *sss* whistling in a quiet lull in the music.

"They're not kissing, they're dancing," Maggie said.

"They're allowed to kiss," said Damien loudly, turning the flashlight on and shining it in Maggie's face. "They're married."

Maggie knocked the light from his hands and both boys scrambled out into the backyard to grab it. "Maggie," Damien whined, "it's gone." "Shut up," Maggie said. The music stopped and suddenly the buzz of the crickets sounded very loud and harsh, as though they were somehow predatory. Maggie heard her father mumble something, and then Connie replied loudly, "Tell me, please, that I'm not hearing what I think I'm hearing."

"Maggie," Damien whined again, his voice faint, calling from the end of the yard. Maggie leaned closer to the screen. "Over my dead body," Connie said, pulling away, but Maggie saw her father's stringy forearms tighten and hold her fast. Connie beat her little fists against his chest, and he laid his sandy head on her dark one.

Damien and Terence were behind Maggie. "You broke the flashlight," Damien said sadly, pushing the switch back and forth with his thumb, which was red and chapped from his incessant sucking. "It's time to go in," Maggie said, and as she moved to the screen door and opened it, the boys could see their parents move apart, their mother smooth her hair. Their father walked through to the kitchen. "Tell your brothers to come in," he said to Maggie as he opened the refrigerator. In its white glow his pale skin was mottled pink. He reached for a beer and held the bottle against his forehead. Terence and Damien stood outside the screen door peering in, seeing him through the wire mesh as though he was on television. "Don't just stand there," Tommy said impatiently as he looked over and saw them, Terence's mouth a little open, Damien's fair skin flushed pinker than his own. "Come on in and go to bed."

When Maggie went into the living room it was empty, and she wondered where her mother had gone. She had not wondered what her parents had been talking about; a distance, filled by the charged electricity of married people on the verge of a fight, had been between them in the car all the way home on Sunday. For the first time Maggie realized it was sensible for her mother to stay away from the Scanlans. Her grandfather Scanlan's house was always full of discord. Her grandfather Mazza's was the most peaceful place in the world. But her mother never came here, either. Maggie supposed that, like other people, Connie saw a cemetery only as a place of death.

As Maggie went back and knelt beside her grandfather, a hearse, familiar as a station wagon, swung past the house and down Nazareth Way to the back plots. Behind it was the flower car, piled high with gladiolus. Angelo Mazza's eyelids drooped. He hated cut flowers, but his emotions were always just a flicker across his face. From inside the lead limousine someone lifted a hand to him. Maggie made the sign of the cross.

"Not so many cars for the old people," Angelo said, as a dozen cars followed, their headlights shining faintly in the bright sunshine.

"What about Mrs. Romano's boys?"

"Two killed in the war, one a heart attack at Mass five years ago. One left, he lives far away."

Across the stretch of lawn Maggie could see people begin to emerge from their cars, the view interrupted only by the DiGenova family's obelisk and the mausoleum with the Good Shepherd stained-glass window in which the Lisa family were buried. A priest, she could not tell which one, took his place and opened his black leatherbound missal, a purple stole slung round his hunched shoulders. "In the name of the Father and of the Son and of the Holy Spirit," he said, and everyone made the sign of the cross in unison.

Two men in dark-gray suits stood apart from the mourners. They turned and looked across at the Mazza house, their hands folded in front of them. ". . . Gives me the creeps," Maggie heard one say, and knew they were talking about her again, and about the unseemliness of children in cemeteries.

"Why did the Romanos go to the O'Neal's funeral home to get buried?" she asked.

"No Italian funeral homes," her grandfather said.

One of the men, the older, balder one, walked across to the road and down it toward them. He wore on his face a carefully arranged smile of welcome. "Angelo," he said, in the voice of a professional greeter, oily and loud, pulling a breath mint from his pocket and popping it into his mouth as he towered over Maggie and her grandfather.

"Hi, Mr. O'Neal," Maggie said. "How's Cathy?"

"She's fine, honey, fine," Matthew O'Neal said, lowering his voice so he couldn't be heard by the group under the tent. "Misses the girls at Sacred Heart, that's for sure."

"Does she like her new school? Mrs. Malone told me there's a pool and tennis."

"There is, there is," he said, sucking on the mint.

"Tell her I said hi," said Maggie, although she disliked Cathy O'Neal, who was chubby and wore her hair in sausage curls and who told patently fantastic stories about the goings-on in the preparation room on the third floor of the O'Neal Home for Funerals.

"I will," said Mr. O'Neal. "And my best to your grandfather," he added, meaning her grandfather Scanlan.

Turning to her other grandfather, who was still kneeling in front of the roses, he said, "Mrs. Romano's son was very concerned about the vines behind his mother's grave. He thinks they really may come right over the stone."

"I will prune," Angelo said flatly.

"The plants are bothersome to quite a lot of people," said Mr. O'Neal. "It's the idea of them." Maggie knew what he meant. People hated to think about what went on underground in a cemetery. When people looked at the lush growth and strong colors of Angelo's plants, they could conclude only one thing.

"Good soil," said Maggie's grandfather, echoing her thoughts, his eyes gleaming in the sunlight.

"Yes." Mr. O'Neal clasped his hands behind him, then in front again. He sighed. He and Angelo had had this discussion before.

The fact was that there were very few of his customers who complained about the luxuriant growth in Calvary Cemetery, just as he had been exaggerating when he had told Angelo years before that people didn't like to see Maggie hanging around, chewing on the ends of her braids, popping up from behind tombstones like an apparition in a gingham blouse and shorts. He was the one bothered by these things. He always thought that the child's odd behavior, her air of watchfulness, was an object lesson in what happened when you mixed blood that wasn't meant to be mixed, although no one could deny that she'd gotten the Scanlan brains, walking away with all the honors in her class year after year. But Matthew O'Neal knew his business, even if his daughter couldn't master fractions, and he knew that cemeteries were not supposed to be turned into gardens, nor children permitted there. Once at a Friendly Sons of St. Patrick testimonial he had made some comments to John Scanlan about how pleasant it was to see Maria Goretti around Calvary and what a change of pace it made. But John had only chewed purposefully at the end of a large cigar and looked at him narrowly, as though he knew that the tone did not match the message. When Matthew O'Neal moved off to refill his drink, he heard John Scanlan say in the sudden silence, "Goddamn ghoul," and then the low murmur of conversation began again.

"Give my best to your grandfather, Maggie," Mr. O'Neal said, as he turned to walk back to the group at the graveside, who were passing their rosaries through their fingers. Without answering him, grandfather and granddaughter bent again over the black soil, the rims of their fingernails edged with earth.

6

HE CHILDREN WERE ALL AT THE TABLE, its mottled red Formica dense with cereal bowls and Fred Flintstone cups, when Connie went out into the backyard to watch the construction crew begin their work. She could sense rather than hear Maggie and Terence squabbling, and she heard the clatter at the sink as Tommy went rooting around on the counter for a spoon for his coffee. She was holding her own cup, cradling it in her hands as though to keep herself warm. The sun was still climbing the horizon behind her, and her knees and elbows felt cool in her plaid shorts and white shirt.

Little by little over the years she had begun to dress more like Tommy's sister and sisters-in-law, more like a Catholic private school girl and less like a girl from a tough public school where the Italian boys wore shirts so starched they could stand up by themselves. Only in her evening dresses and her evening makeup, both always black or red, did she look like her old self. A man waved, circling closer on a big tractor: it was Joey, wearing work clothes and a hard hat, protective plastic glasses on a strip of elastic dangling around his neck. Connie waved back and then turned and went into the house, shivering a little, stumbling on the stones and weeds that gave way to the feeble grass of their backyard. She was still smiling as she came in.

"That's Joey Martinelli," she said to Tommy, dropping into her seat next to Joseph's chair. "Jimmy Martinelli's older brother. I knew him in school. He's the supervisor on this construction project."

"Mommy says he's a friend of ours," Maggie said.

"Not mine," said Tom.

"He says they expect to have the models by the first week in September," Connie added.

"He's nuts," Tommy said, pouring coffee.

"Just three models," said Connie. "There's one that's a ranch house and another that's a split-level and another that's a Colonial like this."

"Not like this," Tommy said.

"Please, Tom," Connie said, "I don't want to listen again to how terrible new houses are. I just thought you would want to know."

"How did he know we live here?" Tommy said.

"He didn't. He came up to use the phone one day and picked our house out of a clear blue sky. I saw him out back before, and went over to say hello and take him a cup of coffee."

Tommy's own mug was half full. "There wasn't enough goddamn coffee for me," he said.

"Tom."

"Don't 'Tom' me," he shouted over the noise from the construction site. "I don't eat any goddamn breakfast. I have one cup of coffee in the morning. I want my one cup of coffee."

"I'll make another pot," Connie said.

Tommy walked to the swinging kitchen door. Then he went out to the hall, took his jacket and tie off the banister, and was gone. The half-cup of coffee sat untasted on the table. The children could not even hear the door slam, although Maggie was sure it had. "Grandpop's right," she said. "Those things are really loud."

Connie did not say anything. She was looking out the kitchen window and washing the coffee pot, but her shoulders rose and fell as though she sighed. She stood there for a long time as the children disappeared one by one, Maggie to the Malones, Terence and Damien to the ballfield, Joseph into the dining room, where he put a ball of crumpled paper into a plastic cup and took it out again.

Connie was tired. She had finally gotten the curtains she liked on the kitchen windows, and now she was afraid she was going to have to pick up and move to some house she had never seen before, a house even farther away from its neighbors than the one she lived in now, even more mired in silence. She would never have enough furniture for a house that size, and she pictured little excursions to furniture stores with Mary Frances, the two of them holding swatches of brocade, her mother-in-law arguing about price.

She realized she had been standing at the sink a long time, washing dishes mechanically, only when the earth movers stopped and the cement trucks arrived outside. Connie could tell by the insignia on the side of their doors that they were from an Italian firm that was one of Tommy's biggest competitors. He always contended that they were owned by the Mafia, as though murder and extortion were the only way Italians could make money, and this enraged Connie, although her uncle Frank said they were Mafia, too. A truck had pulled a long low trailer to one end of the field, and the workmen gathered around it, unscrewing the lids of their thermoses, faint plumes of steam rising from the openings. One passed around a white cardboard box. She could hear the sound of their voices but not their words. Coffee break. She plugged in the percolator and started another pot.

She had tried to talk to Tommy about the new house, but it had been useless. When he was home the children were there, and when the children were asleep Connie had usually fallen asleep, too, her eyes running wild beneath their translucent lids in the fitful sleep of the exhausted.

Celeste had always told her that she had gotten out of her own marriage just in time, even though it had lasted only a year; she had gotten out when they were still talking to one another, even though most of the talking was yelling. It had taken Connie a while to understand what her cousin meant, but now she thought she did. Occasionally in the car she would look over and see another couple in the next lane, sharing the front seat, both of them staring through the windshield, looking straight ahead, saying nothing. Until recently she had not noticed that she and Tommy were doing the same.

It was not that she did not love him. It was just that she felt as if they were in separate cars, metal and glass surrounding them, oblivious to each other's sounds. She assumed they had the same destination, but it seemed futile now even to ask. So much had been left unspoken in their marriage, and now they were speechless. She thought that if they moved to the house her father-in-law had bought, they would never hear each other speak again.

She reached out to touch her curtains. "I'm staying here," she said, as though saying it aloud would make it so, and she felt a surge of rage so great that it seemed ready to cripple her. "Goddamnit," she said softly, and then she repeated it, louder. "Goddamnit. *I am staying here.* I don't care where the rest of them go. I am staying here." Tears began to run down her face, the hot tears of rage. She pictured her husband, her children, the chairs and beds and sheets and towels, carted off to the big new house, and she there, alone, in the empty rooms. It was better than imagining herself in those other rooms, none of them smaller than twenty by fifteen, held hostage by John Scanlan.

After a few minutes Joey Martinelli emerged from the trailer and began to walk across the fields. The workmen stared at his back, and fell silent. Even if she had not seen the coffee mug hanging by its handle on his index finger, Connie would have known he was coming to her house. As he got closer he looked up and smiled at her.

"You didn't have to bring it back right away," Connie said, opening the back screen door and standing aside to let him in.

"I figured you might want it," he said, holding out the mug. "I know you girls. My mother has a row of little hooks inside the cabinets to hang the cups. If one hook is empty, it drives her crazy."

Connie wished her life was that orderly. She could not remember the last time she had bothered to hang the coffee mugs from the little hooks inside her cabinets. "I always liked your mother," Connie said. "She used to bring cake at Christmas."

"She still brings it to your father," Joey said. "She's convinced he's starving to death. She used to bring him over little things, gravy, chicken, whatever. One of her girlfriends passed some remark about how she was trying to catch another husband, so she stopped doing it. She says your girl takes care of him anyway."

"Maria Goretti."

"The skinny kid, right? With all the hair? She looks something like you but not too much."

"I don't know who they look like," Connie said. "Come on in and have a roll."

"I just ate," he said, "but I'll take some more coffee."

He sat down at the Formica table and Connie was sorry to see that it still had rings on it from breakfast. She poured coffee into the mug he had returned and put a doughnut on the plate.

"Your husband is in construction?" Joe said.

"Tommy," said Connie. "He runs a company called First Concrete."

"With the striped trucks. They're pretty good. Expensive. His old man owns it."

"I didn't know everybody knew that," Connie said, sitting down opposite him.

"His old man owns everything," said Joe, wrapping his hands around his coffee cup, and when he saw her face, he added, "Sorry."

"No, it's all right," Connie said. "Tommy's sort of the black sheep. You know. Because of me."

"No, really?" said Joe, who knew that this was true because everyone in his mother's neighborhood said so. He flexed his fingers and studied them as he added, "He got the prize. I know some of the other wives, from dances and stuff. Real Irish girls. Freckles, piano legs, no chest. He got the prize."

Connie felt the flush begin on her throat. Her lips buzzed with the blood inside them. Finally Joey looked right at her and added, "You were always so pretty," as though he dared her to contradict him.

"Your brother Jimmy have kids?" Connie finally said, when her breath came back.

"Three," said Joe, and as if on cue Joseph toddled in from the dining room. "Bear," he shouted, holding his tattered brown bear aloft.

"Thanks," Joe said, reaching for the toy, but the baby pulled it back. "No, no," he said, and Connie lifted him up and kissed his head. "Bear is his security blanket," she said. "He can't go anywhere without Bear. Are you ready for a nap, JoJo?" she added.

"No," Joseph said.

"I gotta go anyhow," Joey Martinelli said, standing and putting his cup in the sink. "When am I going to teach you to drive?"

"You don't have to do that," Connie said. "I wouldn't have told you I didn't know how if I knew you were going to think you had to give me driving lessons."

"No, really, it'll be fun. I taught my brother. I taught my cousins. We'll find a parking lot somewhere and you can drive around in circles. I don't know, we might have to find you a phone book to sit on, but I can have you driving in a couple of weeks if you want."

Connie was surprised at herself as she said, "Okay, if you don't mind. I'd really like to get out more. Just do my own shopping, take the kids places, go and see my cousin."

"So tomorrow at four I'll come and we can start. We'll put the baby in the back seat. Deal?"

Connie smiled. "Deal." He stuck out his hand and they shook, the little boy between them. It was an oddly comforting gesture. "Jeez," he said, looking down, "you have the littlest hands of any girl I ever knew." He opened his big fist and there it was, lying on his palm as though, Connie thought, it was displayed on a pillow. She pulled her hand away and thrust it deep into the pocket of her shorts.

"Tomorrow," Joey said, as he let himself out the back door.

When he was gone Connie hung all the coffee cups on their hooks in the cabinet, and then took Joseph upstairs for his nap. In the upstairs hallway she stood on tiptoe to look at herself in the mirror. All the mirrors were hung at Tommy's height, so that the bottom half of her own face, her mouth and chin, were always invisible. She thought perhaps she should get her hair cut. "I'm staying right here," she said to herself, only half aloud, and wondered as she went downstairs what it would be like to know how to drive, to go wherever you wanted to go whenever you wanted to go there.

7

O N WEDNESDAY MORNING MAGGIE WAS sitting on the front steps when her aunt Celeste arrived. Damien had collected cicadas in a shoe box, surrounding them with tiny tufts of grass and a collection of sticks, and now he wanted to name them. Once he had used up Matthew, Mark, Luke, John, Mickey, Donald and Pluto, he had come to Maggie for help. The two of them argued; she suggested some girls' names and Damien was sure that all cicadas were boys. When Celeste pulled up in front of the house in her red car, the one with the pleated silver fins, Damien appealed to her for support. She took one look at the bugs, their iridescent backs gleaming in the sun, their squat bullet bodies motionless amid the grass and sticks, and said, "Those are male animals." Then she opened the screen door and let herself in. Maggie left Damien talking to the bugs and went inside.

Celeste was not really Maggie's aunt, but her mother's first cousin and closest friend; the two women had been like sisters growing up, the only sister Connie was likely to get, the closest person to her as she grew older. Celeste came once a week in the summer, when business was slow. She brought a shopping bag filled with clothes and costume jewelry for her cousin Connie ("poor Connie," she always said with a sigh) and play makeup for Maggie, which Connie took away and hid on the top shelf of her closet, between the douche bag and the copy of *Tropic of Cancer*. "This is the new you," Celeste would announce, pulling Capri pants and a blouse with low ruffled shoulders out of the bag. Then she would force Connie to put on the clothes and a pair of hoop earrings and walk around the living room until they both would laugh so hard Celeste would cry, "I'm going to pee myself," and run off to the bathroom, little rivulets of mascara running into the lines around her eyes. Maggie never saw her mother wear the clothes Celeste brought after the first time she tried them on; they stayed in her bottom drawer, smelling of sizing. They were not Scanlan clothes.

"What do you think, Mag?" Connie said, twirling around on her tiny feet, forgetting herself.

"I don't know," Maggie said glumly, which was half the truth, the other half being that Connie looked lovely in an odd, eccentric way, like a Gypsy princess.

"Oh, don't be such an old woman," her mother said. "Ce, come here. Your goddaughter disapproves of me."

"Oh my God," Celeste said, smoothing down her skirt as she returned from the bathroom. "My poor bladder. You girls."

Celeste was the only person Maggie knew who was divorced. She had gotten married the year before Connie and Tommy, to a school friend of Tommy's named Charlie Black, who drank. It wasn't the drinking that had made her finally leave, although that was a convenient excuse; it wasn't even the fact that all Celeste's Max Factor pancake could not conceal her bruises on Sunday mornings at Mass. Maggie had heard her once tell Connie that what got to her was the basic boredom of it all, the sameness of sitting around every evening watching Charlie drink beer in his leatherette recliner, his hair flopping over his forehead, his T-shirt yellow beneath the armpits. Every morning Celeste would clean her house, do her laundry, start dinner, talk to her mother on the telephone, walk the poodle, take off her nail polish, put on a different color, watch her little stories on television, and be finished and bored to tears by three in the afternoon. She knew she should have figured this out beforehand; when she thought about it, she had told Connie, she realized that the beginning of life was one great event after another, your first bra and first date and first kiss, your proms and dances and finally your wedding, and then suddenly there was nothing to do for the rest of your life. In the beginning she always went to see Connie in the afternoon, particularly when Connie and Tommy were living in Celeste's mother's house, in Celeste's old room. But after the baby was born Connie was too busy to talk.

Six months after Maggie arrived, Celeste got on the train one day, without a clue as to where she was going, and got off at Times Square. She entered four office buildings, filled out four job applications, and was hired immediately as a secretary. When she got home and told Charlie, he knocked out her right front incisor and threw the poodle out the second-story window. Without a word (she told Connie she couldn't really talk because of the tooth) she packed her vanity case and went home to her old room. Tommy and Connie had moved the month before to Westchester.

Celeste still lived at home, in a kind of extended adolescence in which she spent all her salary on clothes and makeup and spent a lot of time criticizing her mother's cooking. Like Connie, she was a showy combination of black and white, dark hair and white skin, but she was big and getting bigger, a big hefty woman with a big shelf of a bust. When she walked through the garment district to her current job as executive secretary to the president of a blouse company, the Puerto Rican boys who pushed the racks of clothes from building to building would smack their lips and call her "Mama." She pretended not to notice, but she really didn't mind.

"So I think I'm getting married again," Celeste said, settling back in a chair with a cup of coffee.

"Uh huh," Connie said. "Tell me another."

"Honest to God," she said, staring down at the large pear-shaped diamond, yellow as an egg yolk, which she now wore on her right hand and which was the only memento of her last engagement. Maggie had heard one of her Scanlan aunts say that Celeste had the largest collection of yellow diamonds in the world, and when Maggie asked her mother if this was true, Connie only said "That bitch" and slammed out of the room.

"Why do you want to get married? You have everything. You make a good living, have a nice house, privacy, freedom. You've got everything you had in high school except you're old enough to enjoy it. Besides, you hated being married."

"I don't have kids."

"Kids," said Connie. "You're a kid. Besides, it would kill your mother. Can you imagine your mother if you had to be married by a judge or something? Or a rabbi? She'd have a stroke."

Celeste's current boyfriend was a Jew. All of her boyfriends since her divorce had been Jewish. She said it was a well-known fact that Jews did not hit women.

"I know a nice Italian guy I could fix you up with."

"You? Who? Get out."

"Really. Remember Jimmy Martinelli that I used to date? Remember—you were in class with his cousin Anna Maria?"

"The one with the glasses? And the nose?"

"Well, his brother Joseph is working on this construction they're doing here, on the development—"

"Oh Jesus, Con," Celeste said, lighting a cigarette. "My mother is always trying to fix me up with that guy. He's never been married, right? So what's wrong with him? He's like me—can't live with them, can't live without them."

"I think he's shy," Connie said, reaching over and taking Celeste's cigarette and using it to light her own, a gesture Maggie thought was the height of sophistication. She leaned forward to watch her mother pull in on the cigarette, her cheeks filling and deflating like those of a little animal. Connie looked up and saw Maggie staring at her. "Aren't you going swimming?" she said.

"I guess," said Maggie.

"Well, have a good time."

Maggie did not move.

"Vamoose, kid," said Celeste. "I hope you like your lip pomade." She put her cheek out for a continental kiss. "You smell good," Maggie said. "Tabu," said Celeste. "That's what Monica wears," Maggie said. "Shit," answered her aunt. "Celeste!" said Connie.

Maggie went upstairs to get her bathing suit and towel. Her face still smelled like perfume on one side; whenever she turned her head she got a whiff of it, making her feel grown-up and a little bad.

Her room was the nicest one in the house. It had gingham curtains at the window and a gingham spread on the canopy bed, a bulletin board over the desk, and a little dressing table with a gingham skirt. It was like a magazine photograph of a little girl's room; in fact her mother had painstakingly copied it out of a magazine when Maggie was still young enough to be sleeping in a crib. On the floor next to her bed was an old yellow-and-brown striped suitcase filled with the clothes she was taking to the beach. In the middle of July each summer, Mary Frances took all her female grandchildren of a certain age to a seaside town called South Beach. She thought of this as a great excursion they would remember the rest of their lives. Maggie thought of it as sharing a bedroom with Monica for a week. She remembered that there had been times when she was very young when the trip had actually been fun—the restaurant meals, the hotel sheets smelling of starch, the long days jumping breakers on the beach. Now all she could think of was Monica looking her up and down with that smile.

She heard heavy footsteps on the stairs and started to close her door when she saw it was Celeste. Her aunt was carrying a brown bag and grinning. She slipped inside and closed the door. "Santa Claus is coming to town," she said, picking a piece of tobacco from her smile with the end of one long fingernail. She reached inside the bag and pulled out a jumble of green-and-orange print fabric and spread it on the bed. It was a two-piece bathing suit, the top strapless, with small arcs of bone inside so that it looked as if there was a bust in it, even lying there on the bed. Celeste turned the bottom over. The back was covered with row upon row of tiny ruffles. It was the showiest bathing suit Maggie had ever seen, and she could tell by looking at it that it was just her size.

Celeste suddenly seemed embarrassed by her own audacity. She winked at Maggie. "Can't go to the beach looking like Shirley Temple when you're really Lana Turner," she said, while Maggie tried to remember which one Lana Turner was. She looked down at the suitcase open on the floor. "That's the bag your mother took on her honeymoon," Celeste said. "I remember because I filled it with rice. God, she just about killed me. She told me she pulled out her peignoir that first night and the place looked like a Chinese restaurant." Celeste's eyes grew thoughtful. "Anyhow, wear this in good health, kiddo. I'm not sure it's the kind of suit you want to do the breaststroke in. For one thing, you might lose the top. But I can guarantee that everybody will look twice at it." She kissed Maggie on the cheek and moved to the door, crumpling the bag as she went. "Go easy on your old mom," she said. "She's having a tough time these days."

"Why?" said Maggie, holding the suit against her chest.

"One thing and another."

"Grandpop says she has to get on board," Maggie said.

"Sometimes I wish somebody would squish your grandfather like one of those bugs your brother's got outside," Celeste said. "He thinks he can run everybody's life."

"He does run everybody's life," Maggie said.

"I'd like to see him try that shit with me," Celeste said. "Do me a favor—don't tell your mother I said shit, don't tell her we had this discussion, and don't listen to everything your grandfather says." Celeste licked her finger and patted down one of her spit curls. "I'll leave you alone so you can try that thing on."

When she was gone Maggie closed the door again and slipped out of her shorts and shirt. With her back to the mirror she put on the bathing suit, tugging the top into place, exhaling exaggeratedly to find out if it would stay up without effort. Finally she turned toward the mirror. The suit was a perfect fit. The green turned her eyes the color of lime LifeSavers; the ruffles made her look as if she had hips, and the bones in the bodice made her look as if she had a bust. She looked down. If she was careful, no one would be able to tell that there were two inches of open space between the top and her own chest. She held her arms out and twirled in front of the mirror.

Downstairs she heard Damien calling, "Maggie." She ran to the door and threw her back against it. "Go away, Dame," she called, and after a minute she could hear the staccato sound of his sneakers running outside. She went back to the mirror and put her hands on her hips.

From below her bedroom window she heard voices, and looking out she saw her mother standing in the grass, her arms crossed on her chest. She seemed very small, and Maggie felt as if she were looking at her through the wrong end of a telescope. She realized that these days she was always seeing her mother from a distance, as if in pictures—framed in a window, frozen in some pose, her face revealed in some essential way. Just yesterday she had come silently into the dining room on bare feet and seen Connie through the door leading to the kitchen, leaning back against the counter, flushed and radiant. Maggie had suddenly thought that her mother looked beautiful, young, more wondrous than Helen Malone. For a moment she had been stunned by her mother's likeness to someone she could not quite place. And then she had realized that the resemblance was to the picture on her grandfather Mazza's bureau, in the gold frame next to the clothed statue of the Infant Jesus of Prague, the picture of Concetta Mazza at her high school graduation, with black fabric draped round her bare shoulders and a self-conscious happy look on her face, walking in beauty like the night.

Then Maggie had moved, and her mother had moved, and the moment had been over. That was when she saw the man in the kitchen.

"Here's the big girl," he had said, in a false voice. "I'm Mr. Martinelli. I know your grandfather."

"Which one?" Maggie had said, as she sat down at the table and pushed away the coffee cups.

"The Italian one," he said in Italian, and Connie turned and said in the same language, "She can't speak it. You know, they forget. She never hears it." Maggie understood most of what they were saying, but she just sat with her head down, her hair falling around her face.

"I'm going to teach your mother to drive," the man said in the same false voice, smiling at Maggie again, his fingers tapping on a key lying near the edge of the kitchen table.

"Why?" Maggie longed to grab hold of his eyebrows and pull, and reddened at the thought.

"Why not?" Connie said, and Maggie shrugged. She knew that she had cast a pall over the kitchen, but she did not care. "Aren't you finished work?" Maggie said to Mr. Martinelli, suddenly aware that it was quiet out back as Connie began gathering up the dishes.

"I'm leaving," he said. "But I'll see you again."

"I'm going to the beach next week," said Maggie defiantly, but when she looked up and saw his face she realized he had been talking to her mother.

"Is he the one you went to the dance with?" Maggie said after he had gone out the back door, and Connie turned and asked "Who told you about that?"

"Celeste."

"Aunt Celeste. No, it was his brother. Joe was too old. Four years older than me."

"He's really old," said Maggie.

Her mother made a sound like a snort and continued to wash the cups. Joseph shrieked from the playpen on the patio and Maggie went outside to see him. "JoJo, JoJo," she crooned, and the baby grabbed her long hair and stuck it into his mouth. She carried him in on her hip. "He's hungry," she said, putting him in his high chair, and then she saw that her mother was being sick in the sink, and she stood and stared and then got a banana and began to mash it in a bowl for the baby. After Connie had wiped her mouth and taken a drink, Maggie said, "Does Daddy know?"

Connie's eyes looked enormous. "What?" she said.

"That you're going to learn to drive."

"Oh. That. No, I think I'll make it a surprise."

Maggie had looked up from feeding Joseph. "It'll be a surprise, all right," she had said. "When are we moving?"

"What?"

"When are we moving into the new house?"

"We're not moving. This is our house." Connie's face was very pale and there were gray circles beneath her eyes. "I don't know where you got the idea that we're moving."

"Grandpop bought us a bigger house. He gave you keys and everything. He says it has a basketball hoop and a little room over the garage I can have for myself."

Connie dried her hands on a dishtowel. "Whose side are you on?"

Maggie felt she was going to be sick, too, and wondered if it was just the sharp vinegar smell lingering in the kitchen. "I didn't know there were sides," she said.

"Never mind," Connie said. "I shouldn't have said that. We're not moving."

"Are you sure?" Maggie said.

"We are not moving," said Connie in a trembling voice, and Maggie had taken Joseph out of his chair and back to the patio.

Out on the patio now, Celeste stepped into the sun, a Pall Mall glowing white against the blood red of her lacquered nails. She followed Connie onto the lawn, off balance because the heels of her shoes had sunk into the dirt. They had their backs to her, but Maggie could hear snatches of what they were saying. Celeste threw back her head and, her mouth working like a fish out of water, blew a chain of smoke rings into the still air. Suddenly she turned to Connie and said loudly, "We've all gotta grow up sometime, Con."

"So when is it your turn?"

"I'm as grown as I'm gonna get. Here's the God's truth—you're more of a kid than I am, never mind the husband and the four kids and the house. You need to start acting like the mother of a growing girl, not just living in a dream world."

"I was never a kid, Cece. How come I was never a kid? It's not fair."

"You're right," Celeste said. "But you got no choice now, sweetheart. You gotta hold this family together."

"I thought the man held the family together."

Celeste blew more smoke rings. "There's only one thing men hold, and that's when they got to go to the bathroom. All right, sorry,"

Celeste added, seeing her cousin's face. "But sometimes I think you watch too many movies. Your daughter needs you now."

"She doesn't like me, Ce."

"Get out," Celeste said, dropping her cigarette into the grass and rubbing it out with the pointed toe of her shoe. "What's to like? You're her mother. Did you like your mother? Do I like my mother? You need to show her things. Remember how old Rose slapped me when I first got the curse? Boom! 'It's an old Italian custom,' she says. I should have thanked her for preparing me for Charlie."

Connie did not answer. She had her arms wrapped around herself as though she was holding her body together. Maggie could see the construction crew on their lunch break; the two women gave them a little wave, and the men waved back. Maggie moved away from the screen, afraid someone would see her. Celeste put her arm around Connie's shoulder, and they stood that way for what seemed like a long time: Celeste holding Connie, Connie's head of black curls on her shoulder, Maggie holding back the sheer white curtains beneath the pink gingham ones. Then one of the men yelled "Back to the grind!" and the women turned and went indoors. Maggie saw that her mother's face was wet and her long nose a little shiny, and she heard her say softly, her voice breaking, "They're gonna win, Cece. I can feel it. Ten years from now I'll be living in one of their houses, sitting on their furniture, wearing their clothes, and my kids will be their kids. She's already one of them."

"Don't overreact, sweetheart," Celeste said. "You got the ace in the hole. If your husband has to chose between you and them, he'd choose you every time. He already did it when it mattered."

"And what if my daughter has to choose between me and them, Cece? It's not as simple as Cinderella anymore."

"Hey, honey," Celeste said. "This isn't like you. You having your friend, or what? The curse upon you? You and me, we always were on the same schedule."

Maggie heard her mother laugh, high and a little shaky, and saw Celeste smooth her hair.

"I wish," Connie said, with an odd shrillness in her voice.

"Oh, shit," Celeste said, stopping and looking down at her cousin. "Not again. Can't you count?" Maggie wondered what they were talking about, and as she looked down at her mother her eyes began to brim with tears, for no reason she could figure out except that her mother was crying, too.

8

O N THE FOURTH DAY OF THEIR ANNUAL trip to the beach, the Scanlan women had their photograph taken at Cap'n Jim's restaurant. Maggie knew that as surely as her grandmother would disapprove of her bathing suit, and her cousin Teresa would get sunburned so badly she would smell like Noxzema for a month, on the fourth day they would have their picture taken to testify that they were having a wonderful time and were part of a supremely happy family.

While the photographer set up his tripod, Maggie looked around to see what he would see: Monica laughing, her hair shining in the lights; Teresa, who was the same age as Maggie, her eyes pale blue as eucalyptus mints, her face a little vacant; and the twins, a matching patina of pale pink over their faces and arms, staring down self-consciously at their shrimp cocktails. Mary Frances had gone to the ladies' room to freshen her lipstick, which had come off on the rim of her whiskey-sour glass. The picture would cost five dollars, and when it was sent to her at home, Mary Frances would put it in the silver frame that held last year's picture. Maggie had taken the velvet back off that frame one day, and had found seven photographs of the group, starting back when she was six years old, her lips drawn down in an awkward smile to hide the fact that her two front teeth were missing. Monica was eleven in that first picture, and looked, Maggie had been sad to see, much as she looked today, except that there had been the glint of her braces. On Monica, even braces looked good, as if she had jewelry on her teeth.

"Congratulations, Maggie," Monica said now, readjusting the bow holding back her hair. "My father says that your mother is going to have another baby." Monica made the word "another" last a long, long time.

"So what?" Maggie said.

"Really? When? Ooooh," said Teresa, picking up the last shrimp with her stubby freckled fingers. "I hope it's a girl this time."

They were eating by a plate-glass window in the restaurant. It was actually a refurbished tugboat, big and square, with graceless utilitarian lines, which picked diners up at 6:00 and 8:30 from a pier on the bay side of the town of South Beach and sailed along the shore while they ate. Mary Frances took the girls to dinner at Cap'n Jim's each year because she assumed they liked the novelty of it, and each year they mimed excitement and delight, convinced that it was Mary Frances's favorite restaurant. In fact after years of Friday night meatless suppers, Mary Frances hated fish, and she had no stomach for the sea; she usually ate little and drank a good deal. Maggie was like her in this; she usually drank so much soda during these meals that she had to go to the bathroom at least twice, each time thinking of what happened after she flushed the toilet this far from land.

"What are you girls giggling about?" Mary Frances said pleasantly as she came back to the table, although the only one giggling was Teresa. Mary Frances sat down in the middle, between Monica and Maggie, and the photographer fiddled with some dials on his camera. "What a handsome group," he said, and Mary Frances smiled, and the shutter clicked. "All sisters, I presume," he said, and Mary Frances laughed, and the shutter clicked again. It was the same photographer as always, wearing a captain's hat and smoking a cigar. He said the same things every year.

They had spent the day on the beach, where the sound of the sea and the strength of the sun had lulled them all into afternoon naps, even Mary Frances in her rented beach chair. Her magazine would fall open on her lap, her mouth would goggle a bit, and she would doze, waking suddenly, embarrassed, to say, "My, but it's warm." Mary Frances was not entirely comfortable with her granddaughters— she had been the youngest of nine children, and was accustomed to being the baby herself—and she did her best to hide it by playing the role of grandmother the way she expected Billie Burke or Spring Byington would. She affected a sort of breezy elegance, which usually consisted of wide eyes, a half-smile, and the phrase "Well, girls?" all accompanied with a slight sideways tilt of the head. Maggie had once seen a movie starring Greer Garson and had become indignant at the way Greer Garson had imitated her grandmother. It was only in the last year or so that she had realized that Mary Frances herself was doing the imitating.

On the beach, Maggie had listened to the radio and lain on her back on a towel. The air was white with unalloyed sunlight, and her lips tasted like salt from the sea, and from her own sweat. Around her were girls sparkling with baby oil, their hands always busy with their hair, their eyes moving back and forth along the horizon for some boy or another, their nipped-in waists the perfect counterpoint to their bosoms and their hips.

And then there were the littler girls, the ones Maggie had been like the summer before, shrill and jumpy, smelling of Coppertone, wet white T-shirts over their cotton suits to keep them from burning, their plastic buckets beside them on their blankets. And the middle-sized ones, like her cousin Teresa, still digging for sand crabs at the water's edge, still wearing her shapeless nylon tank suit, although she had to slump to keep her nipples from poking its navy-blue surface. Maggie felt as if she belonged nowhere, and to none of them. "Roll over, roll over," the deejay sang every hour, parroting the children's song to warn his listeners to tan evenly, but Maggie stayed on her back, afraid that if she lay on her stomach she would dent the top part of her bathing suit.

Monica was sitting under an umbrella; she tanned only an hour a day because she had read in *Seventeen* that too much sun gave you wrinkles. Occasionally she got up to stroll down the beach, her pink eyelet suit hugging her body, and Maggie would watch her stop at the lifeguard stand and talk to the two young men who sat there, their zinc-oxided noses two white flags on the horizon. Other boys would stop by, and Monica would swivel from one to another. Finally she came back to lie under the umbrella.

In midafternoon, when Maggie was falling asleep, the voice on the radio said, "I've got a special request here from the guys in the sophomore sports club at Fordham. This one goes out to the beautiful, the untouchable, the incredible Helen. No last names, please." Then he played a song Maggie had never heard before, by Johnny Mathis, whose voice kept breaking on the high notes. When Maggie looked up at her cousin, Monica was staring out to sea, her eyes narrowed. "Untouchable my ass," she muttered.

"What, dear?" Mary Frances said pleasantly.

"Nothing, Grandmom," said Monica, and she got slowly to her feet and walked back to the lifeguard stand.

When Monica was gone, Maggie gingerly turned over onto her stomach. She lay flat for a minute, the sand shifting slightly beneath her cheek, and then she propped herself up on her elbows and looked down. Sure enough, her convex top was now concave.

"Oooh," she moaned.

"What, dear?"

"Nothing, Grandmom," Maggie said, pushing out the cups with her finger.

"I love your bathing suit, Maggie," Teresa said with a giggle. "You look like a cancan dancer."

"Watch your mouth, dear," said Mary Frances.

When they were not at the beach, they strolled along the boardwalk, played miniature golf while Mary Frances watched, ate surf and turf at restaurants with imitation fishnets on the walls. Mary Frances told the same stories every year, and over the years Maggie had begun to think there was something sad about them, as though what Mary Frances didn't discuss was somehow different and darker than these pat anecdotes.

Maggie knew very little about her grandmother's past life, except that Mary Frances still mourned Elizabeth Ann, the baby who had died, and Maggie sometimes wondered whether being surrounded by her granddaughters reminded her of her loss. Her aunt Margaret had told Maggie that Mary Frances herself had been born two months after her father had died of tuberculosis and that when she was little she had thought her name was "posthumous child" because so many people called her that. Inevitably the children Mary Frances felt most drawn to were the vulnerable ones. Maggie knew that her grandmother was fondest of Tommy, and she tried not to think about what that meant, for her father and for her. Maggie knew that her grandmother loved her, too, although the rest of the family thought of Maggie as John Scanlan's pet.

After they had had their picture taken, a full moon rose outside the window of Cap'n Jim's, and they looked at the man in the moon as they had cheesecake for dessert. The boat was approaching the pier, and the girls gathered up their white patent handbags and began to follow their grandmother to the door. The guesthouse where they always stayed—"patronized," Mary Frances said, as though she was somehow condescending to the place—was right across the street from the pier. It was a squat, rather pretty white building with white pebbles instead of a lawn, big pots of geraniums flanking the path to the front door, and a porch that ran around three sides where they spent the evening looking over the sea and rocking in their rocking chairs.

"Grandmom, I have cramps," Monica said, as they crossed the road in single file, looking, Maggie thought, like a row of ducks in their yellow and white summer dresses and their shiny white summer dress shoes. "Can I go in and lie down?"

"There's no need to be so explicit," said Mary Frances. "Just go ahead. The rest of us will be out here."

They sat down, facing the ocean, the sounds dying down as the diners moved away from the boat, the sounds dying down to the slow, rhythmical *boom-boom* of the surf, occasionally shot through with a trill of high laughter from the beach.

Maggie mulled over the news about a new baby, which was not

really news after the day she had seen her mother being sick in the sink. One of her most enduring images of her mother was of a headless person, a small torso bent double, making strangled heaving sounds over the sink. For a long time it was the only way she thought of her mother, on those rare occasions when she did think of her when they were apart, although now sometimes there would appear unwanted in her mind the picture of her mother looking like that high school photograph, her face alight, not like a mother at all.

Maggie knew that soon it would be time for Mary Frances to tell stories. Usually when they were at the beach Mary Frances told the story about how she had met John Scanlan. She had been small and pretty, with soft brown hair and hazel eyes, and John Scanlan had looked down at her and said, "You're going to marry me whether you like it or not." It was a great family story, the epitome of what they all liked to think of as the Scanlan directness and determination, character traits that in fact only John and Maggie's aunt Margaret, Sister John of the Cross, happened to possess. But Maggie realized now that the fact that her grandfather had gotten his way said as much about Mary Frances as it did about John Scanlan. For that was how it had happened, really, and even now Maggie could hear it in her grandmother's voice: Mary Frances had not known whether she liked it or not, whether she liked *him* or not; she only knew that John had taken charge of the situation, and that had been that.

And that had been that ever since. In the first ten years she had had seven children, while her husband had become grand, feared and fawned upon by nearly everyone he met. And somehow, over those years, she had come to love him. Maggie could see that it pained her that John let the world know he thought she was silly and childish, although Connie had once said that that was part of the reason John had married Mary Frances, so that he could think she was silly and childish and manage her. Somehow the "whether you like it or not" story always made Maggie feel sad.

"Tell about the lifeguard," Maggie said, looking sideways at her grandmother, who was staring fixedly toward the black void of the horizon.

"Oh, that old story," her grandmother said.

"I love that story," said Teresa.

"Well, as you all know I'm not much of a swimmer," said Mary Frances, whose grandchildren had never seen her do anything in a bathing suit except sit on the beach. "I was with my friend Ruthie Corrigan and we were at the Alden, a guest house down the street here, I think it's called the Grande now. We had a room on the top floor with those dormer windows and just barely room enough for two. Seven dollars a week it was, which may seem cheap to you, but was dear then, I can tell you, especially for me. Not that we were poor. But there wasn't money to burn."

"And you went swimming," said Maggie.

"And we went swimming," Mary Frances continued. "There was a dreadful undertow, one of those where you can just barely stand up. It was dragging us around, but Ruthie was a bigger girl than me, a very big girl, with great big bones and feet, I think they were tens, if you can imagine, and she was staying put and I was all over the place out there. And I was trying to be calm, but finally I said 'Ruthie, I'm drowning, say your prayers and I'll say mine.' And she hollered, oh, did she holler. And before I knew what had happened there was this young man pulling me out by the hair."

Mary Frances stopped to catch her breath, her face as pink as the embroidery on her pocket handkerchief.

"He was as handsome as Francis X. Bushman—"

"Who's Francis X. Bushmer?" said Teresa, who had a mind, John Scanlan always said, "like a sieve."

"Shut up," said Maggie. "An actor. Pay attention."

"He was as handsome as Francis X. Bushman," Mary Frances said, "with beautiful wavy hair and the prettiest teeth. I was all right when he got me up on the beach, only out of breath and a little scared, but Ruthie was screaming like a banshee and finally I had to tell her to be quiet so he could tell me his name. Roderick. Can you beat that? Roderick. Like a duke, I said to Ruthie. And right there on the beach he said, 'May I take you to dinner tonight?' And me still trying to catch my breath, so I just nodded. 'May I take you?' Like a duke, I said to Ruthie."

"But you didn't go," said Maggie.

"I didn't go, no," said Mary Frances with a slight clicking noise, her mouth dry from the whiskey sours. "That afternoon I met your grandfather. And that was that."

Maggie waited.

"He swept me off my feet," Mary Frances said with a sigh.

It suddenly seemed very quiet and the noise of the ocean seemed loud. "I have to go to the bathroom," said one of the twins softly, as though she was a toddler who needed to be taken and helped. "Well, go then, dear, don't discuss it," Mary Frances said impatiently.

"Grandmom, can I go for a walk on the beach?" Maggie asked, as her cousin slipped away.

"In your stockings?"

"I didn't wear them tonight."

"I wish I'd known that. I would have sent you back upstairs. Well, go ahead then."

Maggie handed Teresa her white patent pumps and ran down the stairs. The road that separated the guesthouse from the beach was empty and the sand felt surprisingly cold. The night was so black that Maggie knew she had reached the water's edge only when she felt the sea run over her feet. When she looked for the moon she realized that it must be hidden behind the clouds, and she wondered if it would rain, and what they would all do if it did, stuck together at the beach on a rainy day. To one side she could hear an odd whirring sound, and dimly in the dark she made out the silhouette of someone surf-casting. She began to walk in the opposite direction.

She felt at home walking on the beach. The lonely, empty feeling in her stomach, which seemed out of place in everyday life—at the pool, playing softball, at school, with her brothers—felt suitable at the beach. She walked for what seemed like a long time, and then turned at one of the stone jetties and walked back again, looking for the lights of the guesthouse beyond the dunes. She saw them from some distance away and began to climb to the middle of the beach.

She was perhaps a block away from the house when she almost stepped on a half-naked couple sprawled on a blanket. She drew back and then squinted in the darkness, able to make out the curve of the boy's bare buttocks and the ridiculous welter of clothes gathered around his ankles. "Oh my god," he kept repeating, moving up and down. "Oh my god." Beneath him a girl seemed to be staring blankly at the sky overhead, the whites of her eyes visible even in the darkness. Maggie realized that the girl was staring at her, and that it was her cousin Monica, looking expressionless, grim, her fingernails sparkling on the boy's shoulder as the moon momentarily emerged from the clouds. "Oh my God," he said again, and Maggie drew back and ran across the sand to the break in the dunes.

She kept on running across the street, up onto the porch of the guesthouse; then she sat there hugging her knees for a few minutes before she went upstairs to the room she and Monica shared. One of the twin beds was lumpy with what Maggie knew would be an artful arrangement of pillows. She pulled out her own pillow and turned on her side, feigning sleep when she heard footfalls an hour later. She spent all night wondering what to do, but the matter was settled for her the next morning, as she and Monica walked to the beach together several steps behind their grandmother. Monica gave her a level look, not unlike the one she had given her the night before on the beach, and said quietly, "Who'd believe you? Grandpop says you have an overactive imagination." Then she walked ahead, her carefully oiled calves shining in the sun, talking to Mary Frances.

Maggie lagged behind, and so it was she that Mrs. Polisky, the owner of the guesthouse, reached first as she came trotting up behind them, her fat face red. "Tell your grandmother you've got to come into the house," she gasped. "You've got to go home. Your grandfather's had an accident."

 OHN SCANLAN LAY IN THE HOSPITAL bed, the left side of his face looking as though it was melting into his shoulder, a thick line of saliva edging his jawline. "Wipe his mouth," Mark said to one of the nurses, but as soon as she had done so the spittle crept down again.

Except for the fact that his family stood behind a sheet of glass, kept out of the intensive care unit by regulations that even now her uncle James was appealing, Maggie thought that it looked like one of the deathbed scenes of the British royal family in her book about Queen Victoria. Her grandfather did not look dead; he looked ruined, as though he would have to be renovated from top to bottom to regain any semblance of his former self. Mary Frances was sitting beside his bed, stroking his hand and clutching the cord to the intravenous feed.

"Will he die?" Maggie asked, the only one of the grandchildren left there, the twins having been sent home by cab, Teresa sent to the cafeteria in hysterics, and Monica left in the waiting room with some of the aunts, reading an old copy of *Vogue*.

"What kind of question is that?" Mark asked. "Jesus. Of course not."

Maggie noticed that a tube running from underneath the covers down the side of the bed was bright yellow, and she began to feel sick. She had been in a hospital only twice before, once for stitches in her knee, once to visit her mother when Joseph was born, her father sneaking her in past the nurses' stations, but it had not been like this. Even the smell was different; there was still the odor of disinfectant, but it was overlaid with that of rubber and dirty clothes. She went outside into the waiting area, where her father was talking on the pay phone.

"Did you find her?" Monica was asking him.

"Mind your own business," Tommy Scanlan said, dropping in another coin.

"Maggie, honey, do you have any idea where your mother could be?". Aunt Cass asked.

"At home."

"No, she's not."

"At Celeste's?"

"Your brothers are there, thank God. But Celeste doesn't know where your mother went."

Tommy slammed down the pay phone and said, "She can't even drive, for Christ's sake. She hates the train. Where is she?"

"Did you call Grandpop?" asked Maggie, who thought it was probably a bad time to mention that her mother might be able to drive after all.

"He said he'd find her. How's he going to find her? The closest Angelo Mazza's ever come to driving is riding shotgun in the flower car at a funeral."

"Perhaps she's visiting a friend in the neighborhood," Aunt Cass said.

"She doesn't have any friends," Tommy said, and Maggie flinched. "She has Celeste," she said quietly.

Maggie went back inside and stared through the glass partition. Looking at her grandfather was like looking at the babies in the nursery. Occasionally she would see her grandmother's mouth moving, but no sound traveled through the thick glass, which was crisscrossed with narrow silver ribbons of wire.

Her aunt Margaret was fingering the big black rosary beads that always hung around her waist, although whether it was a prayerful gesture or a nervous one Maggie could not tell. Maggie leaned up against her, something she would not have done with any other nun, or with any of her other aunts for that matter. "Pumpkin, pumpkin," said Margaret, squeezing her around the waist. "Life is tough, isn't it? You know what someone once said? 'Life is a comedy for those who think and a tragedy for those who feel.' " Margaret squeezed her again and Maggie felt the tears fill her eyes, coaxed out by her aunt's warm hand.

"I don't know how anyone could ever think this was a comedy," Maggie said.

Her aunt pulled two butterscotch drops from one of her seemingly bottomless nun's pockets, handed one to Maggie, and sucked on the other herself. Maggie thought her aunt was being companionable, but she also knew from experience that in times of stress Aunt Margaret relied heavily on sweets. She had once told Maggie that she sucked lemon drops whenever she had to teach arithmetic, which was her weakest subject.

Maggie could hear her father out in the waiting room, swearing. "For a religious family, we sure take the Lord's name in vain a lot," her aunt said.

"Do you think Grandpop's going to die?"

"It doesn't look good, does it, sweetie? I don't know, lots of people have strokes and get better. Lots of them don't die. But they're paralyzed, or they can't talk, or something like that."

"Grandpop would really hate that," Maggie said, and she began to feel the pressure behind her nose and eyes that meant she might start to cry.

"I know," said her aunt, turning the big wooden crucifix at the end of her rosary over and over in her hands.

"Do you think that crucifix is too large?" Mark suddenly asked his sister.

"What?"

"The crucifix. Is it too large? We're thinking of scaling it down. I think it's too large. I'd even like to remove the Christ figure and keep a simple wooden cross, which seems more in keeping with Vatican II to me. But Dad says he thinks the nuns wouldn't stand for it. We could cut a good bit off the manufacturing cost of each one if we made the cross half again as big."

"Mark, are we actually having this conversation, here, at this moment?" said his sister, staring at him with her big blue Irish eyes, nearly the same navy as a parochial school uniform. She was wearing what Maggie's father always called her "For Chrissake, boys" look, and Maggie thought she looked very young and pretty.

Her uncle Mark was always saying it was such a shame that Margaret had joined the convent. Once Maggie had asked, very seriously, when she was in one of her religious phases, how her aunt had known that she had had the call from God. "That's a complicated question, sweetheart," her aunt had answered. But Maggie had heard her father say that the call from God was a lot of nonsense, and that when he had asked Margaret why she was ruining her life, his sister had answered a little sadly, "It's quiet, and they'll send me to college."

"So it was your father's fault?" Connie had said, and Tommy had sighed and said, "Yes, Concetta. The flood. The plagues of Egypt. The Second World War. My sister taking the veil. John Scanlan caused them all."

Maggie remembered that she had not been quite sure whether her father was teasing or not.

The door to the hospital room opened and Uncle James came in, wearing his white coat. "They won't let anyone but Mother and I inside," he said, sounding testy. "The director said he didn't care if our name was Kennedy."

"Don't let Daddy hear that," Margaret said. "He'd have another stroke."

"I don't find that funny, Sister," said James, who had called Margaret "Sister" even before she entered the convent. "This is serious."

The door opened again and Connie slipped in. She was wearing shorts and sneakers, and she seemed out of breath. The fluorescent lights overhead turned her the color of skim milk, blue and sickly;

looking around, Maggie realized they all looked that way, except for Uncle Mark, who cultivated a tan while playing golf and had only paled to a light coffee color. "Hi, Con," said Margaret, who liked her sister-in-law.

"Oh, God," said Connie, who had just caught sight of the figure behind the glass.

"Where have you been? Your husband has been worried sick," said Uncle James, putting his hands on his narrow hips.

"Is he going to be all right?" Connie asked, pressed up against the glass, and for just a moment Maggie thought she was asking about Tommy. Mary Frances caught a glimpse of Connie and waved weakly. Maggie realized that her grandmother, who had made good posture her life's work, was slumping in the straight chair. That, combined with the pathetic little whiffle of her fingers at the daughter-in-law she seemed to like least, and the helplessness of John Scanlan in the bed beside her, made it seem as though Mary Frances had suddenly been rendered old and powerless too.

Maggie had spent the ride home from the beach staring at Monica in the seat in front of her, looking for something, anything—a bruise, a shadow beneath her wide, amber-colored eyes, a look on her face— to testify to what she had seen on the beach the night before. Now she began to wonder if her uneventful life had suddenly taken a turn for the worse and would become one impossible scene after another, leaving her, as she was today, so tired she could hardly stand.

"It happened overnight," Margaret said to Connie. "He called James but James didn't realize who it was."

"I thought it was a crank call," said James. "All I could hear was breathing and moaning."

"Oh God," Connie said.

Tommy came in behind his wife, and clutched her shoulders as though he would lift her off the ground. He spun her around. "Where the hell have you been?" he said, his eyes wild. "Where? Everyone was here except for you. You disappeared off the face of the earth." He was speaking so loudly that Mary Frances turned toward them. "He could have died. Where the hell were you?"

"Tom," Connie said, trying to wriggle out from under his hands. "Where *were* you? I got scared."

"Stop it."

"Tell me."

"I went for a walk."

"A *walk?* Who walks in our neighborhood? Who? Even people with dogs don't walk."

"I wanted to be by myself."

"You've been by yourself your whole life. Now suddenly you like being by yourself? Then be by yourself." He let go of her and she stumbled backward, falling against Maggie. Connie looked down at her daughter, as though she was seeing her for the first time. "You're back," she said, and Maggie began to cry.

"Stop it, Tom," Margaret said, stooping to cradle Maggie in her black gabardine arms.

"She shouldn't be in here," said Connie, and she took Maggie's hand and moved away from her husband, turning toward the door. "This is no place for children."

"Where else should she be?" Tommy said. "Her grandfather's dying."

The tears had started to run down Maggie's face, soaking the neck of her cotton shirt. She looked through the glass again and saw that what her father said was true. Mary Frances was staring at all of them, her eyes enormous, but Maggie couldn't tell whether it was because of the dumb show of anger and grief she could see before her, or because of some dumb show of her own playing itself out inside her head.

"Send Maggie out to sit with Monica," Uncle James said.

"No," Maggie said. "I want to stay here."

Connie dropped her daughter's hand and sat down heavily in a straight chair.

"Ah, to hell with it," Tommy said, all the heat and anger gone from his voice, and he leaned his head against the glass and began to cry. Maggie could see Mary Frances's mouth behind the glass forming the word "Tom" over and over again, but there was no sound except that of Tommy sobbing. Finally Connie went over to him and put her hand gently on his arm, his arm with its pale down and tiny freckles.

"Go home, Concetta," he said in a small voice, and then he moved away.

OW DO I SMELL?" DEBBIE ASKED.

Outside, the crickets were so loud they sounded like construction machines; the air was heavy with the heat and the cologne the two girls had put on before they left the Malone house. Debbie had been able to find only her mother's Chanel No. 5, a full bottle Mrs. Malone had gotten for Christmas once and never used; Maggie thought she smelled like a grandmother going to church. Maggie was wearing Tabu, from a little sample bottle belonging to her aunt Celeste. Every time she moved she thought of Monica, and the white flash of bare buttocks on the beach, and she felt hot and then cold, as though she had the flu.

"You smell sophisticated," Maggie said, and she could tell by the look on Debbie's face, with its saddle of freckles and snub nose, that she'd said just the right thing.

The development behind Maggie's house had grown rapidly from nothing into something, more rapidly than Maggie's mother could turn being sick in the sink into another baby. The skeletons of the houses were ranged around the fields, stretching far into the woods at the end of their street. The construction crew had framed in at least two dozen buildings, carved streets in red mud out of the gray-brown earth, left packing crates full of bathtubs and hot-water heaters scattered here and there. The noise was no longer deafening—all the foundations had been dug—but it was persistent and annoying, like the little circular clouds of gnats out back in the late afternoon.

The children had been strictly forbidden to play there, which was one of several reasons why it had become the focus of neighborhood activity after dark. As soon as dinner was over and the sounds of hammering and basso conversation had ceased, anyone over the age of six would slink down the street and around through the woods and swarm over the insides of the skeleton structures, chasing one another up half-completed staircases, looking at the stars through roofs that were nothing more than two-by-fours every two feet, sitting against the concrete in the cool basements and pitching bent nails at one another's ankles. For the first time in their lives they became occupants of houses that were theirs alone.

That first night after Maggie got back from the beach, Debbie had taken her to a split-level house near the edge of the development. It had space for a picture window that would look from the kitchen into the front yard. There was no glass in the windows, and sometimes the lightning bugs and the mosquitoes flew through the rooms and then out again. The little things that lived in the fields had moved back to the edges where the tractors had not yet gone, the rabbits and the field mice and the occasional raccoon that foraged through the garbage cans, only to be taken away in a trap after someone called the ASPCA. The butterflies were still there, but they seemed to be just passing through, settling on a stack of sheetrock and then moving on in a flurry of black-and-yellow ruffles. Only the stream had stayed the same, a narrow sluice of water that ran through Kenwood and into the next town, threading its way beneath the stone abutments of the railroad trestle. Debbie and Maggie had wandered its edges for years, playing with the clay that shone blue-gray in pockets around its banks, lifting rocks and grabbing for the crayfish as they shot out in explosions of silt and water, searching for newts to put in jelly jars, their suction pads pressed to the glass.

The split-level seemed like a big doll's house without furniture, as they sat crosslegged in the master bedroom, a yellow summer moon shining through the square where the window would be. They were waiting for the boys to arrive—the infamous Richard Joseph, and Bruce Stroud, who always went every place with Richard, a kind of Robin to his friend's Batman. The Ouija was balanced on their bony knees and a flashlight lay between them, its beam illuminating the little table from beneath, and sending the heart-shaped shadow of the pointer slanting steeply across the sawdust and the nails lying scattered about the plywood. The air smelled like Christmas trees.

"What is the name of the man I will marry?" Maggie asked darkly, and Debbie giggled. Deep in her heart Maggie had always known that the Ouija only worked if someone pushed it, although at pajama parties she insisted she believed in its magic. Now she wondered why neither of them had decided to push it around to spell out the name of some imaginary future husband.

"Maybe you're not going to get married," Debbie finally said. Maggie lifted her hands and then asked what the future would bring for her parents. "Dumb question," said Debbie, wrinkling her nose and pulling her hands away. "Who cares about the future of parents?"

"I care about the future of your parents. I like your parents," Maggie said.

"I like my parents okay," said Debbie, "but, it's like, they're all taken care of. They know what their future is, who they're married to, how many kids they're going to have, what they wore to the prom. They're sort of finished."

"Something could happen."

"Like what?" said Debbie, and she sounded so doubtful that Maggie could not bring herself to say, What if they start to hate each other? What if one of them starts to love someone else? What if they never talked to each other, or to you? Debbie's life seemed so simple to Maggie; how could she tell her friend that she and her mother didn't even belong to the same family?

They were silent for a minute, the sounds of distant television sets carrying to them faintly through the development, and then Debbie said, "Want to go to Bridget's tomorrow? She's got a Princess phone."

Bridget Hearn was fourteen and lived next door to the Malones. She had taken Debbie up in a desultory fashion in the first weeks of summer vacation, because her own best friend was at the shore until Labor Day, and because she wanted a chance to go through Helen's drawers.

"No."

"She called Richard the other day and asked if he had Prince Albert in a can."

Maggie groaned. "You have to call a store to do that joke."

"But wait, wait, guess what he said? She goes 'Excuse me, but do you have Prince Albert in a can?' And Richard says, 'No, I already let him out.' " He said the perfect thing without even knowing she was going to call."

"She's stupid," said Maggie. "She only cares about boys and clothes. And Helen."

"Her parents go out a lot," Debbie said. "She had Richard and Bruce over one night until midnight. She went down the basement with Richard for an hour and Bruce had to sit upstairs and watch television alone."

"And?"

"And how do I know? She didn't tell me." In the silence, they could hear someone laughing nearby. Finally Debbie said, "She said Richard tried to French-kiss with her."

"And?" said Maggie.

"She said she didn't let him."

"What a lie," said Maggie, whose parents had told her she couldn't hang around with Bridget Hearn after seeing her one day at Mass with a Band-Aid incompletely covering a hickey on her neck. Maggie thought of Monica again. "Do you think Helen has done it?" she asked.

"God, Mag, are you crazy? She's not married."

"So. People who aren't married must do it sometimes."

"Yeah, and wind up like that girl two years ago, what was her name? Who had to go to a home and then her parents moved away? Forget it."

"Maybe doing it is better than we think it is. Our parents do it."

"Because they have to."

"Maybe they want to," Maggie said.

"You're nuts," Debbie said, flicking off the flashlight. Maggie put her hands back on the Ouija. "Let's ask if I'm really moving," she said.

"Doesn't your grandfather say that you're moving?" Debbie picked idly at a scab on her knee.

"He bought us a house but my mother says we're not going to move into it. My father says no, too. Anyway, my grandfather's sick now."

"Sick or not, if your grandfather bought you a house, then you're moving," Debbie said.

Maggie wondered why everyone else in the world suddenly seemed so sure of themselves, and only she felt that every answer was the wrong answer, every situation a strange one. That morning, remembering the scene at the hospital the night before, she had thought about going to see her grandfather Mazza at the cemetery. But she thought of her set of tools, her square of fabric, and they seemed to belong to someone she had once been friendly with but who had since moved away, or gone to another school. This morning she had even felt out of place on the familiar streets of Kenwood. The air had been filled with the buzz of bulldozers, and the familiar curb where she and Debbie had written their initials in wet cement when they were nine had been crushed to pebbles by the wheels of the dump trucks pulling in between two houses. When she finally arrived at the Malones, the front door stood open, as though the place had been abandoned.

On the way over, scuffing her sneakers along the cement, she had begun to think of the summer before, when she and Debbie had lain in sleeping bags in the Malone backyard and listed the things they no longer believed in. They had decided they no longer believed that if you held a Milky Way in front of the open mouth of someone with a tapeworm, the tapeworm would leap out. They no longer believed that someone with four children had done it four times. ("Or someone with six children six times," Maggie had added, not wanting her parents to appear to be the only sex maniacs in Kenwood.) They no longer believed that heaven was in the sky, or that nuns had crewcuts. (Maggie had seen her aunt Margaret's hair one day when they were both in the bathroom at her grandfather's house.)

Maggie had been thinking of that night as she dragged along in the heat, because she was no longer sure what she believed in. She had dreamed about the hospital room, and the plastic tubes winding round and round the bed like the forest of thorns in *Sleeping Beauty*. In the dream Monica was lying there instead of John Scanlan, and her eyes were staring straight ahead; she looked as if she was dead, except that she was smiling. When Maggie drifted up from the dream, the light hazy through her gingham curtains, she wondered how much of what happened yesterday had really happened, and how much was the dream, or something she'd seen on television, or read in a book. She knew the fight between her parents was real because she could still remember how good it felt when she held her mother's hand, and how long it had seemed since that had happened. She remembered her fear and disappointment when Connie let her go.

But when she tried to think of telling Debbie about everything, about her cousin lying on the beach beneath a boy and the moon, about her grandfather lying there drooling, about her mother disappearing and her father fogging up the intensive care waiting-room glass as he sobbed, she could not think of a way to make any of it sound like part of the life they had both known up until then. And she could not bear to think of a different kind of life, a life where things went bad and fell apart all the time, in which people stepped over, trampled really, all the lines she had counted on to give order and shape to every day. She wondered how much of what she felt was her imagination. On the way to the Malones she stared into the sun, as though to burn up what was in her brain; she wondered if she had, as her grandfather Scanlan often said, "spun a bit of a yarn into a sweater."

But when she saw the open front door of the Malone's house, she knew that the one place she had counted on always to stay sane had gone crazy, too.

In the center of the hallway, where someone could trip over them and break a leg if they weren't careful, were two pale blue Samsonite suitcases and a box of books.

Maggie peered into the box: the top two books were *Wuthering Heights* and something Maggie had never heard of called *The Prophet*. The suitcases smelled like new plastic, like Christmas morning, and had the gold initials HAM stamped on the combination locks. Anyone but Helen Malone would have faced ridicule about those initials, but she never even seemed to notice them. Debbie's initials were DAM, of which she was rather proud. With all the rest she had to do, Mrs. Malone could not be bothered dreaming up middle names: all the girls got Ann, and all the boys Robert.

Maggie stood in the hallway for several minutes, alone, wondering whether she should go around and come in the back door as usual, when suddenly Mrs. Malone came running down the stairs. Her face looked bleached in the morning light, and she moved so quickly that her belly bounced and swayed separately from the rest of her body. She scowled at the sight of the suitcases. "The hell of it is," she said, "that I bought her those damn suitcases for a graduation present. I should have bought her the desk lamp instead." She noticed Maggie standing there. "You're back early," she said. "Miss Debbie is upstairs. Ask her if she's flying to Paris this afternoon."

"Helen's moving out," Debbie said, as soon as Maggie opened the door to her bedroom.

While she was at the beach Maggie had missed the two most exciting days in the history of the Malone household. On Monday afternoon, on their way home from the Kenwoodie Club, a striped towel draped around her long neck, Helen had informed Mrs. Malone that she had gotten an apartment of her own. Mrs. Malone had never been considered a stupid woman, but it took her a full five minutes to puzzle out what Helen meant.

It turned out that when Helen had taken a special English literature enrichment course at Fordham that spring, she had met a student who had rented an apartment in Manhattan, near Columbia University. The girl had offered Helen one of the bedrooms in return for half the rent. Helen had cleaned out her savings account and packed her clothes before anyone knew what was happening; her closet was empty except for her Sacred Heart uniform and the long dotted-swiss dress she had worn three weeks before for her graduation. She had given Aggie her jewelry box, and Debbie her dictionary.

"I asked for the bikini but she just laughed," Debbie said.

Mrs. Malone had been wild. For two days, she had slammed around the kitchen late into the night, cleaning the refrigerator, her flip-flops slapping the linoleum as though she was spanking it. Even now Maggie could hear intermittent ranting from downstairs, part of a monologue about how people didn't know when they had it good, how they always wanted what they didn't have, how they would have to learn the hard way. Mr. Malone had found the decision complicated by the fact that the other girl was the daughter of a judge with whom he had long wanted to be on speaking terms. The two men had met at the apartment, turned on the faucets to check the water pressure, talked sternly to the superintendent, and agreed that they would put up with this nonsense until the girls' money ran out, which was expected to happen just in time for the Christmas holidays.

"She's coming," Debbie said suddenly, in the middle of describing all this to Maggie, and they heard the sound of footsteps walking down the hall from Helen's room. The two girls followed her soundlessly, watching her back as she trotted downstairs. Mrs. Malone stood in the hallway next to the suitcases, her hands on her hips.

"Did you take my blue blouse?" she asked.

Maggie stood at the top of the stairs and heard Helen laugh, and behind Helen, through the open door, Maggie could see sunlight. At the curb was a car as blue as the sky. Helen put her arms around her mother's shoulders. She towered over Mrs. Malone.

"Your blue blouse is safe upstairs. I will be safe at 113th Street and Broadway. I will come home soon. I will call every day."

"I don't want to talk to you every day."

Helen laughed again. "I know," she said, "but I'll do it anyway." She looked up to the head of the stairs, and her face glowed pink, as though she'd been running.

"You're back early," she said to Maggie. "What happened—did Monica drown?"

"No such luck," said Maggie.

"Come see me," Helen said, and Maggie wondered if she meant

it. "I'll teach you two how to smoke cigarettes." Mrs. Malone hit Helen on the shoulder and then she started to laugh herself. Maggie could see tears in the eyes of both mother and daughter.

"Oh, you," Mrs. Malone said.

The car at the curb beeped its horn twice, and Helen picked up the suitcases. "Debbie, could you get the box?" she called, and Debbie sailed downstairs, away from Maggie, into the midst of it all. As Helen started to walk out, Mrs. Malone turned and went into the kitchen, her head down. Debbie was already out the door.

Helen turned in the doorway, the sun lighting her black hair. "I left you something in my top drawer," she said to Maggie, and then she was gone.

Maggie ran back upstairs to the bedroom at the end of the hall. On the blackboard Helen had written À BIENTÔT, which Maggie knew was French for something. The single bed had been stripped down to its naked mattress, and the top of the bureau, which had always been a welter of bracelets and postcards and ribbons, was swept clean.

Maggie opened the top drawer. Inside was the California bikini. She held it to her face and smelled the sharp chlorine smell. The color was faded, and the underwire in one of the cups was bent. Maggie felt to the back of the drawer to see if Helen could possibly have meant something else, but that was the only thing left in there. Then she heard the front door close, and feet on the stairs, and without thinking she slipped into Debbie's room and shoved the suit to the bottom of her beach bag, under her towel.

She thought of something Helen had said once about Maggie and Debbie, who had been best friends since first grade, although Maggie was thoughtful and serious and studious and Debbie was often called "pea brain" by the members of her own family: "Debbie likes Maggie because Maggie makes her feel special, and Maggie likes Debbie because Debbie makes her feel normal."

She had thought of that all the rest of the day, and now, as she and Debbie sat in the development house, waiting for the boys to come, it kept running through her head: Debbie normal, Maggie special. She took a deep breath.

She hated the air this time of the summer, the thick heavy air of

July, like something woolly twisted around your head, clogging your nose, making it hard to breathe. Her hair felt like wet wash on the back of her neck. During the afternoon she had made a clover chain and had forgotten to take it off her head. The flowers were browning now, and brittle. Debbie's hair had been cut into a funny kind of pageboy, and each night she took pink foam rollers and rolled the ends over them, so that each morning her hair all around turned under like the curve of a comma, although by night the curve was gone.

"This must be what Helen will do all the time," Maggie said. "She'll just call a bunch of guys and say, 'Come over, we'll watch television. If I like you, you can stay. If not, I'll kick you out. It's my house, I run things. You're not my husband. I do what I want.' "

Debbie looked doubtful. "I don't think even Helen would kick Richard out," she said.

Richard Joseph was the coolest boy in Kenwood. Everyone said so. He was fourteen, but sixteen-year-old girls were interested in him. He was tall and had blond hair and blue eyes and hair on the back of his hands, and a smile that started slowly at the corner of his mouth and then moved to the middle.

"I don't know how Mary Joseph ever came to have that boy with the bedroom eyes," Mrs. Malone had once said about him.

Richard Joseph played bass guitar in a garage band. He had mooned a table of mothers from the high dive at the Kenwoodie Club and managed to convince the manager that the elastic in his trunks had snapped. And once, at a party during Christmas vacation, he had asked Maggie to dance. She was the youngest girl he'd ever noticed, and most of the girls at Sacred Heart thought he had done it just to embarrass her.

So did Maggie. She did not know what to expect from the evening. It seemed as though meeting boys, alone, here, on the second floor, was completely different from seeing them at the swimming pool, or in the rec room of somebody's house. Debbie had told her father she was staying at Maggie's, and Maggie had left a note saying she was staying at the Malones.

"They're coming," Debbie said in a whisper, which seemed unnecessary, since the two boys were singing "She Loves You" in not particularly close harmony, the flats and sharps carrying like trumpet blasts through the still night. Maggie saw a light go on in a house not far from her own.

"SSShhhhh," Debbie hissed, leaning out the window in a great cloud of Chanel No. 5. "Yeah, yeah, yeah, yeah," the two boys sang, playing imaginary guitars on the front of their madras shorts, paying no attention. In a minute their heads came into view at the top of the crude ladder the construction men had nailed into place until they were ready to put in the stairs. "Cool," said Richard, his wavy yellow hair bright even in the dark. "Really cool," said Bruce, who was Richard's permanent audience, a thin boy with spiky light hair and long legs who reminded Maggie of pictures she'd seen of her father at that age.

"We could get in a lot of trouble if they found us out here," Maggie said.

"Jesus, you sound like a nun, you know?" Richard said. "Everybody's out here. The Kelly twins are out here with a couple of girls from Sacred Heart named Kathy or Kelly or something—"

"The two Kathys," said Debbie. "Gross. They do everything together. They get back-to-back appointments to get their hair cut."

"So do the Kellys," said Richard.

"That's true," said Bruce, but no one seemed to hear him.

"Everybody comes out here now. Wait until they turn the water on," Richard added. "I'm going to come out here and take a shower."

"Gross," said Debbie.

"My dad says they'll have to hire a guard soon," Maggie said.

"I like your dad," said Richard. "He's a good guy. You ever seen his jump shot? He has a mean jump shot."

"I like your mother, Maggie," Bruce said.

"Your mother is a babe and a half," Richard said.

"Her mother?" said Debbie. "God! Her *mother?*"

"Monica, too," said Richard. "She's a babe and a half. My brother is friends with her boyfriend."

"She has a boyfriend around here?" Maggie asked.

"What do you mean, around here?" Richard said. "Where else would she have one? I think his name's Donald but everybody calls him Duck. He goes to college with my brother."

Maggie slid down against the wall until she was sitting with her knees in front of her nose. Richard came over and sat down next to her. "Your parents were dancing in your living room just now."

"You peeked in the windows?" Maggie asked, and without knowing why, it made her angry, afraid of what Richard might have seen or heard.

"I don't peek, I look," Richard said, slipping his arm around Maggie's shoulders as though to reassure her. "I look in everybody's windows."

"That's true," said Bruce, staring ruefully at the arm in the half light of the half moon.

"Great perfume," said Richard.

"I can't believe you peeked in our windows," said Maggie, pulling away from the arm, standing up and starting down the ladder, thinking that she was leaving because of the invasion of privacy but knowing she was going for some other, deeper reason that she could not explain.

"Hey," said Richard.

"God, Maggie," Debbie said. She leaned out the window and watched her friend come out of the door of the house. "Maggie," she said again, but there was no answer.

"Maggie," said Bruce, scrambling down the stairs.

"Hey, forget it," said Richard. "I'm not going to go chasing after her." But Bruce's head had already disappeared down the ladder.

"Bridget Hearn was just saying the other day how strange Maggie acts sometimes," Debbie said.

Maggie could hear Bruce calling her as she stumbled across the clumps of dirt and debris that made up the lawn. She walked with her head down, and twice she almost fell, swerving around a framed-in house. "Maggie," she heard him call behind her. "Yo—Maggie. Stop." When she came to a big stack of two-by-fours she sat down on it, her chin in her hands. She kept her head down because she knew there were tears in her eyes.

Bruce came up and sat down next to her, but not too close. For a minute he cracked his knuckles, and finally he said, the timbre of his voice shaky, "He didn't really do it. Look in the windows, I mean. Not really. He always says stuff like that so that people will think he's cool."

Maggie looked up. She could tell immediately that Bruce was lying, trying to be nice.

"It's all right," she said. "I don't know why I did that. Everything's sort of messed up. I can't really explain."

"That's okay," said Bruce. "I feel that way all the time."

"Really?"

"Yeah."

"I never felt that way until a little while ago. Now I feel like everything's crazy."

"I know," Bruce said. He began cracking his knuckles again. "Richard likes you," he finally said. "He told me he really likes you. He said you'll be a babe and a half someday."

"Right," said Maggie sarcastically.

"No, really. He told me."

"I don't see why he's your friend," Maggie said.

"Why is Debbie your friend?" Bruce asked, and Maggie remembered Helen again. Bruce made Richard feel normal and Richard made Bruce feel special. Maybe that was the key to every relationship.

"She just is," Maggie said.

Bruce smiled. Maggie noticed in the dim illumination from the streetlights on the next block that he had hair on his legs. He was looking at the dirt, and, as she watched, he picked up an old nail and tossed it in front of them into the darkness.

He picked up another one, silvery against the tan of his palm, and rolled it around. Wordlessly Bruce handed her the nail. "That looks pretty," he said after a moment.

"What?"

He pointed to her head and Maggie put a hand up and felt the wreath of clover. She started to pull it off. "Don't take it off," he said. "It looks nice. My mother made those things for my sister when she was little."

Maggie lowered her head again. Bruce's mother had died when they were in fifth grade. She felt terrible because she suddenly remembered why Bruce would feel the world was topsy-turvy. "Who cooks dinner in your house?" Maggie finally said, without meaning to.

"The housekeeper," Bruce said. "She cooks dinner and then she leaves. She's not too good a cook. She makes hamburgers a lot."

"I don't know why I asked you that."

"It's okay. Everybody asks me stuff like that. I think people can't figure out what it would be like to have a family that's not like anybody else's family."

"I can," Maggie said, and again she felt as though the words had slipped out.

"Why? You have the normalest family in the world. How would you feel if every time you went to church you could tell that people were pointing at you and saying 'There's the ones with no mother.' "

Maggie didn't know what to say. Bruce picked up another nail. Maggie thought she had never been involved in a conversation with so many silences, except for the ones she had with her grandfather Mazza. Finally Bruce cleared his throat and said, "I remember when you came to my mother's funeral. You had on a black dress with a red tie around the collar. You sent a Mass card. That was really nice."

"The whole class sent flowers."

"I know. That was nice, too. I just hated the way everybody looked at me when I went back to school. Like I was sick or something."

They sat there for a long time, the small night noises clear in the darkness. Maggie suddenly sniffed the air.

"They're smoking cigarettes," Bruce said. "Richard stole a pack of his mother's Salems."

There was a funny clicking sound from inside the development house, and then a little scream. Maggie saw Debbie stick her head out the window. "Come here," she hissed.

"Leave me alone," Maggie said, and her voice sounded loud in the still air.

"It's important," Debbie said, and suddenly behind her there was a flash of orange, like the sun over the horizon of the beach first thing in the morning.

"Oh, hell," Bruce said.

"What?"

Silently he took her hand and pulled her to her feet, and they began to run across the field, leaping over the bigger clods of earth. Maggie stumbled a little. She knew she should concentrate on where she was going, but all she could think of was his hand holding hers.

Inside the development house the smell of smoke was stronger, and a glow was coming from the open square at the top of the ladder. They scrambled up. In one corner a pile of cardboard boxes was burning brightly, the flames hugging a corner of the wall and blackening the two-by-fours of the ceiling. A stray breeze seemed to lift the center of the blaze and send it higher, and in the orange light Maggie could see that Debbie's eyes were dazzled, and Richard was smiling faintly and running his long fingers through his hair.

"Jesus," Bruce whispered.

"I'll get some water," Maggie said, but Richard reached for her arm and held her there, turned toward the fire.

"Don't be a jerk," he said.

"You're crazy," Maggie said. "You're really crazy."

"You're crazy," Richard said, mocking her in a high voice, twisting her arm a little.

"We're going to burn the whole place down," Debbie whispered, but even as she spoke the flames began to shrink, the boxes collapsing into a pile of rose-gray ash, the wood concave where the heat had eaten it away. The four of them stood and stared until finally there was only a great cloud of gray smoke.

"Damn," Richard said. "The wood must be damp."

"You did that on purpose?" Maggie said.

"Wasn't it cool?" Debbie said. "You should have seen it at first. It just went *woosh* like a wave. It almost caught our hair."

"Lighter fluid," said Richard.

"You could have burned the whole house down," Maggie said.

"Jesus," said Richard, "are you always like this? It's not a house. Nobody lives here. Nobody got hurt. Don't you want something to do? Can't you stand a little excitement?" Richard twisted her arm some more. "I give excitement lessons free."

Debbie giggled.

"You're all crazy," said Maggie. She started down the ladder again. "God, is she always like that?" she heard Richard say again.

"I'll walk you home," said Bruce, coming up behind her.

"I know how to get to my own house."

"I want to." They walked together in silence, not looking back, until finally Maggie said, "I wish I could figure out what's going on with people."

"He's easy to figure out. He gets bored."

"That can't be the only reason why people do the things they do. It's got to be more complicated than that."

"I think it's pretty simple."

Maggie could feel the nail in the pocket of her shorts. They walked along in silence until they got to her backyard and then Maggie ran ahead, across the lawn. She thought she heard a small voice call "good-by"; then there was no sound except the crickets. But when she got upstairs to her bedroom, before she turned on the light, she looked out and she could see Bruce still standing at the edge of the yard. She thought he'd seen her, too, because as soon as she'd looked out the window he'd turned and walked back into the development, his head down.

Her door opened, and her mother was standing in the doorway. The light from the hallway fell through the pale folds of her nylon nightgown, and Maggie looked away.

"I thought you were staying at the Malones," Connie said.

"I changed my mind."

"I could hear your voice outside," Connie said, still standing in the half-dark. "Were you with some boy out there?"

"I was talking to a boy I know. Bruce."

"That poor boy whose mother died?"

Maggie winced. Connie added, "Aren't you a little young to be hanging out at night with boys?"

"How old is old enough to be hanging out at night with boys?"

Connie shrugged. She looked tired. The lines from her nose to her mouth seemed deeper than usual. "I don't know. I'm asking you."

"Don't ask me. You're the mother."

"Then I think you're too young."

"I'm getting older," Maggie said, wanting to say much more. "I'm getting a lot older." She expected her mother to ask her what she meant by that, but instead she just sighed. "Yes," Connie said, "I know." She sniffed and Maggie was afraid she could smell the smoke, then realized it must be the Tabu. Connie turned on the bedside lamp and looked at Maggie sadly. Then she smiled. "That's pretty," she said, pointing to Maggie's head.

Maggie took the clover chain off and held it, limp and dying, in her hand. "Where did you get that?" Connie said.

"I made it," Maggie said. "It's easy. You just tie them together. Mrs. Malone taught us. Don't you know how?"

Connie shook her head.

"Your mother didn't teach you?"

Connie shook her head again. "I don't know whether she didn't know how or she just didn't want to teach me."

"I think if she didn't do it, it was probably because she didn't know how. If she could have, she would have."

"Maybe," said Connie. "Go to sleep." Then she ran her hand along Maggie's upper arm. "What did you do?" she asked, and Maggie looked down to see the marks of fingers purpling on the tan skin above her elbow.

"I fell," she said, drawing back. Her mother looked at her for a long minute, and then turned and left, closing the door behind her.

When her mother was gone Maggie stared at herself in the mirror. She looked at the bruises and put the nail from her pocket into her jewelry box, the red leather one Celeste had given her for her birthday. She lay in bed, the moon casting a silver shaft of cold light across the ceiling, and wondered whether in the morning she would be saddled with another dreamlike memory, half real, half incredible. For a long time she kept her eyes open wide in the darkness, and finally, still smelling smoke, she fell asleep.

11

OHN SCANLAN'S HOSPITAL ROOM looked like a committee meeting of the Friendly Sons of St. Patrick. A half dozen men, sleek and florid in their sharkskin and seersucker suits, came in after work to pump his good hand and make jokes about pinching the nurses. Tommy stayed out in the hall, wandering around the nurses' station, buying a bag of M & M's from the vending machine and eating them in the stairwell, reading the newspaper. It was cool in the hospital, and after ten days the nurses were accustomed to seeing the Scanlan family and didn't take much notice of them.

The day before, a student nurse had seen Tommy looking through some papers near her desk and had snatched them from him, her little freckled face as agitated as an infant's. "Mr. Scanlan," she had said, the white cotton curving over the shelf of her bosom, which vibrated with indignation, "that is your father's chart." "Damn straight," Tommy had replied. The doctor had a horrible scrawl—not a Catholic boy, that's for sure, no wonder only the Jews were doctors, the nuns would have their rulers out over this stuff—and the only part Tommy could make out appeared again and again, day after day: "No improvement."

Tommy had been having trouble sleeping. There was a bend in the street just in front of the house, and when a car came by he would watch the diamond-shaped patterns of the lights roll across the ceiling and over the top of Connie's head, like a searchlight. He had black dreams that he could remember only in bits, a rodent face here, a free fall there, a chase, a pursuit, a knife, a gun, but no tale to wrap around them. He would wake with adrenaline throbbing in his chest and look over at his wife, who slept with her hands folded on her chest, her hair fanning out on the pillow. He wondered what was in her dreams.

He was not willing to connect his nightmares to the sight of his father in the hospital bed. He was not even willing to concede that the man was very sick. John Scanlan had turned his hospital room into an office, with piles of invoices and correspondence on the window sill. His former secretary, a square and silent woman named Dorothy O'Haire, who had faded blond hair and dark eyes, came for three hours each day to help him keep up and to read him the newspapers. Tommy knew that Dorothy was there a great deal, but somehow he never managed to see her when he was at the hospital. She had stopped working for John Scanlan nine years ago, when her daughter had been born, but when she heard of the stroke she had volunteered to come back and help. John had told the chief of staff that they would never see another penny of Scanlan money if they didn't discharge him at the end of the week, but the doctors had steadfastly refused to let him go home, and the best the old man had been able to do was to bully them into letting Dorothy in outside visiting hours. "I have my ways," he told his son when he asked about the arrangment. "Mind your own business."

When Tommy was at the hospital, his father seemed much as usual, except that he wore striped pajamas especially bought for the hospital stay. ("Goddamn pansy clothes," he said, when they brought them in. "Sixty-five years and I never wore a pair of these things until now.") During the day, he was at his best: swearing at the staff, demanding more pillows, making the nurse take the crucifix down from the wall so he could determine the model and estimate how much the hospital was paying for its religious articles, bullying Dorothy while she stared at him fixedly.

Tommy never saw his father at night, when he seemed almost as ill as he had been at the beginning, when the corner of his mouth hung low so that his face looked like the masks of both comedy and tragedy; when, although his mother had been dead for nearly half a century, he talked to her about the beginnings of his business and James's whooping cough; when he cried like a baby against the pleated dress front of some night nurse and said, "I don't know, I don't know" over and over again. Even John did not fully remember those times.

Tommy could tell his father was thinking about the more distant past, carrying it with him like a bad taste in his mouth. Occasionally John would lie back on the pillows, his shoulders slipping into the two comfortable narrow grooves worn in the mattress, and then Tommy knew his father was remembering all the others who had dreamed their lives away in taverns, slept them away on sofas in small front rooms, all the men from his boyhood in the tenement buildings who had squandered their lives sitting on stoops, taking their time, telling their stories, being "That Jack, now what a fine fellow he is" and "That Joe, you can't beat him for a good yarn," wasting away from lack of ambition until they were only death's-heads with a lifetime of jokes to their credit. Sometimes John Scanlan thought he owed them everything, because they had haunted him every day of his life, his own old man among them, putting in his time at the Department of Public Works, leaving a life insurance policy just large enough to cover the two-night wake and the plot at St. Ann's. In the hospital they danced in his head whenever he rested, and he would sit up suddenly and begin to add up columns of figures as though possessed, as indeed he always had been. Tommy could tell when his father had been having these spells because John would look at his middle son suspiciously, noticing his resemblance to those hail-fellows-well-met of years gone by.

Tommy came to the hospital every day, apologizing for Connie's absence, saying she was sick, which was true but not the problem. She said she hated hospitals, although she did well enough in them when she was having the kids. She said sometimes that it was a good thing that her own mother had died suddenly, turning a lavender blue one evening at the kitchen table and sliding to the linoleum floor, dead somewhere between the edge of the table and the legs of the chair, because Connie could not have borne being with her in the hospital. Connie could not have borne being with her anyway, Tommy thought.

Margaret was there most afternoons, too, and after a while it occurred to Tommy to wonder how she had so much time on her hands. "It's summer," his sister had said, but that didn't seem reason enough. She had taken to carrying a book with her whenever she came to the hospital, and for the first few days Tommy thought it was the New Testament. Waiting out in the hall for his father's room to empty of visitors, he had looked at the title: *Jane Eyre, An Autobiography.*

"How come you're reading *Jane Eyre?*" Maggie asked her aunt, peeking over her father's shoulder.

"Just for fun," Margaret said.

"You've never read it before?" said Maggie. "It's a great book."

"Is it religious?" Tommy asked.

Margaret laughed. "Tom, honey, underneath this habit—it's me. Average girl. Good dancer. I'm allowed to read books that aren't necessarily religious, or even edifying." Tommy looked skeptical.

"Inside every nun is a woman," she added.

"Do me a favor, Peg," Tommy replied, using her old childhood nickname. "Don't tell Dad that. He's had one stroke already."

After the men had left, all the men who did business with John Scanlan, and all the ones who wanted to, the ones who owned the cement and construction and candle and casket companies, Tommy went into his father's room, his daughter and his sister behind him. Buddy Phelan had brought a fruit basket, which was still wrapped in its tinted plastic. There was a bottle of Canadian Club and two cans of ginger ale on the bedside table.

"That Monica was in here an hour ago," John said to Maggie, "sweet as can be. More there than meets the eye, I bet. She said all you girls were having a grand time at the seashore before I gave you such a scare. What's your problem down there, little girl?"

"I'm tying my shoe," said Maggie, who did not want him to see her face.

"You shouldn't be coming to see me here wearing those sneakers, like you're going to play basketball instead of going to call on your grandfather. You girls don't have good sense. Your cousin Teresa was here yesterday, wearing a scapular under her little shirt. Can you beat that? The Sacred Heart shining through the white of her blouse, like a big stain. The girl's an imbecile."

"She has Sister Luke. She's very religious. She loves stuff like that."

"Nuns," John Scanlan snorted, and Margaret laughed. "The only one I've ever known with the sense God gave her is your aunt. Don't be a nun, girl. Give me your word."

"I don't know, Grandpop," Maggie said, thinking of the scene at the Malones, and the flames licking the corner of the development house. "It sounds kind of peaceful."

"Ha," her grandfather said. "Peaceful. Who gives a damn about peaceful. That makes for a dull life, girl. Remember that. How's your brother?"

"Which one?"

"All of them, for Christ's sake. How the hell am I supposed to keep track of all these children?" He reached into the bottom drawer of the bedside table and drew out a Mason jar that glowed amber in the hospital lights. "They would have killed me days ago if it wasn't for the Scotch," he said. He poured two fingers' worth into a plastic cup and added water from a pitcher. "Don't tell on me," he said to Maggie, as though his children were not there, and drank it down.

"You better watch the booze, Pop," Margaret said.

"You watch your mouth, Sister," John Scanlan said. "I'm still your father even if you are a bride of Christ. I need some time alone with your brother here. Take your niece to the cafeteria and buy her a chocolate bar."

When they were gone the old man leaned back and closed his eyes.

"Jesus, Dad, you're killing yourself," Tommy said, moving empty glasses to the windowsill, but his father just lay there and looked at him, his eyes dull. With the departure of his daughter and his granddaughter, John Scanlan seemed to shrink and grow gray. Tommy sat down in the visitor's chair and waited for some sort of tirade.

"I don't know, Tommy," John finally said, sounding half asleep. "I don't know what the hell to think. I'm tired of this damn hospital. Father McLeod came in here today to talk to me. Scots-Irish, for God's sake. Who the hell ordained him? He says I've had a rare treat in devoting my business life to the business of God. He'd been practicing that one all the way over in the black Buick, right?" The brogue was beginning to creep into his father's voice and Tommy inhaled deeply. The room felt close and smelled of Clorox. "I said 'There's my problem, Father. I should have been devoting my business life to the business of making money.' Now I've got your brother in here, wants to have one of the Manila factories making little blouses for girls. Says that down there in the city the girls are dressing up like fortunetellers and buying embroidered blouses. Big market. I said 'Jesus Christ, Mark, why don't we just change over to dresses?' He thought I was serious. Told me he wanted to discuss that next. Jesus Christ. I've wasted my life."

"Stop," Tommy said.

"The priest asks me if I want the last rites. He said there's nothing to be afraid of, that he knows I know the rewards of life eternal. Life eternal, shit." The old man's face was beginning to redden, his long fingers on the sheets to shake. Tommy came over to the bed. He thought about taking his father's hand, but instead held onto the button that summoned the nurse. "I don't give a good goddamn about life eternal, I told him. I got everything in my life the way I wanted it, everything all lined up right, and I want it to stay that way. Everything. It's not the dying I mind, it's the changing. You see what I mean." He looked up at Tommy, and the younger man began to cry at the terrible light in his father's eyes, as though John Scanlan was seeing visions. "Everything the way I want it. After all this time. You want to keep it just the way it is. Right? Right?"

"I don't know, Dad," Tommy said.

The big head fell, the silver hair looking greasy and gray. John Scanlan reached over for a jelly glass on the bedside table and sipped slowly. "Stop whimpering," he said without looking up. "Your daughter's a funny girl. Takes things too seriously. Always stewing over something. Not like that Monica. She's a slick one, that Monica. She's not pulling anything over on me. I knew a girl just like her once. Went off to Hollywood and took a screen test. Married a man old enough to be her father who owned half of Los Angeles. What was I telling you?"

"Connie apologizes for not—"

"Ah, don't give me that crap, Tommy," said the old man, waving his hand. "Where's your mother?"

"She's coming over later with a piece of pie. Rhubarb pie that your sister Anne made."

"Oh Jesus. The kids must really think the end is near, they're sending me pie." John Scanlan always called his younger brothers and sisters "the kids." He saw them once a year, at a party he held in the reception room of Scanlan & Co. Last year his youngest brother had gotten so drunk that he had approached John, jabbed him in his red boutonniere with his index finger, and said, "I hate your guts." "I know, Jamie, I know," the elder man had said, putting his arm around his brother's shoulder. "And well you should."

"And your mother, too, carting pie from Annie over here," John said now, sipping his drink. "She must be scared."

"Stop," said Tom again.

"Do me a favor," John Scanlan said suddenly, his eyes narrow, shrewd as a predatory bird's. "Help us out in the business or your brother will be pushing ladies' lingerie with the sheenies down on 38th Street. I don't think he knows his ass from his elbow."

"I'll think about it," Tommy said.

"How's the building going, out by you?"

"They're working fast."

"The men are coming this week to clean out your new house. Your mother has them waxing the floors and washing down the walls."

Tommy squared his shoulders, and all the sympathy he had felt evaporated, as though the blood was draining from his body. He was cold with the emptiness of his antagonism and his fear, and he knew how scared he was when he began to wonder if his father's despair and weakness had all been a ploy to lead to this moment.

"We don't want the house," he said. "We're fine where we are. Really. Give it to Joe. He and Annette will be thrilled."

John Scanlan closed his eyes, and Tommy wondered if he had drifted off to sleep. Then slowly the heavy lids came up, and Tommy saw that his father's eyes were like blue bullets, aimed straight to the heart.

"No mortgage payments," he said.

"I can handle my mortgage payments," Tommy said.

"Not without a job you can't," John Scanlan said, and Tommy heard in his voice the word "Checkmate."

"What the hell is that supposed to mean?"

"You figure it out, buddy boy. I've done my part. I gave you a good job at that concrete company, and I'll give you a better one over to the factory, and I bought you and your wife a house fit for a king and queen. I've done my part. It's time you did yours."

"Why are you doing this? I'm a grown man. I run my own life."

John Scanlan let out a great snort, and then began to cough, a cough so long and hacking that Tommy thought he would never catch his breath. For a minute Tommy thought he'd like to just let him choke to death, and then he poured his father a glass of water and handed it to him. Finally John was quiet again, his chest heaving. The two men stared at each other. Tommy knew that his father was going to die, and he knew that John Scanlan had set himself a task before he did so and that that task was to see that the last of the Scanlan boys was exactly where he wanted him to be. He knew, too, that the family would gather round, waiting, waiting, for Tommy to do this one small thing for a dying man, and that if he did it, that which made him who he was would be lost forever, and he would become what he had so often been called: one of the Scanlan boys. One of the old man's sons. A fight to the finish, they called it in cowboy movies, and so it was, and Tommy knew he would lose. Suddenly John Scanlan smiled at him, and Tommy knew that they had both been thinking the same thing.

"This won't work," Tommy said.

"You want to bet?" John said. "I'll bet you a baby grand piano for that new living room."

Tommy stood up. He could hear his mother outside, talking to the nurse. "Why?" he said again.

"I owe it to you, son," John said. "You'd only make a mess of it yourself."

"No."

"Tom," the old man said when Tommy was at the door, "your wife's expecting again, James said."

Tommy nodded.

"Good," said John Scanlan. "I'm happy to hear that."

There was a long silence. Tommy could hear his father's breathing, a rumbling trapped inside the sunken chest. His father's eyes narrowed, and the breathing become more labored. "This one last thing," the old man said, his hand over his heart.

"Jesus," Tommy said, "you're really doing it. Pat O'Brien and the deathbed scene. The old Irish dad and his last request."

"I'm more alive than you are, sonny boy," John Scanlan said.

"Go to hell."

"Listen, Tommy. Let me let you in on a secret. There is no hell. There's no heaven, either. There's only this. You have to make the best of it. I'm going to make the best of it for you. You and your pretty wife."

"No."

"Yes," John Scanlan said. "Now send your mother in. And give your brother a hand before he drives the whole kit and caboodle into the goddamn ground."

12

ONNIE LAY BACK AGAINST THE SEAT OF her brother-in-law Mark's new car and thought that it smelled like the inside of an expensive purse. It looked like the inside of a purse, too, come to think of it, or at least like the inside of Mark's wife's purse. Connie remembered one evening going into Gail's black clutch bag to get some aspirin and discovering that aside from a wallet that looked brand new, a set of keys, a lipstick, and a comb, there was nothing inside, not even a stray bobby pin. Just for a moment it had crossed her mind that the reason Gail was unable to have children was because she didn't leave any crumbs, or pennies, or used tissues floating around in the bottom of her purse. She knew it was a mean thought, and reflexively, the way her aunt Rose had taught her to do when she was small, she had made the sign of the cross.

Gail was driving her home from the party because Connie felt sick. She felt sick all the time now. It was a struggle to breathe in the heavy hot July air, the cannonball of her womb lodged just below her ribs, crowding her lungs. She stared out the window, knowing she must represent some kind of reproach to her childless sister-in-law.

The road was edged with black-eyed Susans; Connie could remember she and her father digging them up not far from here one long-ago Sunday. It had been the summer she was twelve, when Anna Mazza was spending most of her time in Brooklyn. The aunt who had taken Anna in when she came to America was old and sick, her belly grown big and blue from cancer. Connie had been left alone with her father, working with him in the garden for the first time. It had begun with a hollyhock covered in black bugs, its tall stem dirty and withered. It had ended when her mother came home, scowling her disapproval at the grass stains on Connie's clothes. Or perhaps it had been when Celeste came back from the shore, walking up the drive and through the gates, her swelling behind encased in a kind of playsuit in a shiny blue-and-red synthetic print of cowboys and Indians. "Movie star," Connie had said a little disdainfully, kneeling in front of the tomatoes. "Who are you, Lana Turner?"

"Rita Hayworth," said Celeste, who actually did resemble Rita Hayworth, and then she gave her uncle Angelo a big kiss. He drew back as though she had bitten him on the nose, and he looked her full figure up and down with an expression of shock and horror. And then he turned and stared at his daughter and that expression was still there, the kind of look Connie imagined God must have given Eve in the Garden of Eden.

"You all dirty," was all he said.

It was many years later that she had realized that that was the day her father discovered she was female. She had never felt close to him again, and she was convinced that he had never felt close to her.

She thought she saw a shadow of that same look pass over his face when he saw her in her wedding dress, coming down the stairs with her bouquet in one hand. She remembered what she had thought at the time: he's just a man, an ordinary man.

She had thought that, too, when she first saw John Scanlan in the hospital, a vulnerable, ordinary, shrunken man surrounded by white cotton. She even sometimes thought it of Tommy, when she lay beside him at night, although it did not make her angry at him the way it did with his father, and her own. It only awakened her sympathy. When her father had first given her that look, it had made her feel ashamed; now she merely thought that men were somehow afraid of the things they loved best, that they were the real children of the world, without bringing with them any of the joys you had with children, at least for a time.

She knew the contours of her bedroom in the dark as well as she knew anything; the shadow of the two-pronged light fixture like the letter W on the ceiling, the pale-yellow light through the drape of the curtains from the streetlight across the lawn, the odd blotches, like old faces, made by the cabbage roses on the wallpaper, the sliding shadows of the six-paned windows as a car came up and around the street, its engine wheezing in the still night air. Against the wall was a composite picture of her three oldest children: Maggie holding Terence holding Damien, ages seven, six, and one, and then individual portraits of each, the baby a little spastic propped on a platform, the other two wearing fixed, forced smiles. Between the first two and the next two she had had two miscarriages, surges of odd clots that had made her think she was being punished for not loving her children enough, for not believing they were what she had always thought they would be to her. The pregnancies were always difficult, too, kneeling on the bathroom floor, staring into the water in the toilet bowl. The first time she had thought she was dying, or would have a retarded child, a baby with no fingers, or seven fingers, or a mongoloid like Leonard Fogarty. "Listen, kid," Celeste had said, "everybody throws up when they're in the family way. That's how you know you are." Like almost everything her cousin said, it sounded improbable; like almost everything she said, it turned out to be right.

Connie had never had a pregnancy test. One night soon after Maggie was born she had eaten a bad clam at a Coney Island clam bar and had spent the next week wondering how they would afford another baby. It had seemed sort of ridiculous until two months later, when she was sick again and it turned out that she was pregnant with Terence.

Her sisters-in-law were never ill when they were pregnant. Joe's wife, Annette, had played tennis up until the week before she had the twins, although everyone had made such a fuss about it that Connie was more amazed by her ability to withstand the criticism than to rush the net. James's wife had admitted to "a little gas," but quietly and with a guilty manner, as though she thought it might be seen as some reflection on her husband's professional skill.

This afternoon Connie had been at a card party with all of them, at one of the boys' schools just north of Kenwood, a big Gothic building with a Latin inscription over the double doors, and they had all exchanged glances when she had leapt up to find the one women's bathroom in the whole cavernous place. "She really has a hard time, doesn't she?" Jack's wife, Maureen, had said, with an air of assumed sympathy, and they all nodded and thought to themselves: God, the fuss.

But their eyes all seemed to meet in the vicinity of Gail's long, faintly equine face. Then they looked at the cards in their hands, which they busily rearranged. "She certainly does," Gail said, looking around. She often felt that she was unfairly lumped with Connie, that because she had been born Protestant and converted to marry Mark she too was considered an outsider. She made every attempt to show that this was not the case.

"Are you all right?" Annette had asked when Connie came back to the table, her face newly powdered, fresh lipstick dark against the white. She had not been able to find the right bathroom, and had thrown up in a stainless steel sink in the chemistry lab.

"Fine. I'm used to it."

"What about some tea with milk?" Cass had said.

"Nothing. I think I'd better go."

The women had looked around at one another. One of them would have to drive Connie home, and the petits fours had not even come around yet, nor the door prize been announced. The prize was a black cashmere sweater with a dyed mink collar, and everyone had exclaimed over it except for Mrs. O'Neal, who said she already had one, and Mrs. Malone, who said she'd give it away if she got it. "You could give it to Helen," someone said. "It's just the color of her hair." Everyone was quiet for a moment. "Helen's lost her mind," Mrs. Malone said drily, "but I haven't."

Finally Connie said, "Gail, could you give me a lift?"

"Of course," her sister-in-law said, and the others had leaned back and looked at their cards as the two women gathered up their pocketbooks and their white summer gloves. "Tommy looks tired these days," Cass said, as she watched them walk away and they began to play cards again.

"Tommy looks tired these days," said Gail as they drove along in her black sedan, Connie thinking to herself that Gail really did not know how to negotiate a corner properly.

"He *is* tired," Connie said. "He works hard all day and he goes to the hospital a lot in the evening."

"How does he think Dad looks?" Gail asked.

"Like hell." There was silence for several blocks, then Connie said. "Tell Mark to get John to leave him alone. He's driving him nuts with all this about the house and the company. Tom feels bad enough about his father. It's not fair to be holding him up on this now."

Gail touched her barrettes and smoothed back her hair. She had never heard Connie say so much before. "I think Tommy should talk to Mark about it. I don't get involved in his business."

"Oh bullshit, Gail," Connie said, plucking at the fingers of her gloves. She realized it was the first time she had ever said the word out loud, and she liked the feel of it in her mouth, the sound of it, like a powerful and disdainful sneeze. "Everybody's business is everybody else's business in this family. Nobody's made a decision on their own in all the years I've been around."

"That may be how you feel—"

"Who picked out your house, Gail?"

Her sister-in-law's narrow lips tightened. "I did."

"John Scanlan did. He heard it was for sale the day after the old man who lived in it died and Mark bought it that afternoon. So don't tell me about keeping your business private. If you hadn't bought it, he would have tried to get Tommy to buy it. If not Tommy, Joe. Margaret gets passed over because of the convent. Pull over."

"Excuse me?"

"Pull over," Connie said, "or I'm going to throw up on your upholstery."

When she was finished and they had pulled away from the curb, they were both silent again. Finally Connie reached out tentatively and touched her sister-in-law's arm.

"I'm sorry," she said. "I just don't want Tommy to worry. He worries all the time."

"He has to take some responsibility for the family, Connie," Gail said primly.

"Why? Why does he have to? They're all adults. He takes enough responsibility in his heart."

They turned onto Park Street and the trees arched over them, a tunnel lined with brick and stucco façades, closed doors with impenetrable screens. From somewhere they could hear children yelling, and the sound of bulldozers. As they pulled into the driveway, the windows of the car a blur of reflected sunlight and tree branches, Connie thought she saw Terence sitting on the steps of the house, his big shaggy head hanging heavy between his knees. But as he looked up she realized it was Joey Martinelli, and she swung open the car door fast, feeling for the ground with her patent-leather high heels, still a little faint. "I've been waiting for you," he called, not moving.

"Thanks for the ride," Connie said.

"Is that—?" said Gail, and stopped.

"Is that who, Gail?"

"Mark said that you were—friendly with one of the—workers at the construction sight." Gail got the words out as though she was speaking English as a second language, and Connie smiled.

"Now, I managed to figure out that *workers* meant greasy dagos but I'm not quite sure about *friendly*. Does friendly mean I talk to him in the kitchen when he comes over for a drink of water, or does friendly mean I'm meeting him in my slip behind the bulldozers?"

Gail inhaled audibly. "I don't know why you have to be like this," she said. "No one means anything by what they say and yet you take everything as an insult. Any other woman would be thrilled to have her in-laws buy her a big house. It's much bigger than any of the rest of us have, but I don't begrudge it, with all these children. But to have a family that takes an interest, and then to be so critical—I just don't understand it. At the smallest thing you take offense, you assume that somehow you are being insulted, you . . ."

"What does my illicit relationship with the Carpenters' Union have to do with a big house I don't want or need?"

"It's the principle of the thing," Gail said, her face unpleasantly mottled with emotion. "Everything with you is a struggle. What would be just part of life for other people has to be some sort of big complicated thing with you. You isolate Tommy from his family, you make it clear you have contempt for all of us—"

"I have contempt for you? That's a good one."

"No one cares about ethnic differences any longer, Connie. No one thinks about those things."

"How come John says my oldest son has guinea eyebrows?"

"You see, that's just the point. He makes a little joke—"

As Connie climbed out of the car, a favorite expression of Celeste's popped into her head, and without thinking she said, "Button it, Gail." She walked over to Joey as her sister-in-law backed out of the driveway. "Sorry," he said as she approached, pale beneath her powder, her nose beginning to shine. "It's okay," she said, sitting down beside him.

"You're going to get your dress all dirty. Plus your lady friend is still watching you."

Connie looked up and waved at Gail, then put her elbows on her knees and her chin in her hands. It occurred to her suddenly that her heart was beating fast, and that she was having a good time. It was difficult to tell whether it was because of Gail, or because of Joey. When she looked at him she could see herself in his eyes. "I don't know what's come over me," she said, talking almost to herself. "Why were you waiting for me?" she added.

"Time for another lesson."

"I'm not sure I can right now. Are the kids inside?"

"Not so I can tell."

Connie eased her pumps off and stretched her legs in front of her. "My sisters-in-law aren't bad people. They just don't like me," she said.

"I can understand that," Joey said.

"Thanks," Connie said.

"It's an old thing, isn't it?" he said. "Women don't get on with a good-looking woman." Then, as though he'd realized what he said, he ducked his glossy head. "You know what I mean. I even remember my mother and her friends talking about you, how you were the best-looking girl any of them had ever seen." He laughed. "Except that no one would ever notice it because you were a midget princess held prisoner in a deep, dark cemetery."

Connie laughed, too, but she could tell she was still pink and flustered by the compliment. "Your mother's nice," she said, not knowing what else to say.

"I think she always hoped my brother would marry you. She was mad as hell when she found out you were going to marry Scanlan. She said you were just making trouble for yourself." For a moment the two of them looked at each other, and then Connie sighed.

"Let's go in," she finally said.

Inside, the house was perfectly still and smelled faintly of tuna fish. She dropped her shoes on the living-room floor and stood barefoot at the bottom of the stairs. "Maggie?" she called, but there was no answer.

Outside a car stopped, idled, died. Connie opened the door to see Celeste getting out. For some reason she was wearing a picture hat with fake flowers around the brim. She waved, and wobbled up the steps on a pair of stiletto heels, white patent leather with black scuff marks. "Damn," she said, looking down, wetting her finger and balancing on one foot like a flamingo to raise the other and try to wipe away the marks. Connie laughed and held the door open for her. At least Gail had missed this.

"Sorry to bust in," Celeste said. "I got you a blouse on sale." Celeste looked at Connie's navy-blue linen sheath with the white piping. "Don't tell me—let me guess. Lunch with your mother-in-law."

"Very good, Ce, very good. Card party with my sisters-in-law."

"All of them?"

"All of them."

Celeste screamed, clutched her breast, fell to the couch. Then she reached inside her shopping bag. "Next time, wear this," she said. "It's a size four. You're the only person in the world who could wear it." Celeste held up a white lace blouse. Connie could see daylight through it. Joey appeared in the doorway, holding a glass of water. "Who's that for?" he said, his big eyebrows raised.

"Whoops," said Celeste.

"How you doing, Celeste?" Joey Martinelli said. "You remember me?"

"Now that I see you I do," said Celeste, handing her cousin the blouse. "You used to hang out with Bobby, who lived around the block. The one who's a cop now? With the brother who's a cop?"

"Giambone. Bobby Giambone. Yeah, I met you at his house once. You were maybe sixteen, seventeen. I think you were engaged."

Celeste sighed. "I was engaged all the time then. So how come I don't see you around any more?"

"Ah, I don't know. You know how it is—we're all grown-up now. No more parties, no more dances. I never see anybody. I work, I go home, fall asleep. That's about it."

"You ever see Bobby?"

"He moved out of the city. He has a nice place with one of those above-ground pools out on the Island. He hates the city. All the cops, they hate the city."

Celeste reached out for his water glass and sipped from it thoughtfully, leaving a lip print on it the color of bubble gum. "So how's it coming?" she said, jerking her head toward the window, the flowers on her hat moving as though a thunderstorm was coming up.

"Okay. We're having a little bit of trouble with the kids out there. A lot of them are bored with vacation and vandalizing the place in their spare time. They set us back some."

"Kids'll be kids," Celeste said.

"Yeah, well some of them are being a little more than kids. Somebody set fire to one of the models two nights ago. Thank God it didn't do too much damage."

"Which night?" Connie asked, narrowing her eyes.

"Night before last. If it happens again, we got a real problem."

"So you're not done yet," Celeste said.

"We'll be done the models soon. A lot of the others will be finished by October, the rest in November. We sold the first one two days ago."

"You sold one?" Connie said.

"Yeah, to a young couple who live in Queens. He's in business.

They have one kid, a little girl, must be adopted. She's Korean. I think they're Jewish."

Celeste started to laugh, and the flowers on the hat went wild. "What's so funny?" Joey Martinelli said.

"She's thinking about my husband's father," Connie said, and she began to smile.

Celeste let out a whoop. "Bring the old man over here in an ambulance," she said, gasping for breath. "Jews with a Chink kid. Oh my god. He'll move to another state."

"My father-in-law isn't crazy about all this," Connie said. "He's ready to move us to a better neighborhood."

"Hey, I'm always for that," said Joey, grinning.

"So *you* move," Connie said. "I like picking my own neighborhood."

"I love that guy," said Celeste. "He's perfect. My mother says to me last week, 'Father O'Hearn over to Holy Redeemer gave the damnedest sermon yesterday. It was about Jesus and golf.' I said 'Ma, do me a favor. Call the hospital and tell Mr. Scanlan.' "

Joey Martinelli smiled. "That's some hat you got," he said, but his eyes were on Connie, who was stretching her legs in front of her, wiggling her toes, cramped from their afternoon in her good pumps. Her skirt had crept up her legs, and the curve of her thighs shone in nylon stockings. "I like that blouse," Joey said to no one in particular, and Connie crumpled it up in her fist, an edge of white lace falling from between her fingers. Celeste looked from Joey's face to that of her cousin, and then back again. "Fix me a seven-and-seven, Con," she said, her eyes narrowed, and she patted the couch beside her. "Joe," she said, "you come sit here next to me."

13

AL'S WAS A TAVERN A BLOCK AWAY from First Concrete. Its door was set on a diagonal at the corner of two busy streets and thrown into perpetual shade by the elevated subway line. It looked like any tavern in America at the time, with neon beer signs in the window and red plastic seats in the booths and gangly bar stools ranged around a long, long bar filled with old men in the afternoons and working men at night. Above the register hung the first dollar Sal's ever took in, nineteen years earlier. The only thing worth mentioning about Sal's was that they made a spectacular hamburger out of good-grade chuck that Sal D'Alessandro got from a cop who got it as part of his payoff from a wholesale butcher in the wholesale meat market. All the cops ate and drank free at Sal's, and if any of their wives called, Sal always said their husbands had just been there and been called out on some emergency. Tommy usually ate lunch at Sal's. He liked the company and the food.

He took Mark there when, during the last week in July, his brother asked him to lunch. "Jesus, look at this place," Mark said, staring at the retired guys with gray stubble on their faces watching *As the World Turns* on the television. Sal came over after they got their beers, a bar towel hanging from the waistband of his pants. He shook hands with Mark officiously, like the maître d' in a bad French restaurant, and said that Mark looked like his mother. "When was Mom ever in this place?" Mark said, leaning across the table after Sal had left. "You got me," Tommy said. "Dad used to come here for lunch when he was still down the street, but I can't imagine him bringing Mom here." Mark looked around again and said, "Well, she sure as hell didn't come here by herself."

Tommy liked being with his brothers like this, alone, one on one, and he particularly liked being with Mark, who was only a year older than he was, and for whom he felt the slightly condescending sympathy that a man who easily fathers children feels for a man who has been incapable of doing so. ("Maybe it's him," Connie had said one night when they were talking about why Gail hadn't produced a child. "My ass," Tommy had replied, looking like his father.) Not having a family had set Mark apart. Combined with his height, it had diminished him in the family's eyes, and so he was reduced to asserting himself by arguing with his father over the color of embroidery on cassocks. Tommy knew that given a choice between his own position of black sheep and his brother's of barren issue, he'd stick with his own any time.

Gail had once talked about adoption, but John Scanlan had put the lid on that one. "It's not the same," he had said flatly. "You don't know what in the hell you're getting." Then his pale blue eyes had roved over his own family, ranged in their habitual postures of attention and apprehension in his living room. "I don't know," he had added, "maybe you never know."

Tommy had known something was up when he and his brother had met outside their father's hospital room two nights ago and Mark had suggested they get together. "Mark asked you to lunch?" Connie had said, one black eyebrow arched, like some exotic form of punctuation. "What's up?" Of course she knew what was up; it was either the company, the house, or her.

Every year or so someone in his family sat down and talked to Tommy about his wife, as though she was a car that needed a paint job. There was never a question of a trade-in—Mary Frances still asked Celeste how her husband was, even though Celeste had been divorced far longer than she'd been married. "Soused," Celeste always answered with good humor. It was only that they all wanted Connie to run more smoothly, to mix in, to blend in, to be more like them. The worst moment of Tommy's life had been a tenth anniversary dinner Mark had given them three years before, at which Connie had become rather high on fruity whiskey sours, the taste of the liquor lost amidst all the pineapple. There had been a cake with a little bride and groom, and toasts, and Connie had turned to all of them, the bride and groom in her hand, and had said in an odd squeaky voice, "Where were all of you on my wedding day?" And she had said it staring straight at John Scanlan, who stared right back. The effect had been blunted a bit by the fact that Connie had suddenly put her hand over her mouth, and run to the bathroom. Tommy went after her, and when they returned, his parents were gone from the table. "How long has that been going on?" James had said in a professional tone of voice to Connie, whose face was gray-white, and Tommy had said, "Jesus, James, she drank too much." But James had been right after all; she was expecting Joseph at the time, although neither of them had known it.

Now, sitting in Sal's with Tom, Mark said, "So your wife's pregnant again," and the remark lay on the table between them. Then Mark's eyes emptied and he added, "Look, Tom, you're going to need that new house no matter what you say. You'll have five. You need more room."

"We have plenty of room," Tommy said, rubbing the back of his neck. "Let's not start with the house. I don't want to move."

"Your wife doesn't want to move."

"Her too."

"You know she told Gail she wants to live in one of those development houses they're building?"

"Mark, she says those things to get you people aggravated. She's tired of having people make decisions about her life."

Sal arrived with the hamburgers. "Mr. Scanlan, medium," he said, putting the one with the blue stick in its bun in front of Tommy. "Mr.

Scanlan, medium rare," he added, putting the one with the red stick in front of Mark. Tommy wondered where he'd found the little sticks, and how special the occasion needed to be for Sal to use them. Tommy had been ordering hamburgers at Sal's for years and had never had a stick in his before.

Both men ate in silence, ketchup dripping onto their plates. Then Mark said, his mouth full, "People are talking about your wife."

"I don't want to hear this," Tommy said.

"Joe says he went over to St. Pius School to drop off a case of votive candles and he sees her out back with some guy playing hopscotch. She's jumping around like a kid with some big guinea—"

"Hey!" Tommy said, so loudly that two of the men at the bar turned.

"Sorry, sorry, sorry. Anyhow, she waves at Joe like it's the most natural thing in the world for her to be there with some guy. Now, Joe sees her, he makes allowances. Other people are going to wonder what the hell is going on."

Tommy was wondering the same thing himself, but he was damned if he would say anything to Mark. His brother went on talking. "She's always out with those guys who are building those houses," he said. "That's where she was when Pop went into the hospital that day. People have been seeing her out their windows talking to those guys."

Tommy put down his hamburger, wiped his hands on a paper napkin, and sat back in the booth. "She knows the guy who's running the project. He's from her old neighborhood. He's a nice person. She knows his mother. She went out with his brother." He picked up his hamburger. "We're not talking about this anymore. You're all against her. All of you. Always have been."

Tommy was angry and perplexed. That morning he had noticed that the valleys of Connie's face were lavender, the peaks yellow, her eyes as bright as black marbles. She was always ill when she was pregnant, as though it was an early warning. Joseph was beginning to talk in sentences; in a few years he would be saying things she neither liked nor understood. This was the way it was for her, being a mother: a sickness and then a cleaving to her heart, a time of pure love and then the horrible moving away. Sometimes the only way she could love them was to remember them when they were small, pressing her face into the box of flannel receiving blankets in the linen closet, nappy and soft as a baby's head.

Several nights ago, Tommy had been watching the ball game on television, yelling insults at the Yankees pitching staff, throwing pillows at the screen, when he had noticed that Connie was not in the house. Neither were the older children; he was alone with Joseph, who was snoring through a stuffed-up nose in his crib, the night light throwing strange shadows across his fat face. There had been no one on the streets outside, no sound except for the soft murmur of people several houses down talking on their front steps. But in the backyard, just past the dusty bare spot in the center of the grass where home plate had always been, a solitary figure stood looking out toward the development. At first Tom thought it was Maggie, mooning about, but the posture was wrong, the shoulders a little too soft and irresolute, the arms cradling the midsection not angular or awkward enough. It was his wife.

A couple stumbling from the development, a pair of teenagers who lived a few blocks away, nearly ran into her, quiet and small as she was, but they veered off at the last moment, clutching each other's waists, the boy's eyes as blind as a night animal's, his shirttail a crumpled rag outside his chino pants. Connie followed them with her eyes, and then she threw back her head and stared at the stars. Tommy felt afraid.

He went back to the television, back to the armchair, and when she came into the room with a glass of iced tea he pretended she had been with him all the time, just a little out of his line of sight. And she pretended, too. He had told his brother James that she was odd this time, mercurial and withdrawn, even from the children, although as soon as he'd said it he realized she had been that way for some time. Once he'd found her sitting on the floor, just looking at her good china. He couldn't believe that was normal.

"Women have these strange fancies when they're expecting, Tom," James had said, shaking his big handsome head and smiling, and they had left it at that. James had never been the kind of brother to whom

Tommy could confess that he feared his wife's strange fancy was for some guinea with big forearms from the old neighborhood.

He could not believe that she missed that portion of her life. She rarely went to see her father, sending Maggie instead, and he had not found this peculiar. He remembered going for the first time to her parents' home, those two old people, this one lovely, lonely child, and thinking that she was out of the world there, as though she lived in one of those little crystal balls with falling snow inside. He had been amazed that she had even learned to dance, had learned the melody to "Moonlight Serenade," until later, when he had gone to Celeste's house and seen Connie's connection to a normal life. He had always felt a touch of pride at having taken her away from all that, the heavy silent mother with the V cut into one front tooth from biting off thread at the sewing machine, the father who took all his affection outdoors and massaged it into the ground around his beloved plants. Once he had found her, pregnant with their second child, planting tomato plants in the backyard, before one of his sisters-in-law had made a comment about how well Italians did such things, and he had seen tears fall down upon her dirty hands. "I miss my father," she had said, although the old man was only twenty minutes away by car. "Go over and see him," Tom had replied, but she just shook her head. "You don't understand," she had said, sobbing. "Sometimes people are near but they might as well be on the moon." He thought he understood now what she had been saying then.

"How's everything else?" he finally said to his brother to break the silence.

"Come into the business, Tom," Mark said, looking up at him.

"Oh Jesus, not this again."

"Maybe I've been going about it the wrong way. I know your wife is pissed that I've been bothering you—"

"Says who?" Tommy said.

"She told Gail to tell me to lay off."

"Go on," Tommy said.

"But I need your help. Things are changing. There's a lot to be done." Mark stared at his hands. "I've been going over the books,

Tommy. They're not good. The old man moved a lot of money around in strange ways. I don't think we're as solid as he always pretended. Some of the construction companies aren't making money. He mortgaged two of the apartment buildings for that new equipment we got a couple years ago. It's going to take some doing to make things right."

"What do you mean, to make them right?"

"I think the business is in trouble, Tom. I need your help."

"Jesus," Tommy said.

"Jack and Joe are all right, but they're not so smart. I say do something and they do it. But I need a real partner."

"You're exaggerating," Tommy said. "You just want someone to argue with until Pop comes back."

"I need your help. I need someone to work with. It'd be good."

"I have a job," Tommy said, wiping his mouth. "I have a family, I have a house, I have a job."

"The cement company can run itself. Besides, he told me he's thinking of selling it off."

Tommy smiled sourly. "Oh yeah?" he said.

"I figured you knew."

"He'd go that far?" Tommy said.

"He says it's never been a big moneymaker."

"He's full of shit, Mark," Tommy said. "The other day at the hospital he told me he was going to have me fired so that I wouldn't be able to make my mortgage payments and would have to move into that house he bought. He was going to have me fired so that I'd have to work with you to keep food in my kids' mouths. He's got a little chessboard in his head and he's been able to move every piece on the goddamn board except two of them. The last two. Me and my wife. And he won't rest until the game is over, and he's won."

"Jesus, that's a horrible thing to say," Mark said. "Jesus, Tommy, I'm ashamed of you."

"What'd he tell you about me coming into the business?"

The question lay between them as Sal brought coffee and took their empty plates away. Mark took a long time putting milk and sugar in his cup. Finally he said, "The old man told me October first you start as vice president of operations. He says you make five thousand a year more than me."

Tommy laughed. "And you're ashamed of me?" he said, leaning across the table until his forehead almost touched his brother's. "God, Markey, I don't want to piss on your life, but look at you. You're a lackey for him. You don't even have kids because he said adoption was no good. Do you hold it when he takes a piss, too? He's got you just where he wants you. I thought he gave up on me a long time ago, because of Concetta, because I stepped out of line. Now I think he just waited until he knew I thought that, and then he came in for the kill."

"Do you hear yourself? You make your own father sound like a monster."

"You remember when we were kids and Sister Ann Elizabeth asked us to make a drawing of God? You remember? You made him tall and you made his hair yellow and his eyes blue. And so did I. She got such a kick out of that, that our pictures of God looked like the same person. That wasn't just a coincidence, Mark."

"I don't know what you're talking about," Mark said. "I just want you to come into the business with me. You'd be good. We'd be good together. The old man doesn't accept reality. The world is changing. The Church is changing. He's not far off on his jokes about the kaiser rolls. What if they decide to go to using plain pieces of bread at communion? That's a million bucks right down the toilet."

"You're talking to the wrong person about this. Go back to the hospital and talk to the owner of the company."

"He's not coming back, Tom," Mark said.

Tommy felt a chill in his chest and, almost reflexively, his shoulders hunched in, like little wings. "Get out," he said, but his voice was low.

"He's in bad shape. He's much worse than anyone thinks. James says the old man will never really be the same."

"Get out," Tommy said, his voice lower still.

"You come into the business with me, Tom. Take the house. It's a nice house, much nicer than any of those development houses.

Move your wife away from there. It's not good for her. It's not good for you."

"She's fine, Mark. I'm fine."

"No you're not," Mark said.

"Yeah, we are."

"Yeah? Where is your wife right now? Right at this very moment? I can tell you that Gail is at a white sale with Mom and that after that she's going to play bridge with some of her friends and after that she's having dinner with me. Where is Connie right now?"

"She's home taking care of her kids," Tommy said.

"If you're sure of that, fine. If you're sure of that I got nothing further to say. If you're sure of that."

14

AGGIE LIT THE FIFTH FIRE HERSELF.
She felt as though the match jumped
from her hand to the big wet spot
where the lighter fluid had collected
on the plywood wall of the garage.
The house was in the back of the development, up a little rise from
the old creek, and its lumber was still orangy-yellow. It was the spot
on the wall and the fresh look of the wood, she thought when she was
finally alone, that made her think the flames would not spread, even
as they covered the walls like a dazzling cape.

"Isn't it incredible?" said Debbie, who was standing just behind her.

Maggie was struck by several things at once: by the damp smell of
the night, by a persistent trickle of sweat down the back of her head
and into the hollow at the base of her skull, by how hot the flames
became so quickly. It crossed her mind that she was making a memory,
and that she would never in her life be able to communicate the sick
feeling that afflicted her the moment the fire began to leap around
her, the nausea that rose up in her throat as she heard the three people
behind her breathing heavily in the still air. She wondered if this was
the way her mother felt when she was expecting a baby. If it was, she
would never ever have children.

They were out in the development, in a two-car garage. The big square empty space was filled with boxes: a No-Frost refrigerator, a No-Rinse dishwasher, a host of other appliances and fixtures in corrugated brown cardboard. The younger kids had been having a field day, turning empty boxes into tunnels, caves, houses, hauling them out of the big refuse pile to one side of the development and dragging them home as their mothers screamed from the kitchen windows "You take that right back where you found it." Damien had started collecting scraps of Formica, little punched-out circles and half moons where the kitchen installers had carved out holes for plumbing pipes or planed the edge of a counter into a curve. He had a big box full in his room, amid his butterflies and cacti, and sometimes he would take them out and look at them, feeling the smooth surfaces, even sniffing them, and smiling. "You're nuts," Terence said.

Maggie had gone to get Debbie after dinner, but Mrs. Malone had said she was not at home. "Did you two girls have a fight?" she added, frowning.

"Not exactly," said Maggie.

"You come inside and have a Popsicle and tell me about it," Mrs. Malone said, but Maggie had gone off by herself to the development. She knew exactly where to find Debbie and the others. She could smell them now, like a tracking dog; she could smell the accelerant and the sulfur.

The second fire had, like the first, flared and died. The third and fourth had happened when she was not there; one had leveled the walls of a closet, the other had left a black hole the size of the gym's center court mark on the bedroom floor of a house that was barely a frame. She had become accustomed now to not being able to find Debbie when she wanted her, to discovering her at the pool, giggling behind her hand with Bridget Hearn. They would fall silent, their faces flat, as soon as Maggie appeared. It was halfway through the summer, and Maggie felt that the structure of her life had tumbled down around her, her safe haven at the cemetery somehow strange and unsatisfactory now, her invincible grandfather wasting away amid the white of his hospital bed, her parents absent in spirit and sometimes in fact, her best friend a stranger. She had only found out about the third and fourth fires because Joey Martinelli had told her mother one afternoon when the two of them were in the kitchen having coffee and didn't realize that Maggie was in the house. When Maggie had come downstairs for lemonade, quiet in bare feet, her mother had leapt from her chair like a mouse caught in a spring trap, and Mr. Martinelli had been so discomfited that he had asked her how school was. Maggie had felt like an intruder in her own kitchen, and, lying on her bed afterward, had wondered if she would ever belong anywhere again.

She had gone over to the Malones' that same afternoon, and found Debbie in her room, lying on the bed, still pink from a day at the club. Maggie had lain down on Aggie's bed, too, and they had talked in a desultory fashion for a few minutes before lapsing into silence. Finally Debbie had cleared her throat. "I think before you come over you should call and see whether I'm here," she finally said. "And make sure I'm here alone and not already with somebody else."

Maggie had continued to stare at the ceiling. There was a crack that ran across one corner that she knew as well as she knew her own face in the mirror. She traced it with her eyes, back and forth, back and forth.

"Sometimes I might be with other people," Debbie added. "There are things that I'm interested in now that you're not that interested in."

"Like what?" Maggie said.

"How should I know?" Debbie shot back. "Maybe we're maturing at different rates. Bridget says she was friends with Gigi McMenamin for years and years and then they stopped being friends because Gigi just wasn't interested in doing anything. All she wanted to do was hang around the house and read."

"I know what you're interested in," Maggie said. "You're my best friend."

"Maybe I'm interested in other things now. Maybe I'm changing. Bridget says that being out of Helen's shadow has changed me. She says I act more like I'm in high school than most people my age."

"Bridget's a bitch," said Maggie, getting up and walking out.

That was when she had known that the next time there was a fire, she would be there.

But she never suspected that she would strike the match and start the fire. Richard had handed her the box of kitchen matches, his eyes flat, and when he had said, "Your move, Maria Goretti," she knew there was no way back to the way things had been before, to the times of Indian clay in the creek and Ouija boards. She sniffed the air and thought that the scent was an amalgam of what had been and what was still to come, of the old smells of cut grass and plastic toys and stew cooking and the faint ripe odor of standing water, and the new smells of plaster and linoleum, cement and concrete, all nice smells somehow. Sometimes she tried to close her eyes and imagine the field the way it had been only two months before, its reeds hiding the earth and the field mice and the occasional discarded soda can. And when she did, she could envision a field, but it was her imagined idea of one, like an illustration in a book, perfect arcs of gray-green laid on a bias, and not what had really been there at all. She wondered sometimes whether she was doing the same thing to her memories of her own life.

"Your turn," Debbie said.

Maggie knew why Debbie was angry. The day before, they had visited Helen in the city. They had put on summer dresses, because they always wore dresses when they went to the city, and they slipped out of the Malones' front door, which was only used by salesmen and for important parties, while Mrs. Malone was busy warming a bottle for the new baby. Maggie carried an umbrella. It was still wet from the day before, and the day before that. It had been one of the rainiest summers on record, Mrs. Malone said. The weather was making all the mothers feel that perhaps they would lose their minds. "I'll make you a deal," Mrs. Malone had said to the children one morning at breakfast, after Maggie had spent the night. "I'll stay out of your hair until Labor Day if you'll stay out of mine." No one stopped eating. The baby was in a corner, sucking noisily on his hand. He was a large boy, with no hair and an enormous mottled face. It often occurred to

Maggie that what passed as an offhand remark from Mrs. Malone would have been a turning point for either of her own parents.

For days at a time there had been no work on the development, and water ran down the raw brown slopes that stood for lawns in great streams, until ridges were worn into them and piles of silt lay in front of all the new houses. The ones that were only framed in turned a henna color, and the water in the basements grew stagnant on those rare afternoons when the sun shone. Even the negligible little creek, which Maggie and Debbie had been able to negotiate with one good broad jump since second grade, rose and covered its steppingstones, sloshing aggressively up over its banks and whirring around the stanchions of the railroad trestle. After the fifth day, three workmen from the county public works department had come and stared silently at the foot of one of the stanchions, where a narrow groove of earth had been worn away to a depth of three feet. They brought a dump truck full of gravel and filled it in. Maggie was so bored that she went outside to watch; she had put on her yellow slicker, and her wrists poked like sticks from the wide sleeves. She had outgrown it in three months, and outgrown, too, watching workmen shovel stones. Sometimes she took the nail Bruce had given her out of her jewelry box, placed it in the palm of her hand and looked at it, as though at any moment it would turn into something else. When Connie was home, Maggie tried to stay out of her way. When her mother was gone, Maggie stayed in her bedroom, peering out through the window, looking for fires in the rain.

Maggie and Debbie had taken the subway to Helen's building, walking three blocks from the station beneath one umbrella, and by the time they reached the apartment house, an ugly brick rectangle with a keyhole of an air shaft excised from the middle of the yellow-brown façade, their skirts were wet almost to the waist. "Nasty day, ladies," the man mopping the marble floors of the lobby had said pleasantly, eyeing their shiny, skinny legs.

Maggie had assumed that Debbie had asked her to come along because she had realized that Bridget Hearn was a jerk, and that Maggie was a much more suitable companion for such an important excursion.

This was not true. Debbie had told Helen that she might come by, and Helen had said that if Debbie brought Bridget she would not let them into the apartment. "Maggie saves you from yourself," she had said.

Debbie had been to visit Helen three times before, each time with Aggie, and she was affecting an air of great nonchalance, although she was terrified. Nearly every apartment in Helen's building was occupied by the widow of a Columbia professor, and the ladies all bore a great resemblance to one another, all small, slightly hump-backed elderly women with round hats like toadstools and pronounced foreign accents. When they spoke to one another in the elevators, they talked mainly of the price of produce, which they purchased in small quantities each day as part of their daily routine. When they shared the elevator with Helen or her roommate, they usually kept silent, their mouths as tight as the snap closures on their handbags.

One of them, who had herself been an anthropologist in Germany before her marriage, had written several letters in her ornate, rather spindly handwriting to determine how the girls had come in possession of the apartment, and whether they were old enough to be legally permitted to live alone. She was the one who entered the elevator with Maggie and Debbie now, staring down at the puddle on the floor their skirts made. Maggie noticed that the woman was wearing the same sort of shoes and boots that the nuns at school wore, low-heeled, black lace-up shoes with perforated uppers and translucent plastic boots that fitted the contours of the shoes exactly. Maggie's aunt Margaret had once told her that she had found those shoes the greatest impediment to remaining in the convent.

The elderly woman looked at Maggie. "Alone?" she suddenly spat out.

"Excuse me?" Maggie had said.

Debbie giggled.

"You are alone?"

"We're going to visit my sister," Debbie said. "Eight-B."

The elevator door opened. "Ah," the woman said, and stepped off.

"Oh God," said Debbie, when the door had closed.

Helen's apartment was silent. The peephole shone in the yellowish rainy-day glow from the airshaft window. Maggie stood on tiptoe to look inside, but she saw only her own distorted face, her nose as splayed as a bloodhound's. "We came all this way for nothing," Debbie said, pressing on the bell with her thumb. Maggie could hear it ringing faintly inside. Finally Debbie started back toward the elevator. "Come on," she said irritably. "They probably went out to lunch."

Maggie leaned on the bell again, staring back at herself through the peephole. As she walked away, the door opened. A girl with long brown hair and a flowered kimono that barely covered her behind stood there looking down at Maggie. She was holding a cup of coffee in one hand and a cigarette in the other.

"Yes?" she said a little grandly, with a hint of an English accent. Then she saw Debbie skittering down the hall. "Oh, Christ," she said. "Come on in. Helen, it's your little sister."

"Debbie," said Debbie.

"Debbie," the girl called to the back of the apartment.

Maggie walked in and sat down on the daybed, which was something like the sofa in her grandfather Mazzo's house, brown and shiny, its shabbiness accented by an embroidered shawl arranged over the back. The fabric was worn away from both arms. There was no other furniture in the room except for a record player and a set of bookshelves made from bricks and planks. Atop the bookshelves was a plastic version of the *Pietà*, with a rosary hanging around the Blessed Mother's neck. A Rolling Stones album cover was pinned to the wall.

Next to it was a professional black-and-white photograph of Helen. She was wearing a lot of obvious eyeliner and looked older and very beautiful. Her shoulders were bare. Maggie stood up to look at the picture closely as Helen's roommate exhaled and said, "Her Theda Bara look. Wonderful, isn't it?" Maggie nodded. She had no idea what the girl meant.

When Helen came in she was wearing the same kind of kimono as the other girl's, but in a bright salmon color, and her part was lost in the thicket of her unbrushed hair. Maggie thought she looked more beautiful than in the picture, the pale skin of her heart-shaped face pink at the cheeks and chin, her legs jutting out from her robe. "Didn't anyone ever teach you to call first?" she said.

"You don't have a phone," Debbie said, her eyes down, her arms crossed over her chest.

"Sure we do," said the roommate. "We got it last week."

"Don't you tell Mom," Helen said sharply, looking suddenly like her old self as she swept into the kitchen. "Do you want coffee?" she called over her shoulder, but neither of the girls answered.

When she came back into the room, a cup cradled in her hands, Maggie felt as though Helen had been gone a long time. She realized it was only a month since Helen had moved out, and she thought perhaps the other feeling was only because she had never belonged at home, had always seemed about to leave. She did not look at home in this apartment either, although her roommate did, yawning and stretching like a toddler just up from an afternoon nap.

"Mom won't let anybody move into your room," Debbie said, uncrossing her arms. "Aggie begged and begged. She sent in the money to hold your place at Marymount."

Helen laughed, not sarcastically, but with real happiness, her blue eyes alight. "That's all right," she said. "I knew she would. I'll come some day next week for dinner and talk to her after. How's Charles?"

"Okay. He sleeps all the time. Not like Jennifer was."

"Did you tell them about the part?" the roommate said, putting her cigarette out in the milky dregs of her coffee.

Helen smiled.

"Your sister got a part in a revue at a club downtown. It's called *A New World*. Sort of a folk-music thing. I swear she's going to be famous."

"Really?" Maggie said.

Helen shrugged again. "Don't tell Mom," she said.

"You're going to sing in a show?" Debbie asked.

"Don't look so shocked," Helen said. "I have a good voice."

"The face didn't hurt, either," her roommate said.

From the hallway came the explosive sound of someone laboring to clear his throat. Then there was the sound of spitting, and of the toilet flushing. Maggie and Debbie stared, transfixed, as a tall man with awry red hair walked into the living room, his chest and his feet bare, his blue jeans hanging so low on his hips that a small cloud of pubic hair stood out above the waistband. He was scratching his stomach and still clearing his throat. When he saw the girls he looked at them sleepily. "Sorry, wrong number," he said, and walked back down the hall. They heard a door close.

"Ooops," the roommate said.

"I've got to go to work," Helen said.

"The play is during the day?" Debbie asked.

"I'm still waiting tables. The play pays three dollars a performance. I can't buy shampoo with what the play pays."

Maggie was afraid to use the bathroom, but she had to go so badly she was afraid she wouldn't make it home if she didn't do it then. She looked quickly around the corner of the door, but the man with the red hair was not there. The seat on the toilet was up, and the inside of the shower curtain was wet. Maggie wanted to look in the medicine cabinet, but she was afraid someone would see or hear her. She ran the water, and pinched her cheeks to try to make them pink.

"Could you give me a hand with this?" she heard Helen call from a room down the hall, and she waited for a minute to see if the man would respond and then went into the bedroom herself.

It was an odd mixture of things, with Helen's old powder-blue spread on the bed and a silky New York City souvenir scarf thrown over the bedside lamp. There was a poster on the wall of a painting that looked like a pocket watch melting into the sidewalk, and a photograph of a young man who reminded Maggie a little of Richard. "Dali," said Helen. "James Dean." Maggie could think of no possible reply; it was as though everyone in the apartment spoke in code. Helen pointed down her back to a row of little buttons. "I can't reach the middle ones," she said, and Maggie bent over them, scowling.

"You've grown," said Helen. "You'll be as tall as I am soon."

"I'm already taller than my mother," Maggie said.

"But not taller than Richard Joseph. Is he still the *idée fixe?*"

Maggie felt as if they were back to code again. She shrugged. "He's not as great as everyone thinks he is," Maggie said, trying to coax another button through its loop and wondering how Helen would ever get into this dress if no one was around.

"Bravo," Helen said. "I know that kind of boy. All talk and no substance. He's cute, but he's a little too full of himself."

"Debbie still really likes him."

"That's no surprise. You and Debbie are like oil and water." Maggie frowned. She was finished with the buttons, but she fiddled around with the back of the dress to prolong the conversation. "I can tell you exactly what Debbie'll be doing in twenty years," Helen added.

"What?"

"She'll have three kids. She'll live in Kenwood or a place just like it. She'll be married to somebody she met in high school and married halfway through college. She'll say she's going to finish college when the kids are in school. If you ask her if she's happy, she'll say 'Of course I'm happy' and she'll be telling the truth."

"What's wrong with that?" Maggie said.

"There's nothing wrong with it, if that's what you want. It's just that most people don't decide, it just sort of happens to them. That's not what my life will be like twenty years from now."

"Tell me yours," said Maggie, and she stopped trying to pretend she was still buttoning and sat down on the bed.

"I haven't the foggiest. Maybe I'll be an actress. Maybe a dancer. Maybe I won't be good enough to be either and I'll wind up with three kids and a house in Kenwood." She laughed, and Maggie frowned again. "You're right, Maggie, that's pushing it a little. The point is, I haven't done anything yet that will force me in any particular direction. Somebody like my sister, she's already on her way to a decision. In two or three years she'll start dating some guy, and she'll get used to him and he'll get used to her. They'll go a little further each time they park, until they don't have any further to go. And their families will get to know each other and everyone will expect them to get engaged and pretty soon they will. And then they'll be married and the kids will show up and so on and so forth 'til the end of time. How old are you guys again?"

"Almost thirteen," said Maggie, liking the sound of it much better than twelve.

"The decisions you make when you're thirteen can decide who you will be for the rest of your life."

"But can't you change?"

"Sometimes. You can break up with the guy. You can marry somebody else. But after a while, you can't change a thing. Like my parents. Can you imagine one of my parents waking up someday and deciding they wanted to ditch seven kids, or move to a place where they don't know a soul?"

"That's what Debbie said."

"Wait a minute. You've lost me. My sister said these same things?"

"She said parents have no future, that their lives are over."

"Ah. No. That's not the same thing. Your life is over when you're dead. But the _kind_ of life you have—that's settled early, sometimes by accident. Sometimes by character. Like Monica Scanlan. What will she be doing twenty years from now?"

"She'll be married," Maggie said.

"Kids?"

"Only two. Enough to make her seem like an all-right person but not enough to be too much trouble or make her get fat."

Helen grinned. "Kenwood?"

"No," said Maggie. "Someplace with bigger houses."

"California!" cried Helen.

"California?" said Maggie.

"And will she live happily ever after?" Helen asked.

Maggie stopped laughing. "No," she said quietly. "Monica will never be happy, no matter what."

"You're good at this," Helen said. "What will you be doing in twenty years, Maggie?"

"I don't know."

"Husband?"

Maggie thought of her parents dancing, and her parents fighting while her grandfather lay half dead, and of John Scanlan telling Mary Frances he was going to marry her whether she liked it or not, and of the nail in her jewelry box, and the mark of Richard's fingers on her arm. She was wearing a dress with sleeves today so that the bruise marks, a brownish-yellow now, would not show. "I don't know," she finally said.

"Kids?"

"I don't know."

"Kenwood?"

"I don't know."

"I think that's a good sign," Helen said. "Most of the people you know would answer yes to every one of those questions. Just remember that sometimes you drift into things, and then you can't get out of them. Not to decide is to decide."

"Not to decide is to decide?"

"Exactly." Then, in an uncanny imitation of the voice of Mother Ann Bernadette, the Mother Superior of Sacred Heart, Helen added, "I'm so glad we had this little talk, Miss Scanlan." She picked up her purse. "I'm going to be late for work."

"Thanks, Helen," Maggie said.

Helen smiled, her face as clear as though it had just been carved from some pale stone. "Thanks for buttoning me up. Be good. Have you been wearing my bathing suit?"

"It doesn't fit," Maggie said.

"Soon, Maggie. Soon it will."

Out in the living room, Debbie was sitting talking to Helen's roommate. "We have to go," Debbie said. "We have stuff to do." Maggie looked down at her dress. The hem was still a darker color than the rest, and occasionally it clung to her legs. The man had come into the living room again. "Anybody remember where I put my shoes?" he said.

" 'Bye," said Debbie.

" 'Bye," Helen replied.

"*Arrivederci*," said the man with the red hair, from the floor. He was peering under the couch. Maggie was surprised to see him do this; that was where her saddle shoes always turned up when she couldn't find them in the mornings, but she had never known a grownup to lose shoes.

The two girls had ridden down in the elevator in silence. Their train was already on the platform, and they rushed down the subway steps, their damp shoes making slapping noises on the concrete. For a moment as they sat on the plastic seats they were out of breath. Maggie held her umbrella between her knees.

"What were you and Helen talking about?" Debbie finally asked.

"The future."

"Did you tell her what the Ouija said?"

"No," said Maggie, pulling at a cuticle. She did not want to tell Debbie about what would happen to her in twenty years, just as she had not wanted to tell her about the bathing suit. They were silent again as the train rocked back and forth, lulling them into sluggishness.

"Do you think he slept there?" Maggie finally asked, looking up at the advertisements for wrinkle cream and continuing education just above the dirty subway windows.

"That's a stupid question," Debbie had answered, but Maggie didn't know if she meant stupid yes or stupid no. They sped through the tunnel, the air warm and smelling of grease. In the Bronx the train came suddenly aboveground, into the kind of clear white sunlight that Maggie felt she had not seen for weeks. She turned in her seat to watch the tops of tenement buildings go by, squinting into apartment windows, faintly seeing women in light clothing moving around behind the curtains. On a fire escape just opposite one of the stations two boys sat in shorts, chewing gum, and as they saw Maggie watching them they both gave her the finger. She turned around. The two girls were alone in the car.

"Do you really think Helen will be famous?" Debbie said.

"I do," said Maggie.

"I don't think that guy was sleeping there," Debbie said.

"Neither do I."

"Don't tell my mom."

"I won't."

"Don't tell your mom either."

"Don't worry."

They had not spoken again until they reached Maggie's house. It seemed deserted, as it did so often these days. Maggie came back from the bathroom to find Debbie holding the California bathing suit, turning it in her hands as though wondering what it was.

"You stole my sister's bathing suit," she said.

"You went in my drawers," Maggie replied. And suddenly she sucked in her breath, because she realized that Debbie had gone in her drawers a hundred times before, and she had never minded until then.

As though she had read her mind, Debbie said, "I always go in your drawers. But I never stole."

"I didn't steal it. She gave it to me. The day she moved out."

"Liar."

"It's true," Maggie said. "You can ask her."

Debbie looked at her and then threw the suit onto the bed. Maggie wondered whether it would have been better to pretend that she had taken it. She had never really understood, until that moment, how hard it must be to be Helen Malone's sister.

"I'm going over to Bridget's," Debbie said, shoving past Maggie. In the doorway she turned. "I'm getting to be somebody, too," she said, and then she added, "I hope you *do* move."

Maggie had known she would pay—for the time with Helen, for the bathing suit, for Debbie's feeling that Maggie had taken something that should belong to her. Every time she thought about that moment in her bedroom she felt sick, but not as sick as she felt when she found Debbie out in the development that night, daring her to strike a match, her eyes mean, with no vestige of friendship in them. Behind Debbie she could see Bruce, his face pink, and she knew that if he could speak he would say "Don't do it. You don't have to." She wondered why he was there. He didn't seem to shadow Richard so much anymore.

"Do it," Richard said, and the silence was so overpowering that the scrape of the match along the side of the box sounded like an alarm in the room. A tiny flame leapt up in the darkness.

"I saw your mom with that guy today at the high school, Maggie," Debbie said, and there was an edge to her voice. "They were parked in the parking lot. Bridget says—" Before Maggie could hear what Bridget Hearn had said about her mother and Joey Martinelli, she had tossed the match away from her like an unwelcome thought. The corner of the garage burst like fireworks, and a roar swallowed up the echo of the scratch of the match. And they all turned and ran into the darkness.

Maggie came around the corner of one of the raw new roads and thought she heard sneakers behind her, but after a minute the sound faded and was gone. There was gravel on the ground, waiting for asphalt to be poured, and her shoes suddenly skidded sideways, and she fell onto the road; she felt a sharp sting in the side of her calf and on one of her palms. She heard another sound behind her, and then headlights swept the gravel, a car traveling slowly by. She felt caught in the lights, and closed her eyes, afraid the headlights would pick up the pale green of her eyes in the darkness. But the car crept past. In the light from the dashboard, she could see Joey Martinelli behind the wheel. He looked strange, and it was not until he was gone and she had gotten to her feet, blood running down one leg and onto her white sneakers, that she finally figured out that it had looked as if he was wearing a clover chain on his head.

When she got inside her own kitchen she washed her leg and wrapped it with gauze. "Mom?" she called softly, and then a little louder, "Mom?" Finally she heard her father's voice in the darkened living room. When she went in, the ball game was on the television, and the only light in the room was the white light from the screen. "She's not here, Maggie," he said. "She's at Celeste's. Or someplace." There was such an air of quiet acceptance in his voice, and his eyes were fixed on the screen so completely, that Maggie asked no more questions. She went upstairs and cried, using Helen's old bathing suit, limp on her pillow, to wipe her swollen face.

HEN THE TELEPHONE RANG, CONNIE gathered Joseph up off the floor, holding him close as she walked across the hall to the bedroom. She distrusted the telephone, had never been able to see it as anything other than the bearer of bad news. Her parents had agreed to have one installed only after her mother had had a fainting spell one day, but even when it was put in, it sat there silently, like a big black toad, gathering dust on an occasional table, an outsider amid the cheap china figures. When the phone did ring, all three of them had stared at it with amazement, and it was always left to Connie to answer. Tommy had never understood why she liked to make dates with him at the end of the evening, instead of talking later in the week, and she did not know how to explain. What could she tell him: that she lived in a house where they preferred to keep communication at a minimum?

She put Joseph down on her bed and picked up the receiver. The baby stared at the ceiling, fingering the bridge of his nose and rubbing the ear of his old brown bear across his cheek and chin. "Bear," he said.

"Hello," Connie said, rubbing his warm stomach and smiling at him.

"Hello, Connie. It's Monica. Is Maggie there?"

The Scanlan grandchildren did not get away with calling their aunts and uncles by their first names. Connie did not know exactly what to say. Finally she said, "No."

"No, no, NO," said Joseph loudly, talking to the bear.

"I beg your pardon?" said Monica.

"I said *no*," Connie repeated.

Joseph was still babbling, making it hard for Connie to hear. "Would you tell her I called to ask her to be a junior bridesmaid at my wedding?" Monica said.

"I beg your pardon?"

Monica repeated herself, as though she had been practicing the sentence for some time.

"I'm confused," Connie said. "You're getting married?"

"You'll get the invitation this week. The wedding is at the end of the month."

"The end of the *month*? Who's the guy?"

"You don't know him. He goes to Fordham. His name is Donald Syzmanski. His father is a police officer." There was a silence. "A sergeant," Monica added coldly, as though the silence had implied criticism.

Connie did not know what to say. This was the longest conversation she had ever had with her niece. Monica had always reminded her of Gigi Romano, a beautiful girl she had known in high school, who had had an impossibly tiny nose and numerous matching cashmere sweater sets, and whose father was said to be a member of organized crime. She had married an older Italian man and moved to Las Vegas the summer after graduation. There had been 700 people at Gigi Romano's wedding, and her gown had been hand-beaded at a convent in Italy. In high school Gigi Romano had always referred to Connie as "deadbeat" because of the cemetery, and she had always gotten a good laugh out of it. Connie couldn't imagine why she was thinking of that now.

"Have you gotten a dress yet?" Connie finally asked, groping for something to say, and as soon as she said it she realized it was such a non sequitur that she laughed.

"Yesterday," Monica answered coolly.

Connie still did not know what to say. Finally, in the silence, Monica said, her voice cracking, "I assumed that you of all people would understand this. Please just give Maggie my message."

"I think you should call back and ask her yourself."

"No thank you," Monica said.

Connie paused. "I'm sorry, Monica," she finally said.

"Everything is fine," Monica said. "Thank you very much." And she hung up.

"Bear," Joseph said.

Connie lay down on the bed beside him, her hands cradling her lower abdomen. It was only slightly rounded, but it no longer flattened out when she lay prone. Three months pregnant and she had lost three pounds from the nausea, so that her ribs made her naked torso looked like a striped shirt. She knew that it would not make any difference. The baby would be large and healthy. They always were. She had worn a size-four dress the day of her wedding, and yet Maggie had weighed ten pounds. Who could tell what was inside you until it came out?

She felt tiny fingers on her arm. Joseph was patting her softly with one hand while he held his bear in the other. He put his thumb in his mouth and she buried her face in the nape of his neck. He was the only one she could love like this now. The two oldest children always pulled away from her, although it had been years since she had tried to kiss Maggie, both of them squeamish in the face of their shared femininity. And she was wary of Damien, who would climb all over her like an overanxious boy in the back seat after a high school dance. But Joseph was passive and pleased with the attention, and she lay there for a long time.

She felt sorry for Monica, not because she obviously was getting married because she had to, but because she knew the girl would let that fact simmer below the surface of her life, a boil of discontent forever. She would always feel as if she had been trapped, even though she would likely wind up with the same life she would have had whether she had gotten pregnant or not. Connie tried to remember when she herself had realized that, but she did not think she had ever needed to realize it. She had been happy on her wedding day; as she watched the little Tudor cottage surrounded by flowers and tombstones recede through the window of the limousine, she had thought to herself, "Now my real life can begin." She suspected that Monica's real life had been the one she had led up to now, and Connie supposed it would be hard to give that up.

She thought of Gigi Romano again: Celeste had once told Connie that Gigi had no children, only poodles and a midget chauffeur who took her everywhere, moving through the dry warm Las Vegas air in an air-conditioned car. Connie did not think it was going to be easy being Monica Scanlan's child. No, she thought, from now on it will be Monica Syzmanski. She knew it was unkind, that it was true that she of all people should understand, but she couldn't help herself: she began to giggle. Joseph giggled too.

She ran one of her hands up and down the bedspread, a quilted flowered spread made out of some sort of synthetic that was supposed to look like silk. Even in the heat it was slightly cool. She knew it was not a Scanlan spread, that she was supposed to have plain chenille, but she hated chenille, felt whenever she saw the spreads in the Scanlan house that she was looking at spare rooms in a convent or a hotel.

She caressed the spread, up and down, up and down. She loved to run her hands over things, to let sand filter through her fingers or to stroke the tiny fur collar of her winter coat. She supposed that that was what she liked about the babies, too, that for a year or so she could run her hands over their bodies, pale pink as the inside of a conch shell, and feel the thrill of their real silk skins. At a certain point she began to feel bad about it, and she stopped. Perhaps it was the memory of that moment in the cemetery years ago with Celeste and her own father, when she had seen into the sexual chasm that opened up, almost overnight, between parent and child. Or perhaps, Connie thought, it was that for a time touching your babies was like touching the best part of yourself. Connie, raised in isolation amid the dead, had never learned to touch others easily, except for her husband, who wanted to feel her just the way she felt her small children, proprietary and sure in the knowledge that he was stroking an extension of himself. She liked the feel of Tommy, too, but not casually, not out of the blue, only when they were actually determined to touch, in bed at night, which happened rarely when she was pregnant and not at all now. He was sleeping on one side of the bed, and muttering when he did sleep. Feeling her belly, she sighed. The phone rang again. When she answered there was a long silence, and the sound of breathing. "Hello," Connie repeated irritably.

"Oh, I'm sorry," she heard her mother-in-law say. "Is Tom there, dear?"

"He's at work."

"Oh, dear. Has he talked to James?"

"I don't know. I just talked to Monica."

"You did?" said Mary Frances, her voice trembling. "How did she sound?"

"Haughty."

"I beg your pardon?"

"She sounded fine," Connie said, lying back on the bed. Joseph began to chew the telephone cord.

"I don't understand what's going on anymore," Mary Frances said, and to Connie she sounded pitiful.

"I know exactly what you mean," Connie said, and meant it.

"Do you? Oh, good. Oh dear . . . well, I suppose I'd better call Tommy. Is he still at the cement company, or has he started working with Mark already? I don't know; your father-in-law told me he was starting in the business, but he didn't tell me when."

There was a long silence, and finally Connie said slowly, "I don't know exactly where he is. He doesn't know anything about this."

"I know, dear. It's just a help to talk to him. He's a good boy." There was another long silence, filled by the labored breathing, and then Mary Frances said in a rush, "Of course, the boys do marry, and then what have you got? 'A son's yours till he takes a wife, but a daughter's a daughter the rest of her life.' I've heard that many times and the other day it was in Dear Abby, can you imagine, so it must be true. 'A daughter's a daughter the rest of her life.' You should remember that."

Connie felt as though she had walked in on Mary Frances naked, as though for the first time she was seeing beneath the pale bouclé coats and the hats with the little veils. She could remember John Scanlan joking about what a flibbertigibbet his wife had been when he first met her—"diarrhea of the mouth," he once had said, and both James and Connie had winced—but Connie had never known that girl, only the woman who sometimes watched her family with bright, apprehensive eyes as she passed around the cocktail franks.

Finally Mary Frances said again, "Tom was a good boy."

"He still is," Connie replied, her empathy evaporating.

"Of course, dear," Mary Frances said, her voice a little firmer, more like her old self. "I'll call him now."

When she hung up Connie put her hands back down on the spread and stroked it again, up and down. Joseph was beginning to breathe regularly; his black eyes were only slits in his chubby pink face. From below the window came the honk of a horn, then another. The baby's eyes opened slowly.

"Oh, good," Connie said to herself, jumping up and brushing her hair. "Want to go for a ride, Jojo?"

"Ride," Joseph said as she scooped him up.

"Go bye bye," said Connie.

"Bye bye," said Joseph, waving at the bed.

Joey Martinelli was sitting in the car in the driveway, and as she came out he moved over to give her the driver's seat. She put Joseph in the back, where he curled up and began to suck his thumb. "I've never been so glad to see anyone in my life," Connie said, and they drove in silence until they reached the empty parking lot of the public high school, a squat building tinted aquamarine after the misguided architectural style of public buildings of the 1950s. Connie felt that by now she knew the big rectangle of asphalt by heart. She'd done sixty miles an hour on it, stomping on the brakes just short of the grass; she'd learned to accelerate coming out of a curve and had practiced doing a K-turn over and over again. The skid marks in one corner were hers from two weeks before. Now she was working on parallel parking.

Joey got out of the car, took two sawhorses from the trunk and placed them a good distance apart at the end of the lot, just in from the grass. Getting back in, he said quietly, "I'm glad to see you, too." Connie thought his voice sounded strange, but when she looked at him his face was turned away, toward the athletic field and the stand of trees at its edge.

"Could you go and direct me, like the other times?" Connie said.

He looked at her and smiled. "Nope. Your test is next week. Today you do it yourself."

"What if I scratch your car?"

"You won't scratch my car," he said.

The only sound was the breathy snoring of the baby in the back seat. Connie pulled forward, backed up, cut the wheel, pulled in, straightened the car. Then she did it again. Each time she imagined the crunchy sound of the back wheels running over a sawhorse, like the sound a Fifth Avenue candy bar made when you bit into it. She was sure parallel parking was like algebra; she knew she would never need it, but she had to do it to pass the test. After half an hour her arms hurt. "I need a break," she said, opening her door, looking down, and seeing with pleasure that she was only six inches from the grass and that the car was perfectly parallel with the edge of the blacktop. She let her head fall back against the seat, and lifted her hair up off the sides of her face. She could feel her thighs sticking to the leatherette upholstery.

"My niece calls to say she's getting married in a hurry, which means she's pregnant," she said. "Then my mother-in-law calls and starts talking about what she's read in Dear Abby. What an afternoon." She did not add that Mary Frances had suggested that Tommy was taking a new job, a job Connie knew nothing about, a job that filled her with fear and rage. She somehow felt that discussing Tommy with Joey would be disloyal.

Joey laughed. "That doesn't sound like the Scanlan family to me," he said.

"I know. But who knows what really goes on with other people? My father-in-law, who's Superman, is in the hospital. My mother-in-law,

Emily Post, is reading Dear Abby. Tommy's brother's daughter, who has never been seen in public with a spot on her dress or her hair uncurled, turns up pregnant. And my own daughter, who seemed as if she'd stay a kid forever, has two fancy grown-up bathing suits in the bottom of her underwear drawer and goes out at night to talk to boys in those damn houses you're building."

"She does?"

"They all do."

"Ask her if she knows who's setting these fires. They burned down an entire garage last night. If there'd been a breeze, it would have taken half a block with it."

Connie sighed. "My God, what a summer. Will we live through it? I feel like all hell started to break loose as soon as you showed up."

"Hey," Joey said, "don't blame me."

"I don't blame anyone for anything. People just believe what they want. That if you're a kid, you'll stay that way forever. That if you look like a Shirley Temple doll, you're a good girl. You live in a big house, everything's fine." Connie shrugged. "You know who my husband's family thought I was going to be like? Doris Delgaudio."

Connie and Joey both began to laugh. Doris Delgaudio had lived down the block from the Martinellis. She had worn red lipstick as thick as her ankles, crystal costume jewelry, and Capri pants. When she walked, her bottom swayed from one side of the sidewalk to the other, and she made a noise like Oriental wind chimes from the sound of all the crystal knocking together.

"I swear," Connie said, gasping for air, "the Scanlans were all waiting for me to fill the house with crushed velvet and red curtains, waiting to see if I'd stamp grapes with my bare feet in the backyard. I think what bothers them as much as anything else is that I didn't turn out to be what they expected. Their son married a guinea, she ought to at least *act* like a guinea. I think it drives them crazy, that I'm not one thing or another."

"Yeah, you are," Joey said, "you're terrific."

For just a moment, before it happened, Connie could see what was coming, but in the same way she was always convinced people who were hit by a bus froze in the middle of the street, she found herself incapable of doing anything about it. She saw his face move, then his arm and his shoulder, and then he had his arm around her and he was kissing her. Her mouth opened in amazement and she could feel his teeth.

It was the oddest feeling, being kissed by someone who wasn't Tommy. She kissed him back, and her body warmed and she shifted a little in her seat so she was turned toward him. She put her hand on the back of his neck and felt the short hairs, and try as she might, all she could think, while pleasure welled within her, was: This is different from Tommy. And this. And this. He put one hand on her bare knee and she felt a throb inside her groin, and then in her stomach.

"Oh, my God," he groaned, "you are so beautiful."

She imagined this was what she had read about in *Reader's Digest*, an out-of-body experience. She felt that she was looking at herself from somewhere near the inside light of the car, and thinking: Why, it's true. I look wonderful, all white whites and black blacks. Joey ran his thumb over one of her nipples, and the her that was still inside her body felt her joints grow warm. She whimpered softly. She had forgotten all about the baby in the back seat. When he put his hand between her legs she started to slide down, her shoulders jammed between the steering wheel and the seat, and the woman watching it all, the other woman she was, thought to herself, "This is exactly the spot I was in when I got pregnant the first time." She did not know whether it was the power of that suggestion, or the prone position, or the hormones that·flooded her body as her excitement rose, but she suddenly realized she was going to be sick.

She opened the door of the car with one hand over her head and lurched out somehow onto the grass. She gagged a little, and the ground beneath her felt liquid.

When she got back into the car she left her door open because of the sharp vinegar scent of her mouth. Joey was sitting with his head in his hands, and she felt so sorry for what had happened that she started to reach out to stroke his hair and then stopped in midair. She wondered what would have happened if her stomach had not betrayed—or saved—her. When he finally looked up, she could see herself again in his dark eyes; her hair was ruffled and she looked seventeen, and beautiful.

"My being sick had nothing to do with you," she said. "From what I remember about kissing, you're a good kisser." She tried to laugh but no sound came out and he kept his head down. "I always feel sick like that when I'm going to have a baby."

"You're pregnant?" he said, and when she saw how dead his eyes looked she knew that she had been careless and mean without even suspecting it. Marriage had done that to her, she thought. Marriage had made her feel so safe and inviolate that she had felt free to let some man drive her around without ever thinking about how *he* might feel. It had made her secure enough to be surly with her husband and to ridicule his family. Once she had thought being married would make her part of a group, but instead it seemed to have made her a person so complete that she could refuse to look outside her own borders. Or maybe this was how she had become whole, by doing something selfish and wrong, just for herself, just so she could see herself in the mirror for the first time in her life and say: Ah. There you are.

"I thought you knew," she said. "I'm sorry."

She supposed that was how it looked to someone from the outside when you complained about your life, when you were lonely and confused. It looked as if you were ready to leave, as if you were looking for something else. She knew that was how Monica would think of her own marriage, would think that something you were forced to do, something that you hated sometimes, could not be something you might want. But she would be wrong to think that.

In the back seat the baby started making the wet sucking noises that meant he was waking up. Connie closed the door on her side. "I need to get home," she said softly, and she smiled at him.

"You drive," he said, and he looked out the window again, his chin in his hand.

When they pulled into the driveway, Maggie was sitting on the front steps. When she saw her mother she went inside. Connie thought again about how marriage could make you feel safe enough to hurt people without even knowing it.

"I'll come and get you for the test next week," Joey said.

"I don't think so," Connie said. "I think I'll go myself."

"You can't do that. You can't drive without a licensed driver."

"I'll get Celeste," Connie said. "Or Tommy."

"I'm sorry," Joey said. "I really feel like a jerk."

"No, no, no, no, no," Connie said.

"Yeah."

Connie lifted Joseph out of the back seat. "You're not a jerk," she said. "You're a great guy. I meant what I said about being a good kisser, too. You're going to make somebody a terrific husband."

His face hardened, and for the first time that afternoon, he looked mean. "You sound like my mother," he said, and there was no humor in his voice.

"That's a good way to think of me."

"No. I meant what I said. I don't care about the other thing. About the baby."

"It's a pretty major problem," said Connie with a tight smile.

"It didn't feel like a major problem back there," Joey replied, and Connie felt that warmth again.

"I'm a married woman." Connie could hear the quaver in her voice.

"You didn't feel so married back there. Admit it, Connie; you made a mistake. You and I, we're the same kind of person."

"I'm not sure what kind of person I am," Connie said.

"You're the kind of person who should be appreciated. You're not the kind of person who should be treated like some kind of outsider."

"Maybe I'll always be some kind of an outsider," she said. "Maybe that's the kind of person I am." She turned and began to walk into the house. When she looked back over her shoulder, he was staring at her. "Thanks for teaching me to drive," she said.

"That's not enough," he said, starting the engine. He leaned out of the window.

"I'm coming back," he said.

"We forgot the sawhorses."

"I'm not coming back for any sawhorses. I'm coming back for you. I'd worry about taking you away from the Scanlans, but they never had you in the first place."

Connie looked at him levelly. "I'm a married woman," she repeated.

"*Arrivederci*, Concetta Mazza," Joey said, and he peeled out of the driveway, leaving two heavy black stripes of rubber tread behind him.

16

HE FRONT HALLWAY OF THE HOUSE HAD a faint odor, a pleasant mixture of wax, cut grass, and what Tommy supposed was the smell of emptiness, a musky smell that was a bit like the smell of the classrooms in the Catholic boys' high school he'd gone to. Everything he did echoed: closing the heavy oak door, walking across the parquet floor, placing the freshly cut key, its edges still a little sharp, on the white wooden mantel in the living room. The only thing in the house was a bottle of window cleaner on the kitchen counter, left there by the black woman who took the train up from the Bronx to clean his mother's house once a week.

The living room was long and cool even in the summer heat, with four big windows along the outside wall and the brick fireplace across from them, with small flowered tiles laid on the hearth and cabinets built in on either side. Across the hall was a dining room with wood paneling halfway up the walls. The kitchen was enormous, with room for a big table and lots of chairs. Beyond it was a screened porch, and a yard with grass so smooth and green it looked like a golf course.

Tommy had gone to Sal's for lunch and hadn't had the heart to go back to the office, where Buddy Phelan kept looking at him sideways, wondering when he was going to say that he was leaving. He'd had

lunch alone at Sal's, a roast-beef sandwich and a draft beer. He liked
to eat alone, although he never admitted it. It seemed an eccentric
kind of thing, like something you heard murderers had liked to do
before anyone found out they were murderers. But after years of sharing
a table, first with his four brothers and his sister, then with his wife
and children, he found it soothing to sit with the *Daily News* propped
between his plate and his cup and eat his sandwich without having to
talk to anyone.

Sometimes, while he had his coffee, he and Sal would talk. He
thought that Sal must be lonely, living upstairs above the bar in two
rooms, alone since his mother died three years before. Sal was an only
child, and now an orphan. Whenever Tommy tried to think about
that, it was like imagining a man from Mars. Tommy thought how
quiet it must be upstairs, and how Sal must have all night to read the
papers, even the box scores for teams not in New York.

That morning Sal had just looked at him. Finally he said, "Word
is you're getting a promotion."

"Word is sometimes wrong," Tommy said.

"I'd miss you," Sal said, wiping the bar with his rag. "But don't cut
off your nose to spite your dad, Tom."

Perhaps that was why he had driven out here. He had parked his
car down the street and walked up, so that none of his brothers would
see the station wagon and report back that Tommy had given in. Or
perhaps it was that he thought he might discover here how he felt
about everything that was going on in his life, and what that everything
was. Two nights ago he had gone upstairs to bed and heard his daughter
crying behind the closed door of her bedroom, a high and lonely
sound, like the sound the house made when it creaked in a high wind.
He had stood outside for a minute, and then gone into his own room.
For an hour he had strained to hear that sound, sometimes thinking
he heard it, other times that it had stopped. Then Connie slid into
bed beside him, and he fell asleep.

"Connie," he said aloud, as he went upstairs in this big house, and
the word came bouncing back from the clean white walls.

Upstairs there were six bedrooms and four bathrooms. The bathroom off the biggest bedroom had a glass shower stall and a dressing room with big red roses climbing up the papered walls. In the ceiling of the dressing room there was a pull-down door and steps to the attic. As Tommy hoisted himself up he heard tiny footsteps, like fingers drumming on a tabletop, and he thought to himself, "We need an exterminator." He wondered if that thought meant that he was going to live here. For a moment he looked down below him, at the luminous oak beneath his feet, at the edge of one florid rose where the wall met the molding. He wondered if he was looking at the rest of his life.

The attic was surprisingly clean, and empty except for a big trunk, wood banded with metal. He lifted the lid slowly, afraid he'd hear the little feet again. The trunk was full. On top was a manila envelope, and beneath it a welter of lace and satin the color of tea. He could tell it was a wedding dress without even lifting it. Some dried flowers lay to one side.

He slid the contents of the envelope out and sat crosslegged on the unfinished pine floor. There was an old wedding picture, the bride wearing the sort of shapeless veil and straight, midcalf-length dress his own mother wore in her wedding pictures. There was a marriage certificate—Jean Flaherty to Harold Ryan, April 8, 1924, in Most Blessed Sacrament Church, Brooklyn, N.Y. There was a faded white ribbon, a scrap of material, and a postcard from Niagara Falls. Tommy could feel something small and hard in the bottom of the envelope. He shook it and into his palm fell a tiny tooth.

The attic seemed to have been cleaned, and the trunk stood in the center of the floor as though it had been abandoned. Did people think so little of the past? Tommy thought again of eating at Sal's, of a lunch he'd had the week before. A shaft of sunlight had been shooting through the cheap stained-glass fleur-de-lis in Sal's front window, so that bars of red and green and blue fell right across the plate placed in front of the third stool in from the end. Some of the men said that it was enough to give you indigestion, this big spot of color atop your corned beef and slaw, but Tommy liked it. He supposed it reminded him of church, perhaps of serving Mass when he was an altar boy, when he had felt solemn and important as he poured the water from the cruet over the priest's consecrated fingers—his father's cruets, his father's chalice. As he had taken the seat, he thought of what a creature of habit he was, and it made him afraid.

"Penny for your thoughts," Sal had said, and Tommy had found, to his great amazement and shame, that at the words tears welled in his eyes. It was dim in the bar at all hours of the day, and he hoped that Sal could not see.

"Your dad worse?" Sal asked, putting the cream in front of him, making Tommy suspect that the light was better than he thought.

"Ah, who knows," Tommy said, playing with his teaspoon. "The doctors never tell you anything. I don't think they know anything. Half the time he's full of piss and vinegar and the other half he's talking like a baby."

Sal wiped the bar and emptied an ashtray.

"My brother's daughter is getting married," Tom went on, "my niece, very pretty girl, very smart, all the best things. And suddenly my mother calls and says Monica's getting married, three weeks' notice, with her grandfather in the hospital. I understand these things, it happens every day, but jeez, I don't know, maybe it's better that my father can't come. She's marrying a Polish boy, my brother says he's a nice enough boy, but my father thinks that anybody who's not Irish should get out of town, you know?"

Sal nodded. He'd heard about Mr. Scanlan from the Italian guys who worked for First Concrete.

"I guess I figured these things didn't happen anymore, that girls were smarter, that guys were smarter. My brother was figuring on her finishing college, becoming a nurse or something. Now the boy will have to leave school, get a job." It flashed through Tommy's mind that the job would probably wind up being at Scanlan & Co., and that the news of the Polish grandson-in-law was going to be even more horrible for his father than he had at first imagined.

"Remember after the war," Tommy said, "how everybody talked about how tough the changes were going to be? I didn't fight, I was just a little kid, but I can remember everyone saying there would be changes, and there were changes, but they were all good. The wives stopped worrying, everybody bought houses, had a couple of kids, they were damn glad to be home. Now there's no war but there's changes, and they're all bad. You go to Mass, the kids are fooling around, no hats, they're changing the prayers, they're changing the music, the rules. I go downtown the other day for a meeting, and there's two young girls crossing Broadway in front of me, they're wearing dresses as long as one of my shirts. No stockings. No underwear, for all I know." He didn't say that one of the girls was Helen Malone, that he had leaned forward and peered through the windshield incredulously, that when a stray summer breeze had lifted the corner of her short Indian sack dress he had begun to feel very warm indeed and had looked down to see the fabric at his crotch straining visibly, until a car behind him had honked to let him know the light was green. It reminded him of the new bookkeeper in his office, the one with the bleached hair flipped up on her shoulders and the little-girl dresses with the collars and cuffs and the low waists, the one who always rubbed up against him when she passed behind his desk.

Sal reached beneath the bar and brought out the coffee pot. He poured a cup for himself, and a second cup for Tommy.

"You know my sister who's in the convent? I don't know what's going on with her, either. She's reading *Jane Eyre*. A nun! It's a book my daughter read in school. I never read it—I had to read *Moby Dick*—so I asked my daughter what it's about. Some woman is a governess and winds up marrying the man of the house. My sister the nun is reading this? The other day she went to buy a bathing suit. A bathing suit! My sister told me I was behind the times. Maybe that's it. I'm behind the times. I'm still back in the good times."

The two men stared at each other. "Jesus Christ," Tommy whispered, as though he was witnessing a miracle, "that's the voice of John Scanlan, coming right out of my mouth."

"It always has, Tom," Sal said with a smile. "You just never noticed it before. I think that's what parents are for. You need to learn to talk. They give you the voice." In the silence Tommy could hear the television, could hear some woman on one of the soaps say stridently, "Doctor, will I ever be a whole person again?"

"I don't know, Tom," Sal added, pouring himself another cup of coffee. "Nothing ever changes much around here. My mother died. I put the pinball by the door. I got a new TV. On St. Patrick's Day I have corned beef and cabbage on the menu and put food coloring in the beer. Girls get knocked up, old men die. Excuse me, nothing personal. I don't know about nuns. Your sister can't stop being a nun, can she?"

"Who knows anymore?"

"No, forget it, I don't think you can stop being a nun without a whole lot of rigamarole from the pope. But your father—I don't know. It sounds like he's pretty bad."

Tommy looked into his coffee cup again. The sun was moving and he had to move his cup to make it change colors. He wanted to tell Sal that his father was not the trouble. In some strange way he liked talking like his father, thinking like his father. When he thought about running the company with Mark, all he could think of was reining his brother in, telling him to watch it with the crazy ideas. As he watched his father's life ebb, day after day, he began to feel as if his father was flowing into him.

Now he sat on the attic floor and all he could think of was changes, how he hated them, how he wanted them to stop, how he sounded like the old man wasting away in his hospital bed. He looked at the wedding picture in his hand and wondered whether the people in that picture had intentionally left it in the dust, whether they had soured on their old dreams or simply had new ones. Tommy felt his own old dreams slipping away, but he was not sure what the new ones would be. He only knew that they would revolve around his wife. He walked to the edge of the ladder and looked down. He could see his wife in that dressing room, black and white and beautiful amid the roses, in her black bra and black half slip, fixing her hair in front of a mirror that would hang on the one wall.

This house felt too grand for him, like the house of an adult, not the house of an overgrown boy, but he knew she would seem at home here, small and elegant in the large, well-proportioned rooms. He remembered leaving Sal's the other day, driving aimlessly, his eyes clouded by tears, through the Bronx to Westchester, where he was to see about giving an estimate for the foundation for a new wing of the high school. As he turned into the entrance, a sedan had almost sideswiped him, driving too close to the center of the road, and he had yelled "Jesus Christ" and raised his middle finger to the driver before he saw that it was Connie, hunched over the wheel, her lower lip tight between her teeth, with that Martinelli guy in the seat beside her. He had pulled the car over in the parking lot, next to some sawhorses, and rested his head on the wheel until the sick feeling in his stomach had passed.

For hours after that he had driven around, listening to Sinatra on the radio. The day had faded quietly into night, the way it did on these hot August days, and the back of his shirt was drenched with perspiration, but still he drove around, until finally he took a right-hand turn and found himself in the parking lot of the hospital.

"Good evening, Mr. Scanlan," the youngest of the nurses said when he approached his father's room. Dorothy O'Haire was sitting in a plastic chair outside, working on some dun-colored piece of knitting. Seeing her there, Tommy assumed that his father was up and around, raising hell, but when he sat down by the bed he could tell that the old man was in a deep sleep; his eyes were still beneath the blue-veined lids, and his breathing seemed to stop between each inhalation, so that Tommy thought each breath was the last. On the bedside table there was an envelope with "Ryan house" written on it in the old man's florid handwriting, the pride of the nuns at St. Aloysius School; it had been there for weeks, and for the first time Tommy picked it up. As though the gesture had reached deep inside his failing consciousness, John Scanlan's eyes opened slowly, and he stared at his son.

"Something important," he said dully.

"I know," Tommy said.

"You do it for your mother," the old man said, breathing hard on each word.

"Yes."

"Move."

"We'll talk about it when you're a little bit better, Pop," Tommy said, holding the envelope.

John Scanlan shook his head and fell deeper into the pillows.

"No," he said. And then his eyes closed and the slow, measured cadence of his breathing began again.

Tommy had ripped open the envelope and slid the key, shiny as a new penny, into his palm. The one his father had tossed into Connie's lap, that Sunday that now seemed so long ago, had lain on their dresser, untouched, all this time. The freshly cut end of this other one had left a scratch just below Tommy's thumb. He had put it into his pocket, among the small change, and had left it there until this afternoon, when he used it to unlock the door.

Now, coming downstairs, the manila envelope from the trunk under his arm, he took the key from the mantel in the living room and held it again in his palm. Then he took out his key ring and slid it next to the keys to the car, the keys to his house in Kenwood, and the keys to his office. He expected to hear those tiny feet again, but there was only silence, and then the echo of his footsteps as he let himself out and locked the door behind him.

17

HE BRIDAL SALON WAS NOT EXACTLY what Maggie had expected. She had never really thought about getting married, although they had all discussed it enough at school. "If you could marry Paul or John, or any of the boys in class, which would it be?" JoAnne Jessup would suddenly ask her and Debbie at lunch. But that was just fooling around, and actually being married was not, at least as far as Maggie could see. Actually being married seemed so crowded with unspoken rules and odd secrets and unfathomable responsibilities that it had no more occurred to her to imagine being married herself than it had to imagine driving a motorcycle or having a job. She had, however, thought about being a bride, which had more to do with being the center of attention and looking inexplicably, temporarily beautiful than it did with sharing a double bed with someone with hairy legs and a drawer full of boxer shorts. Once she had tried on her mother's veil in the bathroom, a Juliet cap pocked with pearls, its long tail of net beige and tattered. She had locked the door, and placed the little dome on her head, then stood back to survey the effect. But she could not grasp the magic. Perhaps it required the entire outfit. She could not grasp it in the salon either, although she got glimpses of what she was searching for every now and then, in the racks of white dresses, misty as ghosts, hanging along one wall in plastic bags, or in the scratchy sound of one of them being carried across the floor in a saleswoman's arms. Monica had already gotten her dress, and they were there for the bridesmaids—Maggie, two friends of Monica's from Sacred Heart, and the groom's sister, who was unfortunately, as Aunt Cass had confided after Mass on Sunday, "quite large." Neither the fat sister nor Maggie wanted to take off their clothes in front of the others.

Monica sat slouched in a chair in a pale-blue blouse and skirt, her hair in a ponytail, acquiescing to her mother's wishes. If the bridal salon was not quite what Maggie had expected, Monica was not acting a bit like her idea of a bride. She seemed bored and anxious to get on with it.

"What about pink?" Aunt Cass said, and Monica replied, "Fine" in a tone that suggested the answer to What about yellow? Or green? Or blue? would have been "fine" too. The saleswoman brought out pinks of all shades and styles, and finally it was decided that the dresses would be high-waisted, like Monica's, and made from some fabric Maggie had never heard of before called silk shantung. There were little pillbox hats with veils, and the dresses were rather plain, so that the bridesmaids looked very sophisticated, except for the fat sister, who looked enormous.

"Now for the little one," said the saleswoman, a tiny woman dressed all in black, perhaps to better point up the colors of her wares. She spoke with a faint accent and had a bodice dotted with safety pins and needles trailing white and pastel wisps of thread. Maggie realized that the saleswoman was referring to her, and she followed the woman into the dressing room. But she saw at once that the dress there was different, puffed sleeves instead of cap, a big bow at the high waist in the back, even a different hat, like the straw sailors she had always had for Easter, except that it was pink, with a pink ribbon and a gauzy brim.

"Off with the clothes," the saleswoman said brightly, and Maggie turned her back, crimson. She was wearing her slip, the closest thing she had to a bra. She had stuffed the nylon skirt into her shorts, so that she had had lumpy legs all morning. The saleslady clicked her tongue. "You will need foundation garments with this," she said, unzipping the dress. "For the hose. And to give the line to it." But the dress, when it was on, had no line. It fell straight down Maggie's angular body. A carpenter's dream, she thought. Her hair hung in big hanks where her breasts should be.

"It needs *something*," said Aunt Cass, who had slipped in between the dressing-room curtains.

The saleswoman shrugged. "She is a little girl," she said, although Maggie was taller than she was. "It is not the same here"—she grabbed a handful of the bodice—"or here," lifting the skirt and dropping it with another shrug.

"What if we put her hair up?"

"Not with the hat. The hair, besides, is very fashionable today, for the young girls. But it has no style. Perhaps a little lipstick, some rouge." A picture flashed through Maggie's mind of herself on Halloween, when her mother wedged her on the vanity bench in the bathroom and expertly, seriously, her tongue snagged between her lips in concentration, made Maggie's face up. She was good at it, and Maggie always thought she looked wonderful, her lips fuller, deep red, her cheeks flushed with the powdered rouge, her lashes spiky with the mascara, coaxed from its red plastic case with a little brush and some drops of water. But she did not look the way the older girls did, their lips disappearing into their faces in their coats of white-pink lipstick, their cheeks pale, luminous as the moon.

Aunt Cass looked at Maggie in the mirror. Maggie looked back. Her face was hot. "You look fine, honey," her aunt said. She moved the curtains aside and the older girls crowded in. "You look so cute," one of them said, a buxom blonde whose chest had peeked out of the neckline of the dress she had tried on. "God, you're so thin," the fat sister said.

Monica stayed in the chair, playing with a piece of her honey-colored hair, wrapping it around one long finger. Her engagement ring glittered. Her mother moved aside so that Monica could see Maggie, and for the first time that day Monica smiled. "It's you,"

Monica said, narrowing her eyes. "It's really you." Maggie's eyes dropped until she could no longer see Monica's reflection in the mirror, except for one long tanned leg swinging back and forth restlessly over the silken upholstery of the green-and-pink striped chair. Then, with a great effort, she looked up again and stared her cousin straight in the eye. The smile was still there. "I think it's fine," Maggie said, determined to be agreeable. "Besides, no one will care what I'm wearing. Everybody will be staring at Monica. Everyone will be interested in her dress. No one will be able to take their eyes off her."

"It is the bride's day, certainly," said the saleswoman brightly, lifting the hat from Maggie's hair.

Monica rose from the chair and came over to the mirror, and Maggie noticed that she seemed a little clumsy. She looked Maggie up and down and then she went back to her purse and Maggie heard a scraping sound. Her cousin came up behind her, a smile on her face, and held up a lighted match.

"There is no smoking in the salon, miss," said the saleswoman primly.

"Tell my cousin," said Monica as she stared at Maggie in the mirror. Then she blew out the match.

"So I say to my soon-to-be-father-in-law, the New York City police officer," Monica began, circling Maggie, still holding the stub of the match, "I say, Sergeant, what if you had a lovely young girl who had never been in any trouble before and suddenly she joins a band of arsonists. Arsonists! And this is what he says."

One of the bridesmaids giggled nervously. "Monica, you are strange," she said.

"Shut up, Cheryl," Monica said pleasantly. Then she continued, "He says, Monica, my dear, if the local authorities were given such information, the girl in question would go to the local juvenile detention center. In other words, reform school. And I said, my, my, my. If I had such information, should I divulge it? And my soon-to-be-father-in-law said, it is your duty as a citizen. Well, you can imagine how upset I was. I hate to tell tales on people. I think anyone who tells tales on people is a rat." Monica caught Maggie's eyes in the mirror. "Especially about something important. Something that could ruin their whole life."

Maggie had wheeled around, but the saleswoman was kneeling at her feet, pinning the hem of the dress, and she was caught halfway between the mirror and her cousin. She finally managed to turn completely. With a smile, Monica held out the match.

"What is it like to be like you?" Maggie said, staring into her cousin's amber eyes, looking for something inside them.

"Don't play with fire," Monica said.

"I mean it. How can you stand yourself?"

"Maggie," said Aunt Cass, her voice trembling.

"Liar, liar, your pants are on fire," said Monica in an even voice. "Just a warning, Maria Goretti. Anything you can do I can do better. You may think it's Monica, zero, Maggie, one. But you're wrong. We're even now."

"That's not how I am," Maggie said.

"Oh," Monica said in a squeaky little voice. "That's not how I am. I'm a good girl."

"You are a witch, Monica," Maggie said.

"Now, Maggie," said Aunt Cass.

"My, my, my," Monica repeated, her smile tight.

"And you don't fool me one bit," Maggie added.

"I don't fool you," said Monica, and though her voice was low it somehow felt as if she was screaming. "I don't fool you, God! With your family? With your birthday six months after your parents' anniversary? Don't talk to me about fooling. Don't talk to me, Maria Goretti. All I have to do is open my mouth and you'll be in so much trouble you'll never know what happened. Good little Maggie Scanlan. God, if they only knew. You're worse than everyone else because you pretend to be so good."

"Monica, this will stop," Aunt Cass said.

"Can I believe my ears?" said Monica shrilly. "We're defending Maggie? How many times have I heard you talk about how her mother is not our sort, dear? How many times have I heard my father complain that she sucks up to Grandpop so she'll get more of the money? God,

Mother, one night when you were drunk you even called her a wop. Why are we standing up for her now?"

"Monica, you are not yourself," said Aunt Cass, her face crimson, her voice shaking.

"Oh, cut the Mary Frances routine," Monica said, falling back into the chair. "This is myself. This is it. This is me, the real me." She pointed a narrow foot at Maggie. "Who knows who she really is." Maggie looked down at her fingers holding the charred piece of cardboard as though they were strange to her. She threw the match on the floor. "You'd better learn the facts of life before it's too late, Maria Goretti," said Monica. "Or you'll wind up like your mother."

"I'd rather wind up like my mother than wind up like you," Maggie said.

"Same difference," said Monica.

"No," said Maggie.

"May we finish fitting the dress now, ladies?" the saleswoman said.

"I don't think I'm going to need the dress," Maggie said.

"You'll probably be in jail," said Monica.

"No, no, absolutely not, I will not allow this," said Aunt Cass, who seemed close to tears. "You must be in the wedding. It will seem strange to everyone if you're not."

"It will seem strange to me if I am," Maggie said.

"Maggie, please. I cannot cope if you make trouble."

Maggie turned back to the mirror. Her face was white and her eyes were glowing. The salon was completely silent, and in the silence she could hear herself breathing. "What do you think you'll be doing in twenty years, Monica?" Maggie said in a low voice, and she could tell by the look on her cousin's face that the question was first unexpected, then unpleasant.

"I haven't the faintest idea," Monica said.

"I do," said Maggie.

"You can tell the future now, Maria Goretti?"

"I can tell yours."

"Now let us take the dress off," said the saleswoman, and she drew the curtains and left Maggie alone again.

18

I

T WAS BECAUSE OF THE PARKING LOT
that Connie almost turned back, not
because of the hospital. She still found
parallel parking a problem. She had
driven right past her aunt Rose's house
one afternoon because her uncle Frank's car was in the pitched driveway and she would have had to parallel park at the curb. The hospital
lot had head-in spaces: she had tried them at shopping centers twice
and found that if she cleared the car on the right, she wound up with
her front bumper heading straight at the side of the car on the left,
and if she started successfully toward the back of the space, she was
sure to see that one side of the car was in danger of being pleated by
the back bumper of another. Before Connie had known how to drive
she had thought it was a silly adolescent thing, much overrated. She
realized now that she had made herself think that about all the things
she could not do, like swimming and riding a bicycle, and that there
were difficult and elaborate skills the rest of the world had that she
lacked. In a way the knowledge had been soothing; the thought of
some essential inferiority made her feel more at home with others than
her belief in her superiority had.

She had found herself frantic as she drove to the hospital, and she
had thought at first that it was because this was only her second time

out alone. But then she realized it was about Joey, about what had happened in the parking lot. Staring at her bedroom ceiling the night before, she had replayed it all in her head and felt herself flush all over again, flush and burn. And for the first time she had admitted to herself that the baby within her had saved her from committing adultery. She would have done it, in daylight, with Joseph in the back seat, if some combination of hormones and nerves had not forced nausea to triumph over lust.

She had hung around the kitchen all morning, finding odd jobs for herself, and it was not until she jumped at the sound of a truck door slamming that she realized she had been waiting for a visitor, waiting for the visit that would ruin her life.

She had gotten into Tommy's car, then; he had left it in the driveway while he went off with one of the cement-truck drivers, but somehow she saw the fact that it was there as an omen, a sign, and an opportunity to save herself. She did not know why she was here, at the hospital, except that in some odd way she equated her fall from grace with John Scanlan. Just for a moment, on the way there, she had wondered if her father-in-law had planned this, had somehow arranged for Joey Martinelli to be the foreman at the project for this very reason. "I'm off my trolley," she muttered to herself in the quiet of the car.

She found a space all the way at the back of the lot, where there were no other cars, and pulled in, straddling one of the painted white dividing lines. She walked toward the building, its big brick smokestack sending a plume of gray-black up toward the sky. In her straw bag was the *Daily News*, and an airline bottle of Four Roses she had found in the back of the liquor cabinet.

Her heart was throbbing so violently as she crossed the parking lot that she wondered if, beneath her blouse, it looked like a painting of the Sacred Heart, a red oval, fiery like a bull's-eye on her body. All night she had rehearsed what she would say, how she would try to persuade John Scanlan to give up the idea of moving them into that new house, how she would try to talk him out of forcing Tommy into Scanlan & Co. Tommy hadn't told her a thing, but she had known what was happening when she saw the new key on his key ring, and heard from Joey that the word was out that the old man was selling

First Concrete. She had thought at first that she would try to talk to Tommy, but then she had realized that it was useless to discuss the matter with anyone but John Scanlan himself. When she recognized this, she knew some part of her life was over, that she had grown up, and that it was not the liberation she had always thought it would be, but an acceptance of her own powerlessness.

She was relieved, at the visitor's desk, to find that no one else had a pass to be in John Scanlan's room. No one would demand an explanation of why she was stopping by for the first time in her father-in-law's month-long illness, and how she had arrived at the hospital. Standing in the doorway of the room, listening to John Scanlan snore hoarsely, she knew that her carefully rehearsed speech had been a waste of time. Looking across at his beaky profile, the hair slipping over his high forehead, she felt a frisson of fear and dislike, but she knew that he would never again be the power that ruled all their lives. His chest was too sunken, his breathing too tenuous. With a kind of sympathy she looked at the tubes running to and from the bed and realized that he was catheterized, and thought what a humiliating thing that was for a man.

When she stepped to the side of the bed she saw that someone else was there, too, asleep in a chair. It was John's secretary, Dorothy. Connie had only met her once, at a horrid party for John's sixtieth birthday, but she recognized her because something about her stolid face and figure had reminded Connie of her aunt Rose. Tommy had told her that Dorothy was helping out, although the table her father-in-law had been using as a desk was empty now except for a stack of blank Scanlan & Co. stationery.

"Dorothy," Connie whispered, touching her arm lightly.

The other woman slowly raised her head and looked at the bed, then up at Connie. Half asleep, she stared, and then her eyes widened with panic.

"It's okay," Connie said. "You must have fallen asleep. It's kind of stuffy in here."

"We were working," said Dorothy, her fingers, with their big knuckles, twisting round one another like a tangled ball of yarn.

Connie looked down at John Scanlan. It was clear that he was barely capable of consciousness, much less work. She tried to search Dorothy's face for some sign of guilt or fear, but the woman was staring at her hands in her lap. All Connie could see were the big tortoiseshell pins that held Dorothy's hair in an old-fashioned roll at the base of her neck.

"That was nice of you," Connie said.

"I have to go," Dorothy said. "I have to pick up my daughter." Her hands twisted again. "You have a daughter, too," she added.

"Yes."

"Mr. Scanlan likes her. Your daughter, I mean."

"I know."

Dorothy rose heavily. She wore a cameo at the throat of her white cotton blouse. Connie thought she looked out of time, like a visitor from the last century. Her eyes were red. She picked up her purse from the floor, and a paperback book. At the door she turned and looked at John Scanlan.

"He's dying," she said.

"Yes," said Connie.

"I'm glad," said Dorothy, and for just a moment there was a blaze of savagery in her eyes and an acrimony in her voice that made her seem half mad. Then she turned and left.

"Jesus Christ," whispered Connie, sitting down, repelled by the warmth still lingering from Dorothy's body. "What did he do to *her*? How many others are there? Jesus Christ, what a life this man has led." For a long time she sat there and watched him sleep. Twice a nurse came in, glanced briefly at the blue cardboard visitor's pass and at the patient, then left again. The level in the IV ebbed slowly. Connie read the *Daily News*. She left the little bottle of Four Roses in the top drawer of the bedside table. The light outside deepened slightly, from a white to a pale, pale yellow. Finally Connie came to accept that if the key to a prison were on her husband's key ring, he had put it there himself.

She had nearly made up her mind to leave when John Scanlan turned his head on the pillow and opened his eyes. The deep blue was masked by a rheumy film, like the shadow a dog's eyes develop when old age has set in. For the first time that she could remember Connie looked him in the face, eye to eye, and did not flinch, did not look away.

He stretched out his big hand, soft and dry as a snake's skin. The veins on the back were enormous, and by some trick of the light or because of his illness, they seemed to be throbbing.

"Franny," he said hoarsely, reaching for her.

Connie drew back, but he pulled her arm closer and threaded his fingers through hers, engulfing her palm in his own. "Don't be angry, sweetheart," he said, almost as though he was talking to himself. "You're prettier when you smile." And he grinned, a kind of rictus now that his face had been pared down to bone and sinew. Connie thought she had never heard his brogue so thick, even when he was telling stories at parties and had had too much to drink. His grip made the stone on her engagement ring cut into her finger.

For a long time he said nothing, just stared and breathed heavily, as though he had been running. "The children are in bed," he said once. "Good riddance." A few minutes later he winked at her, and said "You're my girl." Connie was pink with embarrassment, although she knew that it was not her he was seeing; she was afraid, too, afraid that he would somehow suddenly snap out of it and be enraged at so revealing himself, be enraged at being duped, even if he had done the duping himself. His lids drooped and he began to breathe more evenly; then they snapped up, like shades that had been pulled at the bottom, and he began to talk as though there was not enough time to get out all the words.

"I'm sorry you lost the baby, Franny," he said groggily, his voice catching on every consonant. "It was the blood that did it. The doctor said it happens sometimes, but there was no blood with the boys. She was a beautiful little thing, but the doctor said 'She won't live, Mr. Scanlan,' and you wanting a daughter so bad, after the three sons, wanting someone you could put in little dresses with the ribbons and things." He fell silent but his breathing was loud. "I remember when you said 'I'm not having any more to break my heart. You have all your boys.' And you didn't want to let me come near, but that kind of thing can't be allowed to last." Connie could hear the sounds of the hospital out in the corridor, the rattling of the gurneys, the footsteps of the nurses. Finally he added, "You can't deny your husband, Franny. That's God's law."

He turned his head away from her and breathed so heavily that Connie was terrified and thought for a moment she should call the nurse. It was a horrible noise, and she wanted it to stop, but she was afraid that if it did he would begin to speak again. She did not want to hear any more.

Finally he turned his head back to her, and Connie saw that the tears were running down his face. He looked at their two hands, linked at the edge of the mattress, and then he looked up, and his face was contorted with grief, his lower lip shaking as though he had palsy, the tears dripping off his chin onto his pajamas, darkening the thin cotton. He pressed the back of her hand to his lips, and Connie recoiled, but he pulled her toward him again, with all the strength of a young man. Connie thought his tears must clear away his blindness and he would see her for who she was, but when he looked up again he only whispered "Please," and she felt the kind of sympathy for him that she always felt for her husband, the sort you feel for a small child, although she never felt it for her own children.

"It's all right, John," she said softly, pressing his fingers. "Everything is all right."

"Say you forgive me," he said.

"I forgive you."

He turned his head away and looked at the ceiling. Then his eyes closed. He dropped her hand, and the snoring began again.

She sat there for a while, and then picked up her purse and left. It was cooler out in the parking lot, and the sky seemed a deeper blue. She knew it must be past dinnertime. She wished she had taken the bottle of whiskey with her; she thought she could use a drink. Driving home, hunched slightly over the wheel, she knew she had learned one thing that afternoon: she would never be alone with Joey Martinelli again. She thought of the old man lying in the bed, of all the business deals and the machinations, and of him saying, last of all, "Say you forgive me." She didn't want to need forgiveness at the end.

That night when her husband came home from the hospital he told her that his father had fallen into a coma and that the doctors did not expect him to come out of it again. "My mother's all upset," said Tommy, sitting at the red Formica table in the kitchen, sipping his beer and staring into space, "because she says the last words he ever said to her were 'This is the toughest goddamn roast beef I've ever tasted in my life' when she brought him a sandwich for lunch yesterday."

"It would be in character," Connie said, knowing that if she did not tell him now she could never tell him, yet knowing that for some reason she could not tell him now. She looked into his face, trying to find the man she thought, so many years ago, would save her. And she realized, without regret, that it had been the other way around, and that she would have to live with that responsibility, even embrace it, for the rest of her life. She realized that for years she had wanted to sit by John Scanlan's side and say "To hell with you." But she had moved beyond the desires of that woman now. She had become a person who could sit there, hand in hand with that awful man, and forgive him his trespasses, whatever they might be. And if her husband knew that, he would know something that would ruin his life even more decisively than his father had tried to do. He would know that his wife was stronger than he was.

"She thought he was going to get better," Tommy said sadly. "She thought he would be all right."

19

N ONE CORNER OF THE BLACK, A TINY zigzag of lightning leapt like a tic in the eye of the sky. Maggie could see it from her bedroom window, just beyond the sweep of gingham below the curtain rod. She was alone in the house. The lights were out. A thunderstorm was coming. Maggie's mouth was dry and full of an awful taste.

The adults were gone again. Maggie often came home in the late afternoons from riding her bicycle aimlessly on the back roads and found the house empty and airless, like a house in a horror movie after The Thing has passed through town and gone. She would go up to her room and soon would hear the idling of a car in the driveway, like dogs growling, and then the heavy sound of the car door and the lighter one of the storm door downstairs. Then the sounds of pots and pans from below, the preparation of dinner.

It seemed to her that all the adults were acting more like children than they had before. The bickering on Sundays, usually the purview of Maggie and Monica and a handful of the younger cousins, was now between Tommy and James, or Margaret and Mark. Mary Frances wept. Old patterns and alliances had surfaced and reasserted themselves, so that her grandmother was dependent upon Margaret, meek with James, and clinging and loving with Tommy. For some reason Mary Frances had decided to reupholster her entire living room in blue damask, and half the furniture was missing. The grandchildren sat on the floor, their patent-leather pumps and saddle shoes making spots of light on the carpet. The atmosphere made them silent and watchful. Monica especially was quiet. She sat at the mahogany dining-room table and read *Life* magazine, her face as white and shiny as the surface of the pages. "God, I wish he'd die and get it over with," she had said last Sunday, fanning herself with a magazine, her honey-colored hair waving wet on her temples. Then she had disappeared into the bathroom, the water running from behind the closed door. Maggie suspected that Monica was crying in there, and this, more than anything else, made her feel everything was off-center. The two of them had not spoken since their encounter at the bridal salon. Maggie was surprised to find herself feeling sorry for the bride, so drawn, so hard-eyed, so brittle in her descriptions of tea sets and china patterns, so joyless two weeks before what Maggie had always thought was supposed to be the happiest day of your life.

The development was quiet. Some of the kids had given up on it, bored and put off by the finished quality of the model houses. Others were worried about trouble. The fires had been in the local newspaper, and the mothers had started to sniff their children's shirts for the scent of smoke. The construction company had hired guards to patrol three times a night; on their first trip out they had picked up some ninth graders in the basement of a split-level house and brought them home while the neighbors watched from beneath their hall lights. A coffee-colored mongrel that had wandered into one of the model homes and become stuck in a crawl space, howling like a mourner at an Irish wake, had been taken to the pound by one of the guards and put to sleep before his owners had figured out where he was. The younger kids swore that his shaggy ghost haunted the house in the middle of the night, howling from below the kitchen linoleum. From Maggie's bedroom window she could see the guards in their tan uniforms, pale shadows with flashlight beams moving at an angle ahead of them. They passed through at nine and again at eleven and, she supposed, at some later time, too, when she was already asleep. In between they checked the doors and windows of the A & P in the next town, the two churches in Kenwood, and the Kenwoodie Club to make sure that no one had scaled the fence to go skinny dipping.

She had spent the day at her grandfather's cemetery, but she and Angelo hardly spoke now. More and more, Damien helped him out with his gardening, and Maggie had lost the knack for being happy there. Until this horrible sweaty season, lines had been drawn, in her house, her neighborhood, her relationships. Some of them were boundaries—good and bad, us and them—and some of them were lines that connected people—mother and father, friend to friend. They had all been rubbed out as surely as if they had been written in chalk, not stone, and Maggie knew she could not live without them. Sometimes she sat for hours with her back against the rough bark of a tree, blowing on a blade of grass between her fingers, wondering what would happen next. Often she cried.

When she got home, she had walked out to the development. She knew Debbie would be there. She had gone to the Malone house the day before because Mrs. Malone had invited her. Charles Malone had been in a bassinet in the kitchen, sucking loudly on the neckband of his T-shirt, little beads of prickly-heat ranged like a necklace around the crease in his fat neck. "That baby is more like a potato than a human being," Mrs. Malone had said, not at all regretfully, as she chopped onions at the kitchen counter. "He just lies there all day sucking on whatever he can get into his mouth. He'll want a beer by the time he's three."

"Aren't most babies like that?" said Maggie, who was sitting at the table while Debbie was upstairs getting dressed. Her long wet hair was dripping onto the seat of her shorts, and even though Mrs. Malone was all the way across the room, Maggie's eyes were tearing from the onions.

"Lord, no," Mrs. Malone said, dabbing at her face with a paper towel. "That Aggie didn't settle down until she was two. Crying all the time unless you carried her around the room on your shoulder. Lifting those little legs and passing gas so loud you could hear her all through the house. It was all I could do not to pitch her out the window." She lifted a corner of her apron and wiped her eyes. "Damn," she said. The baby lost his piece of T-shirt, let out a momentary yell, and had found his middle fingers by the time Maggie got to the bassinet. He had a funny egg-shaped head, like a cartoon character.

The entire house was in a tizzy because Helen was coming home for dinner. It was difficult to imagine what a difference six weeks could make. Helen had become a visiting dignitary from another world, Monica had become engaged and Maggie's mother had become a wraith who evaporated and reappeared without warning in her own home. Mrs. Malone, whose idea of a balanced meal was tuna on toast with a slice of tomato, had planned scalloped potatoes and Salisbury steak for the occasion, bending over cookbooks that had been shower gifts many years ago, their bindings still cracking when they were opened because they had so rarely been used.

Debbie found it all incredibly annoying: her mother dressed in fresh Bermudas and a pressed shirt, her father home early, a cloth on the dining-room table, which was usually reserved for family holidays, and Maggie invited without her permission and against her will. She had wanted to have Bridget Hearn there, too, but Mrs. Malone had said no. "She's not family," she had said in front of Maggie, who had flushed when Debbie said, with an abrupt gesture, "Neither is she." Debbie had gone upstairs to change without asking Maggie to go along, but Maggie had followed anyhow, listening as Debbie railed to herself as she dressed. "Does she think my sister is going to think she turned into a good cook in one month? Does she think my sister will all of a sudden think we eat in the dining room every night?" Maggie suspected that Debbie kept referring to Helen as her sister in an attempt to cut her down to size, but it was all in vain.

Aggie and Debbie had gone downtown with a friend of Helen's from Sacred Heart to see Helen in the revue. While Debbie had said it was "okay," Aggie had been more specific. "She had on this thing like a leotard, you know?" she said, leaning forward, her eyes bright in the beam of a flashlight they had turned on on the floor of the development house. "It was white and it had her heart painted on it like it was bleeding, with drops running down her stomach. And she sang this great song called 'Loving One Another.' And this guy behind us with a beard? He said to this other guy who was with him, 'That's the one I told you about.' And the other guy said, 'You weren't kidding.' " She looked really beautiful. It was really quiet when she sang."

"You could see through her costume," Debbie said.

"You could, a little bit," Aggie said. "Like you can see through my white suit right after I go in the pool? But I think people thought it was just shadows."

"Sure," said Debbie, snorting.

Debbie snorted now as she stood in the doorway of the kitchen. "An apron?" she said. "Oh, hush," Mrs. Malone said, trying to get the smell of onions off her hands.

"You use a lemon," Maggie said. "You rub it on your hands and then rinse them off with cold water."

Mrs. Malone looked over her shoulder in surprise. "Forty years old last month and I've never heard that," she said. "Does it work?"

"My mom does it."

Mrs. Malone opened the refrigerator. "I'll try it next time," she said. "I'll buy a lemon."

Debbie snorted. "Listen to Maggie," she said. "She knows everything." Mrs. Malone had looked from one girl to another and then turned back to the sink when there was a noise behind them. It was Helen, dropping some shopping bags and a big purse shaped like a shopping bag into a chair. She smiled at Maggie, put her finger to her lips and glided across the kitchen. She was wearing pink ballet slippers and a white dress that looked like a slip with pink flowers embroidered on it. Maggie could see that beneath the dress she wore no underwear except for tiny underpants. She had never seen such tiny underpants before.

"Guess who?" Helen said, putting her hands over her mother's eyes.

Mrs. Malone jumped and whirled around. She looked as wiry as an old man next to her soft, slightly rounded daughter. But a resemblance was there, in the clean planes of their faces, in the delighted, dazzled look they both wore.

"You're early!" Mrs. Malone said.

"Early?" Helen said, falling back a bit. "I live here!"

"Not anymore," said Debbie.

Helen whirled around and studied Debbie narrowly. Then she grinned. "You're right, Deb," she said lightly. Her hair was growing longer, and a heavy line of blue beneath her lower lashes made her eyes look even bluer. She stooped over the bassinet and ran one finger along the side of the baby's face. "He looks like a water balloon," she said.

The kitchen had begun to be crowded with Malones. Aggie was asking Helen about her show, and trying not to look down the front of her sister's dress. Some of the younger children were begging to open the shopping bags. Mrs. Malone leaned back against the sink, her arms folded, and stared at Helen. From behind Maggie, Debbie snorted. She went out of the house onto the front steps and Maggie followed her, although she wanted to stay with everyone else.

"You're going to get the back of your dress really dirty," Maggie said, as Debbie sank down on the dusty concrete stoop.

"Who cares?"

"Why are you so mad at me?"

"Don't flatter yourself."

"I'm going to leave," Maggie said. "I'm sorry your mother invited me if it makes you so mad."

Debbie acted as if she had not heard. "She's just like your cousin," she said. "She gets away with stuff because she's pretty. I don't even think she's that pretty. Her nose is really pointy. She used to try to squish it up with her fingers, but it still points."

Maggie sat down, too.

"I hate it when I go to school and somebody goes, 'Are you Helen Malone's sister?' "

"People always ask me if I'm John Scanlan's granddaughter," Maggie said.

"That's completely different."

From where they sat they could hear voices in the living room. The street was very quiet except for the sound of a truck on the next block spraying what was left of the vacant lot for mosquitoes. Small clouds of insecticide rose above the roofs across the street, and a sweet smell drifted toward them. "Certainly not," they heard Mrs. Malone say, and then Helen said with a laugh, "All right, then Coke. I thought you really *meant* 'Would you like anything to drink?' " Then there was a murmur from Mr. Malone.

"I got my dress for the wedding," Maggie said. "It's really nice. I have to get a garter belt to wear under it."

"Bridget says that I'm better-looking than Helen. She says that Helen's eyes are too close together."

"Bridget's a moron."

"Oh, I forgot," said Debbie. "You're Helen's best friend. Who would have figured that out?"

"I used to be your best friend."

"Things used to be different."

Maggie felt her eyes water and hoped it was only the insecticide. She thought she could hear hammering, very faintly.

Behind them the door opened and Helen stepped out onto the steps. "You're going to get your dress dirty," she said to Debbie.

"Who cares?" Debbie said.

Helen looked at Maggie and shrugged. "So do you guys want your presents or not?" Debbie could not help herself; she turned and looked up. From behind her back Helen produced two small boxes. Inside were silver hoop earrings, like little rings.

Maggie held hers in the palm of her hand and touched them with her index finger. "Thank you," she said.

"We don't have pierced ears," Debbie said sullenly.

"Not yet you don't."

The two girls were very still. Finally Debbie said, "They'll kill us."

Helen smiled. "Maggie, if I pierce your ears, what will happen?" she said, in exactly the tone of voice she had used to ask Maggie what she would be doing twenty years from now.

"My mother will yell at me."

"And then?"

"I'll probably get punished. Maybe I won't be able to go to the club for a week."

"It's almost September. The club will close on Labor Day. So what else can happen?"

"Nothing, I guess."

"So you'll get yelled at, maybe punished. But then you'll have pierced ears and new earrings."

Maggie smiled and looked down at the hoops. "Does it hurt?" she asked.

"Only for a minute," said Helen.

"I'll do it," said Maggie, and Debbie looked at her, her eyes wide. "Oh, this is unbelievable," she said harshly. "Maggie Scanlan, who's afraid to do anything wrong?"

"What's with you?" Helen said.

"Forget it," said Debbie. "I know you think she's great, but she's a big chicken. She won't do anything that will get her in trouble. Bridget says she's nun material."

Helen looked thoughtful. "There's trouble, and then there's trouble," she said. She turned and started upstairs, and Maggie and then Debbie followed her. Helen pulled them into the bathroom. There was a needle threaded with white cotton and a bottle of alcohol on the edge of the sink. "Stay away from Bridget Hearn," Helen said as she rubbed Maggie's lobes with alcohol. "She's a jerk." Maggie had smiled, and as the needle went in she did not make a sound. But as they went downstairs, their earlobes tingling, their hair carefully combed forward, Debbie had turned to her and said, "I dare you to come out tonight."

Now, from her window, Maggie watched the guard's car pull away, the pale beige glowing in the half light from the houses. The lightning leapt again, brighter this time, and there was the dim timpani of thunder far away. The lightning flashed and then remained, and as she narrowed her eyes she could see fire pluming from the roof of the house where she and Debbie had once taken up residence. Even at that distance she could see that this one, the eighth one, would be the one that would count, and she understood Debbie's valedictory remark. I won't go, she told herself. I won't go. Afterward, she wondered whether she had gone because of Debbie's dare, because she was worried about her friend, or because she was just as hypnotized by trouble as the rest of them.

She could smell the blaze as soon as she left the house, sharp and bitter, a chemical edge to the natural musk of smoke, a perversion of the autumn smell she'd loved all her life and would never be able to bear again. Trotting among the houses, she began to glimpse the fire, throwing the edges of the building into sharp relief. The house looked much as usual, except that in each of its windows there was a glimpse of waving, gaudy orange, like tattered curtains blowing. The lightning throbbed again, and after the thunder she heard a scream. She went in the front door and saw flames filling the back of the house, turning the walls to nothing, and she saw Richard and Debbie leaping about, laughing. Then Debbie gave a little scream again as the fire moved forward with a roar. "We did it," she cried, her voice shrill. "We finally did it!"

Maggie could see that in minutes the entire building would be alight, and perhaps the ones next to it, too. On the floor there was an empty bottle of Four Roses, its cap filled with cigarette butts, and Maggie wondered for a moment why they'd chosen that to feed the flames. Then she looked at Debbie, who was leaping up and down as though she was on a pogo stick, her hair corkscrewing into little curls in the heat, and realized she was drunk. Her blouse was unbuttoned almost to the waist, and a big bruise purpled her neck just where it met her collarbone. Maggie felt herself flush. She looked over at Richard, and he gave her a slow, sleepy smile and ran his tongue along his lips. He stumbled over and put his mouth against her earlobe, touching his lips to the string Helen had put there until Maggie was ready to wear earrings. Maggie smelled the liquor, a hospital kind of smell, and tried to pull away, but he kept his hand on her shoulder hard, like a vise.

"Hi, sexy," he said. And he looked over at Debbie and then laughed and turned back to Maggie. He was leaning on her, and Maggie suspected that if she stepped aside he would fall over. "You're the coolest-looking girl I know. I love your eyes. Your eyes are so cool."

Maggie shivered. The flames suddenly blazed toward them, leaping toward the ceiling, turning the fresh paint to a pale curdled mess. Debbie yelped and then looked over and said to Richard, "I wouldn't waste my time."

"This is bad," Maggie said. "You guys better get out of here. This is going to burn down the whole house."

"Good thinking," said Richard, who did not move. "Watch it burn with me. You'll like it. Relax. Just for once. You'd be so cool if you'd relax."

"You're crazy. The police will come now. We could all get arrested for this. Look at her. How are you going to get her home like that? What if her mother smells her?"

"She smells good," Richard said, and he ran his hand inside the back of Maggie's shirt. "So what if we get in trouble? Who cares?" He turned his face to her, streaked with soot, smelling of gasoline. "What difference does it make?"

"Deb, don't stay here," Maggie said. "They'll be here soon. You guys are going to get in so much trouble." But Debbie just stood there, staring. "Look at it," Richard said, and he moved toward the burning wall. And then as though the fire had reached out to throw its arms around him, a flame leapt out and flared on his sleeve, played around his hair. Debbie screamed and finally ran from the house, stumbling, and Richard ran behind her, panting, coughing, falling. Maggie knelt down beside him, and by the light of the fire she could see the shriveled red flesh of his hand and arm, and his singed hair and eyelashes.

"Ah, shit, Maggie," he said evenly. And then he began to sob with great wrenching heaves. "I think I blew it."

A few steps away, Debbie was sitting on the ground, her head turned to one side, being sick all over her hair. Maggie went over to her. "You have to get up," she said. "They'll be here soon."

Debbie lay back and stared straight up at the stars. "You tried to take my boyfriend, too," she said, slurring her words.

"Shut up. They could put you in jail for this. Come on." She pulled Debbie into a sitting position and then hooked her arms beneath her armpits. Richard was starting to wail.

"Go away," Debbie said as Maggie pulled her to her feet.

She went limp in Maggie's arms and Maggie dragged her to a house across the street that was almost finished. Gently she lowered her onto the linoleum of the kitchen floor. "Stay here," she said, looking down, but in the dimness she could tell that Debbie had passed out. Maggie buttoned up her friend's blouse and then ran between the houses, leaping over pieces of lumber and discarded cardboard, trying to keep from falling. Her own house was still dark. She saw a light in the window of the construction trailer, and veered toward it. She knew someone was there; she had watched Joey Martinelli's car pull up an hour before, moving with a series of little jerks like hiccups. Maggie had laughed out loud because it reminded her of the way her aunt Celeste drove, swearing at the clutch and the gear shift as she stalled in intersections, her middle finger stuck out the window as other drivers blew their horns and pulled around her. Then the lights had gone on in the trailer, yellow squares reflecting down on the dirt, picking up the little silver trajectories of moths dazzled by the beams. Maggie disliked Joey Martinelli, even though she knew in her heart that he was probably a nice person; it seemed that he was always hanging around, the edges of his mustache wet, half-moons of dirt beneath his square nails. She hated it when he asked about her grandfather. She knew that if her grandfather ever met Joey Martinelli, the man would barely be out of earshot before John Scanlon would start calling him a guinea. One afternoon he had come over to talk to her. "You're almost done over there," Maggie had said to be polite, pointing to the row of model homes.

He nodded. "Shelley Lane," he said.

"You're calling a street Shelley? Like Shelley Winters?"

"Like Shelley the poet," Joey said, his hands in his pockets. "Every street is going to be named after some famous writer. There's a Dickens Street, a Wordsworth Street. The models are called the Emily Dickinson, the Lord Byron, and the Edgar Allan Poe."

"Which one's the Edgar Allan Poe?"

"The ranch."

Maggie shook her head. "I hope no one who comes to see it has ever read Edgar Allan Poe," she said.

"The guy wanted to be an English professor," Joey continued, "but instead he went into construction with his father. He says it shows the best-laid plans of mice and men do something or other. I can never follow half of what he says."

"Weird," Maggie had said.

Now she ran along the tamped-down dirt of the sidewalk until she came to the end of what would be Shelley Lane and knew she had to ask for help whether she liked Joey Martinelli or not. The construction trailer lay across a wide swatch of untouched land, a boundary of grass the developers had planned in the mistaken belief that it would placate the residents of Kenwood, when all it did was to make Tennyson Park seem like another country, like a raw-looking mirage floating over their backyards, distant and unsubstantial, somehow hostile. Maggie could hear music from inside the trailer, the Beatles in harmony, Paul's strained soprano, John's lower, thicker voice as the backdrop. "Things We Said Today." There was a window in the door, and she pulled herself up until she could see through it.

Inside, her mother was standing at a gray table, and as Maggie watched she pushed back her hair with her fingers and looked up at Joey Martinelli, a look of such intensity on her face that Maggie drew back. When she looked again Connie had her head down and Maggie could see that the man was arguing, using his hands, finally putting them on Connie's shoulders. Maggie thought of the feeling of Richard's hand moving softly over her collarbone. On the table was a magazine, the same issue of *Life* Monica had been reading on Sunday, the one with Paul Newman on the cover in an undershirt. Next to it was a half-eaten Three Musketeers bar. As Maggie watched, Joey Martinelli let his hands drop, and Connie looked up again. She took his big fist in her small hand, opened it, and placed something in the palm. For a moment it lay there, under the fluorescent light, and Maggie saw that it was a key. She wondered whether it was the key she had seen on the kitchen table that day she had found out her mother was learning to drive, or the key her grandfather had tossed into her mother's lap, the key to the new house in which they were all meant to live happily ever after.

Joey Martinelli's fist closed around it.

Somehow Maggie was not surprised at what she was seeing, only a little sickened, as she had been the time she had found the dress that was to be her Christmas present on the top shelf of the closet and tried it on, smoothing the skirt until she looked into the mirror and saw her mother standing behind her, her face soft and dark with betrayal and disappointment.

Slowly she backed down the steps and went around to the end of the trailer. The car was parked there, a dark-blue Plymouth sedan, like the company cars that her grandfather's salesmen used on their rounds, anonymous, undistinguished. Her grandfather always said you could pick out plainclothes cops in the city because they always drove cars like this; plainclothes city cops and the priests in the neighborhoods the cops patrolled. "Show me a priest in a Cadillac," said John Scanlon, "and I'll show you a priest who is doing things he shouldn't." Maggie could see in the light from the trailer that the car was empty. She peered in the window on the driver's side. On the seat there was a pink cardigan sweater with little pearl buttons up the front, and another Three Musketeers bar.

She heard the door to the trailer open, and for a moment she was still; then she loped around behind the trailer and made for her own backyard. As she reached the edge of the development, she tripped over a stray cinder block and went sprawling in the dirt, her knees and chin stinging. Turning, she looked back and saw the orange rectangle of the burning development house, and all around began to see lights go on in other houses. From far away she heard screams, and then she realized they were sirens, getting louder and louder. She ran inside the house, upstairs to her own room, and crouched by the window again and watched as the fire engines pulled in, the men shouting to one another to hook up hose after hose to reach the hydrant outside Maggie's house that had been base for tag for as long as she could remember. "We're going to need an ambulance," one of them shouted, and then she knew she no longer had to worry about Richard. Someone stood in her backyard, watching, and then she heard the screen door slam, and footsteps running up the stairs.

"Maggie?" her mother called in the dark. Connie moved to the bed and felt the smooth cover. Then she turned on the overhead light. Maggie was facing the window, and her mother said "Maggie?" again and then stood beside her and looked down at her face.

"Oh no," Connie said. "Not you. Oh Jesus. Not you." Maggie raised her hand to her own hot face and when she brought it away it was black with soot, and even she could smell the gasoline on her fingers.

"How could you do this? How could you? Look what you've done. And you stink of booze."

"Me?" said Maggie. "Me? What have I done? What about you? What about what you've done? You've done worse than I have tonight." Her head dropped onto her knobby knees and the tears streamed down her legs, but instead of cooling her face they only made it hotter. She felt as if she could not breathe and then she raised her head and wiped it with her arm.

"There are rules," she said in a treble voice like Damien's. "There are rules. And if you break the rules you hurt people."

"I haven't done what you seem to think I've done," Connie said softly, and Maggie saw that her mother was wearing a clover chain on her head, and with one movement she rose and snatched it off and held it broken in her hand. Connie didn't move.

"There are rules you can break like that," said Maggie, gesturing out the window at the orange glow. "And then there are the rules that are, are—" She began to sob and the flowers fell from her hand to the floor.

"I wouldn't break those rules," Connie said. "That's not the kind of person I am."

"What kind of person are you?" Maggie said, looking up, and then suddenly she saw herself, and it was as if it was the first time, as if she'd never passed a mirror, never seen a photograph, never looked into her own eyes, and she realized that no matter what she might do with her life, no matter how she might 'twist or turn or move away, it would be for nothing, that she could never escape, not just who she was, but what she had come from.

"I don't know," Connie finally said, and the two of them stood in silence for a long time, watching as the water leapt through the air, putting the fire out, leaving an empty space in the row of new houses.

The noise from the incongruous nighttime crowd—men in black slickers, police with their buttons glinting in the light of the fire, people from the surrounding houses standing in their backyards, barely visible, like a ring of ghosts defending Kenwood—gave way to the faint, unmistakable sound of the last pockets of heat popping into oblivion and the water falling from what was left of the wreckage to the blackened earth. The two women watched in silence. They did not touch or speak or look at each other.

"That's over, the fires," Maggie said finally, her shoulders sagging beneath her white shirt. "I don't want to tell you who, but I promise you it wasn't me. Not this one. I promise you this one wasn't me, and I promise it's over. I promise."

She looked up at Connie and her face was wiped clean, and Maggie knew that her mother did not believe her, although she wanted to.

"I promise you too," said her mother, and Maggie saw that in some sense she might never understand, she had been right to have the suspicions and the fears she had had, and that this day, this night, was the end of a part of her life as surely as it was the end of the new house, now a tumble of glowing debris framed by the square of her window. Silently Connie turned and left the bedroom, turning the light off as she went, and Maggie lay down on her bed in her clothes. When she woke in the morning she was still in her shorts and shirt, but her sneakers had been placed side by side under her bed, and one of Joseph's crib quilts had been wrapped around her.

HEN TOMMY CAME HOME ON THURSDAY night it was already dusk. His dinner was in the oven, the plate covered with foil, and his wife was sitting on a collapsible lawn chair on the back patio, smoking a cigarette and giggling with her cousin Celeste. Tom stood in the kitchen, watching the moths flail against the screens, the fluorescent tube above the counter blinding him, so that when he looked out he could see the bugs and nothing more. He picked at the chicken and beans on the plate, licking his fingers and absently shaking salt over everything. He was not hungry.

After work he had played one-on-one for almost an hour with one of the mixer drivers, running up and down the asphalt court until perspiration falling into his eyes turned him blind and clumsy. Then he had gone to the hospital and driven his mother to church, to a novena to St. Jude, the patron saint of lost causes. Even with the sun down, it was near ninety degrees outside, and Tom felt as if all his energy and hunger and fight had melted into a puddle on the car floor, right between the acceleration pedal and the brake. When he looked at himself in the mirror in the men's room at the plant, a gray room with a persistent smell of Lysol, he thought of the old trick of holding a buttercup beneath your chin to see if you liked butter. Almost always there would be a pale yellow shadow cast by the flower, pale yellow like the color his skin was now, the whites of his eyes, the wet circles on his shirt beneath the armpits.

Down in the basement, below his feet, he could hear the washer going. It seemed as if the washer was always going in his house. He smelled a faint odor of burning and wondered if the vent on the dryer needed replacing again. Then he remembered the fire the night before, already doused and dead by the time he came home from his mother's house. He wished someone would burn the whole damn development down. Outside he could hear more laughter, and looking inside the refrigerator saw that four of his Miller High Lifes were missing.

He did not like it when women drank beer. He even thought it was inappropriate for his mother to have Scotch on Sundays. Whenever they went out to dinner he always ordered a whiskey sour for Connie, and one for himself to keep her company, although he could never taste the liquor in those things. Sal said fancy restaurants didn't use any liquor in drinks like that, only vanilla. He stood inside, drinking his beer, pressing it against his cheek. He did not like it when Celeste spent a lot of time with Connie. The rest of the time he could think of Connie as only his, his wife, nothing more or less. When Celeste came, he felt as though his Connie disappeared, in the way she had taken to doing. He put the bottle down on the counter.

"Tommy?" Connie called, hearing the clink of the glass. Her voice was high and a little giddy.

He walked to the back door, his hands in his pockets, and stood behind the screen like a shadow.

"Come on out," Connie said.

"Hi, Tom," said Celeste, holding the beer bottle by the neck.

"Come out," his wife repeated, and he slid around the screen door, trying to keep the moths from coming in. He knew he looked out of place in his dress shirt, his tie slack around his open collar, his lace-up shoes black and heavy in the heat. Even the lightning bugs were sluggish, blinking on and off in one spot for a long time. Connie's beer bottle was turned on its side on the ground, either spilt or empty.

"We're celebrating," Connie said. "Have a beer."

"Celebrating what?"

"Celeste got married. Today."

Tommy stared at Celeste, who nodded. "At City Hall," she said, with an Ethel Merman laugh. "On my lunch hour. Actually, I took two hours and had lunch anyway."

"To who?" said Tom.

"His name is Sol Markowitz. You don't know him. He runs a hat company on 37th Street. Mr. Mark's Hats. I met him at the deli on Broadway. He's very nice. Fiftyish."

Tommy knew this meant the guy was in his sixties. The last time Celeste had dated someone "fiftyish" he had died of a cerebral hemorrhage when they were at the track together and his horse had won.

Celeste was wearing white toreador pants and a black sleeveless blouse, her hair in an upsweep. "You didn't get married like that?" said Tommy.

The two women started to laugh. "I asked her the same thing," Connie said.

"I wore a dress, for your information," Celeste said.

"Red," said Connie, bursting into laughter and groping on the ground for her beer bottle.

"So?" Celeste said. "I'm not a kid. Besides, he already had the big wedding, the hall, the flowers, the whole bit. Thirty-five years ago. Who needs it?"

"That doesn't make him fiftyish," Tommy said.

"Picky, picky, picky."

"It's not like she wants to have children," Connie said, folding her hands lightly over her stomach.

Celeste shrugged. "Sometimes it's just time, you know? It's time to settle down, get on with your life, act your age."

"Act your age?" Connie said, giggling. "You? Give me a break. Tell me another."

"How many beers have you had?" Tommy asked.

"The enforcer," Celeste said in a deep voice, picking up her bottle and taking a mouthful. Tommy flushed bright red.

"Where's your car, Celeste?" he asked.

"The enforcer," Connie said.

"He's sending a car for me," Celeste said. "Sol is. He had business and I'm going to meet him at home."

"Where's he live?" Tommy said.

"Up in Connecticut. You two will have to come up for a barbeque with the kids. He has a pool. We have a pool. That has a nice ring to it, doesn't it? We have a pool. Seven bedrooms. It's nice."

"Celeste Markowitz," said Connie.

"Oh Jesus," said Celeste to Tommy, "your mom and dad will love that. Don't say anything, okay?"

"Tell you the truth, Celeste," said Tommy, pitching his beer bottle onto the grass, the faint beer buzz he got after a long hot day beginning right behind his eyes, "at this point in their lives I don't think my parents would care."

"Get out," Celeste said. "Your old man would care unless he was half dead."

"He is half dead," Tommy said.

"Tom," said Connie, turning to look him in the face, telling him he was spoiling the party.

"Your father will outlive us all, Tom," Celeste said.

"I think you'll outlive us all, Celeste," Tommy said, and suddenly he smiled. "Let me see your ring."

Celeste held out her left hand so he could see the heart-shaped diamond perched above her big knuckle. It was twice the size of the ring she'd had before. Even in the half-light, Tom could see that it was pale yellow, and he thought again of the shadow a buttercup made beneath your chin.

"That's great," Tommy said. "Beautiful. It must have cost a fortune."

Celeste smiled. Faintly, from the front of the house, a car horn sounded twice. "That's for me," she said, getting slowly to her feet.

"Bring him in," Connie said. "I have cake in the house."

"Sometime," Celeste said. "You can't rush these things." She turned to Tommy and laid one hand, the nails as slick as patent leather, along his hot cheek. "Be nice to your wife," she said, in a throaty, intense sort of voice, and Tommy had a heady feeling of *déjà vu*. Instead of having to root around for it for days, the memory came back to him instantly: Celeste at his wedding reception, shiny in bright blue, dancing with him, looking up to say, her eyes filled with tears, "Be nice to my cousin."

"I'm always nice to my wife," he replied now. "When I can find her."

"Be extra nice to her," said Celeste, and before Tommy could get the last word she had kissed him, and was gone, a cloud of L'Air du Temps lingering over the lawn chair in which she'd sat. Tommy realized it was a new scent for Celeste, perhaps in honor of the new husband. He leaned over and picked up her beer bottle. The top was red with lipstick. He carried the bottle into the kitchen.

Connie followed him. "Tom," she said. When he turned she was standing by the stove, smiling, a misty look in her eyes. It was the booze, he told himself, but still he was excited.

"I have another surprise for you."

"What's that?" he said, running his hands up and down her arms, his fingers encircling her tiny wrists. She pushed her hands into his pockets and his breathing changed, but she only took out his car keys and held them in front of his nose.

"Ta da," she said, and he could tell now that the beer had really affected her. The last time he remembered hearing her say "ta da" was when she came out of the bathroom the first night of their honeymoon in her negligee. He wondered for a moment how she was keeping the beer down in her condition.

Connie walked out the front door, the keys still held in front of her like a carrot on a stick, and he followed. She opened the passenger door of the station wagon and said, "Get in." Then she slid in on the other side and turned the key in the ignition.

"Where's the thing that makes the seat go closer?" she said impatiently, slurring her words a little.

"Are you nuts?" Tommy said. "What do you think you're doing?"

The seat slid forward with a jerk, and Tommy's knees were pinned against the glove compartment. When the lights came on, he saw the grass edging the driveway all sharp-edged and clean, like one of those arty nature photographs. Connie put the car into reverse and backed down the driveway. The bumper hit the street solidly.

"Why does it do that?" she asked, jamming on the brake and adjusting the rear-view mirror.

"This is not funny," Tommy said. "You're going to kill us both. It's bad enough that you don't know how to drive, but you're drunk to top it all off. Just stop."

Connie dug in the pocket of her shorts and handed him a square of cardboard. It was a temporary license from the Motor Vehicle Bureau. It said that Concetta M. Scanlan had brown hair and eyes, did not need corrective lenses, was five feet tall and weighed 103 pounds. Tommy thought she was probably a little heavier than that by now.

Connie was cruising silently down Park Street, holding a little too far to the right, staring a little too intently out the windshield, the way Tommy remembered doing when he had first learned how to drive. At the corner she turned left and went around the block. She went around the block again, and then a third time, before pulling back into the driveway. Part of Tommy noticed that she cut it a little too wide on the turns, but he thought that would iron itself out in time. The other part was so enraged that he could taste the metallic tang of adrenaline on his tongue.

"Ta da," she said again, as she turned off the engine. Without a word he walked back into the house and took another beer out of the refrigerator. He sat down in the living room in his chair and switched on the television. She came and stood in front of it, her arms crossed on her chest.

"Aren't you going to say anything?"

"What do you want me to say?"

"Congratulations would be nice."

There was a long silence. Finally he said, "Where are the kids?"

"Joseph is upstairs asleep. Damien is at my father's. Terence is spending the night at O'Brien's after his game, and I think Maggie is with Debbie."

"Oh, that's convenient," he said sarcastically.

"What's that supposed to mean?" said Connie, turning around to switch off the television.

Tommy just looked at her, his eyes cold, his heart pounding. He looked down and imagined he could see it pulsing beneath his damp dress shirt. The beer was making him feel tired.

"Do you have something going with that guinea?" Tommy finally said.

"You sound exactly like your father," Connie replied.

It was not, he thought, the way he had planned to bring this up. But it was the sight of her behind the wheel that had set him off, so small that it seemed scarcely possible that she could see over the dashboard or reach the brake pedal, like a little girl playing at being grownup. She was exactly the same, and yet she was entirely different. There was no need for her to be able to do this. He could take her anywhere she wanted to go. He went into the kitchen and uncapped another beer, wondering how he could have finished the last one so quickly, but when he came back she was in the same place, with the same hard look around her onyx eyes. Her face and throat were dewy with the heat, and she had faint dark circles just beneath her eyes where her mascara was smudging onto her skin.

"The answer is no," she said finally, breaking the silence, and there was a certain something in her voice that told him that the question had been neither unexpected nor unreasonable.

But it never occurred to Tommy that she might not be telling the truth. She was that sort of person, black and white, who would not lie about what she had done simply because facts were facts and you had to acknowledge them. "I never would have thought this of you," he said slowly. He could think of nothing else but clichés, and he drank his beer to stop from talking.

"Thought what of me, Tommy?" she said, raising her hands in the air. "That I would get tired of not fitting in? That I would want to do the things that other people do? I don't always want to be the strange one. I want to be happy."

"What's happy?" he said.

"I don't know," she said, dropping her hands. "But I know I haven't been it, whatever it is."

Oddly enough, he felt happy now, with just the two of them in their own living room, with his stomach full of beer. He remembered how, one evening in the hospital, his father had asked him to play a game of pinochle, beating Tom as he did all his sons. Then he had fallen back into the pillows, his collarbone like a wooden yoke beneath his pajamas, and said, "There's nothing like a game of cards to make you feel alive."

Tommy looked at his wife now and he loved her, loved how the veins showed blue around her neck just above the little collar of her shirt, how her hair fuzzed out uncontrollably in the heat, how she had joined him to make a life of their own, however flawed, however constraining. He loved all the little things. He did not want her to be like other people. He would never have loved her if she had been. He thought of her pulling into the driveway with such assumed competence, but with her bottom lip caught between her front teeth as she turned the wheel. He began to cry.

"No, Tom, no," she whispered, going to kneel in front of him and cradling his head on her shoulder. "No, no, no. It's all right. It's all going to be all right." Tommy started to choke on it, the hot salt, the booze, the grief, the loss of the father he wished he had had, the death of the world he loved.

"I was afraid . . ." he began, but she didn't let him finish.

"I know," Connie said. "I know. But there was nothing to be afraid of."

Tommy pulled away and looked at her and she smiled, inscrutable and wise. He couldn't tell her that somehow the driving seemed like a great infidelity all by itself, the separation, the pulling away. There was nothing to be done about that now, and he couldn't afford to lose her. He realized that she was the closest he would ever get to not being alone. His parents would die, and the children would change and leave, and there the two of them would be, in their living room, perspiring and talking in fragments.

"I love you," he said, and he started to cry again.

"Yes, honey. Yes, I know."

"Don't go away."

"Where would I go?" Connie said, and she held him for a long time. Slowly, almost in a dream, he began to undress her, there in the living room. It made him remember the first Friday night they had spent in this house, after they had moved from her aunt Rose's. Maggie and Terence were babies, and they had stayed behind in the Bronx while he and Connie came to arrange the furniture, put away the dishes, make up the bare beds. They had had dinner that night on the floor, on a blanket, with a bottle of Rose's Chianti for a kind of celebration, and by the time it was dark they were both drunk. They had pushed everything to one side—he could still feel the scratch of the wool blanket on his bare skin—and fell on each other right next to the dirty plates. Connie's bra had stayed looped around her neck throughout, as if she were a corpse in a *Daily News* rape-and-murder story. There were no curtains on the windows and Tommy had averted his eyes, afraid to see someone peeking in. But when they were finished they walked around brazenly, their clothes on the floor, staying up way past midnight as though they both knew it would be a long time before they would have this kind of freedom again. Tommy remembered walking through the half-empty rooms with one word going through his head: Mine. Mine. He had meant his wife, too. He said it again, now, as he pulled impatiently at her shorts. Their skins stuck together in the heat, and made sucking noises when they pulled apart. As they lay side by side on the carpet afterward, Tommy realized that he had forgotten, for once, that she was pregnant. She, he realized from her response, simply did not care.

"We have to get dressed," she said after a few minutes. "One of the children might come in."

But he was already half-asleep by that time, and he only pulled on his pants and fell into his chair, his head thrown back, his mouth open. She covered him with one of Joseph's blankets, a small square over the middle of his long body, and then she went upstairs to sleep by herself. In the middle of the night he woke up once, his head buzzing with a swarm of hangover gnats, filling his ears with noise and his eyes with little white lights, and he thought suddenly that he had been had once again. This was what his entire married life had been like: long stretches of tedium illuminated by moments, unexpected, when he knew that without her he would be lost. For weeks or months they moved through their separate lives and slept side by side as though they were two strangers who had mistakenly been assigned the same hotel room. And then something would happen and he would find himself staring at her as though he could see the soul of her, looking for an end to his troubles inside the loop of her arms, and he would be snagged with the fishhook of herself, with the barbed hook of his powerless infatuation with something that she seemed to have, some answer that she seemed to offer. She was the one, really, who had always had the power over him, and who always would; his father's bluster was nothing compared to it. He tried to remember all this as he lay there, the aftertaste of liquor awful in his mouth. He wished he had a pen and could write it down, but instead he vowed— perhaps aloud, he thought he heard some muttering in the room—to remember it the next morning.

When he woke again the watery blue of the sky told him that it was dawn. The pressure behind his eyes was enormous. The buzzing had reawakened him, and he pressed his hands over his ears. After a moment he realized that the noise was not inside his head, but in the kitchen, and as he took his hands away Connie appeared at the top of the stairs, her face very pale above the white of her nightgown. He felt embarrassed to look at her.

"Tommy, James is on the phone," she said. When he got up from the chair the room tilted a little. He picked up the kitchen phone and it was only when he actually said "Hello" that he realized he had never received a call this early in the morning, and even before James spoke Tommy knew what he would say.

"He's dead," his brother said.

21

ATES OF HEAVEN CEMETERY WAS NICE, Maggie thought, but not as nice as her grandfather Mazza's cemetery. It had a slight rise and fall to it, little hills and valleys crisscrossed with wide roads. Whole areas were empty, the grass stretching bright green and unbroken for a long way. There were no trees. They took good care of the lawns. Just inside the entrance there was a sign:

NO: PLANTING AT GRAVESITES

       FLAGS

       MILITARY MEDALLIONS

GRAVE BLANKETS PERMITTED ON CHRISTMAS, EASTER, AND MOTHER'S DAY.

NO UNAUTHORIZED VISITORS. PLEASE RESPECT THIS PLACE OF REST.

Maggie thought the last sentence was sort of nice, but the rest of the rules seemed harsh. Strangers strolled around Angelo Mazza's cemetery all the time, and no one thought anything of it. Mrs. Martini left photographs of the grandchildren on her husband's grave, weighted down with small stones. Women were always coming with pots of hyacinths or gardenias. They would kneel with their trowels in front of the headstones and dig a little hole and put the flowers in and then pat the earth around the roots gently, as though they were patting the person beneath. They never worried about the plants dying. Angelo took care of them once they were in the ground. It would have been nicer if her grandfather Scanlan could have been buried at Calvary Cemetery, but Maggie knew he never would have allowed it. She could picture him lying under his shirred white satin blanket, his black rosaries twined around his fingers in the stagy position that would never allow you to say the rosary in real life, thinking to himself, "Jesus, Mary, and Joseph, I'm surrounded by guineas." She laughed a little to herself, and her father frowned at her.

She knew that she should feel sadder than she did, but the fact was that she did not believe that her grandfather was dead, although she had knelt before the coffin and looked down at the waxy hands, still so big and powerful looking. He had made her recite the seven deadly sins just two weeks before. She had forgotten one. "Sloth," John Scanlan had thundered, the violence of the sound bringing two nurses to the door of his room. "And don't you forget it, little girl." Her grandfather had looked better, his mouth less elastic, his eyelids matching, both at half-mast. Sometimes when she would arrive at the hospital he would be sleeping, his breath rippling through his lips like that of an old horse, and when she left he would still be sleeping, even though she had sat there for an hour or two, watching the white light of the sun lay bright rectangles on the linoleum floor. Sometimes they played Parcheesi, and most of the time he told her stories about his childhood, about beating up Billy Boylan behind the garage on Lexington Avenue or being taken into the precinct house by the cops after he stole penny candy from the Greek's place around the corner from the tenement building where his family lived. Some of the stories had been new. Some Maggie had heard before, but they were transformed. For the first time Billy Boylan got some punches of his own in, and was not simply decimated by John Scanlan's invincible right hook; for the first time it turned out that some lemon balls had indeed been stolen from the Greek's. "The cops took 'em, and ate 'em!" her grandfather said loudly, as though consumption was the real crime. Occasionally the stories would be interrupted by her grandfather's doctor, a man named Levine who was ugly and very kind, and who disliked John Scanlan very much but was always cheerful around him. When Maggie first came to the hospital, Dr. Levine and some other doctors would often enter and make her move outside, pulling the white curtains hanging from the ceiling tight around the bed. Their shoes moved at the bottom of the curtain, their shadows made a kind of mime show. But after a few weeks Dr. Levine just felt for her grandfather's pulse, and then left. Maggie had imagined this was because her grandfather was getting better. Now, of course, she knew it had been because he was dying.

"What?" she had said, when her father told her. Tommy was sitting at the kitchen table drinking a glass of Pepto-Bismol, his face gray. "What? Are you sure?" She had gone upstairs to her room to think, looking out over the asphalt shingles of the new roofs to the place where the house that had burned had stood. For some reason she had thought of the picture in the Baltimore Catechism of mortal and venial sin: first the milk bottle with the little flecks of black in it, then the milk bottle dark as a moonless night, and then the bottle pure white again after confession. In some way she felt pure white.

She had not talked to Debbie since that night. She had barely talked to her mother, only watched her walk around the house with the wary eyes of the guilty. Now her grandfather was dead. She felt as though she was bereft of any connections at all. As she lay on her bed, she felt as though she was floating, the motion in her body like the motion of Cap'n Jim's big tug as it plied the Jersey coastline. She looked at the blackened supports of the burned house from her bedroom window, and although she couldn't explain why, she felt that the worst was over. Down in the kitchen, she had watched her mother making macaroni and cheese, to be heated in between visits to the funeral home, and she realized that it was the first proper meal Connie had made in weeks. Maggie wondered if that meant that Connie had come back to them.

The next three days had passed in a welter of small details: the boxes of tissues on every table at the funeral home, the black mantillas laid on the chair in the hallway at her grandmother's house, the holy card with the Sacred Heart on one side and her grandfather's name and the prayer of resurrection on the other. "Accept our prayer that the Gates of Paradise might be opened for your servant," it said. Her grandmother kept changing her mind about whether her husband should wear his blue or his gray suit, as though he was going to a communion breakfast. "For Christ's sakes, Mother," Tommy finally said, "if it matters so much to you we'll dress him in the gray the first night and the blue the next. Can we drop it now?" Mary Frances had started to cry, and been helped up to her room by Margaret. Looking back over her shoulder, Margaret had said quietly to her brother, "Displacement, Tom honey. Thinking about the small things so you won't have to think about the big ones." Maggie had watched with a great full feeling in her throat as tears rose in her father's eyes. For three days, she thought, they were all displacing. She had learned a new word. The only time any of it felt like real life was driving home in the car from the funeral home one night, stretched out on the back seat, her hot cheek against the cool vinyl of the seats. Frank Sinatra was on the radio, and her father was singing while her mother hummed and beat time with the toe of one patent-leather pump. "No, no, they can't take that away from me," Tommy roared happily. When the last few notes died away, he reached across for Connie's hand. Maggie could see their twined fingers in the space between the seats, the lights of the dashboard making blue stars in her mother's engagement ring. Then her father said, "Did they get whoever torched that house?"

"I think one of the boys did it. Mary Joseph's son. He was badly burned. They say he may lose a couple of fingers, and some of the use of his hand."

Tommy whistled. "Police?"

"I think they're handling it privately. The father has a bundle, and he's going to need it. The construction people want $25,000."

Maggie saw her father look over at her mother, his profile sharp against the windshield. "Yeah?"

"I get that from your sister-in-law," Connie said with a wary look. "That's where I heard it. I don't know if it's true."

Tommy grunted, satisfied. "The kid set these fires all by himself?" he added.

"He was the ringleader," Connie had answered.

Maggie stared again at her mother in the limousine stopped in front of the Gates of Heaven sign. Connie's eyes looked clear, her face smooth. This was how she always looked after the baby had settled in, once the bad part was over. The lines of her mantilla melted into the black of her hair. Everyone was stopped behind them, the cars with their headlights on, dim in the sunshine, snaking out onto Westchester Avenue. There were 111 cars in the procession: John's children, grandchildren, brothers and sisters, the workers from Scanlan & Co., the leaders of the unions that represented those workers, the leaders of the dioceses that bought what they made, a great long chain of procreation and commerce. There was one friend, a man named McAlevy who said he'd gone to high school with John Scanlan and had read his obituary in the newspaper. "A helluva pitching arm," the man had told Maggie's father at the funeral home. "Jesus, I'll never forget it. A helluva pitching arm." Maggie had seen the Malone car in the parking lot as she got into the limousine, but she knew she shouldn't wave. She saw it again now, as the limousine inched forward and the family slid from the cars and gathered under the tent that sheltered the old man's bronze casket from the noonday sun.

"I am the resurrection and the life," said the archbishop's representative, a monsignor with a deep, powerful, effortlessly dramatic voice, which alone had ensured his elevation in the church. Uncle James had implored him to say the words in Latin, had hinted at free vestments for the cathedral. The priest had reluctantly refused. The new order was inviolate.

Maggie could not concentrate on the words. A piece of green grasscloth was draped around the base of the casket, but it gapped near her feet and she could see the hole beneath. She knew that they would wait until everyone was gone and then the cemetery workers would lower the straps that let the box down into another box made of some kind of cement. And then they would fill the hole in and place the flowers on top. And by next year the grass would have covered it, and the scar would be gone. There was a largish headstone that said only SCANLAN. The stonecutter would come in a few weeks to finish it. Maggie was struck by the difference between knowing the routine and having it happen to someone she loved.

There was a movement behind her, and she turned to see her cousin Monica, her hand clapped over her mouth, retreat to the lead car, the one in which her grandmother and her uncle James had been riding. Monica seemed somehow to have lost her power, too. At the funeral home they had stood side by side in the ladies' room, and Monica had asked her coldly if she was bringing a date to the wedding. "Elvis Presley," Maggie had said in a monotone. "Paul McCartney. Marlon Brando. James Dean." Monica had smiled. "A comedian," she said. "A real ball of fire."

"Stuff it, Monica," Maggie said. "I'm tired of being afraid of you."

"Remember man . . ." the priest was saying, and Maggie finished the sentence in her mind, just as she would have done for her grandfather if they had been in his living room. Her lips moved: "that thou art dust and unto dust thou shalt return." It was a good feeling, to be able to do that, like knowing the answer in a spelling bee. Maggie suddenly remembered the doorstop her grandparents had kept against the door to the house in summertime. It was a three-dimensional octagon, like a faceted ball, made of milky green stone. Maggie had loved to play with it when she was small, to turn it from side to side to side. One day she had asked her grandmother which was the top and which was the bottom, and Mary Frances had tried to explain that all the sides were the same. "There really is no top or bottom to it, dear," she said softly, not noticing that John Scanlan was standing behind her until he reached clear over her shoulder and took the thing away. He turned it and turned it in his big hand, the hairs on the back catching the light so that they glinted silver and gold, and finally he hit on one side, identical to all the others except that there was a small nick at one edge. He crouched next to Maggie.

"This is the top, little girl," he said, and then he turned to the opposite side. "And this is the bottom. Top. Bottom. Bottom. Top."

Mary Frances had faded away, and Maggie had been happy. She liked answers. When they went to her grandparents' house, after this was over, she would look for the nick. She knew now that her grandfather had been making a point, not telling the truth, but she agreed that the first was more important than the second.

It was nearly time to go. The heat was drying the drops of holy water the priest had sprinkled on the metal lid of the casket. Her grandmother stood with her arm through Uncle James's. The monsignor had turned to speak to her, and she blinked at him as though she could not quite place him.

Maggie followed her parents back to the car. Mrs. Malone stopped to talk to Connie, and Debbie hung back, she and Maggie standing awkward and silent in their black patent-leather shoes, their Teenform garter belts itchy above their pelvic bones. Debbie was wearing her Easter hat, white with black daisies, and a black piqué dress that had once been Helen's and was still too big on her.

"I'm sorry about your grandfather," she said to Maggie softly.

"That's all you have to say to me?" Maggie said. "I saved your life."

"You're nuts," Debbie said. "You got me in a lot of trouble. I fell asleep and didn't get up till two o'clock. I had to go sleep at Bridget's house. Now I'm not allowed to go anywhere. And my mother says you and I can't be friends anymore."

Maggie looked over at Mrs. Malone. For a moment Debbie's mother looked at her, and then she tilted her chin up in a way she had when she was angry, and stared past her. Maggie could not imagine why Mrs. Malone would be angry at her.

"How am I in trouble with your mom for what you did? What did you say?"

"You should have taken me home, Mag."

"You shouldn't have had anything to drink. We're only thirteen. I could see right down the front of your blouse." Maggie stared at her friend's neck. There was a very faint purple mark, ineptly concealed with what looked like Max Factor pancake.

"Oh, grow up," Debbie said. "What are you, my conscience? If you think you can handle everything, then do it. But don't do it halfway. If you're going to save somebody's life, then save it *all* the way."

There was a long silence. The two girls looked down at their shoes, hazy with dust.

"My mother said Richard's father is paying for everything," said Maggie finally, not looking up.

"He's okay," Debbie said. "Bridget says they're sending him to military school. He's going to need plastic surgery on his arm, Bridget said, and one of his fingers was burned off. That's pretty disgusting, but at least it wasn't his face. God, that would have been bad. It didn't even touch his face, just his arm. And it was the arm he doesn't use to write or throw, Bridget said. He'll write and tell me soon. I don't know how I'm going to see him at military school."

Maggie said nothing, only fingered the tissue in her hand. She looked at Debbie, her hair frizzing in the heat, and knew that she would always think of her as her best friend. She looked at Mrs. Malone, who still avoided her eyes, and knew that that was over, too, and she thought that maybe it was Mrs. Malone she would miss most. She would miss having a mother she didn't have to push away, having a mother nothing like herself, having a family with no complications. Her eyes swam with tears, until the sunlight broke into little pink particles and she saw everything as a blur. She had known her grandfather would die. She had gotten used to the idea, little by little over the summer, that he was not invincible. But she knew that she had still believed that some things lasted forever.

" 'Bye Deb," she said.

"God, you're always so dramatic," Debbie said. "That's what Bridget says."

Maggie looked away and saw that now her grandmother had the monsignor on one side of her and Mr. O'Neal on the other. Suddenly her grandmother crouched down and lifted one side of the grasscloth. "Oh, God," Maggie heard Connie say, and the two of them moved away from the Malones and stood behind Mary Frances.

"Could you get your father, sweetheart?" said Mr. O'Neal, wiping his forehead with his handkerchief.

Mary Frances wheeled and brightened. "Maggie, these gentlemen are confused. Go get your uncle James and your father." And suddenly all the boys were there, in their dark suits, looking so alike, so flushed and full of blood. For the first time Maggie saw the family resemblance, and saw it in herself, too.

"I just wanted to know on which side the baby was buried," Mary Frances said, her voice loud enough that people began to look over. "He is under the mistaken impression that there is nobody else in the Scanlan plot." The five men, their hands folded in front of them, turned as one to Mr. O'Neal, who wiped his forehead again.

"Perhaps one of you could show your mother to the car," he said.

"Is there another casket there or not?" Tommy said.

Mr. O'Neal looked at Mary Frances, and then his narrow nostrils flared. "Absolutely not," he said. "And I can assure you that I had a number of conversations with your father about these arrangements over the years and it was understood—twelve places. He and your mother. You five and your wives."

Tommy grimaced. "What about my sister?" he said.

"The sisters make their own arrangements," said Mr. O'Neal, as though that settled everything.

"My parents had a child who passed away at birth," Tommy began. "A little girl."

"My understanding was that at the time she was buried at a cemetery in the Bronx," Mr. O'Neal said.

"And he promised to move her," Mary Frances said, and Maggie could see that her face was beginning to fall, as though the pouchy cheeks were melting just a little. "He promised to bring her up here so that we could all be together." Mary Frances looked imploringly at Mr. O'Neal. Then she took Tommy's arm. He looked around at his brothers, but they were staring down at their clasped hands. Maggie heard her father say, very softly, "He didn't do it, Ma. Maybe he forgot."

He put his arm around Mary Frances's shoulder. A path opened for them through the people who were left, and he guided her to a car and climbed in after her; his long arm was the last Maggie saw of him, pulling the door closed with a loud *thunk*.

"This is not my fault," Mr. O'Neal was saying as Maggie and Connie walked to another limousine. Margaret was already inside, and in silence they drove to the big fieldstone house. There were plates of cold cuts, and Swedish meatballs in a chafing dish with a little candle underneath to keep them warm, and fried chicken and potato and macaroni salad. But Mary Frances never came downstairs. Maggie spent most of the afternoon fetching Mr. McAlevy a fresh drink and listening to him tell a long story about a policeman, a bar in Brooklyn, a colored man, and an Irish gang that seemed to have no point and certainly nothing to do with John Scanlan. She excused herself when she saw Margaret climbing the stairs with a plate of food, and followed her to the door of the girls' room. Across the hall she could see her grandparents' room, neat and empty, her grandfather's gray suit laid out on the bed.

"Have you seen the stone doorstop?" Maggie asked.

"What, sweetie?" her aunt said, balancing the plate of chicken and potato salad on one hand and pushing a piece of hair under her wimple.

"Remember the doorstop? The big round ball with the flat sides that always held the door back?"

"I haven't seen that for years, Maggie," Margaret said impatiently. "Would you go get me a 7-Up with just a splash of Canadian Club in it and bring it here?"

"A cherry?" Maggie said.

"Not necessary," Margaret said, opening the door and taking the food inside.

When Maggie came back, her grandmother was sitting up in bed, eating chicken and patting her face with a tissue. Somehow it was the sight of Mary Frances in the single bed, Elizabeth Ann's bed, that finally got to Maggie, so that when she handed her the drink she began to cry, wiping the tears from her cheeks with the back of her hand until Margaret handed her one of her big plain white cotton handkerchiefs.

"You were his favorite," Mary Frances said, and as Maggie looked at her grandmother, so small and raddled-looking, lying in the small bedroom with the two Scanlan & Co. crucifixes over the two beds, she knew that their lives would never be the same again. On the table next to the bed was a copy of *Wuthering Heights*.

"It's really good," said Maggie, picking the book up and sniffling. "There's some boring stuff at the beginning and end but the main story is great."

"As good as *Jane Eyre?*" Margaret said.

"Better."

"What?" said Mary Frances querulously, eyeing them over the edge of her glass.

"Maggie was asking about the doorstop for some reason," Margaret said loudly, as though her mother was deaf.

"The what?"

"That big stone doorstop we used to have downstairs."

Mary Frances beamed. "You may have it, dear," she said to Maggie.

"But where is it, Mother?" Margaret said.

Mary Frances thought for a moment. "It's in the cabinet to the left of the stove, on the bottom shelf near the back. I put it there last year after your grandfather threatened to throw it out the window. He'd stubbed his toe on it in the dark." Mary Frances patted her face with the tissue again. "I know he'd want you to have it, dear," Mary Frances added.

"Although maybe some time you'll explain to me why you want it," Margaret added, eating potato salad from her mother's plate.

Maggie thought for a moment. "I think it's displacement," she said.

Her aunt Margaret narrowed her eyes, and Maggie could tell that she was trying to decide whether Maggie was being smart or not. Margaret leaned back on the bed, the skirt of her habit hiked up to her knees, her black legs crossed at the ankle. "This family has a future," she said finally.

"What?" asked Mary Frances.

"Nothing, Mother," Margaret said, and she winked at Maggie.

22

I T WAS CONNIE, OF ALL PEOPLE, WHO had taken her mother-in-law to the grave of her daughter, back in one corner of the cemetery where Connie had grown up. Connie had called Angelo Mazza the morning after the funeral, and then she had called Mary Frances, and picked her up in Tommy's station wagon. Mary Frances slid into the passenger seat, clutching her black handbag as though this excursion was the most natural thing in the world. There was no conversation. Mary Frances took out her rosary and said it soundlessly, the silence punctuated by the clicks of her crystal beads on their silver chain. When they drove through the gates to Angelo's little house she let them slither back into the blue velvet pouch in which she kept them.

"This place is very pleasant, Concetta," Mary Frances said as she emerged from the car.

Connie actually thought the flowers looked tired at this time of year, a little florid in their color, like a woman wearing too much makeup to disguise her age. The rose of Sharon and the hollyhocks were ragged, and the daisies had gotten leggy and fell over in untidy clumps. Most of the day lilies were gone, and the handsomest parts of the cemetery were those that had turned a deep green, in a final burst of good health before the early frosts defoliated them. As though he had been thinking the same thing, Angelo emerged from his house carrying a small pair of clippers. He looked neat and elegant in his gray pants and white shirt.

Connie felt as tired as she'd ever been in her life. Part of it was the pregnancy, and part was the heat, and part were the events of the last few days. That morning two police officers had arrived at the front door. They were young, boys really, ten years younger than she was, and they wanted to talk to Maggie.

"I understood that the builders would not be pressing any charges, that they had agreed to receive restitution from the family of the boy responsible," Connie said.

"We have to do our own investigation, ma'am," one of the officers said quietly, and Connie flinched at that last word, and felt very old. She was glad Tommy had gone over to Scanlan & Co. for the day. She called Maggie down from her bedroom. Maggie was barefoot, her hair wet from the shower, and she froze at the bottom of the stairs as she saw the blue uniforms.

"We're particularly interested in the last fire," the officer said.

They sat on the couch and Maggie sat on the floor cross-legged, her shoulders slumped, her arms limp. "Why are you talking to me?" she said.

Connie started to speak, but before she could the officer, flipping through a spiral notebook, answered, "We talked to a Miss Hearn, who said she had no association with the fires. She sent us to a Miss Malone, who said the same. She sent us to you."

Connie could see Maggie only in profile. She had always known that the day would come when her daughter's transformation would be complete, when she would not only be separate but equal, when she would become adult. Connie knew that this could take a long time; she felt that for herself it had happened just the other day, in the parking lot at the high school and in John Scanlan's hospital room. She had expected it to happen when Maggie got her first period, developed breasts, fell in love. But it was happening here, now, horribly. There was a tightness around the square jaw, a hard glint in the eye, that was the look of a woman. It was like that just for a moment, and then it was replaced by the soft vulnerable look of a child who has been mistreated. Maggie's mouth was open, but nothing came out. Then Connie had said, "My daughter was here with me that night. She couldn't have had anything to do with it."

The older of the two cops had looked at her for a long time. Connie was quite sure that they'd heard such a story from a mother a hundred times before. Finally he said, "We're happy to know that, ma'am," as he slapped his notebook shut and rose.

On the ride with Mary Frances to the cemetery, Connie thought of that moment, and of the moment when she saw Maggie's face change and watched the end of innocence right before her eyes. She still did not know how much of it was knowing that Debbie had betrayed her, and how much was what Maggie had seen the night of the fire, the things she had meant when she had said, her eyes blazing, "You've done worse than I have tonight." She did not know whether her daughter had seen Joey Martinelli kissing her in the car, trying to undress her in the construction trailer, or arguing with her when Connie finally had pulled away, empowered by knowledge and not this time by nausea.

Connie wondered, too, what Joey had seen in her own face when she handed him the key to the trailer, what had made him finally crumble and grow still after hours of argument. She knew what she had seen in his: it was that same glaze her daughter had had beneath the watchful eyes of the police, the awareness of the world the way it truly was.

"Life is a terrible thing," she said matter-of-factly.

"Yes, dear," said Mary Frances. "But then, what else is there?" And she slid out of the car as Angelo Mazza came forward to greet her.

Connie realized it was only the third time her mother-in-law and her father had met. Mary Frances seemed to have regained some of her aristocratic manner now that her husband's illness was over, but it was a little weary and worn, like something familiar she had fallen back on purely from fatigue.

"Good morning," Mary Frances said to Angelo quietly. "This is very kind."

Angelo gave a slight bow and then held out his arm. "Shouldn't we drive, Pop?" Connie said, but Mary Frances said, "I would rather walk."

In silence, under a lowered, pale gray sky, the thick air smelling of rain, they trod the asphalt, springy beneath their feet, until they came to a freshly cleared spot by the wall. Connie could see that her father had cut back the wisteria, sinuous and predatory here in the old section, and that some years ago he had planted violets around this stone, their heart-shaped leaves large and plentiful now, the little facelike flowers gone this late in the season. A small square headstone bore only the word SCANLAN, with the disembodied head and wings of a cherub above it. Time's grime, the decades of snow and rain, summer and winter, had left black rubbed deep into the design and the letters. Mary Frances stood with her head down, still holding on to Angelo Mazza's arm.

"I have kept it very good," he said quietly. "Very nice. In the springtime it is always purple, first with the wisteria, then the violets. Very sweet."

"Yes," Mary Frances said. "Thank you."

Connie was sure that there was something strange about this, about the fact that Tommy's sister had been in her own backyard, as it were, even before she first set eyes on Tommy. But it seemed no stranger than anything else she could think of, no stranger than the fact that two people sometimes cleaved together their whole lives long because of something they'd done in the back seat of a car, no stranger than the fact that two people could cleave together their whole lives long, while one thought she'd been made a promise and another that the promise didn't matter much. Or that people could have hard feelings for so long and have them evaporate overnight. Connie put a hand on her mother-in-law's shoulder. "You can have her moved as soon as you want," she said.

"No," Mary Frances said. "This is fine. I just wanted to know where to come. It would be a shame to disturb this."

"Maybe that's what John thought," Connie said.

"No," said Mary Frances sadly, slipping her rosary beads out of her bag. "He just couldn't be bothered. He thought it was a whim. God rest him," she added reflexively.

Connie stepped away from the corner, to give her mother-in-law privacy, and she and her father walked out to the road. Damien was back by the rosebushes, doing the fall fertilization. He had waved to her across the expanse of bushes and headstones, but he had not gotten up from his work. Once she saw his lips move and thought he was talking to a bug.

There were no funerals today, although somewhere across the way Connie could see the garish display of color upon one mound that showed where a grave had been recently filled and all the funeral baskets and wreaths laid atop it. The gladiolus had always repelled her just as they had her father, but she minded them less because they were dead than that they had always been such a symbol of death itself. She remembered shuddering at her wedding when she saw those frilly spears, so unnaturally tall, standing on the altar. Between two rows of headstones she saw Leonard Fogarty running the hand mower, the skin of his flat head pale white beneath the stubble of his brush cut. He would be pleased when he turned and saw her, would come running over with his awkward gait, smiling all over his face, calling "Hi Hi Hi." She remembered him on her wedding day, too, and the sound he had made, like a calling bird: *oooooooh*, as she came out of the house in her pale cream dress, the color of eggnog.

The cemetery was a beautiful place, although she had had enough of the accoutrements of death during the past week to last her a lifetime. It shamed her to know that she was thinking of a new life as well; not the one inside her, but the one around her. They all were. Even Mr. O'Neal had been happy at John Scanlan's wake, although he had done his best to hide it. The family had taken the heaviest, most expensive bronze casket he had for what he knew would be the largest funeral he would handle all year. The Scanlan family had printed up a thousand holy cards in anticipation of the crowd. When all of the nuns from Margaret's convent entered at once, Mark had turned to Tommy and whispered, "Call and get more cards."

"Get the sewing machines converted quick for blouses and table runners," Tommy whispered back, and Connie, overhearing, had had to stifle a laugh. Tommy turned and grinned at her, and then, very softly, he ran his hand over the down of her upper arm. She had shivered and then slowly smiled.

For part of the evening she had found herself alone in one corner with her sister-in-law Gail, who had never become accustomed to the lively air of Catholic funerary rites, particularly the position of the departed at the front of the room like a table centerpiece. Nevertheless she had tried to join in. "He looks good, doesn't he?" Gail had said to Connie.

"He looks dead, Gail."

"You two are certainly taking this hard," Gail said. "Tommy has seemed so moody. It wasn't like him to snap at Mother the way he did."

Connie sighed. "He loved his father," she said, thinking of how little nuance the sentence contained.

"Yes," said Gail piously, adjusting the lapels of her black suit. She looked down at Connie's belly, draped in black wool. "Aren't you hot?"

"It's the only black maternity dress I have," Connie said. "Tomorrow I'll have to wear a blue one."

Gail looked down at her hands in her lap and twisted her wedding ring. "We're going to adopt a baby," she said.

"That's wonderful, Gail," said Connie, feeling a surge of pity for her sister-in-law, her hair so carefully barretted back, her fingers turning, turning her ring. "That's great. You'll love it. It's the most wonderful thing in the world, being a mother." She wondered what it was about this situation that made her say so many things that sounded right but felt suspect. She was afraid that if she stayed here much longer, among the liverish pink and pale green brocades, she would find herself, like the head of the carpenters union now standing behind her, talking of what a good man John Scanlan was, and how much he loved his sons.

"We couldn't have done it while he was alive," Gail said, her voice still lowered as though she was afraid her father-in-law would hear. It was a testimonial to John Scanlan's vivid personality that even Connie, who had no illusions about death, had looked up several times during the evening and momentarily expected him to leap from his prone position and throttle someone who had done him dirty over the years.

"How do you feel about all this?" Gail said suddenly, in what sounded like an accusatory tone.

"Do you mean am I glad he's dead?" Connie asked, and without waiting for an answer she went on, "Not really. I thought I would be, but I think it will probably upset things more than it will help them. And it will be hard to be happy at the wedding on Saturday. But I'm glad for you about the baby."

"Mark can do what he wants," Gail said. "I can do what I want. So can you."

Connie was silent for a minute. She could see John Scanlan's nose, beaklike and fierce, and then two more visitors knelt in front of the casket and blocked her view.

"No one can do what they want," she said, thinking of the look on Joey Martinelli's face when she had given him back the key to the construction trailer.

"I guess I can understand if you're sad," Gail went on as though she hadn't heard. "The way he talked about you—how Tommy was the only one to marry a girl with looks, how the rest of the grandchildren, even Monica, were washed-out from too much Irish inbreeding and your children were the only ones who were halfway decent-looking or had half a brain. If I had had to hear one more word about what great legs you had, I would have screamed."

Connie looked at her sister-in-law for a long time, and suddenly, to her surprise, she felt tears fill her eyes. She felt great pity for John Scanlan, and anger at him, too. "Well, Gail, that's the first I've ever heard of the high regard my father-in-law had for me," she said.

"It would have killed him to say anything nice about anyone to their face. He didn't even kiss me at our wedding. I never heard him say a kind word to Mother. I don't even believe he loved her. I think she was just a baby machine. Excuse me. I didn't mean anything by that."

The man and woman kneeling in front of the body rose, and Connie could see that the woman was crying. She was wiping her face with a tissue, wiping away her rouge so that one cheek was a gray-white, the other a gay pink. It was one of John Scanlan's sisters, the one he always called Fat Marge.

"Who knows how he really felt about anything?" Connie had said, and then she had looked across the room to a corner where Dorothy O'Haire sat lost in the shadows. She was wearing a cheap black suit, clutching a black patent purse. Earlier in the evening, before anyone else had arrived, Connie had come in to make a list of the people who had sent flowers so that Mary Frances could send thank-you notes, and Dorothy had been kneeling at the casket with a little girl at her side. The child wore a beautiful navy blue dress, some gauzy stuff over linen, and a big sailor hat. When she had turned away from the casket, Connie could see that the girl had her mother's dullish yellow hair, but her eyes were of a clear and translucent blue. They were Scanlan eyes.

"Oh, Dorothy," Connie had said.

"Mrs. Scanlan, this is my daughter," Dorothy had said primly. "Her name is Beth." The girl curtsied. "How do you do?" she said, like a little girl in an old movie. On the bosom of her dress her initials were monogrammed in white: EAO. Connie knew that the O stood for O'Haire, and she was just as sure, as sure as if the name had been spoken aloud, that the E and the A stood for Elizabeth Ann. She wondered whether the girl's mother had chosen the name, to stake her claim, or the girl's father, to try to make amends or to live life over. After a few minutes, Dorothy had taken the child outside and put her into a car with someone, Connie could not see who, and then had come back inside alone. "I wanted her to pay her respects," she said to Connie, finding herself that same seat in the corner, and every time during the evening Connie looked over, she had wondered if John had provided enough money for both of them. And she realized she knew another thing she would never tell her husband, and she felt weary with the weight of all the secrets it required to protect those you loved.

Now in the sunlight Connie looked over at her own father and wondered if that's what he had done for her, all these years, if his silence was really protection from a world he found too terrible to live in. He stood silently studying the cemetery, making sure it was perfectly groomed, everything in place. His flawless world, Connie thought, where none of the people are mean or dishonest or careless because none of them are alive. Angelo left her for a moment to say something to Leonard, and then walked back slowly, his shirt glowing in the sun. She was glad she had worn a skirt, even a flimsy cotton wrap one, its ties strained by her thickened waist; her father was offended by women in pants. Her hand went to her hair to smooth it off her forehead.

"Mr. Scanlan is buried," Angelo said.

"Finally," said Connie.

"He was supposed to have the child buried with him?"

Connie nodded. "That's what his wife thought. I don't know whether it was a misunderstanding, or he just ignored her."

"Different things are important to different people," Angelo said. "Most people hate the bugs—your son loves them. Most people talk too much—your daughter listens."

"My daughter is a woman now."

"Of course," said Angelo. "This summer it happened. Anybody could see. When your mother was her age, she was already married. One baby on the way, one baby to come. Children grow fast. Except if they are here." And he looked around him again. Mary Frances joined them, her rosary in her hand, and Angelo escorted her in his courtly fashion back to the car.

Connie was quiet on the drive home, overwhelmed by events. She and Mary Frances fell back on their old ways for much of the drive, the older woman talking in a desultory fashion about Monica's wedding. Connie thought it would be an interesting affair, judging from the fact that the groom's family had wanted his name on the invitations to read Donald "Duck" Syzmanski. As they neared Mary Frances's house there was a long silence, and then the older woman began to speak, almost to herself, so low that Connie had to bend her head to listen.

"No one ever understands what it's like unless they're in it themselves," Mary Frances said. "People look at your children and they see them all in a lump. Even their father, calling them "the brood," herding them into the car for Mass every Sunday morning, making rules to fit them all, about staying out late, about homework, about spankings if they got into trouble, even for Margaret, with her little fanny in white cotton pants, her skirt pulled up. But their mother never sees them that way. Even now, all standing together, men in their suits, too big to hug, you see them all as themselves, clear—Jimmy with his everlasting questions, following you around the house: Why does this happen, Mama, why does that happen? Why does the sun rise and set? And Mark, walking him around the living room in that little row house we had, walking him every night with the colic while he screamed and screamed, the sky so black outside that it was like the end of the world. And Tommy curling like a little shrimp next to me on the beach, pulling a towel over his little shoulders so he wouldn't burn. "Be a man!" John would yell at him, and he'd try to lie still, so still that no one would notice him."

Mary Frances looked over at her. "Do you understand what I'm saying?" she said. "The baby was stillborn and they came at me with a needle to put me to sleep and I said, damn you, give me that child. And I baptized her right there, and she was so pretty, with pink skin like flowers. And I kissed her face and she was real to me, as real as any of the others, even now. More real, maybe. Because you think of what they'll become, and you're always disappointed. Though they're all good boys, all fine, they're never exactly what you dream they're going to be. Only she, only she never disappointed. Even today I dream the same dreams about her as when I kissed her face." She bent her head over her hands, and then lifted it and stared out the windshield. "I kissed her, and then I let them give me the shot."

Connie pulled into the driveway slowly because she found it hard to see through the tears in her eyes, and because she was so overcome to hear Mary Frances put into words Connie's own feelings, the feelings about her children that she had believed were twisted and peculiar and hers alone. She felt the weight of all the wasted years, of the playacting that all of them had done while they lived with that great central figure, that star now dead. Connie supposed that that was the sin for which they would all have to forgive John Scanlan, the sin of forcing them all to play their thankless roles. Her mother-in-law climbed out of the car and then turned back and leaned through the window.

"Tomorrow at the wedding I will tell my son that I want to sell that house his father bought. I will tell him I want the money and he won't be able to argue with me about it. It's not that I mind people trying to arrange other people's lives, but if they do it, they have to do it right." She drew a deep breath and her voice wavered as she added, "The boys say that I can't live here alone, and it could be that they're right. If I had my druthers, I would prefer it be you and Tommy who move in here. Any of the others would drive me crazy. That's not why I'm having him sell the house. I'm not making a deal with you. I just want you to know what I think. I'm tired of keeping my mouth shut. At least you and I wouldn't have to pretend. You could have your ways and I'd have mine." She stopped for a moment. "And I love my son," she added, as though she only had the one.

They looked at each other for a long moment and then Mary Frances began to speak again, and this time her voice was hard and clear. "There are two spaces in that plot in your father's cemetery," she said. "I want the other one. I am telling you and I will tell Tommy, because everyone else will think I'm crazy and they will do what they want in any event. But I'm telling you that it will be your responsibility to see that this time I get my way. The rest of them will want to do what is proper, but you will make them do what is right." Connie leaned over toward her. She wanted to call her something but she couldn't think what and so she simply began, "John said to me in the hospital—" But Mary Frances cut her off. "He did the best he could, dear," she said, sounding more like herself. "A man can't be what he isn't. He did the best he could with what he had. That's something for you to remember. Tommy does the best he knows how."

"I know," Connie said, her eyes filling again. Mary Frances turned and walked into the house and Connie wondered if she should try to tell her more, should try to tell her how sorry her husband had been, although whether it was for the death, for failing to move the baby's body, or for something even more unforgivable she was still not sure. She supposed "He did the best he could" was the best benediction anyone could hope for.

23

AGGIE SAT ON THE BENCH IN FRONT OF her aunt's old dressing table, her long legs hidden beneath the ruffled skirt. Her bridesmaid's dress hung on the back of the closet door. Connie stood behind her brushing Maggie's hair over and over again as though she was painting, coat after coat. Connie was so small that her head just barely topped Maggie's when she stood behind her, so that in the mirror they looked like some strange Indian goddess, one dark head above the other, one set of arms resting in the lap, another rising and falling, holding a brush.

"You two look like sisters," Aunt Cass said.

Monica was in the bathroom putting on her makeup. She looked like the centerfold in one of the *Playboy* magazines the boys had hidden beneath the floorboards of the development houses. She was wearing something called a merry widow, a one-piece lace garment like a very fancy swimsuit, which pushed her bust up and whittled her waist to nothing. "Should she be wearing that?" Connie had said with some concern, but Aunt Cass said that Uncle James said it was fine. Maggie could not imagine Monica modeling such a thing for her father, but she was not inclined to ask questions on this particular day.

Behind her, her mother was humming tunelessly. She was wearing a new dress, a simple red drape in some satiny material. Her lipstick matched. Her hair was in loose, shiny waves over her shoulders. It seemed incredible that she had been so recently to a funeral, but Uncle James and Mary Frances had insisted that the wedding go on as planned, with no sign, even in their clothes, that there had been a death in the family except that the five priests concelebrating the Mass would make mention of John Scanlan during the prayers for the dead. "My father would have wanted it that way," James told several of the mourners at the funeral, who nodded solemnly.

Maggie knew this was not true. John Scanlan would have wanted them to cancel the whole thing, deposit or no deposit. (Actually, Maggie knew, he would have wanted Uncle James to demand that the deposit be returned and to threaten legal action if it was not.) "Give the devil his due," Maggie thought he would say, but she could not quite conjure him up, with his broad white grin and his glittering blue eyes, saying it. She could barely remember his face; she could only remember his hands, big, the hairs on them like a web.

In the mirror her own eyes seemed dead, too, looking inside, and then they came alive as she looked up at her mother. Connie had drawn Maggie's long tail of hair up onto the back of her head, and she was separating it into sections, smiling to herself, as though she had a secret. She picked a thin piece of pink ribbon off the dressing table and began to braid it through one section, her hands quick and sure. Maggie sat silently until her mother had made six narrow braids and pinned them into long loops, chestnut shot through with pink. When Connie was finished she picked up a silver mirror from the dressing table, glancing first at the engraving on the back. "From your aunt Margaret's hope chest," she said, and handed the mirror to Maggie so she could see how her hair looked from behind.

With her hair pulled back, her forehead and cheeks pink, her eyes bright without their dark frame, Maggie felt suddenly shy. "It feels strange," she said, returning the mirror. But then she thought that sounded ungrateful and she added, "It looks nice."

Monica emerged from the bathroom in her merry widow and white stockings, her hair still in rollers, Mary Frances's good pearls around her neck. She had lent Maggie her add-a-pearl necklace; she had not wanted to, but Aunt Cass had insisted. "As a peace offering," she had said, and at that moment Maggie had heard her grandfather's voice loud and clear, saying, "Peace offering my ass." Monica was holding a mascara wand. "Well, well," she said, tilting her head. "The ugly duckling turns into a swan."

"You look lovely, Maggie," said Aunt Cass.

"When you're old enough to wear makeup you just might look like a real girl," Monica said, rearranging her bosom in the boned bodice of white lace.

"She's wearing makeup today," said Connie, "or this pink will wash her right out." Connie opened her purse and began to remove a bottle of foundation, a compact, and a pat of pink rouge. "I'll take that mascara when you're done with it, Monica," she said.

Connie held Maggie's chin in her hand and began to smooth creams onto her face, turning it this way and that and occasionally rubbing something off with a finger she'd touched to her tongue. It seemed to take a long time, with Connie humming and looking at Maggie dispassionately as though she was a piece of furniture being refinished. Finally she let go of her chin, and kissed the top of her head. Maggie almost jumped out of her skin.

"What are you going to do about these?" said Connie, and with her index finger she flicked the limp circle of dingy thread hanging from one of Maggie's earlobes. Maggie inhaled. She had kept her ears hidden beneath her hair for a week. Connie went into her purse again and removed a square of tissue. Inside were a pair of earrings, teardrop-shaped stones, purple-red, dangling from small curving pieces of gold.

"This is going to hurt," Connie said, snipping the strings with a nail scissors and pulling them out. It took her a minute to get the earrings in, and Maggie kept very still, looking into her own eyes again. Her mother stepped back to look at her.

"Ta da," she said.

"Where did you get those?" Maggie said.

"They were my mother's. I found them after she died. It was so strange to see them, because I don't think she wore a pretty thing her whole life, at least when I knew her. Your grandfather couldn't tell me where they came from either. And I wasn't interested in wearing them. They've been sitting at the back of one of my drawers for years."

"You couldn't have worn them anyway," said Maggie, moving her head from side to side.

"Sure I could have. Aunt Rose pierced my ears when I was a baby. I just stopped wearing earrings when I got married. Now the holes are closed up."

"Why did you stop?"

"It used to be something that only girls right off the boat did. Girls like your aunt Margaret didn't have pierced ears."

"And you were a girl like Aunt Margaret?"

Connie grinned. "I tried to be," she said. "I don't think I was very good at it."

"Oh, Connie, what a beautiful job you've done," Aunt Cass said. "Will her hat fit over that hairdo?"

"No," Connie said. "I don't think she'll wear the hat. It's not really her, Cass. And the other girls are wearing hats and dresses that are entirely different."

Aunt Cass narrowed her lips, but she looked again at Maggie's hair, and then she sighed. "Maybe God will count the ribbons as a hat," she finally said.

"Go into the bathroom and see if there's any Vaseline," Connie said to Maggie. "Put a little on your lips and blot it off."

Her mother moved aside and Maggie saw herself in the mirror. She could not believe what her mother had done, how she had managed, with her Touch 'n' Glo creamy ivory and her Autumn Roses cake rouge and her eyebrow pencil, to turn Maggie into a shadow of Connie herself, a manufactured double. She leaned forward but try as she might she could not make the resemblance go away, and it suddenly occurred to her that this was the only difference between the two of them—a little color, a little pressed powder, a few years.

"Thank you," she said to Connie's reflection.

"It was my pleasure," Connie replied, as though the two of them were partners in some antiquated dance.

Maggie drew one of Mary Frances's housecoats tight around her lanky body and staggered into the bathroom in her new dyed-to-match damask pumps. Monica was leaning into her own reflection in the medicine cabinet mirror. The bathroom was strewn with curlers, bobby pins, pots of cream and foundation, bottles of perfume.

"Excuse me," Maggie said, moving past her cousin to reach for the Vaseline on top of the toilet tank. Monica recoiled, and Maggie thought she was about to get nasty again when suddenly she moved toward the toilet and fell to her knees. The retching was painful to hear, as if Monica had a fishbone in her throat; a roller fell from the front of her hair onto the floor. Maggie leaned forward, picked it up, and held back the long curl so it would not get in Monica's way.

The vomiting seemed to go on and on, and Maggie felt stupid standing there, bent over, holding a piece of hair, afraid to move. She had seen the same thing happen too many times to her mother to misunderstand, and this made her feel stupid, too. She remembered saying to her cousin, "You don't fool me one bit," in the bridal salon, and she knew everyone had thought she meant more than she was saying. Perhaps, she thought, her grandfather would in fact have wanted the wedding to take place today, funeral or no funeral. She could see the red welt on Monica's tanned back where the merry widow had pressed into her flesh, and when her cousin finally rose, using the toilet to hoist herself from her knees like an old woman, Maggie saw that her mascara had run in gray rivulets all over her face, making little rivers in the pink of her makeup. Her eyes were bloodshot, her lips swollen, the veins on the part of her breasts spilling from the top of her fancy underpinnings blue and swollen too.

Maggie watched Monica in the mirror as she methodically began to apply cold cream to take off her ruined makeup. When Monica's face was bare, she put out her hand peremptorily, her polished nails pearly, and retrieved the roller. She twisted the long lock of hair back up and began to redo her face, first blotting a single tear that ran down the side of her nose.

"Monica," said Maggie, "I'm really sorry. I'm really sorry it turned out like this."

She knew she had said the wrong thing when she saw the usually implacable face contort. Her cousin whirled round to face her, so close that they were almost touching. "You just don't get it, do you, Maria Goretti," Monica said, her eyes wild. "This is the way it is. This is the way everything is. It's one screw job after another, and then you die. You really think it's going to be like some goddamn little story, but this is what it's like when you grow up. One bad thing after another, and you just have to say 'To hell with it' and go on to something else. But not you. You're going to walk around with that little sad face and those little sad eyes and go, oh, oh, I'm really sorry, you didn't live happily ever after, you—"

"Shut up, Monica," Connie said, standing in the doorway.

"You should be able to fill her in, Aunt Concetta," Monica said after a moment's silence. "I'm going downstairs for my prenuptial crackers, so I don't throw up on Father Hanlon's best vestments."

"You do that," Connie said as Monica put on a robe.

When she was gone Maggie sat back down at the dressing table. "I feel stupid," she said.

"Your cousin is the one who's stupid," Connie said.

"You know what I'm talking about. I didn't even figure out why she was getting married. They probably all thought I was an idiot when we went for our dresses. They were all making little comments about whether Monica's could be let out, and I just sat there listening. You should have told me."

Connie knelt on the floor, lightly, as though there was no belly under the red tent of her dress. She looked up into Maggie's face, her eyes blazing. "Maggie," she said, "there are some things that aren't that important. There are things that seem tremendously important at the time and then years later you look back and think you can't believe you ever worried so much about them."

"You sound like Monica. Everything's silly."

"No," Connie said, smoothing her daughter's hair. "That's not what I mean. It's just that whether you're getting married because you're having a baby isn't as important as getting married and having the baby. Monica's wrong. She's one of those people who sees everything bad. And there are other people who see everything good."

"Like who?"

"I think deep down inside your father is one of them. Your aunt Margaret, too, probably, in a different way."

"What about you?"

"Not good or bad. Things just are."

"And me?"

"I think you'll probably be like me."

The two of them looked at each other for a moment. Finally Maggie said, "Monica said something else to me, too. When we were getting our dresses." She watched her mother's face, but it was very still. "About when you got married. And when I was born."

Connie smiled slowly, but she didn't show her teeth, and her eyes were cold. "She's going to have a hard life, that girl," she finally said, as though she was talking to herself. Then she looked at Maggie and said, "What did I just tell you? There are things that seem important to some people that just aren't important at all."

"You should have told me," Maggie said.

"I wouldn't have known what to say. We got married. We had a baby. I wouldn't change a thing."

"Can I ask you a question?"

"Yes."

"Were you going to have a baby and that's why you got married?"

"That's one way of looking at it."

"That's wrong, isn't it?"

Connie sighed. "What's wrong is if I was angry about it for the rest of my life. Or if you were ashamed." Connie rose and took Maggie's dress down from its hanger. She cradled it in her arms and then she looked Maggie in the eye and said, "It's wrong to light a fire. It's worse to enjoy it."

"I didn't enjoy it."

"I know."

"You don't believe me about not doing it."

Connie was quiet, her face blank.

"It's complicated. I sort of did it, but I sort of didn't. Does that make any sense?"

"Yes," Connie said. "I know exactly what you mean."

"It was hard to think about it while it was happening."

"I know that too."

"Why did you tell the police I wasn't there?" Maggie said.

"Because that seemed closest to the truth."

"Did they believe you?"

"I don't know," she said. "Probably not. Raise your arms." Connie slipped the dress over Maggie's head. She zipped it, and stepped back. "You look beautiful, Maggie," Connie said, and then she corrected herself. "You are beautiful. That's the truth, the whole truth, and nothing but the truth, so help me God."

Maggie looked at herself in the mirror. She stood up and her mother's head behind her disappeared, so that now she only saw herself, and she knew that it was true. "I still feel stupid," she said. She looked at herself again, and behind the mask of the makeup she could see the Maggie Scanlan she used to be, and around her eyes she could see someone else, someone harder to know, harder to understand. She couldn't figure out which of them was worth being, or whether it was possible, just for today, to be both at once.

But later, in church, as she stood to one side of Monica, who was serene and lovely in her high-waisted white organdy, without a hint of belly, she knew that she had learned something. It somehow came as no surprise to her as she came up the aisle to look over and see Bruce in one of the pews with his father, staring at her with his mouth slightly open. It seemed perfectly natural to smile slightly at him and then bow her head to sniff the roses in her nosegay, although she could feel the color rising in her cheeks beneath the artificial pink of the rouge. And when it was time for the vows, Maggie's head came round with a snap as the groom recited his, and she realized that when she had envisioned this moment, thinking about the wedding, she had taken for granted that he would say "I do" in the same voice she had heard say "Oh God" that night on the beach. But his voice was unmistakably the voice of an entirely different person, and after that first swift swivel of her head, she was somehow not at all surprised.

24

OMMY WAS NOT DRUNK. NEITHER WAS he sober. Dessert had been taken away—it was, as was customary, ice cream and a slice of wedding cake that tasted like sweetened cotton balls— and now a gnarled little man with a cart filled with liqueurs had stopped by his table. Tommy looked at the candy-colored bottles and almost sent him on, then thought better of it and, feeling vaguely English, asked for a brandy. Connie shot him a sidelong look, and he laughed. He was having a good time.

Monica's wedding reception was being held at a country club just north of Kenwood and several rungs above the Kenwoodie Club. The banquet room was paneled in knotty pine, and the chairs and restroom walls were covered with green-and-red tartan. It was what John Scanlan always referred to disdainfully as "high Episcopal," and the fact was that James was the first Catholic they'd ever admitted. The membership committee had postponed a decision on his application until after the Kennedy-Nixon presidential election to see which way the wind blew. James had certainly planned a high Episcopalian reception, with mea-ger food and a bad band, all overpriced, but his plans had gone awry. For one thing, the groom's family had persuaded the band, Jimmy Jones and the Lamplighters, to play a number of polkas, which had been received with much screaming, whooping, and lifting of women old enough to know better into the air. For another, the groom's father had taken off his cutaway jacket early in the evening, exposing his service revolver, which, he explained to Tommy, he always wore off duty, "just in case."

"Jesus, in this world, Tom, you never know," he said feelingly.

"The God's truth," Tommy said, having the time of his life and his second Scotch.

Finally, there were John Scanlan's brothers and sisters, all eleven of them. James spent most of the cocktail hour trying to lay blame— and Tommy suspected that he was prime suspect—for it turned out that after the funeral, someone had mentioned to all of them that they were welcome at Monica's wedding. Coming down the aisle to take her seat on the arm of one of the ushers, and already concerned that her daughter was going to be sick at the very sight of Communion, poor Cass had been astounded to see almost two dozen people she had not invited sitting in pews very near the front of the church. She had called the country club from the vestry after the service, and asked that two more tables be set up. It was a tight fit.

Tommy spent most of the cocktail hour talking to his aunts and uncles, whom he had never seen very often. None seemed remotely put out that their brother had given them the back of his hand, except for one cut-rate party a year, for the last forty years. "A prince," John Scanlan's brother Brian, a sanitation dispatcher in the Bronx, kept repeating with tears in his eyes. "If he had been born twenty years later, he would have been the first Catholic president, mark my words, Tom. That smart he was. Our mother used to tell us, 'Boys, when your brother's elected pope, don't do anything to embarrass him.' Little did she know about his way with the ladies. But president he could have had, Tom, if the time had been right."

"He would have made an interesting president, Uncle Brian. We probably would have gone to war with the British."

Brian narrowed his eyes, and then grinned. "You're a great one for joshing, son," he said. "It's a grand affair, isn't it?"

"I'm going to go dance with my wife," Tommy said.

"Bless her," Brian said, staring into the depths of his drink.

"Ten thousand if it's a penny," Tommy said to Connie as they danced to "Strangers in the Night" sung by as bad a Sinatra imitator as Tommy had ever heard. "Country club, open bar, prime rib, six-piece band. For something they threw together in a month, my brother did some job on this wedding."

Connie hummed along with the music, and Tommy pulled her closer. Her stomach felt like a Tupperware bowl placed between the two of them. Suddenly Tommy remembered how the priests had made them slow dance at high school sock hops with a dictionary wedged between their pelvises. If anything, it had increased the consciousness of the near occasion of sin.

"Love was just a glance away, a warm embracing dance away," sang Tommy so loudly that couples near them heard him over the electric din of the overeager organist, and several of them smiled.

"Maggie looked beautiful coming down the aisle," said Connie. "But somebody should have told her to hold her bouquet up around her waist."

"She did fine," said Tommy. "Who did her hair? You?"

Connie smiled up at him.

"It's the first time I've seen her face in three years," he said as the music ended.

Now, adrift in that happy haze somewhere between sobriety and the point at which he started to cry uncontrollably at things like "Danny Boy," Tommy saw his daughter across the room, laughing with a boy in a blue sports coat. The kid was skinny, with dishwater-blond hair that stuck up at the crown and a big mobile mouth full of teeth; he ducked his head whenever Maggie turned to look at him, but as soon as she turned away he would stare at her profile as though it was a crucifix and he a new seminarian. He reminded Tommy of someone, but he could not tell who. Maggie looked strangely grownup, perhaps because he was indeed seeing her face, seeing the lines of her square jaw, sharp now as the baby fat disappeared. "Still flat as a board," he muttered to himself, sipping at his brandy, not meaning to speak aloud. "What?" said Mark, dropping into an empty chair next to him.

Another polka was ending, and suddenly, as if in some primitive hostile response, his aunts and uncles had risen to their feet at their tables, wedged in by the swinging kitchen door, and commenced an a cappella version of "When Irish Eyes Are Smiling." They all had fine voices, and had been well trained in the choir of St. Aloysius School; the singing was so loud that men playing golf on the 11th hole, not far from the huge plate-glass picture window of the banquet room, turned, perplexed, looking for the source of some melodious buzzing that had reached their ears. Tommy could not contain his glee and joined in at the end, hoping the groom's family would not offer some folk song as a rejoinder. But instead the groom's father leapt to his feet with a cheer. "Erin go Bragh!" he cried, clapping his big slab hands.

There was much clapping, and the singers took bows, laughing and hitting one another on the back. "Jesus," said Mark. "Oh, relax," Tommy said, grinning as the band started on "Danny Boy," the Lamplighters recognizing a good thing when they saw one.

"Tom, I need you to help me out," Mark said, lighting a cigar.

"Not now," Tommy said. Mark had been pressing him about Scanlan & Co. since the night of the wake. He thought it was the perfect plan for him to take over John's job and have Tommy take over his own. "I'm thinking about it," Tommy added, as his brother continued to stare at him. "I am giving it serious consideration. Honest to God."

"I need you to look at the books," Mark said.

"I've looked at them."

"What!" Mark said, and Tommy loved the look on his face so much he threw back his head and laughed.

"It's not as bad as you think," Tommy said. "He was careless about some things, but the bottom line isn't as bad as you think. On the other hand, it's nowhere near as good as they think." And he motioned to John Scanlan's brothers and sisters, who were singing "Danny Boy" and sobbing happily.

"How the hell—"

"I took the keys from his dresser and let myself into the office one night after I went to the hospital."

"And it's okay? Everything's there?"

Tommy laughed again, this time without pleasure. "Jesus, Mark, what did you think? That Dad cooked the books? That we were bankrupt? That John Scanlan had been playing the ponies on the side and buying fur coats for his secretary?"

Mark tightened his lips and looked away.

"Holy God!" Tommy said. "You really did. You're incredible. Goddamn incredible."

"Things looked suspicious to me," Mark said.

"So he moved money around a little bit more than he should have. So on some things he robbed Peter to pay Paul. But more than that—forget it. Only in books, Mark. You don't wake up one day and find out that Saint John of the all-cotton cassocks is leading a double life." Both men looked toward the bandstand. Their aunt Marge had just poured a beer all over one of her brothers. James got up from the dais and hurried toward her. Monica's nostrils were flaring. The bridegroom was laughing and she gave him a look that Tommy imagined could turn a man to stone. Something about its intensity reminded him of his father, and he pitied the young man in his rented tuxedo sitting, chastened, next to his niece. "I did always wonder about him and Dorothy," Tommy said absently.

"Jesus!" said Mark. "You think he was doing Dorothy?"

"Ah, who cares now?" Tommy said, watching Marge wave her finger in his oldest brother's distinguished face, knowing as surely as if he could hear her that she was reminding James Scanlan that she had once changed his diapers.

It was the wrong time to tell Mark that the company had been paying Dorothy $1000 a month for years, putting her on the books as a paraffin supplier. Tommy had been oddly unsurprised. Mary Frances already knew. Tommy had been sure of it when he watched his mother seat Dorothy in the third row at the funeral Mass. Connie had met the little girl at the funeral home, and when Tommy saw she was not at the Mass he had asked his wife what the child looked like. "What's her name again?" he asked, and Connie had replied quietly, "Beth." Then she had added, "I think she's like Maggie, a combination of her mother and her father." And Tommy let it go at that. He would keep the checks to the bogus paraffin supplier coming, and he would try not to think about the rest. He had known what his father was really like all those years, but he had never had to stare it in the eye until that moment in the hospital when the old man had tried to suck the soul out of his body as his dying act. Tommy would never choose to look that in the eye again, and he would never expose it to the eyes of anyone else. He looked at Mark and added quietly, "The point is that people are different than you think, but they're not that different. Dad wasn't Dr. Jekyll and Mr. Hyde. He was just the guy you saw, and then the real guy. And they're never the same thing. He did good work. But he wasn't the Second Coming of Christ, like he wanted us all to believe. You'll have some cleaning up to do, some loans to consolidate, some changes to make. But things are good."

"So you'll come?"

"I didn't say that. Besides, maybe I want the top job." His brother's eyes grew big, and Tommy laughed again. "Just kidding you, brother. We'll talk about it soon. But not today." The two of them sat silently as couples whirled around the dance floor. Tommy's uncle Brian and aunt Maureen danced by, both with tears in their eyes. Tommy remembered that even his father, that most unsentimental of men, had sometimes teared up over "Danny Boy." Tommy himself had never liked it; it was difficult to sing along with. James went by, dancing with Margaret, his face red from fighting with his aunt. Margaret was still light on her feet, even in her heavy black Cuban heels, her horrid nun shoes. "Dad's turning over in his grave at that sight," Mark said, but his brother had already moved away from him. Tommy tapped James on the shoulder and cut in, grabbing his sister with a grin. "Oh, good," Margaret said. "You're a much better dancer."

Tommy and Margaret had learned to dance together, in the basement of the big house, with Tommy Dorsey on the radio. Lightly they circled the room. "Are you all right?" he finally said.

Margaret frowned. "I think so," she said. "I think I was going through a little temporary insanity this summer. Or puberty."

"I thought we already had puberty," Tommy said.

Margaret looked up into his flushed and boyish face. "I think our whole lives are puberty," she said. "I think we all have to grow up again and again. Isn't' that depressing?"

"It's crazy, is what it is." Tommy dipped her so her veil hung straight to the floor as the last notes died away. "Leave the convent. Come back and be my sister again."

"You're drunk, Tom," Margaret said, laughing. "Beside, you just want me to move in with Mother. Go dance with your wife." But when the band began to play again, Tommy recognized the song after the first few notes, and shook his head. He kissed his sister, smoothed his hair with his hand, and crossed the room to his daughter. He was just drunk enough to feel like Douglas Fairbanks, Jr.

"They're playing our song," he said to Maggie.

She flushed an unbecoming red and turned to the boy, who ducked his head again. Tommy was surprised when the kid looked up suddenly, his lip with its fuzz of facial hair working, and thrust out his hand. "Hello, Mr. Scanlan," he said. "I understand you are a fine basketball player. Maybe some day we can have a game." Without waiting for a response he turned and walked away, disappearing into the great expanse of tables, chairs, flower arrangements, and drunken Irishmen. Once he looked back over his shoulder at Maggie. "Jesus, what the hell was that all about?" Tommy asked. And turning to Maggie he said, "Isn't that the kid whose mother died two years ago?"

"His name is Bruce," Maggie said.

"Can he really play decent ball?" said Tommy. Then he remembered why he had gone to her and he held out his arms. Monica and her father were already dancing, the bride's train thrown over her arm, a little soiled where it had dragged on the ground on her way into church. Monica looked over her father's shoulder, and he looked over hers. They looked like an illustration in a woman's magazine: That Special Day.

Tommy turned to Maggie and gathered her up, gliding around the floor, circling the other couple with long, graceful steps. Every fourth step he would spin, holding Maggie's fingers in his lightly. He felt good, covering the polished parquet, his shoulders squared. He looked down at Maggie, whose pink dress belled out behind her slightly, but she was looking down at her feet.

"Don't look at your feet," he said.

"I can't follow if I don't," she said.

"Stand on mine," Tommy said. "I can take it."

"Daddy, I'm wearing high heels. I'm too big to stand on your feet."

"Then close your eyes," he said. "Close your eyes and don't think about it."

Maggie tilted her head back and shut her eyes; the lights made copper spots on her hair, and little sparks shone from the amethysts dangling from her earlobes. Tommy kept his arm tight around her waist and turned again, and now she was finally following him. She could not dance like her mother, but she was making a creditable show. As his eyes passed, only half-seeing, over the tables ringing the dance floor, he could tell that people were watching them. He dipped her once, spun, dipped her again, and still she kept her eyes tightly closed and her torso limp and pliable. Tommy began to sing along with the band:

> You're the spirit of Christmas,
> My star on the tree,
> You're the Easter Bunny to mommy and me,
> You're sugar,
> You're spice,
> You're everything nice,
> And you're Daddy's little girl.

He sang all the way through to the end of the song, and when it was over James and Monica walked away from each other and Maggie and Tommy just stood there for a moment. Even after the music ended, she waited a full minute before she opened her eyes.

"You did good," Tommy said.

"I liked it," said Maggie. "Why didn't you ever tell me that before, just to close my eyes and not try so hard?"

"I never thought of it before," Tommy said. Suddenly there was a loud crash, the drummer giving his cymbals a good whack. "It's hokey-pokey time," the lead singer called. "Go dance," said Tommy, and when he got back to his table he saw that the boy had claimed her again, standing opposite her in the hokey-pokey line. He tried to figure out who the boy looked like, but he could not. Tommy turned to look at his wife, who was watching the dancers with a small smile on her face, and then he glanced over at Maggie, who had the fixed and exhausted smile of someone who has been having a wonderful time for hours. "I'm a lucky man," he said out loud, and he finished his brandy, took Connie's hand and led her onto the floor.

25

HEN MAGGIE WOKE UP THE DAY AFTER the wedding, she could hear voices coming faintly from the back patio. From her bedroom window she could see her aunt Celeste and her mother outside, sitting in lawn chairs, coffee cups on the cement at their feet. The clock said noon. Maggie had missed Mass for the first time since she had had the mumps three years ago. She noticed that the earrings, which she'd taken off and put on her bureau, were gone. She put on a pair of old pink shorts to match the ribbons in her hair and went downstairs.

"Hi," she said softly, stepping out into the backyard.

Celeste grinned. "Boy, were you right," she said to Connie, and then to Maggie, "Honey, you look like a million bucks with your hair like that. I can't wait to see the pictures of you yesterday."

Maggie went out the sliding door and sat crosslegged at Cece's feet, her head down. Her aunt was wearing a hot-pink dress that consisted of one tier of ruffles atop another. She had on hot pink plastic earrings and her engagement ring winked at Maggie. "Happy birthday," she said to Maggie. "Your present's inside. It's a diary."

"Celeste!" Connie said. "You couldn't wait and let her open it?"

"What the hell."

Connie went into the kitchen and returned with a small box in her hand, wrapped in silver paper with a pink bow. "Happy birthday," she said, handing it to Maggie.

"God, I remember it like it was yesterday," Celeste said with a grin. "Remember the size of you, Con? I mean, people died when they saw you coming down the street. And then Tommy calling us from the hospital and telling me, 'Celeste, she's the biggest goddamn baby in the hospital.' He said that to everyone. 'Bigger than any of the boys, too.' God he was excited. I just kept trying to imagine ten pounds of baby getting out of your body. Maybe that's what put me off having kids. I remember when you brought her home. I've never seen two human beings look so goddamn happy. You had such a smile on your face, I'll never forget."

Connie looked down at Maggie and smiled. Maggie had finished unwrapping her gift. It was a heartshaped locket with her initials engraved on its face in curly script. "Your first real piece of jewelry," Connie said, taking it from her and leaning over to put it around her neck."

"It's really, really nice," Maggie said quietly, and she didn't say any more. But she fingered the locket as she sat on the ground and each time she felt the little grooves of the engraving beneath her fingertips she smiled.

"Monica just called you," Connie said.

"How? She left for Bermuda this morning."

"She called from the airport," Connie said. "She wants to make sure that you don't throw her bouquet away. She gave me instructions about how to preserve it until she gets back."

"That little witch," said Celeste. "You keep that bouquet longer than two weeks, it'll outlast the marriage."

"I think you're jumping to conclusions," said Connie with a small smile.

"Not because she's expecting," said Celeste. "God, if every marriage that started that way broke up, nobody would be married." Maggie raised her head and listened carefully. "But a man can only take so much and so much of Monica is about two weeks' worth."

"Maybe marriage will change her."

"Ha," said Celeste, and Maggie laughed. "So," her aunt added, "you caught the bouquet. You know what that means."

"She didn't mean me to catch it," Maggie said. "She threw it right at one of her friends but it bounced off somebody's elbow and just landed in my hands. I wasn't even trying."

"It's okay," Celeste said. "I caught the bouquet at your mom's wedding and I was already married. Maybe if you're married and catch it it means you're next to be divorced."

The three of them sat looking over the fields behind them. There were twenty-four houses now: four complete, the rest in various stages of framing and finishing. The remains of the charred house had been razed, and another had already been framed in. For a moment Maggie remembered what the fields had once looked like, and then the memory was gone, and she thought that in a few months she would not even be able to remember what Kenwood had been like before the development started.

"It really looks different back here," said Celeste, who had always been able to read Maggie's mind.

"It's going to change the whole place," said Connie. "They're going to build twenty-four more after these. Some builder has plans for a shopping center just down the road. We'll be surrounded."

"I saw your friend Joe on the avenue yesterday when I was picking up groceries for my mother," said Celeste. "I told him he missed his chance with me. I haven't seen him around here too much lately." Celeste squinted at her cousin in the bright sunlight. She'd always been able to read Connie's mind, too.

"He's busier now."

"Have you finished your driving lessons?" Celeste asked.

"I have my temporary license. My permanent one comes any day now. I drove my mother-in-law over to Calvary Cemetery the other day all by myself. And now at least I have ID if someone in a bar doesn't think I'm twenty-one."

"No small accomplishment," said Celeste, and she arched one penciled eyebrow.

"Give it a break, Ce," Connie said.

"Are you moving?" Celeste asked.

"I think so. It's funny how I just lost all my upset about it. My mother-in-law needs us over there. The question is whether to move into her house or the one down the street. Tommy says they may need to sell the other one to pay some of the bills from the business."

"We really might move?" Maggie said.

"I don't know," Connie replied. "Let's wait and see how your grandmother does."

"Grandmother, Schmandmother," said Celeste. "You'll have five kids soon, and you've got four bedrooms. You'll have to start hanging them from the chandeliers. That's a nice big house the old lady's got."

"Give it a break," Connie repeated.

"How's being married, Aunt Celeste?" Maggie asked.

"It's better this time," Celeste said thoughtfully. "But still it's the same. It's not natural, having someone else telling you what to do all the time. But at least we're not arguing about how much I spend on my clothes. When I was married to your Uncle Charlie, one little blouse and—pow! He broke my nose once over a winter coat."

"Don't tell her things like that, Cece," Connie said. "It'll make her think all marriages are like that."

Celeste lifted her eyebrow again.

"They're not. Look at my mother-in-law. She's a changed person since her husband got sick."

"Probably dancing in the aisles," said Celeste, lighting a cigarette.

"You know that's not true. That man was her whole life. That's the thing the kids don't understand. I was looking at Monica yesterday and thinking, *she has no idea*. It's not just a man. It's your house, your kids, your family, your time, everything. Everything in your life is who you marry."

"That's the longest speech I've ever heard you make, Con," said Celeste somberly.

Connie stared across the fields, her lips still red with a trace of lipstick from the day before. "Somebody moved into one of those houses yesterday," she finally said. "I saw the truck from the upstairs window when I was getting ready to go out."

Celeste shrugged. "Big deal. You know what Sol always says. The more things are different, the more they're the same."

"That doesn't make any sense," Maggie said.

"Yeah it does," said her aunt. "Think about it."

Upstairs a screen was lifted with a sound like fingernails on a blackboard. "Connie," came Tommy's tortured voice. "I need tomato juice."

Celeste laughed. "I'll come in with you," she said as Connie rose. "Put some vodka in it. That'll make him feel better."

Maggie stayed out on the patio and thought about what her aunt had said. The more she thought about it, the more she thought it was ridiculous. She thought about life with her grandfather gone, her grandmother alone, perhaps her entire family living in the big stone house and hanging out in the gazebo. She thought of Monica with a baby and a husband, never again to go to a dance with one boy and dump him halfway through the evening for someone better looking, and of Helen perhaps getting a part on Broadway and having strange men spend the night at her apartment. She thought of Debbie being Bridget Hearn's best friend, or maybe thinking she was until Bridget dumped her, and she tried to think they deserved each other, but instead she got a feeling in her chest as though a rib was broken.

She thought of her mother driving her around during the winter months, while the dark outside and the dashboard lights within made a little oasis of the front seat of the car. She knew that even a week from now things would be different. School would start, and she would spend her days in her green uniform blazer and her plaid skirt, her saddle shoes raising blisters on the joints of her toes and the back of her heels after three months in sneakers and flip-flops. On Tuesday they would shop for school supplies, copy books with their spines still closed tight and pencil boxes that smelled as freshly plastic as Christmas morning. There would be no more nights in the development because she wasn't allowed out on school nights. Soon all the windows of the new houses would be filled with yellow light and the spindly saplings they were planting along Shelley Lane and Dickens Street would grow up to be trees. And soon it would seem as if Tennyson Acres had always been there, and only the older kids would say "Do you remember before they built the development?" and would know what was inside each of those walls. Maggie wondered if someday the people in the last house by the woods would rip up their wall-to-wall carpeting and find the old *Playboys* beneath the floor.

The gold of her locket was warm beneath her fingers. She took a letter from the pocket of her shorts. "Dear Maggie," she read, "I am really glad you are willing to write to me even though we are in the same place and school is starting. I have a lot of things to ask you which are easier to write in a letter than to say to your face. Your face is great but my conversation is not. (HA HA!)" Even now, after reading the letter at least six times, Maggie's breathing felt funny when she got to that part: your face is great. She wondered if Bruce could dance. He had never asked her for anything but the silly line dances at the wedding, perhaps because his father was there. Each time she had looked at him he had looked away and cracked his knuckles. When his father told him it was time to go, he had pressed the letter into her hand, but before he moved away, he had squeezed it hard.

Inside the house she could hear her aunt and her mother laughing. She wasn't sure whether her aunt Celeste was wrong about things changing and staying the same, or whether it was one of those differences between children and adults, like the way they were always saying that time went by so quickly when just to get from June to September seemed to take a lifetime.

Maggie walked through her own backyard to the beginning of the development. The soft ground sagged beneath her feet, and she could see in the cement of the curbs that Terence and his friends had been there, putting in hand and footprints, and leaving their initials: TSS, KAK, RVQ. The asphalt for the roads had not been laid yet, and she could feel the pebbles through the soft thin soles of her sneakers. Up ahead of her was the first house to be finished, a ranch house with sliding picture windows in almost every room. Maggie remembered that Richard and Bruce had written their names inside the doors of the kitchen cabinets the day they'd been installed.

Maggie approached soundlessly, close enough to see into the living-room window. A man and a woman sat on a couch against one wall. He was bald, with his shirt sleeves rolled to the elbow, and she had a short cap of black hair, like a bathing cap, and tiny black eyes. They held round glasses, almost like bowls, filled with dark amber liqueur, and they sipped at it as they looked around them. Their furniture looked as if it had elbows, it was so angular, and on the wall above the couch was what Maggie was sure must be modern art, a soaring splash of fuschia dotted with black and gray. It was pretty, really, and the gray matched the couch. The man rose and Maggie leapt back, her heart pounding, but when she looked in again she could see that he was only adjusting the picture, and she imagined they had just hung it, hung it before they unpacked any of the cardboard boxes stacked at the far end of the room, before they began putting away their dishes and discovering names written in pencil inside their brand-new cabinet doors.

The woman rose and stared at the picture, a hand on her hip, and then she said something to the man and stood tapping her foot while he made the smallest adjustment. A voice in Maggie's head said stridently, "I'd bet my bottom dollar they're Jews," even though Maggie herself was thinking that they looked mostly Italian, and Maggie recognized it as her grandfather's voice. And she knew that for the rest of her life, from time to time she would hear that voice within her head.

She wondered if this was what it was like to be haunted. Or perhaps that was what heaven was, the eternal life of your own point of view fired off, every now and then, inside the skulls of unsuspecting friends and relatives. Maggie thought that her grandfather would live that way in her mind, until the day when she died herself, when there would be other people around to remember her. She looked back at the houses of Kenwood, old and familiar, and she looked around her at Tennyson Acres, and the two seemed to her to be the past and the future. She heard her grandfather's voice again, saying, "There's the here, and then there's the hereafter." That was how it looked to her, the two parts of the neighborhood, like here and hereafter, like what had been and what was to come. Her grandfather was finally having his hereafter, but he was here, too, inside her head, and she was glad of that.

It wasn't only the dead that lived with you that way. When she closed her eyes she could hear Helen say "Not to decide is to decide," and her mother saying, with a great throb in her quiet voice, "Not good or bad. Things just are." She knew that twenty years from now she would still hear all those voices in her head, and she knew that as long as they stayed there she would be able to do all the things she had to do, to make all the choices she had to make. But yesterday, as she had walked down the aisle, looking into the curled heart of the pink rose at the center of her bouquet, she had heard another voice, telling her to lift her chin, to keep her shoulders square, to walk slowly. And suddenly it had come to her, as she was dancing with her father, the stars of darkness exploding inside her closed lids, that the voice she was hearing was her own, for the first time in her life.

One True Thing

For Prudence M. Quindlen

PROLOGUE

Jail is not as bad as you might imagine. When I say jail, I don't mean prison. Prison is the kind of place you see in old movies or public television documentaries, those enormous gray places with guard towers at each corner and curly strips of razor wire going round and round like a loop-the-loop atop the high fence. Prison is where they hit the bars with metal spoons, plan insurrection in the yard, and take the smallest boy— the one in on a first offense— into the shower room, while the guards pretend not to look and leave him to find his own way out, blood trickling palely, crimson mixed with milky white, down the backs of his hairless thighs, the shadows at the backs of his eyes changed forever.

Or at least that's what I've always imagined prison was like.

Jail was not like that a bit, or at least not the jail in Montgomery County. It was two small rooms, both together no bigger than my old attic bedroom in my parents' house, and they did have bars, but they closed by hand, not with the clang of the electric, the remote controlled, the impregnable. An Andy Griffith jail. A Jimmy Stewart jail. Less Dostoyevsky than summer stock, a jail for the stranger in town who brings revelation in the leather pack he carries slung over one shoulder and has a thrilling tenor voice.

There was a shelflike cot arrangement, and a toilet, and a floor with speckled linoleum, so much like the linoleum in Langhorne Memorial Hospital that I wondered if the same contractor had installed both. When the door was locked the policeman who had brought me down the long hall after I was photographed and fingerprinted left, his eyes more than a little sympathetic. We had once been in the same beginner's French class at the high school, he to eke out another C in his senior year, me to begin the diligent study that would culminate in the Institut Français prize at graduation. After the sound of his footsteps died away the place was very quiet.

From up front, where the police dispatcher sat, there was the sound of someone typing inexpertly, the occasional animal honk from the police two-way radios. From above there was a hum, a vague, indeterminate sound that seemed to come from electricity running through the wires just beneath the acoustical tile ceiling. Above me were those plain fluorescent tube lights.

Sometimes now, at work in the hospital, I will look up at a certain angle and I see that ceiling again, those lights, and the sense of being in that small space once more is overwhelming, but not really unpleasant.

Sitting on the cot, my hands clasped lightly between my knees, I felt relief. The lockup, I repeated in my head. The slammer. The joint. All attempts to scare myself, all those cheap slang terms I had heard come from the nasty fishlike lips of Edward G. Robinson as I watched *The Late Show* in the den, the house dark, the screen gray-blue as a shark, my father and mother asleep upstairs. The can, I thought to myself. The Big House. But overlaying them all was a different thought: I am alone. I am alone. I am alone.

I lay on my side on the cot and put my hands together beneath my cheek. I closed my eyes, expecting to hear a voice in my ear, a cry for help: for a cup of tea, a glass of water, a sandwich, more morphine. But no one spoke; no one needed me any longer. I felt peaceful as I could not remember feeling for a long time. And free, too. Free in jail.

For the first time in days, I could even stop seeing my father, with his smooth black hair and his profile a little dulled by age and fatigue; I could stop seeing him spooning the rice pudding into my mother's slack mouth, like a raven tending to the runt in the nest, all wild, weird tufts of head fuzz and vacant, glittery eyes. Spoon. Swallow. Spoon. Swallow. The narrow line of his lips. The slack apostrophe of her tongue. The blaze of love and despair that lit her face for just a moment, then disappeared.

I can still see that scene today, play it over and over again to reduce it to its small component parts, particularly the look in her eyes, and in his. But, back then, during my night in jail, for a few hours it disappeared. All I was aware of was the hum.

It reminded me of the sound you could hear if you walked down the street on a summer day in Langhorne, particularly where I lived, where the big houses were. There was always the hum. If you were attentive, stood still and really listened, you could figure out that it was the hum of hundreds of air condition-ers. They were pushing cold clean beautiful air into cold clean beautiful rooms, rooms like ours, where the moldings teased the eye upward from the polished surface of the dining-room table or the cushions, with their knife creases left by the side of someone's hand, on the big brown velvet couch across from the fireplace and the Steinway.

That was how I thought about it, although that was not how it had been for the last few months of my mother's life. That was how it looked before the couch from the den had been crowded into the living room to make room for the hospital bed. Before the furniture had all been moved back against the walls to make room for the wheelchair. Before the velvet nap of the couch had been disfigured by vomit and drool.

Inside the lids of my eyes I could see a kind of dull reddish light, and it reminded me of the light on those streets at the end of the day, particularly in autumn. In the magic hour the cars, so distinct, so identifiable, would come down our street, to turn into driveways or continue to some of the small streets and culs-de-sac farther on. Dr. Belknap the pediatrician, whose patient I had been all my life. Mr. Fryer, who worked in the city as a financial consultant and was obsessed with golf. Mr. Dingle, the high school principal, who could only afford to live on our street because his wife had inherited the house from her parents.

And then, late at night, after the streetlights buzzed on, with their own hum, a few others came. Always last was Mr. Best, the district attorney. My brother Brian used to deliver his *Tribune* every morning, just after sunrise, and Bri said that every time he pedaled his bike up the driveway to the sloping sward of pachysandra that set the Best house off from the street, Mr. Best would be standing there. Impatient at dawn, he would be tapping his narrow foot in leather slippers, wearing a corduroy robe in the winter and a seersucker robe in summer. He never gave Brian a tip at Christmas, always a baseball cap that said MAY THE BEST MAN WIN, which was what Mr. Best gave out in election years.

An election year was coming up when I was in jail.

The police officer came by my cell. I knew his name was Skip, although his name tag said he was really Edwin Something-or-Other Jr. I had seen him last at the town Christmas-tree lighting ceremony in December, when my mother's tree was the nicest tree, with its gaudy decorations and big red bows. He had been on the high school basketball team and had sat out every game. His broad back had been a bookend on the bench, a short kid named Bill on the other side, both of them waiting for the team to come back from the floor so they could feel again the nervous jostle that made them part of the action for a few minutes. My brother Jeff probably knew him. He was one of the boys who lived outside of town, in one of the Cape Cod houses that punctuated the corkscrew country roads.

The county had a lot of them, out where the corn grew in summer taller than any farmer, and tomatoes and zucchini were sold from little lean-tos with a plywood shelf out front. Sometimes, in August, the zucchini would be as big as baseball bats, and, because no one wanted them, the kids would use them to beat the trees in the softer light of the surrounding forests. The only zucchini worth having, my mother always said, were the tiny ones with the blossoms still attached.

Montgomery County had acres and acres of farm and forest, and then a wide avenue of junk, auto-body shops and Pizza Huts and discount electronics places and mini-malls with bad Chinese takeout and unisex hair salons. And at the end, when you'd come through it all, you arrived at Langhorne. It was the perfect college town, front porches and fanlight windows, oak trees along the curbs as big around as barrels, azaleas in the spring and hydrangeas in the summer and curbside piles of leaves in the fall. Langhorne had a shoe store full of loafers and a jewelry store with trays full of signet rings; it had a bookstore run by an elderly couple named the Duanes, Isabel and Dean Duane, who had retired from a busier life in the city and who seldom consulted *Books in Print* because they already knew everything that was in it. They were rather like the people in Langhorne, the Duanes—they knew everything about what was going on in their little world.

The jail was not in Langhorne proper. That was how the people who lived there always referred to it, "Langhorne proper," so that you would know who lived on one of the oak-lined streets and who lived in the slapdash houses and trailers outside of town. The jail was over by the gas stations, the storage facilities, the Acme and the Safeway.

The policeman, Skip, who had played in one quarter of one game his senior year, came in to check on me that night because he was concerned that I might be terrified, lonely, weeping. He was concerned that I might be unhinged by the fact that I had been in jail for nearly four hours and my father had not arrived to post bail, to say "Dark day, darling?" in that way that made my few friends go wild about him, his blue eyes, his arch and charming manner, his aphorisms. When the police had first put me here they had waited for him to come bursting in the door, with his long stride, swearing in Englishisms: "What in bloody hell is going on here, may I ask?" My father was the chairman of the Langhorne College English department and he was famous for his Englishisms; they went down exceptionally well when he would speak at the Langhorne Women's Club or the Episcopal Book Club on *David Copperfield* ("Minor Dickens, Ellen, strictly minor—*Bleak House* is too rich for their systems") or *Pride and Prejudice*. My father had called me Little Nell when I was younger.

My mother sometimes called me Ellie.

But my father did not come to bail me out, and so the young policeman came to watch over the scared woman he expected to find in the cell. He was apparently amazed to find me asleep beneath the fluorescent lights, my knees drawn up to my chest, my hands joined beneath my cheek as though I was praying. Or at least that's what he told the *Tribune*.

I saw the story after my brother Jeff and Mrs. Forburg agreed that it was best for me to know what was being said about me. "Shocked," the story said Skip was. "Disbelief," they said he felt. He said that in school I had always been a cold person, superior and sure of myself, and he was right. He said that I was smart, and that was right, too.

But he was smarter than I was about some things, and he knew that a girl in jail, a girl just barely old enough to refer to herself as a woman when she wanted to make sure that you knew she was not to be trifled with, should be rank with fear and adrenaline, up all night contemplating the horror of her position. Especially a girl charged with killing her own mother.

Instead he found me sleeping, a faint smile on my face.

You can see that smile in the pictures they took the next morning, after I appeared in court, charged with willfully causing the death of Katherine B. Gulden. The courtroom artist didn't capture it when she drew me, with my court-appointed lawyer at my side, his pale-blue suit giving off a smell of sizing as he sweated in the small, close room.

(I remember thinking that anyone represented by a man in a pale-blue suit was doomed for sure. And his dress shirt was short-sleeved. "Going up the river," I thought to myself. "In for the long haul.")

But in the late afternoon, when the strip mall across from the municipal building was in shadow and my bail had been arranged—$10,000 cash and a pledge of a four-bedroom Cape with a finished basement—when I finally left the Montgomery County jail, the smile I had had while asleep was still on my face, just a little half-moon curve above my pointed chin and below my pointed nose.

On page one of the *Tribune* I smiled my Mona Lisa smile, my dark hair braided back from my forehead, my widow's peak an arrogant *V*, my big white sweater and a peacoat flapping over dirty jeans, a smudge faintly visible on one cheek. And I knew that even the few people who still loved me would look and think that here was Ellen's fatal hubris again, smiling at the worst moment of her life.

Some of them did say that, as the days went by, and I never answered them. How could I say that whenever I went out in public and someone leapt into my path, a Nikon staring at me like a tribal mask on an enemy's face, all I could hear was a voice in my ear, an alto voice over and over, saying, "Smile for the camera, Ellie. You look so pretty when you smile."

And my mother spoke, alive again inside my brain, edging out Becky Sharp and Pip and Miss Havisham and all the other made-up people I had learned so long ago from my father to prize over real ones. She spoke and I listened to her, because I was afraid if I didn't her voice would gradually fade away, an evanescent wraith of a thing that would narrow to a pinpoint of light and then go out, lost forever, like Tinker Bell if no one clapped for her. I listened to her, because I loved her. She'd asked so little of me, over the course of our lives, and I wanted to do this one small remembered thing, to smile for the camera.

At the end I always did what she asked, even though I hated it. I was tired to death of the sour smell of her body and the straw of her hair in the brush and the bedpan and the basin and the pills that kept her from crying out, from twisting and turning like the trout do on the banks of the Montgomery River when you've lifted them on the end of the sharp hook and their gills flare in mortal agitation.

I tried to do it all without screaming, without shouting, "I am dying with you." But she knew it; she felt it. It was one of many reasons why she would lie on the living-room couch and weep without making a sound, the tears giving her gray-yellow skin, tight across her bones, the sheen of the polished cotton she used for slipcovers or the old lampshades she painted with flowers for my bedroom. I tried to make her comfortable, to do what she wanted. All but that one last time.

No matter what the police and the district attorney said, no matter what the papers wrote, no matter what people believed then and still believe, these years later, the truth is that I did not kill my mother. I only wished I had.

PART ONE

I remember that the last completely normal day we ever had in our lives, my brothers and I, was an ordinary day much like this one, a muggy August-into-September weekday, the sky low and gray over Langhorne, clouds as flat as an old comforter hanging between the two slight ridges that edged the town. We'd gone to the Tastee Freeze for soft ice cream that day, driving in Jeff's battered open jeep with our arms out the windows. My brothers were handsome boys who have turned into handsome men. Brian has our father's black hair and blue eyes, Jeffrey our mother's coloring, auburn hair and eyes like amber and a long face with freckles.

Both of them were tanned that day, at the end of their summer jobs as camp counselor and landscaper. I was pale from a summer spent in a New York office on weekdays and house-guesting at Fire Island weekends, spending more time at cocktail parties than on the beach, where melanoma and Retin-A were frequent talking points among my acquaintances.

Afterward I wondered why I hadn't loved that day more, why I hadn't savored every bit of it like soft ice cream on my tongue, why I hadn't known how good it was to live so normally, so everyday. But you only know that, I suppose, after it's not normal and everyday any longer. And nothing ever was, after that day. It was a Thursday, and I was still my old self, smug, self-involved, successful, and what in my circles passed for happy.

"Ellen's got the life," said Jeff, who'd been asking about the magazine where I worked. "She gets paid to be a wiseass for a living. You go to parties, you talk to people, you make fun of them in print. It's like getting paid to breathe. Or play tennis."

"You could get paid to play tennis," I said. "It's called being a tennis pro."

"Oh, right," said Jeff, "with our father?" He sucked the ice cream from the bottom of his cone. "Excuse me, Pop? Mr. Life of the Mind? I've decided to move to Hilton Head and become a tennis pro. But I'll be reading Flaubert in my spare time."

"Is it possible for one of you to make a life decision without wondering what Papa will find wrong with it?" I said.

My brothers hooted and jeered. "Oh, great," said Jeff. "Ellen Gulden renounces paternal approval! And only twenty-four years too late."

"Mom is happy with anything I do," said Brian.

"Oh, well, Mom," said Jeff.

"Jeffrey man," someone called across the parking lot. "Brian!" My brothers lifted their hands in desultory salutes. "What's up?" Jeff called back.

"I'm history here," I said.

"You were history here when you were here," said Jeff. "No offense, El. You're a hungry puppy, always were a hungry puppy, and the world don't like you hungry puppies. People are afraid you're going to bite them."

"Why are you talking like a cracker radio commentator?" I said.

"See, Bri, Ellen never relaxes. New York is her kind of place. An entire city of people who never relax, who were antsy in their own hometowns. So long, hungry puppy. Go where the dogs eat the dogs."

The light was dull yellow because of the low clouds, like a solitary bulb in a dark room. The asphalt was soft in the driveway under our feet, the smell of charcoal drifting over Langhorne the way perfume hung over a cocktail party in the city. Our father came in late in the evening, but we were used to that: he stood in the den for a time, leaning against the doorjamb, and then he trudged upstairs, oddly silent.

Not odd for the boys, with whom he had the strained, slightly mechanical transactions that many fathers have with their sons. But odd for me. I had always felt I knew my father's mind, if not his heart. Whenever I came home, from college and then later, on visits from the city, he would call me into his study, with its dark furniture and dim sepia light, would lean forward in his desk chair and say, simply, "Tell."

And I would spin my stories for him, of the famous writer I had heard read in a lecture hall, of the arguments about syntax I had had with editors, of the downstairs neighbor who played Scarlatti exquisitely but monotonously on the small antique harpsichord I had once glimpsed through the door of his apartment.

I often felt like someone being debriefed by a government apparatchik, or like Scheherazade entertaining the sultan. And often I made stories up, wonderful stories, so that my father would lean back in his chair and his face would relax into the utter concentration he had when he lectured to his students. Sometimes at the end he would say "Interesting." And I would be happy.

Our mother was in the hospital that day, and as it always did, the house seemed like a stage set without her. It was her house, really. Whenever anyone is called a homemaker now—and they rarely are—I think of my mother. She made a home painstakingly and well. She made balanced meals, took cooking classes, cleaned the rooms of our home with a scarf tying back her bright hair, just like in the movies. When she wallpapered a room, she would always cover the picture frames in the same paper, and place them on the bureau or the bedside table, with family photographs inside.

The two largest pictures in the living room were of my mother and father. In one they are standing together on our front porch. My mother is holding my father's arm with both her own, an incandescent smile lighting her face, as though life knows no greater happiness than this—this place, this day, this man. Her body is turned slightly sideways, toward him, but he is facing four-square to the camera, his arms crossed over his chest, his face serious, his eyes mocking.

Back when we were still lovers, Jonathan had picked up that picture from the piano and said that in it my father looked like the kind of man who would rip out your heart, grill it, and eat it for dinner, then have your wife for dessert. Allowing for the difficult relationship between Jonathan and my father, the relationship of two men engaged in a struggle for the soul of the same woman, it was a pretty fair description.

I wonder if my father still has that picture there, on the piano, or whether it's put away now, my mother smiling dustily, happily, into the dark of a drawer.

Next to it was another picture of my mother hanging on to my father's arm. Wearing a cap and gown, I am hanging on to his other one. In that picture, my father is squinting slightly in the sunlight, and smiling. Jonathan took that picture. I have it on my dresser today, the most tangible remaining evidence of the Gulden family triangle.

My mother would be saddened by my apartment now, by the grimy white cotton couch and the inexpertly placed standing lamps. My apartment is the home of someone who is not a home-maker, someone who listens to the messages on the answering machine and then runs out again.

But she would not criticize me, as other mothers might. Instead she would buy me things, a cheap but pretty print she would mat herself, a throw of some kind. And as she arranged the throw or hung the picture she would say, smiling, "We're so different, aren't we, Ellie?" But she would never realize, as she said it, as she'd said it so many times before, that if you are different from a person everyone agrees is wonderful, it means you are somehow wrong.

My mother loved the hardware store, Phelps's Hardware, and the salesmen there loved her. My father would always tease her: "Once again, she has paid the Phelps's mortgage for the month and alone of all her sex has cornered the market on tung oil and steel wool!" My father always teased her. I was the one he talked to.

It was a charmed day in the charmed life we lived, my brothers and I, that day we went to the Tastee Freeze. I see that so clearly now. We lolled on the grass in the backyard afterward, cooked and ate some hamburgers, watched television. And then the next morning our father came downstairs, his khakis wrinkled, his blue shirt rolled back from his wrists, and told us all to sit down. He leaned back against the kitchen counter as I sat opposite him, sipping a glass of orange juice. My two brothers sat in the ladderback chairs at either end of the kitchen table. My mother had caned the seats. I don't include those details by way of description, but in tribute. Things like this were my mother's whole life. Of this I was vaguely contemptuous at the time.

When I was a little girl, she would sometimes sing me to sleep, although I always preferred my father, because he made up nonsense songs: "Lullaby, and good night, fettuccine Alfredo. Lullaby and good night, rigatoni Bolognese." But my mother sang a boring little tune that was nothing but the words "safe and sound" over and over again. It put me right to sleep. My father always jazzed me up; my mother always calmed me down. They did the same to one another. Sometimes I think they just practiced on me.

I remember. It's what I do for a living now, how I earn my keep, make my mark, through memories. I remember well. I can remember the orange juice on the table, and Brian, his torso jackknifed between his knees, throwing a ball into a mitt over and over. The glass was half full; the table was oak, a big round moon of a top on a sturdy pedestal with predatory claws at its base. My mother had rescued it from a junk shop, stripped and refinished it, waxed it with butcher wax until the muscles in her arms stood out like pale polished wood themselves.

"Cancer," my father said as we sat ringed around it. There had been certain vague signs, certain symptoms. She had felt sick for a long time. "Your mother procrastinated," he said, as though she was somehow to blame. "First she thought she had the flu. Then she imagined she was expecting. She didn't want to make a fuss. You know how she is."

The three of us looked down, all three embarrassed by the thought of our forty-six-year-old mother imagining she was pregnant. I was twenty-four. Jeff was twenty. Bri was eighteen. You looked at the numbers and you could tell we were planned children. We knew how she was.

My brothers were leaving for college that weekend. Their stereos were packed up, their suitcases standing open in the center of their rooms. And I had come back from the city for four days for a visit. I hadn't even unpacked, just pulled clothes out of a duffel bag on the chest at the foot of my bed, not putting anything away, leaving the drawers of my dresser empty and clean, lined with flowered paper. Four days seemed enough for the occasion. More, and I would miss a book party and lunch with the editor of an important magazine. A week in the hospital, she had told us. A hysterectomy, she had said. It had seemed unremarkable to me in a woman of forty-six long finished with childbearing, although every day that I grow older I realize there is never anything unremarkable about losing any part of what makes you female—a breast, a womb, a child, a man.

Funny, how the imagined pregnancy jarred us at first more than the cancer, which we could scarcely comprehend. And how I suddenly realized why my mother had seemed so joyous the month before, in town to take me to lunch on my birthday, her pale translucent redhead's skin flushed with pink. A forty-six-year-old woman aching to ask her sophisticated city-daughter where you could buy attractive maternity clothes. It makes me hurt now, just to think of what was going on in her head, before she finally discovered what was going on in her body.

"Chemotherapy," my father said. There were verbs in his sentences but I did not hear them. "Liver. Ovaries. Oncologist." I picked up my glass and walked out of the room.

"I'm still speaking, Ellen," my father called after me.

"I can't listen anymore," I said, and I went out and sat on the front porch, on a wicker rocker with a cushion that, of course, had been made by my mother.

The things they sold at antique stores in my New York neighborhood were like things my mother had bought years ago—square old chests made of russet-colored cherry wood, patchwork quilts, wicker settees painted white. We lived on the nicest block in Langhorne but in the smallest house, a white clapboard farmhouse left over from the days when the surrounding hills were farms and the college was the estate of Samuel Langhorne, who had made his money in machine parts on the cusp of the industrial revolution.

Our house looked like a pony that has somehow nosed its way in among the horses, a painted miniature to their murals. But it was as beautiful as any inside because of my mother's hard work. She had married a man who would never be rich, but she said she had not minded, because she knew he had a vocation instead. Lapsed Catholic that she was—or perhaps not so lapsed, in her heart—she had said it exactly that way, as though my father had become a priest, or at least taken vows, when his seven sacraments were only "Introduction to Victorian Poetry," "The Romantics and the Seasons of Love," and other such offerings in the college catalogue.

Even on its nicest block, where most of the residents were too rich to work at the college, Langhorne had the odd feel of a town that is about something other than itself. Washington is like that, and Orlando, Florida, which has Disney World. And Boston. When I went to college in Boston—or Cambridge, as all Harvard students learn to say—I was convinced it was because I wanted a larger pond, a more cosmopolitan setting, blessed release from the bell jar of Langhorne, where everyone knew my name and my class rank, which was number one. And of course I wanted to sleep with Jonathan whenever I could and he was at Harvard, so I went there, too. I was always afraid that if I wasn't in bed with Jonathan, keeping his cold feet warm, it was a cinch someone else would be.

But the truth is that Cambridge and Langhorne are in many ways very much alike, and not just because so many of my father's spiritual colleagues are in Cambridge, roaming the streets with the *Times* tucked under their arms, in cuffed chinos with the knees bagged out. All college towns are essentially the same. There is something strange about the roots of people settled in a place where everyone else passes through.

I sat on the porch and looked across at the Buckley house as I had done so many times before—Tudor, stucco, rhododendrons and a perennial garden fading fast, losing its pinks and whites and blues, nursery colors. They had gotten balloon shades in the living room since the last time I was home.

There were no shades on the windows in my apartment in New York. When my mother had visited the month before, it had been not only to have lunch but also to figure out which items of furniture, stored in the cellar, would fit nicely in my two small rooms. "You have no window coverings!" she had said. "The whole world is watching you undress!"

"Oh, Mama, big deal," I said. "Everyone in this neighborhood is gay." I was damned if I'd tell her that the first time I pulled off my shirt in my bedroom I'd looked across at the amber lamps lighting other people's lives and clutched the cotton to my chest. Or that since then I'd dressed and undressed in my windowless bathroom, like a virgin on her honeymoon.

But I was damned, too, if I'd put up balloon shades, or lace curtains, or those narrow venetian blinds. One of the things I loved about having my own place was the spill of white light across the scratched wooden floors each morning, the wave of mellow light that snuck slowly across the futon on my bedroom floor in late afternoon and early evening, the moon rising outside my window.

The light and sun and stars belonged to me in that place where anyone, looking in the window, would find a stranger, an unknown. Not Ellen Gulden. Not little Ellen, who, when she was eight, was dressed for Halloween as a princess in blue net and star-shaped sequins. Not Ellen Gulden, who met Jonathan Beltzer in A.P. English and became inseparable from him when she was seventeen. Not Ellen, who graduated from Harvard with a magna—*"Non sum summa est?"* said my father, who did not speak Latin and had only been a magna himself, but I got the message anyhow—and then went to work for some big magazine in New York as an editorial assistant and sometime reporter.

As I sat on the porch of my mother's house I was in a place where almost everybody knew, not only my name, but all those things. A shadow crossed my lap, and I knew it was my father.

"My train is at six-ten," I said, my voice trembling.

"Ellen," said my father, "your mother needs you. She is coming home Tuesday and she won't be well for long. The disease is apparently advanced. Soon she may not be able to bathe herself. In a month or two she will not be able to cook or clean."

"We can hire a nurse. That's what the Beldens did when Mrs. Belden's mother was sick." But even as I said it I knew how preposterous it sounded. In the Gulden household, the ethos was do it yourself, for everything from Christmas gifts to floor sanding.

"Your mother didn't hire a nurse when you had your tonsils out. She didn't hire a nurse when you had chicken pox or when you broke your arm. She wouldn't want strangers in her home. She won't even have a cleaning woman."

"Papa, I have an apartment. I have a job. I have a life."

The shadow lifted. The screen door slammed. A delivery truck slid by with a rumble as it changed gears and so I did not hear my father's muffled footsteps when he returned, when he came across the porch in his deck shoes. My linen jacket sailed into my lap, and my straw hat, and then my purse came down hard on the wooden decking, my wallet bouncing loose. My duffel bag landed at my feet.

"You"—he said, throwing a book atop the pile—"have"— and then my running shoes—"a Harvard education"—then my loafers—"but"—and the glass of orange juice rolled unbroken atop the mess, soaking the shoes—"you have no heart."

My father says this all the time, usually about writers. Pound's problem, he says, is not that he was an anti-Semite but that he had no heart. Fitzgerald's work is fatuous and second-rate because he had no heart. And now I was part of this motley crew, the geniuses and the almost-rans, all those smart people who were irredeemably flawed because they lacked something many people said George Gulden had never had at all. Something I'd spent my whole life trying to win from him.

My possessions lay strewn around me, the bright detritus of another life, and I stared at them and at the glow of the juice glass, its curving surface shining iridescent silver in the late-afternoon sun.

There were ghosts everywhere on the pavement and beneath the trees. Kate Gulden pulled Brian in the red wagon up the hill as Jeff and I dragged the quilt and the picnic basket behind. Kate Gulden tacked a sign that said CONGRATULATIONS across the porch posts, so that I covered my face when the principal brought me back from the state capitol after I won the essay contest. She planted bulbs around the porch lattices, painted the shutters Williamsburg blue, heaved groceries out of the back of the car, lived a domestic life double time.

I pictured my mother marooned in the living room, some cheery woman in a white uniform making her tuna sandwiches and folding her underthings, the house silent and a little dusty. But there was no story to go with that picture. When I'd written a false paragraph in a story my friend Jules would say, "This one just doesn't parse."

Kate Gulden and a hired nurse did not parse.

All my life I had known one thing for sure about myself, and that was that my life would never be her life. I had moved as far and as fast as I could; now I was back at my beginning. All my life my father had convinced me, almost by osmosis, rarely with praise, that I was gifted, special, that there were things other people could not do that I could do effortlessly. But I had never imagined this was one of them.

I packed up the pile of my jumbled belongings and carried it inside, the empty orange-juice glass balanced atop it all. But when I got to the door the glass rolled sideways and fell, shattering into innumerable shards, bright in the sun.

I think that the people I know now believe I went home to take care of my mother because I loved her. And sometimes I believe that was in my heart without my knowing it. But the truth is that I felt I had no choice. I felt I had to be what my father wanted me to be, even if it was something so unlike the other Ellen he'd cultivated and tutored for all those years, even if it meant that I had to go from his brightest student to his demi-wife. I had to prove that, unlike Pound and Fitzgerald, I had a heart.

I carried my things back upstairs to my bedroom. When I came downstairs, my father was in the den, talking on the phone. I waited in the doorway until he was finished. Then he turned to look at me, his silhouette black against the light coming in through the window. He looked as big as he had when I was a little girl, when I would watch him rise and rise and rise from the side of my bed at night until from below, his head, with its carefully brushed black hair, would blot out the light and make it nighttime as surely as if he had his finger on the switch to the moon and sun.

He had always been able to read me; if I had good news I had never been able to hide it past the moment when he saw my face, and if I had bad news his own face would settle, even before I spoke, into vertical planes of disappointed expectation.

"I'll be back Tuesday morning," I said, and he nodded.

"To stay," he said, a declarative sentence.

"I don't know about that," I said. "There are other options. Maybe you could take a sabbatical. It's been four years since you took one for the book."

He pressed his lips together, and the lines grew long down either side of his face. "It seems to me another woman is what's wanted here," he said. I've never forgotten the way he said that sentence. My father's syntax was often peculiar, as though he'd absorbed the Victorians whole when he made them his area of expertise, taken them in as you do an oyster. But for once it seemed to me he could have said "I want" or "I need." He could have paid me the compliment of necessity, or indispensability. But no: "It seems to me another woman is what's wanted here."

We looked at each other and I thought I saw something relax in him, in his eyes and shoulders, and I knew that he knew I would do what he wanted. "We'll see how it goes," I said.

"Ellen," he said, "this is not something that can be decided piecemeal. It's important that we settle this for the duration. Your mother will need someone to take her to the hospital for chemotherapy. I have no idea how debilitating that will be or how many other things she will no longer be able to manage. The doctor says she will need someone with her during the day. And a sabbatical is out of the question for me right now."

"A sabbatical is out of the question for me right now, too."

"Ellen, will you do this or will you not?"

"I don't know," I said. "I'll be back on Tuesday." And I turned to go.

"Ellen," he called when I was at the door. I watched as he passed his hand over his jaw. "This is a difficult time," my father said, and the effort of that sentence, within it the shadow of an apology, seemed to shake him. We were not in the habit of apologizing to one another. There had never been the need; neither of us ever disappointed. He sat down in a chair and let his head fall back, his hands slack along the upholstered arms. He looked old.

"I need to get the broom," I said. "I broke something." And I went to the kitchen and stood for a time, my head against the broom-closet door, a dustpan in my hand, and then went outside to clean up.

And so it was that I came back to Langhorne on a Tuesday morning, drove back in a rented car with a burgeoning sense of claustrophobia worse than if I'd been caught in an elevator between floors. I turned off the highway and drove through the more modest parts of town, the parts where the small houses were only an arm's length apart and the bigger ones had been chopped up into apartments for students and staff.

The green in front of the Town Hall was planted thick with asters in an early autumnal rusty orange. I always thought the town green looked best in spring, glorious with daffodils, hundreds of them. When a breeze moved across them they bowed, together, like dancers in a Busby Berkeley musical.

It seemed a long time until April, that day I drove back into town.

My few New York belongings were in the car—the futon, an old trunk, and a portable electric typewriter. As I pulled into the empty driveway, our house looked as though it was abandoned. Next door I saw a curtain rise, then fall.

I had quit my job at the magazine and sublet my apartment. The people I worked with had tried to be sympathetic, but they were incredulous. "My mother is sick," I said to the managing editor, a stout, short man named Bill Tweedy, flushed from high blood pressure and hard drinking, who had worked in newspapers and had contempt for himself and for the rest of us because we had the luxury of having six days from start to finish in which to put out a publication.

"Ellen," he said, "not to be crass, but a sick mother means three weeks off and a very nice arrangement of flowers sent by the staff. You were doing good here. You did that nice short thing on the gay cop, the story on the girl who got murdered on Madison Avenue, that was a good piece. You did all the research on that kids-and-summer guide. If you quit, there's no guarantee."

"I have to," I said.

"How about if I gave you a promotion?" he said. "More money?"

"Mr. Tweedy, do you honestly think someone would come in and say their mother was dying of cancer to get a raise?"

"Ellen, this is New York."

My friend Jules, my only real friend at the magazine or in New York, took me to lunch. Jules was fragile, physically and psychologically, too, but no one ever noticed because of the enormous aureole of black curls around her small pointed face, and the resonant timbre of her deep rich voice. Both made her seem like a big person, invulnerable and sure; the misapprehension that we shared those qualities had drawn me to her when we first met.

But I came to know the real Jules, the one who pulled that hair back from her face and leaned forward to peer suspiciously at herself in the mirror, who fell in love, was broken by it, sat alone for weeks feeding herself on yogurt and show tunes, and fell in love again. I knew the Jules whose mother from her earliest memories had told her that she should never be disappointed by failure because failure was all you could expect.

"This is a woman who would have told Abe Lincoln not to pursue a law degree," Jules told me once.

Jules loved me as I'd never been loved by a friend before, with full knowledge. She'd once been told by someone who had been a year ahead of me at Harvard: "Ellen Gulden would walk over her mother in golf spikes to succeed." "Well," Jules had replied, "I'm not her mother." After I'd cleaned out my desk at the magazine she took me out for lunch and held my hand across the table.

"Let them think we're dykes," she said disdainfully, glancing around at the buttoned-up men in deceptively wide and wild ties eating something tartar at the tables around us. "With the guys I meet, I only wish we were." When I started to cry she passed me Kleenex filled with lint from her leather backpack. There was a green M & M stuck in one corner of the tissue. Jules was incredibly, proudly disorderly. There were often odd bits of old food and half-empty coffee cups on her bedroom nightstand. "Eat it," she said of the M & M. "It will make you feel better."

"You have to do this," she added, rubbing my fingers as though I was a child who had come in from the cold. "You would want your daughter to do it for you."

"Jules, what about my life?"

"What about it? It's not forever. Look, Ellen, I understand. Do you think in a million years I would want to move back into my mother's apartment in Riverdale and listen to her go over all the ways in which Marvin and the floozy screwed up her life? But the truth is that she's your mother, and she needs you for a while, and you get your life back at the end and you've done the right thing."

"My mother and I—"

"Please," said Jules, "okay? Just please. Your mother and you have a difficult relationship? Excuse me, but why wouldn't you? Why should you be different from every other daughter in the world? Besides, she sounds like the only halfway decent mother in the world. Has she ever told you you need to lose weight?"

"I'm a good weight."

"You see, there you go. The fact that you would think that you have to be overweight to have your mother suggest you need to lose weight shows the ways in which you are clueless about how bad this relationship can be. The fact that you could say that you are a good weight is a measure of what a sane upbringing you had."

"You don't know my father."

"I don't need to know your father. I know Jonathan."

Jules did not like Jonathan. It was one of the only sore spots in our friendship.

"Don't start," I said.

"Agreed," said Jules, pushing her curls back with her fingers.

"I'm just afraid."

"I know you are. But when you come back here you will have done something really important."

"If I come back."

Jules squeezed my hand so hard I winced. "This is not *Peter Pan*," she said. "Your brothers are not the Lost Boys. They can learn how to run a microwave. Your father can learn where the Goddamn dry cleaner is. But no one," she ended, and her eyes filled, "can help your mother with the shit she'll be going through but you."

"Hire a nurse," Jonathan said when I called him at the data-processing job he worked two nights a week to pay for law school.

"She didn't hire a nurse when I had bronchitis," I said.

"Oh Ellen, did Papa George come up with that line? It's so—so self-sacrificing. It sounds just like him."

"Fuck you, Jon," I said.

"Oh, you will," he said, his voice silky, and he described in detail how I would when next he was in Langhorne, which seemed like years from now.

That was what I was thinking of as I tugged the futon from the back seat of the rental car—all the times we'd laid atop it and worked away, trying to find the places that would drive one another half mad, feeling half mad when we succeeded. Like a mummified prom corsage or a lock of hair, the stains on the futon were the memoirs of our life together. There was no place I could possibly imagine putting it that would not disturb the perfect prettiness of my mother's house.

It would be conspicuously out of place in my room, which was sponge-painted a pale blue, its windows veiled in flowered chintz. Over my desk were my diplomas, framed and matted, and the certificate from the state essay contest, handed to me hastily by the commissioner of education as the cameras made their *nick-nick* insect sounds. I had written a glib and self-righteous defense of euthanasia, and the conservative Catholic governor, who usually awarded the $1,000 prize, wanted nothing to do with me.

I spent the money on a hiking trip in Colorado and a leather jacket for Jonathan.

So I rolled my futon into the garage. Whenever I saw it there, over the next few months, whenever I went out to get a can of oil or a screwdriver, its misshapen bulk in the corner made me tingle, like a spinster peeking into the master bedroom of the house next door, all grim mouth and warm crotch.

I don't know how much my mother knew about my sex life, or the rest of my life, for that matter. I don't know how typical our relationship was, either. Perhaps I know the wrong sort of woman, overcerebral and nervous. I only know that I can tell from the timbre of Jules's voice on the telephone, edgy and a little higher than usual, that she has just seen or spoken to her mother. I only know that one day I went in to see my adviser at Harvard, a woman who had appeared on television news programs more than once in the role of a Valkyrie, brandishing her almost incendiary intelligence, and found her with her head in her hands. "The tenacious umbilical cord," she said lightly when I asked if I should come back another time, but her posture had given her away.

When I considered her dispassionately I knew that, as my friends said, I was lucky in my mother. It was simply that I rarely considered her at all. My mother was like dinner: I needed her in order to live, but I did not pay much attention to what went into her.

My father was dessert. He exhibited the kind of dim general interest in my brothers that fathers had in the television shows of the 1950s. But he did not play catch, and he did not fish. He read, and he taught. Sometimes he let me correct his blue books for freshman English. Sometimes I think he got his reputation as a savage grader from me, although I might have inherited my predilection to judge harshly from him as well.

The most potent memory of my childhood is the sound of the door opening in the evening as he came in. It always reminded me of that moment in *The Wizard of Oz* when Dorothy opens the door of the house and the black-and-white world of Kansas turns Technicolor.

As I opened the same door, that Tuesday morning, the house was dim and gray, quiet, seemingly empty. The air smelled of some flower, very sweet, and I saw a pitcher filled with freesia on the gateleg table in the hall. In the living room there was a slender glass vase filled with blue iris, bright against the yellow-and-white striped walls. On the silver tray on the piano were the cards: "From the faculty and staff of Langhorne College," "Get well, Kate—Skip and Caroline Byers," "From the Buckley family with our love."

And then I turned and she was there, on the stairs, in blue pants and a shirt, the color lighting up her red hair like a flag. "Ellie," my mother said, in surprise and gladness. "You're home!"

I did not know whether it was my imagination, but her shoulder blades seemed sharper, little wings jutting from her back as I pressed her close. She smelled of bath powder, but of something more chemical, too, and when I squeezed her I thought I felt her wince, although it was I who pulled away first, as I always had.

"I'm fine," she said, sitting down in one of the big wing chairs. "I am. I weighed myself this morning, thinking I'd be pounds lighter, but I'm still the same. It must be all this water I'm holding. But the water's supposed to calm down, and meanwhile I have to take it easy. 'NO painting,' said Dr. Cohn, my new doctor, who is, you'll love this, a woman. 'NO papering, no stenciling, no upholstering.' I had to stop her and say, 'May I needlepoint and sew?' 'Yes,' she said, 'if it doesn't include a ladder or a staple gun.' "

She went on like that for so long that it seemed she would run out of air; she talked about the doctors, the flowers, the food in the hospital, the food her friends had brought to the house in casserole dishes. And then suddenly her face stilled, sagged. Her eyes lost their shine, and she took a deep breath. She seemed to marshal her strength, and then her eyes lit up again like lanterns that had momentarily guttered in the wind of her thoughts.

"I don't know why I'm talking about all that," she said. "The important thing is that I'm all right. That's why you're here, isn't it, to make sure I'm all right? And I am. I never want you or the boys to worry about me. I feel good. I feel fine. I sleep more than I used to. But I'll be myself before you know it. It would kill me if I thought you were worried. I can live without a staple gun." And we both laughed.

"You look great, Mama," I said, and it was almost true. She looked so good that I remember wondering whether, by the end of the month, I could throw out the grad student who'd sublet my apartment and get my old job back.

"Well, I didn't know you were coming or I'd have something in the oven," she said, touching her hair. "I don't know how good any of these things people brought over will be. Like bringing coals to Newcastle, I thought, to bring us food. So we'll have dinner out tonight at the Inn. Jeff drove Brian to school and your father has some meeting or other. So the two of us will have an early dinner, and then we'll go to Duane's and get some books. You'll tell me what's good and I'll read instead of paint. I have to have something to read anyhow while I'm having the treatments. You know how the hospital is—two hours waiting for five minutes pricking the end of your finger for some blood. Or whatever they're going to do to me now. How long can you stay?"

I looked at her, at her long-fingered hands with their nails kept short for the sake of her projects, and I realized that she did not know why I was there. It was how it had always been. My father made the decisions, and she learned about them later and lived with them. Improved on them, usually.

"I'm home for a while, Mama," I said. "I'm back in my room upstairs for a while."

"Home?" she said. "Here?"

I nodded.

"Oh, no, Ellen. What do you mean? What about your friends and your little apartment? What about your work?"

"I've taken some time off," I said, but I could not keep my eyes from giving me away.

"Oh no," she whispered. "No no no no no. Not to be a nurse-maid to me, to take care of this house, to take care of my house. You'll hate me."

"That's absurd," I said.

"Oh God, Ellen," she said, as though I had not spoken. "You have to go back. We can have dinner and then you can take the train in the morning. Or the last one tonight. There's one tonight late, isn't there?"

"Mama," I said. "Mama, you're going to need help. I can sit with you while you have the chemotherapy"—and when I saw her lips begin to work I added—"the treatments. I can take care of the house and do some of the things the doctor says you can't do until you're feeling better."

"Oh Ellie," she said sadly, "I'm not a fool. Don't talk about it as though I have the flu. I said to Doctor Cohn, 'Well, I can't do this and I can't do that, but can I at least commit to doing one of the Christmas trees around the green for the caroling evening?' And she says, 'Well, Kate, it's a long way until December.' And of course your father starts to hum that song about it being a long time from May to December. And Dr. Cohn shot him such a look. 'Well, Doctor, I'll make you a Christmas ornament,' I said. 'I'm Jewish, Kate,' she said. 'Well, then I'll make you a menorah.'

And I will. Doing that does NOT include a ladder or a staple gun."

My mother looked around the room and slowly came back to me. "I know why you're here," she said. "I know what's going on."

"I'm staying."

"I see that," she said. "Whose idea was this, your father's?"

"Both of ours. All of ours. Mine. It's just for a while, Mama."

"This will never work," she said. "He should have known it would never work. He knows you."

She was only saying what I'd already said to Jules a hundred times. But I wanted her to think better of me than I'd thought of myself.

"That's not fair," I said. "I can help. I can do things here for you. I can do things with you. I come home and you're not even happy." I sounded petulant but I did not care.

My mother put out a hand lightly to touch mine. "Ellie, I'm always happy when you're here. But I don't want you out of pity."

"It's the right thing," I said.

"For who?" she said, and when she saw my face she sighed. "This is hard for your father."

"Him? What about you?" What I really wanted to say was: what about me?

"I'm fine," she said. But her smile was bleak, without light or warmth. And for the first time I thought of what it must be like to know that you were going to die, that the trees would bud, flower, leaf, dry, die, and you would not be there to see any of it. It was like standing too close to the fire; my mind leapt back.

My mother's face was calm but empty; I realized she looked like my Grandmother Nina, who never showed anything on her face, even, my mother said, when her only son was killed in Vietnam and the chaplain came to the door of their apartment on Broadway.

My mother liked to tell the story of how two men—"boys really, kids"—had come into the dry cleaners her parents owned one day and demanded the money from the register, and how her mother had spit Polish curses from between her clenched teeth, her face expressionless, while they reached across the counter and stuffed bills into the pockets of their jeans. I imagined that my mother's face now was much as my grandmother's had been then.

"Do you want some tea and a piece of cake?" my mother asked evenly, as she had asked so many times before. And without waiting for a reply she got up, tentatively, and went into the kitchen, and soon I heard the kettle whistling.

W ell," my mother said the next day as we sat at the oak table in the kitchen drinking tea, "what should we do?"

"Do?" I said.

For of course I thought we would not do anything much except drift, that she would feel sick, although she did not look or act sick at all, and I would be miserable, although I would hide it and deny it. That we would see one another, as we always had, across a divide.

But when I first arrived home she still behaved as though she was Kate Gulden in her own safe haven. And Kate Gulden had always had something to do, some project, some plan, dozens of them at once, so that it seemed a sin, if she was knitting, for her not to have a pot of something or other simmering on the stove.

"We need a project," she said that morning. "Something the two of us can do together."

Had there ever been such a thing? I was the one who ran in and out of the house; she was the one who stayed inside it. Somehow it made the peculiar intimacy of our situation so stark, that Kate and Ellen Gulden were finally together, alone, searching for something they could do in tandem.

"I guess I could use the staple gun and you could guide me," I remember saying in a lukewarm fashion.

"No no no," my mother said impatiently, and she bent her bright head down to the mug of tea, blowing into it, a wreath of steam around her face. "Something different." She looked off for a moment, and then slowly she said, "A book group."

Then and now, there was something about the tone of her voice that made me know that she had come up with the idea earlier and was pretending that it was new. "A book group?"

My mother laughed, an artificial trilling sound that had a certain impatience about it. "Ellie," she said, using the diminutive that only she gave me, "are you going to repeat everything I say as though it's the most startling thing you've ever heard?"

"No, I—I'm sorry. A book group. Fine. Who else should we have?"

"Oh, no one else, I don't think, do you? The two of us will read books and talk about them. I've always wanted to belong to a book group, but there are only two of them in Langhorne, and I never really fit into either one. One is that group of younger women from the country club who read junk, and the other is the one the faculty wives have. They always seem to be reading books I've never heard of, by writers I've never heard of. I suppose they're relevant."

"Relevant?" I said.

"There you go again."

So that became our project, what my mother named the Gulden Girls Book Group. We went down to Duane's Book Store that afternoon, one of those September afternoons that feel like deepest August, warm and dank and slightly overcast, the trees dipping to meet the dusty sidewalks. We bought two paperback copies of each of three books: *Pride and Prejudice, Great Expectations,* and *Anna Karenina.* And when we came home we arranged them carefully on the shelves in the den, both of us stepping back for a moment to see how they looked, as though they were a sort of still life.

Those books gave shape to our days, those first few months. They were distinct from the chemotherapy regimen, although we always took books with us when we went to the hospital to wait, and my mother often read while she was lying on the recliner as the chemicals dripped slowly, tiny raindrops into the tributaries of her body. And when I had spent sufficient time each day on the small everyday chores of laundry and vacuuming I found so tedious, she would call out to me: "Time to read."

"What a great thing," said Jules when we talked on the phone. "She trumped you at your own game. Not to mention the professor."

"Jules, the thing you do that I hate is that you read a hundred times more into everything than it deserves. We bought books. We're reading books. We'll talk about books. So what? I never said she was stupid."

"Thanks for sharing that, hon. I never thought she was. And what I meant was that she probably figured you'd be bored and she'd look at you being bored and it would remind her of why you were there. But instead she found something that will guarantee that you won't be bored. Very smart. Very smart."

I wish Jules had met my mother, but somehow I had never arranged for them to get to know one another. Both of them were smarter than I was about people. But they only spoke once on the phone when I was out grocery shopping. I remember afterward that I asked Jules what they'd talked about. "Tie-dyeing," she said. To this day I am not sure whether she was kidding.

One afternoon my mother and I packed our books, took a picnic up to River View Park, and spread an old quilt on the grass on a rise from which you could see all of Langhorne. The Montgomery River ran below us, a sluggish strip of brown with ailanthus trees growing on its banks. Off to one side, behind a stand of pines, were the public tennis courts, always cracked, always crowded. Across the river was the campus of Langhorne College, concentric circles of construction—the stout Gothic of the thirties, the characterless hotel architecture of the fifties, the newly built science building a blinding wall of glass. At their center was the enormous red brick turreted mansion that had once belonged to Samuel Langhorne, where he had lived with a stout and rather jolly-looking wife whose portrait, black satin and pearls, hung over the mantel in the reception area of the administration building. Her name was Minnie, and they had no children, which, as a child, I had thought rather sad. But that was how the college came to exist, its motto being something in Latin that, in translation, meant "all our children."

The classroom buildings hung over the river from a high and stony bluff. Behind them the campus fell away to the dormitories, a scattering of ugly little houses, and a rock quarry out of sight just beyond the back gates. Two footbridges and a one-lane bridge for cars linked it to town, and when the admissions office gave directions to prospective applicants and, more important, their parents, they always brought them that way instead of the direct route off the highway and past the quarry and a truck-storage depot. Langhorne was a fine but somewhat obscure small liberal arts college, a kind of poor relation of the Swarthmores and the Haverfords, and driving through Langhorne proper was more calculated to win hearts and minds.

Sitting cross-legged on the quilt, we ate chicken sandwiches and cucumber salad with red onion. Except for the hint of scalp beneath her sunlit hair and some lines that had appeared around her mouth, my mother looked fine. She took my arm when, as now, we had to walk over rougher ground, but she did it lightly, affectionately, to make it seem companionable rather than necessary. When we'd eaten blueberries I lay on the blanket rereading *Pride and Prejudice* and my mother worked on a needlepoint design of sunflowers on a blue background. Then she took out her book and I took a nap.

It was a beautiful day, the day of that picnic. The sun warmed our arms and legs, but there was a breeze, too, that ruffled the pages of my book. A tennis ball, bright against the tumbled browns and deep greens of the hillside, skittered by and bounced away over the edge of the outcropping, down toward the river below.

I woke as it went past, sweaty and cramped, curled on the quilt in the fading sun. I thought of the time Jon and I had gone skinny-dipping just below this spot one summer night, then made love beneath the low-hanging branches of some bush. There had been a full moon, and after I was finished but before he was, as he still moved above me, his half-breath half-grunt the only sound in the still night air—*uh uh uh uh*—I lay with my head turned sideways and saw stray balls all around, tennis balls, a Wiffle ball with its plastic scored by plastic bats, even a golf ball from the driving range past the tennis courts.

There was nothing erotic about the memory. I had had twigs in my hair, and an old knotty root made a tear on my thigh, and when I mentioned the balls afterward Jon became sulky, accused me of being sexually remote. But I felt lonely remembering it. I looked out across the river to the college and wondered where my father was now, and knew that if I asked my mother she would know, would have memorized his class schedule as she did every semester.

But she was the one who brought him up and broke the silence. She was staring across the river, her eyes vacant. Then she said, "I remember this book. I was reading it when I met your father. I remember admiring it but being a little put off by it, too, because it does that cheap thing that people do, it makes the sister who is sweet and domestic and good a second fiddle to the one who is smart and outspoken. Jane and Elizabeth. I remember them now. It didn't seem fair to me, that Jane was so good and yet Elizabeth is the one who is admired."

"I suppose that's Austen fighting back. She was that kind of woman and she knew that it was the sweet and good girl who was esteemed in society, not the one like Elizabeth who speaks out."

"But Jane Austen should have known better than to make women into that kind of either-or thing—"

"Do you really think she does that?"

"Yes, I do. It happened in another book, too." She looked out over the river again. "*Little Women*," she said after a moment. "There was the sister who was the writer, and the one who had babies."

"Jo and Meg," I said.

"It's all the same," she said. "Women writers of all people should know better than to pigeonhole women, put them in little groups, the smart one, the sweet one. Women professors do it at the college, too, at faculty teas and things." My mother pitched her voice low and looked from under her brows. " 'Oh, you keep house—how turrrribly innnnterresting.' " She laughed, but I did not.

"Perhaps Austen just meant them as prototypes," I said.

"No, they're real enough, both of them, Jane and Elizabeth. Jane admires Elizabeth, and Elizabeth admires herself."

"Not true," I said. "Elizabeth admires Jane plenty."

"Really? Where? When you're reading it this time pay attention to that, show me where, tell me if you still believe it when the book is done."

"I thought you'd said you'd already read this book."

As though I had not spoken she went on: "I remember how relieved I was to see that they all had names I could pronounce. I'd just finished reading some Russian novels and the names drove me crazy. There'd be these long names in *War and Peace* and I'd just skip over them. Does that surprise you?"

"I think most people do that."

"I didn't mean about the names. I meant that I read the Russian novelists."

"No," I said. It did.

"When I was your age, or a little earlier I suppose it was, because when I was your age I already had you, I used to go over to the library at Columbia when I wasn't working at the dry-cleaning shop. I'd read for hours. My parents gave me off from ten to two most days and I went over there and studied. I think in the back of my mind I thought it would be a substitute for not going to college. I found a reading list for freshman English once and I read all the books on it, although afterward your father said most of them were no good."

"But you didn't meet him in the library."

"I met him at the cleaners. He had one sports jacket, a navy blue blazer, and he brought it in. It had a big spot of tomato sauce on it from the Italian restaurant on Amsterdam Avenue, and my mother made that clicking noise with her mouth she used to make when a customer brought in something really dirty. He told a funny story about taking a girl to that restaurant, the daughter of his thesis adviser I think it was, and having her father walk in the door and hitting his fork with his elbow and getting sauce all over them both. That episode killed the romance. Or I did."

"Grandma and Grandpa must have been wonderful chaperones."

"All your grandmother said when he brought the jacket in was 'Ready Tuesday.' But I kept reading in the library until he recognized me and then I kept reading in the library until he took me out to the Hungarian bakery for coffee and I kept reading in the library until he took me to the Italian restaurant. His hair was all black then, and he was thinner, but not much. He was very handsome."

"Still is."

"Yes." My father's regular features had lost flesh in some places, sagged in others, his rather thin mouth becoming more of a liability as the parentheses of middle age appeared around it. He was the male equivalent of that handsome woman about whom people say, "She must have been a beauty when she was younger."

"And he was so smart," my mother added. "The moment he opened his mouth you knew how smart he was." She looked from the river to me and she smiled, a smile so full of remembered joy that it hurt my heart to see it. "I leaned across the restaurant table and said, 'I would be the ideal faculty wife.' And when I leaned back, all red in the face, or at least that's what George said, hair red, face vermilion, he said, I leaned back and the entire front of my pink turtleneck was covered with tomato sauce."

"You never told me this!"

"You never asked."

"Oh, Mama, that's a smartass answer," I said.

"Was it?" my mother said, brightening. "Smartass?"

"Definitely smartass. And are you saying that that's it, that that's why he married you, because you asked him?"

"Oh, Ellie," she said ruefully, as though she was surprised I didn't understand something so simple, "I imagine he married me because I reminded him of his mother."

I thought back to my Gulden grandparents, who had run a summer camp in the mountains of New York State. Both of them were dead now, but when I was a little girl I had gone to them for the two weeks before school started, after the children from Long Island and Manhattan and Connecticut had gone home from camp, sunburnt and covered with mosquito bites. I had wandered through the reeds around the horseback-riding paddock picking up the arrows gone astray from archery and bringing them to my grandfather, a strong, quiet man with forearms that stretched the seams on his short-sleeved Banlon shirts so the stitches showed.

My grandmother was different. She looked like my father, lithe and fine-featured, and she sat on a rock while I hunted for crayfish in the creek and let me bake baking-powder biscuits with a thumb-print filled with jam in the center of each one. She smelled of roses and flour, sang Christmas carols at bedtime, braided my hair each morning and tied it with bits of yarn left over from arts and crafts.

"I guess I can see that," I said.

"I remember liking what I read of *Pride and Prejudice,* only wishing that it could be told from Jane's point of view. Your father said that would have made for a very dull book. Your father never really liked to talk shop when he got home. Except with you, of course, but that's different. I think he thinks of that as part of your education. Sometimes when I listen to the two of you I feel like a Little League player listening to the Yankees."

"Oh, come on."

"I don't mind. It's interesting."

"That's not how I would describe it."

"How would you describe it?"

"It's tiring," I found myself saying, "staying on top of your game."

The breeze was stronger now, blowing the pages of the book and lifting one corner of the quilt. Downstream I could see two children playing beneath the footbridge as I had done when I was small, pitching stones into the water.

"It's a mistake to base your entire life on one man's approval," my mother added quietly.

"It was the way women lived when you got married," I said.

"I was talking about you, Ellie," she said.

"Jonathan and I don't have that kind of relationship."

"I wasn't talking about Jonathan," she said.

We grew quiet again. The carillon across the river that Samuel Langhorne built to foster a sense of spirituality on campus rang out "Amazing Grace." When it stopped, "was blind but now I see," hung in the air for a moment like a cloud.

"Why didn't you finish the book the first time?" I finally said, the notes dying like the sun going down.

My mother wrapped her hand around the paperback in her lap and held it to her chest. Her knuckles gleamed like four round white stones in the pale yellow light. "I left my copy at City Hall the day I married your father," she said. "It was a library book, too. I had to pay to have it replaced."

"I'm not sure how this book-club thing works," I said. "When we're done, do we set up some time for discussion?"

"Wasn't that what we were just doing?" my mother said.

"No, I mean about theme and character and that sort of thing."

"Wasn't that what we were just doing?" she repeated.

"So we talk as we go along?"

"Why not?" my mother said.

"And when do we move on to the next one?"

"Ellen," she said, laughing, putting the book down and picking up her needlepoint, "for an intelligent girl you need an awful lot of direction. We'll go on to the next one when we're finished with the one we have."

My parents met and married in 1967, and though we later came to think of the 1960s as a time of great upheaval and liberation, the truth was that for them the upheavals came later, in their everyday lives. They were married at City Hall, took the subway downtown to Chambers Street, and were back in time for my father's four o'clock tutorial.

My mother went back to work in her parents' dry cleaners on Broadway, but after she locked up that night she went up to my father's one-room apartment at 135th Street, climbed into his bed, and next morning began to make curtains out of sheets. She cooked casseroles on a hot plate. They even had dinner parties, my mother once told me, chili and garlic bread balanced on the laps of half-a-dozen starving students.

By the time the Upper West Side was rife with consciousness-raising groups and faculty members were shedding their twin-set Smithy wives in favor of graduate students with short skirts and long hair, my parents were on their way to Princeton and then Langhorne, one a place in which change came slowly, the other a place in which it came hardly at all.

I was a clever child, with the ceaseless goad stabbing away deep inside me that comes from being the eldest child of a clever parent. While my mother drove us to swimming lessons and taught us to string stale cranberries for the Christmas tree and scolded us for using vulgar language and laughed at our knock-knock jokes, my father's distance was as seductive as his smile.

Nothing changed when my mother became sick. If anything my father was more distant than ever, and more mannered in his manner when he arrived. "What ho, crew?" he would say, putting his briefcase on the bench near the door. Or "You've never looked lovelier," he would say to my mother, bending over her hand, and she would reply, as she always did, "Oh, Lord, Gen," the pet name she had invented years before, shorthand for Gentleman George. Often my mother was already in bed when he got home. Sometimes, when I heard him quietly close the kitchen door long after night had fallen, I felt as though I was losing both my parents at the same moment, although I did not feel in the slightest like a child. I saw them with the cold eye of the adult now.

One night shortly after my mother and I had had our picnic and formed our book club, my father and I found ourselves together in the dark and sweet-smelling living room, with its bowls of homemade potpourri. Looking up from *Pride and Prejudice* and the circle of golden light cast by the reading lamp, I finally said, "Why am I doing this alone?"

"Doing what alone, may I ask?"

"Tending to your wife."

His mouth got very thin, and his voice very English, a prelude to meanness. "My wife? My wife? That woman is your mother. I have sat here hundreds of times watching her do for you, care for you, cook for you—"

"And for you," I said, refusing to be shamed.

"Ellen," he said, "I have to earn a living. To pay the mortgage. To pay the medical bills. Your mother understands."

"Is reconciled, you mean."

"You know nothing about it." He picked up my book and raised his eyebrows. "Haven't you read this a hundred times?"

"Apparently this is the book your wife gave up to marry you," I said.

"You've lost me."

"We've formed a book club. Mama wanted to read *Pride and Prejudice*. She started it at Columbia and stopped reading it the day you two got married."

"I don't recall that she liked Austen very much."

"That's not really accurate. She thinks Austen is condescending to women. Especially women with more conventional characters and expectations than those of Elizabeth Bennet."

My father shrugged. "Jane Bennet is as satisfied with her lot as any young woman in nineteenth-century fiction, as you well know."

"I'm not sure I remember," I said. "Now that I'm a housewife I've got other things to think about. Floor wax. Ironing. Which brings us back to our original discussion."

"Which seemed to me particularly futile. You and I have different roles to play here."

"I don't like mine."

"It won't last forever."

"That is a low blow," I said.

"Ellen, there is no reason for the two of us to be at cross-purposes. Your mother needs help. You love her. So do I."

"Show it," I said.

"Pardon me?"

"Show it. Show up. Do you grieve? Do you care? Do you ever cry? And how did you let her get to this point in the first place? When she first felt sick, why didn't you force her to go to the doctor?"

"Your mother is a grown woman," he said.

"Sure she is. But wasn't it really that you didn't want your little world disrupted, that you needed her around to keep everything running smoothly? Just like now you need me around because she can't. You bring me here and drop me down in the middle of this mess and expect me to turn into one kind of person when I'm a completely different kind and to be a nurse and a friend and a confidante and a housewife all rolled up in one."

"Don't forget being a daughter. You could always be a daughter."

"Oh, Papa, don't try to make me feel guilty. What about being a husband?"

"That is none of your business. That is between your mother and me." He rubbed his eyes with the flat of his hands. "These days at the beginning of term are very tiring. And I don't have the energy for anger." And he disappeared into the dark of the hallway and up the stairs. His voice came out of the black, disembodied, a kind of Cheshire Cat without the smile. "Don't forget," he added, "I take the night shift."

As I stood up to turn out the lights and go to bed I glanced at the picture of the three of us on the piano. I saw my mother's glowing face, and thought of how she had made it possible for my father to believe that his world would be effortlessly cared for because she had, seemingly effortlessly, cared for it. I was beginning to understand the effort in the care now, and that made me angry, to know how she had pretended that he had a job and she had something so much less. And it made me fearful, too, of the future. The essential differences between my mother and me seemed less essential, now that I could see her sitting in the library at Columbia, reading her way through the classics. She had given that up for my father, and she had deferred to him ever since, it was true. But now I understood how easy it was to do what he required, particularly in the service of what seemed a worthy cause.

I looked down at the three of us in the photograph, frozen in brilliant color beneath a sunny blue Cambridge sky. And I wondered how much I, too, had made possible my father's unthinking primacy. Or was it their marriage I safeguarded, my mother ever sweet-tempered without the demands of my father's intellectual arrogance, my father still enamored of his wife because he had another companion for his life of the mind? How providential that most children left home when they did, before they were wise enough to understand their parents.

"You'll feel better in the morning," I said aloud, and as I stared at the picture it became abstract, a blur of color and light, subject to a hundred interpretations. Then I stepped back and it rearranged itself into what it had always been, a still life of happiness. My eyes were dry and sandy. I felt tired and sapped, as though I had been living here like this my whole life. As indeed I had, looking for myself in the space between the two of them.

I felt undone by that night's exchange with my father, as undone as I had been the day, years before, when I first began to understand that it was not only his work that kept him on the Langhorne campus long after classes were done for the day. Langhorne, too, had a library, though not as large and distinguished as Columbia's. There was something churchlike about it, with its long and narrow stained-glass windows commemorating Shakespeare's heroines and its plain benches flanking the big oak tables. I, too, went there to fill in the gaps in my public school education with ambitious social studies projects and papers on Conrad and Melville that were half cribbed from literary criticism texts.

I don't know what brought my father to the library one afternoon when I was working there, at a table with a gaggle of girls doing a group project deconstructing T. S. Eliot's *Four Quartets*. But I heard them clearly once he had stalked down the center aisle and into the stacks: the divine Professor G, one said, and who is it now, said another, since his teaching assistant went to Colby?, and I'd do him, said one with curly black hair and a big gap between her front teeth.

No, they squealed, and a boy scratching away at a legal pad with a stack of reference books in front of him turned to glare at them. He's old, he's married, he grades so hard, they whispered.

He's my father, I thought.

I could imagine the man he was to them, because I had seen that man myself, though rarely at home, where, it occurred to me, he rested up for the hard work of becoming that George Gulden, the lover, the dazzler, the charmer. I find it difficult to talk about my father's charm today without reducing it to something akin to a snake in a basket and a fakir with a flute, talking about it the way you talk about drinking when you've been sober for years and all you can remember about a beer is what it was like to wrap your arms around the toilet at three A.M. and catch the sanctifying smell of bowl freshener as you threw up.

But it was a real true thing. My father was cordial to men, albeit intent on making his word known, his word law, but to women he was courtly and so warm he appeared to be courting even the elderly and the very young. "My dear Mrs. Duane," he would say as he stepped to the counter in the bookstore, "where might I find *In Cold Blood*? Your help will serve, not only me personally, but an entire generation of impressionable students who think of Truman Capote as a guest on *The Dick Cavett Show*. And, by the by, if the jacket of that new Norman Mailer stacked in the window fades, will you consider pitching them all as a service to mankind, or, in deference to the head of women's studies, who buys those copies of Germaine Greer you persist in ordering, a service to humankind?"

Mrs. Duane was a sophisticated woman, the widow of a former State Department official who had remarried and moved to the country from an apartment on one of the museum blocks off Fifth Avenue. But she was helpless before the stream of pleasantries that my father could pour from the pitcher of that personality. I had watched her once shift a huge stack of *The Canterbury Tales* from one wall to another because my father had complained about finding them in the short-story section. "I would say, George, that you had the gift of blarney if only you were Irish," she had said more than once. "I have gemütlichkeit," said my father, "that's what it is, whatever it is, be it some rich fruit dessert with clotted cream or a disease of the pancreas, I have it and it is yours. Have you the book?"

"I have," Mrs. Duane said. And if she hadn't, she would have gotten it.

He did this with me, too, when he remembered, although never once after I had come home to care for my mother. I can still remember how he taught me the ABCs in the evening before bed, when we were living in a small two-bedroom apartment on a back street far from the university in Princeton and I saw him on weekdays only when I was bathed and brushed and perfect in my long eyelet nightgowns. (My mother made those nightgowns. "I cannot for the life of me find a decent nightgown for a little girl anywhere!" she would say to her small group of faculty wives, who were perfectly satisfied to put their own children into Mickey Mouse pajamas or Doctor Dentons.) "*A* is for Aaaah-aaaah-aaaah-CHOOOOOO!" he would sneeze. "*B* is for blunderbuss. *C* is for cancan dancers kicking up their heels for Toulouse-Lautrec in the fin de siècle." And so on until we got to *Z*, which was for Zsa Zsa Gabor. No one said Zsa Zsa like my papa.

Sometimes, particularly if one of my girlfriends was in the car, he would sing "Let's Call the Whole Thing Off" or recite slightly dirty limericks or compliment the girl extravagantly on an ACT LOCALLY, THINK GLOBALLY T-shirt ("Can human understanding surpass the sentiments now beating within—whoops, atop—your breast?") Of course, they loved it all. "My father sits in the car and farts and tells me to shut up while he gets the sports scores off the radio," said Jennifer Buckley, whose father owned a company that built supermarkets and public schools. "Your father knew one day that I was wearing Giorgio. Excuse me, but no contest."

But a man who can identify perfume on an eleventh grader sitting in the back seat of his car may have certain shortcomings as a father. One night in December, home for Christmas my first year at Harvard, I went to his office, high in one corner of an old limestone building that houses the English department and its classrooms. Grandma Nina had called from Florida, telling my mother in Polish that Grandpa had had a stroke and that the doctors believed he was going to die. The phones at the college were out of order because of a winter ice storm, some cables down, and so I took the footbridge, holding tight to the railings as the wind made the walkway sway, trying not to look at the cold river below, the water high on its banks.

The guard waved me through, and when I got to the fourth floor the office door was closed, but I could hear sounds from within, moans, the thump of the old springs on my father's shabby leather couch. "God, Beth," I heard, even through the closed door. "Jesus Christ, Beth." Beth was the name of a fierce feminist American history professor who was visiting from Rutgers. This is so banal, I thought to myself, using one of my father's favorite words, so banal, people do this all the time. Carefully and quietly I took a sheet of stationery from the desk of the department secretary and wrote "Your wife wants you." But I stood there and listened for a long time before I slid it under the door. Even now, all these years later, it gives me a sick feeling to think of it.

I don't know whether my father knew I knew. Our relationship underwent a change after that. I was less supplicant, more judge, and I was a person who, when called upon to judge, always judged harshly. A girl once dropped out of our creative writing seminar at Harvard because we had to read aloud and then talk about one another's work, and after four sessions she could not bear, she told the instructor, to hear what I would do to her stories, based on what I had done to others. I was unrepentant when the instructor told me this. "That's her problem, isn't it?" I said.

I judged my father just that harshly, or maybe more so because I'd imagined he had adjudged me wanting for so long and in so many ways. But nothing seemed to have changed between my parents, then or ever. And it was much later that I made the connection between what had happened and my enduring love affair with Jonathan, in which I wanted and hated him in relatively equal parts. When we went back to Cambridge after that Christmas vacation, Jonathan was amazed to discover the things I had now decided to do when we were in bed together. And not just in bed—I once slid my hand into his lap and inside his fly during an art history lecture, an explication of the Arnolfini wedding portrait, those two whey-faced people in elaborate robes preparing for a tedious eternity together. It is amazing to me now how far I was willing to go to mimic my father. It would make an interesting case for any psychiatrist.

We never spoke of what had happened, my father and I. The closest we ever got was when I came home six months later for summer vacation. I told my father of an encounter I had had with a professor in the Harvard graduate English department, who was also a novelist of some note, after I sent him some stories of mine. He had not liked the stories, I could tell by his careful and rather empty comments, although he had told me he had never seen brown eyes quite as dark as mine—"really, truly black!" he fake-marveled. I knew after only a year at school that this was clumsy code for "Be friendly and I'll take you to dinner and to bed."

I told my father of how, looking at my name at the top of each page, he had said, "There was a George Gulden in my grad school group. He was a smart guy but kind of a pain in the ass. He just dropped off the face of the earth after he got his degree."

We both knew what that remark was code for, my father and I, as we sat eating vegetable lasagna and Caesar salad, but he did not flinch and I told the story casually. My mother turned away, turned to the stove, and Jeff and Brian gaped. My father smiled thinly and said, "He's a very poor writer, and he was a very poor doctoral candidate. Did he like your stories?"

I didn't answer, and my father smiled again, knowing what that was code for. I remembered I had answered the writer in my mind, had imagined saying, with hauteur, turning away his offer of another beer, "He's my father. And you're an asshole." I imagined myself stalking out and leaving my manuscript on the table. Instead I had ducked my head and said nothing, took my stories and walked home in a driving rain, so that the manila envelope was the consistency of cereal by the time I got inside my dorm room. Jon was waiting on the bed in his underwear, reading a biography of Jefferson. "Did you sleep with him?" he asked. "You are a pig, Jonathan," I said, dumping my ruined manuscript in the basket. "Yeah, but I'm your pig," he said, crooking his finger at me, and over I went again.

Hospitals are a little like the beach. The next wave comes in, and the footprints of your pain and suffering, your delivery and recovery, are obliterated; the sheets are changed. But transient as it all is, if I went to Montgomery Medical Center today it would be a kind of homecoming, although one of the small desires of my life is that I never ever see the place again, its awkward red-brick bulk, its tiered parking garage and automatic double doors.

For four months it was our sometime world, where my mother saw her doctor and had what she still preferred to call her treatments. Its floors were covered with gray linoleum speckled with white and black so aggressively ordinary as to be offensive; its intercom interruptions and the glass-fronted cabinets filled with pointed things became the backdrop of our life together.

Off one of the corridors that fanned out from the lobby we waited in molded plastic chairs to be ushered into a cubicle where the closest thing my mother had to salvation, before morphine became her saving grace, could flow slowly into her veins and try to kill off the cells run amok. They'd wanted her to check herself into the hospital for the chemotherapy but she'd refused, and so I brought her every three weeks and we spent the day amid the sharp smells and clamor of the outpatient unit.

They'd made it pretty, the chemo cubicle, with flowered wallpaper and a bright blue leatherette recliner. Even the chemicals were somehow decorative, the crystalline bags glimmering silver in the overhead light of the windowless room. It took almost the whole day to get it all in, drop by drop by God-please-let-it-work drop.

Oh yes, I prayed in that cubicle and in the hallway outside and in the cafeteria, where I went as much to shake off the feeling of being buried alive that I felt in that tiny room as because I really wanted another cup of coffee. But I prayed to myself, without form, only inchoate feelings, one word: please, please, please, please, please.

My mother made me wait outside when she was examined by her doctor. She was a rather fierce-looking woman, Dr. Cohn, with the strong and handsome face that you see on old coins. She wore simple sheath dresses of slate blue or taupe or dull prints, as though they were bought mainly because they were unobtrusive beneath a white coat. I remember how firm her handshake was, so definite, like everything else about her. I thought she was rather cold, but since then, since I've gotten to know more oncologists, I realize that she only had the slight wariness that so many have, faced as they are so often with certain failure.

Certainly Dr. Cohn was kind to my mother. She always came downstairs to visit during her chemotherapy, took her hand, and talked with her quietly about her symptoms as the chemicals did their methodical drip-drip dance.

"There's platinum in this stuff, Ellen," my mother said, smiling, during the second round, "just like in my wedding ring. That's why my mouth tastes like tin."

"Is it working?" I said.

"I can't say how well it's working yet," Dr. Cohn said. "I'll be doing some tests and I'd like to hear how well you felt, Kate, after the first time."

"She threw up the entire next day. Everything. Every bit of food she ate. And when that was gone she had the dry heaves. Plus her hair is starting to come out all over her pillow."

Dr. Cohn's smile was so faint that it was little more than a pucker at the corners of her mouth. "Those aren't unexpected side effects. But I'd like to hear from Kate about how she's feeling."

"It's not too bad. I do hate the tinny taste. I'm losing weight, although I never thought I'd see that as a problem. And my hair looks pretty awful." My mother ran her fingers through her thinning red curls.

"Oh, come on, Mama. You must have thrown up ten times the last time."

"Any pain?" said Dr. Cohn.

"Nothing to speak of," said my mother.

"Are you sure?" I said.

"Ellen," said my mother.

When Dr. Cohn left I followed her out into the hallway. Her stride was long, and I had to hustle to catch up with her.

"Doctor, I really feel at a loss here. I don't know enough about what they found during her hospital stays. I don't know enough about her prognosis, about what to expect. I really need ten or fifteen minutes of your time."

She put a hand beneath my elbow. "Come," she said, and walked me back down the hall.

"Privately," I added.

"I won't do that," she said evenly. "This is your mother's illness. She deserves to be part of any discussions we have about it." She pushed open the door and walked over to the cubicle.

"Kate," she said, and my mother opened her eyes and smiled. "Ellen has some questions about your condition and I wonder whether you'd like me to answer them now or to see you both upstairs later?"

"What kind of questions?" my mother said, and for a moment I could not answer.

"About where the cancer started. About whether it's spreading. About what comes next."

My mother looked into Dr. Cohn's eyes and not mine as she answered. She recited like a child called to give an answer in class. "The scan showed it was in the liver. And maybe in the ovaries, too, although they can't find that on the scans. There's something in the blood test that makes them think maybe the ovaries are involved. The doctor in the city who looked at the pictures and the slides and gave us a second opinion said that's highly unusual but not unheard of. Do I have it right so far?"

"Exactly," said Dr. Cohn.

"What else, Ellen?" my mother asked.

"I just feel as if I need to be filled in."

"On what?"

I knew what I would have said if the doctor and I had been in the hallway together. I would have said: how long? I would have asked: how bad? I would have wanted a blow-by-blow of disintegration, the road to death. But I could not ask the questions with my mother there. I suspected she already knew the answers, that she'd wanted the same ones I did, and wanted to keep them to herself.

"That's all," I said. "I'm going down to the cafeteria for coffee." Dr. Cohn followed me out.

"I'm the kind of person who likes to know things," I said.

"So is your mother," the doctor said. "Why don't you ask her about some of them?"

Suddenly I stopped and snapped my fingers. "I just thought of something," I said. "My mother's parents owned a dry-cleaning shop. Do you think the chemicals there could have caused this?"

"Your father asked the same thing," Dr. Cohn said.

"And?"

"And your mother said 'What does it matter now?' "

The only time I saw my mother break down during those weeks was when we were passing through the lobby just as a woman was rising from a wheelchair at the automatic doors, turning to take a sleeping newborn from the arms of a nurse to carry it out to a waiting car. The baby's hand was splayed on the swaddling, a pink star, and my mother's mouth began to work as she stood and watched mother and child move through the doors. "Ah," she breathed, and she pressed a tissue to her face.

Within weeks she knew the names of all the nurses, their family backgrounds, the ages of their children. As she waited they would smile and say her name: Good morning, Kate, how are you? Just a moment more and we'll get you in. And naturally, the county being what it was, they knew us. One of them had a son who had gone to school with my brother Jeff. Another had a daughter on scholarship at Langhorne. "She says your father is one of the best professors there," she said. "She says when you get an *A* from him it really means something."

"She is absolutely right," my mother said.

"I remember when you won the essay contest," said a nurse named Gina as she ran a needle into the catheter the doctors had implanted just above my mother's heart so that the nurses wouldn't have to hunt around for veins. "The Port-A-Cath will be a lifesaver later," she'd said to me. "For the morphine."

"The morphine?" I'd asked.

"Well," she'd said, looking down at a tray of instruments, "maybe not."

Usually the two of us were alone, but one morning, I remember, there was an elderly woman who described in detail her hip replacement and the subsequent convalescence which had cast a long shadow over her life. Finally, almost as an afterthought, she asked my mother why she was there. "I need a chest X ray for a life-insurance policy," my mother replied.

"If I had told her the truth, I would have been there forever," my mother said after her treatment was done that day.

The woman could not have been from Langhorne, or she would have known about my mother's illness. Everyone in town did. They were all a little too bright, a little too chatty when she went to Phelps's hardware or the supermarket. "How nice that Ellen's home," they said, but no one asked what I was doing there, because they already knew. "How well you look, Kate," they lied. Lord, I thought, what a shock it would be if any of them ever had the guts to lean across a counter and say, "How's the cancer?" But despite the scarves and hats my mother began to wear over the ruin of her pretty curls, despite how thin she became, I never heard the word "cancer," not ever, until after the cancer was gone.

The only person who used the word was Mrs. Forburg, my senior English teacher. One day soon after I came home I received a note in the mail addressed to me in her angular vertical script. It was short and straightforward, just as she was. "Ellen dear," she wrote, "I think of you fondly and often, not only because of your mother's illness but because of your own responsibilities. Would you come to dinner soon? My own mother died of cancer when I was young and perhaps we could be of help to each other. All love, Brenda Forburg."

I tucked it in a corner of my desk blotter and took it out from time to time to call. But there never seemed to be the time.

For despite the chemotherapy, and the days afterward when I could hear her heaving pitiably in the master bathroom, despite the weekly blood tests and exams, I suspect that my mother would have said that those were wonderful and full months for her. She and her daughter finally had the relationship she had always imagined would accompany the canopy she had made for the four-poster bed in the attic bedroom, the scrapbooks she kept of report cards and literary magazine poems, the hours she spent on birthday parties and Care packages to college and camp.

We went to the movies, took a day trip to the beach, ate lunch a few times at little restaurants whose ads she had clipped from magazines and newspapers. She got tired very easily, and once or twice the way she breathed made me frightened. But she refused to be housebound, or to let me be.

"What exactly are you doing all day?" Jules asked one night

when she called to regale me with the stupidity and arrogance of the Yale man who had my former job.

"I'm being a girlfriend," I said.

"Picking over the perfidy of men?"

"Shopping," I replied.

I suppose today that I should say that those months were wonderful for me, too, a chance to make amends for a lifetime of taking for granted. The truth is that while it was happening I tolerated it, and when I thought about it I hated it all. In the beginning I thought it was because of all that I was missing, because of the life just an hour away that was passing me by, in the city where you could become yesterday's girl in a weekend.

But it was more complicated than that, and simpler, too. As my mother guided me to the right sort of wax for the cherry bowfront chest or sent me out to buy cheese or berries, I felt as though I was sinking beneath the weight of a life I had always viewed with something even more dismissive than contempt, a life I had viewed as though it were a feature in *National Geographic*, the anachronistic traditions of a distant tribe.

It was a world without men, too, with my brothers gone away and my father scarcely there, letting my mother take care of her own disintegration as she'd taken care of her house, her children, the life which she had devoted to him.

"I know what you're saying," I told Jules. "I know someday I'll be able to walk away from this. But what if I just get back into it again? What if I marry Jon and it turns out that what he really expects is a suburban matron who knits sweaters for his children?"

"What Jon will want in his first wife is the kind of woman who runs charity luncheons and hires good staff. His second wife will be the trophy wife, the one who designs jewelry or something and wears leather pants."

"You've just reduced three lives to a set of clichés," I said. "And one of them is mine."

"True clichés, El. And I'm betting that one of them won't be yours. I know you don't like me to cast aspersions on Jon, but how often has he called you? How often has he written? When will he come to visit? Your mother needs you and you need him and he's nowhere to be found."

Jules was right; Jon had called only twice since I had come home. But I did not care much. The Ellen Jon knew was the other Ellen, the one who always shone with the luster of success. The Ellen who sat in the hospital corridor with Kate Gulden was inevitably a loser; after all her triumphs, this endeavor was doomed to failure.

One afternoon in early October we went to the big mall outside of town and across the racks at one store my mother saw a woman who had once been part of the group that decorated the village green for holidays—the Minnies, they called themselves, after the childless Mrs. Langhorne.

"Oh, Ellen, do you remember Sheila Fenner? She was in the Minnies when you were in high school."

"And I miss it," said Mrs. Fenner. "But I'm a working woman now, and there's no time for anything but the grandkids and Bill's dinner, and even that comes out of the microwave. But look at you, Kate, you're a shadow. When did you lose so much weight? You're a bone."

"Oh, you know," said my mother shrugging. "Running around. Keeping up with Ellen."

"Weight Watchers?" said Mrs. Fenner archly.

My mother looked at me sideways. She knew what I would say if left to my own devices: "No, Mrs. Fenner, it's the chemotherapy plan. A delicious shake for breakfast, one for lunch, an IV in your chest at teatime, and before you know it you weigh ninety pounds."

"No," said my mother, "I hate those plans. The food is just awful."

"Well, it's nice to see you," Mrs. Fenner said. "And Ellen. Jill said she saw your byline in a magazine a while ago. That must be terribly exciting." I smiled. "Jill's husband is at Cornell Medical

School. I wish he'd finish up so they could get out of the city. I just worry terribly. Where do you live?"

"Greenwich Village," said my mother.

"Lovely. And how are the Minnies?" added Mrs. Fenner, in the slightly condescending way we speak of the lives whose usefulness we have outlived.

"I'm having them over for lunch next week," my mother said.

How I remember that lunch for the Minnies. Years later, when I was on call at the hospital, when my scalp began to feel rank and gritty and my face slack after a night of screaming and suffering and pleas for painkillers on the medical wards, I would try to gauge my fatigue and always I would come back to the same basis for comparison: I was as sweaty and drained as I had been at the end of the day I cooked for those women, the day I learned how much work it took to make lunch for ten, or at least to do it the way my mother did.

The day before, she sent me shopping, and when I returned she laid her ingredients out on the kitchen counter: the chickens, the zucchini, some cream, some carrots, I can't recall exactly what else. I was in the basement loading the dryer and I heard her making clanging noises, pulling pots and pans out of the lower cupboards, the tympani of my childhood. I could conjure up winter evenings at my desk, writing in my journal or taking notes on index cards, hearing that *crash-bang* and knowing that the engine of my world was running smoothly.

"I can do that," I said, as I came upstairs. My mother was squatting, the top half of her inside a cabinet, looking for a lid in the back. When she emerged she was clutching it triumphantly. "I should have redone this kitchen years ago," she said, getting to her feet, using the edge of the counter for support, panting a bit.

"I can do that," I repeated.

"You can make a chicken paillard and zucchini soup?" she said. She lifted her big stockpot onto a back burner and began to fill it with water from the tea kettle. "I should have redone it years ago," she said, as though to herself. "At least I would have had a sink deep enough to put a pot in." Then she turned, hand on her hip, narrowed her eyes and looked at me.

For just a moment she looked hard, calculating, as though she was sizing me up. Then she wiped her hands on a dish towel and sat down in one of the chairs at the oak table. She was wearing a big blue butcher's apron; she untied it, pulled it over her head, and handed it to me.

"The torch is passed," she said. "Take the chicken and put it into the pot with a carrot, some peppercorns, a stalk of celery and a handful of parsley and cover it with water. And put the kettle on for tea. You can't cook without tea."

It took me all afternoon to make that meal. She sat and gave instructions. I leaped back and screamed the first time I fed zucchini into the food processor and it let out a *chi-chi-chi* sound that made me think it would chew up my fingers. I mistakenly poured a mug of hot tea into the chicken stock. My mother just laughed. "At least it wasn't sugared," she said. "Leave it alone. They'll think it's some exotic new recipe if they notice at all."

At some point, I remember, I dropped into the chair opposite her, my face damp from the heat of the stove. "If you don't mind my asking," I said, "isn't there an easier way to do this? Don't people buy chicken broth in cans? Can't you get prechopped zucchini or something?"

"I don't think you can get prechopped zucchini, although you can certainly get chicken broth in cans," she said. "But I've always liked doing it this way. It tastes better and it makes me feel productive."

"Lord, Mama," I said. "You're the most productive person I know."

"Well, if you think that, it's because of all the things like this I did."

"But how did you do this when we were little? How did you have the time? Didn't we get in the way?"

"Not so much," she said, sipping at her tea. "You and Jeff were usually off someplace outside. And Brian would sit right here, on the floor, and cook with me. I would give him some flour and some water and he could sit here for hours and stir the whole mess together and sing 'Waltzing Matilda.' "

"I remember that," I said.

"The only problem I had was that you used to run away so often. That was mostly when we lived in Princeton. I'd be making stew or something and a squad car would pull up. After a while I got to know all the policemen. Do you remember that?"

"Not really," I said. "I remember you talking about it."

"One of them said to me, 'Well, Mrs. Gulden, this little girl is just on her way to somewhere else.' " She turned and looked at me, her eyes so bright, and then she smiled ruefully. "But Brian just sat and stirred his mess." There was a popping sound from the top of the stove. "You've got your stock too high," she added, and I sighed and got to my feet.

"I like the book club better," I said.

"So do I," my mother said.

"The Gulden Girls Book and Cook Club," I said, and she laughed. She looked so happy. But I noticed that when she lifted her mug of tea her hand trembled. You could hear her breathing a room away. And often, almost unconsciously, she rubbed at her lower back as though she had a pain there.

It was a good lunch; I remember that, too. Someone said that the soup had an unusual taste, and both my mother and I choked. "It's Ellen's secret recipe," my mother said.

The annual plan for the Christmas trees was made at that meeting; it took almost as much time as my stock to simmer and settle. Each year the Minnies decorated the twelve blue spruces that stood in a cluster at the end of Main Street. Each year they made dozens and dozens of balls and figures and garlands, and then they rose on ladders, all those women, like a construction crew, and turned the trees into the focal point of the town green. The mayor lit them and a choir sang carols.

The trees were a Langhorne tradition and were taken very seriously: if you lived in Langhorne and did not attend the tree lighting ceremony, everyone assumed you were too sick to stand, which is what I sensed the Minnies feared would happen to my mother in the six weeks before Christmas. One year a group of high school boys had picked the trees clean of their decorations in the middle of the night, and when school was dismissed that day there were two squad cars outside in the circular driveway. By next morning all the decorations were back on, and back on exactly where they had been when the Minnies had put them on.

"Now, what are our colors?" Linda Best, the district attorney's wife, said as she leaned her shelflike bosom on our mahogany dining-room table.

"I think red and gold this year," said Isabel Duane, eating her chicken in the European fashion, the tines of her fork turned down and her knife pushing bits of food onto their sharp silver points.

"Oh, not again," said Mrs. Byers. "Wasn't it just the year before last that we had red and gold?"

"You always do this, Caroline," Mrs. Duane said. "You always lump them all together. We haven't had red and gold for years."

"Oh, Kate," said Mrs. Byers, turning to my mother at the head of the table, "wasn't it just two years ago? Remember, because you used those angels with the big red robes and the gold trumpets? It was the year before last."

"Isabel's right," my mother said, a hand atop Caroline Byers's to cushion the blow. "Last year blue and silver; the year before was red and white. We haven't had red and gold since the year Ellen left for Harvard. I remember because I was making angels the first Thanksgiving she was home."

"How many years ago, Ellen?" Mrs. Best said.

"Five. Or six."

"So red and gold it is," Mrs. Duane said, with a little nod that said she'd known it would be so. Mrs. Byers frowned. "It seems done, somehow," she said with a sigh.

I could almost feel my mother relax at the other end of the table. She loved the tree decorating, and she had been deeply unhappy one year when some Minnie, now gone, moved to Florida or somewhere equally distant spiritually and physically, had prevailed upon the others to embrace a color scheme of blue and green. "Ugh," she had said whenever she sat down to work on her decorations that year.

My mother had one tree to do by herself, as she had for many years; she would not be moved by faint suggestions that she oversee the entire project. I thought of Dr. Cohn and her menorah. She would get one, I knew, made by my mother from a pattern in some magazine. Or she would get some other token, a sampler or a needlepoint pillow. I could imagine Dr. Cohn telling people who came to her office that a patient had once made it for her.

"Is George taking some time off?" Mrs. Best asked as they stood to leave after coffee and dessert.

"George?" my mother said. "He has more work than ever, with this new faculty tenure committee. And he's working on an article. You know how he is."

Mrs. Best's mouth narrowed to a thin line of bright coral lipstick. "Well, yes, so is Ed, but under the circumstances—"

"Linda, you will be late for the library meeting," Mrs. Duane interrupted. "And so will I, and I just won't." Mrs. Duane hugged my mother, and I saw my mother wince and wondered where it hurt. "Lovely lunch, Kate," Mrs. Duane said. "Lovely lunch, Ellen." And she cut her blue eyes toward Mrs. Best and made a horrid face. Then they all were gone.

"I'll clean up, Ellie," my mother said, but ten minutes later I found her asleep in the living room and I cleared the table and did the dishes myself. It had been a lovely lunch, but it had tired her. I hated Linda Best.

The leaves turned and floated down, commonplace to all but the children, who scuffed through them along the curbs in their school shoes on the way to the bus stop. We made Halloween treats, a quarter and a Tootsie Roll and a plastic witch riding a broom, all tied up in an orange napkin with a black ribbon. I learned how to make beef burgundy, although I nearly ruined it, and to fold napkins into swans. The tasks were both tedious and challenging, like diagramming complex sentences. "In the unlikely event that I become the overseer of an elegant household," I said, "I will have one company meal."

"Don't forget your zucchini soup," my mother said.

She told me stories of going to public school in New York when the schools were still good there, about riding a Schwinn her father bought secondhand in Riverside Park, about being forbidden to go to City College, which was all the dry-cleaner's daughter could afford, first because her father wanted to protect her from the Jews, then the blacks. She took out her past lives as though to look at each, fold it carefully, and put it between tissue paper in some cedar-scented bottom drawer.

She told me of how her brother Stevie, older by two years, had gone to Fort Benning on a bus to join the Army and how she had envied him the excitement, the trip down south, the communal life instead of the airless apartment with the tiny spotless kitchen, and finally the tissue-thin letters with the strange exotic stamps. She told me of how they finally brought him home from Vietnam in 1965.

"My mother said to the funeral-home director, 'Open the box.' Stevie's dress uniform was perfect, I don't think he'd worn it more than once or twice, but his poor face was so swollen that it was hard to tell it was him. And they'd powdered it over, but you could still see that it was a funny blue color, like a bruise. My mother looked at him and she said 'Steven' very quietly, and she touched his hand."

That was the only time my mother cried during October, that and in front of the television. At night sometimes we went through the television listings with a pencil, picking out old movies. We watched them with a bench in front of us, bowls filled with Styrofoam balls, pins, ribbons, sequins, so we could work on the Christmas decorations.

We watched *Waterloo Bridge*, saw Vivien Leigh jump to her death after descending into prostitution. We watched *Dark Victory*—Bette Davis blind—and *Now, Voyager*—Bette Davis beaten down. We watched *Stella Dallas* three times.

And cried and cried and cried and cried, blowing our noses into the tissues that stood amid the finished decorations. Or sometimes we cried at tragedies on the news shows, toddlers, as yellow as young pumpkins, who needed new livers, girls who left home to become Broadway hoofers and wound up as decapitated hookers, former child stars photographed with hidden cameras as they picked food from dumpsters. Mass murders, earthquakes, floods, fires—all took our minds off real tragedy for at least a little while.

We finished *Pride and Prejudice* and turned to *Great Expectations*. My mother thought Pip's admiration for Estella was unconvincing. "It's the weak link in just about every book I've ever read," she said one day, lying on the couch with the book on her lap, her raspy breathing punctuated with a barking cough. "They set up a very smart, very thoughtful, very nice character, and then have him fall in love with someone that anyone could tell is a horrible human being."

"But in real life nice smart people fall in love with horrible people all the time. More often than not, in my experience."

"Well, you should know," my mother said, and then immediately added, "I'm sorry."

"Apology accepted," I said.

"Believe me, Ellie, I understand sexual chemistry. Understand it perfectly. From experience." My mother's face began to turn a deep rose color against which her eyes looked very brown, but she seemed determined to go on. "It's a powerful thing."

"Mama," I said, "are we about to have that little sex talk we never had when I was thirteen?"

"I beg your pardon! We did have that little sex talk. For God's sake, I practiced for it for two weeks. And we had it when you were eleven, when I first noticed that you had"—she made a pointing motion with her index fingers—"poking out the front of your swim-team tank suit."

I frowned. I vaguely remembered something about tampons and fertilization, but it was as murky as the water in the pool where we practiced for swim team, with its yeasty smell of overchlorination, a smell I had realized some years later in Jon's car was second cousin to the smell of semen.

"Please don't tell me you don't remember," she said.

"I kind of remember."

"I even had a little pamphlet about the female sex organs, and then all you cared about was the math. What about twins, you said, and I explained that there were two eggs. What about trip-lets? I think you got all the way up to octuplets. That was the first time I'd heard that one, octuplets. And finally I told you how the egg and the seed got in the same place at the same time and you said, without missing a beat, 'How does it feel?' "

Suddenly it all came back to me. I remembered how on that day, too, my mother's face had flushed bright, and she had run a hand distractedly through her hair, and then my father had come into the hallway unexpectedly, noisily, ebulliently, with some great news—a sabbatical? a publication in some scholarly journal?—and she had never answered the question. But I had known the answer by her face, and, later, by her manner some Sunday mornings at the breakfast table, bemused, sleepy, and self-satisfied.

"Of course I told you the truth," she said now, completing the memory the way it ought to be. "I don't think you were a bit pleased. You just looked at me in that sizing-up way you had when you were young and went upstairs. I wondered what you were thinking. I always had a hard time figuring out what you were thinking."

"I know," I said.

"I didn't do a very good job of dealing with that," she added, looking down at her hands and turning them in her lap. "Figuring out what you were thinking. Your father was better at it. Much better." She looked at me and added, "I'm sorry."

"That's all right," I said, a little mystified because I was not sure what the apology was for. For so long I'd thought about myself as a girl who'd walked away from her mother's life that it would be a long time before I would start to think about the other part of the bargain, how easily she'd let me go.

One morning I awoke confused from a dream in which Jonathan and I were biting at each other at the front of a large lecture room filled with students. I heard high cries from the bedroom below, and for just a moment I thought that there was a baby somewhere in the house, waiting to be changed and fed. Then my father called my name. When I got to their bedroom he was sitting on the edge of the bed, a towel around his waist, and my mother was crying without tears.

"She's in horrible pain," he said. "She says it's her back." And he turned to her. "All will be well, Katydid, shh, shh, shh. All will be well. Shhhh."

"A heating pad," my mother said, her voice shrill.

"She's been up most of the night," my father said. "I couldn't find a heating pad but she insisted I shouldn't wake you."

"Let Ellen sleep," my mother said querulously, as though she had been repeating it all night long.

I brought a heating pad down from my room and together my father and I pulled my mother upright, one on each arm. With the quilt rolled back and her nightgown slipping off her shoulders and twisted up around her thighs I could see how much she had hidden from me until now. The skin on her upper arms hung down in wrinkled sacs; her collarbone stood out like the beams that hold the house up. Her legs were narrow stalks, bruised. I was reminded of a girl in our house at Harvard whose diet consisted only of bananas and Evian and who left at midsemester, still insisting as her size three leather skirt slipped down her bony hips that what she really needed was to run another mile each morning.

Six weeks we'd lived so close together and yet she had insulated me from much of the disintegration she saw whenever she removed her nightgown each morning. Insulated me when she kept me out of Dr. Cohn's office, when she talked to me in gentle code of works of fiction and past lives, when she shut the door of the bedroom and bathroom and mustered her gay smile on our excursions. "Let Ellen sleep," she had insisted, and I knew why. She was not yet ready to let her child be the grown-up in the house. She had had one great calling, as a mother, and she would not be forced from the field.

When we laid her back down on the heating pad, my father and I, she was breathing as though she'd run up the stairs herself.

"You have a nine o'clock," she said to him, without opening her eyes.

As I was calling the doctor I heard the door open and close, and knew that he was gone. I wondered what he thought when he looked at the wreck of her body, whether he was sad or repulsed. I wondered what she thought as she watched him look. I wondered what life was like on the night shift, whether she was able to say and feel the things in the dark of their bedroom that she kept from me in the light of day, whether he was a better man than I now thought him.

I called Dr. Cohn at the hospital. "I know you guys don't make house calls anymore," I said, and before I could go further she said, businesslike, "I'll be there in half an hour." And in half an hour the blue Volvo with its MD plates and baby seat in the back was in the driveway, and I made a pot of coffee.

"Oh, Doctor, I've done something to my back, a disc or something," my mother said plaintively. "The pain is awful."

I watched Dr. Cohn fill a syringe, feel softly around the lump in my mother's upper chest, then inject something into the catheter lodged beneath the skin. Almost immediately my mother relaxed, and her lids began to droop.

"Better," she said, lying back with her arms at her sides.

The doctor rolled her over and lifted the blue flannel nightgown with its pattern of tiny flowers. I held my hand to my mouth and turned away, my head against the cool white jamb of the door.

"Ellen?" my mother said faintly, half asleep, and I tried to reply but my throat had closed around the knot of my fear and grief and no matter how I worked I could not make it open and let my words out. Although what I could possibly say, except "Mama," like a baby, a good child, I did not know.

"She went downstairs to fix me another cup of coffee, Kate," said Dr. Cohn.

"Oh, wonderful," my mother replied, and in a minute I heard her breathing slow and deepen. The doctor had pulled down her gown, rearranged the quilt, and was taking her pulse.

Downstairs we sat together at the table, that old oak table, with its golden surface. Dr. Cohn drank her coffee without speaking. After it was finished, she took a pad out of her bag and began to write. She had nice even script, and when I said so she laughed dryly. "People have been thrown out of med school for less."

She handed me the prescription. "She didn't throw her back out," she said.

"I'm not stupid, Doctor."

"I know that, but as you may have realized by now, intelligence is not what's needed here. Empathy is. Your mother seems to be in a great deal of pain. It's hard to tell how much because, as you well know, she is an uncomplaining patient. Perhaps to a fault. Her cancer is progressing far more quickly than I think any of us would have suspected. I wouldn't be telling you that if I hadn't already told her during our last visit. One of the most important things at this point will be the management of her pain. I've given you morphine pills. Depending on how she does, we may go to a pump that will dispense morphine directly through her catheter. Have you and your father discussed hospice care?"

"Doctor, I can't predict the future, but I can tell you this. No hospice, no hospital. I had a good job in the city and a nice apartment and friends and places to go and people to see and I junked it to take care of my mother. And I am going to take care of my mother. I will do what is required."

She began to write on her pad again. "Are you seeing someone?" she asked as she wrote.

"A shrink?"

"Actually, we in the trade prefer to call them psychiatrists. But yes. I think you need someone to talk to."

"I talk to my mother."

"You need someone to talk to *about* your mother. And about how your mother is making you feel about yourself. And your mother could use someone to talk to about how it feels to be dying."

"My mother is fine. My mother can talk to me."

"Can she? Has she said she's terrified to go to sleep because she's afraid she'll never wake up? Has she told you she imagines sometimes how the rest of you will go on with your lives and forget her? Has she told you that she wants to have sex with her husband but she's afraid he doesn't want her? Look at the stenciling around the ceiling of this room, at the quilt on her bed. Look at the trees outside this house and the wreath on your front door, which I assume she made. Has she told you how it feels to lose it all?"

Doctor Cohn pulled the second sheet from her prescription pad. Side by side they lay on the oak table. "Morphine sulfate," said one. "Jessica Feld," said the other, with a phone number under it.

"You need to talk to someone, Ellen," she said, standing up.

"You need to talk to someone and you need to give her the pills every eight hours to help her get through this next part. Don't let her chew them and don't crush them. I'll send over a wheelchair. She may experience difficulty walking soon. I'd like to see her tomorrow if she's up to it. I'll let myself out."

Before she'd even pulled out of the drive I took the two prescriptions upstairs and stuck one under the edge of my desk blotter, beneath the note from Mrs. Forburg I hadn't answered yet. When I went to the pharmacy with the other, Mr. Sellinger filled it without pleasantries, except to say as I left, "Give our love to your mother." And I did, and the pills. For a while, they helped.

My brothers came home the Tuesday before Thanksgiving. Brian burst into tears when he saw her. But she only pulled him down next to her. He knelt by her chair and put his head on her chest, next to her heart. "No, no, Baba," she said as she had so many years ago.

Jeff stood looking down at them, a crooked smile on his freckled face. "Ma, you look like hell," he said.

"It's Ellen's fault," she replied.

"Nah, it's not. You haven't been eating your vegetables. You've been out dancing all night long. There's an empty six-pack behind the shoe rack in your closet. I know your kind."

"Oh, Lord, Jeffie," she said, and he ruffled her hair.

But I think our mother's appearance was not as big a surprise for either of them as mine was for Jonathan, when he arrived at the house unexpectedly on Wednesday. I heard steps behind me and there he was, handsome in a blue sweater and gray flannel pants, his eyes hidden by his mirror sunglasses. It was when he took them off that I saw the surprise in them, saw him look me up and down in a way that, under different circumstances, would have been flattering. I was wearing a red-and-white checked apron that said KISS THE COOK on its bib, and I had pushed my hair up into a haphazard bun on the top of my head. I was making biscuits, and my hands and the front of my apron were covered with flour. I hugged Jon and kissed him hard, and when I finally pulled away I had left him blotched with white, his sweater, his pants, even the part of his hair that hung heavy like a butterscotch parenthesis over his forehead.

"Oh, hell," he said, looking down at himself.

"Love you, too," I said, and playfully—or spitefully, I'm not certain which—I put a floury thumbprint in the center of his chest.

"Ellen!" he yelled. After I'd washed my hands and taken off the apron he wrapped his arms around me and kissed me for a long time in the quiet house. "You smell like butter," he said, but he didn't sound that happy about it.

Both of us pulled apart as we heard slow footsteps on the stairs. My mother came into the kitchen. "Jonathan," she said brightly, and he bent to kiss her cheek, pale yellow skin stretched over sharp bone. I left them talking about law school. But after I had taken a shower, when the two of us were out in the car, he leaned back against the seat and let his breath out, long and hard: *Whhhhooooo.*

"How do you feel?" he asked.

"As little as possible."

"I see what you mean," he said.

He didn't, of course, because instead of putting off feeling, Jonathan never really felt things at all. I liked to think he loved me in those days, but loving a woman was not truly part of his constitution. No Jessica Feld, no "what we in the trade call psychiatrist," was necessary to explain this to the laywoman. Jonathan's mother had left when he was just two and she just twenty, had decided her spur-of-the-moment teenage marriage was a mistake and left behind its most tangible asset, the little boy who, once grown, would never be able to say "I love you" without believing that the sentence was a prelude to a farewell, an abandonment, a kick in the teeth.

She lived in California now, had another family, a house with a pool. Once, when he was twelve, he had managed to get his mother's phone number out of his grandmother and had called her and heard a little boy answer the phone. "How could somebody just leave their kid?" he told me he asked her when she came on the line, and she replied, still with a broad streak of Brooklyn in her voice, "I just did."

"You could almost hear the shrug," Jonathan said.

Not long ago I saw Jonathan on Madison Avenue with a really lovely-looking woman, with blond feathers of hair around her face and sharp intelligent eyes. I knew that she was smart and interesting, someone you could take anywhere. Jonathan appreciated her, I'm sure, just as he appreciated me, appreciated my quick mind, the determination and ambition, the ardor and the lack of inhibitions. But love? I don't think so.

His father had been a police officer in New York City, taken retirement after the requisite twenty years and what the cops called a tit job as chief of security at Langhorne College. He and his son moved into an ugly modern house just outside town which was, Jon once said, four times the size of the Brooklyn apartment they'd shared with his grandparents.

He had stared openly at me in English class, and afterward I heard him ask Jackie Belknap who I was. "Gulden?" said Jackie. "Study, study, study, bitch, bitch, bitch."

"Just what the doctor ordered," said Jonathan.

He was good-looking in an odd kind of way, with eyes a little too close together and dirty blond hair, a strong jaw and surprisingly full and feminine lips, very red. These last gave him a powerful aura of sexuality which was not in the least misleading. But we were a match as well, both of us quick and anxious, driven and oblivious to the effect we had on other people. Hungry puppies, as Jeff would have said. Jeff would have said that someday we would wind up eating one another up. But I wouldn't have listened.

Jonathan's father had remarried when we were in college, to a secretary at Langhorne. That Thanksgiving, he and his wife—"call her my stepmother and die," Jon said to me early on—were three hundred miles away at her daughter's. We walked in the door of the house and began to remove our clothes before it was even closed.

In movies there is always something sexy about such a thing, about the sight of gray flannels, red turtleneck, flowered panties, gray socks, in a Hansel-and-Gretel trail leading to the bedroom. But as I was struggling with hooks and eyes as though it was the most important thing in the world that I be naked, there was something so driven and desperate about it that by the time I was on my back on the bed all pleasure had vanished. I almost said aloud, "All I really want to do is sleep." But not to Jonathan. Not ever to Jonathan.

It had been a long week leading up to the holidays. Sometimes my mother would twist in the chair and I would know that something was gnawing at her belly and her lower back. Certain lines about her mouth, once only smile lines, began to deepen with her grimaces. Her hair was wispy, the thin and awry fuzz of an infant, and each morning she wrapped her head in a scarf and pulled a few strands from beneath it to soften the sharp bones that showed so clearly now in her face.

And the rages began. The worst was the day when I brought the wheelchair out. Once the pain came in earnest she was like that, turning from time to time into a person I had never seen before. She raged against several members of the Minnies who wanted to make her honorary chairman of the tree ceremony and spare her the work of decorating. She raged at the way Mrs. Duane had rubbed her back in the bookstore, "petting me as though I were a dog." The outbursts seemed so different from her usual self that I sometimes felt as though the cancer itself had a voice, and I was hearing it. Or it was the voice of the morphine.

"I am not an invalid," she cried when she came down from a nap and first saw the wheelchair folded in a corner. "First you dope me up and then you want to turn me into an invalid." She sat down heavily on the living-room couch, holding a pillow to her belly like a shield, and raged at the wheelchair and at me. "Put it away right now, Ellen. Put it away or I will roll it down the street." She picked up a Styrofoam ball and with shaking hands tried to push a gold sequin into it with a drawing pin. "It's humiliating," she said, and the sequin dropped to the floor.

"I just want you to be comfortable," I said.

"You want me to be dead. You want me to die so you and your father can get on with your lives."

She was wrong. I had hoped the wheelchair would give her back some of her dignity, not take it away. And I'd hoped I'd get her back, too, for a few weeks more, another book perhaps, another series of lessons in her old familiar domestic life. But I knew the only thing that would restore her to her old self, bouncing on the balls of her feet, baking the day away with flour in her hair, keeping her dark feelings inside, was the clean slate of death. Then that Kate Gulden would live always in my mind. I was frightened of this other Kate, this enraged and dessicated impostor. She was right about that; I did want that angry stranger gone. For so long I had wondered why she was not angrier at my father, at her lot in life, at the bargain she had made. But as I saw her rage, felt it like a black thing with teeth and claws, I blessed her tranquillity, and yearned for it.

I tried to tell Jonathan all this. Dr. Cohn was right; I needed someone to talk to. After we made love I lay staring up at the ceiling fan, tears running down the sides of my face, and said, "If I had any guts at all I would hold a pillow over her face."

"Don't say things like that," Jonathan said.

"Oh, Jonathan, you don't know. You're drinking coffee in the cafeteria and working on your moot court arguments and I'm watching this woman start to slowly disintegrate before my eyes, and all I can think is, this is my last chance to know her, to be her, to not kiss her off because she doesn't work or she didn't graduate from an Ivy League school or she doesn't think the world rises and falls on whether or not there was really a Dark Lady behind Shakespeare's sonnets. And the days slip by. She hates Elizabeth Bennet, can you believe it? Just hates her."

"Who the hell is Elizabeth Bennet?"

"*Pride and Prejudice.*"

"Oh, well, then, that explains it," Jonathan said, leaning up on one elbow, his face caught in the last bit of daylight shining through the blinds in his bedroom. "Listen, Ellen, you need some rest. You are going to go crazy with this. Can't Papa George give you a break so you can spend the weekend with me?"

"I can't go anywhere, Jonathan. I can't tell from day to day whether she'll be all right or not."

"I think you're being too hard on yourself."

"There's no such thing as being too hard on yourself, Jon."

"Is there such a thing as being too hard?" he said, moving quickly from death to sex, his favorite subject, as he pushed my head down.

Afterward we dressed and drove back to my house. "Do you realize that during the entire thing we never kissed?" I said.

"Oh, Christ, Ellen, calm down," Jon said, sated now and irritable.

I spent the rest of that evening creaming onions, peeling yams, making stuffing exactly as my mother directed, producing a great groaning board of dishes just as she always had. After Jonathan brought me home, as I stood in the kitchen in my nightgown slicing celery, I realized that I was doing it all for the sake of stability, to make it seem as though this Thanksgiving was no different from any other. I was maintaining, abetting, creating a kind of elaborate fiction, just as my mother had, with gravy and pumpkin pie and heavy cream. The fiction that everything was fine, that life was simple and secure, that husbands did not stray and children grow, that the body did not decay and finally fail, that the axis of the earth passed dead center through the kitchen and the living world and the world kept spinning, our family unchanging, safe and sound.

My mother looked horrid on Thanksgiving morning; she had made up her face elaborately, as though somehow she could create her own fiction with blush and eye shadow, the fiction that she was well, that she was blooming. But my brothers did not collaborate; instead of making the rounds of friends' houses that afternoon, they stayed at home, wandering in and out of the kitchen, talking of school and asking about home. They settled into the couch with Jonathan for the football games. My father sat with them, reading and making derogatory comments. "The greatest single collection of future car-dealership owners and fast-food-restaurant franchise magnates in the United States," he said.

"So Rod Laver is a teaching pro at a country club right now," said Jeff. "Big difference."

"Tennis has finesse," said my father. "Tennis has style and grace."

"The sport of kings," said Jonathan.

"Come off it, Jon," said Jeffrey. "You love football. The only thing I've ever seen take your mind off yourself is the Super Bowl."

"And Wimbledon," Jonathan said. "And I wasn't agreeing. I was commenting."

"Sucking up," muttered Jeff.

"God, I hate that expression," my father said. He turned to me, then looked into the kitchen. "Where's your mother?"

"She's upstairs with Brian."

"Don't make her feel superfluous, Ellen," my father said.

"And don't make me feel guilty."

I basted and rearranged the cheesecloth that was draped around my turkey like a shroud. I was beginning to talk about food the way my mother did: my stuffing, my yams, my turkey. My zucchini soup. It would always be my zucchini soup, with a cup of tea in it.

Upstairs my mother was settled in the big chair by the window in her room, her feet up on the ottoman. She was wearing a handsome plum-colored dress with big brass buttons which I had bought her at the mall; when she saw that the label had been cut out she was so pleased. "A bargain!" she said. "How much?"

"None of your business," I said with a grin, as though I had gotten the dress for next to nothing. In fact it had cost seventy dollars, and I had taken the label out because it read MOTHER AND CHILD. Maternity clothes, my mother needed now, to accommodate her poor swollen belly.

When I went up to check on her, Brian was sitting crosslegged next to the ottoman, a book in his lap, reading aloud. As I came in he slid the book beneath the ruffled skirt of the chair.

"What have you got there, Bri?" I asked. "*Tropic of Cancer? Peyton Place? Story of O?*"

"Much worse," my mother said.

Brian slid the book out again and held it up. It was a Gothic novel, with a cover illustration of a woman in ruffled petticoats being pressed to the highly defined pectoral muscles of a man wearing only jodphurs. "Your father will call the police," my mother said, giggling.

"The thought police," said Brian. "They would all be wearing tweed jackets and they would deprogram you by making you read the *Oxford English Dictionary.*"

"Oh, honey," said my mother, giggling again, "don't make fun of the *OED.*"

"They take you in a room and put headphones on you and make you listen to Orson Welles read *Silas Marner*," I said.

"Now, there's a real mystery," my mother said. "How someone wrote a book as good as *Middlemarch* and then wrote a book as boring as *Silas Marner.* Jeffrey would say she was all over the map."

"Oh, Ma," said Brian. "The person who wrote *Silas Marner* was a guy. George Eliot."

My mother and I screamed and held our heads. "Oh, my God, Bri," I said, "if Papa heard you you'd be on the road with your thumb out, on your way back to Philadelphia. George Eliot was a woman. It was a pen name. Her real name was Mary Ann Evans."

"Are you sure?" said Brian.

"Honey, it's okay," I said. "You're going to major in political science. Just don't let Papa hear you. That and this"—I nudged the paperback with my foot—"would finish him off. I can see it: PROF KILLED BY BAD LITERARY TASTE: SON HELD."

There was a knock at the door and when my father looked in, we all began to laugh.

"What's so funny?" he said.

"A case of mistaken identity," I said.

When the food was on the table in the dining room, on the mahogany table with its matching breakfront and china closet and chairs that had once belonged to my grandparents, my mother took Brian's and Jeffrey's hands and said, "I want to say grace." And for the first time in years we did:

"Thank you for the world so sweet, thank you for the food we eat, thank you for the birds that sing, thank you, God, for everything."

When I raised my head and dropped my father's hand I looked at him and there were tears in his eyes.

For dessert I had made pumpkin pie, and as I was in the kitchen cutting it my mother came in. She looked tired and she'd eaten all her lipstick off, leaving only the edge of it, like false wax lips from Halloween.

"I need a pill, Ellen," she said.

"Mama, I gave you one just after lunch. It's only been four hours."

"Ellen, I need a pill. Where are they?"

"They're in the cabinet in the powder room. Can't you wait until after dessert?"

"Get me a pill, please, Ellen," my mother said, so loudly that all conversation stopped in the next room. "And remember that this is still my house." I could hear the edge of one of those rages in her voice, and as she returned to the table I went to the medicine cabinet.

I heard her say to Brian, "Now—I want a full report on the roommate and any suitable girls."

"And you can tell me when we go out later about all the unsuitable ones," Jeff said.

But Brian did not go out with the rest of us. He helped my mother to bed after we'd had our coffee in the living room; he sat in her room after she'd dozed off, listening to her breathe in the dark. "Don't fall asleep here," I whispered, but he didn't reply, and I knew he'd be there until my father came up. I remember thinking that if they gave any of us an aptitude test for taking care of Kate Gulden when she was mortally ill, Brian, sweet and earnest Brian, would have aced it. Jeff once had described us all: "The food chain is that Ellen lives up to Pop, and I live up to Ellen." A little plaintively Bri had said, "What about me?"

"You don't have to live up to anyone, kid," Jeff said. "You and Mom just have to get up every morning and be present on the planet."

So predictable, that it would all begin to unravel in a bar. That was where we went after the dinner dishes were done, Jonathan and Jeff and I, to a bar called Sammy's, named in honor of Samuel Langhorne, who was about as much a Sammy as Thomas Jefferson was a Tommy or John Adams a Jack. The place was one of those dark English-pub imitations, with cheap, mass-produced stained-glass windows and a big dark wood bar with heraldic nonsense fixed to its front. It was full of town kids home for Thanksgiving break and the community college kids, who wished they were. Jeff had to wade through a sea of glad hands and big smiles. One girl ran her hand up his khaki leg from knee to thigh and said, "Come over to see me."

"Who was that?" Jonathan asked.

"A very happy woman," said Jeff. "Name of Jennifer."

"They're all Jennifers," I said. "When our mothers were young, they were all Kathys and Pattys. In ten years they'll all be Ashleys and Taras."

"Aren't you tough!" said Jeff.

"My middle name."

"Yeah, you put on a good show, El. But I see through you."

"Deep down inside a romantic?"

"Deep down inside a softie."

"This conversation is like a Kahlil Gibran sitcom, for Christ-sake," said Jonathan. He smiled over at Jennifer, who smiled at him. I slipped my hand into the back pocket of his jeans.

"I'll cut it off, Jon," I whispered as we sat down at a table, a slab of heavy varnished wood with a round red votive candle winking at its center.

I hadn't had a drink since the day I'd come back to Langhorne. It didn't feel right; it didn't parse. Neither had the seal of sex I'd felt between my legs as I'd cooked and cleaned the night before in my mother's house. I thought about it as the need to be in control, to be there for her in every way, in case of some crisis, some emergency. I thought about how terrible it would be if she was left to suffer alone while I took my forays into pleasure in Jonathan's boyhood bedroom with the pennants still tacked over the bed, if she called out and I was too muddled by wine to hear.

But now, when I analyze my own behavior, I think I felt obliged to deny myself anything carnal, a frisson of lust, the blur of a shot of vodka, to help pay for her pain, as though pleasure was an affront to her.

That night in Sammy's, with Jonathan smiling that promising smile across the table at me, the red light making amber shadows on his face, I forgot all that. I had two beers, then something called a Samuel Sling, fruit juice and a muddle of different liquors, one of those drinks that go down so easy and make your head swim so fast. Under the table I ran my foot up the inside of Jonathan's thigh. The two men talked about the football, their course work, their professors. In the middle of a sentence I cut Jeff off.

"He just kills me," I said.

"Who?" said Jon. But Jeff knew.

"My father. He just kills me. He sat there and let you guys clear the table. He didn't say a word to me about dinner. And he goes off before she's even asleep and says he has work to do in his study. As though we were servants. As though we're there to serve him. Jesus." I signaled the waitress across the room. "We need another round," I called.

"The hell you do," Jeff muttered.

"This is what it's been like from day one, Jeffie," I said. "He is literally never there. I literally do everything."

"Does your mother complain?" said Jonathan.

"That's not the point," I said loudly.

"El, the entire bar doesn't have to share this with us," said Jeff. He shrugged and looked at Jon. "My mother never complains about anything."

"Exactly," I said. "And now she can't because he's never around."

"He was never around before," said Jeff.

"She was never dying before," I said.

"Everyone deals with bad stuff in their own way," Jon added.

"Well, that's the point, isn't it, Jon?" I said. "Whenever one of you guys says people deal with bad stuff in their own way, it means you don't deal with it at all. You just wait for it to go away. You don't help. You don't listen. You don't call. You don't write. WE deal with it in our own way. WE deal with it. We girls. We make the meals and clean up the messes and take the crap and listen to you talk about how you're dealing with it in your own way. What way? No way!"

Jennifer at the bar was staring at our table. So were her friends. I gave them the finger and Jeff pulled my hand out of the air. "Whooa,' he said. "Should we get out of here?"

"I am not your father, Ellen," Jon said as the waitress brought our drinks. He took my glass from the tray and put it down on his side of the table.

"No you are not, Jon," I said, reaching across the table to get it. We pulled in opposite directions; the glass toppled and my drink ran into his lap. "Jesus," he said, standing up.

"Let's go," Jeff said.

"I'm ready," Jon said, "and Ellen sure as hell is. Do you want us to drop you at home?"

"I'm going with him, Jon," I said. "It's been a long day. A long week. A long month. It's very tiring, being my mother."

"Ellen, you have lost it. You are not your mother. You have never been your mother. There is no one in the world more different from your mother than you are."

I took my jacket from the back of my chair. "That was the stupidest thing you've ever said, Jon. And I am leaving."

"I haven't seen you in almost three months."

"Whose fault is that?"

"Oh, Christ," said Jon.

"Cool it, Jon," said Jeff. "You got laid yesterday, you'll get laid tomorrow, and you'll probably get laid Saturday."

"Hey, Jeff, my sex life is none of your business. And neither is hers. She's a big girl."

"Ah, hell, she's not as big as everybody thinks."

"If everyone could stop talking about me as if I wasn't here, I'd like to go home and just go to sleep," I said. "I'm drunk and I'm tired and I'm sick of all of you. And I don't want a ride because I want to walk home just so I can be alone for a change."

And I was alone, walking home in the cold November night with my nose and eyes running, leaving Jonathan angry, locking eyes with Jeff and with Jennifer, whose lip gloss and tousled bangs seemed a world away to me. I felt like a very tired housewife, and I looked like one, too, in my corduroy slacks and cotton sweater. When I got home my mother was sitting in the living room, reading. "You didn't have to wait up for me," I said.

"My back hurts."

Next morning the boys left me to sleep late, and when I woke up and heard war whoops from outside the window I looked out to see Brian letting my mother roll down the street in the wheelchair, with Jeff stationed down the gentle slope to stop her. The look on her face reminded me of the first time we ever put Brian on a sled at River View Park, the commingling of fear, excitement, joy, and terror. "Go for it, baby!" Jeff yelled as he put out his arms to catch her. "Bring it on home."

My head hurt and my tongue felt too big for my mouth. I climbed back beneath the quilt and slept until almost noon, and when I awoke and went downstairs my mother was sleeping on the couch in the living room, her hands beneath her cheek, a throw over her legs. A note from my father on the kitchen table said "Catching up at the college." In the den my brothers were talking, their voices rising, falling, breaking. I went out on the porch and sat hugging a sweater around me until the sun began to disappear and a chill to descend. Then I went inside to make turkey sandwiches.

Jonathan did not call that evening, and I didn't call him. When he called on Saturday it was to say that he was going back to Cambridge early to get some work done and that he wanted me to think again about coming up soon to spend a weekend with him. "There's no way, Jon," I said, and we hung up with no plans to talk, to meet, no "I love you," not even any salacious suggestions for the future. Jon, I remember thinking to myself, was not of this time and this place; he was something I would come back to when I came back to being the other Ellen.

It would not be until months later that I would learn, from both their sworn testimonies, that he had spent Thanksgiving night and most of Friday morning in bed at his father's house with Jennifer. So predictable, all of it. So unsurprising, so somehow apt, along with all the other things that happened that winter.

The first part of my mother's illness had been a kind of childhood for me, the kind of childhood I might have had, had I been a different sort of girl, my mother a different sort of woman, and both our needs to woo my father less overwhelming. Holiday cheer, Thanksgiving side dishes, stories of childhood, girlhood, and marriage—all of these were handed down to me, now, with a certain air of urgency, as though it was a school assignment on which she'd fallen behind, this chance to reclaim the daughter she might have had, the one who, like Brian, would have been happiest sitting at her feet, laughing up at her own laughter.

But once she began to use the wheelchair our relationship was reversed, she the child, I the mother. Perhaps it was why she had resisted it so strongly. It was difficult for her to get around the house alone; the doorways were narrow, the rugs a beautiful impediment in shades of crimson and deep blue. But although I moved the furniture closer to the walls, I did not even ask if I could roll up the old Orientals. What she needed now was for the things around her to be as lovely and familiar as possible. So much else was shifting and becoming ugly.

One day she decided we should go downtown on foot—"and on wheels," she added—to pick out three more books at Duane's. She put on a blue pea jacket that had always fitted her perfectly, sleek and elegant, and it concealed how thin and concave her chest was now, like the breast of a baby bird.

"What about a little makeup?" I said. "Just in case we run into someone."

"Somehow I don't think your father envisioned you having a career as a cosmetologist."

"And why not? I could wind up in the *Tribune* that way." My mother liked to say that every engagement announcement in the local paper was of a cosmetologist engaged to a man "associated with" a construction company. It drove my father crazy when she read them aloud, but crazier still when she read about the weddings, all the detailed descriptions of someone's point d'esprit dropped waist, bishop's sleeves, and cloudburst tulle headpiece.

"Oh, Ellie, you've been in the *Tribune* more than anyone except Ed Best and the mayor. Go look in my scrapbook upstairs. Girls' State, the Spelling Bee, the Essay Contest, your graduation speech. You're always in the *Tribune*."

"It sounds like you're keeping a running count."

"You bet I am. And why shouldn't I? Now go ahead and put a little makeup on me, but don't get carried away."

It was more difficult than I'd imagined. When I had smoothed on foundation, penciled in eyeliner, and brushed on mascara and blush, my mother looked a little like the kind of pictures I'd drawn of her when I was five, all round red cheeks and eyelashes like spiky black spiders. I had not gotten the effect I wanted, which was the impossible illusion that Kate Gulden was just as she always had been.

"It's very difficult to do this on someone else's face," I said.

My mother leaned on the chest of drawers in the hallway and

peered in the mirror. "You've never worked on a redhead before," she said. "That's your problem." She took a small sponge from the bag of cosmetics I was holding and scrubbed her face for a moment.

"Much better," I said.

"Your career as a cosmetologist is over before it began," my mother replied.

"As a cosmetologist, I'm a great writer."

"You are a great writer," said my mother, my fan club, my burden, as I buttoned her pea jacket and pulled on her beret.

With her bony face and pallor, she looked like an aging fashion model. She'd always been a pretty woman, my mother. Unlike so many other women, whose wedding photographs are more like pictures of their daughters than of themselves, she had kept her looks and her bright eyes.

I put on my down jacket and brought the chair backward down the front steps—*clunk, clunk, clunk*—in a technique I'd learned from watching mothers in the city with their strollers. My mother came down the steps slowly and carefully and sat down.

"I feel stupid in this thing, but I want to go out," she said. "I feel like I've been a hermit. You too. You haven't been out since your brothers left after Thanksgiving."

We came down the street slowly because I was afraid of losing control of the chair on the slope and because I could tell, watching her head swivel from side to side, that she was looking around carefully, sight-seeing in her own neighborhood. "Look, Ellie, the Jacksons already have a tree up in their living room," she said, and "Claire Belknap had better put something over those roses or she'll lose them if there's an early frost," and "Why did the Bests paint their house that color? It was so nice when it was white." It was as though she was seeing for all it was worth that day, all of it, every single insignificant trivial marvelous detail of it, every one.

At the bottom of the hill we turned onto Main Street just below the green. The flowers that usually ringed the flagpole were gone now. The twelve big evergreens stood alone, the sweeping angel wings of their branches so beautiful.

"They never quite know what to do with that planting area after they take the asters out but before the trees are decorated," my mother said. "Our first year here, there was this new woman, I think she was the provost's wife, who donated dozens of poinsettias. Public Works put them all in, no questions asked. Not one person seemed to know that poinsettias are tropical plants and have to be kept indoors in a cold climate. Next morning it was the saddest sight you've ever seen, like a battlefield. All those plants had just keeled over. Your father came home thinking this was a wonderful story and I told him I had known when they were putting them in exactly what would happen. But we were new here and I didn't know who to tell, or if I should tell, and so in the end I just kept quiet. Your father thought that made the story even more wonderful, that he had a wife so clever that she'd known how ridiculous the whole idea was. So he told it around at every Christmas party, although in the telling I kept getting cannier and cannier and meaner and meaner. Your father got a very good story out of it. But the provost's wife was chilly to me for years."

It was cold that day, but we stopped at least a dozen times so my mother could talk to people she knew. It was difficult to maneuver the wheelchair up and down the curbs and over the uneven pavements, and sometimes she became impatient. When she wanted to go into the Langhorne Shoe Shoppe, I struggled with the chair at the door, holding it open with my hip, trying to steer and force the big rubber wheels over the ridged floor mat in the doorway.

"This is exactly like dealing with that damn double stroller I bought when Brian was born," she said. "I'd be heaving and hoing it through the door and you'd be halfway out into the street with me screaming after you."

She used the armrests to help herself stand up and walked inside, leaving me to back out and set the brake on the street. I watched her through the display window, glimpsed her profile between a pair of tassel loafers and some hiking boots. We had the same sharp noses. She was talking to one of the salespeople, and then she sat down. I stood on tiptoe and could see her slipping off her flats, and then someone emerged from the back room with a tower of boxes.

"Ellen?" a voice said behind me.

It was Mrs. Forburg, my English teacher. "Couldn't you call me Brenda now?" she said.

"To be honest, I'd rather not. I think you should remain Mrs. Forburg forever. It's a kind of honorific."

She laughed. In her parka and gray pants she was as small as a ten-year-old, but she had the dried-apple skin and white-gray hair of a grandmother. "Is your mother inside?" she said.

I nodded. "She appears to be buying shoes. I didn't know she needed shoes."

"Does any woman really need shoes?" Mrs. Forburg said, looking down at her own gray walking oxfords. "Buying shoes always gives me a lift, like buying new stationery or a new purse. It makes you feel as if there's something to look forward to." She reached across the chair and touched the back of my hand. "Did you get my note?" she said.

"I did, I did, but I've been so busy I haven't had time to call you. Jeff and Brian were home for Thanksgiving, my mother and I are doing a lot of things together. The house. You know."

"I didn't mean it as a command performance. I just wanted you to know that I'd always be happy to feed you some spaghetti and listen to your troubles."

There was the high rattle of the bells over the shoe store door, and my mother came out with a bag. "Beautiful new loafers," she said as she sat down heavily in the chair. She looked up. "Mrs. Forburg!" she said.

"It's good to see you, Mrs. Gulden." My mother slipped the shoe box out of her bag and showed off the loafers, gleaming cordovan leather with tassels. She showed me how the black flats she was wearing were slightly down-at-heel. It was quite a performance, but I could tell by the look in her eyes that Mrs. Forburg recognized it for what it was. It was the same look she had once given me when she handed me back a B paper savaging Charlotte Brontë, a paper made up almost entirely of my father's opinions. "Original thought next time, Ellen," she had said quietly that day, but it had sounded less like a rebuke because of the sympathy in her gray eyes, and a certain tone to her voice, the same tone she had now. She saw things, Mrs. Forburg.

She had always been my favorite teacher—Jeff and Brian's, too, although neither of them had been as mesmerized by English literature as I was. Mrs. Forburg had deftly steered me through fiction and verse, gently edited my poetry, which was clever but not at all deeply felt, and made me keep a journal my senior year, although I think she sensed that she was getting the expurgated version of my life. "She is still the best English teacher I have ever had," I said one night when I was home during my last year at college. "Then you are taking the wrong courses at Harvard," my father had said dryly. I had been shocked into silence, but my mother had not.

"You're just jealous, Gen," she said evenly.

"Jealous? What do you mean?"

"Ellen can have more than one teacher," my mother had said without looking at him. There was a sharp scraping sound as he had pushed back his chair.

"You misjudge me, Katherine," he replied.

On the street outside the shoe store my mother smiled up at Mrs. Forburg and took her hand. "I'd like to invite Ellen to dinner, Mrs. Gulden," Mrs. Forburg said. "To get reacquainted. Would that make life difficult for you?"

"No! Absolutely not! She's cooped up in the house all the time with me and she gets antsy, although she doesn't say it. I'll make her call and arrange it with you." And so we continued down the street.

"I didn't know you needed shoes," I said.

"I don't," my mother replied.

It was a busy afternoon. We stopped at Phelps's and Mr. Phelps hugged my mother, swaying back and forth, his eyes glistening. "Oh, don't go getting mushy on me," my mother said, smiling at him brightly. He gave her the name and number of a young mother who had been in to ask about stenciling flowers on a crib. "I wanted to have you talk to her, but I wasn't sure how you would feel about it," Mr. Phelps said. "I'll call her when I get home," my mother promised.

At Duane's, both Mr. and Mrs. came from the back room to discuss what we should be reading next, and I saw Mrs. Duane drop a Gothic novel with a cover illustration of a tortured-looking woman in a hoopskirt into our bag. The wives of two faculty members came over to tell my mother how well she was looking, and she leaned down out of the chair to speak to their children, toddlers and one gangly girl of eight or nine who stared hard, perhaps remembering her parents whispering about something terrible—"Kate Gulden . . . so young . . . George's wife . . . just awful"—in the kitchen. A woman who lived several blocks over from us began to talk of homeopathy and herbal medicines, but my mother smiled and said, "Not now, Frances." Then we went down the street and got an ice-cream cone and I pushed the chair home with one hand while I licked away.

"Good thing you looked nice," I said. "I felt like I was with Jimmy Stewart at the end of *It's a Wonderful Life*."

"They're all just sorry for me," my mother said.

"Oh, please," I said. "That wasn't what that was all about. They were all so happy to see you. Everyone likes you."

"I know that. They just didn't have to think about it until now."

"That's terrible," I said.

"You can't judge, Ellen. People are different. People love in different ways. Sometimes hugs and kisses, sometimes something else. And sometimes they can't feel it, they're just made that way."

"Like who?" I said, afraid.

"My mother was like that. She was very poor as a child, and things were hard, and I've never been sure how she came to marry your grandfather, but it wasn't what either you or I would think of as a love match. And I think some part of her shriveled up and died from not being used, not being exercised. The closest she came was loving my brother, and look how that ended. The closest thing she has to a son is a flag all folded up into a triangle that she's never unrolled once, and a rubbing of his name from the Vietnam Memorial that one of her nephews sent her after he took a trip to Washington."

I turned the chair into the flagstone path to our front door. We never used it, always went in through the kitchen, but there were six steps there and here it was only three to the porch and a shallow sill into the hall. "It's almost time to decorate the house," my mother said, as I came around to face her and help her out of the chair.

And she raised her arms to me to be lifted up, and I wrapped mine around her. She pulled me closer and I could feel her body like sticks in a bag, the slightness of her now, her ribs like some fragile musical instrument beneath my hands.

"Thank you, Ellie," she said.

"We'll go downtown again next Saturday," I said. "You can buy some more shoes. Everyone will be so happy to see you."

"I'm happy to be home. I'm so tired I'm going upstairs to bed as soon as I have some tea." We walked up the stairs together, arm in arm. "I can make it myself," she said.

"Do you need a pill?"

"I'll get one myself. Ellen?"

"Huh?" I said, bumping the wheelchair back up the steps.

"Call Mrs. Forburg and arrange to go to her house for dinner," my mother said. She moved slowly into the kitchen, her fingertips feeling along the walls, itsy-bitsy spiders yellow-white against the wallpaper, as though she was blind as well as lame.

I lay on the couch for a while and finally I fell asleep, almost as tired from the afternoon as she was. When I finally woke I could see the streetlights shining amber through the looped drapes of the living room, and hear my mother in the kitchen. In my mind's eye I could see her sitting at the oak table, her upper arms as round, her skin as pink and clear, her eyes as serene as they had been six months before.

"Here's the most important thing to remember," I heard her say in her authoritative "Ellen, you will not wear that dress to play in Buckley's backyard" voice. "You must tap most of the paint off the brush before you begin. You want an almost dry brush, not a wet brush." And then: "It's definitely a girl? Oh, that's wonderful. I have one daughter and you can't imagine . . . twenty-four . . . yes, she is . . . well, I do, too . . . oh, I know, but you get used to it . . . well, that's wonderful. What design did you choose?"

The woman who wanted to stencil the crib. Of course. I stared at the streetlamp and thought I saw snowflakes falling against the scrim of its glow. Claire Belknap had better mind her roses. Ellie Gulden had better wax the runners on her sled. Ellie Gulden's sled was still in the garage, a Flexible Flyer with her name painted in red script on the crossbar, next to Jeff Gulden's sled and Brian Gulden's sled

Kate Gulden had painted the names. My father had never pushed us down the hill at River View Park and never pulled us up. There were no snow days at the college, where everyone could tumble out of bed and into classroom buildings. There were no weekends for a man who wanted to be a department head, or later for a man who was one.

But I could see her, standing at the place at the bottom of the hill where there was a dip and then a bump, yelling up at us, a cap pulled down over all but the smallest divot of eyes and nose and mouth, "Not so fast. Not so fast. Slow down. Oh, my lord, Jeffrey, you'll give me a heart attack." All of life like a series of tableaux, and in the living we missed so much, hid so much, left so much undone and unsaid. Jeff had broken his arm once on that hill, and she had taken her tempera paints and painted a toy soldier up the entire length of his cast. He had been mortified.

A few minutes later I heard my father come in the back door, and her cry: "George! So early." She sounded much as she had that day I first came back: "Ellie! You're home."

"Come outside and see the snow," I heard him say softly.

"There's snow?"

"Just a little." And then the kitchen door opened again, and closed with a click, and I went up to bed and heard no more. In the morning there was no snow at all, except in my mother's memory. "I caught it on my tongue," she said. She laid her hand on my father's at the breakfast table. "It was beautiful."

"Yes, it was," he said, and smiled back at her.

No one knows what goes on inside a marriage. I read that once; the aphorism ended "except for the two people who are in it." But I suspect that even that is not the truth, that even two people married to each other for many many years may have only passing similarities in their perceptions and their expectations. I think I read somewhere, too, that social scientists interviewed couples and found that they had vastly different ideas about everything from their spouse's favorite dessert to their preferred sexual position.

Sometimes I feel limited now by how much life experience I have to extrapolate from books and research articles.

But I know from experience that those least capable of truly assessing any marriage are the children who come out of it. We style them as we need them, to excuse our faults, to insulate ourselves from our own expendability or indispensability. I remembered the great relief I felt when I first read about Oedipal theory, the relief of knowing that the triangle in which I found myself was archetypical.

So that when I saw my parents together day after day during that winter I could not truly say whether their relationship was changing or whether I was really seeing it for the first time because I was seeing my father for the first time.

One day early in December he asked me to have lunch with him in a steakhouse several miles from campus, the kind of dim and faintly pretentious out-of-the-way place I imagined you would take someone for an assignation.

"Come here often?" I said, as the waiter brought drinks and steered us toward the salad bar.

"Most of the time I'm far too busy for lunch. I eat at my desk while I work."

"I'm flattered," I said.

"Ellen, I had several agendas when I asked you to meet me today. But one of them is certainly to find out why you are being so hostile. I know this is not the optimum situation for any of us, but you and your mother certainly seem to be managing well. I'm perplexed as to why I'm met with coldness or overt hostility whenever I enter the house."

"Give me an example," I said.

"Oh for God's sake," he said, "this is not a debating contest. You know exactly what I mean. Do you need more help? Should I have a nurse come in?"

"A nurse didn't take care of me when I had chicken pox."

"This is not chicken pox and if you need an example of what I'm talking about, the sarcasm in that sentence is sufficient. Do you want salad?"

"Not if it's iceberg lettuce and canned chick-peas."

"I'm quite certain it is."

The waiter took our order, and there was a long silence broken by the sound of someone in the kitchen throwing pots and pans around in a fit of temper or extraordinary clumsiness. The brother of a member of the college board of trustees stopped by our table to say hello.

"Look, Papa," I said. "I don't want to fight with you. I'm under a lot of pressure. I don't need any more from you. I'm just getting through this day by day."

"I understand that completely, Ellen. And I understand that whenever we talk about what is going on, we talk about you, about how you are feeling, about your unhappiness. I think this time should be about your mother. It calls for a little empathy."

"Empathy is the one thing I never really learned," I said softly. "You never taught me empathy."

"Learn it now," he said peremptorily.

"And you? Where is your empathy?"

"I told you before—"

"I don't want to hear about the mortgage. The college would give you a leave any time you wanted. You've taken sabbaticals to write books and you can certainly take one to participate in the most important thing that's ever going to happen in your God-damn life."

"Keep your voice down."

"Oh, fuck that, Papa. I'm the one who is behaving appropriately here, to use your expression, and you're the one who's not. She needs you to be with her."

"Did she tell you that?"

"She doesn't need to tell me that. She shouldn't need to tell you. Yesterday she sat for twenty minutes with the Goddamn Christmas wreath on her lap before I could put it on the front door. She kept feeling it as if she were blind, as if the meaning of life was in the pinecones she'd wired to that wreath. I asked her if she needed help putting it up and she just said, 'This is pretty, isn't it?' Sometimes she goes into her room and pretends to sleep and instead she goes through all these boxes of stuff she has, swim-meet ribbons and pictures we drew years ago and old papers from when she was in high school. She just stares and stares at them. Why should she have to sit by herself and look at pictures of her life when she could have the real thing? Why should she sit around conjuring up her memories of your life together when she could be with you making real memories? Everything has changed in that house, everything, from my level of empathy to her level of agony. But you don't know about either because you're behaving as though life goes on as usual. Life as we knew it is over. Done. Finished."

My father sawed away at a bloody steak without looking at me. Finally he said, "You're giving her the morphine?"

"And I'm going to keep giving her more and more. If the pills turn out not to be enough, I can get a little pump that will deliver it into the catheter they put in her chest. But I'm not you. And I can't deal with all the pain in her head. She can only go so far with me. She still thinks she has to protect me, or baby me, whatever. You're her husband. She needs to talk to you."

He stared at his food, making it into a kind of still life: a piece of dry gray-white baked potato, a red wedge of meat. Another. Another. It looked as though he was playing chess with his lunch as he moved it in mysterious patterns. As he cut and arranged he spoke quietly, so that he could not eat unless he stopped. And could not stop until he had finished.

"Sometimes I think about how I first saw her at Columbia, and how eager she was," he said. "But you know that because you know how she is. So eager, as though she wanted to see and understand and know everything, but not in that way the students had, to catalogue and dissect and then eventually dismiss or internalize it. But in the way she had of seeming to want—" he stopped sawing at the food, searching for a word in the still and murky air above our table—"wanting just to soak it up. There was a kind of life there, as though if you felt her cheek she would be warm. And she was. Still is. She's never changed much, all these years. There's still that, that—avidity. And I wonder sometimes where it will all go. It seems impossible that it will simply go out, like a light. All fiction takes as its great central mystery death, mortality, but it seems to me now that all of it misses the point."

He looked up at me, his empty fork poised in the air, like a small weapon or a signal of surrender. "I can't imagine the light going out," he said.

"You're talking about her as if she was already dead," I said.

"I've known her all my life," he said, and his eyes were puzzled, dull, like the eyes of a sick animal.

"Me too."

"Yes," my father said. "I suppose it's even truer of you children. But you'll go on. I have a difficulty imagining a life without your mother."

He ate then, slowly but with gusto, as though he'd completed some exhausting task. When he was finished he looked up again, his eyebrows sardonically lifted, his everyday self. "So much for the soliloquy," he said. "It's merely that I can't bear the thought that she's in so much pain. Sometimes at night she's awake for hours with it."

I sighed, and said what he wanted to hear. "I can take care of that," I said.

"I will try to give her more of an opportunity to ventilate," he said.

"Papa, we're not talking about an opportunity to ventilate. If she needed to ventilate, I'd send her to this shrink Dr. Cohn recommended. She needs you to talk to her, to listen to her, to let her know that it's all right to talk back to you, to confide, to unload. Tell her some of the things you've just told me."

"But she knows all that."

"Sometimes people need to hear things said out loud before they become real," I said.

Coffee arrived, bitter and tepid. A secretary from the English department bent over the table and told me that I was a very lucky person to have such wonderful parents. She twinkled at my father and waved over her shoulder as she disappeared into a dim corner of the restaurant, and I wondered if she had slept with him. The cheesecake tasted like heavily sugared spackle. I remembered I had to pick up strings of white lights to loop around the azalea bushes by the porch. I remembered we needed milk and toilet-bowl cleaner. I spilled coffee on the front of my sweater but luckily my mother had taught me the month before how to get coffee stains out with baking soda.

"I think we need to begin discussing funeral arrangements," my father said.

"Papa," I said. "You ask too much. You always have." I went to the bathroom and when I came back he was finishing his coffee and talking to the brother of the board member again. "Gotta go," I said, and I left for the mall and the supermarket.

When I got home my mother was asleep on the living-room couch, her mouth open, her lids fluttering as though someone was chasing her in her dreams. In the kitchen I sat at the table, littered with little notes—the one that said "lights for bushes" I threw away—and some stencil patterns of rocking horses and flowers. I telephoned Dr. Cohn's office and her nurse said she would call another prescription in to Sellinger's. But five minutes later, as I was still going through the notes—"shop for Xmas presents for J. and B.," one said, and I wondered how we would manage that—the phone rang.

"Ellen," said Dr. Cohn, without preamble, "how are we doing on that dosage? When does she get breakthrough pain?"

"First hour the stuff doesn't help, second and third hours she feels great," I said. "Fourth and fifth she dozes. About the sixth hour her back starts to hurt. Sometimes I cheat a little and give her something then."

"Good. You go ahead and do that. I think if we play around with this a little bit we can keep her comfortable and maybe lessen the sedation some, although that may be the disease and not the medication. Make sure she keeps taking it with the laxative. How are her spirits?"

"Depends. Quiet and thoughtful now, a lot of the time."

"Cogent?"

"Yes." I picked up the rocking horses. "Giving stencil advice on the phone."

Dr. Cohn laughed, a surprisingly deep and throaty sound. "I find your mother amazing," she said.

"Me too," I said, and I held my hand tight over my mouth so no noise would come out, no sobs.

"Ellen?"

"Fine, fine, I'm fine."

"I want to send you a nurse. Once a week. Blood pressure, heart sounds, that kind of thing. And to keep a watch on the catheter so that if we need it later for morphine it's in good shape. She can give you a break, let you get out, maybe help your mother bathe or dress."

"She can bathe and dress herself."

"Whatever."

"No nurse," I said.

"I insist."

"No."

"She'll come Monday."

"Ellie?" my mother called from the living room.

"I've got to go," I said. "I'll get the prescription later. Thanks for your help."

I sat at the table and looked down at a sheet of paper. Morphine, morphine, I'd written over and over. The phone rang again.

"El?" Jonathan said. "Guess what? I got the job."

Jonathan had applied to the district attorney's office in Manhattan for a summer internship. Sleek and full of himself in a gray double-breasted suit and red tie, he'd interviewed the Wednesday before Thanksgiving. He sounded more surprised than I was at his good fortune.

"We'll get a sublet downtown, near your old place. It'll be perfect for me and from there you can look around for something permanent. One of the women in my Con law class says she knows an NYU instructor with a one-bedroom on MacDougal who may be going on sabbatical. Maybe I can even get a magazine piece out of this." From time to time Jonathan threatened to write something to prove that he was at least as good as I was, a fact about which I had no doubt.

"Can you ask Jules whether she knows of anything or if she can ask around? She's got to know someone who's going off for the summer and wants to rent out their apartment or have someone house-sit their cat or something," Jonathan went on. "I am so psyched about this. The money is for shit but the contacts and the résumé value are great. And naturally the living arrangements will be superb even if the apartment's a pit."

"It's great, Jon."

"We'll celebrate at Christmas. My father is going to love this. Love it. It's the closest a lawyer ever gets to being part of the NYPD."

"It's great."

Silence. "Are you okay?" he finally asked.

"Just working on my morphine dosages here. I had lunch with my father and he wanted to discuss funeral arrangements, but before he could get to burial versus cremation I left to pick up toilet-bowl cleaner. And I'm reading *Anna Karenina*. I have this sneaking suspicion that this time around, she's going to stay with her husband and have a miserable life." More silence. "I'm pleased for you, Jon."

"And we'll get a place."

"I can't leave here."

"Yeah, but by June, El . . ." Silence again, longer this time.

"Jonathan, I'm not going to look for an apartment on the assumption that I can get rid of my mother in time to spend the summer in bed with you."

"I didn't mean that," he said.

"Yes you did. You thought to yourself, well, Mrs. Gulden will be dead by summer and then I can split the rent with Ellen and get laid in the process."

"Look—bottom line? Next time I have good news to share I'll call somebody else."

"Bottom line? That's a good idea. Because good news does not compute for me right now." I don't know which of us hung up first. I was the one who cried afterward. I'd been with Jonathan for nearly a third of my life and it ended over a summer sublet. Or at least that was what I would say when I made it flippant and amusing for Jules. I should have felt angry or bereft or heartbroken. But those emotions seemed luxurious to me, like a long hot shower or a bubble bath. I could not afford them.

I heard a shuffling sound and looked up to see my mother leaning on the doorjamb. She was wearing a pair of my old leggings and a shirt of my father's, its lower buttons pulling slightly over her distended belly. And for just a moment I thought to myself: you have ruined my life. You have ruined my life with your damn selflessness, your damn accommodations, your damn illusions, your damn husband, and now your damn death. Perhaps a shadow of all that passed over my face, for her voice was plaintive, almost childlike, when she spoke.

"I need a pill, Ellen," she said, the trace of a whine in the ebb and flow of her inflection.

I handed her the vial. "What would I do without this stuff?" she said, and she took one, her head tilted back and her throat working like a bird drinking from a puddle. "I'm so tired," she said after it had gone down. "I'd like some tea."

"I'll make it," I said.

"Please," she said as she went back to the living room. I put the kettle on to boil, and then, as though by rote, I put bread in the toaster and mixed sugar and cinnamon together in a small bowl and took the butter dish out of the refrigerator. It was almost like waking up from a dream when I finally looked down and saw, on the pretty lacquer tray, the mug of tea and the plate with two slices of cinnamon toast cut in triangles. It was the snack my mother always made us when we came in from sledding, playing in the snow, skating down at the pond behind the public library.

I carried it carefully into the living room and put the tray on the coffee table. The room was dim, and my mother was asleep on the couch, her breathing raspy, her eyes sunk into the concavities of her skull. One hand was held to the side of her face, as though to shield it from view.

"Mama," I said softly, but the only answering sound was the rattle of her breathing. I sat down on the ottoman and drank the tea and ate the toast and it was as though the house was breathing, too, all three of us breathing in tandem, dying in tandem, trying to keep body and soul together as the wind shook the storm windows in their metal frames. A leaf blew down the chimney and lay shivering on the stone hearth, and in a few minutes I took the tray into the kitchen and then came back into the living room to sit with her and watch her sleep.

By Monday morning I had forgotten everything about my call from Dr. Cohn except what she'd said about the morphine. Three or four hours after she took the medication my mother was groaning with pain, sometimes keening as though she was chief mourner at her own wake. More morphine given more often helped that, although it meant she slept more and sometimes she talked to herself in a monotone I could hear from her bedroom. Maybe there were things she needed to speak aloud that she could not say to anyone else.

So when the front door bell rang, the carillon of my childhood, *bing-BING, bing,* as it had not done for so long—"they all think cancer's contagious," my mother had said wearily one afternoon of her friends—I was unprepared for the slender dark woman who stood on the steps in a bright red jacket with a big canvas bag slung over her shoulder.

"Ms. Gulden?" she said, careful to use the more modern honorific, the dissonant sound of bees buzzing. She had a slight accent and her teeth were very white against her dark face and

hair. Above the *V* of her coat a white tunic jumped out like a surprise.

"Yes," I said, pushing at my hair, which I had not yet found
time to brush or barrette back.

She put out her hand. "I am Teresa Guerrero. I will be helping
you and your mother."

It was so deft, the way she said it, and I wondered if they taught
them etiquette in some hospice training class: do not say you are
there to take care, to treat. Say that you are there for both the
patient and the family. Make yourself an assistant; do not try to
run the show until later.

"Oh, Ms . . ."

"Guerrero. I am Ecuadoran originally, although for quite some
time I have been an American citizen."

"Ms. Guerrero, I told Dr. Cohn I didn't really need any help.
I'm caring for my mother myself."

"I appreciate that, Ms. Gulden. For today I will do nothing but
meet your mother and monitor her vital signs, her heart rate, her
respiration, her blood pressure. Later you can decide whether and
in what ways you wish to use me."

I looked at Teresa Guerrero for a long time, but unlike most
people she did not attempt to fill the silence that grew between us.

"I don't know about this, Ms. Guerrero," I said.

"We will find out."

"I am Ellen," I said, unconsciously adopting her speech patterns.

"I am Teresa." I stepped aside and let her in.

In the living room my mother was working on her needlepoint
pillow, the background half finished. Her clothes hung loosely
from her shoulders, and I had been able to tell for several days
that she wore no bra, although I was not sure whether it was
because she could not put one on or because she felt, with her
poor deflated breasts, that it was superfluous.

Teresa put down her bag, which made a clinking sound. "Mrs.
Gulden," she said, "my name is Teresa Guerrero and I am the

nurse sent by Dr. Cohn to monitor your vital signs." Vital signs, I thought, she keeps saying vital signs. Perhaps it is to make the patient feel vital. Will she ever say she is here to monitor dying signs? I watched my mother smile up at her, her bright company smile, and wondered whether she would offer refreshment.

"I appreciate that," said my mother. "Would you like a cup of tea?"

"No, thank you," Teresa said solemnly. "I never drink on duty. I don't eat on duty either."

"Do you laugh on duty?" I said.

"If something is funny," Teresa said. Turning back to my mother she asked her to push up her sleeve and unbutton the top two buttons of her shirt. "Knock knock," she said.

"Who's there?" said my mother.

"Banana."

"Banana who?"

"Knock knock."

"Who's there?"

"Banana." Her slight accent made the word sound exotic and very beautiful, almost erotic.

"Banana who?"

"Knock knock." She inflated the blood pressure cuff and consulted her watch.

"Who's there?"

"Banana."

"Banana who?"

"Knock knock."

My mother giggled. "Who's there?" she said.

"Orange."

"Ah! Orange who?"

"Orange you glad I didn't say banana?"

We all laughed. "I thought these children had told me every knock-knock joke under the sun, but I've never heard that one," my mother said.

Teresa was listening to my mother's heart. "Shhh," she said.

She moved the silver disc of the stethoscope from place to place, stopped to run her fingers gently over the catheter beneath my mother's skin.

"Is it still beating?" my mother asked.

"Loud and clear," said Teresa, who took a clipboard from her bag and began filling in a form.

"Do you have children?" I said.

"No," said Teresa. "I have not yet married."

"So where'd you hear the knock-knock joke? Not from Dr. Cohn?"

"No, not from Dr. Cohn. From the daughter of a woman I also visit. She is five and thinks that joke is very funny. I have heard it from her perhaps twenty times."

"What's wrong with her mother?" my mother said, buttoning her shirt.

"Mama, I'm sure they're not allowed to go from house to house talking about their patients."

"Her mother has breast cancer, Mrs. Gulden," said Teresa. "I have been seeing her for three months. Her own mother cares for her some of the time but she is not able to do certain things for her."

"And she has a five-year-old?"

"And a seven-year-old."

"Oh, Lord, that poor girl," my mother said, her mouth trembling.

"If the two of you were together in this room you would have a great deal to talk about," said Teresa.

"Yes?" said my mother.

"We can talk more about that. In the meantime what can I do for you? Is your pain under control? Can I help with your diet? Would you like help with bathing or dressing?"

"Oh, I'm having a terrible time getting in and out of the bathtub. But I can't have you coming to bathe me."

"Mama, you didn't tell me that," I said.

"Oh, there are so many things to worry about, Ellen."

"I can help you."

"No. Not with that."

"Oh, Mama, I've been in a million locker rooms."

"It's different," my mother said.

"Let's go upstairs," Teresa said. "I can show you some of the ways that coming in and out of the tub can be made more comfortable. And I would like to irrigate your catheter and you should be lying comfortably for that."

"Will it hurt?" said my mother.

"Compared to what I imagine you are used to, not very much."

My mother's lips quivered again as she replied, "What I'm used to is awful."

"Yes," said Teresa, and she took my mother's hand. "It is important that you not hurt." My mother's head dropped, an orange daisy in a drought. Tears fell, *plop, plop,* on their joined hands. I felt like a voyeur, a stranger. They stood together, Teresa helping my mother to her feet.

"Excuse me," said my mother, pulling a tissue from her sleeve and dabbing at her face. "I'm usually better than this."

"Better and stoic are two different things, Mrs. Gulden. You have a right, even an obligation, to express your feelings." She reached into her bag and brought out a folder. "You may want to read these," she said to me. "Not all of them are suitable for all patients but Dr. Cohn seemed to think you should have them, particularly the more technical information." Then she offered my mother her arm. Through the white bones of the banisters I watched them disappear, head, torso, knees, feet, as though they were ascending to heaven.

In the folder was "The Dying Person's Bill of Rights" and some pharmaceutical pamphlets about morphine. There were sixteen tenets to the Bill of Rights, and I got through "I have the right to be treated as a living human being until I die" and "I have the right not to die alone." I did not break until the last one: "I have the right to be cared for by caring, sensitive, knowledgeable people who will attempt to understand my needs and will be able to gain some satisfaction in helping me face my death."

"What satisfaction?" I sobbed, and the tears ran hot down my face and I cried into a pillow until my face was as swollen as I imagined my mother's stomach must be beneath my father's shirts.

I don't know how long Teresa was there, but she never touched me or made any noise. When I finally looked up, she was standing with her stethoscope around her neck. She began to rummage in her bag, to pull out instruments and swabs in sealed silver packages.

"This is why I told Dr. Cohn we did not need a nurse," I said to her, still shaking. "Having a stranger in the house is too upsetting. I cannot afford to fall apart."

"Falling apart is curling up into a fetal position and staying in bed for a week," she said. "What you were doing is having the emotional response an individual has to the loss of someone they love. We cry to give voice to our pain."

"That's very poetic, Ms. Guerrero, but it doesn't make me feel any better."

"You are not going to feel any better for a long, long time, Ms. Gulden, and you know that far better than I do. But I refuse to believe that keeping your grief bottled up makes you feel better than crying."

"Like a five-year-old," I said, blowing my nose.

"The five-year-old who provides me with jokes never cries, Ms. Gulden. She does not understand what is happening. But you do."

I shook my head. "I can help her," Teresa said, and went upstairs again. In a few minutes I heard a cry, a short sharp one, from the second floor, and then the long murmur of voices, and I got up and went to make two cups of tea. I sat at the table in the kitchen and drank one while the other grew cold on the counter, a tan skim of milk congealing on its surface. From above came another sound. I went to the living room and looked upward, and then I heard it again, the sound of a belly laugh. Teresa came downstairs swinging her stethoscope.

"What was that all about?" I asked.

"She'll tell you," she said, as she began to pack up her things. "I've taught her ways to sit on the edge of the tub and then slide in in stages, but it's going to make it easier if you buy one of those rubber mats with suction cups and fasten it to the side so she feels more secure. Then she will not slip."

"Should I help her bathe?"

"She is embarrassed by the condition of her body, but it may become necessary. Does she have an odor?"

"God, no."

"That may come and when it does you will have to talk with her again." She zipped her bag shut and for the first time since she arrived she smiled. She was very beautiful.

"How old are you?" I asked.

"Twenty-three," she said.

"Jesus. I'm twenty-four. Why do you do this kind of work? You could be working in the hospital nursery, bathing babies."

"Anyone can bathe a baby," Teresa said. "Not everyone can do this."

"You're good," I said.

"That's what Dr. Cohn said about you, Ms. Gulden."

"Ellen," I said.

"Ellen," she said. "I will be back next Monday, unless you need me sooner." She handed me a card.

I put the kettle on and brought my mother a fresh cup of tea. She was on the floor in her bedroom looking through a long brown box, the kind lawyers keep documents in.

"Do you remember the Halloween the boys went as a set of dice and Brian fell over downtown and Jeff wouldn't help him up because he got such a kick out of seeing him waving his arms and legs around. Jeff said he looked like a turtle on his back. Oh, I could have killed him, but the idea was very funny."

"Don't tell me—you've got the costumes in there."

She held up a picture of the two boys standing side by side on the front lawn, the light dying behind them so that there was a bright disfiguring star of last sunlight in the upper right corner.

Jeff was showing number two, Bri a five. Lucky seven. "I lent the costumes to someone and they never gave them back. It was a good one."

"Is that what you were laughing about?"

"When?"

"I heard you laughing upstairs when Teresa was here."

"Oh," my mother said, laughing again. "No. It's another joke: a little boy comes into the classroom and his teacher says, 'You're late. Where were you?' And he says, 'On top of Blueberry Hill.' And a second little boy comes in and the teacher says, 'You're late. Where were you?' And the boy says, 'On top of Blueberry Hill.' And a third little boy comes in and the teacher says, 'You're late. Where were you?' And he says, 'On top of Blueberry Hill.' And a little girl comes in and the teacher says, 'I suppose you were on top of Blueberry Hill too.' And she says, 'I *am* Blueberry Hill.' "

My mother giggled. "The five-year-old told her that?" I asked.

"The seven-year-old," my mother said.

"If I had told you that joke when I was seven I would have spent the afternoon in my room."

"*Autres temps, autres moeurs,*" my mother said, her fingers moving in a stroking movement to the bump of the catheter beneath her skin.

"Voltaire, I think," I said.

"Really?" my mother said. "I thought your father made that up." And she laughed again and looked back at the box. "Remember the Halloween when you were Bo-Peep?" she said.

"And I had to carry those sheep you made and kept spilling my candy?" I said. "How could I forget?"

"I remember it all," said my mother, "every bit of it."

On the morning when she went to decorate her tree we threaded red ribbon through the spokes of my mother's wheels, the way my mother had threaded red, white, and blue ribbons through the wheels of our bikes on the Fourth of July when we were children, ribbons and playing cards—but only the red ones, for the color—attached to the spokes with clothespins so that we made a noise when we rode like old engines, Model Ts in movies.

But none of the Minnies, even Mrs. Duane, who talked to us for a long time about a little girl who'd been kidnapped in Texas—tragedies! Oh, we loved our secondhand tragedies!— mentioned the ribbons. I suppose if they had acknowledged them it would have meant acknowledging the wheelchair, and if they acknowledged the wheelchair it would have meant acknowledging my mother's fragile sloping shoulders and the way her hands shook when she lifted them from the armrests.

And that would have meant acknowledging the disease, and the fears, and the dangers, and the death. Better than anyone I understood why they didn't want that to happen. Better than anyone except maybe my mother.

Imagine having to dictate your prose to someone else when you are writing a novel, or telling someone where to place the cerulean and how to mix it with white for the edges of a cloud in your landscape, and you can understand what it was for my mother to have to sit in her chair in front of the blue spruce, grown now to twenty feet all these years after its planting as a seedling, and direct my clumsy efforts to place her ornaments exactly where she wanted them. There were hundreds of them; both of us had sore calluses and little pin dots of dried blood on our fingers from pushing in the sequins and aligning the hanging wires. All red. All gold. Gold and red striped, gold and red spotted, random patterns of red and gold. And big red ribbons shot through with gold and stiff with wire, to be cosseted into bows.

"No no no, Ellen," she called from below as I attached a bow to a branch. "It's supposed to ripple." With her hand she sketched a shallow wave in the air, and the winter sunlight seemed to illuminate the blue veins on its back like miniature rivers, tributaries from her heart.

"That ball right near your hand . . . no . . . no . . . there! It's hanging too low. It needs to be tucked under there more tightly . . . higher . . . that's it . . . and then there should be one just below it . . . no, lower and over a little." It was like trying to scratch someone's back, finding the right spot, except that it was bigger than any back and the effort seemed to go on forever.

Mrs. Best had the tree next to us; her ribbons were gold, her ornaments red and gold wooden soldiers. "Where does your mother get that ribbon that holds its shape?" she asked me with her lips pursed.

"She just seems to have things like that," I said. "She's the kind of person who can go upstairs to the linen closet and dig up some silver stars if you need them."

"Oh, Linda, don't worry," my mother called to the two of us on our abutting ladders. "Yours looks beautiful already."

The truth was that even with my shortcomings at spacing, grouping, and tying, I thought the Gulden tree was the handsomest, although Mrs. Duane was swathing hers in some gold stuff that looked like fourteen-karat insulation, which was magical if strange. "Some of them never learn that with a tree this size in a public park, gaudy is key," my mother had said when I remarked that our ornaments looked like plump chorus girls in a second-rate summer-stock production of *42nd Street*.

As I stepped back to look at her tree, I could see she'd been right. The more tasteful decorations, including Mrs. Best's, seemed to disappear amid the ice-blue branches of the big trees. And when the switch was thrown on the red lights the public works people had threaded through the day before, the quieter efforts would completely disappear. "These will reflect!" my mother had declared triumphantly, turning her sequins in her shaking hands.

"Ellie, there's a bow on the other side that's much too close to the end of a branch," she called, fingering the ornaments in a box on her lap.

It took us nearly three hours to decorate that tree. By the time we were done, though the temperature was in the low thirties, I'd laid my jacket on the grass and discarded my gloves, my fingers alternately numb and aching from the pine needles and the wire hangers. "My back is killing me," one of the Minnies said loudly, clinging to a ladder with one hand and rubbing the small of her back with the other.

Mrs. Duane went down the street to the deli and brought back coffee and sandwiches for us all, and I sat at my mother's feet, my shoulders sagging, and ate roast beef and drank my coffee black. She ate nothing at all, only sipped at a cup of milky tea.

"How are you holding up?" I said very quietly.

"There's a problem. I don't know exactly what it is, but I can feel it."

"What?"

"It's something about the bows. Maybe they need to face down a little more."

And back up I went, as Mrs. Best stood with her arms crossed on her chest and looked from her tree to ours and then back again. She sighed. "Kate, you do have an eye. You simply have an eye. And with an eye, you either have it or you don't," she said.

What a dope, I thought to myself as I tilted bows downward.

"Linda, you're being silly," my mother said, but from the gay tone of her voice I could tell that she agreed completely, with Linda Best and with me, too. "It looks beautiful, and the children will love the soldiers. Do you have any more?"

"Tons," said Mrs. Best.

"Load 'em on," my mother said, as I cut my finger on one of the wires. "More is more."

I wasn't sure why she seemed so indefatigable that day, whether it was the brilliant weather, the pleasure she took in making things pretty, the return to something she'd done for so many years, or the competition—"the Super Bowl of home decor aficionados" my father had called it that morning at breakfast. Certainly my mother seemed a good deal happier at Mrs. Best's chagrin than was charitable, and at the improvement in the Best tree as Mrs. Best hung soldiers from every bare inch of branch.

Or perhaps it had been that she had gone out with my father the night before, dressed in her cranberry shift, the gold brooch of a bow with pavé diamonds at its knot pulling down one shoulder of the dress, which had already grown far too big for her. She'd made herself up painstakingly, but because her hands were unsteady her lipstick was, too, and her eyeliner looked a little like the stuttery lines on some hospital monitor.

She timed her morphine carefully so that the hours when she got most relief and least sleepiness would come during dinner and the chamber music concert they planned for later. She wore her fur coat and bent her head to rub her cheek against its soft collar.

When she and my father had driven away I sat on the living-room couch with my hands in my lap and tried to make a plan for my own evening. I had been so busy arranging for her dress, her medication, where her wheelchair would go in the car, that I had forgotten that for the first time in many months I would be alone. I called Jonathan, but he was not home and I left a breezy message on his machine: "Just called to check in. Call me if you have a chance." When I heard the recording of Jules saying, "Can't come to the phone right now . . ." I hung up.

But after I found *All About Eve* on a cable channel, ate some ice cream from the container, and had a light beer, I felt more like my old self, the Ellen Gulden who had walked around her little downtown apartment touching things her first night—sink, stove, bathroom taps—thinking "Mine, mine, mine."

Jonathan was not coming home for Christmas. He'd be doing three fulltime weeks of data processing; it would pay for his summer sublet. He had plenty of schoolwork to do, too, he'd said. And perhaps he had a first-year law student who loved the way he ran his tongue over his upper lip and made impudent eye contact as they talked about torts.

The pressure and pain behind my eyes and in my jaw was intense, maybe from the beer, and I wondered how morphine would go down with alcohol. On the TV Eve Harrington became a big star but sold her soul to that dandy of a devil, Addison deWitt. I'd never thought it seemed like such a bad bargain, although I'd have known better than to cross Bette Davis, with those mean sleepy eyes and that hard fish mouth.

The next movie was *High Noon.* I hated Gary Cooper and Grace Kelly—"so white bread," Jules and I would always say in unison—and I turned the television off just as a car door slammed outside.

Even before they got in the house I could tell that my parents' evening had not gone well. I could hear my mother arguing outside in the drive, and when my father opened the door with her clinging awkwardly to his arm, his face was white, his eyes dark.

". . . they were all looking," I heard her say as he helped her over to the couch, where she lay down slowly, in careful stages, her pumps left on the floor like a memento.

"I'll get the chair," I said.

When I came back in, my father had turned on the lamps and was in the kitchen. I could tell from the sounds of cabinet doors and canisters that he was making tea. My mother's eyes were closed, but she was biting her lower lip. When she opened her mouth there was lipstick on her teeth. Mascara was gathered at the corners of her eyes, smudgy shadows.

"Disaster," she whispered.

My father came in with a mug and handed it to her. She raised her head and shoulders to sip, then put it on the coffee table and fell back.

"I am never going out again," she said.

"Oh, nonsense, Kate," my father said. "A thousand people have dozed off during chamber music in the chapel. The president has done it nearly every time in my memory. Why shouldn't you?"

"Because I never would have before and they all knew why I did it tonight. I remember the Vivaldi and a little of the Mozart and then the next thing I know I'm waking up with spit all over my chin and everyone staring—"

"No one was staring," my father said. "They were getting ready to leave and gathering up their things."

"They were staring. At the restaurant people stared, too. And then you made the fuss about the chair—"

"The doors should be wide enough to accommodate wheelchairs. It's the law. The restaurant was negligent."

"—and you used that word," my mother continued, the pitch of her voice climbing. "You used that word!"

"I'm sorry," my father said.

"I am not handicapped, and don't you forget it. Either of you. I am not handicapped. I'm just weak. And woozy. I get woozy. That's why I need this thing."

"I said there were laws about accommodating the handicapped. I did not suggest that you were handicapped."

"Don't say that word," she said. "Don't say it."

"I'm sorry," he said again.

I went into the kitchen and made myself a cup of tea. But when

I went back to the living room, my father was kneeling beside the sofa with his head in my mother's lap and she was smoothing his hair. They were talking to one another, but I could not hear the words, only the plaintive tones of one and the murmurings of the other. I went back into the kitchen and poured the tea into the sink, threw away the empty ice-cream container, took two aspirin for the pain behind my eyes, and decided to go to bed. The house was quiet except for the faint hum of the furnace from the basement, just discernible through the floorboards.

I went through the hallway to the stairs, past the watercolor portraits of Brian at six, Jeffrey at eight, Ellie at eleven with serious eyes and mouth and a pink ribbon holding back her dark hair. But my parents were there ahead of me, my father three steps up, carrying my mother, who had her head on his shoulder.

"I'm so tired, Gen," she said quietly, without ever knowing I was there.

"I know, dear heart," he replied.

The next morning my father said the dinner had been a fiasco. "If she were a child she would have been described as playing with her food," he said, then drained his coffee cup, picked up his book bag, and left for his nine o'clock class before she could come downstairs. Yet when she did come down she was all lit up, dreamy, smiling, with the lines softened around her mouth and on her forehead. And she stayed that way all that day.

My father, before he went to work, had been merely distracted; his hair was awry, and there was a spot of blood on his collar to match the nick on the underside of his chin. All the lines on his face looked deeper, as though he'd had a bad portrait done, or an unforgiving black-and-white photograph. "What class do you have?" I'd asked as I handed him coffee.

"Women in Dickens," he said.

"Miss Havisham and Estella? Or the wimps, Little Dorrit and Dora and David's sainted mother?"

"All," he said, standing up.

"What about his wife and his mistress?"

"Only the work, not the biography," he said. "Ellen, the buttons have broken on the collars of two of my shirts. I put them on the chair in the bedroom. Could you see that they're replaced? And I'd rather we had the skim than the whole milk. Or get both and give the whole milk to your mother. Your brothers will be home on Thursday afternoon so they'll need plenty to eat."

"But how can you separate the work from the biography?"

"What?"

"Dickens. How can you illuminate the work if you separate the work from the biography?"

"You know the stock answer to that," he said, distracted. "The work stands alone. Does the nurse come again soon?"

"Monday."

"Your mother liked her. She said last night that she found her helpful."

"She's good," I said.

"The doctor has decided to discontinue the chemotherapy," my father said.

"What?"

"She spoke to your mother the other day at the hospital, when you took her over. She told me last night. Dr. Cohn decided that it's not having much of an effect." He went into the hall for his briefcase. "I'll meet you at seven here for the tree ceremony."

"That's it? That's all? No more chemo? End of sentence? End of discussion?"

"What more is there to say?" my father said, and left for work.

The night they lit the Christmas trees on the green was a perfect night of its kind in Langhorne. In summer there would be those dark nights with a cool breeze blowing faintly and the passing scent of petunias in the air, nights that veered between hot and not so hot so that when you went skinny-dipping in the reservoir you would get out and then jump back in because the water felt warmer than the air.

In fall there were the sweater days, football days, when the sun shone clear but light yellow, the color of white corn, and as you walked down the street a leaf would pirouette to the sidewalk right before your eyes, almost brushing your nose, and late at night the rumble of the furnace would suddenly shake the house like a snore.

And spring, what there ever was of it, was all beautiful, the pure smell of wet and fresh and the daffodils sashaying on the green, in our yards, in hidden wild patches on the hillside sloping down to the river amid the damp grass.

And in winter there were nights like the one when they lit the trees that year, when the sky hung down like black silk punched full of holes so that the bright light behind could shine out in tiny points, thousands of them. The air burnt your tongue a bit with its cold, and the bony fingers of the bare tree branches reached up to lay hands on a full moon. It was bright outdoors, silver-bright, with the long black shadows of shrubs, houses, people walking down the sidewalk and staring up at the moon as though it was moving the tides of their lives and they could feel the ebb and flow inside them.

Usually on a night like that in Langhorne you'd only know how perfect it was when you went to take the garbage out and were dazzled, or came in late from work or a movie and stopped to marvel. After dark people stayed home in Langhorne, not because there was anything to fear, but because our houses—our kitchens, our dens, our bedrooms—were where our lives took place.

If a stranger walked the streets, which had never happened in my memory, he would see from the sidewalk one imagined oasis after another of yellow light and easy love: a woman's head at a kitchen window, her arms moving in slow and steady patterns as she washed dishes; children passing to and fro in their rooms looking for pencils or turning down the stereo on command; men dozing in big comfortable chairs. Outside on the cold streets you would see no one, except perhaps some child walking home from a friend's house after working on a school project, the pyramids in papier-mâché, a disquisition on *Romeo and Juliet* and family discord. You would hear nothing except for the faint sounds from within those houses, of piano practice and the water running and the commentators from *Wide World of Sports*.

But the night they lit the trees was different. Whole families, their collars turned up against, not the cold, but the idea of cold, of how cold it ought to be in the shadow of Christmas, came down the street to the green. From inside our house we could hear the murmur of their voices outside, a drone like that of bees around the hydrangea bushes on one of the perfect summer days.

My mother was upstairs getting dressed, and I was packing a

bag with her pills, extra gloves, and four Christmas ornaments that we had not put on her tree, just in case, she said, although it was hard to tell what "in case" meant. She'd put on an old pair of wool slacks, cinched tightly under a red turtleneck and the red sweater with reindeer leaping across it that she wore every year to the tree ceremony. She came down the stairs slowly, holding tightly to the banister, then settled herself in her chair and pulled her beret over what little was left of her hair.

"No coat?" said my father.

"I don't need a coat," she said. "I'm layered. Besides, I want to show off my sweater."

I was wearing red, too, and my father a green loden coat, and together we made a festive group, with our beribboned wheel-chair. My father pushed the chair and I walked alongside. The moon touched the handles and made silver pools of its own reflection. My mother tipped her head back to look up.

"Beautiful night," she said softly.

The road around the green was packed with people, the crowd so large that some stood on the streets that fanned out from the hub. But we were able to push right through because my mother and the other Minnies were given a place at the front, next to the podium from which the mayor gave the signal to light the trees.

"Hey, Mrs. Gulden?" said Hetty Belknap, who for all her child-hood had been known as Hugh and Sophie Belknap's change-of-life baby, a scrawny little girl with freckles and sandy hair that looked as if she'd cut it herself, perhaps with manicure scissors.

"What, sweetie?" my mother said.

"I like how you decorated your wheels," she said, and her father gave her a stern look. "I didn't say anything about her being sick," Hetty whined as he led her away.

"Hey, Ellen," said a young police officer keeping the crowd back, whose name I couldn't quite recall until months later when I saw him at the municipal building.

"Well, how are you?" I said brightly. "Look at you in your uniform."

"Ellen's imitating me, Gen," said my mother, giving me a wink.

The Presbyterian choir stood in their red robes with songbooks under their arms, and Amanda Bollan, who'd been in Honor Society with me, waved and then turned to say something to the woman next to her.

"Is Brian home yet?" one slender girl with fur earmuffs asked me, ducking her head.

The mayor shook hands with us all. So did Mr. Best, wearing one of his MAY THE BEST MAN WIN hats.

"Linda says you gave her good advice on her tree," he said to my mother.

"Oh, Ed, she didn't need it," my mother replied.

"You're looking well," he added. "And you, too, Ellen."

The Minnies usually stood in a semicircle behind the podium, but this year they grouped themselves around my mother's wheelchair. The mayor read their names amid the sounds of mothers *ssshusshing* their children and one little girl wailing loudly, the sound fading, like an ambulance turning a corner, as she was carried away into darkness.

I'd been a little girl here once, riding on my father's shoulders, clutching at his hair while my mother held Jeffrey awkwardly against her hip, to one side of her bulging stomach. The year she had first been a Minnie I had looked every morning in the basket in the hallway to see what she'd made for her tree the night before. But I'd never helped decorate before that morning. She'd never asked. I'd never offered.

"Happy holidays, Langhorne," the mayor said, a change from the "Merry Christmas" of years gone by because of the complaints of a Jewish professor of economics at the college that had occupied page one of the *Tribune* for a week two Januaries before. He raised his hand and the trees came alive, sparks leaping from amid their branches, the sequins on my mother's tree winking red and gold. The crowd burst into applause and the choir began to sing.

There was a moment of silence as the last deep sonorous note of "Silent Night" died away. My father's eyes were fixed on my mother; his lips were held together tightly, one to the other, but when she looked over, he smiled broadly.

"Which one did she do?" he asked, as though the tables and countertops of his home had not been littered with sequined ornaments for weeks.

"Third from the left," I whispered, smelling the lemon of his cologne and the musty wool of his coat. "Papa smells," I called them when I was a little girl, along with the smells of shoe polish and leather shoes.

"I suspected as much," he said.

The choir bounced through "Deck the Halls," their consonants as sharp as could be, punctuated with little white bursts of warm breath on the cold night. The Minnies hugged one another, and the mayor thanked them, and the crowd surged forward to look at each tree closely. For a moment I lost sight of my mother as she disappeared amid a circle of neighbors. The young cop smiled across their heads at me, then turned away, his pale face a moon above the children pushing through the crowd to find their friends.

"Are you Ellen?" said a woman with blond hair held back from a high forehead with a red velvet band dotted with silk holly leaves and sequined berries. She had on a black wool cape that swung open when she moved. She was very pregnant.

"I'm Halley McPherson," she said, shaking my hand. "We just moved here from Atlanta. My husband is comptroller at the college. This is such a nice thing, isn't it?"

"It is, but it must seem sort of small town after Atlanta."

"Well, everything really is small town, anyhow, isn't it? My husband always says there are no big ponds. Although your mom says you're a New Yorker, so maybe you wouldn't agree."

I smiled noncommittally. I didn't.

"Well, I just wanted to meet you because your mother has been such a saint to me. I told the man at the hardware store that I was looking for a decorating book to do the baby's nursery and he said that I didn't need a decorating book if I talked to your mom."

"Oh, you're the crib person. How'd it turn out?"

"It's beautiful. Nobody can believe I did it myself."

The crowd around us moved aside and there was my father, pushing the wheelchair. My mother smiled and put out her hand.

"Oh Halley, there you are in person." She looked down at Halley's midsection. "You look wonderful."

"Fecund," said my father.

"I'm due a week from Friday," Halley said.

"Mama, how did you know it was her?" I said.

"She talked me through making the headband, too," Halley said, raising her hand to her hair. "That's how she was going to recognize me. And soon she's coming to see the crib."

"Very soon," my mother said.

As we walked back up the hill, children eddying around us, adults calling greetings across the street to all three of us, my mother looked up at the moon again and said, "I do love Christmas. It's always been my favorite holiday. I used to decorate the whole apartment with construction-paper things when I was little." She took my hand as we walked. "Ellen, we need to get a tree," she said.

"No, no," I cried, and people turned around to look. "Please, Lord, not another tree to decorate. Let this cup pass from me."

"Just one more," my mother said, laughing. "Only eight feet tall or it won't fit in the living room."

"One more," I said. "That's my limit."

"And the boys will be home in two days, and we'll have ham for Christmas dinner. Much easier than turkey."

"Turkey wasn't so bad."

"And it's good to know how to make a turkey, just in case."

"In case of what?"

"Oh, you," my mother said.

"The Gulden tree was the most beautiful one," my father said.

"I know," said my mother.

The moon was as perfect and bright as a dime, and from some of the houses bits of colored lights shone out, the lights on Christmas trees whose outlines were lost in the dark of sleeping houses, empty houses, houses whose people were still winding their way up the hill. There was a slight wind, and the outdoor evergreens made a sound like hands rubbing softly together.

My mother shivered. "You're cold," said my father sternly. "You ought to have worn a coat."

"I'm not cold," my mother said.

A little boy in a red cap pulled low ran past us, crying "Mommy!" and faintly, from the bottom of the hill we could hear a group of people singing "We Wish You a Merry Christmas" in stops and starts, searching aloud for the words.

"I love Christmas," my mother said with a sigh.

My father leaned down so that his head was close to hers. "And Easter," he said. "I have it on good authority that Easter comes early this year. Very early. And that nice young woman will surely need you to teach her how to paint eggs or weave baskets."

My mother put her hand to my father's cheek, and then she looked up again at the moon. "No, Gen," she said. "Easter was never my holiday. To hell with Easter."

The second time Teresa came to the house Jeffrey and Brian were home from school. They had climbed out of Jeff's leaky jeep sopping wet, caught in one of those dreadful soaking winter rainstorms just outside of Philadelphia but determined to make it home for dinner. Our mother was asleep upstairs when they first arrived; the night after the tree lighting she had woken up crying with pain soon after she went to bed and then had woken again, after I gave her more morphine, weeping incoherently about the babies and a thunderstorm and a tree splitting in the front yard and falling on the house. I stood in the doorway of their room while my father tried to calm her, undone by her blank eyes and senseless rant. He held her arms and repeated, "You are having a nightmare, Kate. It is a nightmare. A nightmare. There is no storm. There are no babies."

"No babies," she said.

"No."

"I'm here, Mama," I said.

"A nightmare," she said.

"Yes."

Finally he eased her back and pulled the covers around her shoulders. Like a light turned off, her lids went down and she began to breathe heavily, as though she had a bad cold. My father got out of bed in his boxer shorts. While I looked away, leaning against the doorjamb, he pulled on last night's pants and shirt.

"I cannot sleep after that," he said. "Are hallucinations a side effect of the medication?"

"I don't know," I said. "What if they are? I'd rather have her hallucinating comfortably than suffering from the pain."

"I'm not suggesting that she should suffer. I'm suggesting that we should not administer medication without knowing all its side effects."

"Oh, Papa, who gives a shit? Who gives a shit if it makes her skin turn purple and blood come out her nose if it stops her from hurting? This is not an intellectual exercise. This is day-to-day let's get through this."

"Just ask the doctor," he said, going downstairs.

"You ask her," I said.

But instead I asked Teresa when she arrived with her bag. Jeff had been out with his high school friends until nearly dawn, and he was in the kitchen in bare feet and running shorts when the bell rang.

"My public," he said, holding a peanut-butter-and-jelly sandwich in his fist and throwing open the door.

"It's Teresa," I said, looking over his shoulder. "Come in, Teresa. She's upstairs and the area around her catheter seems a little red. She was hoping you would look at it and at some lumps she has on her sides."

"Certainly," Teresa said as Jeff held the door and watched her pass. She laid her coat over one of the wing chairs in the living room, took the small pouch from her duffel bag and went upstairs. In a moment I heard her call, "Rise and shine."

"Give me a clue," Jeff said.

"The nurse."

"The nurse?"

"I told you. Dr. Cohn wanted to send a nurse once a week. That's her. Teresa Guerrero."

"Teresa?"

"Jeffie, hon, I have a floor to wash and three loads of laundry. Dr. Cohn sent a nurse, her name is Teresa Guerrero, and I too have noticed that she is extremely young and attractive."

"When you said a nurse I pictured someone who looked like a dinner roll. Round. White. Fluffy. Comforting."

"Well, this is what you get instead."

"My stars," said Jeff, eating his sandwich. "Sakes alive. Well I'll be."

Before Teresa came downstairs Jeff had put on a pair of jeans and a rugby shirt. "Even shoes," I said. "My stars."

"Put a sock in it, Ellie," my brother said.

"I'm really glad you guys are home," I said.

"Me too. Especially for Brian. He's having a really hard time at school. Hates his roommate, hates his adviser, hates his courses. I think it's basically because he hates not being here. He even talked about transferring to Langhorne so he could be near Mom."

"Dad would never stand for it. Besides, if he doesn't do it next semester, he won't have to do it at all."

"You think?" Jeff said.

"Yeah. Unless there's some kind of miracle, I think we'll be coming into the home stretch soon."

"Ah, shit," Jeff said. "How soon?"

"I'm like an alcoholic. I take it one day at a time. I can't tell you what next week is going to be like."

"I saw Jon in Cambridge a couple of weeks ago. I went up to see the guys at BU and had a drink with him. He told me he wasn't coming home for Christmas."

"I don't think he can deal with the idea of someone losing their mother."

"Yeah, well, that's very understanding of you, but I think he needs to play out his little personal psychodrama at some other time, when someone he allegedly cares about doesn't need him quite as much. I think his behavior sucks."

"And you told him that."

Jeff smiled. "Is the Pope Polish?" he said.

"And?"

"He's not the kind of guy you need in a tough time," Jeff said.

"No," I said.

"On the other hand," Jeff said, "a year ago I would have said the same thing about you."

Teresa was swinging her stethoscope when she came downstairs. She had on big gold hoop earrings and a dress this time, with a long full white skirt that almost swept the ground, and she was carrying a small box, wrapped in red with red-and-green striped ribbon. All week I'd been delivering gifts while my mother slept, to neighbors, to nurses, to Dr. Cohn, who took out the small needlepointed pillow on the end of a ribbon that said OY VAY and hung it on the doorknob of her office. "The oncologist's creed," she said. "I believe that was the thought behind the gift," I had said.

Teresa held up her little box and smiled. "What a lovely woman she is," she said.

"You have any more jokes?" I said.

"No, no more. Those children are fixated on Blueberry Hill, Blueberry Hill, I believe because we told them it was vulgar. The boy keeps repeating the word, vulgar, vulgar, as though he loves the idea."

Jeff stuck out his hand. "Jeff," he said. "Gulden." Recovering a bit, he added, "All County Soccer, All County Lacrosse, eldest son, power serve."

"I believe your mother already told me all that," Teresa said cooly. Turning to me, she added, "I don't see any real problem with the catheter site. I've irrigated it again, and taken a blood sample, which Dr. Cohn wanted. When was her last medication?"

"I'm not sure."

"She seems very very tired to me. I don't believe the adjustment on the dosage or frequency is exactly right. May I speak to Dr. Cohn about it?"

"Sure. She naps in the morning and the afternoon now, but she doesn't plan them so much as she just drops off. Sometimes she'll fall asleep on the couch while she's reading or in her chair when the TV's on. Then she'll be fine for a while and then she'll start to fade again. She's particularly tired this week because she had a bad night Tuesday. My father wants to know—does the morphine cause hallucinations?"

Teresa looked up the stairs, then at Jeff. "Can we sit down?" she said.

"There are a variety of opinions about hallucinations and the use of morphine," she said when we were in the living room. "Many physicians will tell you that it does not happen. Others will say that it is one possible side effect. Some nurses will tell you that what happens are not hallucinations at all. When did this happen?"

"The other night she woke up crying about babies and thunderstorms."

"Well. There are several possibilities. One is that it was a nightmare and she had a more acute reaction than you or I might have because of the medication. The other is that it was a true hallucination. But she also may be working out some matters mentally that would emerge in that fashion. I know that is very vague, but we think some people we see have things that they want to think about or talk about and that the people who care for them can only see those things as hallucinations."

"Like?"

"I have an older woman dying of cancer of the pancreas who constantly accuses her husband of infidelity with a variety of their acquaintances. Very vividly and in considerable detail, I might add. I've learned a few things I did not know about sexual congress."

"Oh, shit," said Jeff.

"Are we sure he's not?" I said.

"We are sure he is not," said Teresa with a slight smile. "It is my theory that she is contemplating his life without her and that her anger and fear leads her to rehearse it in that way."

"Babies and thunderstorms?" Jeff said.

"I am not a psychiatrist, Mr. Gulden, and I am told that Ellen does not want to consult one. But perhaps you are the babies and this"—she swept her arm around the house and brought her hand to rest on her bag and its welter of medical equipment—"is the storm."

"Maybe you should think about psychiatry," Jeff said. "That's pretty credible."

"Perhaps you can discuss her dreams with her, Ellen."

"I wish I could just take your stethoscope and listen to her heart. Really her heart, not the beating, but inside."

Teresa took the stethoscope from her bag and handed it to me. "Maybe it will help. Any intimacy will help. I can get another one." She stood up. "I think I will come again soon if you are not opposed."

"Any time," said Jeff.

"Mind your own business, Jeff." I slung the stethoscope around my neck. Sometimes, afterward, I've thought of that, how that was the first time I'd ever handled a stethoscope and how I hung it around my neck, just like the doctors and nurses did. I've thought about how Teresa gave it to me and how I kept it even though I knew I should offer to hand it back.

"My mother likes you, Teresa," I said. "Come as often as you think necessary, or helpful, or whatever. I have a feeling she may need you more often now."

"Yes," Teresa said, picking up her coat.

"How long?" Jeff said.

"I cannot say for sure," Teresa said. "It's more important that you take advantage of the time you have than that you worry about how much time there is."

And that was exactly what we did over the next week. The boys took her out in the jeep, wrapped in scarves and blankets against the cold, to see the Christmas decorations all over town, from the austere white lights in the bushes and trees outside some of the largest houses in our neighborhood to the small Cape Cod on a narrow county road ten miles from town, which had big plastic choirboys with 200-watt bulbs inside their pink heads singing on the lawn, a sleigh and eight reindeers in tortured postures on the roof, and a blinking sign that said JOYEUX NOËL covering the garage door.

The three of them came in that night howling because of Jeff's description of what he called "La Maison de Billion Lumières" and the electric bill of the family that lived inside. I could hear them in the den as I made cocoa and set out Christmas cookies on a plate in the kitchen.

"How can we possibly turn in without calling them and, as politely as possible, saying, 'Monsieur, Madame, why French? Why?' " Jeff cried. " 'To add a touch of class to the Little Rascals with their plastic choir robes? Because—get this, folks—it's not working!' "

I brought a tray in and Brian added, "Geez, El, if you could see this place. And Jeff is driving real slow, real slow, and doing this description of all the stuff they have, and Mom is saying, 'Jeffrey, they will hear you!' But he can't hear her because she's laughing so hard she's making little squeaky noises."

"He was very mean," said my mother, laughing.

"I was just as mean about how constipated the Byers' house looked, with the white candles in each window. I'm an equal opportunity mean person. No one can call me a snob."

"You're a snob," said Brian.

Jeff grabbed him in a half nelson. "You're toast," he said. "You're through."

My father stepped into the den from the hallway, his hand over the telephone receiver. "Will you all please be quiet!" he hissed. "I am on the phone to Cambridge!"

"Jesus," Jeff whispered. "Cambridge! I almost interrupted a conversation with someone in Cambridge."

"Jeff," said my mother.

"All right, Little Ma. The cookies are supreme, as always."

"Talk to your sister, dear. She made them."

Jeff stared at me. "Picture it," he said. "Ellen Gulden actually putting flour and water in the same place at the same time—using the Mixmaster—the spatula."

"What the hell do you think I've been doing around here all this time?" I said. "Who do you think runs the vacuum and does the laundry and makes all the meals? Who do you think shops and cleans and makes the beds?" My voice began to break and there were tears in my eyes. I stopped and turned away, back to the kitchen. "Shit," I heard Jeff say, and my mother did not reprimand him.

We watched all of the Christmas movies, *Miracle on 34th Street* and *It's a Wonderful Life,* and when George Bailey's brother called him the richest man in town we sat there sobbing, and even my father cried silently. On Christmas Eve I made shrimp and opened champagne. "Betty Crocker! Sit right here by me," said Jeff, and this time I did not lose my equilibrium. We watched *A Christmas Carol,* the old black-and-white English version with Alastair Sim.

"There has quite literally never been a good film made of one of Dickens's novels," my father said, peering at the screen over the top of his reading glasses, *The New York Review of Books* open on his lap. "It's not possible. The backbone of Dickens is physical description. It's the description that fails them. Look, now, here's the party scene when Scrooge is an apprentice and nothing, absolutely nothing they can do in the way of casting or dialogue for the character of, say, a Fezziwig, can touch what is in the book."

"I bet that's just what Mario Puzo says about *The Godfather,*" said Jeff.

"Listen to the dialogue, Ellen," my father said. "The rhythm's been completely eradicated."

"Oh, put a sock in it, Gen," my mother said, and we all burst out laughing, all except my father, who colored slowly, from chin to forehead. Jeff had gone to get a copy of the book from my room, and he was reading along with the movie dialogue, which was remarkably intact. "I'm sorry, really," my mother added, "but you can't be condescending about *A Christmas Carol.* Not tonight."

"My point was—"

"I know. But I want to watch the movie."

I think at any other time my father would have continued the argument, or perhaps at any other time my mother would never have begun it in the first place. But he fell silent and read while the rest of us finished one bottle of champagne and opened another.

"Are you still angry at me, Gen?" my mother said during a commercial break. "I was never angry at you," he said.

But when we discovered she had fallen asleep, after Scrooge had learned to keep Christmas, he would not carry her upstairs. Perhaps it seemed too intimate a gesture to make while his three children stood around. Or perhaps, I thought, remembering how happy my mother had been the morning after their disastrous dinner, carrying her upstairs promised something afterward that he did not want to give. We woke her—"It's over? It's over?" she asked, like a small child who'd fallen asleep at the circus—and Brian led her upstairs.

Next morning she was up at seven, earlier than she'd been in weeks, to lie on the couch and open her presents. Jeff gave her a silk scarf with big bunches of purple grapes all over it, enormous and luxurious, and she slung it around her shoulders. Brian gave her a copy of Gibbon's *Decline and Fall of the Roman Empire.* She said brightly, "I've been meaning to read this for years," and the two of them laughed until they choked and had to be pounded on the back. Brian leaned toward me and whispered, "It's another one of those romance novels. The Duanes gave me the *Roman Empire* dust jacket."

I gave her a set of walkie-talkies, so we could communicate when she was in a different part of the house. My father gave her a platinum band of small diamonds in one perfect circle. It caught the light and turned it blue and pink, and though it fell down to her first knuckle when she moved, no one suggested she get it in a smaller size.

"It's called an eternity ring," said my father, almost shyly.

"I know," my mother said, the small stones brilliant against the dark blue of her velour robe. "It's beautiful, Gen. It's the nicest thing I've ever gotten."

Jonathan sent me a datebook, one of those thick leather ones that very busy women take out and put on the table at lunches, filled with phone numbers and memos to themselves and a page for each day of the year and a map of the London Underground, as though they ever traveled by anything but cab. The whole year to come moved like playing cards under my fingers, empty and clean, February, July, November.

I paged through, sitting on the floor beside the tree. My birthday in August was on a Friday, my mother's a Tuesday at the end of June. Easter did come early, at the end of March.

"Subtle, isn't he?" said Jeff as he looked over my shoulder at the empty white pages.

I still own that datebook. I use it every day now; I'd be lost without it, without all the phone numbers, the slips of paper with scribbled notes about times and consults and medication, the notes about where I have to be next Tuesday, next Friday, next month. Sometimes I feel if I lost it I would lose the linchpin of my life. But of course I remember that in one way I lost the linchpin years before, not long after I acquired the datebook. It was not an even swap.

When the year is done I take its pages, its scrawled and sloppy and often unintelligible record—what did "11—DMC" on May 12 mean, anyhow?—and put them in a small manila envelope, seal it, and put it in a shoe box. Jules, who has things thrown in boxes in every closet in her apartment, bank statements and telephone messages and old junk mail and family photographs, says I am anal and do this to bring surface order to a spiritually chaotic life. But by now, five years after the habit began, it has simply become one of those things you do, like the way you fold or ball your socks or whether you eat corn on the cob from left to right or right to left.

I never open the envelopes to look at those old pages. And no one, looking at them after I am gone, will know much more about me than they've known before, except perhaps, if it was not already manifest, that I am a very, very busy woman and that I like to use a fine-tip marker pen with black ink, not blue.

But what would surely perplex anyone who ripped open the yellow envelopes and looked inside are the first two months of the first year. I remember well that they are completely empty.

The datebook sat on my desk through January and February. I wrote Jules's number in it, which was unnecessary, since I knew it by heart. I wrote in Jeff's and Brian's addresses at school. I did not write in Jonathan's address; he had done it himself. In blue ballpoint. The only blue ballpoint entry in the book.

"Do you like it?" Jon asked. "I was going to get you the one with a week on a page but I figured it would never be enough, with all your running around. The day-on-a-page version makes it pretty fat, but I figured the trade-off would be worth it."

"It's great, Jon," I said.

"It was calling your name," he said.

And it was, it was calling the name of the old Ellen Gulden, the girl who would walk over her mother in golf shoes, who scared students away from writing seminars, who started work on Monday after graduating from Harvard with honors on a Thursday, who loved the moments in the office when she would look out at the impenetrable black of the East River, starred with the reflected lights of Queens, with only the cleaning crew for company, and think of her various superiors out at dinner parties and restaurants and her various similars out at downtown clubs or cheap but authentic places in Chinatown and say to herself, "I'm getting ahead." That Ellen Gulden, the one her boss suspected of using the dying-mother ploy to get more money or a better job title, would have covered every inch of these pages with the frantic scribble of unexamined ambition.

For two months I wrote nothing in it. I had no need. The big event of January was when the hospital bed was delivered and we moved the furniture from the den into the living room to accommodate it. The home of Kate Gulden was being dismantled bit by bit, going to that place where past perfect lives dwell, perhaps to live there side by side with the former Ellen Gulden, who ate ambition for breakfast and anyone who got in her way for lunch.

The last good afternoon I remember was when I learned to make bread. I kneaded and folded and patted down and covered up with a dishcloth and my mother and I talked about Teresa and what she did. As the bread rose we sat in the living room with our fat copies of *Anna Karenina*. I lost myself in the book, in Levin's scything under the hot sun, in Vronsky's self-absorption, in the romances and the intrigues and Anna's palpable misery and obsession. It was only when the light died in the room and I could no longer see the letters properly that I looked at my mother, who was looking at me, the book held open with her hand.

"I'm glad we did this one," I said in a rush, "because I'd really like your opinion. The last time I read it was for a course on women in literature and we had this young woman professor who said that the fatal flaw of the book was that it was written by a man and that Anna would have left her husband for her lover but that she never would have left her son, that if a woman had written the book she would have known that. I tried to talk to Papa about it once, but he kissed the whole idea off—I think he said that Anna stood for the body and Kitty for the spirit or something like that, which I suppose is right. But what do you think? Do you think she was right, that Anna would have stayed for the sake of the child?"

There was a long silence, and I thought she was thinking about what I had asked. And then quietly she said, "I can't see the words."

"I know," I said, "it's getting so dark." I turned on the table lamp. "You should have told me to turn it on earlier."

She shook her head, a shower of red glints, and she let the book slip from her grasp and onto the rug. "I can't see the words on the page anymore. I can't read anymore. My eyesight is going.

Like an old woman." She sighed deeply and then there was a sound, like a bone caught in her throat.

We sat in silence and finally she said, "It's hard for me to believe that any woman would willingly leave her child."

"Not for love?"

"That is love," she said. She reached down and picked up the book.

"I'll get you a magnifying glass," I said.

"A pill," she said. "I need another pill."

Later I told Teresa about my mother's eyesight, and she told me she was not surprised, that it might be some unusual side effect of the medication and the deterioration. "We had a book club," I started to say, and then I made that same sound my mother had, that swallowed sob.

"You will have to move on to something else," Teresa said.

"I'm scared shitless," I said, putting my face in my hands.

"Of course you are," Teresa said. "You are doing all of the right things. And that is the right thing now."

"I can't stand this much longer," I said.

It was quiet, so that I could hear the hands of the kitchen clock clicking round their inexorable orbit. Teresa waited a long time, and finally she said softly, with the first hint of sympathy or real softness I had ever heard in her voice, "You will stand it as long as you need to."

If it had not been for Teresa Guerrero I am not sure that I ever would have bathed or dressed. Like Baby Jane and her poor sister, my mother and I would have sat in the living room, in bathrobes and greasy hair. But because of Teresa, because I needed to make myself seem all right for her, I rose early, showered, cleaned last night's detritus off the kitchen counter, the plate from the leftover meal my father had taken from the oven faintly warmed by the tiny blue pilot, the plate from the cherry pie I had eaten before bed.

I was getting heavy; the only pants that fit anymore were the ones with the elastic waists. But my father looked just the same, drawn and distinguished, although some days he seemed better than others, and I always wondered if those were the days after the nights when he had had some associate professor, some administrative aide, on the creaky leather couch in his office. When I wondered that an anger as powerful as pain jumped in my gut, but I put it down because I could not afford it. I needed all my energy to get through the days now, now that my mother had begun to die in earnest.

Perhaps I was being romantic, but I think she made it happen herself, the slide, after the boys left. I remember how she had said "To hell with Easter," and I think that maybe for a long time she had struggled toward Christmas, toward the old traditions and the time together, that she had made up her mind she would marshal her strength for that time, in its way the apogee of the kind of life she had tried so hard to construct in that small and pretty white house, the life of family meals and pleasant rituals and pretty things.

She was so often gay during those two weeks, that sort of feverish gaiety they say people sometimes wrap around themselves for a moment's warmth before they put a gun into their mouths or step into the long tunnel of air from roof to pavement. I think that when Jeff had loaded his army surplus duffel next to Brian's in the back of his jeep, after he grabbed the roll bar and vaulted into the front seat, both of them packed in down and wool against the gray January morning, after my mother had held Brian's head on her shoulder, smoothing his tears away with the flat of her hand, after we two stood and waved good-bye—I think it was then that my mother gave herself permission to give up.

"I think she's lost the will to live," I said to Teresa one day a week later. "Is it that simple?"

"It is," she said with that faint curve of a smile, which in the beginning I believed was distant and a little condescending and now I saw simply as a dignified expression of understanding. "Your mother has been able to lead at least part of her life these last few months in the way she is accustomed to and loves. Perhaps now she realizes that is no longer true, that more and more she will become an invalid. They teach us there are stages in terminal illness: denial, anger. At the end comes reconciliation."

"Fuck reconciliation, Teresa."

"Not for you, Ellen. For her. I would not expect you to be reconciled."

Teresa came three times a week by then. One day Jules called when she was there, and when I called Jules back I told her I'd been with the nurse.

"Oh, that must be a day at the beach," said Jules, who had just broken off with a painter who said she was too needy because she complained when he tried to pick up waitresses at the restaurants where they ate together.

"No, she's great, Jules," I said. "She's like a combination shrink-priest."

"Some combination," said Jules. "And she takes good care of your mom?"

"She takes care of me, too. She talks to me. She keeps me sane. Sometimes I wonder which of us is her patient, actually. You and she are my links to the outside world. Or maybe you're my link to the outside world and she's my link to the inside world."

"You sound like you're in therapy," Jules said, chewing on something on the other end of the phone.

"Oh, please," I said, imitating Jules herself, who always said you could tell the people in therapy by how crazy they were.

"I think I might be changing my mind about that," Jules said softly. "I think I might need someone to talk to."

"You can talk to me."

"I know, sweet. But I can't tell you my troubles because my troubles are no troubles compared to your troubles." In the silence I could hear Jules chew and swallow. "Relative troubles, that's what we're looking at here. Does Teresa listen to your troubles without telling you hers?"

"I don't really think Teresa has troubles."

"God bless her," Jules said. "What a life."

Instead Teresa told me about other people's troubles in a way that was strangely soothing, that made me feel part of a great sorority of pain and suffering. She told me of how the woman with cancer of the pancreas had died in her husband's arms in bed, how the woman with breast cancer and the two small children had had a remission and didn't need Teresa anymore. "Will you have to go back to their house someday?" I said, wanting, like Scrooge, to see some scene of happiness connected with a death, and Teresa said with her eyes suddenly burning, "I pray not." Sometimes I forgot that there were other lives entwined with hers as intimately as were our own.

"Do you see someone?" I asked her one morning.

"I am seeing a man who lives in the city," she said. "But it is difficult to have a relationship at such a distance."

"Tell me about it," I said. "How did you meet him?"

"At church. My mother knows his mother. Until two years ago, I lived not far from him in Brooklyn."

"You used to live in the city? I had no idea. How did you wind up out here?"

"There is a camp for disadvantaged children about thirty miles from here. It is called Camp Dream. I went there when I was a child. Once we came to Langhorne for the movies. When I looked at it from the bus window I thought it looked like the sort of place I would like to live someday."

"So you just picked up and came here?"

"There is a shortage of nurses everywhere."

"But why did you leave the city? I love the city. When I slept in the city for the first time in my apartment, I remember feeling as if I was home for the first time in my entire life. Sometimes people say, oh, how can you sleep, all the noise? I listen to the horns and the ambulances, and it's like, life. Real life, right outside."

"Yes, I know."

"So why did you leave?"

"How you love New York? That is how I hate it. The noise, the dirt. The real life. I have enough real life. When I am in my apartment here, I can hear the trees moving in the night. I will never go back to the city."

"Not to visit?"

"There is no one to visit. My mother died when I was eighteen. And the answer to your question is no, not of this illness and that is not why I do what I do. She was hit by a gypsy cab on Nostrand Avenue while she was on her way to work. The driver was very, very sorry, and so was I, and I left the city and came here. If the man I am seeing is interested enough, he will follow. If not, not."

"We have something in common. Our mothers, I mean."

"My mother was a hard woman who had lived a hard life."

"In what way?"

"I think I will leave that alone for now. There is no good way to tell people that they are lucky in their relations."

"I know that," I said. I looked over the living room, the piano and the prints and the framed photographs on the piano.

"I have never met your father," Teresa added. "I imagine he is an interesting man."

"Don't you ever wonder why you haven't met him?" I asked.

"He is at work when I am here."

"But don't you ever wonder why he isn't here, why he doesn't at least come by to meet you?"

"It sounds as if you are doing the wondering for both of us. And one of the things that it is important someone in my job understand is that illness brings out different qualities in different people. Some are enriched by it—yes, I know, you do not want to consider the possibility, but it is true, and I have seen it. Some people have a talent for it and some rise to the occasion. And some are diminished by their fear. They often deny, or withdraw."

"Jeff is right—you should be a shrink."

"Your brother is a very interesting person. I imagine your father is much like him."

"You imagine wrong. My father is much like me. Or I am much

like him. Or at least I was. Right now I'm not much like myself, if you know what I mean."

Teresa smiled again, such a small smile that sometimes you saw it in her eyes before her mouth, like something on a hospital monitor. "Suffering transforms," she said.

"Suffering sucks," I said.

"I agree. With both conclusions, actually."

No one came to see us. No one, except for the UPS man when Jules sent me books from the office, and manuscripts, too, so I wouldn't lose my editing touch. I stacked them in the corner of my bedroom and continued with *Anna Karenina,* even though I knew very well how it ended. I felt as though I had an obligation to go on until the train thundered out of the station.

Sometimes, when I went out to buy groceries or some books or a bouquet of daisies, because such things gave my mother pleasure out of all proportion to the act, I would run into some old friend, one of the Minnies, a faculty wife, and I could almost see the sentence forming in their minds before they said it: "I've been meaning to stop by, but . . ."

Another small spark of anger would flare in my chest, then die through lack of oxygen, except for the afternoon when I went into the bookstore to buy a magnifying glass. Teresa said she thought it was the medication affecting my mother's vision. But I think it was just one more part of her too tired to go on.

When Mrs. Duane began to say she'd been meaning to stop by,

I looked into her clear blue eyes, the color of sky, wise and so aware of the duplicity of what she was saying that they darted away from my own, and without thinking I interrupted, "Then do it. Don't tell me about it. Don't regret that you didn't. What she has is not catching."

"Ellen—"

"Don't," I said, my voice getting higher and louder. I realized that people in the store had stopped to listen but I didn't care. "No one has come to see my mother since the week before Christmas. She's lonely and she's sad and she thinks that everyone's forgotten her, and all because it's too uncomfortable for anyone to deal with anything deeper than winter ski plans and shopping for dinner." And I picked up my packages and left without paying.

I came home and put the magnifying glass on the table in the living room next to *Anna Karenina*. But I saw no evidence that it was being used. Still, I would not put her book back on the shelf with the two others. I would not declare the Gulden Girls Book and Cook Club defunct.

The next day Mrs. Duane called and asked if she could come over for lunch. I fixed chicken sandwiches and she and my mother ate at a properly laid table in the dining room—"placemats, Ellen," my mother had said. Mrs. Duane scarcely met my eyes. She gossiped with my mother about whose children were doing what and the January slump on Main Street.

I noticed that she assiduously avoided discussing the shortcomings of men, perhaps the greatest talking point when Jules and I had lunch together. And I wondered whether that was yet another difference between women of my mother's age and women of my own, or whether it was a difference between women who were single and women who were married and therefore had much, much more invested in their men than we did. Or perhaps it was because of how her friends felt about my mother and what they knew about my father. I wondered whether Mrs. Duane and the women like her had always done that around my mother, or whether they did it as a matter of course, not certain that any of their marriages were safe from being served up with the spinach salads and the iced tea.

My mother let me help her from her wheelchair into the dining-room chair in which my father usually sat, the one with arms, and that was where she was when Mrs. Duane arrived. She was wearing a sea-green turtleneck with a crewneck sweater in the same color, but the collar of the one and the bulk of the other could not quite hide her frailty.

The morning after her "lovely lunch," as she called it when she spoke of it to my father, she slept late and I was in the kitchen cleaning when I heard her faint footfalls on the old pine floors above me. There was the sound of the water running, the faint wailing of our pipes like a small and halfhearted banshee, the muffled closing of drawers and doors and then silence.

I sat down at the table with one of my mother's magazines, looking at spring perennials, although where I was going to plant perennials and why, when gardening bored me so, I could not have told you. I read the recipes and the instructions for making a bedskirt for a crib. Perhaps my mother was saving it for Halley, whose daughter must be overdue. From above me I heard a sound that I thought at first must be the pipes again, or a child calling from down the street, or perhaps a sudden bad-tempered fit of winter wind whipping around the dormers. It came again and I lifted my head. Again, and I went to the foot of the stairs.

"Ellen," came the cry.

I ran up those stairs as I had not run up since I was in high school, running to see if my father was in early, to tell him news and make it real—"I got into Princeton!" "I won the essay contest!" "I'm valedictorian!" How many times had I run in, banging doors, breathless, to tell him something and had to settle for her instead? How plain had it been on my face?

"Ellen," came the cry again.

Her bedroom was empty, the covers thrown back. Before my mother was sick I think the only time I had seen my parent's bed unmade was when they were in it, when I came in frightened after a bad dream, when I stuck my head in to tell them I had gotten home safely at one in the morning. A pair of knit pants and a tunic were on the chair, which had been moved closer to the bathroom door so that my mother could walk, stopping for a handhold as she went, from bed to table to chair to bath. The bathroom door was closed, and I knocked softly.

"You have to come in," my mother said with a catch in her voice.

The room was warm and smelled rank, the smell of perspiration and something sweeter, deeper. My mother lay in the tub, her arm across her eyes, perhaps practicing the child's fiction of believing that if she could not see me I could not see her.

"I can't get out," she said.

Silently I picked up the towel that was on the bench just next to the tub—she had made the bench from a kit, I remember, then painted it and sanded some of the paint down so it would look old—and hung it over my arm. I took her by the hands and tried to pull, but her legs scrabbled helplessly in the water, slick with bath oil, finding no purchase on the smooth porcelain of the tub. Then I reached around her chest and, with one great tug, pulled her over the edge and onto the bench. I was panting and the front of my denim shirt was wet with bathwater and, perhaps, perspiration. She weighed nothing, but felt so heavy.

I had never before and have never since set about a task which required me so completely to act without thinking. My mother leaned her elbow on the edge of the tub and her head on her hand and wept as I toweled off her poor ravaged body. I took it piece by piece, bit by bit, because I knew that if I allowed myself to really look at her, at what she had become, I would be done for.

But she knew, and while I couldn't speak, she couldn't keep silent. Suddenly she wiped her face with her hand and said, "I never wanted you to see me like this. I should have just stayed there until your father got home. I couldn't figure out what was worse, having you see me like this, or him."

"I would have come up eventually," I said, drying her shoulders.

"I would have died before I would have let you see me like this. Just . . . rotten. That's what I look like now, like a peach when it's all rotten. Like bad fruit. Why can't I just die and be done with it? It's a crime for a human being to have to live like this. Rotten like this." And she let her head drop down again.

It was an apt description. Her skin was slack on her body in places, like soft fruit when it's past its prime, on the insides of her thighs, her upper arms. But most of her flesh was stretched tight over her bones, a faint shroud for the skeleton: the two long bones running parallel beneath the skin of her arms and legs, the cage of pelvis and ribs. In her face every bit of skull was visible where the flesh had gone, leaving only the clear outlines of the understructure, the yawning *Os* of the eye sockets, the sharp peaks of the cheekbones, the hinge of the jaw, from which all the padding had disappeared. Her breasts were flat and sagging, like those of old women I'd seen in pictures of primitive tribes, and her pubic hair was nearly gone.

I went behind her, and, hooking my hands under her armpits, pulled her into a standing position. She held my arm tightly and shuffled into the bedroom. I helped her on with her underpants and her pants, her tunic, as she held on to the edge of the dresser. But I never touched her, not really, never patted her, much less held her close. And if I told you today that I've wondered about that a hundred times since then, whether I should have wrapped my arms around her instead of the towel, whether I should have rocked her as she had done so many times for me, I would be lying about the number, because it has been many many more.

I never try to remember how she looked that morning. I remember that I never touched her, and I never looked her in the eye. When I was done she moved slowly to the bed, like a blind person in an unfamiliar room, and she lay down on her back, staring at the ceiling. For the first time I noticed that the scarf Jeffrey had given her for Christmas had been slung over the mirror atop her dresser, so that a spill of glossy purple grapes and green grape leaves and the sinuous twist of vines hung in place of any reflection.

"I'm going back to sleep," she said.

That January, when they delivered the hospital bed, leaving the den in disarray and the living room crowded with furniture, leaving a long scratch in the oak floor of the hallway because they were careless with a metal side rail, she didn't say anything. She just got in and turned on her side so that she was looking out the window, out the window that looked out on our driveway and the side of the house next door. It was as though something was broken, but I think it broke in the bathroom, on that bench.

At the end she was both child and mother, both teacher and student, both strength and supplicant. At the end she lay in the den, in the bed with the high bars on the side, so that she would not roll out at night. Sometimes I would stand in the doorway in the dark, quiet and observant as a Peeping Tom, and watch her thrash and cry and talk, bits of disconnected things, about my father, about her babies, always babies. About people whose names meant nothing to me, who might be ghosts, figments, or regrets and missed opportunities. When she talked to her brother Steven one night, her eyes open even though their glaze made their blindness as clear as a white cane, that was when I stayed until the sky outside began to lighten. Somehow I thought if she talked to her brother, dead so many years ago, it meant she was seeing another country in her mind's eye and that her heart was hammering toward its inevitable full stop.

Often I watched with tears dripping down my face onto the front of my nightgown, but it was as though they were an inert function of my body, like a runny nose. There were no sobs, none of the heaves that you associate with a crying jag. There was no sound but my mother's thick and arduous breathing as I stood across the room, bleeding tears.

Once, when I came downstairs, the side of her bed had been lowered, and my father was wedged uncomfortably next to her. He and I looked at one another in the darkness, but I turned and went upstairs and if he followed afterward I did not hear him.

That room had white pine paneling on the walls and flowered curtains at the windows, a rose-and-green print I can still evoke in memory. The green couch had been carted into the living room, the hospital bed positioned in front of the wall of bookshelves so it faced the television. But all of the light and prettiness evoked by the decor was negated that month by the light, which was dim and gray, the dour grudging clouded sunshine of January and February. Now, today, I feel my heart begin to sink on New Year's Day and lift only—inevitably, ironically—when Easter is on the horizon. My miserable anniversaries.

One night the branches of the Douglas fir at the corner of the house lashed my windows and hers all night long, and by morning the snow was falling thick and fast, so that there was no light in the room at all and I had to turn on the lamps in the middle of the day. The snow began to drift until finally it reached almost to the windows. My mother kept her head turned to the side all day, except when she drank her soup, lifting the spoon to her mouth in a long slow arc, dropping her mouth open when the spoon was only halfway there, as though she could no longer trust herself to coordinate her motions more precisely. "The snow is so beautiful," she said, handing me back the mug, and then she fell asleep.

Beneath the rich yellow light of the lamp I read and, when my eyes became tired, went into the kitchen to judge the progress of the storm by the thickness of the blanket in the back, ripples and hillocks where it covered small bushes, a rise in the yard that marked an azalea I had protected with an upturned peach basket and a burlap bag. The phone in the kitchen rang like a scream in the quiet house, and when I went to answer it I saw that the day had slipped away and it was nearly seven. Only the light told me the time, and the light had been disguised all afternoon.

"Ellen," my father said, "I cannot possibly get home in this. The security people have closed off both the footbridges and no one has been able to get out to plow. I will sleep somewhere here."

"In your office?"

"I don't know. Several of the other people in the department have pullout couches. If I can find someone who's already gone home, I'll use theirs. If you try me here and there's no answer, that's what I've done."

"Uh-huh," I said.

"How is your mother?"

"The same."

"Tell her that I'll see her tomorrow."

"Yes."

"Are you all right?"

"Fine."

I think I remember that when I put down the phone there was a flicker of the thought that if my mother died during the night, with the snow falling thick outside, while my father was marooned on a sofa bed with some erudite honors graduate of a Seven Sisters college with strong opinions on Henry James and a soft spot for narrow handsome married men, that he would suffer with the memory the rest of his life. Or perhaps that was how I remembered it afterward, when memory plays so many tricks.

In the den my mother's eyes were open, looking at nothing. "Who was that?" she said softly.

"Your husband," I said in what I thought was a voice without expression. "He cannot seem to find a way to get home, so he is staying at the college. He says he will see you tomorrow."

"It's a bad storm," my mother said, looking out the window again.

"It's not that bad," I said.

"Ellen," she said, and her voice was stronger than it had been in days, "put down the book." In fact her voice was stronger, sterner, than I had ever remembered it, except the day that I mocked the little girl with Down's syndrome who once lived at the foot of our hill and my mother turned cold and pitiless in a way I had always thought only my father could. She was like a sprinter now, at rest until those brief necessary moments when she would become herself for just a few minutes.

"What has happened between you and your father?"

"What do you mean?"

"You have been very angry with him since you came home. If you're going to be angry at anyone about all this, you should be angry at me. I'm why you're here, not him."

"Mama, this is not about you. And it's not something we should discuss. I have my own differences with Papa that have nothing to do with you."

"They do have to do with me, especially now. He's all you'll have."

"Stop. Just stop." I raised my hands, palm out, as though to push the words away.

"No, you stop. You and your father will need each other. And you and your brothers. And I hope he can have more of a relationship with the boys, too, if I'm not there to get in the way. But you and he already have such a bond. You're so much alike."

"Please don't say that."

"Why? Because he's not perfect? Because he's not the man you once thought he was?"

"Mama, I can't talk to you about this."

"Ellen," she said, struggling to turn toward me, her hands like pale claws on the railing of the bed, her legs scissoring away the white sheets, "listen to me because I will only say this once and I shouldn't say it at all. There is nothing you know about your father that I don't know, too."

The two of us stared silently into one another's eyes, and I think that after a moment she gave a little nod and then lay back.

"And understand better," she added.

"All right," I said.

"You make concessions when you're married a long time that you don't believe you'll ever make when you're beginning," she said. "You say to yourself when you're young, oh, I wouldn't tolerate this or that or the other thing, you say love is the most important thing in the world and there's only one kind of love and it makes you feel different than you feel the rest of the time, like you're all lit up. But time goes by and you've slept together a thousand nights and smelled like spit-up when babies are sick and seen your body droop and get soft. And some nights you say to yourself, it's not enough, I won't put up with another minute. And then the next morning you wake up and the kitchen smells like coffee and the children have their hair all brushed and the birds are eating out of the feeder and you look at your husband and he's not the person you used to think he was but he's your life. The house and the children and so much of what you do is built around him and your life, too, your history. If you take him out it's like cutting his face out of all the pictures, there's a big hole and it's ugly. It would ruin everything. It's more than love, it's more important than love. Think of Anna."

"Anna?"

"In the book." She gestured toward the end table where my paperback copy of *Anna Karenina* lay.

"But you didn't finish reading it."

"I'd read it before." She looked at the snow falling, tiny floating ghosts tapping against the window, spinning in and out of the blue-black beyond. "I'd read them all before. I just wanted a chance to read them again. I wanted a chance to read them with you."

I leaned over the rail of the bed, its metal cold and hard against my chest, and took her hand in mine, her grip strong, painful almost, and then lax. I slid the railing down and I put my head on the sheets, atop the cage of her pelvis, no fat or flesh to protect it. I cried until the sheets were wet, and she stroked my hair, over and over, the dry flesh making a faint sibilant sound, like the smallest whisper. Then in a softer voice, she began to speak again.

"It's hard. And it's hard to understand unless you're in it. And it's hard for you to understand now because of where you are and what you're feeling. But I wanted to say it, I didn't say it very well, I'm no writer, but I wanted to say it because I won't be able to say it when I need to, when it's one of those nights and you're locking the front door because of foolishness about romance, about how things are supposed to be. You can be hard, and you can be judgmental, and with those two things alone you can make a mess of your life the likes of which you won't believe. I think of a thousand things I could teach you in the next ten years, and I think of how everything important you learned the first twenty-four you learned from your father and not me, and it hurts my heart, to know how little I've gotten done."

"No, Mama," I whispered.

"Yes, yes, yes, yes, somebody let me speak the truth, somebody let me," she cried. "Your father says I'll only upset myself, and you say, please, no, Mama, and only Teresa lets me speak. Saying it is the only thing that makes me feel better, even the drugs aren't as good as that. All the things we don't say, all the words we swallow, and it makes nothing but trouble. I want to talk before I die. I want to be the one who gets to say things, who gets to think the deep thoughts. You'll all talk when I'm gone. Let me talk now without *shushing* me because it hurts you to hear what I want to say. I'm tired of being *shushed*."

"What do you want to say?" I said, lifting my head and pushing my damp hair aside. "Go ahead and say it."

"I just said everything I wanted to say, except that I feel sad. I feel sad that I won't be able to plan your wedding. Don't have a flower girl or a ring bearer—they always misbehave and distract from the bride. And don't have too many people."

"Mama, I don't know that I'll ever get married."

"Don't say things like that, Ellen. Think about what I just told you."

"All right. What else?"

"I feel afraid that when I fall asleep I will never wake up. I miss sleeping with your father."

"Should I tell him that?"

"I already have."

"What else?"

"If I knew you would be happy I could close my eyes now and rest." Her voice was beginning to sink and die, as though it was going down the drain, rush of words to trickle of whisper. "It's so much easier."

"I know it is. I wish you could."

"No, not that. The being happy. It's so much easier, to learn to love what you have instead of yearning always for what you're missing, or what you imagine you're missing. It's so much more peaceful."

"I'll try," I said.

"It doesn't work that way." And suddenly she was asleep. Her mouth hung open and her hair was scraped back from her forehead, lank because we had not washed it for several days, not since the last time Teresa had come. The lines across her forehead were cut deep, as though someone had done them with a ruler and a pencil. The sheet over her midsection was dark with my tears.

Everything you know, I know, she'd said, and it was true. I was the ignorant one. I'd taken a laundry list of all the things she'd done and, more important to me, all the things she'd never done, and turned them into my mother, when they were no more my mother than his lectures on the women of Dickens were my father.

Our parents are never people to us, never, they're always character traits, Achilles' heels, dim nightmares, vocal tics, bad noses, hot tears, all handed down and us stuck with them. Our dilemma is utter: turn and look at this woman, understand and pity her, like and talk with her, recognize that she has taken the cold cleanliness of the spartan rooms in which she grew up and turned them, within her considerable and perhaps wounded heart, into a life-long burst of cooking and cosseting and making her own little corner of the world pretty and welcoming, and the separation is complete—but when that happens you will have to be an adult. There is only room in the lifeboat of your life for one, and you always choose yourself, and turn your parents into whatever it takes to keep you afloat.

Just before midnight she woke. She licked her lips slowly, twisting and turning her arms on the sheets, then turned her head.

"Is it morning yet?" she said.

"No."

"I need pills," she said.

It was a new vial, nearly full. She gulped one down, her throat working; coughed and then sipped again, her whole body moving with the effort. She sighed and it rattled deep in her throat, half groan.

"Help me, Ellen," she whispered. "I don't want to live like this anymore."

We stared at each other in the half-light of the lamps.

"Please," she said. "You must know what to do. Please. Help me. No more."

"It'll be better in the morning."

"No," she said, and groaned again. "It will not. It will not." She sounded like a tired and irritable child. She wrapped her fingers around my wrist, the wrist of the hand that held the pills. Her grip was surprisingly strong, and for some reason I thought of those people who lift Volkswagens off babies pinned beneath, of people trapped in caves and found alive, saved by a diet of snow, long past the time when they should have died.

"Please," she said. "Help me. I don't want this." But I could tell that the pill was already beginning to take effect, or perhaps that the effort of the words, the request, the hand on my arm, had put her under. She looked at me sadly from beneath lids that began to drop like those of some wise old bird. "Help me," she whispered. "You're so smart. You'll know what to do." Then her eyes closed completely. "Please," she whispered once more.

I slept that night in a chair in the den, fell asleep as the snow continued to fall. It covered everything without any sound except the scratch of the pine branches against the side of the house. I woke to the ugly fluorescent brightness of a world deep in fallen snow, covered with pitiless whiteness. It was a world changed forever, a world in which I found it difficult to meet my mother's eyes.

It must be terrible to bury someone you love in early May, when the ground is beginning to thaw and stretch and turn bright green and the smell of lilacs tumbles down from the bushes like a little benediction. Or in September, when the noon sun is still warm on your face but the evenings are cool enough for flannel and an extra blanket dragged up from the footboard in the middle of the night.

Or at Christmas. It must be terrible at Christmas.

February is a suitable month for dying. Everything around is dead, the trees black and frozen so that the appearance of green shoots two months hence seems preposterous, the ground hard and cold, the snow dirty, the winter hateful, hanging on too long. At the beginning of the month I had bought my mother anemones at the florist on Main Street, paid fifteen dollars for a tiny bunch because they seemed, with their fragile lavender and bright red, to represent something that seemed as distant as the moon. I put them on the table next to the window, so that when she looked out she saw, not just the gray piles of old plowed snow at the edge of the driveway, like slag from some quarry, not just the side of the neighboring house and the big oak groaning in the winter winds, but those frail and beautiful things, bending their heavy heads toward her. But after only two days they fell, drooping almost to the dusty tabletop, their stems defeated, perhaps by a draft from beneath the sill. And I threw them away.

"Lovely, Ellie," she whispered sometimes, even when they were gone. "Lovely flowers."

Teresa came one morning and attached the little machine, like a tiny tape recorder with its red digital numbers, that would pump morphine into my mother's catheter whenever she pushed a button on its side. Teresa programmed it and taught me how to do it, too. "We will have to say how much is enough, and for how long," said Teresa.

"Could she overdose with this?" I said.

Teresa looked at me, one brow raised slightly. "Not likely," she said.

My mother winced when Teresa lodged the needle in the catheter, but when it was taped in place and the little box placed at her side she said she felt nothing except the pull of the tape on her tender skin. "I can retape it, Mrs. Gulden," said Teresa, smoothing her hair, held back from her face with a black band. "Perhaps it is too tight."

"No, Teresa," my mother said. "It's fine. Thank you."

We sat by her side for almost an hour without speaking, Teresa and I, she making notations in the small log she always carried, me finishing the background on the sunflower pillow. As she slept, my mother pulled fretfully at the diapers she now wore. Three times in the past week she had soiled the bed, and I had called Teresa, who was not supposed to do such things—they had a health aide to change beds, someone not as skilled or as salaried as a nurse—but had insisted that this was no time to have someone new and foreign in our home. After Teresa cleaned my mother and helped her onto the sofa, I gathered up the sheets with a great deal of bustle and carried them to the basement, holding my breath so that I would not gag.

"I'm so sorry," my mother said each time.

Finally Teresa had taken her hand and sat on the side of her bed. "Mrs. Gulden, I would like to catheterize you," she said.

My mother's hand came up slowly to touch the small mound on her chest, above her heart.

"A urinary catheter," said Teresa. "So you need not use the bedpan or depend so much on Ellen."

"Oh no, Teresa," she said. "I don't need that."

"I think perhaps you do."

"No, no."

"Then I think perhaps you should wear protective pants."

"Oh no," she said, and lay back on the pillows. Tears began to slide from beneath her eyelids down the furrows from eyes to nose and nose to chin. "This is too much."

"I know it is upsetting," said Teresa softly, stroking the back of my mother's hand. "But I believe it will be easier for you. And for Ellen, too."

But whenever my mother dropped off to sleep she pulled at the diapers as she did now, as though when she was unconscious they became the tangible reminder of the pain, the disintegration, the life that had become a half life.

She ate nursery food when she ate, which was not often. She ate oatmeal, applesauce, puddings, yogurt. Her lips were cracked and dry, and several times a day I smoothed petroleum jelly over them so that they would not peel or bleed. It had become difficult to tell whether she was awake or asleep under the thin blanket of consciousness, or simply lying with her eyes closed, thinking the unimaginable thoughts that anyone must feel when they are standing on the bluff overlooking the abyss.

"How are the boys getting on?" she said slowly after Teresa had gone.

"Fine, I guess. Jeff is his usual wisecracking self. Brian has a new roommate and seems to like him better than the old one."

"Good. I worry about Brian."

"Do you want me to bring them home, Mama?" I asked.

"No, Ellen," she said clearly.

That last afternoon I gave her cream of tomato soup for lunch, but after three spoonfuls she shook her head, perhaps because the act of moving the spoon from mug to mouth was so slow, so torturous, so messy that I had to put on a new top sheet afterward. She wore her velour housecoat, its nap flattened by the days in bed, and from beneath it her legs were sticks.

"I look like those people in the films about the camps," she whispered, looking down.

I tucked the clean sheet, with its nice fresh smell, in around her, and pushed back her hair. On the metal cart in the corner that held her pills, her water, a box of tissues, now her soup mug, was a tiny picture in a heart-shaped frame of a newborn, its face the color of your skin after a hot shower. Her tiny fists were balled up and thrown over her head as though she was surrendering, and her face looked like an uncooked biscuit with raisins for eyes. The dome of her head, atop which there was only fuzz, was off-center and misshapen. Halley had had her baby and had brought over the hospital picture to give to my mother. At the door I said that my mother could not have visitors, but then a voice had called faintly, "It's all right, Ellie," and I had brought Halley in for a few minutes at my mother's bedside. She was nursing, she said, and could not stay long because her milk was coming in. But at the door she hugged me and said, "I'm so sorry, so sorry," as she wept. There were dark circles under her eyes and her hair looked nearly as unkempt as my mother's. Ground down by maternity, the two of them, I thought.

"This must be so hard on you," she had sobbed, trying to muffle the sound with a tissue she pulled from her pocket.

"It's almost over," I said.

When I came back into the room my mother had been staring at the photograph. "That baby is no beauty," I said.

"Babies are never beauties, especially first babies. They're a long time coming out, and they get knocked up in the process."

"The little mother doesn't look so good, either."

"She'll be fine," said my mother. "It's hard work, but she'll

manage. When I think of the people I've known who've had children who had no business even owning a cat—well, they all get
raised somehow."

"You were a good mother," I said.

"I worked hard," she had said.

It was around four when she woke up and started to turn
toward me. Then, remembering, she reached up and pushed the
button that released the liquid morphine into her catheter and
from there to a vein. She closed her eyes and her breathing
became hoarse and very loud, like the noise a stick makes when
you run it down the length of a fence and it hits the pickets, one
by one, with that surprising carrying sound. I paced my breathing
with her own, the two of us raising and lowering our chests in
unison to keep ourselves alive. "That works better," she said after
a few minutes. Her hand found the medication machine again and
pressed, but I knew nothing would come out. Perhaps it had a
placebo effect, for she slept again for another hour. I turned on
the lamps around the room after I saw her eyes glittering in the
half darkness.

"I love you, Ellen," she said.

"I love you, too, Mama."

"I've always known it," she said, and she smiled, the old smile,
so warm and full that it was like the moon laid on its side. It was
in her eyes, too, and her whole face, so that all the devastation of
the last six months fell before it, her whole soul shining out at me.

I tried to smile back but my mouth and chin quivered uncontrollably and my eyes blinked as though I had a tic.

"Gen?" she said. "Is your father here?"

"He has a late class today, doesn't he?"

She closed her eyes and her forehead furrowed deeply. Then she
nodded. "I hope he's home soon," she said.

"I'll call him," I said, as I'd said before, but this time she did
not try to stop me.

Inside the kitchen I dropped down at the table, my hands shaking, and pushed the buttons on the phone. Twice I misdialed and

when I finally had the number right it rang and rang and I could see it, the office with its wall of untidy bookshelves, the books shoved wherever they would fit, stacked atop one another, spilling onto the floor near the big heavy desk with the narrow drawers down each side, books under the two nondescript chairs where the students sat, books climbing one side of the scratched and creased brown leather couch on which there was one pillow, needlepointed by my mother, that said, CALL ME ISHMAEL.

"Come on, Papa, come on," I whispered, but there was no answer and something inside me said, of course not, of course, there never is, there never was, just the incessant ringing, come home, come here, talk to me, tell. Tell. Tell. But there was no answer.

"Gen?" my mother called with that plaintive tone in her voice again.

"I'm going to campus to get him," I called. "There's something wrong with his phone."

I took my down jacket from the peg near the back door and fished in the pocket for my keys. It was the first time I had been outside for three days, and the cold was shocking, the sort of still and bitter cold that freezes all the soft and vulnerable parts, the membranes inside your nose, the end of your ears, the tips of your fingers. At first the car coughed and would not turn over, and again I said, "Come on, come on." I could not have explained my urgency except that my mother had never before called for my father at work—"bothered him during the day," she called it—except for the day when her father had had his stroke. Good news or bad, we waited until he came home, until he had taken his leather case from the back seat of the car and come up the steps and into the kitchen, until the door had closed and he had joined the family.

At the green the streets were almost deserted, the store windows impenetrably covered with a gloss of steam, heat within and freezing air without. The gears made a grinding sound as I climbed the road along the river to the small bridge that led from the town to the campus. The bridge was slick with ice, and I downshifted when the back end of the car began to fishtail. But still I kept my foot to the gas, desperate to give my mother what she so clearly wanted. I was afraid that when I came back to the house she might already be dead. I knew that if that happened I would never forgive my father, nor he me.

The end of the bridge sloped down sharply to a set of stone pillars, each with a plaque: LANGHORNE on one, COLLEGE on the other. I drove past the parking lot of the new science building, past the stolid gym and the two nondescript language classroom buildings to the old gray stone building with the word ENGLISH in capitals square as shoe boxes above the double doors. As I parked the car in the fire lane out front, the campus lights, tall poles with vaguely Victorian globes atop them, came on, and yellow lights twinkled all over the dim walkways like something on the London streets in the days of Dickens.

"Name, Miss?" said the security guard.

"Professor Gulden's daughter," I said, and ran past him up the stairs four flights, until on the last landing my heart rang in my ears.

The door to my father's office was closed and the lights in the waiting area outside off. By the red glow of an exit light and a low-hanging fluorescent in the hall, I could see a piece of paper taped to his door. But it was only a sign-up sheet for conferences for freshman English students, those hapless dozen assigned to what had always been the class my father most loathed teaching.

The door of the office was locked. The rest of the hallway was dark and the only sounds were the faint ones of cars and the occasional calling voice from outside and below.

"Goddamnit," I said aloud.

Downstairs the guard sprawled, legs apart, in a chair next to the sign-in book. "You still need to sign in, Miss," he said unhappily.

"Have you seen Professor Gulden?" I said.

"He came down and left about ten minutes before you got here," he said. "I tried to tell you, but you went too fast."

Without answering I ran back out to the car and started the engine. The radio was on, perhaps had been on all the way over without my noticing it. There was an outbreak of civil war in the Sudan and a budget deadlock in Washington. In Texas a twenty-year-old man had been executed in the electric chair, and five children had died in a school bus accident. The forecast was for colder weather overnight. I hit the stanchion of the bridge with the right front bumper of the car, slammed on the brakes, backed up, and kept on going. The street lamps cast round moons of pure white light on the black asphalt of the streets. As I came around the circle, I could see the Duanes locking up the bookstore. It was such an ordinary night in Langhorne. From outside, through the lace cotton curtains, our kitchen looked as safe and warm as it always had.

Inside, my father's book bag was on the table. In the den he bent over my mother, lifted the small canister that fed the flow of morphine into her veins, smoothed back her hair. "Where the hell were you?" he said softly without turning.

"At the college, looking for you."

"Why?" he said, turning.

"She was asking for you. She wanted you."

He turned back and ran his hand over the surface of her hair and down her raddled neck to her collarbone, its line a shelf above the downward slope of her chest. "You and I must have just passed one another," he said. "I could have killed you when I arrived and the house was empty."

"You were on your way here and I was on my way there," I said. "Like an O. Henry story."

"Comedy of errors," he said. "I should have known. It was just the shock of finding her alone. How has she been?"

"Not good."

"Has she eaten?"

"Not much."

My father touched the machine with a fingertip, as though he was afraid of it. "This is a pump version of her medication?"

I nodded.

"Is it helping?"

"I think so."

"My poor Kate," he said softly, and as if she heard him she stirred, plucked at the mass of paper wadding at her crotch one last time, and slowly opened her eyes.

"Gen," she said.

"Yes, dear."

Both of them turned and looked at me, my mother slowly, as though it required great effort. She smiled. "Go take a rest, Ellen," she said.

I'm not sure, even now, even after I've been asked more times than I can count, exactly how I spent the next few hours. I only know that as long as I heard the murmur of quiet conversation from that room I did not intrude, and I heard them for longer than I could have imagined possible. Once I heard my mother's voice raised, thought I heard her crying, thought I heard the word "Please!," one soprano note of entreaty. Once I heard my father's voice raised, thought I heard him curse loudly and hit the surface of something hard with his hand. But much of what I heard was the sound of two people talking quietly a room away, that murmur that sounds like pigeons in the park, wood doves just beyond the line where the lawn meets the trees.

I did take a shower, and I lay on my bed, soaking my pillow with my wet hair, and I think I dozed off for an hour or so. The house was very quiet and a half-moon was visible outside my window, the clouds moving across its profile.

When I went back downstairs the door to the den was open and in the light, the floor and walls thick with shadows that rose and fell and wavered with slow synchronized movements, my parents were sitting facing one another. My father was in a straight chair, with a plain china bowl in his lap, and my mother had the back of the hospital bed canted almost all the way up, so she seemed to be sitting upright.

Her head was angled far from her chest, her mouth open, her

eyes dull, except when he finally finished his slow arc of filling the spoon, lifting it to the level of her mouth, and bringing it forward. Slowly she would bring her lips together and apart, and then with a visible movement of her neck and jaw muscles would swallow, her head falling back.

She looked like a baby bird and he like someone feeding a baby. The motion went on, head forward, spoon forward, spoon in, head back. Each time they made contact her eyes would blaze, but I believe now, having replayed the scene so often in my mind, in the sepia tones that I believe lit it even then, that she was looking not at the dollop of rice pudding but past it at him.

Over and over I would see him lift that spoon in the lamplight. It was the most vivid way in which I remembered my parents together after I had lost them both, and in memory I tried to decipher it, to deconstruct the movements, the motives, the emotions, the truth. Although my idea of truth now is not what it once was.

I passed on from the doorway of the den into the living room and sat there reading the same page of *Anna Karenina* over and over again, the one in which Anna rides on horseback in a black habit, her hair in curls. I still remember that, as though it's yet another picture on our piano: the horse, the habit, the dark curls. And I thought of how my mother had already read this book, and both the others, how she had formed the book club to break through the reserve of her own daughter, to find something that the two of us could talk about before it was too late for the two of us to ever talk again. How deft she had been. "Tell," she'd said, and I had. But she'd done it without ever saying the word.

After about an hour my father came into the room, pushing his hair back with his hand. His eyes were edged sharply in red.

"No one should have to live like that," he said.

"How was she?"

"No one should have to live like that," he repeated. "No one."

"That's what she said."

"I know," he said, his mouth working. "She's right. She

shouldn't have to live like that anymore." He rubbed his eyes with the flat of his hand. "She wants me to sleep with her in there," he added. "I can't. I can't. Not tonight. I'm going upstairs."

"I'll stay up for a while," I said.

"That's not necessary, Ellen."

"I can't sleep anyway," I said.

"Let her be," he said.

For another hour I sat in the living room, looking around at all her handiwork: the big brass bowl on the cherry chest of drawers against one wall, with the old map of Langhorne framed and hung above it, the pillows needlepointed with big blowsy roses on the velvet couch, the coffee table that had been a desk before she cut its legs down in the garage, cutting herself with the saw, holding her hand to her mouth as she came into the kitchen for the first-aid kit that was kept in the second drawer next to the sink. Her blood always looked so bright against her white redhead's skin.

I stood in the doorway of the den for a long time and watched her after that, tired as I was. But she was not restless that night. There were no sentence fragments, no muttered names, no pushing at her hair or the hated diapers with her fingers. Her mouth hung open and she breathed in and out through it with a deep soughing noise, almost like a growl, and between those breaths a great silence hung in the air, a silence like forever.

When I sat down at the side of the bed I took her hand in mine. It was cold, and I could feel the bones, like little brittle sticks in my own warm and sweaty palm. I began to breathe in tandem with her, and when I inhaled it felt as if whole minutes went by as I waited for her to let the air out again and let me do the same. In. Out. In. Out. Perhaps it was because the breaths were so far apart, perhaps I was faint, but after a long while I began to feel as though I was watching the two of us from some corner of the ceiling, looking down on this evaporated woman with her red hair thin and dull now, her hands lying palm up on the sheet as though in some gesture of entreaty, and her daughter next to her, her rather square face hung about with a curtain of dark hair, her free hand plucking at the knee of her old black pants.

In. Out. In. Out. They breathed in unison, and as I watched them I wondered which would stop first. And then one did, the mother, and the sound brought me back to myself, out of the daze into which the slow repetitive sound had allowed me to fall. There was a sound like that a car makes when it won't start on a cold morning, an *eh eh eh eh* deep in my mother's throat, and I held tight to her hand as though I would crush it in my own long strong fingers. A shudder shook her body, and then the sound once more: *eh eh eh,* and one last long inhalation of breath.

I waited for her to exhale, waited for so long, holding her fingers, feeling them small under my own. I laid my head down near the foot of the bed but I did not let go until I could tell by a faint shift of the black outside that it was almost morning. Her hand was cold when I finally laid it on the sheet. The sheets were still as the snow had been after it stopped falling, still and clean. And when I looked at her face there was nothing of her there, nothing at all, as though she'd tiptoed out in the middle of the night when I'd dozed, just as she used to do when I was a little girl and fell asleep while she crooned "Safe and sound."

I was still sitting there at sunup when my father came down the stairs heavily and stood in the doorway, shivering, with cold or something else. "How is she?" he said.

"She's dead," I replied. "I'll go make the coffee."

PART TWO

I had not acquired much during the five months that I had lived in my old room, tracing the marching flowers of the stenciling around the edge of the ceiling in the dark, lulled to sleep finally by the familiar shape of the dormer window, awakened sometimes by the crying from the floor below, living and breathing and finally dying in tandem with my mother. There was the datebook, still on my desk, still empty. There was the bulky oatmeal-colored sweater my parents had given me for Christmas: that was how our presents were always labeled, although we always knew our mother bought them. There was a pair of jeans Jeff left behind at Thanksgiving that I had pirated, and a new pair of boots I bought at the mall because my mother had so wanted me to buy myself something one day in October.

And there was the navy-blue suit I bought for the funeral, to wear with a pair of old black patent pumps I found in the back of my closet, left over from high school graduation. I would not be taking that suit with me. I would not be wearing it again.

So when I packed my duffel two weeks after my mother died,

a week after she was buried, there was little more to put in than I had taken out—less, actually, because two pairs of cords were too snug now and I left them in a drawer.

I didn't prepare to go right away. I stayed one morning to oversee the dismantling of the hospital bed and the return of the wheelchair, folded like an empty suit, its plastic leather seat slumping dejectedly. On another I rearranged the furniture and called someone in to shampoo the upholstery and the rugs. The silver needed to be polished. I finished the background of the sunflower pillow and took it to a shop where they would fill it and sew on a velvet back; they knew what to do from all the other times my mother had picked out the shape, the fabric, the edging. As I was turning to walk out and heard the little bell on the door jingle above me, like the one Jimmy Stewart hears at the end of *It's a Wonderful Life,* my umbrella half opened against a cold and heavy winter rain, I stopped and told them to send the pillow, when it was done, to Jules's address in the city. I had decided I wanted to keep it.

One morning as I made coffee I told my father that I would be willing to clean out the closets in his room. He did not look up from his bran and his *New York Times* as he said, "No. Absolutely not."

But after he had gone to the college, wearing the same turtleneck he'd worn for three days, I went upstairs and pushed aside the white louvered closet doors, running my hands over the rainbow of clothes, the bright blues, the summer whites, the tartans, the purples and reds. And then, without thinking, I reached out my arms and hugged them. I smelled lilac eau-de-toilette and Jean Naté and Joy and attar of roses all jumbled together, the day perfumes and the night ones, the bath oils and the face lotions. Over them all was the smell of something else, but remote, musty, so dead that it was worse than it had been when I stood in the cemetery next to the oak casket, so clean, so shiny, like the table in the kitchen.

"This house is terribly empty," my father had said as he ate his breakfast the morning of the funeral, and it was true. Just as my mother's body had seemed inconsequential to me when I realized that the heat and light that lived within it had disappeared, so her house seemed hollow, a random collection of things, objects, as empty as a display room in a furniture store.

Jules called me so often that I began to laugh at her. "Just checking in?" I said, and she responded, "Oh, go to hell." She was all packed, ready to take the train down for the funeral, when I told her to stay where she was. I wanted to see Jules, to feel her fingers kneading mine, to tell her everything while the two of us curled up in opposite corners of the big old burgundy velvet couch in her tiny living room, our shoes on the floor beneath us. She would pick tendrils of horsehair out of the corner where the velvet had worn away; I would reach over and slap her hand. But not yet.

"I don't want you here now," I said on the phone. "I want to come back there and have it all be the same, different from this, not part of what's been going on here."

"Untouched by human hands," she said.

"Exactly."

"The magazine is sending a deputation."

"Please, Jules, tell them no. I just don't want it. All this is one thing and my life there is something else and I want to keep the two of them separate."

"Can't I be the exception?" she said softly.

"No. Not even you."

"I have that nice black suit that we bought on sale in Bendel's."

"You'll wear it to dinner when we go out to celebrate my new job."

"What? What job?"

"Got me. But when I get a job we'll celebrate."

Jules was quiet for a minute. "I don't know," she finally said.

"Please, Jules," I said.

"What are you wearing?" she said.

I laughed long and hard, longer and harder than the remark required. "That's the kind of thing I need from you," I said.

"You need a bottle of wine and a good cry," Jules said, and I could tell by the slightest tremor in her deep contralto voice that she was crying. I took a breath and let it out in a sigh.

"Later," I said. "I promise."

I wore a navy-blue suit, my father wore a navy-blue suit, and the boys wore navy jackets. Wasn't it Diana Vreeland who once said that pink was the navy blue of India? But wasn't it true, I said at the lunch afterward at the Duanes' beautiful, rather austere home on a hill street parallel to our own, wasn't it true, I said, as I wolfed down chicken salad and pound cake, that navy blue was the black of college towns?

Of course no one laughed, and Mrs. Best said, "Always joking, Ellen." They all remembered that moment, over the next few months.

At the funeral luncheon my father was not himself, not the man who had taught me to say things like that. He was not the wit that day, smelling of white wine and lemon cologne, the bereaved wit talking of how my mother would have loved the chamber music and the chapter from Corinthians and Isabel Duane's eulogy. Instead he stood by a table clutching a mug of coffee and listened as others came up to condole and reminisce.

His hands shook, and his face was gray. He looked more ill than my mother had, those months ago, when he had come out onto the porch and told me I had no heart. He did not recognize Dr. Cohn when she took his hand, and when she bent near to say something in his ear his eyes were as glazed and blank as those of those people you see whiling their lives away in a mental institution. It was as though his soul had flown, too.

She asked me to walk with her out to her car, Dr. Cohn, in her black wool coat and a hat with a brim turned back from her strong face. She looked exactly like one of the Orthodox women I had seen on the Upper West Side on Saturday mornings, herding gaggles of small children, girls in dresses, boys in jackets and yarmulkes, to temple. Glibly I asked, "Do you go to all your patients' funerals?"

"The ones I particularly like," she said.

She opened the front door of the car, slid inside, and gestured for me to join her. She looked straight out the windshield at the old snow, in ugly piles along the curbs and driveways, as though we were driving somewhere and she was concentrating on the next turnoff.

Finally she said flatly, "I don't know whether to say this or not. But I will. The pathologist found something wrong during the autopsy."

I made a sound, half snort, half laugh. I was a little drunk and very tired. "News flash, Doctor," I said. "I guessed that there was something wrong with my mother."

"Don't be flip, Ellen. I mean they found that the cause of death was an overdose of the morphine."

"The pump?"

"Someone's already looked at it. It's fine."

"The pills?"

"I don't know. I just know that the toxicology reports showed that she had enough morphine in her to be fatal. More than enough. A great deal."

"So? So what? She took morphine all the time. You know that. And Teresa will tell them that my mother was in agony, she was like an animal by the very end, wearing diapers, drooling, never knowing what day it was, never able to get up. Who cares how she died? She should have been put out of her misery weeks ago. If she had been a dog they would have."

"Ellen," Dr. Cohn said, "you should watch what you say."

"I don't care what anybody thinks of me."

"Don't you wonder who did it?"

"Did what?"

"Are you listening to me? Someone administered a fatal overdose of morphine to your mother."

"Did you tell my father?" I said.

"We had to tell the district attorney."

I snorted again, louder. "Oh, God, Mr. Best," I said. "Who cares? Did you tell my father?"

"I tried," Dr. Cohn said. "But he seems so vague. I didn't quite feel that he was completely present, if you know what I mean."

And she was right. He did well enough in class, I heard, but he seemed abstracted and fatigued otherwise. The president had offered him a sabbatical, but he had replied as he had when I offered to clean the closets: No. Absolutely not.

And I wondered whether, as he drove across the bridge over the Montgomery River to the gray stone building where he held court in that corner office, as he handed out reading lists and oversaw senior theses, perhaps even as he was offered dinner and a good dry martini by some assistant professor still looking for a life companion and knowing, at least, that a widower had not been opposed to marriage as a matter of course, I wondered whether all was obscured by a vision of his hand holding a spoon with a small seashell pattern on the handle, my mother's second-best dinner setting, carrying rice pudding from the bowl to her mouth. After the funeral, after Dr. Cohn told me about the morphine, even before I really understood that someone was going to be hell-bent on finding out how it came to be in my mother's raddled body, I began to think about the pudding.

I wondered about it as I packed up, the silver clean, the furniture back in its original position. I heard a whine, a hum, from the lower floors, and for just a moment I thought it was the wheelchair, moving from the living room to the kitchen. But it was only the furnace tuning up. I thought I heard a high cry from below, plaintive, tortured, alive. But it was some bird, knocking against the kitchen window at its own seductive reflection, falling in love with its own image in a case of mistaken identity. *Knock, knock. Knock, knock.* It went on and on as I filled my vanity bag with aspirin and Vaseline and my diaphragm and some tubes of lipstick. There was an empty plastic container that had once held morphine tablets and I dropped it into the trash as I had the one that had stood on the table in the den, that morning after, as my father sat and whispered to my dead mother, his dead wife, his voice so soft and intimate and finally broken that I had gone into the other room and put on Vivaldi, loud, so I could not hear him, before I made a pot of coffee in the kitchen.

Knock, knock, went the bird again, but the timbre was different this time, and I went down, my bag in hand. The train schedule was on the table in the hall. The 6:10, I thought. The 6:10 that I had last taken that day in September, after I drank the orange juice and smashed the glass and vowed to show I had a heart.

They were knocking at the door, two men in suits, their knocking an echo of the bird, a cardinal it was, smashing himself so determinedly against the window that there were now smears of some sort of mucus and a trace of blood. The two men stood on the doorstep and when I opened the door neither moved, but the older one, the one with the brown suit, said pleasantly, with a half-smile, "Miss Gulden." It was not a question.

Officer Patterson, and with him Officer Brown, in the brown suit. If I could raise my father from his torpor it would be by telling him that, by telling him that it was a cheap faux Dickensian trick, telling him how Officer Brown worked the knot of his tie back and forth just before he asked a question, as though someone had created him on the page determined to give him some defining characteristic. Officer Patterson said, "Nice house." Officer Brown said, "We'd like to ask you some questions." Officer Patterson refused coffee. Officer Brown asked if I could come downtown.

"What's that noise?" Officer Patterson said.

"A bird bashing his head into the kitchen window," I said, and they looked at one another.

My duffel was on the floor by the gateleg table. The train schedule was tucked beneath a blue-and-orange Chinese bowl. Everyone admired it, including Officer Brown. My mother had been jubilant about that always, because she had purchased the bowl from a grocery and kitchen supply store in Chinatown for $25, having bargained the proprietor down from $35 and demanded a bag of fortune cookies thrown in into the bargain. "A good housewife makes a happy home," one of the cookies had said, but it was I who got it, and wrinkled up my nose as I read it aloud.

As I walked out to their black sedan I could see my futon in the garage, ready to be thrown into Jeff's jeep later in the week and carted back to Jules's apartment. After we were gone, two other police officers came, with my father, and searched the house, and they found the empty pill vial in the basket, and another at the bottom of a trash bag in the garage, and the diaphragm, and the train schedule, and the duffel bag. It said in the papers later that I had been preparing to flee. "I was catching the six-ten, for Christsake," I said to Jeff in a diner over a club sandwich and a chocolate milk shake after he and Mrs. Forburg bailed me out. "I was going back to where I really live." Someone heard me say it, and that was in the paper, too.

Officer Brown asked me what my mother ate, what she drank, how she slept, how she looked, whether I liked her, whether I loved her, whether I was anxious to stop nursing her and get back to the city and a life of my own. He asked me about morphine dosages, administration, side effects, pills, and pumps. I knew all about it, and I told him so, and the stenographer took my words down, and the sun had set outside the windows of the municipal building and Mr. Best was waiting anxiously in his office and the 6:10 had just pulled out of the station when they arrested me and charged me with killing my mother.

"You've got to be kidding," I said, and that was in the paper, too.

That next morning, after I'd spent my night in jail, the hum of the electrical lines lulling me to sleep, after I'd appeared in court and moved carefully through the clot of reporters at the front entrance, after I'd climbed into Mrs. Forburg's old beige car and taken off with her to meet Jeff at the Greek diner two towns over, I told her that I couldn't wait to tell my father about Officer Brown in his brown suit, about the Grand Guignol of the court- room, so very Evelyn Waugh. And it was then that it occurred to me that he hadn't been there, not during the night, not in the morning. "He has an early class on Thursdays," I said.

"I could beat that man with a stick," Mrs. Forburg said.

I didn't see my father again for eight years, except for one afternoon down the long gray high-ceilinged corridor of the county courthouse, both of us yet again in navy blue, both of us knowing that the illusion of our inseparability, our fused identities, crumbling these many months since he had said I was heartless and I had set out to prove to him that I was not, that the illusion was now blown apart forever.

It was either him or me. For the last time, after they arrested me, I chose him.

It was the summer when I had just turned eight that I went to stay with my Gulden grandparents for two weeks and it rained without ceasing. It was that thick gray chilly rain that sometimes grips the northeast in August and sends the children of summer colonies and beach towns into sporadic fits of Monopoly, bowling, Old Maid, hide-and-seek in the closets and the basements of houses pungent with damp, sends them finally to driving their parents crazy, until their mothers let them play in the rain as one last desperate diversion.

My grandmother taught me War during those days, both of us with sweaters over our summer clothes; I remember the lamps, turned on to make a show of light against the gray outside, glinting off her wedding band and the buffed surfaces of her nails as she laid the cards down. Although I had long outgrown them, we played Chutes and Ladders and Candyland; although I played clumsily, we played Risk and Parcheesi.

My grandmother said my grandfather would teach me chess, but he never did. Even as the rain poured down outside he went about his normal round of seasonal activities at the camp, turning off the water to the cabins, caulking windows and floating empty plastic bottles in toilets, putting antifreeze in the pool lines. He came in for lunch and dinner, hung a yellow waterproof parka, streaming with water, on a peg near the back door, ate and then went back outside, ate, and then sat in the lamplight himself in the evening for an hour or two, reading books about the Civil War or watching baseball players in sunny cities flicker by on the television while my grandmother knitted, her needles, too, catching the light.

A bottle of beautiful amber-colored whiskey sat on the little table next to his chair, and a tumbler that always had an inch or so of amber in it. It did not make him garrulous, brilliant, or mean, the way it did my father. A deeply silent man, it merely made him more silent. I can remember the words my grandfather said to me one by one, like trees on a plain, there were so few of them.

When we ran out of things to do, my grandmother took out her scrapbooks—tooled leather covers held together with rawhide ties, thick, rough black paper covered with pictures held in place with little tan triangles, the pictures with the wavy edges and flat black-and-white vistas of my grandmother's girlhood. The picture I remember best was one of my father and his father standing side by side in front of the lake that was the southernmost perimeter of the camp.

Perhaps what first caught my attention was the date, which showed my father to be the same age in the photograph as I was at the time. But what I remembered afterward was how puny he was, a slight boy in a checkered shirt and dark shorts, his knees big knobs in the ungainly line of slightly bowed legs, his hands on his hips, his arms akimbo and shoulders squared as though he sought to take up more space in the frame than his body would normally dictate. His father was a big man, tall and square—*stalwart* is the word that comes to mind—with curling dark hair and a square jaw, with big arms and big hands, but he looks even bigger next to his son, some great dark evergreen next to a pale-green blade of grass. Both of them had fixed expressions on their faces, and I could almost imagine my grandmother telling them to smile, smile, smile, as my mother had always told me, and their expressionless faces only becoming more grim as they stood silently without complying. In her efforts to include all of my father in the picture, my grandmother had nipped off perhaps two inches of her husband's head.

My father had been like the boy in that picture in the two weeks after my mother died: diminished, overshadowed, frozen in some posture out of his customary place in the world. Perhaps his children contributed to that, for when they arrived home, the evening of the day on which she died, my brothers ignored him. Not in any mean way, but as though their connection to him had always been a secondary one, by means of the woman he had married and they had loved. If our family had been a wheel, a perfect round thing moving in perpetual motion down an easy road, she had been the hub and the route all at once. We were directionless, he as much as we three. He more, actually.

It was why, waking in a strange bed in a strange house the morning after I had been arrested and arraigned, I was the only one who was unsurprised that my father had not come to rescue me. He seemed so small now, so shrunken, that I could not imagine him capable of such a thing.

Besides, the others did not know what supporting me would require him to do, to admit, to confess. The rest of them had not watched him feed his wife rice pudding, the spoon sweeping through the air like a pigeon with a message, coming home. The rest of them had not heard her whisper "Help me." In a square and drab room with a single bed, a dresser, and no pictures on the walls I closed my eyes and saw him again, lifting, spooning, lifting again. The rest of them were wondering where the morphine had come from, but I believed I knew. My mother had made perfect order in her home in large part because her husband craved it, and then she had disordered it—the undusted tables, the wheelchair, the night terrors, the hospital bed, the smell of rank perspiration and chemicals. Perhaps he could not bear it. Perhaps he felt sorry for her.

Perhaps he even loved her. Perhaps she had asked of him, that last night when I heard them talking, what she had asked of me and he had had the courage and the love to do what I had not. For that possibility alone I believed he deserved my protection. At least that is how I think I felt when the woman I am today analyzes the one I was then.

"There's coffee, Ellen," said Mrs. Forburg, turning off the radio when I came out into the little kitchen in the same pants and sweater I'd slept in in the little cell in the Montgomery County jail.

In silence I sat at a small white table and looked down at its surface, drawing patterns with the side of my spoon. After a moment Mrs. Forburg sat opposite me.

"No school today?" I said.

"I took a personal day," she said.

"Personal, all right," I said.

"You can stay as long as you like."

"How much money did you pay to get me out?" I said.

"Ten thousand dollars. Ten percent of your bail. I get it all back unless you leave town."

"Skip town," I said.

"What?"

"That's what they always say in the movies. Skip town. Don't worry. I'm not going anywhere."

"That's why they say they arrested you, because you were getting ready to flee."

"Well, I guess that's one way of putting it. I was packing my duffel bag to go back to New York. Two guys showed up at the front door, told me they wanted to ask me some questions at the police station, and the next thing I knew I was under arrest."

"Ellen, you knew what the autopsy found. The doctor says she told you last week, after the funeral. Why didn't you do something?"

"Do what?"

"Get a lawyer. Talk to someone. Come to me. Didn't you understand what would happen?"

"I didn't do it," I said simply.

How many different ways were there to say it? When the investigators at police headquarters had asked me, sitting in a room the color of my palms on the same kind of molded plastic chairs my mother and I had sat on as we waited for one of the nurses to clear a room for chemotherapy, I said it over and over again. I didn't do it. Did I give her the pills? No. Did I know why the vial was empty? No. Did I love my mother? Did I hate my mother? Did I resent my mother? Did I want my mother dead?

"If you had seen my mother and you understood what she once had been, you would have wanted her dead, too," I said, enraged.

Did I kill her?

No.

But I could see the spoon go up and over, into her mouth and out again, her eyes glittering in the light from the lamp. I never said anything about the spoon. I never have, all these years.

That summer when I was eight my father drove me to his parents' house, a cabin on the grounds of the camp, screened from the kids and the counselors by a row of enormous pines my grandfather planted when my father was just a baby. "Georgie's trees," my grandmother called them. It was a long drive, three hours and then some, and we stopped at a restaurant in a town called Liberty and had club sandwiches and iced tea. The rain had already started, although they were saying on the radio that it would end the next day. But I didn't care. As we drove my father recited poetry in his changeable actor's voice, Shakespeare and John Donne and even Edna St. Vincent Millay:

> What lips my lips have kissed, and where, and why,
> I have forgotten, and what arms have lain
> Under my head till morning; but the rain
> Is full of ghosts tonight, that tap and sigh
> Upon the glass and listen for reply,

And in my heart there stirs a quiet pain
For unremembered lads that not again
Will turn to me at midnight with a cry.
Thus in the winter stands the lonely tree,
Nor knows what birds have vanished one by one,
Yet knows its boughs more silent than before:
I cannot say what loves have come and gone,
I only know that summer sang in me
A little while, that in me sings no more.

The words, the sentiments, which I did not understand, seemed to fill the car, the end to reverberate—"that in me sings no more"—and there was a long silence afterward that seemed longer because of the small intense sounds of the woods which surrounded us on either side—the high incessant trill of some bird, the long whirr of what I assumed were bugs. Then my father looked at me and shrugged.

"Even second-rate poetry is better than no poetry at all, Ellen," he said. I remember the sense of relief, almost a physical feeling, that I had waited for him to speak first, to tell me what to feel, that I had not told him immediately how beautiful I thought the poem was.

"You are an exceptional child, Little Nell," he said, when he looked over at my dazzled face.

Deeper and deeper into the woods we drove, the inside of the car dark because of the great old oaks and elms that arched their branches to touch one another across the narrow country roads. We went for miles without seeing a house, a car, anything more than wild-eyed rabbits and the fat and sluggish groundhogs that grazed on the sparse grass that grew along the roadsides. It was what the parents wanted for their children when they sent them to camp, this isolation, the sense that they were being set down in the real America. But it was difficult to imagine my father here, poring over Aesop's *Fables* by the light on his old desk, riding the school bus twelve miles to the nearest town and its stolid red-brick elementary school, leaving here with his bags packed for prep school, where the trees had been thinned and light poured in.

We were not far from the big wooden arch that marked the turnoff for the camp when the doe leapt in front of the car. For a moment I could see her face turned toward me, the muzzle soft-looking even from that distance, the eyes black and round, those enormous ears outstretched to know the road just an instant too late. The impact when we hit her was tremendous, and flecks of black and red spotted the windshield as my father veered sharply onto the shoulder and jammed on the brakes. Afterward, when I looked into the medicine cabinet mirror in my grandparents' cabin, I realized I had hit my head on the dashboard. There was an abrasion and a bump.

"Holy shit," he said.

The deer was on the verge across the road, making a scrabbling motion with her narrow pointed feet. But she could not stand or even push herself along, and she only turned her body slightly, this way and that, her neck arched so it looked as though her head would touch her long, beige-gray silky back.

My father got out of the car and went around to look at the front bumper. "Damn," he said, his face tight with rage, glancing across the road, then back at the car. "Damn."

The noise the deer made with her feet was like someone using a typewriter: *staccato, stop, staccato, stop.* For a moment she would rest and her arched neck would fall and I could see her face, her nostrils working in time with the ragged rise and fall of her sides.

My father got back in the car and put it into gear. "Don't say a word," he said. I was even afraid to turn in my seat to look as we drove away.

My grandparents were outside when we pulled in at their house, past the cabins, empty as old shoe boxes, past the paddock and the pool. Through the trees you could see a sliver of lake, just below the rise on which their house sat.

"I need a drink," my father said to his mother when he got out of the car, and he told her what had happened.

"Oh, George, what a terrible thing," she said as she held his arm, walking him toward the house.

"The animal?" my grandfather said in his guttural voice, which clotted around the consonants.

"It's done for," my father said.

"It's by the road," I said.

My grandfather went into the house and came out with a shotgun. He put it into the back of his old station wagon and pointed at me. "Show me," he said.

"Nature will take its course," my father said. But my grandfather started the car and reached across to open the door for me.

"For God's sake, I'll come," my father said, shrugging off his mother's arm. My grandmother's face looked like the doe's, eyes bright, mouth soft and trembling. I was already in the front seat and my father tried to pull me out by the arm, but I hung back next to my grandfather and shook my head.

"How many Goddamn deer do the townspeople shoot every fall?" he muttered.

When we got back to the place in the road, with its curly ribbon of black skid marks, the deer was still alive, still moving its legs fruitlessly. My grandfather pointed the gun at her head, and for a moment she arched away, turned to look, then lay still. His shoulder jerked back just a bit as he shot her. I cried all the way to the cabin, my face in my hands. My grandfather patted my shoulder and my father looked out the window.

"I need a drink and a new car," he said to my grandmother as the two of them went into the house.

That and the photograph of him and his father together, those were the two things I thought of most often as I slept in Mrs. Forburg's guest bedroom and drank coffee at her kitchen table. That afternoon Jeff came to the back door, cutting through the woods so he could avoid the local reporter and photographer who were sitting outside Mrs. Forburg's house. He tapped on the glass of the kitchen window and peered in, his eyes framed by the yellow café curtains.

"This is like a bad spy novel," I said.

"I have some calls to make in my room," said Mrs. Forburg.

Jeffrey and I sat and looked at one another across the kitchen table. "You look like hell," he said.

"I know, but what can I do? I've been wearing the same clothes for two days and I'm out of moisturizer."

"I have your duffel in the jeep. I'll bring it in if those guys outside leave."

"They'll get bored sooner or later."

"They're not going to get bored. Tomorrow there'll be ten of them, then twenty. This is what they call a headline grabber. That's why that asshole Best had you arrested in the first place—not because he can make a case, but because he can make page one for days and days, making speeches about mercy killing and justice for all. There are people in town saying this never would have happened if you hadn't written the essay for the contest. Between that and the doctor who keeps hooking people up to an IV drip and the nurse up in Canada who pulled the plug on all those people last month, this is a big story."

"It'll pass."

"Not soon, sweetheart. Not soon."

"What else are they saying in town?"

Jeff bent his head, and the glints of red in his hair made me see my mother for a second. "Some of them say that you were justified in what you did," he said.

"And the others?"

"That you weren't."

"Is there anyone who believes that I didn't do it?"

He shook his head.

"You?"

He looked up in surprise. "El, you have a lot of character failings, the most profound of which at this point seems to be the mistaken impression that people are sane and sensible. But you've never been dishonest in your entire life. To a fault, I should add."

"Brian?"

"Bri's really fucked up. He calls from school and just cries and cries. I don't think he cares what killed her, just that she's dead. That's what these fools messed up with this thing—our right to just deal with the fact that she's gone, instead of how she got that way. Cancer killed my mother. Our mother. That's what I say."

"When are you going back?" I said.

"I'm staying here until this is over."

"In the house?"

"I'm there as little as possible. Pop and I have some difficulty communicating."

I thought of my father, quiet and shrunken, in the house that Kate built, imagined his hand with the spoon in it going up and over, up and over, into her mouth and out.

"He really wants to see you, El," my brother said. "Every morning at breakfast he says, 'I must speak to your sister' and every night at dinner he says, 'Have you spoken with Ellen?' He says the two of you need to talk. He wants me to arrange a time here when you can be alone together. He says he understands if you won't come to the house."

"I need to not talk to him right now," I said. "And he needs to not talk to me."

Jeff squeezed my hand. "He won't take no for an answer."

"He'll have to," I said. "Tell him it's impossible."

"His lawyer told him he shouldn't see you until after the grand jury meets," Jeff said, "but he insists you have to talk."

"He has a lawyer?" I said.

"Yeah. And you need one. A good one."

"Maybe I'll call Jon for a referral," I said.

"Jon?"

"F. Lee Beltzer. Mr. Jurisprudence. My nominal boyfriend." At the funeral Jon had worn navy blue, too, but he had only taken my hand at the church after the service and had not come to the Duanes' afterward.

"Haven't you read the papers?" Jeff said.

I shook my head. "Shit," Jeffrey said, and he got up and looked in the refrigerator, closed it and then opened it to look again.

"Jon is your problem," he said. "After Mom died he told his old man that you'd been saying you wished she'd die. His old man heard about the autopsy and went to Best to get extra tests done. Jon nailed you."

"Jon?"

"Yeah."

"He gave me up?" I asked.

Jeff nodded.

"Pretty extreme way to end a relationship," I said.

"Cut that crap, Ellen. He screwed you, big time. He's scum and he always was scum and now you're going to pay for your shitty taste in men." Jeff took my hand again. "I know what happened," he said. "Don't you think I know what happened? There's only one person you'd ever do this for."

"I'm doing it for her," I said.

"Who?"

"Mama," I said. "I'm doing it for her. Jeffie, I can't talk with you about this any more. Not one more word. I just can't. Will you get me a lawyer?"

"What should I tell Pop?" he said.

"Tell him I understand," I said. "Tell him we'll talk sometime. I just don't know when."

"And if I run into Jon?"

I thought for a minute, my hands in my lap. I thought of Jon calling his mother in California, asking her how she could have just walked out one day and left him behind, left a two-year-old to grow up with a hole in his heart. I thought of him hearing her reply, "I just did." I thought of his hands on my lower back and my breasts, his mouth on my belly, of the datebook and the apartment he had probably already sublet, with a big double bed. My head hurt.

"Tell him to go to hell," I said.

"It's a deal," Jeff replied.

When my therapist asked me to keep a journal dissecting the events of that year, she wanted me to particularly deal with the emotions I experienced immediately after I was arrested, before the grand jury heard and decided my case, decided whether to indict me or not. For a while I thought about doing what I had always done for Mrs. Forburg when I wrote compositions or poetry in her class, spinning synthetic emotions out of the silky yarn of intelligence. I was more likely to scam my therapist than Mrs. Forburg, who was far sharper and harder than her often twinkly manner would suggest. She would send my poems back with the dismissive "Clever . . . but!" or the softer "Nice language, but where are you in here?"

It was difficult to tell my therapist, as I finally did, that I felt very little during the weeks after I was charged with my mother's death, although if I had known as much about psychiatry as I do today I would have realized that this was an eminently acceptable answer, easily classified as "lack of affect." At the time I assumed it was because I had lapsed, like an alcoholic or a mental patient who must be recommitted, that I had made a stab at being my mother's daughter and had now reverted convincingly to being my father's, my emotions pickled in a solution of cynicism and self-involvement. Sometimes I wondered whether all children had to choose in that fashion. I pictured my mother sitting watching a toddler, looking for the early signs: which would it be, his or hers? Like embroidered hand towels. I wondered if that was why there were three children, to break the tie. On numbers my mother had been the big winner, but perhaps not on sheer strength of devotion, at least not until the end.

It was difficult to explain how ordinary your life can be, even when extraordinary things are happening around you. Jeff was right; the number of reporters outside Mrs. Forburg's house grew in the next few days, then ebbed, then grew again when new reports surfaced that the prosecutor was asking for help from a famous pathologist in Florida, that my former boyfriend was expected to appear before the grand jury, that the school board was considering disciplinary action against Mrs. Forburg, who walked into the glare of television lights and a half dozen flashes every morning when she left for school.

"Let them fire me," she said, making coffee the morning this last appeared in the *Tribune*. "I can get my Social Security and maybe it'll teach my students something about doing the right thing."

"I still don't entirely understand why you're doing this," I said.

"A mind is a terrible thing to waste," she said.

"Seriously."

"Seriously, you needed help and I was in a position to provide it. There's no mystery in that."

"You're playing the Shirley Booth role in this movie."

"I always hated Shirley Booth," Mrs. Forburg said. And then she left and you could hear the noise, a hum and then a fusillade, lousy with fake intimacy: "Brenda, are you going to lose your job?" "Can you tell us how Ellen is doing?" "Have you talked about what she did?" Then the noise of the car turning over and scattering gravel as she pulled out of the driveway, and the questions died away.

That was the only peculiar thing about my life, that and the way people looked at me in the supermarket or at the mall, the sidelong glances and the stares. After the first two weeks the reporters outside drifted away, waiting for the next hearing, the easy drama of the courtroom. But the *Tribune* kept running the picture of me leaving the courthouse after my arraignment whenever Mr. Best would make a new announcement, and I had only to smile slightly when a little girl lifted her skirt over her head in a grand gesture in the produce aisle or I thought idly of something my mother had once said about mall rats, and someone was sure to narrow their eyes and peer at me. Yes . . . I'm not sure . . . yes, it is . . . that's her.

"Her mother," you could sometimes hear them whisper. The little girl would drop her dress and move closer to the stroller in which her baby brother slept, mouth open, chubby legs bowed on either side of a great diaper bulge.

In the Safeway an elderly woman pressed a little book of daily meditations with a rose on the cover into my hand. "God bless and keep you, dear," she said.

"You're better looking than your pictures," said the checkout girl.

And the telephone answering machine in Mrs. Forburg's dining room was full of messages. The *Tribune* reporter, Julie Heinlein, was tireless in her pursuit of me, scenting the sort of break that would take her away from Langhorne and on to somewhere bigger, better. Her voice wheedled and coaxed on the tape—an interview, an off-the-record conversation, a first-person account. Once she said, "I've been told that you, too, are a journalist." And I remembered Bill Tweedy's disgusted judgment one night over boilermakers in the Blarney Stone downstairs from the magazine offices: "A journalist is a reporter who worries too much about his clothes."

There were the nut cases, of course, offering to marry me or to hold me down and kill me painfully so that I would fully appreciate my sins. And there were the advocates. The Center for the Right to Die had taken up my cause and offered to provide me with a lawyer.

"It is time for every one of us to realize that family members know better what is right for the terminally ill than the courts, the police, or the medical personnel who would keep them alive at all costs," said a man who identified himself as the executive director.

"I didn't do it," I said to the machine.

"You have become a symbol to millions of people of how caring family members are victimized by a system that offers no hope to their loved ones," he continued. "You could be an important voice for the movement to allow people to die with dignity and, if necessary, with assistance."

"I didn't do it," I said again.

The next message was from a man who said that he knew a variety of sex acts that I would enjoy. I listened to the messages myself because I didn't want Mrs. Forburg to have to hear them, but afterward I felt sick, as though I had stomach flu. I lost weight during those weeks. I could not keep food down.

Every few days on the machine there was a voice I knew as well as my own, that in cadence and timbre was much like mine. "Ellen?" my father would say. "If you're there, would you kindly pick up?" In the silence I would hear his breathing, a little ragged, as though he'd been running. "Ellen?" There was never more of a message than that, my name and the demand that I respond, until one afternoon he began to speak.

"Ellen," he said quietly, "I would like to talk about what happened. I know it's difficult for you. But we cannot leave this unsaid." There was a long pause. The tape made a clicking sound as it moved around its eyelike spools. "I didn't know what they were doing at the police station," he continued. "I had no idea they would arrest you. I would have come. I didn't know. I wouldn't—" there was a choking sound, a sharp breath. "We should talk," he said. "We need to talk." And then there was the noise, so final, of the receiver being put down.

That was the last message I got from him.

Apart from that, the days were ordinary, almost tedious. I think now the only real manifestation I had of what was happening around me, in the newspapers, in offices at the courthouse and the municipal building, was a feeling not unlike the homesickness that always filled me for the first few days when I went to stay at my grandparents' house, and even, I was stunned to discover, during the first few months of my freshman year at college.

It was not really the home my mother had made that I yearned for as I wandered through Mrs. Forburg's rooms; I remembered how empty it had seemed after the hospital wagon came and the attendants efficiently, almost magically, took the body away. But I was sick in my soul for that greater meaning of home that we understand most purely when we are children, when it is a metaphor for all possible feelings of security, of safety, of what is predictable, gentle, and good in life.

During those weeks in Mrs. Forburg's house, much of my life was predictable. In fact it was much like the life I had lived those last few months tending my mother, and yet it felt so empty by comparison. There was no center to it, no point. It was an empty housewife's routine of sweeping floors, folding laundry, even watching soap operas. I cooked and cleaned and read; I simmered casseroles and made pies. But there was no one, nothing, around which all this activity revolved. It was simply the white noise of my life, the way to make the time go by least painfully. I was like a mother whose children have been killed in some horrible accident and yet who continues to put a pan of brownies on the table on a trivet every afternoon at three.

One night I went to put out a bag of garbage, to leave it at the end of the short drive off the graveled country road where the McNulty brothers would get it in the morning. They would throw it into the back of the truck they took to the dump, where they were as constant a sight, with their low foreheads and dirty watch caps, as the big oily-feathered birds who picked with sharp beaks at the orange sections spotted with coffee grounds, smeared with mayonnaise and lettuce.

I had put another bag there earlier, and by the light of the nearly full moon I could see a racoon with its pointed snout buried in one corner of the glistening green plastic. It whirled to greet me, baring its little yellowish teeth, nothing cute or cartoon-ish in its ratlike eyes and scrabbling hands, and then it ran across the road and into the dark. I saw that it had spread its booty around the mailbox post, an untidy heap of bones cleaned to gray whiteness like the moon, a tuna can, a small jar that had once held tartar sauce, a half lemon now reduced cleanly to a bowllike bit of yellow peel, two greasy paper towels like dying flowers.

I began to work off the twist tie of the bag I was holding so I could put all the things inside it, but as I stooped to pick up the first bone, my ankle went awry, slipping sideways, and I fell heavily into the grass and dirt and began to cry, long rattling gasps that held my chest down like a hand on my sternum. I sat and wept, my face lifted to the sky as though the moon might warm it. A chicken bone, the fragile ribs and cartilaginous center bow of a breast, was beneath the heel of my hand, and I picked it up and threw it with all my might, hearing no sound as it landed in the scrubby weeds on the other side of the road.

"Goddamnit," I cried, and I tried to get to my feet, but Mrs. Forburg was behind me, bending stiffly to put her hands on my shoulders.

"It's just the Goddamn mess," I said. "Look at it." I moved my hand in a wobbly arc and finally brought it up to my chest, feeling my breathing catch and slow, catch again.

"Go inside," she said. "I'll do this." And I did.

Sometimes I helped her with her homework, editing senior essays with a red pen, grading the true-and-false tests. True, they said, Shakespeare began a sonnet "Death Be Not Proud." True, they said, Mr. Darcy is a character in *A Tale of Two Cities*. True, they said, *Silas Marner* was written by a man named George Eliot.

It's funny, isn't it, what will make you break? Your lover moves to London and falls in love with a news reader for the BBC and you feel fine and then one day you raise your umbrella slightly to cross Fifty-seventh Street and stare into the Burberry shop and begin to sob. Or your baby dies at birth and five years later, in an antique store, a small battered silver rattle with teeth marks in one end engraved with the name Emily lies on a square of velvet, and the sobs escape from the genie's bottle somewhere deep in your gut where they've lain low until then.

Or the garbage bag breaks.

Wrong, wrong, wrong went my big red checks on the test papers, and then I got to *Silas Marner* and George Eliot and I pressed my hand to my face, trying to keep everything inside where it belonged. I walked, head down, to the one small bathroom in Mrs. Forburg's house.

"You can't keep it all bottled up," she said when I came back out.

"Sure I can," I said.

"Do you want tea?"

"No. What I really want is a drink, but that way lies disaster."

"Amen," said Mrs. Forburg, who went to Al-Anon meetings twice a week in the basement of the Lutheran church, as she put a bowl of peanuts on the table. "Don't get grease on my papers."

"You guys always do that," I said, struggling with a smile. "Even at college, you always call them 'my papers.' Why are you so fierce about the possessive?"

"I never thought about that before," Mrs. Forburg said, eating a handful of nuts. "Maybe it's because they're the only tangible part of teaching. Except for you guys, of course, the finished product, but even that's ephemeral. You watch the students work in class and you know that what you're doing is taking hold, but there's nothing really to show for it except this." She held up a paper covered with red ink. "Bad example, but you understand my point. You look at the papers and you can see what sticks and what doesn't. It's one visible manifestation of how well you're doing what you do. That, and occasionally you'll get a letter from one of them that lets you know you did a good job."

"I should have sent you a letter like that. I was full of what you taught me. I mean, I lived on what I'd learned from you through four years of English lit."

"Thank you, my dear. That's what you always hope will happen, but it doesn't really give you much to hold on to. I suppose in a way it's like having children. No one really knows how good a job you've done unless, paradoxically, you've done a bad one and a child goes wrong. Otherwise, you've spent years on this work with precious little credit."

I don't know what I would have done without Mrs. Forburg during all those weeks. It was like living with a softer, more gentle version of my father, ever anxious to discuss the link between literature and life but not judgmental about opinions that diverged from her own. In the evening we had dinner together, watched the evening news, and talked for an hour or two afterward at the table in the kitchen, with the blinds always shut tight. When she went out to her meetings I watched television sitcoms and read mystery novels and talked to Jules on the phone.

"People aren't supposed to ask about AA things, are they?" I asked one night after Mrs. Forburg had come home from her meeting.

"I don't know about people," she said. "You can certainly ask me about Al-Anon."

"Why do you go?"

"Because it helps me to understand why I do some of the things I do," she said.

"Sorry, I put that badly. You usually go to Al-Anon if you have a family member who is an alcoholic. Who's the family member?" I raised my arms, palms open, as though to indicate the empty house, empty of photographs or mementos, too, so different from my mother's house. "Sorry," I said, "that was a nasty way of putting it."

"Have you noticed you apologize a lot these days?" Mrs. Forburg said.

"Is that a way of evading my question?"

"No, it's something you might want to think about. The answer is that my ex-husband was an alcoholic. My father was an alcoholic. And my mother was an alcoholic. And I was, in the vocabulary of the addiction, the enabler who made it possible for all of them to go on drinking. I took care of my mother when she was drunk and then when she was dying, and I adored my father and made excuses for why he did what he did."

"And your husband?"

"Oh, he was my father all over again—charming, smart, and crippled. You can find my story in any handbook on alcoholism. But knowing that you're typical doesn't go a long way toward making you feel better in your day-to-day life."

"How long have you been divorced?" I asked. I could not remember Mrs. Forburg ever being married.

"Twelve years," she said.

"It takes you that long to get over it?"

"That's a naïve comment from someone as intelligent as you are. It takes your entire life to get over some of the people you've loved, and some you never get over."

"You always do that. The intelligence thing. It's as though if you're smart, you will understand yourself."

"You're right. That's naïve of me. Particularly of me."

"Is your father still alive?"

"He died three years ago. But if my head counts for anything, he'll live forever."

I understood that. I thought of my father all the time during those weeks. When I did not think of him, I dreamed of him. People were chasing me in those long, attenuated, slow-motion chases that are so common in dreams and, perhaps, more than we ever understand, in life. Sometimes my father would be one of them, sometimes he would be a bystander, sometimes he would try to help me but let go of my hand as I went by, our fingers slipping past one another like fish swimming parallel for a moment, then off in opposite directions.

When I was twelve or thirteen, I remember, I went downstairs for a glass of milk and found him and my mother sitting at the table, the round oak table, beneath the sampler of our family tree: George and Kate in cross-stitch below a stylized line of grass and flowers, and then the three of us in the branches, full names, careful script in straight stitch.

My father had had a big balloon glass of brandy in front of him. I could smell it, sharp but with that lingering sweetness. He was wearing an Irish fisherman's cardigan, bulky with cables, and his sports coat hung on the back of the chair. He was leaning back on the back legs, which we were never allowed to do because my mother said it was bad for the chairs.

"Ellen, an opinion," he said, letting down the chair with a clunk and leaning forward to cup his brandy in his hands. "Did you see the story in today's *Tribune* about the apartment complex they are proposing to build down from the college?"

"No," I think I said. Was I thirteen then, or fourteen? Did most girls my age read the paper?

"Here," he said, handing me a section of newspaper that had been on the floor below the table. "Background." His words were very crisp, in the way they were when he had had a good deal to drink.

The story said that the state was proposing to build a complex of twenty-four apartments for low-income residents, on a wooded site directly behind the quarry.

I looked up.

"Your mother," my father said, "finds this perfectly acceptable."

"That is not what I said, Gen," my mother had said.

"Perfectly acceptable. Here you have a lovely wooded area which will be raped for the sake of building some crackerboxes for people who, within weeks, will have left old cars on the lawns and written their names all over the walls. Your mother does not find this troubling."

"That's not what I said, Gen."

"Well, what was it you did say?"

"I said that everybody has to live somewhere."

"There you have it, Ellen. Words to live by: everybody has to live somewhere."

"I'm going to bed," I said.

"So am I," said my mother.

"No one wants to engage in civilized debate in this household," my father said.

Do I remember this correctly or do I remember it now as I wish it had been? When I remembered those occasions in those weeks, I remembered myself aligned with my mother against my father. Can any of that be true? Or was it just the trick of the light, that when she was alive shone on him alone and now shone only on the place where she had once been, nothing but Jesus rays and dust motes and a circle of silver on the ground? All my stories have alternate endings now, like "The Lady or the Tiger." There is the ending where I am brittle and clever and he looks at me over the rim of his half glasses, the blue of his eyes bisected by tortoiseshell, and his mouth curves just a little at the corner and I know that I have done the right thing. And there is the other ending. My mother's ending.

"There you are," he said, "words to live by—everybody has to live somewhere."

"I'm going to bed," said my mother.

"And you, Ellen?" he said.

"I'll stay down here for a while," I said. "Do you want another brandy?"

One night I had a dream that I was driving our car, sitting on a telephone book so that I was high enough to see over the dashboard, and that I hit the deer and he said, "Very careless, Ellen," but you could tell by his smile that he was not really angry. And my grandfather got the gun and we went back but the deer was gone and in its place was a woman in a nightgown, her face turned away. "Who's that?" my grandfather said, but neither my father nor I recognized her.

I liked my lawyer. Not my first lawyer, the one who stood beside me at my arraignment, when the edges of my fingers were still black with the ink the police used to fingerprint me. Not the lawyer whose name, as nondescript as his clothes and his observations, was Smith.

But the lawyer who took over my case, who was paid for by Jeffrey with money that I only realized afterward, when the need for lawyers had long passed, was equal parts the money left Jeff by our Gulden grandparents and contributions from a handful of families in Langhorne who had been friends of ours and who believed that I should not be prosecuted. Most of them, I think, believed that I had killed my mother, but they believed I had done it out of kindness. Jeff told me that Mrs. Duane would only repeat, "If you had seen her pushing that wheelchair . . ." as she wrote him a substantial check on the bookstore account.

The money was not enough, I knew that. Jonathan had once told me he could expect to bill out at $300 an hour if he made partner in the firm he most coveted, the one with the atrium full of ficus trees and the private dining room with the nouvelle American chef. And I knew that Robert Greenstein would spend hours on this case even before it came to trial. His office had no atrium, no chef. He ate chicken salad from paper bags on the green blotter of his desktop; I ate with him on a few occasions.

But he was still a respected criminal trial lawyer, and the $25,000 my brother gave him was not enough. I told Jeff we should pay him in food, bring in the lasagna in disposable foil trays, the crockpot soups, the pineapple upsidedown cakes and the brownies that still littered the counters in my mother's house and filled the freezer so that it was impossible to open it, Jeff had told me, without having some funeral meats fall at your feet. Let him eat cake, I said.

"You'll give me the rest when you sell your story to television," Bob Greenstein said, "like that girl upstate who had her father killed because she didn't like her curfew and he didn't like her nose ring."

"Fat chance," I said, my mouth full of chicken salad.

That was one of the things I liked about him, that there was none of the hush, the reverence, that accompanied conversation with most people on the subject of my mother's death, no matter how they thought it might have happened. Even the reporters would talk in funeral home tones, what passes for understanding when people talk about death. "I know this is probably a difficult time, but if you could give me a half hour," they would say on the messages on Mrs. Forburg's home machine. "We do hair and makeup," said the assistant to a producer at a television station. "In case that's a concern."

But Bob never dropped his voice, never leaned toward me with concerned brown eyes beneath lowered brows. He was in many ways an unattractive man, short and squat, with only a fringe of hair, a tonsure that looked as though it had been drawn in with an eyebrow pencil. His shirt fronts stretched tight and dully white across his paunch, and his office smelled of cigar smoke, although for some reason he never smoked in front of me. His desk was a

mahogany reproduction piece, perhaps of something at Monti-
cello or Mount Vernon, and its big surface was scratched, the
finish worn off here and there by a cigar that had been allowed to
burn low, taking the veneer with it. One wall was lined with file
cabinets, with files piled untidily atop them, and behind him was
a breakfront with photographs of a boy and girl, stiff school portraits with fake rustic backgrounds.

"Wife?" I said when I first sat in the chair across from him.

"Left," he said.

I enjoyed communicating with someone like that, without
explanation or recriminations, without psychologizing or pontificating, just clean and pure, almost like math: Wife. Left. I was a
client to Bob Greenstein, a case, a problem, a fact pattern, a task
to be mastered. I liked that, too. It was a great relief to be with
a person who did not want to know my soul, my deepest secrets.
Quite the contrary.

Jeff would drive me in the jeep up the interstate to a small city
that rose just beyond the highway the way all the others did, the
shabby houses beneath the overpass ranged around the ramps, and
then the center of town, and then just beyond it the homes of
those with money and position. In the years to come, when I traveled more, I would realize that every American town was so con-
structed, that only New York was different, the rich and the poor
hopscotching across the horizon, Park Avenue one way in the
eighties and another in the hundred and twenties, Riverdale and
the South Bronx only a long, long short walk away from one
another.

I don't know where Bob lived, although I had his home phone
number in case, although I was never entirely sure what in case
was in this case, whether the police might come in the middle of
the night or the judge revoke my bail without cause. I imagined
him in a bare apartment somewhere, his wife living with the children in one of the Tudor houses just beyond the center of town,
so like the ones in Langhorne. Although for all I knew he had a
splendid contemporary on a swath of open land ten miles away,

with a Jacuzzi that provided a view of the woods and lots of
action in the evenings.

I didn't need to know much about him, nor him about me,
except for the story. I told him of how the police had brought me
to the station for questioning a week after my mother's funeral, of
how they arrested me after talking to me for four hours.

"And you talked to them?" he said.

I shrugged.

"Never asked for counsel?" he said. "Answered all their questions? Cooperated fully?"

I nodded.

"You went to Harvard?"

"I didn't go to the law school," I said. "My boyfriend did."

"Yeah, your boyfriend. Some boyfriend. You watch television,
Ellen?"

"Not much. Old movies, mainly."

"Don't talk to the police. The police are not your friends. If
your cat is up a tree, then you want to be nice to police officers.
If you are under suspicion in a murder case, you do not. They are
on the other side. They are not interested in the search for truth.
They are interested in the search for you."

That's when you could see what Bob Greenstein would be,
when he made a speech like that. He came on like a nightlight, a
faint and steady glow of something not quite conviction, something closer to what carny salesmen used to do when they sold
patent medicines and Bibles.

"You're cynical," I said quietly.

"I'm realistic," he said, shaking his head. He kept shaking it
as he looked through a pile of papers on his desk. He lifted the
blurred Xerox of a newspaper piece, and when I saw the headline
and picture I winced.

"Yeah," he said at the gesture. "I bet you are very sorry you
ever wrote this essay, or at least that you won with it."

"I'm not sorry I wrote it. I'm only sorry it's not better."

" 'A fifteen-year-old dog lies on a metal examining table,' " he began to read. " 'His breathing is ragged. Behind him a veterinarian fills a needle with clear fluid to do what needs to be done—put the animal out of his misery.' "

He stopped and peered up. "Where'd you see them put the dog to sleep?" he said.

"I never did. I made it up."

"Age of the dog and everything?"

"And everything," I said.

He sighed. "Blah blah blah blah," he said, a stubby finger running down the article. "Blah, blah, blah, here, 'It seems outrageous that those humans suffering just as much as animals, even those who say that they are tired of life and want to end it, are kept alive by extraordinary means. What are feeding tubes and respirators but playing God on the part of men? What is keeping people alive when they would be better off dead than extreme cruelty?' Blah blah blah, 'participate in decisions about our own deaths,' blah blah, 'truly, mercy killing is an apt name.' Yow."

He looked at me again.

"What can I say?" I asked, shrugging. "I was seventeen years old and I knew nothing about the subject. It's glib, it's self-righteous, and it's badly written."

"You wrote it?"

"Yes."

"Did your mother ever read it?"

"Yes."

"Did she disagree with your conclusions?"

"We didn't discuss it." Actually, I think she said, when I was mailing it in, "It's a horrible subject." Or perhaps that is only my reconstructed memory.

"Your father?"

"There's a grammatical mistake near the end. A 'that' where a 'which' should be. He was livid. We didn't discuss the content."

"I'm curious about your father. He's been the mystery man in this case. Do you talk to him."

"No," I said.

"Why not?"

Again I shrugged.

"Why didn't he bail you out?"

"Ask him."

"He's been asked. He says he didn't know they were holding you until the next morning, by which time you'd already been released by your English teacher. Is that possible?"

"Yes."

"He was sleeping when your mother died?"

"Yes."

"He was not alone with her the night before?"

I paused. I did not know what my father had told the police. As though he read my mind, Bob added, "That's what he says."

"Right," I said.

"But you were with her. She was in a completely helpless state. And when she died you didn't call him, you just sat with her until morning."

"Yes."

"Why?"

"I didn't want to let go of her hand," I said, and he nodded. "Good," he said. It was the right answer. It was true as well. I felt as though I'd won an office pool, some sort of lottery. Correct and accurate.

"What was the last thing she said to you?" he asked, but I could not remember. I could only remember the endless silence of that night, rubbed raw with the sounds of breathing.

We went over everything I had gone over with the police, the morphine pump, the settings, the mostly full vial of pills. And all the time I saw the spoon with the rice pudding going in her mouth and out again, my mother's eyes glittering like topaz: I saw her mouth work until the food went down, saw the death's-head on the pillow as we breathed in tandem. Bob took notes on some sheets of paper. Then he leaned back, rocking slightly in an old wooden desk chair with a pillow placed at the small of his back.

"Here's the problem with what's appeared in the papers so far," he said. "And I say that because I'm getting a whole lot more on this case from the *Tribune* than I am from Ed Best, who is playing this very close to the vest. Maybe that's because he only did it in the first place to get himself in the papers so he can be attorney general or run for Congress. His wife, by the way, says you were cracking jokes at the funeral. Anyhow, you put it all together, and people will see this one of two ways. Best case scenario is that you did give your mother the morphine, but that you had justification for doing so, that it was the right, even the moral thing to do."

"Uh-huh," I said.

"The other is what will be the prosecutor's case, and that is that you are a very tough, very hard young woman who got tired of being tied to this dying mother and gave her the morphine so you could go on about your business."

"Well, that's the view of me that conforms more closely to reality."

"Now, you see, that's the sort of thing that you say that is counterproductive in this context. It's very Upper East Side, but it's like telling the police that anyone in their right mind would have killed your mother if they had a chance—"

"That's not what I said."

"All right."

I folded my hands and looked down at them, the veins seeming bigger, bluer, knottier than they had before. "I know people like to make up little stories about life," I said, "that they like things to have a certain shape. Daughters who adore their mothers and would lay down their lives for them. Daughters who hate their mothers and kill them. Noble gestures, grand passions. The right thing. The wrong thing. Made for each other, happily ever after."

I looked Bob Greenstein straight in the eye and continued, "Everyone makes up their little stories and then they wonder why their own lives aren't like that. It makes life so much simpler if they can get rid of all the loose ends. Ellen is such an angel, loved her mother so much she couldn't bear to see her suffer. Or, Ellen is such a witch that she walked over her mother in spikes to get what she wanted. I can't be responsible for other people's little stories. I have enough trouble making sense of my own."

"That's very poetic, but here's my trouble, and I'll lay it right out for you. I need some little story to go into court with, because experience tells me that if I don't have one you are in big trouble."

"I'm already in big trouble," I said.

"A trial and a possible jail term will be bigger trouble. Much bigger. You have no idea."

"I'll tell the grand jury that I didn't do it and they won't indict me," I said, almost believing it.

"Very bad idea for you to appear. Very bad. I don't envision having you testify."

"I'm testifying," I said. "I need to testify. I insist. Absolutely."

Bob Greenstein leaned back and sighed. "Oh, what a prize I got with you, kid," he said.

Being in therapy always reminded me of being in Bob Greenstein's office, of watching someone try to make my little story into a coherent whole. Sometimes I wished my therapist would just lean forward, her hand splayed over her notebook, and say with feeling, "Oh, what a prize I got with you, kid." Sometimes now at work I think it myself. What a prize.

Easter did come early that year, before the gray sticks of the azalea branches had begun to soften with a pale-green haze, before the crocuses and snowdrops were anything more than sharp points lifting improbably from soil still hard. The little girls would be disappointed, their flowered dresses hidden at church beneath their worn winter coats, their white straw hats incongruous above the wool collars, their white patent shoes incongruous beneath. Mrs. Forburg went to visit a cousin in Philadelphia. Brian came home for the weekend, but he didn't call and he didn't come to see me. Jeff went to stay with a girl he knew from school.

Bob Greenstein had told me to stay close to Mrs. Forburg's house, to keep a low profile in Langhorne, to live like a nun. But I felt so lonely that weekend, after I'd waxed Mrs. Forburg's linoleum and washed her curtains, that I ignored all his advice and went out on Good Friday. I drove alone to Sammy's in Mrs. Forburg's beige Chevy sedan, drove through the thick rich blackness of the cold night until the bar sign sprang from the darkness of a corner just shy of the center of town, its neon profile of a cor-

pulent gentleman in a red stock tie bright against the starless sky.
There were few cars parked outside. I'd combed my hair but I was
damned if I was going to put on lipstick just so the auto mechanics and retail clerks of Langhorne wouldn't talk about how I'd lost
my looks.

"Where is everybody?" I asked the bartender, a guy named
Mark who had graduated from high school four years before I
did, one of those guy who always wore a baseball cap in a vain
effort to disguise premature baldness.

He shrugged and brought me a beer. "Easter's one of those
vacations kids don't come home for. Too short, I guess."

"So where are all the Langhorne kids?"

"There's a dance there tonight. The place has been dead since
the lunch crowd left." All but one of the tables were empty, the
red glass globes burning steadily in their centers. Against the wall
four men somewhere between senior year and middle age were
hunched forward over their candle, their chins red in its reflected
glow, reminding me of the game we once played with buttercups,
looking for the yellow to tell us who liked butter. One man met
my eyes across the room and let his drop conspicuously. I turned
around.

"You haven't been in in a while," Mark said, putting a bowl of
Goldfish crackers in front of me.

"Christmas holidays, I think," I said.

"You still at Mrs. Forburg's?" he said.

"You'd read it in the paper if I wasn't."

"All I read's sports," he said.

"Bull," I said. "Even if that's true, you'd hear it in here twenty
minutes after I pulled out of the driveway."

"She's a nice lady," he said.

"Nobody could agree more," I said.

"Yeah, well, if you think she's so nice, why'd you go and get
her in trouble? They've got a committee investigating her, some
parents have transferred kids out of her classes, the other teachers
are giving her a hard time."

"Who says?" It took me a moment to remember that Mark's mother was one of those large and faceless women in hairnets who worked the steam table in the cafeteria. One of the nice ones, too, the ones who gave double mashed potatoes and big slabs of cake.

"That guy Murphy on the school board, who's hated her since she stood up for the kids on the newspaper when they wrote that poem making fun of the superintendent? He's been telling people she's a dyke, that the both of you are dykes. Didn't she say anything?"

"Maybe she doesn't know."

"She knows," he said.

"She says she doesn't care."

"She cares,' he said, wiping off the bar.

Another man slipped onto the stool next to mine. He was short and stocky, broad through the shoulders and torso, with the kind of build that would have guaranteed him a berth on the wrestling team in high school. Familiar strangers, I'd always called them, the dozens of people a year or so older or younger than I whose faces I knew from the halls of the high school but whose names I could rarely immediately place, so that my mother had become accustomed, during college and afterward, to those times when I would come back from shopping and blurt out "Lauren McNulty" or "Jim Bettman" at the dinner table.

This one ordered a shot and a beer, looked down one end of the bar and up the other, taking pains not to meet my eyes. He raised a glass to the four men in the corner, but they were of no help to me: "Hey" is all one of them called across the room. I thought he was older than I was, a year or two, and the longish hair meant he was a townie, probably a working man; all the college boys wore their hair short now. He kept his shoulders high so his head sank down between them, almost disappearing in the blanket plaid of his coat, like a turtle or an old man.

"Hi, Ellen," he finally said, throwing back his longish hair with a peculiar twist of his head, and I thought about how much easier this would be in the city, where everyone wanted to establish their bona fides: perhaps you don't remember? we met at the Lincoln Center party for the anniversary of the magazine. I was with a friend of mine who's at Jensen, Jensen and Bates, I think you knew his fiancée from college. The litany was endless—tangential relationships, friends of friends, restaurant near-misses—"I was just at Le Besoin last Tuesday!"

But not in Langhorne. "How are you?" he asked, and then he ducked his head and asked Mark for another shot of Wild Turkey. That Wild Turkey was the prettiest color in the muted bar light, the amber-brown of beautiful eyes. "I'll have one of those, too, Mark," I said, but when I put more money on the bar the man picked the bills up, folded them in half, and put them beneath my beer mug. "Chris," I thought suddenly, and it was all I could do not to say it aloud. "Chris Somebody." He lifted his glass of Wild Turkey and sipped for a second, then threw it down.

"Ah," he said, a short burst of breath, and then grinned, still looking straight ahead, so that I could see the grin only in his eyes reflected in the mirror over the bar. The bottom part of his face, his mouth and chin, was blocked out by the wall of bottles, of Stoli and Bushmills and Courvoisier, another pretty color, darker than the Wild Turkey. Even the top of his head, his hair, was cut off because the mirror over the bar at Sammy's was edged with college pennants, Langhorne hanging cheek by jowl with Michigan, Stanford, Yale, Penn, to show how important it really was. The little college that could, the last president had called it sometimes, and when he did my father had always rolled his eyes extravagantly. I lifted my own shot glass, and, closing my eyes, drank it off. A shiver shook me, the kind my mother used to tell me meant someone walking over your grave. When I opened my eyes Chris Somebody was looking at me in the mirror, and he winked, an insouciant gesture so obviously foreign—he did it too slowly, for one thing—that for some reason it made me feel warm, and my eyes filled. Or maybe it was just the Wild Turkey.

"You don't remember me, do you?" he said, talking to my reflection in the mirror, as though secondhand was safe enough.

"Yeah, I do," I said, feeling the Wild Turkey moving to my stomach, my groin, my joints. "Chris."

"Chris Mortensen," he said. "I was one of the guys who put the lights on the trees this year."

I couldn't remember even seeing the guys putting the lights on the trees. "Were you one of the guys who put in the poinsettias that year they all died?"

We were still talking in the mirror. Mark had moved down the bar and was arguing with two town kids who had produced fake ID. Only the stupidest or most naïve tried to get a drink in Langhorne, where everybody knew your high school class. Most of them went two or three towns away to drink, or had someone go into the state store and buy them a big bottle of sangria to drink sitting in the car or wrapped in blankets beneath the bridge. Jon had always stolen vodka from his father, poured it in a jar and then added water to what was left in the bottle.

When I asked about the poinsettias Chris ducked his head again, like I'd caught him in something.

"Long before my time," he said. "But my cousin was on that crew. He said he knew they'd die but he just put them in anyhow."

"The provost's wife wouldn't talk to my mother for years after that. She knew they'd die, too. My mother, not the provost's wife."

Chris looked down at his empty shot glass, then raised it so Mark could see. The bartender nodded down the length of the bar. "I'm not serving you no matter what, so you might as well go home or drive over to Montgomery Heights," he said, and swearing under their breath, the kids left.

"You want another?" Chris said.

"Sure," I said.

It went down easier for both of us the second time, and the beer felt sharp and tingly on my tongue right afterward, like needles on velvet. "That stuff is the prettiest color," I said.

"Yeah, huh?" he said. His hands were laid flat on the bar, as though he was bracing himself. They were like the rest of him, compact, thick. Across the back of one was an enormous scar, raised and pink, a bright ugly worm of a thing. I put out an index finger and touched it lightly, then looked at him in the mirror. He looked down.

"It was a real stupid thing," he said. "I was cutting Christmas trees out at one of the farms for that big lot downtown, the one in the back of the market parking lot?" Everything he said was a question, as though it was up to me to correct him, to insist that there was no farm, no market, no lot. "The chain saw just slipped and *zipp, whoa,* there it was." This he seemed surer about, but not as sure as I, seeing the blood, the white bone, smelling the sweet smell of gore and the medicinal tang of the emergency room, the little plastic bags sealed with the sutures inside, a made-up memory more real than a true one.

I shivered again. "Jesus," I said.

The men at the table were arguing about the upcoming baseball season and a skinny woman at the end of the bar was trying to talk Mark into selling her a six-pack. She had bad skin and her clothes hung loose on her, a pink sweater and jeans. "He'll kill me," she kept saying while Mark wiped the bar without looking at her and shook his head. Finally she left, the open door letting in fresh cold air, sweeping away the smoke and the warm stuffiness for a minute. I was beginning to feel very drunk, so drunk that when I looked toward the door and saw Jon come in, the collar of his down jacket pulled high around his neck, I thought I was imagining him, until I saw him stiffen at the sight of me. You could tell by the way his eyes moved, just for a minute, that he thought about turning around and going out again. But when we looked at one another I knew he'd never let himself do it.

"Ellen," he said as he walked down the length of the bar and took a table near the back.

"Jonathan," I said.

I looked at Chris in the mirror. He looked sad.

"Want another?" he said.

"Sure do," I said. That one I sipped, but it didn't really make much difference.

"Your boyfriend from high school, am I right?" Chris said.

I nodded.

"I sort of remember you from high school," he said, "but you were pretty much younger?" Again the question mark.

"High school wasn't exactly the high point of my life," I said, probing with my tongue to see whether I could still feel my gums.

"I liked high school," Chris said, running one finger over the scar on the back of his hand. "It was the closest to being an adult without any of the bad things about being an adult, like rent and taxes and just responsibilities, if you know what I mean."

"That's how I felt about college," I said.

"Oh, well, college," he said, shrugging.

I had to go to the bathroom so badly that it was like a pain in my midsection, but I'd have to pass Jonathan's table to get to it. Finally I slipped off the stool. The light in the bathroom hurt my eyes, and I leaned into the mirror over the sink after I'd washed my hands and looked hard at my own reflection. "Oh, Ellen," I said out loud.

As I went back to the bar, Jonathan called my name again, this time with urgency, but I just waved him off over my shoulder.

"You want to get something to eat?" Chris said.

"Here?"

"Somewhere else?"

When we went out into the night it was so black we could scarcely see each other, which was just as well. In the cab of his truck he tuned in the radio before we drove away and the little yellow-green backlights from the tuning bands lit up his scar so it looked lavender, like a ribbon.

"I'm not really hungry," I said.

"No? Me neither."

I don't remember much about the ride, except the cold, how my fingertips ached, how our breath came puffing out white in the closed cab even though the heat was on, making my toes burn. I sang along to the radio, loud. It was as if I was alone when I did it.

I remember a trailer, a double length made over to look like a ranch house, with shutters and even a little porchlike thing appended to the front, and Chris saying that his father was gone— "Good riddance and sayonara and all that," he said, but there was nothing blithe in his voice, I do remember that—and his mother had moved to California and left it all to him. I think he said that proudly and then tentatively, still with the questions in his voice. He gave me a drink, and then another, vodka this time, with no color to it at all, clear as ice.

The only thing I remember really clearly is the quiet in the trailer, as though nobody lived there, the quiet outside deep in the pinewoods, and my own voice as he got on top of me in the bedroom where the double bed filled nearly every inch of space, so the bureau served as kind of footboard. I turned my head away from his face as it came closer, closer, and on the edge of the bed I could see his hand, the one with the scar, and at some point I said, "I just want to feel something." I thought I was thinking it, but it came out in words, and in that way they do when you're drunk, the words vibrated in my head. I heard them as though from far away, and they seemed to hang in the air like mobiles, each one turning slowly over the bed. "I just want to feel something," I said again, and I did feel something, but it was happening far away, down nearer to the foot of the bed, where the bureau was.

It was just before dawn when I woke up. The pain was starting behind my eyes, and my tongue was fuzzed. I lay for a moment and tried to remember where I was. The windows in the trailer were squat and narrow, so that only a sliver of sky, still dark but beginning to lift just a little, was visible between the trees. The room smelled of sex, used sheets, and space heaters. I got up and went to the bathroom, drank two glasses of water and stared at myself in the mirror. Then I put on my old underpants, the ones with the run in the back, and my cords and my sweater. My bra was in the living room. I put it in my purse, thought for a moment, then picked up the keys Chris had laid on a small table by the door, the kind of little table that Langhorne High boys sometimes made in shop class, with bright brown stain and a high gloss coat of polyurethane. There were two framed photographs on the table, a portrait of Chris in a tie and plaid shirt that had to be his high school graduation picture, and a hand-tinted old-fashioned head and shoulders of a girl who had his eyes and mouth.

I went out to the truck and started the engine, but it was sluggish because of the cold. Twice I had to pump the gas pedal to stop it from idling low and then dying. The second time I heard a knocking noise and jumped when I saw a face on the other side of the steamed glass. Chris was wearing only his pants, and the hair on his chest sprang up from the goose bumps.

"Where you going?" he said. "It's five o'clock."

"I have to go back," I said. "I shouldn't have fallen asleep."

"Well, hey," he said, moving from one foot to another on the cold ground. "I mean, hey, who wouldn't?"

I gunned the engine.

"You want to go to the movies tonight?" he said.

"No," I said.

"Dinner maybe?" The pain behind my eyes was getting worse.

"Look," I said, "my life is strange now and I don't have the energy or the patience to turn a passing conversation in a bar into some big enormous deal. Because it's not." You could see him flinch, almost as though I'd hit him, and I knew that that was exactly what he'd done, that in between that first shot of Wild Turkey and the moment when he'd pulled my sweater over my head he'd probably spun himself some homey fantasies about dinner, conversation, confidences. It had to be lonely, nights out here alone in the trailer, the paneled walls of the tiny bedroom with no pictures. It was deep dark out here, like the inside of a closet when you were playing hide-and-seek and the others had stopped looking for you. Later, when I thought about it, I imagined he mainly wanted the sex for the sake of the company.

"My truck?" he said.

"I have to go back to Sammy's and get my car. I'll leave the truck there with the keys under the mat." It never occurred to me to wonder how he would get there himself, and he didn't fight with me about it. I rolled up the window and pulled out of the narrow opening in the trees that led away from the trailer. In the rearview mirror I could see him standing, hands in pockets, still dancing from one foot to the other.

In a place like Langhorne I would have known if he had told anyone about that night, but I never heard anything, not from Jeff, not from Mrs. Forburg or my lawyer, not secondhand through Mark or Jon or those faceless men who watched in silence as I staggered out of the bar. Chris Mortensen acted like a nice guy that night, and I suspect he probably was. Which made me something much worse than I'd even felt that day, driving his truck through the gathering morning between black rows of pines, leaving him to stare at the four walls of his bedroom.

Let me be honest," said Jules, who had left the magazine to be an articles editor at one of the fashion journals. "The utter degradation you're describing so vividly is all in a night's work for your average New York career woman."

"I know," I said. "It just feels different here."

"Different how? Because everyone knows everyone else's business? Because everyone is interested in yours?" Jules had quit in large part because James had demanded she write a first-person memoir of our friendship. She had called him a fucking slug and emptied her desk before Bill Tweedy had heard of the assignment and killed it. "You ARE a fucking slug," someone told Jules he'd said to James, who replied that a real journalist—bad choice of words, but James had never understood the boss—used his life to enrich his work. "So does a black widow spider," Bill had said.

"I feel like my mother's watching me, judging me, like she sees everything I'm doing," I said.

"Oh, honey," said Jules, "I've always felt that way about my mother."

"But now I feel like she has the right."

"Oh, honey," Jules said.

By the beginning of April the grand jury had heard a dozen witnesses. Jonathan had been in town Easter weekend for his appearance. When I told Jeff I had seen him in Sammy's that night, he said that he imagined Jon wanted to talk to me.

"Did you throw a drink in his face?" he said.

"The thought never crossed my mind."

"Before I die I'm going to break his nose," Jeff said.

"You have my permission," I said.

Jeff took me to the cemetery several weeks after Easter. He waited in the car while I wandered between the rows of stones like a tourist, reading all the familiar names, the names in the Langhorne phone book, on the high school class rosters, on the war memorial in the middle of the town square, on the brass plaques to one side of the doors of the lawyers' offices and doctors' suites, in the engagement and wedding announcements in the *Tribune*. James, Benson, Warren, even Best, Mr. Best's mother, aged eighty-nine. They always said that he had been unusually devoted to her. Perhaps that was my bad luck. Or perhaps it was all the imagined slights over the years, the way I had always looked half amused at his wife's dithering, the skating and swimming at the lake from which I had excluded his children, the puerile graduation speech criticizing the town fathers for their insularity. "Holden Caulfield couldn't have said it better himself," said my father, who was as contemptuous of Salinger as I'd been of the soft and pudgy Best children, improbably named Allegra and Herbert after some long-dead relatives. KATHRYN, said Mr. Best's mother's stone. Again my bad luck. Or perhaps he merely thought he was serving justice, or pouring the concrete footing of a midlife shift to politics. Perhaps there was nothing personal in it for him at all.

My mother's stone was already in place, a small gray rectangle of granite. KATHERINE B. GULDEN, it said. 1945–1991. I knelt and put my hands against it. I looked back and saw Jeff's head turned away, the sunlight making a bright stripe in his auburn hair. Faintly I could hear a guitar riff from the jeep's tape player.

From the pocket of my jacket I took a trowel and began to dig two shallow troughs. The ground was cold and friable, with limp stringy remnants of yellow grass just below the surface. The deeper I dug the warmer it became, and I imagined that six feet under it was warm as toast. Warm as toast, I said, to soothe myself. Warm as toast. I looked at the stone and imagined the line beneath the dates: HER LAST MEAL WAS RICE PUDDING.

The stripe in Jeff's hair was just the color of her own, a warm red-gold, as though the sun was always shining on it. The dirt beneath my nails was a shade darker than her eyes. The Wild Turkey had been just a little lighter.

I had gone to a farmers' market to buy seeds and cold frames for Mrs. Forburg's house, to plant her a perennial border and a vegetable garden. Moving toward the big stall where an Amish woman with silver-blond hair and almost colorless blue eyes had always sold bulbs, I saw a woman with red-gold hair wearing a navy peacoat. Her back was turned to me; she was picking over bulbs, leaning forward to look at the small photographs of flowers that were spiked above each bin, leaning in to ask the woman, in her white bonnet with a virginal frill framing her long oval face, some question about a small knotty tuber on the palm of her outstretched hand.

So foolish, I thought to myself as I edged around people carrying hanging plants and flats of flowers, brushing by women with big pots of garish red tulips like rapacious mouths swaying on their pale green stalks. So stupid, as she moved away from the bulb stall, still with her back to me, and on to a circular wire display of Burpee's seeds, looking at the Big Boys and Better Girls. She went over to a corner of the big warehouse building where peat and fertilizer were stacked in fifty-pound sacks, and out a side door into a blue car with some unreadable college sticker on the back windshield. I think she flashed a glance at me in her rearview mirror, and then she was gone, her hair still curving just above the navy collar of her coat.

Years after, I remember, I read a monograph on grieving that studied bereaved children and found that many thought their mothers had moved away, gone to a new house, a new life, new children. "We are all children," I said aloud as I read it, feeling foolish, foolish and correct, too.

The troughs were finished and I took from my pocket the assortment of bulbs I had gone back and bought after the car had driven away, twenty-four in all: a dozen tiny grape hyacinths and a dozen dwarf tulips, small sturdy things less than a foot tall that would have ruffly pale-pink petals like improbable little birds. I dropped them randomly into the holes and patted them softly into place, planting them out of season.

"You're not allowed to do that," said a man walking by in gray work clothes and a checked wool jacket stiff with dirt.

"So arrest me," I said, picking the soil up in small handfuls and letting it drop onto the bulbs until they finally disappeared. When the holes were filled, I put some mats of dead grass on top to keep the bulbs warm until the earth thawed, and wiped my hands on my pants.

Jeff took me out to a diner on the highway afterward. We ate burgers with cooked onions and greasy fries and chocolate shakes and he talked about the handball game he had once a week with Mr. Duane and how difficult it was to tread the fine line between giving the older man a good game and not going all out and trouncing him. "Plus," Jeff said, his mouth full, "aside from the question of leaving him with a shred of dignity, there's the very real possibility that if I run him around enough he will keel over with a coronary. Pop's in much better condition than Mr. Duane and he starts to get windy on me pretty early on when we play tennis these days."

"How is he?" I asked.

"Ah, you know Dean Duane. One story about the glory days of the bull market after another. When giants walked the hallways of

Dean Witter Reynolds and the corporate raiders were in the full flower of their manhood."

"I meant Papa," I said.

"He's the same," Jeff said. "Maybe a little better. I think he really misses the both of you. It's like he had these two great things going and now they're both gone. He's stopped asking me to talk you into seeing him."

"Do you guys talk about me?"

"Never," said Jeff.

"Mama?"

"Nope. Nor will he discuss Edith Wharton or Jane Austen with me, or the shortcomings of the modern English major. It doesn't leave us with a whole lot to talk about over our TV dinners."

"Not really TV dinners?" I said.

"Nah, I just wanted to make your skin crawl. Actually, it's a lot of pizza and takeout. Have you ever had the Chinese food from the place in the mini-mall just past the Safeway?"

"I don't think so," I said.

"Unfuckingbelievable, El. It is the worst stuff you've ever tasted in your life, but if you pick it up late all the guys who work there are sitting around eating bowls of what looks and smells like Chinatown food, great fish and vegetables and sauce. So one night I point to this guy's bowl and I say, 'Gimme that' and they all start talking to one another in Cantonese dialect or something, and when I get the stuff home, it's moo-shu pork and fried rice. It's Caucasian discrimination, like they think real Chinese food is too rich for our blood."

"Did Papa get a laugh out of that?"

"I didn't tell him. He doesn't really resonate to that kind of thing, if you get my drift."

"You just don't try with him," I said.

"And the feeling is mutual, dear, unless you've forgotten."

"You could have felt the same way about me."

"I did. But there's more to you than meets the eye. Besides, you know many attractive women who can be introduced to me.

Speaking of which, I saw Teresa the other day on Maple Lane. She was visiting Bobby Jackson's dad, who has lung cancer."

"Wow," I said. "For us, Mama was her only case. But for her, it's one of so many."

"Yeah, but she has a special spot in her heart for you still, I think. She told me to tell you that she's not seeing the guy anymore, and to ask you why the gorilla crossed the road."

"Because he thought he was a chicken."

"*Whooa*," Jeff said, "you are good. Very good."

"That means the lady with the kids and the breast cancer has breast cancer again." I shook my head. "It never ends."

"She said just the opposite. She said to tell you she thinks of you often and it will all be over soon."

"I know. She called me that night after she saw you. She sounds good, although she says she has two patients now who are fading fast."

"Are you going to go see her?"

"Maybe," I said. What I didn't say was that when I had asked Teresa whether I might take her to dinner to thank her for everything she'd done, she replied quietly, "The hospital has asked me not to see you until after all this is settled."

"*Et tu*, Teresa," I said.

"That is not fair, Ellen," she said evenly. "I want very much to see and talk with you and I am very concerned about you. But it is important to other people that, for now, I keep this job."

"I'm sorry," I said.

"We will talk after," she said. "For a long time."

I made no social feints, no more trips to Sammy's. I knew why Jeff chose a restaurant fifteen miles from home and then chose a booth with no other diners seated around it. My voice had automatically taken on a quieter timbre, the better to avoid being overheard. There were fewer messages on the machine, but the assisted suicide and euthanasia zealots still pursued me, and a psychic from Missouri called twice to say that she had talked to my mother, who was very happy and forgave me.

The huge bruise shaped like an open mouth on my left breast had turned from blue-purple to yellow-green, then disappeared, but I had never been able to reconstruct precisely how it had come to be there. Sometimes I would be reading or watching television, *How Green Was My Valley* one night, *I'll Cry Tomorrow* the next, and a momentary tableau would be there before me, a tangle of limbs, frantic movements, loud cries, and I would put my head in my hands.

"Do you remember a Chris Mortensen?" I asked Mrs. Forburg one night when she was correcting essays on *Pride and Prejudice*.

She nodded. "Nice boy," she said. "His father used to bounce him and his mother around a good bit and his mother was an alcoholic, and not a recovering one either, but somehow he turned out very sweet, the kind of boy who'd help you get your car out if it got stuck in the snow in the parking lot. I'm surprised you know him."

"I met him in passing one night."

"He comes to Al-Anon sometimes. I think he goes to meetings himself, too, although I can't say for sure."

"AA, you mean?"

She nodded again. "Whether he inherited it from Mom or started in because of Dad, I'm pretty sure he had a problem. Although maybe he's working on it now."

"Oh, Christ," I said.

"Things are tough all over," she said. She passed me a sheet of looseleaf with a single sentence on it. "The girl named Elizabeth in the story is a snotty bitch!" it said. "What should I reply?" she asked with a small smile. "It's true," I said. "But reductive," she said. "Write that," I said, " 'true, but reductive.' That'll knock him for a loop."

"Why do you assume it's a boy?"

"The bitch part. I don't know. The snotty stuff. It sounds like the cute girl with the locker next to his is ignoring him so he projected onto Jane Austen. Write: Please see me after class and we can compare and contrast the courting rituals of nineteenth-century England with your difficulty getting dates."

"True but reductive," Mrs. Forburg said.

"Are you going to lose your job because people think you're harboring a lesbian murderer for carnal purposes?"

Mrs. Forburg started to laugh. She was wearing a bright red sweater, and her face above it, red-cheeked and shiny, made her look when she laughed like the bride of Santa Claus. She even shook when she laughed, like a bowl full of jelly, although I would never tell her so because she was more sensitive than she pretended about her weight.

"I'm serious."

"I know, it just sounded so much like a cheap television tabloid show. Ellen, I'm sixty-three years old. I've been teaching for thirty-two years and I've been at Langhorne for twenty. I've been asked a hundred times why I don't get a job at the college and I've always had the same answer—"

"That George Gulden wouldn't hire you."

"That may be true. I suspect your father would think I'd irreparably sullied myself by teaching slow fifteen-year-olds. But I like teaching slow fifteen-year-olds. They need me more than the A.P. kids do, who think they've invented the sexual undercurrents in violence when they read *Macbeth* or start writing poetry without capitals, and, in most cases, without meaning, after they've read cummings."

"You've just described Ellen Gulden, class of eighty-five."

"Yes, I have, and if that was all I remembered about Ellen Gulden, class of eighty-five, she wouldn't be here."

"The girl named Ellen in the story is a snotty bitch."

"True, but reductive. I remember meeting your parents at an open school night when you were a sophomore, that year you were taking senior A.P. English and we were trying to figure out how to keep you occupied for the next two years. And I suddenly understood the pressure you must be under, trying to emulate this extraordinarily cerebral and remote man on the one hand

and this extraordinarily warm and nurturing woman on the other."

"It never occurred to me to emulate her."

"Then what have you been doing for the last six months?"

"I haven't a clue."

"Oh, that answer is really beneath you. You know exactly what you've been doing. You've been doing the right thing at enormous personal cost. And now at the end to somehow be blamed for it—it's a Goddamn outrage and I'll tell anyone who asks me. They say that no girl becomes a woman until her mother dies, but all this is ridiculous."

"In my case it should be father."

"Well, father then. Your father's dead to you, isn't he? You never see him. You never talk to him. Wasn't your image of your father always just . . ." she looked up, narrowing her eyes, as though she was searching for the word on the wall of the living room that held a print of Andrew Wyeth's *Christina's World,* the attentuated arms and yearning posture always reminding me of how my mother had looked that day when we'd had our picnic above the college. "Wasn't your image of your father always just refracted through your mother's belief in what he was? Wasn't he really just her creation?"

"He has a very strong personality," I said.

"Does he? He has very broad mannerisms, I'll agree, but that doesn't necessarily mean a strong personality."

"I feel like I'm in analysis," I said.

"Self-analysis," Mrs. Forburg said.

"You still didn't answer my question about your job."

"Sure I did. I said the best part of my job is dealing with the kids who need me most. And I'm eligible for Social Security. And if some of the parents of this town are dumb enough to boot me because a twerp like Ed Murphy wants to see empathy as a sexual perversion, they don't deserve me. And you've avoided my observations about your family."

"My father is not dead. He's in my head all the time. He's a running commentary, that voice of his, like subtitles."

"And your mother?"

"Her, too, but no commentary. Just a presence. Like God. There's not a whole lot of room for me in there."

"Oh, honey," said Mrs. Forburg, and she sounded just like Jules. "That *is* you."

The Montgomery County Courthouse was past its prime. It sat just beyond the green, up a small hill, behind a narrow swath of parkland planted with flowering fruit trees where people often ate their lunches in the warmer months. The library stood across upper Main Street from it, an old red-brick mansion with big square rooms that made for a rabbit warren of reference books, old texts, current bestsellers, and heavily used children's classics. The courthouse was white-gray, with columns along its front, a heavy urnlike light fixture suspended from chains above its ornamented doors, and at the cornice line, just below the front roof, a quote from Shakespeare, BE JUST, AND FEAR NOT.

The courthouse had been built at the turn of the century, and looked not unlike the building in which the Langhorne English department was housed; the same architect had designed them both. The smaller houses around it had been transmogrified into law offices and title companies. But all the time we'd lived in Langhorne there had been constant complaints about the old courthouse, that the courtrooms were difficult to heat and air-condition, that the judge's chambers were not large enough. Most of all there were complaints that the old courthouse was too great a distance from the offices of the prosecutor and the police, built some years before in one of the commercial developments that had insinuated themselves amid the corn and bean fields and stretches of undevelopable stony land far from Langhorne proper.

The courthouse looked like the sort of courthouse habitually used in movies, and there had been a huge uproar when I was in junior high school and a television production company had come to town to film a pivotal scene in a true-crime drama on the shallow steps that led up to its columns and front door. The *Tribune* had run stories on page one about the movie, about the leading actor, about the use of Langhorne locals as extras. It had been one of the biggest stories I could remember, but not bigger than my own.

But still there were complaints about the old building, although those who had lived in Langhorne all their lives held out against change, even when Ed Best was elected district attorney and made the construction of a new, more modern facility the linchpin of his campaign, along with more DWI crackdowns. His chief opponent was the assignment judge, a forty-year veteran of the bench named James P. Hallorhan who lived two blocks from the courthouse and had the biggest office in the building, a corner one with mahogany paneling and a small ornamental fireplace.

After he died his fight was carried on by his widow, a deceptively fragile-looking woman named Alice who took her exercise each day by walking to the courthouse, roving the halls greeting old acquaintances, some of them judges in the middle of hearing a case, and then walking home. But Ed Best, dim as he sometimes seemed, dreamed up a way to get Alice Hallorhan on his side, and that was how the county came to break ground, the year before my mother died, for the James P. Hallorhan County Justice Building on a cul de sac off the highway, a cube of glass and stone that would hold prosecutors, police, and all court functions.

It was only half done, having run into all manner of construction troubles, from the ventilation to the substructure, and so on the day I testified before the grand jury charged with deciding whether I had killed my mother, I did it in the old courthouse, which was as easy and familiar as almost any building in Langhorne to me. In tenth grade we had had a kind of rudimentary moot court competition on the death penalty, and I had been the judge. I had sentenced the defendant to life without parole after usurping the privilege of the Supreme Court from the bench and ruling the death penalty unconstitutional. I liked the view from up there. I liked the power.

Thank God no one had remembered, or, remembering, told the newspaper and television people. The day I testified before the grand jury the *Tribune* ran a profile of me which began on page one and was spread over a full page inside. They used my high school graduation picture, a photograph taken in the statehouse the day I won the essay contest in which I held my certificate to my chest in much the same manner I had held the ID board when my mug shots were taken, and, of course, the picture taken as I left the courthouse after I'd been bailed out. GOLDEN GIRL, said the headline, and below it in smaller type A LIFE OF STELLAR ACCOMPLISHMENT ENDS IN A MURDER CHARGE.

"Ends?" I said to Jeff that morning on the phone. "Ends? I'm not dead. I'm not even indicted yet."

"Count your blessings," he said. "There's not a single Angel of Death reference in the whole thing."

The truth was that it wasn't a bad piece. It was accurate as far as that went, except that it said that my mother's parents had emigrated from Germany and that my father's had operated a resort in the mountains, an error that made me conjure up my grandfather Gulden in a sun visor and plaid Bermudas instead of overalls. It quoted from the same sections of my mercy killing essay that Bob Greenstein had picked out in his office, and from my graduation speech: "Authority must earn the right to lead, and we owe ourselves the right to refuse to follow if they do not." "Oh, shit," I said, but even though I could remember standing at the podium on the lawn of Langhorne High School pontificating in a high voice, more frightened than I would ever have admitted, my mother's eyes hidden by her sunglasses, my father's eyebrows raised so slightly only someone who knew him as well as I did could have seen it, I could not remember speaking those words. But they sounded like me.

They'd talked to Jonathan's father, who said that he was confident that the jury would understand what I'd done and take into account how worn down I'd been by caring for my mother— "insanity defense" I said aloud—and to several of the Minnies, who talked of how tired I'd looked the day we decorated the tree. They'd talked to Halley McPherson, who showed them the crib with tears in her eyes and recounted my words "It'll all be over soon" when she visited before my mother's death. They talked to several anonymous nurses at the hospital, who said that I seemed unusually well-versed in medical techniques. They talked to high school classmates who did not like me, and high school classmates who said they liked me but could understand if others did not. There was a sophomoric poem I had submitted to the literary magazine, which had held up publication for several weeks while it was decided at the highest levels whether the word "fuck" could be rendered as F*** or whether the poem would have to be removed. "We all knew Ellen would have made a fuss about that," said my P.E. teacher Mrs. Schultz, who for some reason had been on the faculty board of the student publications.

God, it was a bad poem. And the *Tribune* rendered it as (expletive deleted).

Julie Heinlein, she of the soft-voiced phone messages, had written the story in a workmanlike fashion. But she had not talked to Jeff or my father, to Jules or Teresa, to Mrs. Forburg or Ed Best. When I read the profile all I could think of was what I had told

Bob Greenstein about people wanting their little stories neat, tied up with a ribbon. The newspaper article was accurate, as far as it went; it just wasn't exactly true, from the air of lugubriousness that seemed to hang over recollections of our family life to its rendering of me as a woman of steel, with neither qualms nor conscience.

"She didn't do it," said Bob Greenstein, in the third paragraph of the story. "That's all you need to know."

"I've known Ellen since she was reading the Nancy Drew mysteries," said Isabel Duane, if Julie Heinlein's description was to be believed, with some asperity, "and it has never for a minute occurred to me that she would have hurt Kate in any way. She loved her so much. If you could have seen her pushing her wheelchair when they came in here—nobody who saw them could believe it."

It was a lovely thing for Mrs. Duane to do, except that I'd always hated the Nancy Drew books.

Bob was furious about it when he came to pick me up that morning in the low-slung red sports car that he drove, I was convinced, only to prove he was capable of getting out of it. "Why do you think it's in there this morning?" he said. "Best leaked them the date of your appearance. It's bad enough you insist on doing this, without a whole mess of reporters and photographers there when you do it."

"But I thought the grand jury proceedings were all secret," I said.

"In theory they are, my friend, but in practice I would not put it past that shit to up his public profile with a well-placed word to someone from the *Tribune* at the Kiwanis." He shot a glance at me sideways. "Do us both a favor," he said. "Don't smile this time."

"Don't worry," I said.

When we got to the courthouse—BE JUST, AND FEAR NOT, I read aloud, and Bob just sighed—he swung around to a back entrance and tapped on a steel door, tried the knob, tapped again. A guard opened the door a crack, spoke to him, looked from him to me, and shook his head.

"We've got to go in the front," Bob said. "Don't answer any questions."

As we came up the steps I shivered. I was wearing the blue suit I'd worn for the funeral; Jeff had brought it from the house. My hair hung long and loose around my face, and for the first time since Thanksgiving I was wearing makeup.

The reporters were in the lobby, in the circular rotunda with its mosaic floor laid in the pattern of an enormous bronze and gold sun. One of them, a radio reporter with a tape recorder tucked under his arm, saw us first, and a kind of muted cry went up, and then like some grotesque animal they all moved together, cameras, notebooks, pens, and microphones held high like weapons. I could not pick out one question from another: Why have you decided to testify? What are your plans? What do you want them to know about what happened?

We pushed through but they moved with us to a bank of elevators at the back of the building, the elevators Bob had hoped to catch in the basement instead of on the lobby floor when he knocked at the door outside. Some of the questions were for him: Why did you decide to have her testify? Will she testify at the trial? I looked down at the toes of my pumps, which my mother had bought for me. We'd worn the same size shoes. I thought there was a little mud around the edge of the soles from the last time I'd worn them.

Bob guided me into the elevator and then stood in the doorway so no one else could get in. He held the door and leaned forward, his square bulk blocking me from their sight. "You tell Ed Best he could lose his license for a stunt like this," he hissed, and there was an infinitesimal moment of complete silence, and in it I heard the voice of someone, faintly, as though from far away, asking plaintively, "Well, who is it?" And the doors closed.

"That was smart," I said, "the way you did that."

"Yeah? Tell me why it was smart."

"Because now instead of focusing on me testifying, they'll focus on you threatening Ed Best," I said.

"You're smart, too," he said. "Just remember that smart helped get you into this mess and smart isn't going to get you out. You've reached the limits of smart."

"I know," I said.

I remembered from the day of the moot court competition in high school that the courtrooms had long narrow windows and burnished paneling like fine furniture around the bench, the jury box, along the walls. The courtroom ceilings had been high, and the symmetry of justice had been written in the seating arrangements, the judge above it all, the jury to one side, looking on, passing judgment.

The grand-jury room was nothing at all like that. It was less than half the size of one of those courtrooms, with two small windows along one wall that let in so little light that someone had put on the overhead fixture, a rectangular fluorescent light that flickered every now and then. Bob had told me that there were twenty-three jurors, but he had not told me that we would all sit in such close quarters that I only recognized the prosecutor, an assistant in Mr. Best's office, because he was the one wearing the suit and tie. The others were in less formal dress, ranged on hard chairs in a loose semicircle around a small table. In the beginning I tried not to look at them, as though eye contact would put them on the spot. I was sworn and I found something soothing about it, as though I had said a prayer for my own soul. I intended to tell the truth, although perhaps not all of it, depending on the questions.

But as the prosecutor began to ask me how I came to nurse my mother and how she had deteriorated and who had been alone with her the last day of her life I began to look, not at him, a man perhaps ten years older than I with a shaggy haircut and a shirt collar at least a half-size too small, as though he was finding it difficult to move past the person he'd been at twenty-five. I began to look at the people ranged around me.

Part of it was that I wanted them to understand what had happened, but part was simply curiosity. It was difficult for me to believe that there were nearly two dozen people in Montgomery County I didn't know by name, hadn't been served by at the five-and-ten or the luncheonette, hadn't seen in the parking lot of the supermarket with one of my classmates in the car.

The truth was that several of them looked familiar, not familiar enough to put a name to but familiar enough to know that I'd looked across the pumps at the gas station, perhaps, and seen him pumping gas into his truck, or walked by the beauty parlor that stood across the street from Sammy's and seen her under the dryer, bought tomatoes at a roadside stand from this one or seen that one shoveling a walk in front of some house across town from my own.

But there was one woman I thought I knew from the moment I first looked at her, although the longer I stayed in that room—and it was a long time, almost two hours, if you counted those times when I was sent out and invited back in again, the prosecutor with his lips pressed together over slightly protruding teeth—the more I realized I didn't know her so much as apprehend her, perhaps understand her. She was in that middle ground between aging and elderly, a thin woman with silver hair worn handsomely in a short bob swept to one side, eschewing the fuzzy permanents of her kind. She wore a medium-blue knit suit with a skirt that just covered her knees, and she held her hands clasped in her lap, narrow white hands dappled with the dark spots of age. From time to time she turned the two rings atop each other on her left hand. I could imagine her living in one of the pretty small houses just to the south of ours, the widow of a middle manager or even a Langhorne administrator.

But it was her posture that made me tell everything, after a while, to her and her alone, the face in the audience an actor chooses to emote to. She sat very straight but she seemed to yearn forward just a little bit, her shoulders ahead of her hips, and she looked into my face with a searching look in her blue eyes, as though she was waiting for me to solve the puzzle she'd been working slowly these many weeks, to tell her what really happened.

"Miss Gulden," said the prosecutor, whose name was Peters, "I'd like you to read something." He handed me a copy of the essay I'd written for the essay contest—the original copy, it appeared, for it was stamped with a date six years before and the *e* in the words was slightly lifted, something my electric typewriter had always done after I'd knocked it off my desk one day.

"You wrote this?" he said after I'd read it aloud.

"I did," I said.

"And won first prize in the annual state Young Writers' Competition?"

"Yes."

"Do you still agree with the sentiments in that essay?"

"Yes," I said, "as far as they go."

"What do you mean by 'as far as they go'?"

"I still believe that people are kept alive long past the time when life is of any use to them. But when I wrote that essay, I knew nothing about the subject firsthand."

They were all looking at me now, except for a young man, almost a boy, really, who was staring conspicuously out one of the windows.

"And now you do."

"Yes."

"From your mother's illness and death."

"Yes."

"Did your mother agree with the sentiments expressed here?"

"We never discussed it," I said.

"Not when you won the contest?" he asked.

"No."

"Not when you were caring for her, doing the things you've described, watching her deteriorate, in your opinion."

"No."

"Miss Gulden," he said, tapping the palm of his hand with a

pencil in a gesture so reminiscent of a movie gesture that I almost smiled, except that I heard Bob Greenstein's voice saying, "Don't smile, don't smile."

"Miss Gulden," he said, "did you believe that your mother's life in her final days was worth living?"

"That's not how I would put it."

"In your words?"

"I think my mother had lost her dignity, her place, all the things that made her life happy. She was wearing diapers. She was sleeping almost constantly. And for a woman like her, who'd always been so capable, so full of life, so lively—it was a terrible thing. It was terrible for her and it was terrible for me."

"Miss Gulden, did you tell police officers Brown and Patterson that if they had seen your mother they would have thought she was better off dead?"

"Yes."

"Did you tell Jonathan Beltzer that if you were a good daughter you would put a pillow over her face and suffocate her?"

"I don't remember if those were my exact words. I said something like that."

"Had you been drinking?"

"No."

"Did you know what constituted an overdose of your mother's morphine tablets?"

"Yes."

"Did you know that if you crushed or broke those tablets they would become even more toxic than they already were?"

"Yes."

The woman in the blue suit was leaning toward me, as though she wanted to say something, to ask me her own questions, perhaps to stop me.

"Do you recall what your mother's last meal was?"

It was the first time I had stopped during my testimony. I frowned and looked down at my hands in my lap and saw again his hand, elegant, graceful, with the silver spoon held in its fingers, up, down, and over, up, down, and over.

"I don't remember."

"No idea?"

"I hadn't had any sleep for several days. It was probably one of several things, either some cream soup, some applesauce, some pudding, maybe some yogurt. She couldn't eat anything that wasn't the consistency of baby food."

"You would have fed her."

"Sometimes she fed herself. It didn't go very well. I had to change the top sheet."

"Did that annoy you?"

"I was well past being annoyed, Mr. Peters."

That was a mistake. "How far past, Miss Gulden?" he asked. It was a rhetorical question.

"At the risk of repeating myself," he continued, "I want to go back. You believe that there are times when someone's quality of life is so compromised that death, whether natural or assisted, would be preferable."

"Yes," I said.

"You believe that your mother's quality of life was horribly impaired at the end of her life?"

"Yes."

"And did you give her a fatal overdose of morphine?"

"No."

"Given what else you've said, I've got to ask—why not?"

"Why not what?"

"If you believe in what you wrote and you believe in what you've said, it would be logical for you to have given your mother an overdose. You even told the police that that's what they would have done."

"Let me try to explain," I began, trying not to let my voice rise or harden, and I looked right at the woman in the blue suit, who was sitting perfectly still. "Maybe it's the difference between saying you're for capital punishment and being willing to sit there and pull the switch on the electric chair. In theory, I meant these things. But when it's real, when it's a real person—it's different. I was so busy keeping her clean and making her food and making sure she had her medicine, I never stopped to think about anything bigger than how we were going to get through the next hour. Maybe it was like having a baby in that respect. Everyone talks about how wonderful it is, how fulfilling, but I've always thought it seems like one little piece of drudgery after another, a feeding, a changing, a bath, and maybe it's only afterward that it seems wonderful. I didn't have time to think about anything more than all those little things, taking care of my mother. It's so much easier to know just how you feel about things, what you believe, when you're writing it on paper than when you really have to do anything about it or live with it."

"Could you have done it if you wanted, Miss Gulden?" he said.

"Yes. But I didn't."

He was finished with me, but she wasn't, I'm sure. They sent me out into the hallway where Bob sat, looking through some files. He looked at me over the half-moons of his reading glasses but neither of us spoke as I stood outside the door that said GRAND JURY in faded gold stenciling. It was a thick wood door, some narrow-grained wood, and no sound came from the other side. After a few minutes I heard noises from the end of the corridor, and looking down it I saw my father come around the bend and stop. He lifted his hand and waved, and it was when I saw him that I remembered how I had looked at them both that last night.

"Go take a rest, Ellen," I said to Bob Greenstein, and I started to shake.

"What?" he said, still looking down the hall.

"You asked me about her last words. She said 'Go take a rest, Ellen.' She wanted to be alone with him."

"Your father?" he said.

"Yes."

"Did they ask you about that inside?"

"No." I wrapped my arms around myself, and he put an arm around my shoulder.

"She sent me away," I said.

"He blew you a kiss," Bob said.

"What?"

"Your father," he said. "He just blew you a kiss."

"He waved."

"Looked like a kiss to me," Bob said.

The door opened. "Ms. Gulden," the prosecutor said. His hair was ruffled, as though he had been running his hand through it, and as I followed him back into the grand-jury room and sat down he turned his back on me.

"Miss Gulden, I have one last question. Did you love your mother?"

It was not what I had expected. When I had looked at her and she had looked back at me, the woman in the blue suit, with a question in her eyes, I had thought that question was the one which would most require me to lie. I had waited the two hours, in this wooden chair with curving arms, to be asked whether I had any idea who had done it. But to this question I could tell the truth if only I knew how to do it. "Jesus, kid," I could almost hear Bob saying, "the answer is yes. Simple. Elegant. Yes. Nobody needs poetry here."

But she was looking at me so fixedly, almost as if she'd asked the question herself. Bob had told me that any of them could tell the prosecutor they wanted a question asked, and that he was obliged to ask it unless he could dissuade them, that in theory he was there only as the jurors' agent. I looked at her and I was sure that the prosecutor had not wanted to ask the question, that it was she who had made him ask it.

"The easy answer is yes. But it's too easy just to say that when you're talking about your mother. It's so much more than love— it's, it's everything, isn't it?" as though somehow they would all nod. "When someone asks you where you come from, the answer is your mother." My hands were crossed on my chest now, and the woman in the blue suit turned her rings. "When your mother's gone, you've lost your past. It's so much more than love. Even when there's no love, it's so much more than anything else in your life. I did love my mother, but I didn't know how much until she was gone."

"Did you kill her?" the prosecutor asked.

"No I did not," I said. "I couldn't do it."

I guess, if the movies are to be believed, that when a jury is ready to tell you what they've decided you've done, or didn't do, you get to your feet in front of them and they tell you plainly, publicly, with the kind of ceremony that, in most of our lives, is reserved for confirmations or weddings. In the old days they executed you that way, too, but no more.

I was on my way home from the Safeway, from buying cubed meat, carrots, and tiny onions for a stew, from buying yeast and wheat flour for bread and shortening and pureed pumpkin for pie, when I turned on an all-news radio station and discovered that the grand jury had decided not to indict Ellen M. Gulden for the death of Katherine B. Gulden. Frozen in stone still, both of them were: the Harvard honors graduate, the wife of the chairman of the Langhorne English department. We had been distilled to our component parts long ago, Mama and me. Like the last veteran of some old war, I felt as if I was the only one left who knew us as we used to be, as we really were.

It was a chilly day but there was a little bit of warmth rising from the ground, so that you could imagine, if you took a good long sniff, that from this soil in the foreseeable future would come lilacs, then hollyhocks and roses. The Belknaps' perennial border would soon begin to come back from the dead. The grape hyacinths, those baby fingers of purple panicles, so small you had to search for them amid the grass, would unfurl slowly from the ground around my mother's headstone this time next year. The tulips would follow. Long after people had ceased to talk about me at parties and in the aisles between the Duanes' oak bookshelves, the hyacinths and tulips would revive, thrive, yellow, die, sleep, revive again. And she would never, ever see them. Even the flowers went on without you, so fierce was death.

"No bill" was what they said on the radio, "no cause." No case, no trial. No nothing. No nothing. I felt nothing as I drove over the curving back road that led to Mrs. Forburg's house, or perhaps what I felt was that odd sense you have when you are barreling down a street and you discover it is a cul de sac, a dead end.

I came around the S-curve and before me one of the small valleys surrounding Langhorne was spread, a patchwork of different greens, deciduous and evergreen, in the afternoon light. At the bottom of the hill was the house that had bailed me out two months before, and in front of it and across the road, too, I could see a coven of cars and a van with a satellite dish. I made a U turn and drove down the road behind, parked on the shoulder and hiked through the woods, laden with grocery bags. They saw me, some of them, as I emerged from the line of trees and sprinted to the back door; I could hear someone shout and then the others begin to move, like a battalion on the battlefield. But I was in before they had time to shoot me.

The red light on the answering machine glowed in the dimness of the closed house, with its blinds drawn tight for so many days. "Ms. Gulden, this is Nancy Barrett at CBS. This—" and with a push of a button it was gone. Gone was the *Time* magazine reporter with the name that sounded as though it had come off a headstone in Boston's oldest cemetery, the *Times* reporter, who sounded as if she had a cold, and Julie Heinlein, her voice weary: "If by any chance you want to talk to anyone it could be completely on your terms." With the push of a button I made them all disappear.

Jeff sounded jubilant. "Don't go anywhere," he said. "We're coming to get you."

I could hear the reporters outside, one of them taking a coffee order for the others, prepared to drive all the way downtown to the luncheonette. "Regular or light?" he said. "Betts—I asked you a question. Regular or light? And a roll? What the hell do you think this is, a restaurant?" Two of the men were talking about their children, about how much trouble they were causing now that they'd learned to walk. "Wait until they're fifteen," someone else said.

I browned the meat. I rolled the crust. I kneaded bread dough and put it aside to rise in a bowl that Mrs. Forburg said had belonged to her mother. The phone rang, the machine picked up, and I heard her voice, "Ellen, if you're there—"

I picked up the receiver, leaving flour on the mouthpiece, the dial. "I'm here," I said.

She must have been in the pay phone just outside the gym. I could hear a babble behind her, dozens of voices in a fractious harmony, a shout or mock-scream punctuating it all. "Hello?" I said.

"It's noisy here," Mrs. Forburg said. Then there was silence again and I could tell by her breathing that she was crying.

"I'm making your dinner," I said.

"You just leave it there for me on the stove," she said, "and you pack your bags and you get as far away from there as fast as you can for as long as you can."

"They must have believed me," I said.

"They damn well should have," she said.

"Yo, Michael," someone shouted in the background, then said, "Oh, sorry, Mrs. F."

"You'll get your money back on the bail," I said.

"Lord, Ellen," Mrs. Forburg said, "you think of the most irrelevant things. Is Jeff taking you to the city?"

"I think so."

"When you get settled you call and give me your address and I'll come and visit."

"I'll miss you. Thank you." And after a time from the other end there was the echo, "I'll miss you. Thank you." When we hung up, the phone rang again immediately, a reporter from the Associated Press, but the machine just took the message while I sat down at the kitchen table and wrote out instructions on how to finish making the bread and when to take the stew out of the oven. Then it rang again and I heard a soft and slightly accented voice: "Ellen, this is Teresa Guerrero calling." There was a pause as though she knew I was listening. I don't know why it was only when I heard Teresa's voice that something inside me broke just a little, and I began to cry.

"Hello, Ms. Guerrero," I said.

"I am happy today, Ms. Gulden," she replied evenly. "And many of my patients will be, too, fellow sufferers who followed this with personal interest."

"How is the woman with the breast cancer and the kids?" I asked.

"Not so good."

"Teresa, I just want you to know something," I said. "I didn't do it."

"It is not important."

"It's important to me. It's important to me that you believe it. Especially you."

"I always have. But it was never important. You have many more important things to do. So much work. So much work. I pity you, friend."

"I have no job."

"Ah, Ellen," Teresa said, "you know quite well that is not the work I mean."

"Will you come and see me in the city?"

Teresa sighed. "Only for you would I go there. Only for you."

When Jeff came to the back door, his face pink with pleasure and the exertion of sprinting across the yard, my duffel bag was already packed.

"The last time I tried to do this, the cops came," I said.

"So we won't take any chances," Jeff said, and he grabbed my hand and together we ran across the backyard to his jeep, parked next to Mrs. Forburg's car, and jumped into our seats. The reporters were eating in front, eating and having their afternoon coffee, too, and they never even saw us sneak away, hand in hand, like Hansel and Gretel.

"Haul ass," I said quietly.

"Not yet," Jeff said, and he headed downtown, toward the town square and Main Street, the courthouse rising above it all. I thought of the woman in the blue suit, of how she'd seemed to lean just a little forward. "They must have believed me," I said as Jeff tried to tune in the all-news station.

The next day the papers said that maybe they hadn't, maybe they'd believed, as so many others had, that I'd done what I was accused of doing because of love or duty, that the prosecutors had gone too far. But just for that afternoon, as Jeff whipped around the curvy roads, I thought that maybe someone had believed what I said.

". . . Gulden, a former Harvard honors student, with the murder of her mother, Katherine. Mrs. Gulden, the wife of the chairman of the English department at Langhorne College, died in February and an autopsy . . ." the radio bleated, and then the signal wavered and a Brahms concerto took its place. We rounded a corner and heard a fragment of Ed Best talking, and then the weather. Tomorrow would be sunny, highs in the seventies. Spring had arrived.

No one had planted flowers in the tubs at the bottom of the porch steps and the azalea by the side of the garage looked as though it had died, although a few green leaves on one stem had made a valiant effort. Jeff turned off the engine. "I thought you might want to go inside," he said. I stared at him, then back at the house. "Pop will be here in fifteen minutes. He called me when he heard. The first thing he said was 'Perhaps now I can see your sister.' Not 'isn't it great.' Not 'whoopdedoo.' Just like that: 'Perhaps now I can see your sister.' I'll never understand him. Never, no matter how hard I try."

Jeff opened the door of the jeep. "I can't, Jeffie. Especially not right now."

"You sure?"

"Perfectly sure." I looked back at the house, my home. "Is it dusty?" I finally said.

"He's got a cleaning lady from the college coming in once a week."

"That's not enough. Has he changed anything?"

"No."

"I can't," I said again.

Jeff climbed out of the jeep. "Okay, wait," he said, and he went toward the kitchen door, and I could see the table in my mind, unpolished, untidy.

"Jeff," I called, and he turned back to me. "I want something."

When he came out of the house he had it under his arm, the glass in the frame glittering as the sunlight caught it. He laid it on my lap, the photograph of my father, my mother on one arm, I on the other, at my college graduation. I unzipped my duffel, wrapped a nightshirt around the picture, and shoved it deep in the bag.

"Isn't there one of you and her alone?" Jeff said.

"No," I said, "I don't think there ever was one."

He drove down the hill, past the shoe store and Phelps's Hardware and the Duanes', and I thought I could see the shadow of Mrs. Duane's pale hair through the window, past the displays of books. The daffodils stood straight on the green, so many of them. If I squinted there was only a yellow blur beneath the flagpole.

"Which way are you going?" I said.

"Train station," Jeff said, and he grinned.

And there on the platform was Jules in her city clothes, her long gauzy black skirt, her cowboy boots, her black leather jacket and black sunglasses, her black backpack and black hair curling wildly around her head. I got out of the car and she ran, her boots making tapping sounds on the platform and the stairs, and grabbed me so hard we both listed to the left.

"I told you to stay in the city," I said, holding her and looking at her, holding her and then looking again. She was thinner than I'd remembered, and her eyes looked different.

"I had eyeliner tattooed on," she said, blinking. "It hurt like a bitch but it's one less thing to do in the morning."

"Oh, Jesus, Jules," I said.

"You were on the AP wire," she said. "They spelled your name wrong. They made you Golden."

"Yeah," I said.

"You are Golden," Jules said, and she climbed into the jeep.

"I just didn't think you should be alone for the ride," she said, once I was in back and she next to Jeff.

"Excuse me, but what am I, the chauffeur?" Jeff said. "Yes, Miss Julie, ma'am, where we going, Miss Julie?"

"Oh, you know what I mean," she said.

Every news station had something about the grand jury, and so we turned on a music station and played it loud. Jules decided we should put the top down, and our hair whipped around our faces, sticking to our lips and teeth, blinding us. We rode for an hour like that, singing along with the radio. When Jules turned around to talk to me I leaned forward, one hand on my duffel so it wouldn't blow away.

"I found a new place, two blocks from mine!" she shouted, the only way she could be heard. "It's prime, honey. A fireplace, two bedrooms, a bathroom with a window." I'd almost forgotten how much a window in the bathroom meant in New York City.

"How much?" I said.

"Only three hundred more than I'm paying now. Let's do it, El. I have to make a decision tomorrow or let it go—you know how they are. You'll find a job and three hundred will be nothing."

"Or I'll sell my story to television."

"So you'll find something. C'mon."

"I don't know, Jules. No guy right now? No hot prospects?"

Jules held back her hair with her long fingers. "There was a guy, now there's not a guy, then there'll be a guy, then no guy, guy gone. You know the routine."

"I do," I said.

"That shithead," Jules said, and we both knew who she meant.

"Yeah, well," I said.

"Yeah, well, nothing. If I run into him I'll take him apart."

"No men for me right now," I said.

"So let's take this place."

"All right," I said, and Jules bounced up and down in her seat like an excited child.

"You're the best, Julie Julie Boboolie," Jeff said.

Jules leaned toward me until her hair touched my arm softly. "If only he was a little older," she said.

"I heard that," Jeff yelled. "That's completely and totally unfair. Younger men are happening. Younger men are a trend."

"Oh, stop," Jules said. "You can't settle down with a trend." Jeff accelerated and we came over a rise in the highway and there, poking into the air like a quiver full of arrows, was the island of Manhattan, the Emerald City, a glorious mirage.

Jules turned around and smiled at me. "Click your heels together three times and say there's no place like home," she said.

"Yeah, and if I do where will I wind up?" I said. And over the ramp and through the tunnel all of us were silent, until on the other side we came into the center of it, came out next to a hotdog cart with a yellow-and-blue umbrella and steam rising from the square hole in its center, to a young black man with a squeegee, the skin tight on his facial bones, who jumped back and yelled, "Hey, motherfucker!" when Jeff turned on the wipers, shifted gears, and took off down Ninth Avenue.

"I'm not sure where I am," I said.

"I know, honey," said Jules. "Welcome to the island of lost souls."

"You two are a pair," Jeff said.

"I'd marry her in a minute if I could," Jules said, turning around to smile at me and pat my knee.

"There's no place like home," I said. "There's no place like home."

"We're not in Kansas anymore," Jules said.

"There's no place like home," I said again as we headed south to the Village.

EPILOGUE

My beeper went off during the second act of a new musical about children in a tuberculosis hospital at the turn of the century. All down the row of velvet seats in the rich darkness of the theater, I saw heads turn and eyes glisten out of the black disapprovingly, as the tinny birdsong issued, muffled, from between my wallet and my checkbook. I reached down into my purse, switched it off, and looked at Richard, smiling ruefully. "Always, always," he whispered, squeezing my upper arm and sending me up the aisle, crouched a bit so as not to disturb the audience, to call the hospital.

It took me a long time to find a job after I moved in with Jules that spring eight years ago. Perhaps I could have found another berth in journalism, even had my old job back at the magazine. But I would have been hired as an oddity, a talking point, book-party gossip.

Besides, I knew too much about the business now from the other side of the notebook. It was not just the stories that had been written about me during the investigation, and afterward, too, nor the fact that Jon sold a first-person account of our relationship to a magazine which put it on the cover along with the omnipresent photograph of me, the inappropriate effect of my Mona Lisa smile.

It was the idea of facing a future skimming the surface of life, winging my way in and out of other people's traumas, crises, confusions, and passages, engaging them enough to get the story but never enough to be indelibly touched by what I had seen or heard. Jules left, too, went into book publishing because she said that hard covers had a dignity that slick glossy paper and flimsy newsprint did not. Every New Year's Eve she offered me a million dollars to write the story of my recent life, and every New Year's Eve I called her a fucking slug, and then we got drunk together. I love Jules. Every New Year's Eve she says if I were not a woman she would marry me tomorrow. She says when they change the laws we should do it anyway.

Afterward some people said—and a few wrote—that it was inevitable that I would go to medical school, but the truth was that I did not think about it until I began visiting AIDS patients at the hospital around the corner from my apartment. I stayed with Jules for six months and then got a place of my own, paid for it with temp work and an evening job as a waitress at a fairly famous bar and grill, where I waited on young Wall Street types with incipient paunches beneath their custom-cut shirts, as well as the occasional up-and-coming movie actor.

I slept with a lot of men during those months, just to feel something. Several of them reminded me of Jonathan, but not one of them reminded me of Chris Mortensen. Perhaps that's why I had no regrets about them. When Jeff told me nearly two years after that Easter weekend that Chris Mortensen, from high school, remember him?, short guy, had been killed in a head-on collision between his pickup and the McNultys' dump truck—the McNultys, naturally, were not even scratched, although they folded their garbage collection business because the younger lost his license for driving while intoxicated, something the elder had done the year before—I searched his face carefully for something hidden there. But he looked guileless. Maybe it was just a bit of Langhorne gossip. Maybe not.

I was lonely, that first year back in New York. Except for Jules, I had only two kinds of friends—those who had abandoned me because of what had happened and those who took me up only because of it. I was also approached by those who wanted me to champion the right to die, assisted suicide, passive euthanasia, to become a poster girl for the cause, as though there had been no denials, no dropped charges, no insistence that I had not done what they believed I should be so proud of doing. One doctor devoted to helping people with multiple sclerosis die by hooking a hose to a car's exhaust pipe came in person to my apartment, hose in hand. I closed one of his fingers in the door.

My decision to become a doctor had nothing to do with any of that. Not long after I moved into my own place, a studio with a stove and small refrigerator hidden behind louvered doors in a closet, the man across the hall, an actor, began to lose flesh from his long bones, in a deadly progression that seemed so natural to me that I scarcely registered it at first. When I went to see him in the hospital in October, bright blotches now disfiguring the face that had once brought him soap-opera roles and coffee commercials, I was importuned by the head nurse to visit some of her other patients. When she asked me twice to spell my name—Gulden? Gulden? Oh, like the mustard—something relaxed inside me.

I did it for myself, the visiting, because I was so lonely. And perhaps for Brian, too. After our mother died he avoided me, and I assumed that it was because he, too, disbelieved my denials. But then one day he came into the city from Philadelphia on the train. I met him on the platform at Penn Station, the air warm and faintly tinged with gray, as though we were lovers in some old movie coming together again after many years, crowds eddying around us as we caught one another's eyes. And we did catch one another's eyes, staring full into each other's faces, and then he smiled, that sweet bright smile, and I held him for so long a time that people would have been justified in thinking we were lovers.

"Oh, El," he repeated over and over again.

At dinner that night at the restaurant where I worked, where they fed us free, he told me that he was gay, that he thought sometimes that his quiet all his life had been a way of holding back the words that frightened him so. All the time I thought he hated me for something I hadn't done, he believed I would be repelled by what he was doing. It was joy, knowing both of us were wrong.

Even today he has still not told our father. But that night, as we sat for hours over coffee, this seemed less important to him than the sure knowledge that our mother would have accepted him.

"She wouldn't have cared," he said.

"No," I said, "she wouldn't."

That's not exactly true, of course. My mother would have cared very much, would have cared that her best beloved baby was assigned a path that might cause him pain and ridicule, that his life might be harder because of it. She would have cared very much about the daughter-in-law she would never have had—quiet, pretty, so dear, she surely would have imagined her—and the grandchildren there would never be. But it was simpler to say that she would not have cared. We made her simpler after she was dead. No, that's not true, either. We'd made her simpler all her life, simpler than her real self. We'd made her what we needed her to be. We'd made her ours, our one true thing.

It's all anyone wants, really, to make life simple. Sometimes people have wondered why I'm not more bitter about what happened to me. And I was bitter for a long time, but at base I understand. Death is so strange, so mysterious, so sad, that we want to blame someone for it. And it was easy to blame me. Besides, when people wonder how I survived being accused of killing my mother, none of them realizes that watching her die was many, many times worse. And knowing I could have killed her was nothing compared to knowing I could not save her. And knowing I'd almost missed knowing her was far more frightening than Ed Best and his little army of shrunken suits.

In all that time in New York, finding my way again, inventing a new one, I never saw my father. In the beginning it did not seem to be deliberate. I no longer celebrated holidays; he rarely came into town. For a year he was a visiting professor in England; for my last two years of med school I worked so hard that I sometimes went for days seeing no one but my classmates and whoever happened to be admitted to the hospital.

I have never gone back to Langhorne. I don't believe I ever will.

Jeff did not attend his own college graduation. He said that he thought ceremonies were stupid, but I wonder whether he wanted to keep my father and me apart. A month after Jeff graduated I received a letter addressed in that familiar sprawling angular hand. I was on my way to work when I picked up the mail and I put it in my backpack to read later; for days it haunted me amid the detritus at the bottom of my bag, the ChapStick, the spare change, the keys. Then one day I went to look at it, to hold it in my hand and consider slitting it open and letting the words tumble out. And it had disappeared.

I searched my tiny apartment, but could find it nowhere. I pulled books from the shelves and flapped them wildly, hanging on to their spines. I looked in the crippled folds of my pullout couch and in the kitchen cabinets. But I never found it.

Perhaps I pulled a subway token from the bottom of my bag as I ran toward a turnstile, and the letter fluttered to the cement floor and from there to the tracks. Maybe I took out my wallet, distracted in the delicatessen, and it dropped down between the ice-cream case and the counter, to be found and discarded during a remodeling years later.

As we psychiatrists like to say, there are no accidents.

I see my brothers often, and perhaps they see my father but do not say. Brian left Penn and runs a framing store in Philadelphia, and seems happier than he ever did, although he is still looking for someone to love. Jeff went to summer school after I was cleared, or exonerated, or whatever you call it when no charges are brought against you for something everyone really believes you did. He went to law school and now he is a prosecutor in Manhattan.

Neither of us misses the irony of that, although I like to think he did it because he wanted to make sure the right people got indicted. It's the same office in lower Manhattan where Jon worked that summer, but although he performed well Jon was not offered a job at the D.A.'s office, nor did he get any of the clerkships for which he applied.

In the newspaper accounts, which I read one summer day on microfilm in the New York Public Library, just before I began med school, when I was between a temporary receptionist's stint and two weeks playing handmaiden to the executive vice president of an ad agency, he had said that his legal training made him understand keenly the moral need for him to come forward when my mother's death was ruled suspicious. But Jeff told me that many of the lawyers in his office had thought it was "low rent," as one put it, to testify against your lover, no matter what she might have done. Besides, they found his ambition fearsome. "Walk over his mother in golf spikes," one said.

Ah, Jon's mother. How his life would have been different had she reconciled herself to boredom in Brooklyn and carted him to PBA picnics and the Aquarium at Coney Island. He is at one of the big firms now, although not the one with the atrium. I presume that no one there much cares that he ratted me out. There walking over your mother in golf spikes is probably a term of art. There he puts in his seventy hours a week.

I put in mine each week now, too. I am as driven as I was before those months I spent at home; I am simply not as sure of myself or of all the things I once believed. When I enrolled in medical school one of the tabloids put my picture on page five, a photo of me sitting in the cafeteria that was obviously taken by one of my fellow students. ANGEL OF DEATH NOW A DOC? the headline read, and although there was a flurry of protest and a visit with the dean, I was allowed to finish. After a while people seemed to forget.

I never forget. My remembering has gotten more vivid as the years go by. I never considered going into oncology. I knew enough, after my rotations, to know that my mother was in every way a typical patient except that she died more quickly than many with her kind of cancer. But she would have died nonetheless. If I had been her doctor I would have treated her just as Dr. Cohn did, with precisely the same results. I would have asked for the autopsy, too, just as Dr. Cohn did, the professional curiosity that so changed all our lives.

"As her daughter, would you have behaved differently?" my therapist asked once, with an unaccustomed gleam in her eye. And the answer is that, knowing then what I know now, I would have. I would have given her more opportunities to talk, to complain, to fantasize, to weep, to speak. But that is what I am in the business of doing now, and it sounds easier in retrospect. I did the best I could at the time. We all did, I think, even my father, with his distance, his terror, his spoonfuls of rice pudding.

Sometimes still I think I see her in crowds, see that shiny crown of burnished hair bobbing along just a few heads away, just a little too far away to reach. The other day, thoughtlessly, I bought an old recording of *South Pacific*. I remembered that we had watched the movie one night when the pain in her back was especially bad, but somehow I had forgotten being a small girl, sitting in front of the stereo while she taught me to sing: "I'm stuck,/like a dope,/with a thing called hope,/and I can't get it out of my heart . . ."

Sometimes things leap out at me now, a funhouse of memory, some forgotten, others supressed. Even at the theater that night, just before my beeper went off, a few bars of music had made me think that I should call her when I got home. Sometimes I even pick up the phone and begin to dial. The sunflower pillow is on my couch. "Do you needlepoint?" the occasional female guest asks. "No," I say.

"George Eliot!" my brothers and I yell, when it's late and we've had too much to drink, and we all laugh. They help me remember, and I help them.

Most of my patients are young women embarked on a quest for perfection, eaten up by it. Early on, one of them, a brilliant girl who had tried to starve herself to death the summer between Exeter and Yale, said to me in the middle of a session, when she was getting a little too close to some personal truth, "My mother says people say you killed your mother."

"Does she?" Her mother was an extraordinarily beautiful woman, the trophy wife of a financier who had herself recently been shed for a younger trophy. She always had swatches of fabric in a big velvety leather bag, and gold pens, and gold-bound books with room layouts on graph paper inside them and her name embossed in gold on the covers. Once it crossed my mind that, had my mother been wealthy and idle and cold, she would have been this woman. But if my mother had been wealthy and idle and cold, she would have been someone else entirely.

"She said you got off on a technicality."

A slight tilt to the head, a nod. That's what I do when I want the patient to go on.

"I can understand why you'd want to. I'd love to get rid of my mother."

I looked at her poor transparent arms, sticks in the sleeves of the T-shirt she wore as a rebuke to the silk blouses in her closet, and thought that the person she was trying to kill was surely not her mother.

"But if you did it," I said, "what next?"

"What?"

"Your mother is disappeared, dead, gone, however you put it. What then?"

"Like how?" she said.

"Just think about it," I said.

When I was in therapy as part of my training I told my therapist that since my mother had died I no longer knew who I was. I felt as though I had lost my connection to the past. The future seemed to me, as hers had been, the blink of an eye.

The irony was that before she was ill I had been so sure of who I was, of what I wanted. I was George Gulden's daughter and I wanted to make him love me. And in many ways I am still very much like him. But I am also the last living member of the Gulden Girls Book and Cook Club, and I will never forget it, nor ever be the same for it. I will never again be able to think that Anna did the right thing when she closed the door and ran after Vronsky; I will always think of little Seryohza shivering in the hallway, waiting for Maman to return, as I sometimes wait for mine, pausing with the telephone receiver in my hand to make a call and then remembering that the woman I need to speak with has been dead for nearly a decade.

My mother left her mark on me at the very end, so that perhaps now I see my father as she did, admiring and covertly pitying at the same time. My father is not a bad man. He is only a weak one. And he only did what so many men do: he divided women into groups, although in his case it was not the body-and-soul dichotomy of the madonna and the whore but the intellectual twins, the woman of the mind and the one of the heart. Elizabeth and Jane Bennet. I had the misfortune to be designated the heartless one, my mother the mindless one. It was a disservice to us both but, on balance, I think she got the better deal.

Jules always says that someday I'm going to write a big blockbuster self-help book, that we'll call it *Women Who Love Men Who Love Themselves*. My last year of medical school I fell in love with an intern named Jamie, a Californian with white-blond hair and hands so skillful that he was a cinch for surgery and infidelity. It took me six months to discover what everyone else knew, that his mood swings were a function of methamphetamines and his favorite position was with a nurse in an empty single.

I like to think he was the last of the string.

Richard is an orthopedic surgeon, the medical equivalent of a carpenter. He has been my friend for a year and my lover for another and now he wants to be my husband and he will be, I suspect, if I can overcome the fact that I feel about him much the way I feel about my brothers. Once when I was fitfully cruising the living room of the chief of surgery's apartment at a party, drinking too much wine and pretending not to notice the powerful chemistry between Jamie and the chief's third wife, the one in the black strapless dress, Richard said to me roughly, "My problem is I'm too nice to you."

"It's my problem," I said.

"You bet your ass it is, sweetheart," he said, folding his brawny arms over his chest and kicking at the carpet.

He is nice. The night we went to the theater he had tickets for a Knicks game. I only knew because I found the tickets in the drawer in his kitchen where he keeps the scissors. And when my beeper went off, a dozen different men, even other doctors, would have frowned or fidgeted. He only squeezed my arm and sent me off. An adolescent psychiatrist does not have the same interruptions as, say, an obstetrician. But there are emergencies nonetheless. I am accustomed to them now.

There was only one pay phone in the lobby of the theater, off behind a column. A man in a double-breasted suit was using it. When he saw me standing behind him, he took a cellular from his pocket. "On the fritz," he said with a mixture of ire and apology. And he began talking numbers, money, dealmakers and breakers with someone on the other end.

I paced a bit on the theater's Oriental-patterned wall-to-wall and looked at my watch. Two minutes and I would tell him I was a psychiatrist with an emergency. Even an investment banker would hang up. People always did, envisioning a man on a rooftop, a girl with a razorblade at her wrist. I paced a little longer, standing in front of the glass doors to Forty-sixth Street. On the other side, smoking a cigarette, stood my father.

He tossed the butt onto the ground and put it out deftly with his toe, then turned slightly toward the lobby and saw me there. He tilted his head—is that where I got it, that gesture I thought was only mine?—and then gave a half-smile, part recognition, part ironic distance and parted the glass doors with his elegant hands.

"As you've doubtless noted with great disapproval, I've substituted cigarettes for liquor," he said, without preamble.

"Great—keep the liver, lose the lungs. A winning equation."

"Age does not wither nor custom stale your sharp tongue."

"Actually, it has. That was the old me talking. I think you should give up smoking but I also think giving up drinking is an excellent idea."

"Your medical opinion."

"Yes."

"I never imagined you would be a doctor," he said, looking at me closely, as though it would have changed my face. Or perhaps he was looking for my opinion of him in my eyes. Instead I wore the studied neutrality of my profession.

"And an alienist," he added.

I threw back my head and laughed, and so did he, and for just a moment I thought nothing has changed, nothing.

"Only you would use that term," I said. "So Victorian."

"And you work with children," he said.

"Adolescents," I said. "Depression, suicide, other manifestations of despair."

"The stuff of fiction," he said.

"No, not really," I said. "On paper you can make them do what you want. In practice you have to convince Anna not to throw herself in front of a train."

We stared at one another. "You're looking well," he finally said.

"And you," I replied.

"You like the play?"

"Not much," I said. "I'm surprised you're here."

"I have a friend who studies set design," he said. "Her teacher did the scenery."

The banker hung up the pay phone. "It's all yours," he said to me. "Emergency," I said to my father as I lifted the receiver.

It was not much of one: a young woman who'd tried to drink herself to death at a small liberal arts college in Ohio and who'd just begun taking antidepressants wanted to double the dose because they weren't working. "I told her it takes a while for them to take effect, but she won't settle down until she's heard it from you," said one of the nurses on the psychiatric floor.

"Tell her I will see her first thing in the morning," I said. "And tell her the antidepressants should begin to work by the end of the week or I will change her dosage or her medication. And remind her that I'd assigned her to read *Wuthering Heights* along with the medication."

He was still there when I got off the phone. I knew he was. I would have felt it if he had left. His eyebrows were raised.

"You assign the Brontës to the mentally ill?"

"It will help her understand compulsion," I said, "and it will take her mind momentarily off her own. And despite what you think, I always liked the Brontës." I smiled. "I have to get back to my seat."

"I would like to say one thing," he said, and the look on his face was stripped, frozen, like the look on his face that day we hit the deer.

"It's not necessary," I said.

"I would like to," he said. "It's important that you believe what I said in my letter. That I never, ever blamed you. I would have done what you did in your position. Perhaps I should have."

"What?" I said.

"I never blamed you for what you did. It was the right thing to do. It took a good deal of courage. Real courage. Valor. I couldn't say that at the time because of the circumstances. Perhaps I said it badly in the letter. I never blamed you. I wish I'd done it myself."

I looked into his face and there was nothing there, no guile, no subterfuge, nothing except the truth of what he was saying.

"Oh, Papa," I said.

"I admire your courage."

From inside I heard the first plangent strains of a violin sketching out the beginning of a love song. Two fools, I thought, looking at him. Two brilliant fools: he thinking it was me, me believing it was him. Like an O. Henry story, except that it had blighted both our lives. Suddenly it seemed incredible that all this time I had thought him either courageous or cunning enough, depending on his motives. It was too dirty, too real life, those crushed pills, that bowl of custard, that crystalline moment of decision. Neither of us could have managed it.

But in the end what was important was not that we had so misunderstood one another, but that we had so misunderstood her, this woman who had made us who we were while we barely noticed it. Sometimes I try to reconstruct it now. Maybe after I heaved her from the bath she began to horde her pills, to ask for them when she did not need them, to keep them in a cache beneath her underwear or in a box with her anniversary pearls, so that some winter morning, when the light was gray, she could gulp them down and sleep easy.

Perhaps it just came to her, that afternoon, when I went out to find my father and he was on his way home to her and she found herself alone. Perhaps she pulled herself to the table by the window where I kept the vial. Perhaps she bit them, chewed them to bits, and waited for dark to fall.

Maybe they were even in the rice pudding after all; maybe her last domestic act in that pretty kitchen was to grind the pills to a powder and mix them in the little container that she knew, eventually, would make her last dessert. Now that I know, now that I'm not so blind, I can imagine her thinking to herself, as surely as I made this little world with my own two hands, with the turpentine the paint the yarn the floor wax the tung oil the flowers the kindness the care the need the fear the love so I will leave it.

"What then?" I'd asked my patient about the fantasy death of the woman who'd made her out of her own body, and now I had to begin asking myself all over again. The only thing sadder than life, Edith Wharton once said, is death. But sometimes it seems she had it backward.

My father looked old and empty, like the skin of a cicada, the illusion of the thing. I suppose in some strange way he honored me with his assumption and I was damned if I would tell him otherwise. Let him think of me as a heroine from some little story. He became part of the crowd that night, the great throng that believed speaking the truth was inconsequential, a cover for what I had really done. It was easier when I believed I was covering for him. Now I would have to reinvent him.

And her too. Sometimes now I say to myself, logically, that I could not have known, that the knowledge that she had asked my help convinced me that she could not help herself, that at the end I had every reason to believe that she was too sapped, too weak, too far gone.

But the truth is I didn't really think she had it in her. And being so wrong about her makes me wonder now how often I am utterly wrong about myself. And how wrong she might have been about her mother, how wrong he might have been about his father, how much of family life is a vast web of misunderstandings, a tinted and touched-up family portrait, an accurate representation of fact that leaves out only the essential truth.

I wondered as I made my way back down the aisle in the theater, and I've wondered since, who I should tell about what I now know. Bob Greenstein wouldn't care; if my job is to search for truth, his is to seek scenarios. I wonder whether knowing what really happened would help Jeff smooth over his differences with our father. But perhaps those differences go back much, much further than any question of pills or responsibility, back to those days when the two of us, my father and I, would move into his den and leave the boys on the porch, leave them to the love of their mother.

Mrs. Forburg? Teresa? When I see them now, we never talk about the past. We talk about Mrs. Forburg's travels around the country, where she teaches retired adults about the Great Books in elder hostels. We talk about Teresa's daughter Gina and how hard it is for her husband the pediatrician to make time to see the little girl when he is spending so many hours each day taking care of other people's children.

If I could tell anyone what I know now, perhaps it would be the woman in the blue suit. Somehow I feel that she deserves to know it, so that the story for her can have a beginning, a middle, and an end.

And someday I will tell my father. Someday soon, I imagine, although there is a great temptation to leave the man I once thought the smartest person on earth in utter ignorance. When we parted he had asked, "May I call you?" like a suitor. And I had handed him my card, as though our meeting was a piece of unfin-ished business.

It never occurred to me, in the dim light of the theater lobby, to blurt out the truth as I had suddenly discovered it. I have learned my profession well. Before I tell him what really hap-pened, as far as I know it, I need to understand it myself. I need to understand how, learning as much about my mother as I did during those long days we spent together, I had somehow missed her essence. And he, the person who should have known her best in all the world, had missed it, too. Or perhaps she had only duped him, with the deft and docile ways she found to make his life just what he wanted it to be, duped him into thinking that there was less to her than met the eye.

I will find a way to make it parse, as Jules still says. Doing what I do now, I surely should understand that all our lives have some mystery at the core, and many of them go unsolved. If I had not come to that play on that evening, if I had gone to the Knicks game with Richard instead, if my patient's medication had taken effect, if the nurse had not called, if the banker had not been on the phone, if my father had not taken up smoking, if, if, if, if, my own story would have ended with a different sort of father, a different sort of mother, and, of course, a different sort of daughter.

When I went back to my seat Richard took my hand and smiled in the darkness. When the lights came on after the curtain call, he kissed my cheek. As I looked at him I realized that, while I would never be my mother nor have her life, the lesson she had left me was that it was possible to love and care for a man and still have at your core a strength so great that you never even needed to put it on display. I realized that Richard was nothing like my father but very much like my mother. And I thought that I would marry him very, very soon and take my chances with all the rest. Perhaps then I could afford to know my father again, to fall within the now truncated circle of his thrall.

"Everything okay?" Richard asked.

"Is everything ever okay?" I said.

"Is it really true that a psychiatrist can only answer a question with another question?"

"I don't know, what do you think?" I said. I squeezed his big hand, walking out into the night air, and then I added, "The patient is fine. I prescribed Cathy and Heathcliff until her medication kicks in."

We stopped on the sidewalk. The audience eddied around us, dissecting the play, but I did not see my father again.

Richard reached down and checked my pulse. "And how is my patient?" he said.

"Have you ever had the feeling that you had things all figured out and then suddenly you find yourself back to square one?"

"I've never felt that I had things all figured out," he said.

"You are a better person than I am."

"Simpler."

"Better."

"Have it your way," Richard said, and we began to walk. A black man with rheumy eyes asked for a quarter. "No change," I said. Richard dug into his pocket and gave him a dollar. "Get a cup of coffee, guy," he said.

"Life's a bitch," I said.

"Yeah," Richard said, "but consider the alternative."

"Is that George Burns or Émile Zola?" I said.

"I thought it was me, actually. C'mon, I'm starved; let's go eat."

"Food," I said. "That's what I need."

Black and Blue

For Quin Krovatin
From one writer to another,
with admiration and enormous love.

The first time my husband hit me I was nineteen years old. One sentence and I'm lost. One sentence and I can hear his voice in my head, that butterscotch-syrup voice that made goose bumps rise on my arms when I was young, that turned all of my skin warm and alive with a sibilant *S*, the drawling vowels, its shocking fricatives. It always sounded like a whisper, the way he talked, the intimacy of it, the way the words seemed to go into your guts, your head, your heart. "Jeez, Bob," one of the guys would say, "you should have been a radio announcer. You should have done those voice-over things for commercials." It was like a genie, wafting purple and smoky from the lamp, Bobby's voice, or perfume when you took the glass stopper out of the bottle.

I remember going to court once when Bobby was a witness in a case. It was eleven, maybe twelve years ago, before Robert was born, before my collarbone was broken, and my nose, which hasn't healed quite right because I set it myself, looking in the bathroom mirror in the middle of the night, petals of adhesive tape fringing the frame. Bobby wanted me to come to court when he was testifying because it was a famous case at the time, although one famous case succeeds another in New York City the way one pinky-gold sunset over the sludge of the Hudson River fades and blooms, brand-new each night. A fifteen-year-old boy from Brooklyn was accused of raping a Dominican nun at knifepoint and then asking her to pray for him. His attorney said it was a lie, that the kid had had no idea that the woman in the aqua double-knit pants and the striped blouse was a nun, that the sex was consensual, though the nun was sixty-two and paste-waxing a floor in a shelter at the time. They took paste wax from the knees of the kid's pants, brought in the paste-wax manufacturer to do a chemical comparison.

The lawyer was an old guy with a storefront in a bad neighborhood, I remember, and the kid's mother had scraped together the money to hire him because Legal Aid had sent a black court-appointed and she was convinced that her son needed a white lawyer to win his case. Half-blind, hungover, dandruff on the shoulders of his gray suit like a dusting of snow, the kid's attorney was stupid enough to call the kid as a witness and to ask why he had confessed to a crime he hadn't committed.

"There was this cop in the room," the boy said, real low, his broad forehead tipped toward the microphone, his fingers playing idly with his bottom lip, so that his words were a little muffled. "He don't ask none of the questions. He just kept hassling me, man. Like he just keeps saying, 'Tell us what you did, Tyrone. Tell us what you did.' It was like he hypnotized me, man. He just kept saying it over and over. I couldn't get away from him."

The jury believed that Tyrone Biggs had done the rape, and so did everybody else in New York who read the tabloids, watched the news. So did the judge, who gave him the maximum, eight to fifteen years, and called him "a boil on the body of humanity." But I knew that while Tyrone was lying about the rape he was telling the truth about that police officer, because I lived with that voice every day, had been hypnotized by it myself. I knew what it could do, how it could sound. It went down into your soul, like a confessor, like a seducer, saying, "Tell me. Tell me." Frannie, Frannie, Fran, he'd croon, whisper, sing. Sometimes Bobby even made me believe that I was guilty of something, that I was sleeping with every doctor at the hospital, that I made him slip and bang his bad knee. That I made him beat me up, that it was me who made the fist, angled the foot, brought down a hand hard. Hard.

The first time he hit me I was nineteen.

I can hear his voice now, so persuasive, so low and yet somehow so strong, making me understand once again that I'm all wrong. Frannie, Frannie, Fran, he says. That's how he begins. Frannie, Frannie, Fran. The first time I wasn't your husband yet. You were already twenty, because it was the weekend after we went to City Island for your birthday. And I didn't hit you. You know I didn't hit you. You see, Fran, this is what you do. You twist things. You always twist things.

I can hear him in my head. And I know he's right. He didn't hit me, that first time. He just held onto my upper arm so tight that the mark of his fingertips was like a tattoo, a black sun with four small moons revolving around it.

It was summer, and I couldn't wear a sundress for a week, or take off my clothes when my sister, Grace, was in the room we shared, the one that looked out over the air shaft to the Tarnowskis' apartment on the other side. He had done it because I danced with Dee Stemple's brother and then laughed when he challenged me on it. He held me there, he said, so that I couldn't get away, because if I got away it would be the end of him, he loved me that much. The next night he pushed back the sleeve of my blouse and kissed each mark, and his tears wet the spots as though to wash the black white again, as white as the rest of my white, white skin, as though his tears would do what absolution did for venial sins, wash them clean. "Oh, Jesus," he whispered, "I am so goddamned sorry," And I cried, too. When I cried in those days it was always for his pain, not for mine.

As rich and persuasive as Bobby Benedetto's voice, that was how full and palpable was his sorrow and regret. And how huge was his rage. It was like a twister cloud; it rose suddenly from nothing into a moving thing that blew the roof off, black and strong. I smell beer, I smell bourbon, I smell sweat, I smell my own fear, ranker and stronger than all three.

I smell it now in the vast waiting room of Thirtieth Street Station in Philadelphia. There are long wooden benches and my son, Robert, and I have huddled together into the corner of one of them. Across from us slumps a man in the moth-eaten motley of the homeless, who smells of beer and vomit like so many I've seen in the waiting room at the hospital, cooking up symptoms from bad feet to blindness to get a bed for the night, an institutional breakfast on a tray. The benches in Thirtieth Street Station are solid, plain, utilitarian, like the pews in St. Stanislaus. The Church of the Holy Polack, Bobby called St. Stannie's, but he still wanted us to be married there, where he'd been baptized, where his father had been eulogized as a cop's cop. I had never lived in one place long enough to have a real home parish, and I'd agreed. Together we'd placed a rose from my bouquet at the side altar, in front of the statue of St. Joseph, in memory of Bobby's father. It was the only memory of his father that Bobby ever shared with me.

The great vaulted ceiling of the train station arched four stories over us, Robert and I and our one small carry-all bag, inside only toothbrushes, a change of clothes, some video-game cartridges and a book, a romance novel, stupid, shallow, but I had enough of real life every day to last me forever. Gilded, majestic, the station was what I'd believed the courtroom would be like, that day I went to court, when my husband took the stand.

State your name.

Robert Anthony Benedetto.

And your occupation?

I'm a police officer for the City of New York.

The courtroom in the state supreme court had been nothing at all like Thirtieth Street Station. It was low-ceilinged, dingy, paneled in dark wood that sucked up all the light from low windows that looked out on Police Plaza. It seemed more like a rec room than a courtroom. The train station in Philadelphia looked the way I'd always imagined a courtroom would look, or maybe the way one would look in a dream, if you were dreaming you were the judge, or the accused. Robert was staring up at the ceiling, so high above that those of us scattered around the floor so far below were diminished, almost negated by it. At one end of the huge vaulted room was a black statue of an angel holding a dead or dying man. I thought it was a war memorial, and under normal circumstances I would have walked across to read the inscription on the block beneath the angel's naked toes. But whatever the opposite of normal circumstances was, this was it. I shivered in the air-conditioning, dressed for July in a room whose temperature was lowered to April, my mind as cold as January.

The statue was taller than our little house down the block from the bay in Brooklyn, taller than my in-laws' house or the last building where I'd lived with my parents, the one in Bensonhurst, where, in the crowded little bedroom, I'd dressed in my wedding gown, snagging the hem of my train on a popped nail in the scuffed floorboards. The sheer heroic thrust of the station made me feel tiny, almost invisible, almost safe, except that my eyes wandered constantly from the double glass doors to the street at one end to the double glass doors to the street at the other. Waiting, watching, waiting for Bobby to come through the doors, his hands clenched in his pants pockets, his face the dusky color that flooded it whenever he was angry about anything, which was lots of the time. I'd been waiting for Bobby to come through doors most of my life, waiting and watching to gauge his mood and so my own.

A finger of sweat traced my spine and slid into the cleft where my underpants began. The cotton at my crotch was wet, summer sweat and fear. I'd been afraid so many times that I thought I knew exactly what it felt like, but this was something different altogether, like the difference between water and ice. Ice in my belly, in my chest, beneath my breasts, between my eyes, as though I'd gulped down a lemonade too quickly in the heat. "Brain freeze," Robert and his friends called it when it happened to them, and they'd reel around the kitchen, holding their heads.

"Wait on the bench by the coffee kiosk," the man had said. He had driven us from New York to Philadelphia in total silence, like a well-trained chauffeur. As we got out of the old Plymouth Volare in front of the train station, he had leaned across the front seat, looking up at me through the open passenger door. He had smelled like English Leather, which Bobby had worn when we were both young, before we were married. Bobby had worn it that time when I was nineteen, the first time. Or twenty. I guess it was right, Bobby's voice in my head; I guess I'd just turned twenty, that first time. Maybe he was testing me then, to see how much I could take. Maybe he did that every time, until finally he had decided that I would take anything. Anything at all.

"What?" Robert had said, looking up at me as the man in the Volare drove away from wherever he came from, whoever he was. "What did he say? Where are we going now? Where are we going?"

And there was the coffee kiosk, and here was the bench, and here we were, my ten-year-old son and I, waiting for—what? Waiting to escape, to get gone, to disappear so that Bobby could never find us. I think Robert knew everything when he saw me that morning, cutting my hair in the medicine-cabinet mirror, whispering on the phone, taking off the bandages and throwing them in the trash, putting all the recent photographs in an envelope and addressing it to my sister, Grace, so that Bobby wouldn't have good pictures to show people when he started to search for us. "Where are we going?" Robert had asked. "On a trip," I'd replied. If Robert had been an ordinary ten-year-old he would have cajoled and whined, asked and asked and asked until I snapped at him to keep quiet. But he'd never been ordinary. For as long as either of us could remember, he'd been a boy with a secret, and he'd kept it well. He had to have heard the sound of the slaps, the thump of the punches, the birdcall of my sobs as I taped myself up, swabbed myself off, put my pieces back together again. He'd seen my bruises after the fact; he'd heard the sharp intakes of breath when he hugged too hard in places I was hurt. But he looked away, the way he knew we both wanted him to, my husband for his reasons, me for mine.

It was just that last time, when he came in from school and I turned at the kitchen counter, his apple slices on a plate, his milk in a glass, my face swollen, misshapen, the colors of a spectacular sunset just before nightfall, my smile a clownish wiggle of a thing because of my split lip, that he couldn't manage to look away, disappear upstairs, pretend he didn't see. "Mom, oh, Mom," he'd said, his eyes enormous. "Don't worry," I'd replied before he could say more. "I'll take care of everything."

"Mom," he'd said again. And then maybe he remembered, remembered the secret, remembered all those mornings after the horrible sounds and screams, how his father would sit at the table drinking coffee from his PBA mug, how I'd come in from running and go up to shower, how everyone acted as though everything was just as it should be. So the wild light in his eyes flared, flickered, died, and he added, "Was it an accident?"

Because that's what I'd said, year after year. An accident. I had an accident. The accident was that I met Bobby Benedetto in a car, and I fell crazy in love with him. And after that I fell further and further every year. Not so you'd notice, if you knew me, although no one really did. On the outside I looked fine: the job, the house, the kid, the husband, the smile. Nobody got to see the hitting, which was really the humiliation, which turned into the hatred. Not just hating Bobby, but hating myself, too, the cringing self that was afraid to pick up the remote control from the coffee table in case it was just that thing that set him off. I remember a story in the *Daily News* a couple of years ago about a guy who kept a woman chained in the basement of the building where he was a custodian. Whenever he felt like it, he went down the concrete steps and did what he wanted to her. Part of me had been in a cellar, too, waiting for the sound of footfalls on the stairs. And I wasn't even chained. I stayed because I thought things would get better, or at least not worse. I stayed because I wanted my son to have a father and I wanted a home. For a long time I stayed because I loved Bobby Benedetto, because no one had ever gotten to me the way he did. I think he knew that. He made me his accomplice in what he did, and I made Robert mine. Until that last time, when I knew I had to go, when I knew that if I told my son I'd broken my nose, blacked my eyes, split my lip, by walking into the dining-room door in the dark, that I would have gone past some point of no return. The secret was killing the kid in him and the woman in me, what was left of her. I had to save him, and myself.

"Where are we going, Mom?" he whined in the station, but he did it like any kid would, on any long trip, and it almost made me laugh and smile and cry, too, to hear him sound so ordinary instead of so dead and closed up. Besides, he knew. He knew we were running away from his father, as far and as fast as we could. I wanted to say, Robert, baby, hon, I'm taking you out of the cellar. I'm taking you to where there won't be secrets anymore. But that wasn't exactly true. They'd just be different secrets now.

There are people who will do almost anything in America, who will paint your house, paint your toenails, choose your clothes, mind your kids. In Manhattan, at the best private schools, you can even hire a nitpicker if your kid gets head lice. And there are people who will help you get away from your husband, who will find you a new house, a new job, a new life, even a new name. They are mysterious about it because they say it's what they need to do to keep you safe; when she goes on television, their leader, a woman named Patty Bancroft, likes to say, "We do not even have a name for ourselves." Maybe that's why I'd felt I had to whisper when I talked to her on the phone, even though Bobby was long gone from the house: to keep their secret, my secret. There are people, Patty Bancroft had said, who will help you; it is better if you know no more than that.

I looked down at Robert, hunched over on the bench, bent almost double over a little electronic game he carried with him everywhere. Ninjas in glowing green lunged forward and kicked men in black masks; the black masks fell back, fell over like felled trees. The ninjas bowed. The number at one corner of the screen grew larger. Robert was breathing as though he had been running. I ran my hand over his dark hair, cut like a long tonsure over his narrow, pointed skull. My touch was an annoyance; he leaned slightly to one side and rocked forward to meet the ninjas, take them on, knock them down. He was good at these games, at losing himself in the tinny electronic sounds and glowing pictures. My sister, Grace, said all the kids were, these days. But I wondered. I looked across the station at a small girl in overalls who was toddling from stranger to stranger, smiling and waving while her mother followed six paces behind. Even when he was small Robert had never, ever been like that. Grace said kids were born with personalities, and Robert's was as dignified and adult as his name. But I wondered. When Robert was three he sometimes sat and stared and rocked slightly back and forth, and I worried that he was autistic. He wasn't, of course; the doctor said so. "Jesus, talk about making a mountain out of a whatever," Bobby had said, reaching to lift the child and never even noticing the way in which the small bony shoulders flinched, like the wings of a bird preparing to fly, to flee.

"We're going on a trip," I'd told Robert that morning.

"Where?" he'd said.

"It's kind of a surprise."

"Is Daddy coming?"

Not if we're lucky, a voice in my head had said, but out loud I'd replied, "He has to work."

Robert's face had gone dead, that way it does sometimes, particularly the morning after a bad night, a night when Bobby and I have gotten loud. "Is that why you're wearing glasses?" he said.

"Sort of, yeah."

"They look funny."

In the station he looked up from his video game and stared at me as though he was trying to figure out who I was, with the strange hair, the glasses, the long floaty dress. The ninjas were all dead. He had won. His eyes were bright. "Tell me where we're going," he said again.

"I will," I said, as though I knew. "In a little while."

"Can I get gum?"

"Not now."

Around the perimeter of the station were small shops and kiosks: cheap jewelry, fast food, newspapers, books: the money changers in the temple. The voice of the train announcer was vaguely English; there was a stately air to the enterprise, unlike the shabby overlit corridors of the airports. No planes, Patty Bancroft told me when we first talked on the phone two weeks before. Plane trips are too easy to trace. The women she helped never flew away; they were not birds but crawling creatures, supplicants, beaten down. Trains, buses, cars. And secrecy.

When I'd first met Patty Bancroft, when she'd come to the hospital where I worked, she'd said that she had hundreds of volunteers all over the country. She said her people knew one another only as voices over the telephone and had in common only that for reasons of their own they had wanted to help women escape the men who hurt them, to give those women new lives in new places, to help them lose themselves, start over in the great expansive anonymous sameness of America.

"What about men who are beaten by their wives?" one of the young doctors at the hospital had asked that day.

"Don't make me laugh," Patty Bancroft had said wearily, dismissively.

She'd given me her card that day, in case I ever treated a woman in the emergency room who needed more than sutures and ice packs, needed to escape, to disappear, to save her life by getting gone for good. "Nurses are one of my greatest sources of referral," she'd said, clasping my hand, looking seriously into my eyes. It was the most chaste business card I'd ever seen, her name and a telephone number. No title, no address, just a handful of lonely black characters. I put the card in my locker at the hospital. I must have picked it up a hundred times until, six months later, I called the number. She remembered me right away. "Tell me about this patient," Patty Bancroft had said. "It's me," I said, and my voice had faltered, fell into a hiss, a whisper of shame. "It's me."

"Where are we going?" I had asked her when we spoke on the phone two days before the man in the Volare had picked us up at a subway stop in upper Manhattan, two weeks after Bobby had beaten me for the last time. My voice was strange and stiff; my nose and jaw had begun to heal, so that if I didn't move my mouth too much the pain was no more than a soft throb at the center of my face.

"You'll know when you get there," Patty Bancroft said.

"I'm not going away without knowing where I'm going," I said.

"Then you'll have to stay where you are," she replied. "This is the way it works." My hand had crept to my nose, pressed on the bridge as though testing my resolve. I felt the pain in my molars, the back of my head, the length of my spine. I felt the blood still seeping from between my legs, like a memory of something I'd already made myself forget. "The bleeding will stop in a week or so," they'd said at the clinic. Pack plenty of clean underpants, I thought to myself. That's what it comes down to, finally, no matter how terrifying your life has become. A toothbrush. Batteries. Clean underpants. The small things keep you from thinking about the big ones. Concealer stick. Tylenol. My face had faded to a faint yellow-green in the time it had taken me to plan my getaway. Bobby had been working a lot of nights. We'd scarcely seen one another.

"What will happen if you leave and then your husband finds you?" Patty Bancroft had said.

"He'll kill me," I answered.

"He won't find you if you do what we say." And she'd hung up the phone.

The station public-address system bleated and blared. "Mom, can I have a Coke?" Robert said, in that idle way in which children make requests, as though it's expected of them. The video game and his hands lay in his lap, and he'd tilted his head back to look up at the ceiling.

"Not now," I said.

A line of people in business suits had formed at the head of one of the stairways leading to the tracks. Two of them talked on cellular phones. A woman with a handsome leather suitcase on a wheeled stand left the line and walked toward the coffee kiosk. Her heels made a percussive noise on the stone floor. "Café au lait, please," the woman said to the girl behind the counter.

She looked at her watch, then turned and smiled at me, looked down at the floor, looked up again. "You dropped your tickets," she said. She handed me an envelope she stooped to pick up from the floor.

"Oh, no, I—"

"You dropped your tickets," she said again, smiling, her voice firm, and I could feel the corner of the envelope, a sharp point against my wet palm.

"Metroliner!" called a uniformed man at the head of the stairs, and the woman picked up her coffee and wheeled her suitcase to the stairway without looking back. I sat down heavily on the bench and opened the envelope.

"God!" groaned Robert, hunched back over his game.

"What?"

"Nothing," he said.

Inside the envelope were two tickets to Baltimore on the 4:00 PM Metroliner. I looked at the big digital clock and the wall timetable. 3:12, and the next Metroliner was ON TIME. There were other things in the envelope, too: bus tickets, a driver's license, Social Security cards. For a moment I was blind with confusion, and then I found the names: Crenshaw, Elizabeth. Crenshaw, Robert.

I had not liked it when Patty Bancroft gave me orders on the phone, but now I felt a powerful sense of gratitude. She had let me have my way in at least one thing: Robert had gotten to keep his own first name.

And I was to be Elizabeth. Liz. Beth. Libby. Elizabeth Crenshaw. Seeing myself reflected in the glass of the coffee kiosk, I could almost believe it. There she was, Elizabeth Crenshaw. She had short blond hair, a pixie crop that I'd created with kitchen scissors and hair dye in the bathroom just before sun-up, just after I heard the door shut behind Bobby as he left for work. She wore a pair of gold-rimmed glasses bought from a rack at the pharmacy, clear glass with the kind of cheap sheen to the lenses that turned the eyes behind them into twin slicks of impenetrable glare. Elizabeth Crenshaw was thin, all long bones and taut muscles, because Fran Benedetto had been running for more than a decade and because terror had made it hard for her, these last few years, to eat without feeling the food rise back up into her gorge at a word, a sound, a look. "Skin and bones," Bobby said sometimes when I was naked, reaching for me.

It had taken me a while, that morning, to decide what to wear, but I was accustomed to being concerned with my own clothes, even though I didn't care about them much, not like Bobby's mother, who was forever seeking discount silk and cashmere, trousers cut perfectly to her tiny frame, jackets and skirts with good linings and labels. Much of the time I wore my nurse's uniform, the white washing out my thin freckled skin and making a garish orange of my hair. But let me change into anything snug, or short, or low, and I would see Bobby's eyes go narrow and bright. Although it was always hard to tell exactly what would offend until the moment when he put his head to one side and looked me up and down until my pale skin flushed. "Jesus Christ," he'd say in that voice. "You wearing that?" And I would feel like a whore, me, plain Frannie Benedetto, who had been up half the night with her little boy who had a stomach bug, who had been on her feet all day carrying syringes and gauze pads and clipboards and pills, calming down the drunks and hysterics, stopping to talk to the children, placating the doctors. Fran Benedetto, who had never been with a man other than her husband. But let her wear a blouse whose fabric suggested the faintest hint of slip strap, and all of a sudden she was a slut. Slip strap over bra strap, of course, for if I wore a skirt and didn't wear a full slip, the way Bobby's mother always had, there was no telling what Bobby might do. It was funny, after a while: I could tell you what Bobby liked and didn't like, what might set him off and how much. But I couldn't have told you as much about myself. I was mostly reaction to Bobby's actions, at least by the end. My clothes, my makeup: they were more or less his choice. I bought them, of course, but bought them with one eye always on Bobby's face. And his hands.

But Beth Crenshaw I would create myself, without reference to Bobby. I started to create her even before I found out her name in the waiting room at Thirtieth Street Station. Beth Crenshaw wore a loose, long flowered dress I'd found in the back of my closet from two summers before, the sort of dress that Bobby always said made women look like grandmothers. Bobby's own grandmother, his father's mother, always wore black, even to picnics and street fairs. "C'mere, Fran," she'd yell across her daughter-in-law's white-on-white living room, where she sat like a big blot of ink on the couch. She'd fold herself around me and cover me in black, make me feel small and safe. "Aw, God bless you, you're too thin," she'd say. "She's too thin, Bob. You need to make her eat." She'd died just before Robert was born, Bobby's Nana. I missed her. Maybe it would have happened anyhow, but I think Bobby got harder after that. Harsher, too.

"The reason you hooked up with me," I said to Bobby once, when we were young, "is because my red hair and white skin look good next to your black hair and your tan."

"That was part of it," he said. That was a good day, that day. We played miniature golf at a course owned by a retired narcotics guy in Westchester, had dinner at that Italian place in Pelham, made out in the car at a rest stop on the Saw Mill River Parkway. Both of us living with our parents, he in the Police Academy, me in nursing school: we had no place else to go. The first time we had sex it was in a cabana at that skanky beach club his mother liked; a friend of his from high school who vacuumed the pool let us stay after closing. It didn't hurt, I didn't bleed. I loved it. I loved how helpless it made him, big bad tanned muscled Bobby Benedetto, his mouth open, the whites of his eyes showing. It made me want to sit on his lap the rest of my life.

He talked about getting a tattoo on his shoulder, a rose and the word *Frances*. I said I'd get *Yosemite Sam* on my upper thigh. "The hell you will," he said. It turned out I didn't need it; Bobby tattooed me himself, with his hands.

"Red hair is too conspicuous," Patty Bancroft had said on the phone. It had been the only conspicuous thing about me, all these years. Smart, but not too. Enterprising, but not too. Friendly, but not too. The kind of girl who becomes a nurse, not a doctor. The kind of nurse who becomes assistant head, but not head nurse. The kind of wife—well, no one knew about that.

"There's still some good years left on her," Bobby would say when his friends came over, and they'd laugh. It was the way they all talked about their wives, and I wondered, looking at their flushed and friendly faces, if they were thinking of bones that had not yet been broken, areas that had not yet blossomed with bruises.

And they looked at me and saw a happy wife and mother like so many others, a working woman like so many others. Fran Flynn—you know, the skinny redhead who works in the ER at South Bay. Frannie Benedetto, the cop's wife on Beach Twelfth Street, the one with the little boy with the bowlegs. Gone down the drain that morning. Transformed, perhaps forever, by Loving Care No. 27, California Blonde. Hidden behind the glasses. Disguised by the flapping folds of the long dress. California blonde Elizabeth Crenshaw, with nothing but thin milky skin and faint constellations of freckles on chest and cheeks to connect her to Frances Ann Flynn Benedetto. A bruise on my right cheek, faded to yellow, and a bump on the bridge of my nose. And Robert, of course, the only thing I'd had worth taking with me from that tidy house, where Bobby liked to walk on the carpeting barefoot and I cleaned up the blood with club soda and Clorox before the stain set. Beth. I liked Beth. I was leaving, I was starting over again, I was saving my life, I was sick of the fear and the fists. And I was keeping my son safe, too, not because his father had ever hit him—he never ever had—but because the secret inside our house, the secret about what happened at night, when Daddy was drunk and disgusted with himself and everything around him, was eating the life out of Robert. When he was little he would touch a bruise softly, say, "You boo-boo, Mama?" When he got a little older he sometimes said, narrowing his big black eyes, "Mommy, how did you hurt yourself?"

But now he only looked, as though he knew to be quiet, as though he thought this was the way life was. My little boy, who had always had something of the little old man about him, was becoming a dead man, too, with a dead man's eyes. There are ways and ways of dying, and some of them leave you walking around. I'd learned that from watching my father, and my husband, too. I wasn't going to let it happen to my son.

Frances couldn't. Beth wouldn't. That's who I was now. Frances Ann Flynn Benedetto was always watching and waiting, scared of her husband, scared he would turn on her, hit her, finally knock her out for good. Scared to leave her son with no mother to raise him, only a father whose idea of love was bringing you soup after he'd broken your collarbone. Frannie Flynn was gone. I'd killed her myself. I was Beth Crenshaw now.

Beneath the rippling skirt I could feel my legs trembling as an announcer with a sonorous voice called out the trains. But I could feel my legs, too, feel them free. No slip. I'd left that goddamn slip behind.

Frannie Flynn—that's how I'd thought of myself again, even though my last name was legally Benedetto. The name on my checks, on my license, on the embossed plastic name tag I wore on the breast of my nurse's uniform. Frances F. Benedetto. But in my mind I'd gone back to being Frannie Flynn. Maybe Bobby knew that. Maybe he could read my mind. Maybe that was part of the problem, that he could read my mind and I never had a clue what was going on in his.

Frannie, Frannie, Fran. I heard his voice saying my name, like the ringing in my ears, when he brought his open hand hard against the side of my head in a dark corner of the club foyer, that time I argued with him in front of his friends about whether we were staying for another round of beers at a retirement party. Fran. I can hear his voice in the sound of the train moving south down the tracks. I'm coming, Frannie. You can't get away. You're mine, Fran. Both of you.

I still can't figure out why everyone in New York talks about Florida as if it's a cross between Paris and Lourdes. The pilgrimages to Disney World, the fabled retirement condos in Lauderdale. "Moira Doherty, now she's got a life," one of the cop wives said at a barbecue. "Kevin put in his time and now there they are, not even fifty yet, in Boca, both of them working part-time. She gave me her rabbit jacket. I won't be needing it, hon, she said. Nice and warm down here, even in January. What a racket."

Maybe Moira's lying on a lounge chair watching the sun on the water, but Robert and I wound up in a garden apartment court in a dusty town called Lake Plata, almost an hour's drive to the ocean. Or that's what I'm told; I don't have a car, so I wouldn't know. There's an irony for you: I went from Brooklyn to Florida and wound up trading down, exchanging a house with the Atlantic at the end of the block, shimmering between two rows of attached imitation brickfronts like a mirage, for a square of gravel studded with gnarled bushes, no water in sight except for the pools that sit outside the motels on the highway. There's a flatness to Florida, or at least this part of it. It makes me feel like I'm in one of those rooms in a horror film, where the ceiling lowers and lowers and the floor rises, trapping you, squishing you flat. Although, come to think of it, that's the way I'd felt in my own living room for a long time, whenever I heard the sound of Bobby's Trans Am pulling into the garage beneath the couch and the carpeted floor.

When we got to Florida and Robert and I stepped inside the apartment Patty Bancroft's people had arranged for us, I'd realized it reminded me of the apartments I'd lived in when I was a kid. I could almost smell the bland steam that was the smell of cooking in my parents' house. I could almost hear the soft *woosh* of my father sucking oxygen hungrily through the heavy black rubber mask. And I could almost see the notes my mother left for me next to the stove in her angular handwriting and then in Gregg shorthand once she'd made me take the secretarial course at Queen of Peace: white wash, ham butt, drugstore. Frannie's "To Do" list. My mother had needed to work for as long as I could remember. And so, as a result, had I.

Robert had known the worst as soon as we stepped inside the place, as soon as he looked around at the dim *L*-shaped living room with a wood-grain dinette in the short arm of the *L*, seen the nubby tweed couch, the kind that's supposed to be stain-resistant but couldn't possibly look any worse with a stain or two. He tried to pull up the blinds and I told him sharply to get away from the window. "Are we going to Disney World?" he'd asked, back when we were taking the IRT from Brooklyn to Manhattan and then again as we drove from Manhattan south to Philadelphia in the old Volare, its driver wordless behind the wheel. Now he knew the answer.

On the train from Philadelphia to Baltimore he'd fallen asleep open-mouthed, his face mirrored in the window, and he'd slept on the bus we took from Baltimore to Atlanta. The bus tickets had been tucked into the envelope behind the Metroliner tickets.

"Mom, where are we?" Robert had said when we got off the bus in Atlanta, his eyes dim with sleep and fatigue.

"You must be the Crenshaws," said a short woman whose car was parked at the curb, a minivan full of children's car seats. "Yes," I said, and Robert had looked at me as if I'd lost my mind. "Where are we going?" he'd said again, more insistently. The woman ignored him, glided over his words with her own as though she was used to doing it. "I've got a nice snack for you in the back," she said cheerily.

She was kind, that woman, although she talked for three hours straight about her show dogs, corgis, just like the ones the queen of England had. She was nervous, but she'd brought some juice, some crackers, and an apple for Robert, and a blessed thermos of coffee for me. Robert got carsick twice, throwing up on the shoulder of the highway while I rubbed the sweet spot between his shoulder blades and the dog breeder called, "Hurry up, hurry up!"

"How did you get into this work?" I'd asked after Robert had fallen asleep again, after the woman had finished feeding me on the false biography to go with my new name, finished filling me in on the made-up life in Wilmington, Delaware, and Robert Crenshaw, Sr., the estranged husband who was an accountant. "How do you know Mrs. Bancroft?"

She'd turned on the radio. "Didn't they tell you not to talk about any of that?" she said.

"They didn't tell me much of anything."

"That's for the best," the woman said. "There's a box of doughnuts in the back. Here's your house key."

I don't know what I'd expected when I opened the door of No. 7 Poinsettia Way, its aluminum painted dark brown, its peephole glowing like a glass eye. I was just glad to stand still, to stop moving, to stop running. "Where are we, Mom?" Robert had said for what seemed like the hundredth time, and what could I say to him? We're home? His home was on the bay in Brooklyn, his room carpeted in a blue so thick and vivid that it was like walking through the sky, his shelves and drawers filled with everything he'd ever wanted: stuffed bears, battery-powered robots, plastic Supermen, electronic games, so that he could sit in his room for hours and not go out where things were scary. Out on the streets, his father said. Out in the kitchen, I thought, where there were loud voices and sharp noises and sometimes crying, too.

Numbers were singing in my head. 153 49 5151. That was Elizabeth M. Crenshaw's Social Security number. $1,256. That was how much had been in our joint checking account, and half of it was in a wad at the bottom of my purse. And Gracie's phone number. If only I could talk to my sister, the way I had in the half-light of our bedroom when we were girls, the streetlamps shining in a divot of yellow across our twin beds, the car wheels a hiss outside on the city streets. I'd never hidden anything from Gracie, at least until after I was married. She was six years younger than I was, my baby as much as my mother's, probably more, me pushing her around the neighborhood in my old stroller when she was a toddler, telling her the names of things, singing "Old MacDonald," always interrupted by people making comments about her burning bush of curly hair, like mine but brighter, wilder. If only I could talk to Grace the way I did when we were older, lying in the darkness, listening to her questions, answering them as best I could. How come the nuns can't get married? How old were you when you got your period? How many feet in a yard, yards in a mile? What's our address now? Eight apartments I'd lived in with my parents before I'd married Bobby when I was twenty-one, in six of them I'd shared a room with Gracie. There was never any discernible reason for why we moved; we never moved up, or even down, just from one shabby two-bedroom in Brooklyn to another. As suddenly as the weather changing, we'd get dressed one Saturday, the first week of the month, and load the couch and the easy chair and my father's oxygen into a U-Haul and lie down to sleep that night a dozen blocks away. What's the point of hanging pictures, my mother always said, the sound of my father's wheezing a counterpoint from in front of the television. The mirror was always sitting atop her bureau, propped against the wall.

They'd given me low expectations, all those places. All I wanted was a house that felt like home, where the furniture matched, where the carpet was clean and a color I liked. I wanted to sit in a big chair in a den somewhere, with my feet up on an ottoman, and look around and think: this is my home. I wanted to be able to picture myself in that same room thirty years in the future, with my kids grown and my grandchildren babies and the smell of my cooking so familiar that no one even noticed it anymore. It didn't seem like too much to ask, and there was a while there, with Bobby, when I thought I had it nailed. I'd had a neighbor who kept the key to my house in case I locked myself out, a butcher who knew that I wanted loin of pork with the bone out, a school at the end of the street, a climbing rose working its way up the supporters of the deck out back. I'd had roots. I knew how deep they'd gone.

Knew it so powerfully when we stepped into that fugitive apartment, my boy and I, my eyes burning as we stood on the

threshold. It was not an anonymous apartment, this narrow du-
plex somewhere in central Florida, miles and miles from the
coast. That would have been bad enough. It was, like those others
where I'd spent the years before I married Bobby, redolent of the
lives of dozens upon dozens of strangers who'd smoked cigarettes, fried chicken, taken showers, slept late, risen early. It was a
transient place, right down to the ubiquitous sound of the tap
dripping into the scarred stainless-steel sink. When I entered that
apartment I hated Bobby Benedetto with a ferocity I had never allowed myself to feel while I was living with him. I hated him on
behalf of my lost life, on behalf of my bedspread and dust ruffle,
my landscape over the couch and my guest towels in the powder
room. Forced back into the rootless life I thought I'd left behind
when I married him, I hated him so that, in that moment, I
thought if we ever met again, I'd be just as likely to murder him as
he me.

But after two weeks the feeling dulled, and I kept thinking I
should count my blessings. Isn't that what Daddy always said,
coughing in his recliner, when I complained about not being able
to go away to college or take a job at the beach with my girlfriends
in the summers because then Grace would have no one to look
out for her? Count your blessings. My nose no longer hurts. The
bleeding has stopped. And four doors down in the horseshoe of
our little apartment court is a family named Castro, and among
their five children is a ten-year-old boy who has mastered the
sixth level of Double Dragon, whatever that is. "You know the
finishing move?" Bennie Castro asked Robert the third horribly
bright morning we had been there. The games kept them
grounded, so that Robert was either upstairs or on the front
steps, he and Bennie shoulder to shoulder bent together over the
flickering screen. Bennie has two sisters, twelve and four, and

brothers who are seven and five, and it is a great luxury for him to be almost alone, with no siblings demanding his attention or his toys. So every day now he comes to our apartment and he and Robert sit upstairs, the ninjas punching one another incessantly. Mrs. Castro just smiles and nods and says in pidgin English that this is very nice of me and acts as though there is nothing note-worthy about the fading bruises on my face. With her round cheeks, her hair scraped back into a ponytail, her Tasmanian Devil T-shirt and dimpled knees, she seems younger than any of her children. "Good-boy," she says, nodding at my son.

Occasionally the two boys go outside to ricochet around the quadrangle of stunted grass and cement, and I stand guard and watch their every move, flushed and sweating in the Florida heat. Sandy, the youngest Castro, shadows them as Gracie once did me, running back and forth on the ragged pavement that makes a broad *U* around the perimeter of the garden apartment complex. Occasionally she stumbles and falls on a piece of concrete heaved up by a tree root, sees narrow red pinstripes begin to form on the yellow-brown skin of her knee. She wails, shrieks, forces enor-mous tears from beneath her spiky lashes, and calls for Mama as though she is drowning and her mother is on the boat. A moment later there is the thin sound of chimes in the muggy air: "Ice cream," the little girl shrieks, tears still glittering on her cheeks as she dances and claps. The definition of redemption.

My son scarcely ever cries. And his smile comes so seldom that it's like bright sunshine on winter snow, blinding and strange. It's been this way for as long as I can remember. "Robert's an old soul," Grace used to say, maybe because she knew I needed to hear it, to think Robert's silence, his preternatural self-possession, were inherent, not acquired, not the equivalent of covering your ears, hiding your eyes. But when Bennie's little sister hugs Robert's legs, he always smiles down at her. I had a kid in a coma once, when I was working med-surg instead of ER, and I remember the look on the face of his mother when he blinked his eyes and muttered "water" after he'd been close to death for a month. That must be the look I have as I watch Robert smile down upon the shiny ebony head of Sandy Castro, the look of a woman whose child has come back to life.

"This isn't a vacation," Robert had said in a low shaky voice when we'd first entered the apartment, and he must have seen the look on my face, because he went up the narrow stairs and didn't come down again. I lay on the couch, exhausted, the cheap fabric scratchy against my face, and all at once I was asleep, a sleep as deep as unconsciousness. When I woke most of a day had gone. The place was as quiet as if it was still empty, and I took the stairs two at a time to the bedrooms, calling Robert's name, and found him asleep yet again. I stood over him and looked down at his splayed legs, the hands let loose from their habitual half fists, the big bottom lip like his father's, the light coffee skin. I'd breastfed him for almost a year, an excuse to hold his warm body close. "Who'd have thought, and you as small as you are," my mother-in-law had said, eyeing the exposed breast disapprovingly. On the beach on summer Sundays I'd taken my time rubbing on his sunscreen, feeling the stalk of his spine beneath my fingers, vertebra after vertebra, loved by me. At night in his room I'd read him *One Fish, Two Fish* as he curled into the semicircle of welcoming torso. "You baby that kid," Bobby said, sometimes with a sweet smile and a hand on my arm, sometimes with a sneer, a snort.

"Hey, big guy," Bobby always said to Robert, and he'd cuff the boy lightly, playfully, as though to prove that Robert had nothing to fear from his father's fists. Once one of the cop wives asked me why Bobby didn't wear a wedding ring, asked me in a way that suggested that maybe my husband spent time in the bars and clubs of Manhattan passing himself off as a single guy. And maybe he did. But the reason he'd stopped wearing his ring was because it had once split the skin when he punched me in the shoulder. I guess you could consider it considerate, that he didn't want that to happen again. But of course it implied that there would be an again. And there always was.

The second day after we'd arrived in Florida, when Robert still hadn't spoken, I sat down on the edge of his bed as evening deepened into night and talked to his back as I rubbed it.

"We're going to stay here for a while. Maybe for a long time."

He was curled up on his side, his hands, with their long fingers, pressed together between his knees. "This isn't a vacation," he had said again, but this time with the dull flatness of fact.

"We're kind of hiding, Ba," I said. "No one knows we're here. No one knows who we are."

"Who from?" he said, even though I knew he knew. "Why?" "What?"

"Who are we hiding from? Why are we hiding?"

I took a breath and looked at my nails. They'd grown long, too long for a nurse's nails. But I hadn't been able to go to work in almost two weeks, not with my face every color, blue and yellow and green, like the faces we'd worked on in the emergency room, shrugging our shoulders and scrawling comments on the chart. Poss DA. Possible domestic abuse. It had always come over me, a weakness in my legs, when I wrote that on some other woman's records. I should know.

"From Daddy. We're hiding from Daddy. You know that. You know he hurt me. You saw my face. I know that's hard for you, but Daddy hit me, Ba. He really hurt me. More than once. A lot more than once. You know that. You saw me. You saw what

I looked like. Lots of times. This last time was bad. Really, really bad."

And suddenly he was up and at me. His black eyes were big and his face flushed, and I reared back and then tried to reach for him as I saw the ghostly curlicues where tears had dried on his cheeks.

"No he didn't. You said he didn't. I heard you tell the people at work that you fell. And Aunt Grace. And Grandmom. You said you fell down, or got sick. Stuff like that. I heard you on the phone."

"Ba," I said, his baby name, Ba Ba Black Sheep shortened to Ba Ba and then to a single syllable, explosive with love. I reached out my hand but he pulled back, curled up, and turned away, his raised shoulder like a fin, a blade, a wall. How many times had he lain in bed at night just like this and heard the sound of hand against flesh, shoulder against wall, the sound of the arguments, about dinner, disrespect, adultery, a trip to Dorney Park, washer fluid for the car, no garbage bags, no rye bread, the wrong kind of mustard.

"I lied," I said. "I lied so people wouldn't know. I was ashamed. And I was afraid. I was afraid of Daddy." I took a deep breath. "I'm still afraid of him."

His sobs shook him and me and the flimsy bed, no more than a cot, not like his loft bed at home, with the desk and the computer beneath it, the Yankees season calendar on the bulletin board. Would it be so dangerous if I found another Yankees calendar somewhere and put it on the wall? Was there someone out there looking for us already, looking for a woman buying a Yankees calendar in July, more than half the months of the year already gone? More than half her life gone, too, thirty-eight years of it, much of it devoted to tending her wounds, hiding but never healing them. All I'd ever wanted was to be an ordinary woman, an ordinary wife and mother. Now all I wanted was an ordinary divorce, one of those sad, shamefaced affairs in which the children carried duffel bags from one parent's house to another amid the sounds of bickering about the support check. Even that was denied me. "You're not going anywhere, Fran," Bobby had said more than once. And he meant it.

"Mommy, why can't we go home?" Robert had cried, turning and reaching for me. And I didn't know whether he was mourning his familiar room, and his Little League team, and his friend Anthony from kindergarten and his grandmother's gravy on Sunday afternoon and his old familiar school and block and park and car and his beloved father. Or whether he was wishing for something more, all those things overlaid with the sense of safety and security I'd never managed to give him and had run away to try to find for him. For me, too.

"I know, baby," I said, holding him warm and sticky against me, smoothing his hair and crying myself. "I love you, Ba. I love you so much. You are the best boy."

The next morning he'd met Bennie, and that was that. We hadn't spoken about it since. I had to let him get used to things by inches: new town, new school, new friends. No more accidents. No more pretending that that was what they'd been in the first place. How do you tell your son his father did things you can't always believe yourself? Sometimes I think of Bobby pushing me into the wall, or backhanding me in the car. And for just a minute I think I've got to be exaggerating, which is just what Bobby wanted me to think. But then I can taste blood in my mouth again, and I know it's all just as I remember it. I even started using a soft toothbrush so I wouldn't have to taste blood in my mouth more often than I already did. How do you tell that to a kid who loves his dad?

One evening two weeks after we'd gotten to Florida I was kissing Robert goodnight and he reached up and touched my cheek. The old cotton spread was pulled up to his chin, the air conditioning laying a light chill and the smell of mildew over the thick, humid air. His hair was getting long, flopping over one dark eye. In the dim light from a small window he looked more like Bobby than ever, but the Bobby I'd always loved, the sweet soft boyish Bobby. I kissed his forehead and smoothed back his hair, and instead of stiffening or pulling away he smiled.

"Your face looks better now," he said. "Can we go to the movies sometime?"

I went into the bathroom, the only place in the house where there was a mirror, which I figured was no accident. The tenants of this particular place wouldn't want to look at their own reflections, see the bruises and the scars and the grief and humiliation looking back from their own eyes. When I was a little kid I'd stood on a shoe box in front of my mother's bureau when Gracie was taking a nap in our room, and stared into my own eyes in the mahogany-framed mirror. I don't know why I did this; maybe just to really see myself, to try to figure out who was looking back at me out of those hazel eyes. I seemed more real to myself if I could see my own face, not walk behind it. Maybe that was why I'd avoided mirrors the past couple of years, because it was so strange to me to see the look on my face, alert and oddly empty all at the same time, like the face of a blind person moving around a dangerous corridor, her arms outstretched.

I didn't look that way all the time. Not at the hospital, where I was never afraid, even with the blood and the screams and the crazies. Not when I was with Robert alone, when I walked him home from school or took him to the movies, when it was just the two of us. But the rest of the time I was afraid. In my own home. With my own husband. It made me ashamed, to live behind that face, to think of myself as a person who looked that way. I left to be that person all the time, every day, every night. Twenty-four seven, as the kids say.

But it was almost as bad going as it had been staying. Everyone I loved was lost to me. There was country music on the radio downstairs. It had already been tuned to the station when we'd come to this godawful place, with its scrubby trees and its strangers. The good thing about country music is that you can cry when you listen to it, pretend it's the music you're crying about.

I checked the locks on the windows after I came down from Robert's room. I checked the windows every day. They were still locked. In the closet I had found two boxes of clothes, women's size eights and boy's size twelve, T-shirts and jeans mostly. There were some half-used bags of sugar and flour in the cabinets, some tea bags and a jar of peanut butter, and I wondered who Patty Bancroft's people had last sheltered here, where that woman had gone, whether her husband had found her and talked her into coming back, back home where her own clothes hung in the closet. Maybe he was like Bobby, that shadowy husband, devoted to the notion of the happy family even as he shattered it with his own hands and his words and his dark, dark eyes. "I'm leaving you, Bobby," I'd said once after he'd grabbed me by the hair, and another time after he'd pushed me down, and another time, and another, and another. "No you're not, Fran," he'd said. Real flat, just the way Robert sounded sometimes. His father's son. Once when I wouldn't let Robert buy a game at the mall he'd pushed me away, hard, and I'd felt the echo of his father's big hands in his small ones. Robert had said he was sorry in the car on the way home. But Bobby always said he was sorry, too.

The venetian blinds were closed. The neighbors must think we're vampires. Or perhaps they're used to it. Perhaps all the women who lived for a time in this apartment kept their blinds down.

From a mailbox on a corner in Manhattan I had sent Grace an envelope of family photographs. Inside was a scribbled note: "Don't worry. We'll be fine." She must have gotten it by now. Her phone number sang in my skull as I stood in the small kitchen. And it was like I was still chained in a basement somewhere, only this time I'd just stay here forever, alone. I felt so alone that if I'd looked out the windows and seen nothing but black all around me, I wouldn't have been surprised. But upstairs my son was sleeping with a soft look on his face, a gentle curve to his mouth, that I hoped could someday be the legacy from me to him. And I was going to get through every day so he could have that. I ate stale cereal from the box with one hand and felt my face with the other. Bruise or no bruise, it still hurt deep in the bone, where only my fingers could find the damage. And all I could think was that if I hadn't gone to one particular Brooklyn bar on one particular night when I was just a kid myself, knew next to nothing about men or marriage or shame or pain, I wouldn't be where I was. But then I wouldn't have had Robert. And Robert was all I had that mattered.

I didn't begin a new life; it began me. A letter came informing me that Robert was enrolled at the local elementary school, that he would be in class 5-C and that he needed No. 2 pencils and a three-ring binder on the first day.

Together we walked through the flat, stifling streets of Lake Plata to stand and look at the school building. His school, I called it when Robert and I talked, but it seemed so strange to us both. The architecture was strange, and the plants and shrubs, too, so that there was nothing to remind us of our former life except each other. Robert even took my hand as we stood across the street from the school, a low stuccoed building ten minutes from our apartment, beige plaster, red tile roof, stunted palms at all four corners. P.S. Hacienda, I called it to myself. P.S. Taco Bell, grades K through 6. When I called the principal's office the secretary said they'd already received Robert's documents from his old school. It was all I could do not to ask them where that might have been, and whether he'd been a good student there. All Patty

Bancroft had told us, at the hospital, was that she had people working for her who were able to create paper trails. Work histories, school transcripts, passports. "I won't be more specific than that," she'd said.

A few days before school started Robert had taken out his black-and-white marbled composition book and sat down at the dinette table angled between the kitchen and the living room. I stood behind him as he wrote "Robert Crenshaw" in the little box that said "This book belongs to." I made him do a page of "Robert Crenshaw"s until I realized that it was like a punishment, like writing "I will not talk in class" 100 times, the way the nuns made Grace and I do when we were young. And he'd been so good, Robert—too good, I thought sometimes, going to bed as soon as I asked, although I'd been letting him stay up later than usual to keep me company, to keep the walls from bearing down on me and the sound of the moths batting against the screens from sounding too loud. I could tell that he thought if he was good enough I'd take him home. Maybe that's why he'd always been so quiet and clean as a kid. Maybe he figured if he was good enough his father wouldn't hit me anymore.

"This is kind of hard, isn't it, hon?" I'd said, looking over his shoulder. "A new school, new friends. Plus the name, and the story about where you're from and everything. I wish I'd come up with some other way to do it. But I couldn't. I'm sorry."

Robert silently put his composition book in his new backpack. School supplies, a backpack, a new polo shirt: the little wad of bills in the bottom of my bag was melting away. It was like my boy and I were playing a role in some phony TV show. Everything felt artificial. I went into the kitchen for a glass of water and stayed there for a minute, trying to figure out whether I could go through with it. The phone was on the wall. Grace would have plane tickets waiting in Tampa before dinner. I don't know what I might have done at that moment, if I hadn't stumbled and brought the glass up against one of my front teeth with a sound, a feeling, I never wanted to hear or feel again. I couldn't go back to Bobby now without Robert thinking that that was all right, that what would come afterward was the natural order of things. He'd traded one set of secrets for another. But this second set was nothing compared to the other.

"It's phonetic, Crenshaw," I said, handing him a cookie. "You can just sound it out. And you remember about Daddy not being a police officer, and not talking about New York or Grandmom or anything when you talk about family stuff. We're from Delaware. Are you sure you can remember that? It's that real teeny state on the map, the one just down from New Jersey."

"Mom," Robert said, "kids don't talk about that stuff that much. They don't talk about their last names or where they moved from that much. Only grown-ups talk about that stuff."

At times like that, I did count my blessings. We'd arrived only three weeks before school began, only three weeks of aimless summer emptiness for my son in this still-strange place, and those weeks filled by Bennie, who was to be in the same class with Robert. Once in a while I felt the presence of someone behind all this, moving us artfully around the chessboard of this strange expatriate life. For that I was grateful.

Children need structure. That had always been my motto, had been from the time I set up story time and park visits and bath before bed for Grace, when I was little more than a kid myself, my mother secretary to the head of the municipal worker's union, my father signing over his disability check the third of every month. Gracie and I left home at the same time every day, the redheaded Flynn girls, one carroty as a cartoon character, the bigger girl more auburn. "Knowledge," I'd say. "Unpleasant . . . mythic." Spelling words on Friday mornings before the test. Times tables on Tuesdays. And every afternoon, as we met on the corner, I'd say before anything else, "What'd you get?"

"A hundred," Grace almost always said, student outstripping teacher. Structure. With structure there was no room for doubt, mistakes, sadness, loneliness. Except occasionally, for me, at night, when I could tell by her breathing that Gracie had drifted off to sleep. Ah, Bobby. I was so ripe for you when I first saw you, saw you glowing in the darkness of that Brooklyn bar like a fire on a cold night.

Now Robert would have structure every day, the hours in school, the hour of homework, not too much time left over to think, to brood. He had Bennie to go with him on the bus every day and a poster of Don Mattingly in pinstripes over his flimsy bed upstairs. There would be sports teams to join and practices to fill the hours. Now only my own day would lie before me, less like a life than like the interruption of one, the part on an old record when it skipped, one chord over and over. When Bennie and Robert were playing upstairs I allowed myself one soap opera on television, an hour of family feuds, impossibly grand weddings, suggested sex. I took the boys on long trips to the Home Depot, a twenty-minute walk for a can opener and a pot holder. I counted my money at least twice a day. I was so worried about going broke that one day I picked up a job application from Kmart, then put it in a drawer in the kitchen, baffled by how to fill in the section on previous job experience. I bought a pack of index cards, intending to tack them up on the bulletin boards at the supermarkets: Will clean your house. But out on walks with Bennie and Robert, looking at the flat, cinder-block ranch houses and dolled-up aluminum-sided trailers planted on concrete slabs on the side streets, I wondered if anyone in Lake Plata could afford a house cleaner. And when I looked at the phone in our living room I saw that there was no number on the dial, and realized I knew no phone number to put on the index card, no number at which I could be reached. I would be reduced to asking for my own telephone number the next time I talked to Patty Bancroft.

My one luxury was a fat collected edition of some of Agatha Christie's mysteries that I picked up off a remainder table at the Job Lot store. I read while I listened to the spoken song of an afternoon radio talk-show host, who appeared to hate Hispanics, Democrats, and homosexuals in equal measure, but who enjoyed his hatred so much that it was almost a pleasure to hear. He always said the word *influx* as though it was gum and he was popping that *X* between his molars. Big John Feeney, his name was. I always turned him off when the boys came downstairs.

I still had $402 of the money I'd brought from home. From home. Would I ever learn to stop thinking that way?

"What if the principal at your new school is a giraffe . . ." I said the Friday before school began as Robert and Bennie were eating Blimpies, a special lunch I'd arranged as a treat, along with an hour at an arcade in a strip mall on the highway.

". . . and she keeps banging her head going into the classrooms . . ." Robert replied.

". . . so she wears a football helmet all the time . . ."

". . . and plays quarterback on the team, which has a winning season . . ."

Bennie was looking at us big-eyed, open-mouthed. "It's a game we play," Robert said. "My mom made it up. It's called 'What If?' "

"What if," I'd say to Grace Ann when she was on the swings, "we had a house in the country . . ."

". . . and I had a horse and you had a horse and Daddy had a big car with no roof . . ."

"A convertible, they call that. And what if we had a governess instead of school . . ."

". . . and she made us eat worms!"

Or, when we were older, walking to the bus stop, she on her way to Queen of Peace, I to nursing school: "What if you fell in love at the hospital with a doctor with blond hair and blue eyes . . ."

"And you fell in love with a writer with an apartment in the Village . . ."

"And you and your husband got the apartment next door to us and you both worked at St. Vincent's Hospital . . ."

"And you became a full professor at NYU . . ."

"What if," I said to Robert as he was eating his breakfast on the first day of school, "you went to school today . . ."

"And got the desk next to Bennie's . . ." he replied.

"And had a really really nice teacher who liked you a lot . . ."

"And got picked for the soccer team . . ."

"What if it turned out you really liked it here . . ."

"I have to go get Bennie or we'll miss the bus," Robert said, picking up his backpack.

Every first day of school he'd ever had I'd gone with him: carrying him whimpering into nursery school, walking hand-in-hand to first grade. Don't let anyone tell you New York is a big city. "I know you," said the cop outside P.S. 135 in Sheepshead Bay as we passed him on our way to St. Stannie's. "You look just like your dad."

"I know," Robert had said, so faintly you could scarcely hear him. The school at St. Stannie's was red brick, an unadorned box in the shadow of the Gothic church, all the flourishes and frills used up in the service of the tabernacle, the stained glass, and the carved limestone apse. The only thing distinguished about the school was a long brick pathway to its door. Robert had trudged up it on his way to Mrs. Civello's first-grade class, with that strange defenseless look a dress shirt gives a little boy, wheeled and run to me, holding tight to my legs, pressing his face into my belly. Then he'd turned and run inside, his navy uniform tie whipping around behind his skinny neck. Some of the other kids hadn't lost their baby fat yet, round thighs emerging from the plaid parochial-school skirts, bulbous cheeks above gap-toothed grins. But Robert was always a wraith, narrow and bony, a chest like a fledgling, his eyes taking up half his face.

By third grade I'd been ordered to stay half a block behind him, while he walked with Anthony and Sean and Paul and his other friends. But I'd never wanted to be with him so much as that first day of fifth grade in Lake Plata, and instead there was the yellow bus at the corner, on which no parents were allowed. Robert shoved Bennie into the seat by the window, so that he was even further away from me than the thin yellow skin of metal and glass. "It's vacation time for Mom," the bus driver shouted over the raucous sound of the engine and the kids.

" 'Bye, Mrs. Crenshaw," Bennie called, then turned away to talk to Robert.

I made it to the school building almost ten minutes before the bus did, and checked to see that no one was watching the school from the parking lot. I peered into the lobby, even looked around the corner down the hallways and saw nothing but the occasional teacher whisking by. I went back outside and stood behind a minivan across the street and waited for Robert's bus. The driver was a heavy woman in a Dolphins hat, who counted heads aloud as children spilled down the steps. Robert was the nineteenth, disappearing into a river of dark and light heads moving toward the doors. "And that's twenty-seven and I'm outta here," I heard the bus driver say. When she'd pulled out I could see the door of the school, could see a little girl in a pink dress being wrestled away from her mother and led wailing into the building by a man in khaki shorts and a polo shirt with a whistle around his neck. "She'll be fine," he called back to the mother, who was wiping her eyes. Another little boy had turned in the doorway to look back at his father, who was standing on the sidewalk with a video camera. The kid was squinting, one eye shut so tight that it pulled the rest of his face up into the kind of grimace I'd seen on stroke patients. People kept bumping into him, hurrying into the building.

"What do you want me to do now?" he said to his father.

"Wave and say 'good-bye,'" his father said.

"Good-bye," the kid said, without waving. He carried a lunch box shaped like a Mickey Mouse head, even though they served lunch at school. I knew because I'd asked Bennie a dozen times, finally satisfied when I saw the menu in the local paper. Today they were having chicken nuggets, green beans, and tapioca pudding.

"Jason is now officially in third grade," said the dad with the video camera in a phony weathercaster's voice. Next to him a knot of mothers were talking about overcrowding in the kindergarten.

"Poor Jason," said a woman who'd been standing next to me, shading her eyes with her hand.

"Dad goes a little overboard?" I said.

"They had to ban that sucker from the school with that camera of his," the woman said. She was wearing pink linen shorts and a matching blouse, white sunglasses, and pink nail polish. She sounded like an actress playing Blanche DuBois in summer stock, looked and smelled as though she'd groomed herself as pains-takingly for this morning as I had the morning I got married. A drawl and Diorissimo, or something that smelled a whole lot like it.

"First grade, he filmed Jason on his first field trip, Jason giving his report on alligators to the class, Jason trying out for peewee soccer, which, by the by, he's not real good at. Last year he tried to film Jason taking some standard reading test they were giving. I figure that was the last straw. He's not allowed inside the school with the camera anymore. Came close to suing, too, I heard, 'cause of infringement on his constitutional rights. Does the Constitution guarantee you the right to be a weenie?"

Both of us looked toward the school. The sun made such a glare on the windows that they looked like one-way mirrors; we couldn't see a thing. But I could feel Robert inside, feel him sit-ting at his new desk looking furtively around the room, trying to get used to this, trying to scope out who mattered and who didn't, who it was safe to approach and who would backhand him with a word, a look. I could feel him watching the teacher, trying to pay attention to what Mrs. Bernsen was saying while every hair on his body was vibrating to the atmosphere in the classroom the way the new kids' did. Or at least the way mine had when I'd been the new kid. And, along with it all, he'd have to remember his last name as though it was fractions, or division, something difficult he'd barely been introduced to. I could see Robert taking a test, writing in his crabbed script a capital *B* to begin his last name. I could see him erasing the *B*, his tongue snagged between his front teeth, writing a capital *C* instead.

Or maybe not. Maybe when you were a kid you were so unsure of yourself that every school year was a time of reinvention;

maybe only adults were stupid enough to think they knew exactly who they were. "Hi," I said over and over in my head sometimes in the morning as I was making coffee, or in the evenings as I fixed toast and eggs for dinner. "I'm Beth Crenshaw." I practiced writing it the way I'd once written "Mrs. Robert Benedetto" in the margin of my notebooks in nursing school.

"If a man who says he is Robert's father comes to the school, you have to call me immediately," I had said on the phone to the school secretary.

"We already know that, Mrs. Crenshaw," she said wearily, as though her entire life was made up of custody disputes and parents' paranoia. And again I felt an invisible hand at work. It was a hand that made it impossible for me to ask questions, for surely there would be something peculiar about a mother who didn't know who had given the school fair warning, about a mother who asked where her son's school records had come from and who had sent them, about a mother who asked the office, "By the way, do you know our phone number?" "Guardian angels" Patty Bancroft always called the members of her invisible nameless network, and I was grateful. But at times it felt less celestial than intrusive, almost suffocating, for other people to know more about me than I knew about myself. It was as though I existed in someone else's imagination. I glanced at the narrow-hipped, narrow-shouldered woman next to me in the parking lot, and wondered whether our conversation was accidental or whether the clothes I wore every day, those charity size eights, had once belonged to her.

"Beth Crenshaw," I said a little irritably, sticking out my hand, watching for a reaction.

"Oh," she said, "sorry. Cindy Roerbacker. You new?"

I nodded.

"What grade is your kid in?"

"Fifth."

"Which class?"

"Mrs. Bernsen."

"Good. Mrs. Jackson is an idiot. The sweetest woman in the world, but my two-year-old could teach her social studies."

"What about yours?"

"Fourth." She sighed. "Her name's Chelsea. My little one's Chad."

"Your husband Charlie?"

"Craig," she said. "Isn't it awful? I got carried away, and now I'm stuck with it. If we have another girl we'll have to name her Caitlyn, I guess." The man who'd led the screaming child into the school emerged from the double doors in front and walked halfway down the walk, looking from one end of the road to another. He was still wearing the whistle and carrying a clipboard, and his face was as flushed as my own.

"Vice principal," Cindy said, her arms folded on her chest. "Mr. Riordan. Nice man, but a little—" she whiffled a slender hand through the air like a bird. "Maybe not. I can't tell."

"You never can," I said, grinning. I remembered the day at the hospital I pulled an aide into the supply closet and gave her hell for telling one of her friends as they were unloading lunch trays that Dr. Silverstein smelled like a fairy. "Jesus," I said to my friend Winnie afterward, "if a man dresses nicely and has the littlest bit of drama about him, everyone has him written off as gay."

Winnie had patted my hand with her own, with its square nails and short fingers. "Fran, I love you dearly," she said, "but Dr. Silverstein's been living with an architect named Bill since he was in medical school. You need to pick your fights."

I missed Winnie, the head nurse in the emergency room at South Bay Hospital, who could calm a rape victim just by rubbing the back of the woman's hand as I combed her pubic hair for evidence, Winnie who made me feel afterward, as I cried in the bathroom, that I'd done good instead of harm. I missed Mrs. Pinto, our neighbor, who left Baggies full of ripe tomatoes on my steps during August and September and called Robert "handsome man," making his olive skin darken to a dull red-brown. And God, how I missed Grace, missed talking to her on the phone every blessed day, about her students, about my patients, about nothing at all, where to buy cheap sneakers, what mascara didn't irritate your eyes. "Where were you?" she'd say if she couldn't reach me in the morning. God, how she must miss me.

I wished I missed my mother more, but after my sister had gone away to college and my father had died, she'd moved in with her sister Faye and out of our lives into a life of day trips to factory outlets and Atlantic City, of communion breakfasts and bingo games. It was as though her marriage and children had been only a brief interlude in her real life, Marge and Faye, two sisters watching the Weather Channel and bickering about the verisimilitude of their girlhood memories. I had talked to my mother once a week, said less than I'd just said to Cindy Whatever-her-name-was, a complete stranger squinting at her watch in the merciless sun.

"You going to work?" she said.

I shook my head. "What about you?"

"Not until this afternoon," she said. "I sell Avon part-time. In this weather the lipsticks melt half the time. Sometimes I keep everything in the fridge—they don't like it if you do that, but darned if I can sell cream blush that's as soupy as paint." She sniffed down the front of her blouse. "Lord, I wish I could get inside into the AC. The first year with Chelsea I had to sit in the kindergarten for half the day and then sneak out when she was at music. That's how I wound up doing PTA. First grade we tried to make her go cold turkey, but she cried so hard I had to stay out in the hall where she could see me at least until circle time. Second and third grade I stayed around for the first hour until January. Volunteered in the library and all that. This year, I said, Chelse, honey, it's time to cut the cord. But she asked me to stay outside where she could see me out the window for just half an hour the first day. Craig said, first it's half an hour, next thing you know it'll be until lunch. I don't know." She shrugged. "Do you think I'm crazy?"

"Nah," I said. "It's hard being a kid, never mind a mother. I can't ever figure out whether I'm doing things because they're good for him or because they make me feel better."

"That's it in a nutshell," she said, fanning herself with her hand. "Although I'm still wondering where she got all this fear stuff from. Like she'll ask whether you can get your shoelaces caught in the escalator at the mall. They'll be earthquakes or tornadoes on television and she wants to know where you could stand or how you could hide to get away." She shielded her eyes and looked toward the school. "Our house got struck by lightning once, when Chelsea was three. All it did was char the side of the chimney, but who knows with kids what sticks in their minds? You have one of those real fearless boys?"

I shrugged. "He's a boy. He keeps his fears inside."

She nodded. "Boys," she said, and I looked at her, at her glossy dark hair and painted nails, and wondered what she'd say if I replied, Yeah, that and the fact that his father used to beat the shit out of me and he figures he'd better be quiet and nice or the whole world will blow up. What would she say if I replied, Your kid wants to see a natural disaster, she should have seen my face after the last fight?

What if, I thought to myself, I'm talking to myself the rest of my life? What if I can never say what I'm thinking to anyone ever again? I looked back at the school building, and then grabbed Cindy by the arm. "What?" she said, and turned to see the two patrol cars, white and red and blue, pull up outside the school. Men in uniforms were stepping out of the cars, loping up the path and into the building, stopping just inside the door to talk with the man in the khaki shorts. Telling him, telling him. Next, one of the cops would pull a photograph from his breast pocket, the picture of Robert taken last year at St. Stannie's, sitting on the steps beneath the statue of the Blessed Mother, wearing the same polo shirt he'd worn as we traveled from New York to Lake Plata. I'd given a copy of it to my mother-in-law; she kept it in a gilt frame on her bedside table, with the tissues and the Sominex. I could see her handing it to Bobby, see him taking it into the photo shop to have copies made, see him finger his big lower lip as he tried to figure how best to deal with me when he found us.

The men were moving inside; I could almost see the three of them bent over a sheaf of manila folders in the office. I imagined them looking through the files for new students, walking to the fifth grade classroom, seeing Robert, whispering to the teacher, taking him out of class. It all came to me, like one of those flip books Robert had gotten for Christmas, all the little pictures moving fast, making a story, the story of the beginning of the end of my life.

"What are those two cops doing going into the school?" I said. The only woman in America terrified at the sight.

"They always come here the first day," Cindy said. "They talk to the kids about not talking to strangers, not taking a ride from anyone, only going with someone you know, the usual." She squinted across the lot. "That one's Officer Bryant, I think. I don't know about you, but I hate knowing the police are younger than I am."

"You're sure?"

"Positive," she said. "He's a good ten, twelve years younger than I am. The other one, I can never remember his name, but he's even younger than that." She looked at me. "Are you okay? You want to have a cup of coffee?"

It sounds stupid, saying how I felt at that moment. Maybe it was the sheer chemical relief, the balloon deflating in my stomach, the buzz subsiding in my head. Maybe it was knowing that the police officer would see my boy as nothing more than another face in a crowd of children and that this woman saw me as nothing more remarkable than one of the moms. Maybe it was the way Cindy talked about her daughter, that combination of fear, ego, and love that oozes out of a good mother like perspiration when the kids are small, the fuel that had stoked my fires for a decade. Or just the way she stuck one pinkie under the white sunglasses to wipe away a raccoon circle of mascara from beneath one blue eye. Maybe it was that cornpone accent, so different from my own. Or the sense of relief I felt knowing that the police were there to tell the kids to be careful, although the attentions of a stranger toward my boy took a distant second place to my fear of a rental car parked at the corner and his father with his arm right-angled out the driver's side window, saying "Hey, buddy," in that rich, persuasive voice.

Or maybe it was me remembering female friendship, what I had with Winnie and with Gracie, too, as much friend as sister. What I had with Bridget Foley in elementary school, until her

parents moved to the Island, and with Dee Stemple in high
school. I hadn't had too much of it; I'd never been the kind of girl
who traveled with a big boisterous pack. Maybe that's why I'd
been pulled so powerfully toward Bobby, because there was always a circle around him, faces turned toward his, listening,
looking, laughing. I'd had too much to do always, filling jelly
doughnuts at the bakery to earn money for nursing school,
helping Grace with her papers, taking my father in a taxi to the
doctor's office, waiting for a plumber when the heat cut out on a
January day. But I'd always had one good girlfriend, and looking
at Cindy Roerbacker, hearing her easy confidences, I remembered how much that friendship had meant to me, that way you
could just open your mouth, sitting on a bench in the park, lying
across your twin bed, standing over a sink in the girls' room,
pulling the phone into the closet—just open your mouth and let
your whole self out, all those small mosaic pieces of self that felt
barely held together with plaster of personality half the time.
And then it had been wrecked for me by Bobby, who didn't like
my girlfriends, called Dee a tramp, Winnie a dyke, Grace a
bleeding heart, and who gave me a secret so big that it might as
well have sat in the middle of the friendship like a wild animal,
ready to tear it apart.

"So how's Bobby?" someone would say.

"Good. Good. Fine. Busy, you know?"

"Everything okay?"

"Sure. Everything's fine."

So much of my life was stuck in my throat like a bone, and I
could never, ever let it out. But I had gotten used to that. Bobby
had given me one secret about who I really was, and now I had
another. Or Fran Benedetto had a thing she couldn't tell, not over

a beer, a burger, a cup of coffee. But Beth Crenshaw could talk about her life all she liked. Lies were so much easier than the truth. Maybe I'd be good at this.

It was clear to me in only a few minutes that our meeting was chance, that Cindy wasn't a Patty Bancroft construct. In the minivan she said her best friend had moved to California over the summer, commiserated with me over the difficulty of divorce, apologized for the juice box and the cracker wrapper beneath my seat. In her kitchen she made decaf and put out a plate of mini-muffins, and something about the way she talked and laughed and sometimes stared out the sliding doors to the deck and the pool told me that she needed company as much as I did. Her life sounded more like an itinerary than an existence, Gymboree with Chad two mornings a week, lunch every Wednesday for the se-niors at the Baptist Church, Chelsea's ballet and gymnastics, Sunday school, selling Avon. But it seemed like the patches stretched a little long once she got back here to her own kitchen table.

"I got a bunch of stuff I cleaned out of Craig's mom's house when they moved to a condo," she said. "It's just sitting in the basement, if you're short anything. Curtains or chairs or what-ever. I had a girlfriend from high school, she was so busy holding on to the big pieces, the armoire and the entertainment center, that she didn't even notice till after her husband was gone that she hadn't saved one single chair. She was standing around in her own place for the better part of a week."

"It's all right," I said.

"Sure, now?" Cindy said. "There's a mess of stuff down there. Go look if you want. Some of it's real nice. Well, not *real* nice, but presentable. And clean. Craig's mother's a real clean person."

Our kids give us courage, I think. The only way I'd gotten through Robert's first day of first grade had been to remember the stalwart set of those little shoulders, and the thing that kept me in my seat during soccer games when the coach yelled at him was the dignified way he'd lift his bony pointed chin. And I thought of how he'd refused to let me unearth his fears about a new school, a new name, a new life, of how he'd decided to swim in alone in the stream of children I'd seen that morning, with only Bennie and his backpack as life preservers. He was beginning a life, a life as Robert Crenshaw, making a place for himself. And so would I. Goddamn Bobby Benedetto, so would I. Maybe I was supposed to hide behind my blinds, to make myself invisible. Maybe that was what Patty Bancroft thought would be safest. Maybe that was what most of the women did. Not me. I'd changed my hair and my clothes, my name and my address, so that I could live, really live. I needed a job, and a friend, and a shot at changing that closed-up little apartment, with its thin carpeting and colorless couch, into someplace that seemed like people lived there, lived ordinary uneventful lives.

"Actually," I said, "I could use some curtains."

"Couldn't we all?" said Cindy Roerbacker, laying on the drawl plenty thick, her eyes bright, smile big, a smudge of lipstick on her teeth. "Girl, let's decorate."

Robert started his second week of school, liked the kids, liked his teachers, slept less, spoke more, although not as much as another kid would have done. And I splurged on a gallon of butter-yellow paint, to mark a month in Lake Plata, living through it, learning to let some of the fear out of the tight muscles in my shoulders. That's how small the living room of the apartment was: one gallon of paint was enough. I'd hung a sampler in the kitchen that I'd found in Cindy's basement: in cross-stitch it said, "May you be in heaven an hour before the devil knows you're dead." Mrs. Roerbacker's old multicolored afghan hung over the back of the couch, and some throw pillows were plumped up at either end. From Cindy's basement I'd taken an old oak rocker, a seascape in a maple frame, a chenille spread with blue and yellow pompons, a set of café curtains with cherries printed on them, and some drapes with stripes so bright they made you dizzy. "You sure about those?" Cindy said when we put them in the back of the minivan. She didn't try to patronize me when she helped me carry all the stuff into the apartment on Poinsettia Way. She just looked around and nodded as though it was what you could expect from a divorce, a dislocation. That's how she was, realistic but never grim. "You can work with this," she said. It didn't take long to paint the place, it was so tiny. But when I was done with the downstairs it looked like a feature in a woman's magazine on decorating on a budget. Except that the venetian blinds were still closed tight. The overhead light stayed on all day.

"It looks different in here," Robert said when he came home from school and dropped his backpack on the table.

"You don't like it?"

"It looks different." At dinner he slumped over his buttered spaghetti, mumbling. School was fine. Bennie was fine. Mrs. Bernsen was fine. The spaghetti was fine. *Fine* is a kid's way of telling you he doesn't want to talk. I'd watched parents ignore that in the emergency room; fine, fine, fine, the kid would say, and Mom and Dad would probe deeper, like dentists with those little sharp silver instruments. Kids used *fine* as the Novocain.

"It smells like paint in here," Robert said.

"The smell'll be gone in a day or two."

"I guess if you painted we're going to stay," he finally mumbled. His voice was hollow, deep, with grace notes of tears.

"It'll get better, Ba. You'll see. You'll make more friends, play sports, figure out the fun things to do around here. Maybe once I get a job we'll find a bigger place."

"Can I write to Anthony?"

"No," I said. I rubbed my hand along his arms. There was yellow paint around my cuticles, faint autumn moons. "This is really hard, I know. You're being so good about everything. And maybe someday things will be different. I don't know yet."

"I have homework," he said.

"I know, Ba, but I want to talk for a while."

"I want to do my homework first."

We sat together on the couch after dinner, watching situation comedies, families fighting and making up in the span of a single half-hour, while an unseen audience laughed at everything they said or did. Direct conversation had never been the way to engage Robert; I had always had to wait through the silences for his words to swim up at me. It was like the time Bobby and I had spent a week in the Bahamas and gone snorkeling off a steep reef, how the bright fish would appear from the dark navy shadows of the sea, dart past, disappear. That's how Robert's words were, small pretty fish swimming up at me and then disappearing into the depths. After we put our dishes in the sink, two cheap china plates, two forks, a saucepan, Robert sat next to me, my arm around him. From the time he was a little boy he had rubbed a strand of my hair idly against his cheek when we sat side by side. It was an automatic tic, a habit like thumb-sucking or nail-biting; it had driven Bobby nuts. "It's fucking weird, Fran," he said. Now that my hair was short Robert couldn't do it anymore, but I dipped my head down close to him, so that at least my hair was near, so he could smell it, sense it. I was letting it grow a little bit, as much as was safe.

"Bennie's parents came from Cuba," he said, his eyes bright in the glow of the TV.

"A lot of people came here because the government was bad for them. A lot of them came to Florida. It's the farthest south you can go in the United States before you get to Cuba."

"His mother can't speak English that much. Like Mrs. Pinto, the way she mainly spoke Italian."

"It's really hard to learn a new language if you're older."

"Jonathan in our class says people in America should only speak English. That's stupid. Everybody in Brooklyn speaks another language. Or lots of people."

"I wish Bennie would teach me some Spanish."

"How come you don't know Italian?"

I shrugged. "I know how to say 'What a beautiful face' because every lady in the neighborhood used to say that about you when you were a baby." He wasn't looking at me but I could see that he was smiling slightly.

"Jonathan says he has a pool in his backyard."

"The lady I had coffee with the other day, the one I told you has a girl in fourth grade? They have a pool, too."

"Above ground or in ground?"

"What?"

"Jonathan said his pool is in ground. He said above ground pools were cheap."

"The lady I met, Mrs. Roerbacker, her pool is sort of both. Because it's built into the deck in back of their house but it's sort of above the yard. You'll see. She wants you to come swimming."

"Jonathan is kind of a jerk," Robert said, leaning into my shoulder, his hooded eyes at half-mast, black onyx glinting from beneath the lids and the heavy fringe of lashes.

I could hear his breathing deepen, could hear the second hand of the old kitchen clock jerking around, hear the faint sound of a car out on Poinsettia. Both of us started to nod off. Sleep had become a refuge in which, for at least a few hours, the world seemed less uncertain. Both of us, I think, could imagine that we were still where we belonged. Or had once belonged. Maybe Robert dreamed of everyday life, dreamed of those mornings when he'd come downstairs to the sunshine splashed across the linoleum in the blue-and-white kitchen in Brooklyn, on one of those mornings when Daddy was eating bacon and eggs, pushing his food around the plate with a half piece of toast, and Mommy was standing at the stove with not a mark on her.

"No offense, Mom," Robert has said several times, trying to make things the way they used to be, "but you look better without glasses."

Both of us flinched when the phone rang. The sound seemed so loud, so strange in the quiet room, and we stopped as though we were playing "Red Light, Green Light," and whoever was It had wheeled around to catch us moving. But I was paralyzed, not so much by the sound, but by the look on Robert's face. It was transfigured by a combination of hope and fear so strange and strong that it made me want to look away, the way you look away when someone's weeping. I did not know who was on the phone, but I knew who Robert imagined it was.

"Answer it, Mommy," he finally said.

There was the sound of background noise: the screech and honk of a public address system, the sharp *bing* as coins hit the insides of a pay phone, the insect clicks as the phone recognized and accepted the payment. *Clang, clang, click:* I knew who was on the other end. Patty Bancroft always says she fears any attempt to trace her women. That's what she calls them, her women, as though she oversees a harem, or is a madam in a bordello. My body must have relaxed at the noises, for when I looked up at Robert I could see by his face, blank again, that he knew it was not his father on the phone. "Christ, does that kid know how to read you," Bobby had said sometimes. Sometimes I thought he was jealous, when he said that.

"We've arranged a job for you, Elizabeth," Patty Bancroft said, as someone called a flight in the background.

"Beth," I replied.

"Pardon?" said Patty Bancroft.

"Beth. Beth Crenshaw."

A silence. "All right, then," she said. "We've arranged a job for you, Beth. As a home health-care aide. Unfortunately you can't work as a nurse without a nursing license, and that was difficult to arrange. This was as close as we could get. The wages aren't bad. No benefits, sorry to say, but it's the best we could do. They'll call tomorrow."

"Thank you," I said. "I wondered. I'm going a little crazy here, with nothing to do."

"You must be patient," she said. "We know how to do this."

"I don't even know my own phone number," I added.

"Well, that was an oversight." She read the numbers to me slowly. "Don't give it to more people than you must," she added.

Secrecy, Patty Bancroft had said when she came to speak at the hospital, was the hallmark of her organization. No stray piece of paper, no phone number, no newspaper clipping, could give her volunteers away as they spirited women out of their own homes and into the anonymous America where Robert and I were now living. Along the main stretch of highway in Lake Plata, or what I've seen of it without a car, is a Burger King, a storage place, a drive-through bank, a Taco Bell, an International House of Pancakes, an enormous supermarket with a salad bar just inside the automatic doors, a Toys 'R' Us, a Kmart, and a Home Depot. The only way I'm certain we're in Florida is the license plates on the cars; otherwise it might be September in Colorado or California or either of the Carolinas. Generic America, 97° and sunny. "Thank you for stopping at Burger King," says an older man with a Spanish accent when I take Robert out for lunch every

Saturday, hoping that the sameness of the bun, the burger, the decor, the logo, the greeting, will make this strange and unfamiliar life feel less strange, more familiar.

"Is there anybody who lives in Florida who's really from Florida?" I said to Cindy as we sipped at decaf.

"Well, me, actually," she said apologetically, as though it was a character defect.

Secrecy, Patty Bancroft had told us at the hospital, is the secret of her success. I know all about keeping secrets. There is no one in the world who knows the topography of my injuries, who knows all the secrets of my body. There is no one in the world who knows that my husband twisted my wrists, pushed me down the stairs, broke my collarbone, and, finally, my nose. Not my mother, who seemed to lose interest in me after I married, as though I was her responsibility only until I could be handed on to someone else. Not my sister, who saw me only when I could arrange it, which is to say when I could lift a sandwich without wincing. Not my friend Winnie, although she had treated more women like me than either of us could count. Only Bobby knows it all, but he always said I exaggerated. Mountain out of a molehill. That's one of his favorite expressions.

My son knows some of it, but he knows it in his own peculiar way, in some closed-up closed-down corner of his mind. I'm afraid over the years he's developed a strange kind of color blindness. At some point he stopped being able to see black and blue.

Secrecy, secrecy. As I listen to the sound of her voice on the phone I can picture Patty Bancroft adjusting the triple strand of pearls she wears on TV, wore that day at the hospital, that hide the lines around her neck and complement her pretty pink-and-white skin. Winnie had invited her to South Bay in February to talk to the senior staff. We'd had three women die in our emergency room in a single year. One had fallen out of a window when her boyfriend came at her with a box cutter, another had had a bottle broken over her head by her husband, and a third had been shot with a Saturday night special by a man she'd divorced the year before. All three women had had restraining orders against the men who finally killed them, legal papers saying that the men had to keep away. Maybe they were the last three women in New York to know what all emergency-room nurses know, and cops' wives know, too: that restraining orders are a joke, made, as they say, to be broken. One of the tabloids did a big story about the three women, about the hospital and what it had done for them, and what it had failed to do.

"Here's a story about the hospital," Bobby had said, shoveling in his eggs before going out on an undercover narcotics assignment. He'd sipped at his coffee, glanced up and seen the look on my face, thrown the paper down and then his fork, too, so that it skipped across the surface of the china and landed tines down on the tablecloth. "You take yourself too fucking seriously, Frannie," he'd said, putting on the army camouflage jacket he wore when he was supposed to be a druggie. "You didn't used to be like that."

God, how many conversations I had with Bobby Benedetto inside my own head, so many words bouncing around, fighting, dying to get out and instead dying on the vine like one of the squash he planted in our little backyard after the black bugs got to them. I didn't used to be like that because you didn't used to hit me quite so hard, Bob, I'd say silently. I didn't used to be like that because I didn't have to call in sick or stay away from my own sister, with her sharp eyes and sharp mind. Or see my son look at a welt on my arm, a welt like the shadow of a hand, and see the question form in his mind and watch as he shoved it back into the closet where he keeps his fear of his father and his fears for his mother. And for himself.

Talking to myself, always talking to myself. I didn't used to be like that when I was younger, Bob, twenty and twenty-one and full of dreams and plans and love, because the good times overwhelmed the bad and your hands were gentle more often than they pushed and jabbed. You'd take me out to that restaurant on City Island and you'd talk to me, not about anything important, just like you thought I was your friend. You'd tell me about the lady you met who'd been standing naked, all 320 pounds of her, in her kitchen on a hot, hot New York City afternoon when some young guy with burglary tools tried to climb in her window. When you told her to cover up she said, "Well, I figured I shouldn't be touching nothing at the scene of the crime." And we'd laugh until the tears ran down our cheeks into our shrimp fra diavolo. Or you'd tell me how you shoved some punk up against the wall, a kid who'd grabbed a television set from the old Jewish man who'd said he'd never move his appliance store from the old neighborhood, and how you'd discovered the punk had enough warrants to really put him away, not like the other times, the times when you finished your paperwork and then cruised by the projects and saw the guy you'd busted just sitting out by the hydrant with a big smile on his face. And I'd look at you, with your dark skin and eyes and heavy brows and big bottom lip, the inside the color of a red grape, and think what I'd thought when Tommy Dolan introduced us at that bar down by the water my first year in nursing school, when I was nineteen, when Tommy said, "You got to meet Frannie Flynn. Everybody likes her." I'd think that you were the best-looking man I'd ever seen.

And, maybe seeing that thought in my eyes, seeing yourself in my eyes, so big and strong and sure of himself, that Bobby

Benedetto, always a crowd around him at the bar, listening to his
stories, buying him drinks—seeing yourself like that in my eyes,
you'd take my hand across the table. And you'd even listen to a
few of my stories, too. Although that stopped after a while; you
gradually stopped listening and I stopped talking the last couple
of years, when you were so angry all the time instead of just occasionally. When you'd been passed over for a couple of promo-
tions and there hadn't been another baby, when you'd wrecked
one car and talked your way out of a DWI, given a free ride by
the two young cops at the scene after they saw your badge. A
thousand small disappointments, a half dozen big ones, and you'd
stopped talking about the people trying to keep their sons out of
trouble in the projects, the teenage girls taking good care of their
babies, and started talking all the time about the spics and the jigs,
the people you busted and I patched up. They live like animals,
you'd say, and you'd look around our house, with the flowered
couches and the flowered drapes and the flowered canisters lined
up on the kitchen counter, flour, sugar, coffee, tea. You always
liked things to be so neat, just like at your mother's. "The baby's
got fingerprints all over this coffee table," you yelled upstairs
one Sunday morning before your friends were coming over for
football and lasagna. "You know where to find the Windex," I
yelled back.

What possessed me? What possessed me, after the guys were
gone, to say, "When Jackie Ferrin chews, you can hear him in the
next room."

"Jackie's a good man," you said.

"He still eats like a pig."

"Yeah, God forbid anyone should offend your ears, huh,
Fran? Plus he scratches himself sometimes, right? That's it, let's
take him off the guest list. Jackie Ferrin's got God knows how

many goddamn decorations for bravery, but he scratches his balls and chews with his mouth open."

"I'm going to bed," I'd said. "I'll do the dishes in the morning."

"We'll have roaches all over the goddamn kitchen. And with the new carpeting we got no money left over for an exterminator."

And on, and on, and on, about nothing, until finally he shoved me into the kitchen table so hard I fell and cracked my collarbone. "Jesus Christ, Fran, I was just a little lit," he said the next day, but it was past the time when he would take me in his arms to say it. The Bobby he saw in my eyes now was no hero. My eyes had become a funhouse mirror that reflected back a grotesque. For two weeks he laid off the beer and came home early from work. He even took Robert out a couple of times by himself. "The boys'll go to the park and give Mom a rest," he said. Things were good there for almost a year. It was my first broken bone; I think maybe that scared him. But I knew he'd try again, and again, and yet again to wipe that look off my face, that reflection of himself in my eyes.

"Women who have had this happen need to understand that domestic violence has nothing to do with them, with what they did or didn't do," Patty Bancroft had told the hospital auditorium full of doctors and nurses, advising them on how to treat their patients, how to get them help. It was like listening to an oncologist give a case history when you were rotten with cancer. I spent so many nights listening to the sound of Bobby's breathing in the dark and trying to figure out what had happened, whether it was his mother or his father, Robert's birth or envy over the big collar some other guy had made. Or the booze. Or the raise I got that meant I was making $900 more than he was every year, 900 lousy dollars they could have back at the hospital for all I cared.

"Hey, Frances Ann," he said, doing our taxes at the desk in the little den overlooking the alley behind the house, "you make more money than I do." And a shiver went all through me. I could read his voice as well as I could read an X ray.

I think that was the night I realized I could never merely divorce or leave him the way other women could leave their husbands, knew he would never let me go. I was packing Robert's school lunch, making a peanut-butter sandwich with no jelly, quartering an apple, and he was sitting at the kitchen table, drinking a beer.

"What, the kid can't eat an apple like everyone else?" he said, watching me.

"He likes it cut up."

"You baby him." That's what Bobby always said about Robert. "You baby him."

The phone rang, I remember, and he sighed because he thought it was someone from work, and it was, but mine, not his. "Hey, nurse," Ben Samuels had said. That's how he always greeted me, at the hospital. Hey, nurse. Hey, doctor. He was a good doctor. He always touched the patients when he talked to them. He always looked into their eyes.

"Hi," I said, looking at Bobby.

"Remember that book on spiritual healing we talked about a couple of weeks ago?" Ben Samuels said. "There's a documentary about it on PBS tonight. In about a half an hour. I thought you'd like to take a look at it."

"Thanks," I said. "See you tomorrow." I could tell by the silence that he was puzzled by my brusqueness. I had my back to Bobby as I hung the phone up. Every phone call was like espionage by that time.

"That was Winnie," I said. "About some documentary on spiritual healing on TV at ten."

"What the hell is spiritual healing?"

"The idea that the power of the mind can overcome illness as effectively as medical treatment. We've been talking about it at the hospital."

"Sounds like bullshit to me," Bobby said. He went to the refrigerator, opened another beer, rubbed against me as he went back to the table and sat back down, lifted his beer in the Bobby Benedetto patented lift, drank deep. His sweat smelled like beer at night, his sweat and his breath. He looked up at me. "Who did you say that was?" he said.

"Winnie."

"It didn't sound like Winnie from where I was sitting."

At ten I turned on the television and sat down on the couch. Bobby dropped into his lounge chair. "Give me the remote, Fran," he said. He had another beer in his hand. Two minutes of narration and he shook his head. "Can the human mind control the human body?" said a voice, and Bobby switched to the Sports Channel. Ah, what a rare pair we were.

"I'm going to bed," I said.

"You didn't really want to watch that shit, did you?" he called after me.

"Actually, I did."

"Bring me another beer, all right, Frances?"

I carried another bottle of Bud into the living room, leaving fingerprints on the icy bottle.

"You couldn't open it?"

"For God's sakes, Bobby, it's a twist-off cap. Even if it wasn't, you could probably get it off without an opener."

"What the hell is that supposed to mean?" I'd carried the empty back into the kitchen and didn't answer. When I turned from the trash he was standing in the doorway. He looked good when he was drunk. I'd noticed it when he was younger. His eyes glittered and his mouth went slack in a way that had once made me warm and willing and now made me very, very careful. Most of the time.

"Who'd you say that was on the phone?" he asked.

"Oh, for Christ's sake, Bob," I began.

"Oh, for Christ's sake what, Fran?" he said in that low, slow voice, his eyelids at half-mast. He put down the bottle and moved in on me, and I didn't know which was worse, my first thought— that he was going to make me do it in the kitchen, pressed back against the edge of the white Formica countertop—or my second, that he wasn't going to be able to do it himself. I could feel that he couldn't, could feel him feeling it.

"You need to put a little weight on, Fran," he'd said, pushing against me. "You're nothing but skin and bones." He kissed me hard, more holding my mouth down with his face than a kiss. I couldn't breathe, and I tried to slide my face away from his but he had a hand at the back of my neck, and finally I had to push him, had to, I was suffocated, smothered, fighting for air. He tried to push his mouth back down on mine, although I was gasping, and I slid sideways and he fell forward, bumping his chin into the cabinet door. It was like one motion, the fingers lifted to his own face, the backhand to mine, so that I fell and cut my head on the pointed corner of the cabinet by the window, felt the blood warm in my hair and on my neck.

When I'd imagined marriage, when I was standing at the altar of St. Stannie's the week after I'd turned twenty-one, I'd never imagined staring at the ceiling, the back of my hair matted with blood, willing my husband to get done and get off.

We'd written our own vows: "I will follow you," Bobby said, his voice making it sound as though it was in bold italics, "to the ends of the earth." And he would. I knew it as he snored beside me that night, he smelling of Budweiser, me of blood.

That night I got pregnant again, but I lost the baby after four months, and for a week he gave me a massage every night, working the muscles in my shoulders with his strong hands, straddling my body. Maybe it's hard to understand, for a woman who has never had it happen to her, never watched her husband sob in contrition with those choking sobs that sound like he's swallowing glass. He made me feel cared for, Bobby did, at times like that, cared for the way no one had ever cared for me. Babied the way I'd never been babied, even by my own parents. He reached me somehow, reeled me back in, rolled me over and said, "I love you so much, sweetheart," and touched me so softly all over that I reached for him, although the doctor said to wait, and got pregnant again. And lost that one, too. For the best. For the best.

When we were dating, I thought it would stop when we were married. When we were married, I thought a baby would help. After the baby, I thought if we had another child he'd feel better. And when Robert was two I couldn't leave because those were the formative years, although maybe I didn't think enough about what we were forming, Bobby and I. And when Robert was starting school I couldn't leave because school was a big adjustment. And I couldn't leave in May because I'd screw up our family summer vacation, and I couldn't leave in November because it would screw up the holidays. So I stayed, and stayed, and stayed.

And then those three women were killed, and when I read their stories I realized that all of them had left, the way everyone expects you to when he hits you, beats you up. They filed the papers, got the restraining orders, said, "No more." But two had been enticed back, over and over again, and one had never managed to get away even after the divorce. Her husband had kicked in the apartment door, showed up at her office, grabbed her at the bus stop in front of a dozen witnesses who watched him lay into her. Then finally killed her. All dead, all three of them, even though they left, even though they tried to break away. They were the ones who wound up broken. And I could hear Bobby's voice, begging, begging, breaking me down. And I could see him following me on my morning run, sitting three seats away on the bus to the hospital, talking Robert into letting him into the house. That's when I realized that I wasn't going to be able to leave the way other women left their husbands. I wasn't going to be able to leave at all. I was going to have to disappear.

I looked around the apartment as Patty Bancroft talked. Maybe, then, this was the ends of the earth. But at least it had curtains.

"They'll give you uniforms," Patty Bancroft said about my new job after she'd fed more quarters into the phone.

"Do they know?" I said.

"What?"

"Do they know who I am?"

"They know you're Elizabeth Crenshaw," said Patty Bancroft. "You have excellent references. There's no licensing requirement in Florida. It's one reason you're there. They'll send you out on a case or two next week."

"Beth," I said. "I've decided on Beth."

"Everything will be fine, Beth," she said, "if you do what we say."

"You sound like my husband."

"Excuse me?"

"You sound like my husband. Everything will be fine if you do what I say."

There was a silence in which I could hear people talking and laughing, walking through what must have been an airport on their way to somewhere else, traveling, not fleeing. "Make no mistake about it," Patty Bancroft said. "He is looking for you right now."

Scut work was what the agency gave me, work for an orderly, not a nurse. Cooking, cleaning, shopping. But it was fine. It was wonderful. Places to go, people to see. My first visit was to a thirty-year-old woman with cerebral palsy in a blank-faced apartment complex for the handicapped. Her name was Jennifer, and she told me what she needed by tapping on the keyboard of a computer with a long straight stick harnessed to her quivering hand. She looked like a bird, her head rising and falling as though she was eating instead of just telling me what she wanted to eat, her eyes rolling above a slack mouth that appeared to smile. "Instant oatmeal," she wrote my first day. "Quart skim milk. Jell-O pudding cups, chocolate. TY." TY for thank you.

She said it, too, although it sounded more like a growl or a throat clearing than a word. When I came back with the groceries I could hear the printer attached to her computer humming. After I'd changed the sheets on the single bed in the tiny back room, she used the stick to point to a stack of papers in the printer tray. Eleven pages of painstaking notes, including dates of all her hospitalizations. The first sentence was "My name is Jennifer Ann March, and I was born in Atlanta, Georgia, at 6:14 AM on Tuesday, November 7, 1967. The attending obstetrician was not available and an obstetrical resident, Dr. Gregory Littel, performed the delivery with high forceps."

"The forceps," I said aloud, not really meaning to, and she made the growling noise again and bobbed her head, as if to say, yes, yes, that's why I am the way you see me today, because of damage done by the forceps and the resident. If not for those high forceps I would be a thirty-year-old woman playing tennis at the public courts and working evenings as a waitress at Daisy's on the highway. Or maybe, given the intelligence and diligence of the medical history I held in my hands, a thirty-year-old woman finishing her doctoral dissertation on single-celled organisms or nineteenth-century chamber music. Everyone needs a way of making sense of their deformities, and a difficult birth was as good a way as any of explaining CP, of explaining to herself why she was slumped sideways, imprisoned in her own body, proffering these single-spaced pages as a way to make me see her as human.

"Is this for me?" I asked, and her head bobbed again. On her computer screen words appeared like magic, messages from people jousting with one another verbally in a chat room. "The meteor showers this weekend were stupendous," said the last line on the screen. "From Manitoba they looked like silver fireworks."

"I'm going now," I said. "I'll be back Tuesday. Can I bring anything with me?"

Her wobbly head swayed from side to side. Her hair was cut short, perhaps an inch long all over; I knew a nurse dressed her in the mornings. Count your blessings, my father always said. It shames you, to count yours by the hardships of other people. That noise again, deep in her throat.

"You're welcome," I said, closing the door behind me, stepping outside into the heat.

Maybe Patty Bancroft was right; maybe Bobby was looking for me even as I put pudding and milk into Jennifer's refrigerator. But I was looking for him right back. I walked to my jobs by a different route each time, peering into parked cars, turning around if someone came up slowly behind me. Cindy and I volunteered in the school library for the first hour of every day; she could tell Chelsea she was in the building and I could keep an eye on Robert and on the door to the school, just opposite the library double doors. We traded in sweating in the parking lot for reshelving and covering books under the querulous direction of old Mrs. Patrinian, who called each of us "Mommy." The school secretary got to know me, to expect to see me around. "If Robert has any problems, you'll call?" I asked one day when I brought her an iced tea from the cafeteria. "Absolutely," she said, tapping an envelope of Sweet'n Low into her cup with a long nail painted pink and white.

Most days Cindy and I had coffee after, unless Chad had Gymboree. "All first-time moms, who talk about the baby falling off the bed like it's the *Titanic*," she said dismissively. "If I hear one more debate about putting tubes in for ear infections, I will spit." Then we went to work. Cindy loaded her black imitation leather display cases into the minivan and I went to see my patients. There was Jennifer twice a week, and a dialysis patient from the local hospital named Melvin, whose skin was as yellow as margarine. He never even looked away from the television as I took his blood pressure and listened to his heart. He watched the stock ticker on the financial network and made notes on a legal pad. "He's not taking this well," said his wife. He was a long-distance trucker waiting for a kidney transplant. In the meantime he played the stock market on paper, buying and selling in his head, GM, Textron, IBM, The Gap. Every morning he sent his wife to the 7-Eleven for lottery tickets. "You think it's wrong to pray for a transplant?" said his wife, whose name was Ada.

"Why would you think it was wrong to pray for a transplant?"

"I offered to give him one myself, but the doctor said it was no good. Otherwise someone has to die. I mean someone has to die for him to get a kidney. It seems like a hard thing, to pray for someone to die."

"Don't worry about that, Ada," I said.

I saw Melvin twice a week, too. I couldn't warm to him, although I felt sorry for Ada, who washed his sheets every day in Clorox to get out the sweat stains. But my main job, and my favorite one, was taking care of the Levitts, in a building called the Lakeview on the other side of the highway from our house. It was a good long walk, about twenty minutes, the twin towers of the senior citizens' complex rising before me like a mirage amid a sea of small white stucco houses with red tile roofs, vibrating with window air conditioners. Some days I would sit down on the steps of one small house or another, scraggly flowered bushes shielding me from view, and wipe my forehead with a Kleenex. Sometimes I stopped at the 7-Eleven myself for a Big Gulp. "Hot out there," the Asian man behind the counter always said, making it sound like one big polysyllabic word, an idiomatic expression he preferred, along with a big grin, as the price of doing business in this crazy, crazy country. It seemed possible that I was the only person in Lake Plata who didn't travel in an air-conditioned car. Since we'd arrived in Florida my face had been crimson most of the time, all the blood visible through my thin skin, my hair in spikes every which way.

The first day I went to the Levitts had been a school holiday, Faculty Development Day, and I'd reluctantly entrusted Robert to the Castro family, slowly, loudly asking Milagro Castro if she could look out for him while I was gone.

"Let me tell her," Bennie had said, turning to his mother. A birdsong of Spanish from the boy, then a series of manic nods from his mother, then more Spanish and another emphatic nod.

"She says she will take care of him the same way she takes care of the rest of us. She says he is a good boy."

Mrs. Castro poured forth a torrent of words, her head and hands dancing.

"She says Robert will have lunch with us and it will be a pleasure to have him. She says he is a good boy and she will not let him out of her sight. All right, Ma, that's enough." Bennie had turned back to me. "She's saying a lot of praying stuff. Well, not praying exactly, but God stuff. That's okay, Mommy, she understands." And the two boys had trudged into the Castro apartment, arguing about which comic superhero was more indestructible, as Bennie's mother and I bowed and grinned like dolls on the back of a car dash. Women's work, they seemed to say with their retreating backs. The screen slammed. Then Robert came back out, pulled me aside as Mrs. Castro smiled upon us both and whispered, "When are you coming back?"

"Around four," I said.

"Four in the afternoon?"

"Are you sure you don't want to come with me? I said you could come with me and sit in the lobby."

He shook his head. "I just want to know." He turned back to Bennie, and I turned toward the Lakeview and the Levitts.

"Look, Irving," Mrs. Levitt said the first time she opened her apartment door to me, as I stood outside in a hallway that smelled like Lysol and old people. "Look," she said, after standing on tiptoe and peering through the peek hole. "They sent a new one."

The Levitts lived in a one-bedroom apartment with a kitchen so small that Mrs. Levitt and I could not make iced tea and sandwiches in it at the same time. It had one of those balconies so many apartment buildings in New York had, just big enough to stand on, small, ugly, and useless, the appendix of modern architecture. Mrs. Levitt used it only to check for a storm coming when she heard the warning on the Weather Channel, and to hang her hand washables. Sometimes, as I got close to the building, I could tell which apartment was the Levitts' by the assortment of corsetry baking in the still air.

The apartment was as plain and simple as the inside of a box, but it was full of rococo furniture, sideboard next to highboy, a big sectional with old brocade pillows worn soft as baby skin, an assortment of sepia photographs displayed in Lucite frames on a bureau pushed into one corner. There were dining-room chairs but no dining table, end tables with geometric inlay and flimsy plastic tray tables. The Oriental rug was tucked under at one end, six inches too long for its surroundings. One corner of the living room was crammed with a hospital bed, a card table with medications and spray cleaners and adult diapers, and a large oil painting of a dark forest in an elaborate gilt frame. When I was a student nurse I'd done home visits to a seventy-year-old cancer patient, a retired furrier whose small efficiency had been much the same. "Their lives shrink as they get older, but their furniture stays the same size," my clinical supervisor had said.

"That color washes you out," Mrs. Levitt said the first day I went there, as she opened the door and looked at the blue polyester zip-front shift that I wore on the job, which fomented and held perspiration like the plastic weight-loss wraps I'd seen in women's magazines.

"And hello to you, too," I said.

"Uh-oh, Irving," Mrs. Levitt said. "This one's got a funny bone."

There wasn't much for me to do at the Levitts, really. Mrs. Levitt and I turned Irving over; he had had a stroke that left him incontinent, mute, and largely paralyzed except for the occasional wild spasm. Together we changed Irving's sheets and his pajamas. Mostly we drank tea after feeding Irving pureed peas and broth through a straw and changing his diapers.

"Can I use the phone to call my son?" I said that first day. "It's a local call."

"Mom, I'm fine," Robert said, impatient. "We were in the middle of something."

"I'll be home soon," I said, hearing in his voice, in his breathing, impatient little snorts, that he didn't care, that part of his great slow sinking into normalcy was to go about the business of being a boy with everything that was in him.

"I'll be honest, sweetheart," Mrs. Levitt said in her accented English. "I can sure use the help with Irving here. But it's also a pleasure to have someone to talk to. Not that Irving's not someone. But you were never a wonderful conversationalist, even before, were you, Irving?" She winked at me, lifted a hand to her woolly hair, stippled white and gray, which looked as though it had been permed and then left to get by as best it could for the duration. "Florida, Florida, he says as soon as he starts thinking about retiring. Everybody's going to Florida. What am I going to do in Florida, Irving, I say, but next day we woke up and there was a foot of snow. Oh, boy, I said to myself, that's that.

Next thing I know, he's got the house on the market. Look at this." She heaved herself out of a mahogany chair, using the beautifully carved and curving arms for leverage, and motioned me over to a broom closet in the hallway between living room and bedroom. Inside there was a vacuum cleaner, a quilted gold garment bag that smelled of mothballs, and a set of golf clubs.

"You golf?" Mrs. Levitt said. I shook my head. Lots of cops golf, a slightly more athletic variation on the theme of sitting together out on the patio talking about how the transit cops are morons and the patrol cars all need new shocks. Bobby lifted weights instead. His forearms felt like a boneless rib roast before defrosting. God, he had a beautiful body. "You got nothing to complain about, Fran," one of the cop wives had said to me once at a PBA clambake in Hampton Bays, looking from Bobby to her husband. "Baby likes beer," her husband used to say, patting his belly.

Mrs. Levitt gave the golf clubs a kick with her bedroom scuff. "He says he's going to take up golf. Seventy-one years old and he thinks he's, what was his name, Arthur Somebody, big golfer. Weren't you, Irving? All that handicap nonsense you picked up from Bernie Meerson and his gang at the swim club. Do you think I should put an ad in the paper, try and sell them?"

"The golf clubs?"

Mrs. Levitt nodded, went back to her chair, the tea and cookies. She leaned toward me and lowered her voice. "What would happen is this," she said, squinting at me. "Somebody'd buy the clubs, Irving would wake up or come out of this"—she waved her hand toward the corner as though to indicate the whole mess, the adjustable back of the bed, the box of diapers, the catheter bags—"and he would say, Selma, where the hell are my clubs? You sold them? What, Selma, you thought I was going to die?" She shrugged, her pillowy torso rising and falling with certainty and resignation. I looked over at Irving, a yellow mummy with rheumy dark eyes, his fingers twitching, his breathing the closest he came to conversation. The bed was angled so he had a panoramic view of the cluttered random landscape of Lake Plata, one small roof after another broken only by the skeleton supports of the water tower and the boxy sprawl of the Wal-Mart and Kmart, but he seemed to see nothing, hear nothing. Perhaps he could still feel the drumbeat of his heart beating in his body; who could tell? It was hard to imagine him demanding his nine iron.

"Never mind," Mrs. Levitt said. "What do you think about this girl went missing in Orlando? The boyfriend killed her, you take my word for it." Oh, I believed that.

Listening to Mrs. Levitt talk about Irving was like sitting out back at a barbecue talking to the other cop wives the way I'd done dozens of times during my marriage. Sometimes, on those summer afternoons, I'd think Bobby was right, that I exaggerated things. I'd sit in the backyard of Bobby's friend Buddy's split-level out on Long Island, and listen to Buddy's wife, Marie, and her sister, Terri, who was also married to a cop, and Marie's neighbor Annmarie, whose husband was a firefighter, and they all made it sound like marriage was the Stations of the Cross, like that was the natural order, trial by husband.

"He can sit out there like Father of the Year, but God forbid he should bathe one of them or buy them a pair of shoes," said Marie.

"A pair of shoes?" said Terri. "What are you, dreaming? A pair of shoes? What about putting the goddamn mayonnaise away after he makes a sandwich?"

"He makes his own sandwich?" said Annmarie, and we had to laugh. Had to.

Oh, lord, the stories they told, and all of them funny and sharp, like Mrs. Levitt's. About how Terri was so tired from the kids one night that she fell asleep in the middle of sex. About how Buddy showed up at one of the girls' birthdays drunk and passed out on the couch, where the party carried on without him, around him, how someone put a butter-cream rosebud on his nose and he never even stirred. About Annmarie's husband, Kevin, and the toast he gave at his brother's wedding that was so full of profanity and references to the groom's previous girlfriends that the bride burst into tears.

"Honest to God, it's like having five kids, and the girls are easier," Marie said.

The working girl, they all called me. Hey Fran, they'd say, what's up in the real world? And I'd tell stories about the hospital. About the girl who came into the ER ten centimeters dilated and named her baby Benedetto because she kept staring at my name tag, yelling and cursing and using her long toes against the laminated footboard of the bed for leverage while she pushed. About the gunshot victim who tried to grab the bullet as a resident held it high on the blade of his retractors and raised a ruckus when we wouldn't let him have it for his collection. "I got five of those suckers on the headboard of my bed, man," he moaned. "Five, all lined up nice. Gimme that one." About the couple who came in hemming and hawing and finally managed to say that somehow the condom got lost. A female resident put on rubber gloves and retrieved it. "You're supposed to unroll it as you put it on," she said to the guy.

"Damn," he said.

We'd sit in the kitchen and I'd tell those stories and they'd howl, those women. Never the men. The men sat on the patio under the awning in the summer and downstairs in the finished basement during the football season. They got the big screen TV, we got the kitchen table and the fridge.

I don't think I exchanged more than five words—"Fine, thanks," and "Take it easy"—with Buddy in all the time I knew him. We were barely inside the door, Bobby and me, before he'd go in one direction and I in the other, to the kitchen with the women. It was like we were different species.

None of the women worked. None of their husbands wanted them to work, they said. They all said it as if they were a little curious, like they wondered how come Bobby let me, like they'd discussed it among themselves, like they were waiting for me to let them in on the secret. None of them knew that there were ways in which Bobby made me pay for the luxury of working my butt off at South Bay five, sometimes six days a week.

"I got enough to do around here," said Marie.

I remember wondering whether that was it, whether if I stayed home and made silk-flower wreaths and decoupage boxes Bobby wouldn't be so mad at me all the time. Except that it didn't seem that Bobby was mad at me, exactly, just that he was mad, and I was the one who happened to be there.

Annmarie went home early one evening, before the rum cake and the coffee, and Marie leaned toward us and said, "That poor girl, I tell you. He's had someone on the side for two years now. She thinks his family is still pissed about that toast at the wedding, but they can't look her in the face because he knocked the girlfriend up."

"Get out!" said Terri.

"Swear to God," said Marie.

"Why doesn't she leave?" I said.

"Where would she go?" said Terri. "She should screw up her life because her husband is a pig? She just repainted the whole house. She papered the hallway."

I told them about Patty Bancroft, too, when she came to the hospital. They'd already seen her on television, talking about how a woman could get lost in the great expanse of America with a little help from the right people. "We're better than the Witness Protection Program," she said on one afternoon talk show.

"All Buddy would have to do would be to raise a hand to me once, and I'd knock him on his ass," Marie said.

"You don't know," said Terri, and I looked at her, looked at her brown eyes with their thick fringe of mascara, like spiders around them. She didn't look back at me, and I wondered. But wondering was all any of us would ever do. We'd put on silky cocktail dresses and blow-dry our hair and walk into the weddings and christenings and confirmations, our husbands checking the coats, slipping the tickets into the pockets of their suit jackets, and we'd look like happy couples, and some of us maybe were, and lots of us likely weren't, but none of us would ever talk about it. I'd been stupid when I got married, figured it was just like an extended dating relationship, one dinner and movie after another, sex in a real bed or even on the kitchen floor. I should have known by the way the photographer made us behave for the wedding pictures—"Now look down at the ring . . . look up at him . . . hold up the flowers"—that a lot of it would be putting up a good front, day after day, week after week. Until if we were lucky, if there wasn't cancer or a car wreck, our grandkids would someday toss us a fiftieth anniversary party in a catering hall and toast us, their eyes wet, for the simple fact of our stubborn marital longevity, confusing it with love.

And yet, and yet. At Robert's First Communion party Bobby and I sat side by side at the table as our son thanked everyone for coming, solemn at age eight in his little navy blue suit and his first tie, red-and-blue striped, and my right hand found Bobby's left, and I looked at him and saw the father of my son, the beginning of my grown-up life, the person who slept every night on the right side of my double bed, whose shorts I'd folded in a plastic basket for fifteen years. It was like there were two Bobbys, two Frans, two couples, and one was sitting at that table, knee nudging knee, breathless with love for our child and so, by some process of osmosis, for each other. The other Bobby and Fran stayed home, waiting for nightfall, she afraid of saying the wrong thing, he— well, I never knew what he felt.

Sometimes when I went to Cindy's house I looked at the pictures of her and her husband, Craig, and wondered whether there were two of them, too, the daytime and the nighttime couple, like masks of comedy and tragedy. And Mrs. Levitt and Irving. And strangers I saw in cars, sitting next to each other at stoplights, looking straight out the windshield, never at each other, living parallel lives.

"That princess and prince now?" Mrs. Levitt said. "There's a marriage that spelled trouble from the very beginning. And now, all of a sudden, here's the girlfriend and who knows what else."

"Remember how wrinkled her wedding dress was when she got out of the coach?"

"The princess?" Mrs. Levitt raised her hands to the sky in mute entreaty to some greater power. "I said to my friend Flo in Chicago, I said, Flo, you sit on silk and look what happens."

If Irving hadn't had his stroke only three weeks after they'd moved into the Lakeview, if she'd had time to make friends with the other women in the building, Mrs. Levitt would have gossiped about the super and the single woman on the ground floor, the dry cleaner and his nasty wife. Instead she talked about the people in the papers: the princess and her divorce, Streisand and Sinatra— "not a happy woman," Mrs. Levitt said about one, and "not a happy man" about the other—the president and the first lady. Mrs. Levitt got the tabloids when Mrs. Winkelman down the hall left them with her recycled newspapers; she would listen on Tuesday evenings for the sound of the Winkelman door and then sneak down to the incinerator and ease the *Star* and the *Enquirer* out from the twine bundle. "Look, Irving, here's that one you liked from *Dallas*," Mrs. Levitt would call across the room. "She's not holding up too good."

"Irving," she would say as she smoothed the blankets, "you remember how you lost all our vacation money in Vegas on half an hour at the blackjack?"

"You think I didn't see you that time with Mamie in the wet bar of their place?" she said as his mouth gaped.

"You were always cheap, Irving," she mused as she went into the drawer and took out fresh pajamas, laundered so often they were soft as silk. "Twelve years it took me to get a decent stove. And even then I had to hear about it for the next twelve."

Sometimes Mr. Levitt made a sound like a groan or a wheeze, and she would say, "Yes, yes, yes." And something in the way she said it made me believe she had been saying it for years, that she had said it when her husband said, "Look at how fast that crazy man in the Chevy is driving," or "It's gonna pour any minute," or "This is one tough piece of meat," that Mrs. Levitt had replied "Yes, yes, yes" just as she did today. I hate to say it, but the two of us ignored Mr. Levitt, paid him less mind than the television set or the coffeemaker. But I had the feeling Mrs. Levitt had been doing that for quite awhile.

"You listening, Fran, or am I talking to myself?" Bobby would say sometimes, late at night. God, how I wanted to say, you're talking to yourself, Bobby. But I wouldn't have dared.

"He was a good worker," Mrs. Levitt said as I irrigated and then reconnected Irving's catheter, both of us looking dispassionately at her husband's slack penis. "He made a good living. Sales. He sold automobile parts. I never even learned to drive. Too busy to teach me, right, Irving?" She smiled. "Something like that," she said. "You want tuna on toast for lunch?"

"You don't have to go to any trouble for me," I said.

"It's no trouble. I made lunch for the last girl, and she was colored. Not that I minded, but I think Irving wasn't so happy about it." She opened the refrigerator and took out a loaf of wheat bread. "Were you, Irving?" she called into the other room, and put the bread in the toaster. "But I have to say, she wasn't rude. We had one before her, she handled Irving like a sack of potatoes. I called the agency, I said she had to go. I think they sent me the colored girl for spite. Not that we minded, right, Irving?"

"Do you need anything?" I said as I was leaving each day, and Mrs. Levitt said no until I'd been there two weeks. I suppose by then she'd decided she could trust me. She put her head to one side, a girlish gesture, put one finger beneath her chin. Then she reached for her purse, a black tote bag with big white polka dots. "I'll give you the money, you'll bring *People* magazine," she said.

"I'll get it," I said. "Don't worry about the money."

"And some other time you'll bring a Big Mac," she said. "Big Mac is Irving's favorite fast food. Big Mac and senior coffee. A large coffee and only a quarter if you're over sixty-five. Which we are, right, Irving?" She straightened his covers, tucked him in as though he was a child. No children, Mrs. Levitt had told me, making a vague motion toward her midsection and moving on to some movie star's marriage. Just her and Irving, forty-eight years and counting.

The supermarket on the strip up the street from our apartment was as big as a football field, so brightly lit that it bleached out the skin of even the tannest women pushing their kids around the aisles in carts. Jets of water sprayed the peppers and plums so they seemed irresistible, more like art objects than produce. In one corner was a pharmacy, in another a bank, in a third a bakery section that gave off the smell of cinnamon unexpectedly as you came upon it, like one of those perfume inserts in a magazine. It was as though they'd put an entire American small town in an airplane hangar and then arranged and lit it to best advantage. It made me think of how I'd imagined heaven when I was a kid, white light and something for everybody. People were always hollering to their kids to find a second cart, as though they had been seduced into soup and cheese and instant pudding without meaning to be.

Robert and I could only buy as much as we could carry, but for the two of us that was usually plenty, and I was careful about how

I spent my money. We'd been in the apartment for almost three months and I still hadn't paid any rent, didn't even know how much it was. It was another one of Patty Bancroft's mysteries; "We'll take care of that end of things" she'd said when I asked how long the rent would be taken care of. So I opened a credit union account with the home-care company, putting away some money every week just in case. I wore my uniform and my hand-me-downs; mainly I spent money on treats for Robert, trips to the arcades with Bennie, weekend fast-food lunches, sometimes a shirt or a comic book. I didn't want him to feel deprived, to feel poor as well as rootless. Twice he'd had nightmares and I'd sat with him until he fell back suddenly into sleep; he couldn't, or wouldn't, say much about the dreams, just that there were bad guys, that he was running, that there was darkness, falling, fear. Twice he'd asked to stay home from school with a stomach ache. Once beneath his bed I found a piece of looseleaf paper: "Dear Dad" in his scratchy, back-slanting penmanship, "I bet you are very surprised to—" Then, nothing. Perhaps I'd told him dinner was ready, knocked at his door. Perhaps he'd heard Bennie calling from downstairs. I threw the paper away.

"You hungry?" I said as I found a cart whose wheels worked. Robert shrugged. He shrugged a lot, too, these days. Are you tired? Shrug. Do you want to watch a movie? Shrug. How could he care about anything at all, when in an instant it might disappear, when the outlines of our life were as faint and transparent as the picture on the old television in the living room. It was like that Etch-a-Sketch he'd gotten from Santa, year before last. You drew the picture and then turned the toy over, and the image was gone, nothing but gray, waiting for the next one, just as fleeting.

I didn't know how much I'd be able to buy him for Christmas this year, or how in hell I'd ever get through it, get through the tree and the meal and the goddamned carols. I pushed the cart and stopped thinking. I'd gotten good at that, at just cutting thoughts off, as though I was changing channels. From Christmas to chicken cacciatore.

The one thing I wouldn't scrimp on was food. Once the heat began to wane a bit in what, up north, passed for the beginning of winter, once I began to feel the least bit at home in the windowless kitchen in the apartment, I'd begun to cook the Italian food that Ann Benedetto had taught me to make years before. I figured it would make Robert feel more at home, the way it had made me feel as if I was making one, really making one, all those years ago.

"My mother needs a daughter," Bobby had said, "and you need to learn to cook a decent meal." Every Sunday he dropped me off, when we were first married, at his mother's house, in his mother's kitchen so clean that a spot of red sauce looked like blood. I took a shower before I went, did my makeup, but sometimes I thought she could smell it on me, what we'd been doing before, while Ann was at nine o'clock mass.

Her cooking was a list of don'ts: don't buy cheap cheese, don't put the sauce on too high, don't use garlic salt instead of real garlic, don't layer the lasagna more than three times no matter how deep the pan. A list of don'ts, a list of Bobby doesn'ts: Bobby doesn't like the hot sausage, Bobby doesn't like the thin spaghetti, Bobby doesn't like the bread from Emilio's bakery, only from Marie's. Most Sundays she had a new shirt for him, a soft, fine double knit with a collar in a dark color. "I was at the outlets," she always said. Later she bought things for Robert, polo shirts and oxford button-downs. "Rags," she called T-shirts and blue jeans. "Garbage," she called frozen food.

"She came from nothing," Bobby's grandmother hissed when Ann went to the bathroom. "You just remember that. Don't take any crap from her. She's half Polish, for Christ's sake. My son, God love him—she gave him such a time." Bobby's grandmother always liked me, until the day she died. She gave me her cameos, that I'd had to leave behind in the rosewood jewelry box on my bureau. God, I'd thought to myself, Bobby'll really kill me if I take Mama's brooches. Mama, we always called his grandmother. Ann, I called my mother-in-law. She never asked me to call her anything else.

But she made me a cook, and so I could make Robert meatballs and braciola, pasta e fagioli and lasagna, little pieces of home at this flimsy table 2,000 miles away. He invited Bennie for dinner, and the two of them hunched over their plates without speaking until finally their mouths were shiny with tomato sauce and grease. Bennie's mother did the same for Robert: beans and rice, chicken with a sauce of tomatoes and onions. Bless our boys, talking with their mouths full.

"You want chicken cacciatore?" I said as Robert and I traipsed down the endless meat aisles in the supermarket, and he nodded, bent over another video game, which he'd traded his old one for to some boy at school. This one was soldiers and kickboxing. It made little grunting noises when one man hit another with his booted foot. *Unh. Unh. Unh.* We went past pork and beef to poultry. At the front of the store a bulletin board held flyers with pictures of missing children. The faces changed twice a month. I knew because I always looked at them while I was pretending to get a cart with wheels that really worked. All the kids looked happy in the pictures, as though they didn't care that they were missing.

"Don't put mushrooms in it," Robert said.

"You don't have to eat the mushrooms."

"Can I go look at the comics?" he said without raising his head from his game.

"Where?"

"I don't know. They're over there. I'll find them."

"I'd rather you stayed with me."

"Mom, I'm not a baby. I'm all right. Just let me go."

"You come back to me in ten minutes," I said as he trotted away. I still hated to let him out of my sight. Each afternoon when I heard the school bus pull up I stood behind the screen, a peeping Tom of a parent, making sure he got off the bus and in the house safe and sound. Sometimes I wanted to hold Bennie and say, thank you, thank you, over and over again, thank you for being an ordinary boy, for making my boy seem ordinary, too, for going everywhere he goes.

"Where's your father?" I heard Bennie ask Robert one day, but nicely, softly. There had been a long silence from the bedroom, or maybe it just seemed long because I was holding my breath. Then Robert's voice came, low: "He and my mom are split up."

"Jonathan's mom and dad split up last year," Bennie said. "Allyson lives with her mom. I don't know where her father is. Sean, too. His parents got divorced when he was real little. He stays with his dad every weekend in East Preston." It was as though he would go on and on with his litany of fractured families, of kids walking on the broken glass of their parents' lives. "Your mom cooks good," Bennie had said after a moment.

"I know," said Robert. "She cooks really good at Christmas." I held the back of my hand against my mouth and a little saliva ran over my fingers with my tears. Everything we'd lost, everything I'd forced him to leave, seemed somehow to be in that simple sentence. She cooks really good at Christmas. In that moment I thought of going back, of walking in through that familiar door just so I could see the look on Robert's face. All my life I'd tried to make my boy happy, and now to keep him safe I had to make him sad. And angry, too. I could see that in the set of his mouth, sometimes. I'm not sure he knew who he was angry at. One night, doing his homework, he'd thrown his math book onto the floor and hit the wall with his pencil and I'd stood up from the couch, but stopped, so still, because the jerky choreography of violence and rage was so familiar to me that I couldn't come any closer, even when the object was long division.

"This is so stupid," he'd shouted. "This is all different than what we learned last year, and besides, it doesn't make any sense, the way they want us to carry things. And she makes us show all our work, and there's not even enough space on the page."

"What about using another piece of paper?" I said quietly.

"We're not allowed, Mom," he screamed, and tears were beginning to run down his face. "You don't understand. We're not allowed. We have to do it on this sheet or we get points off. This is so stupid." And he pushed over the chair, ran upstairs, slammed his door so hard that I swear I felt an answering vibration in the living-room floor, like the aftershock from an earthquake.

"You want to talk about things?" I said that night as I sat on the edge of his bed.

"Nah," he said.

"It might make you feel better."

"I feel okay."

"You didn't seem okay when you were doing your math homework."

"It's really stupid, the way they do it here," he'd said.

I watched him walk away in the supermarket, his head still

bent over the video game, skirting the carts intuitively, the way I imagine a blind man negotiates his living room. The long bones in his legs had begun to grow, so that he had that Tinkertoy look a boy has as he becomes a young man, sticks and knobs precariously held together. He would be taller than his father, and better looking, too. He had my nose, not the hawk beak that made Bobby look so terrifying sometimes, his black eyes predatory above it. What else was it that boy, Tyrone Biggs, had said from the witness stand? "That cop, man, he scared me."

"Did he threaten you?" his stupid defense attorney had thundered, breaking the rules, asking a question he didn't know the answer to.

"No, man. He just looked at me. Looked at me real cold."

The way some mothers look at their kid for birth defects when they're babies, try to suss out signs of stupidity as they learn to walk and talk, so I watched and waited to see that dark, lowering look on my boy's face, the look the sky has before the rain comes down in gray sheets. Three months I'd watched him for signs of colic, finally relaxed into motherhood when the danger period passed. It'd take longer this time, looking not for gas but for the early signs of rage. It was why I tried to draw him out, so that he could vent that way instead of the other. "Use your words," I used to say when he was little, and most of the time he did. But once, walking away from St. Stannie's in the morning, I'd heard a group of boys calling him Robert the Hobbit, of all things, no more than a silly singsong following him down the street, Robert the Hobbit, Robert the Hobbit, as he trudged along the pavement with his head down. And then, almost without breaking stride, he'd turned and hurled himself at them, his arms pinwheeling, his eyes big. "Shut up!" he shrieked as he hit and hit and hit, the other boys stunned, backing away, putting their hands up palms out. "Shut up!" until I pulled him away, screaming myself, "For God's sake, Robert, stop. Stop it!"

"Daddy said you have to fight back," he'd said as I hectored him on the way home. And when I complained, Bobby just waved his hand and shrugged. "The trouble is, Fran, that you don't know about boys," he'd said.

Moving away from me down the long market aisle, Robert looked just as Bobby might have as a boy, except that there was something defenseless in the way he held himself, a kind of roundness to back and shoulder. And I wondered whether Bobby had ever been like that, defenseless, before biceps and bravado and badge. Before me. Or whether Robert had learned to walk like that from me, from all the years that I'd made myself small, trying not to attract notice, give offense. Suddenly, as though he'd felt my eyes on his back, Robert looked over his shoulder and smiled, a smile that on that dark pinched face was more than a smile, was a hand, a hug, a kiss. That was the smile Bobby had had, too, when he saw me when we were both young, that made my spirit levitate, warm from the inside out.

"You know what, Frances Ann?" Bobby had said, sitting next to my bed in the single room on the hospital's maternity floor, Robert's misshapen little head cupped in his palm. "We got everything."

Jesus, I loved him. There, I said it. It makes me feel stupid, sometimes, feeling my scars, the spots where you can just make out the damage and the ones where the bruises and hurts live on only in my head. I loved Bobby, and he loved me. Anyone who heard him say it once would never disbelieve it. In the beginning I loved him, loved him, loved him pure and simple. And then after a while I loved the idea of him, the good Bobby, who came to me every once in a while and rubbed my back and kissed my fingers.

And I loved our life, the long stretches of tedium and small pleasures that marked most of our time together. Our life was like a connect-the-dots drawing, and those were the lines, the bad things only the haphazard arrangement of dots they connected.

And now all the love goes into what's left of that life, one boy, his basketball shoes too big for his little body. I watch him and I'm afraid my face looks the way Ann Benedetto's face looked when she watched Bobby, like a hungry cat when it hears the can opener, all eyes and appetite. I'm afraid that I'll wind up the way she did, with nothing but the casual, almost charitable, almost condescending affection that a grown man has for his mother once he's moved on to another woman, another source of intensive care. Alone in that spotless house, with the photographs on top of the television, Bobby at four, his foot tucked under him, his chubby fingers wrapped around his knee. Bobby at twenty-six, in his dress uniform. Across the living room, on the wall unit, was the photograph of her husband in his own police blues.

"My old man was some piece of work," Bobby always said. He'd been shot, Robert, Sr., by a junkie who didn't know how to wave a gun around during a bar robbery without having the thing go off. It was two months after we started going out, and I cried at the funeral, not for Lt. Benedetto, who I'd met only once, but for his son. The sound of the bagpipes was like strange birds, and the cops were like an army, blue with black swipes of elastic over their badges.

That's all he ever said, *some piece of work*. Never an anecdote, or a word of affection or even anger. His father was the stone in Bobby's heart. And maybe his own father would be the stone in Robert's. The patterns, the patterns, as inviolate as a clan tartan. Red, green, black, blue, father, son.

I'd been standing staring into the depths of a half-filled cart, and when I looked up a tall man had stopped Robert at the end of the aisle and was putting a hand on his shoulder. Suddenly I felt my stomach empty out, felt as though I might faint. I pushed forward, but there were two elderly women crowding the aisles, peering at coupons, and by the time I got past them Robert wasn't there. The man was looking at chickens, or pretending to. Looking too hard, I thought, like a bad actor, so that he didn't look up until I'd planted myself in front of him.

"Excuse me," I said. "What were you saying to that child?"

"What?"

"That boy? The one with the dark hair? What were you saying to him?" I realized the two women with the coupons were looking at me. My voice was too loud, even to myself.

"Robert Crenshaw? I teach him PE. At the elementary school."

The relief in my posture, the surrender to the safe and commonplace in my shoulders, head, face, must have been so profound that he peered at me perplexed for a moment, then smiled. "You're Robert's mother," he said. "And I just scared the heck out of you. I am really, really sorry."

"No, no, forget it. It was silly. It's just—"

"—that you have to be more careful today than when we were kids. Hey, in my job I know." He stuck out a big hand, thick-fingered. My own disappeared inside it, then reappeared as I pulled away, like a small fish released from the maw of a big one. He was a bigger man than I'd thought, seeing him across the parking lot and lawn of the school that first day, big and bulky, flushed and friendly, with thinning blond hair and light eyes behind aviator glasses. What kind of animal does your gym teacher remind you of? I'd ask Robert walking home, another game we played. And the answer would be something good-natured, plodding, big and big-hearted. A bear maybe.

"Mike Riordan."

"Beth Crenshaw."

"I know," he said. "You and Mrs. Roerbacker work in the library."

"Sorry. I missed meeting you somehow."

"I'm a gym rat," he said. "I'm practically mildewed. You from New York?"

"No," I said, feeling my shoulders tighten again. "Delaware."

"You sound like New York," he said. "I've been meaning to call you about Robert."

"Why?"

"Hey, he's fine. You know, he's new. He'll open up more when he gets used to the drill here. There's no problem. I just want him to play on our soccer team. No big deal, no high pressure, two practices a week and they're before dinnertime. I never yell and scream, and I give them off the day before a big test. But we start next week and he'd need to stay after school and either walk home or have you pick him up. He's new and he didn't seem too sure it would be okay with you. Bennie Castro's playing, if that makes a difference."

"I'll talk to him. It's fine. It would be good for him."

"Great. Great." He paused. "I'll send home a permission slip and some more information. You can call me if you have any questions. I'm the vice principal, too, whatever that means. Call about anything, the school, the homework, whatever." He hesitated, looking into his cart. "Would you mind if I asked you something?"

I shook my head.

"How much do you know about chicken?"

"Chicken?"

"Cooking chicken."

"I've cooked a lot of chickens, if that's what you're asking."

"You know those things that you can put inside the chicken, sort of holds them standing up so they cook faster? They've got them back with the pots and pans and things. They're metal, shaped kind of like a big golf tee. Do those things work?"

I laughed. "I don't know," I said. "It never occurred to me to buy one. A chicken only takes an hour anyhow. Why rush it?"

"That's what I thought. Thanks," he said, staring into the meat case.

Suddenly I heard Gracie's voice, as clear as if it was coming over the loudspeaker instead of John Mack Carter's tips for using exciting, exotic cilantro in a variety of dishes with an international flair. Where were we sitting, Grace and I? Was it that coffee bar on Lexington Avenue, where the counterman always called her "Professor," or the Greek restaurant in the Village with the homemade pita that made us both so full we would groan all the way to the subway? The Greek place, I think, and Grace talking about the tall man she kept running into at D'Agostino's, who wanted to know about tarragon, about potatoes, about sour and heavy and light cream. "As though I wouldn't know that asking a woman about how to cook is the oldest pick-up line in the book," Grace said, shaking her head.

"I didn't know that," I'd said.

"When was the last time somebody picked you up?" she said.

"Almost twenty years ago," I'd said. Bobby, in the bar where Tommy Dolan had introduced us. Bobby, one black apostrophe of hair over his forehead, saying, "Hey, Fran Flynn. I guess if everybody likes you I might like you too." Bobby, leaning against the bar, a perfectly natural pose, his elbows back, his big forearms knotted, his pelvis thrust forward, which was the whole point.

"Well, good luck," I said to Mike Riordan, and then felt myself turning hot, and red, the same way I'd colored that first time I met Bobby. I felt foolish as I strode off to pick up parsley, tomatoes, and garlic. Soccer season. Rules, practices, uniforms. Maybe while Robert was at practice, after I got home from the Levitts, I would do something to his room, cheap bright curtains and a new quilt, some more posters, a desk. I thought there had been an old desk in one corner of Cindy's basement. Vermicelli, chicken stock, tomato paste. The cart was getting too full; Robert would complain about the weight of the bag all the way home, particu larly if he had a comic he wanted to be reading instead. It was time to check out, head home. A stockboy sent me seven aisles over, to where the comic books shared an aisle with greeting cards and paperbacks, but only one elderly woman was there, reading birthday cards with her face close to their gaudy surfaces. I walked slowly, snaking through aisle after aisle, thinking about how big the market was, bigger than any I'd visited in the city, looking for Robert. Looking and looking. I began weaving through other shoppers, past cans of soup and coffee, cases of Coke and Pepsi, stacks of paper towels and toilet paper, back to the comic aisle, empty now. Part of my mind kept thinking that I needed paper towels, and the other part was saying, shouting, screaming over and over again, "Robert? Ba? Baby? Where are you?" I turned in aisle sixteen, dairy, and made my way back again. "Have you seen a boy, about ten, in a green T-shirt with a tiger on the front?" I began to ask the other shoppers, and "No," they said, no, sorry, no I haven't. Of course they haven't, thought one part of my mind, because he's in a car now, driving down the highway, saying, hey Dad, I missed you Dad, how's Grandmom, where we going, when are we going to go back and get Mommy?

I was moving so fast that I bumped into someone's cart and knocked a box of cereal from it. I came around the corner in frozen foods and almost collided with a man holding a box of macaroni and cheese, reading the back, and I saw that it was the gym teacher again but I suddenly couldn't recall his first name, only that he wanted Robert to play soccer, that I needed paper towels, and that my son was gone. He knew right away, as he looked up, saw me, smiled, then frowned, that something was wrong.

"I can't find Robert," I said, my voice an octave higher than usual, almost falsetto.

"Calm down," he said. "Calm down." He took my arm at the elbow and led me toward the front of the store, leaving our two carts next to the freezer cases, glass and chrome and foggy windows like the cases in the morgue at the hospital, where we nurses tried never to go if we could help it. I could tell by the feel of his hand at my elbow that he was used to taking charge. "He can't have gone far," he said, like it was something he'd said before. At the window where they cashed checks he stuck his head inside. "Excuse me," he called, and then I remembered that his name was Mike. A heavy girl with bad skin came to the window. CUSTOMER SERVICE, said the sign over her head.

"I'm on break," she said.

"We've lost a child," Mike Riordan said. "Can you do a page or something? Robert is his name, Robert Crenshaw."

"I can't page without the manager."

"Where's the manager?"

She called into the back "Where's Lenny?" and there was a

mumbled sound, and then she came out of the booth and I started to cry, my hands over my face. "Kids get lost in here a lot," she said, as if to be helpful, and then, calling over to the closest register, "Pete, where's Lenny?"

"Hold on," Pete said. "I got a price check."

"Where's the paging equipment?" Mike Riordan said pleasantly.

The girl pointed back toward the booth, and he said, "Use it right now or I'm going to go in and use it myself."

"Don't have a spas, mister," she said. "Your wife should have been watching him."

"There's Lenny," Pete called, and Mike turned toward a dark man in white shirt and pants. HERE TO SERVE YOU: LENNY said the tag on his shirt.

"Please," I said.

"They want me to page for their kid," said the girl. "They can't find him. I told them I couldn't page without you saying so."

"He's ten," I said. "He was supposed to be in the comic aisle. Where the cards and magazines are."

"Skinny kid?" said Lenny. "Dark hair, green shirt?"

"Yes," I said, knowing the worst, knowing what Lenny would say next, describing the man who'd left with the kid as dark, nice-looking, big through the arms and shoulders, looked like the kid, looked like his dad. And Mike Riordan would want to call the police and I would want to die, right here in the supermarket, rather than go home to that apartment alone. Or back to Brooklyn.

"I just threw him out on his butt. He's probably still out in the parking lot."

"What?" Mike Riordan said, but I was already halfway to the doors. The pavement between the store and the parking lot was full of people loading groceries into the backs of their cars, but off to one side, where the gum machines and the little automated horse ride stood, Robert was sitting on the ground, his arms held tight around his knees, his head down as though he was one of those little black bugs, the ones that roll up into a ball to protect themselves when they're disturbed.

I ran to him, touched his arm, and he jumped, then jumped at me, almost knocked me down as he threw his arms around me. Neither of us spoke and I just held him, held him tight, saying nothing, trying to stop the shaking in his back and shoulders. Then I heard a voice behind me say, "Hi, Robert. You okay?" But Robert shook his head and kept it pressed to the front of my body, although his arms had fallen to his sides.

"That bastard, excuse my French, says that he thought Robert was alone and that they have a rule against unsupervised kids in the store," Mike Riordan said from behind me. "Apparently they've had some problems with vandalism, shoplifting, and he just throws kids out if they're by themselves."

Robert's head snapped up, and spit flew from his mouth as he cried, "I told him and told him that my mom was there and I could find her. I told him I wasn't unsupervised. He just kept saying sure, sure, she'll find you outside. He wouldn't listen to me."

"Oh, sweetie," I said, holding him tight, but he pulled away.

"He wouldn't even let me look for you. I told him where you were, and then you weren't there. Where did you go? Where did you go?" He was so loud now that an elderly man came over to peer at him, at us, as though to save him from being abducted by the woman in the faded blue shorts and white polo shirt, the man in the blue button-down and the aviator glasses. "He's fine, he's fine, he's just upset," Mike said.

"I told him," Robert said, crying, and I reached for him again but he pushed me away. He slumped back against the big glass window at the front of the supermarket.

"I told that guy I'd be writing to the head of the supermarket chain," Mike Riordan said. "That was the most stupid, sadistic thing I've ever seen. All he had to do was walk him around the market."

Robert mumbled something, and I leaned in to listen. "I don't care what you said," he said. "I told him that my dad would kill him. I told him that he'd shoot him with his gun."

"Let's go home," I said.

"I'll drive you," Mike Riordan said.

That night Robert and I had frozen pizza for dinner. We'd left all our groceries in the store; so had Mike Riordan. "I hate this place," Robert said, and I did not reply.

I was frightened then, and no amount of paint, no optimistic plans, no hours in the school library, no TYs from Jennifer nor "Sit, Mrs. Nurse" from Mrs. Levitt could take that feeling away. No framed prints hung between the windows could change the fact that the blinds were drawn, sullen and mute. That moment in the supermarket, when I was certain Robert was gone, saw only emptiness in the space where he had been, was like a dress rehearsal for disaster. Afterward, adrenaline was always in my blood, as though I swallowed it down every morning with my vitamins. It was like those times years ago when I went to police funerals with Bobby, and felt, as the sound of taps floated over the cemetery, as though I was rehearsing the agony of losing him. It was the greatest pain I could imagine. But I was young then.

Coastal storms blew across the state all through the end of October, and the dried and yellowed branches of palms would slither across the roof over my bedroom sometimes late into the night, the wind blowing gravel from the center courtyard with a sound like bullets spraying the brick walls outside. The storm windows shook in their frames, and I lay on my back staring at the ceiling, waiting for the surreptitious sound of the front door opening. I went over it every night in my mind, how it might have been different, how I could have saved us all: me and Robert and Bobby, too. Sometimes I'd lull myself to sleep with memories of the two of us pushing Robert in his stroller around the neighborhood, Bobby's brawny arm brushing against my own, the hair rising on both, his black and thick, mine pale and downy. Or I'd see Bobby in my mind in the backyard in September, picking tomatoes, looking at each one carefully before he put it into a colander Robert was holding solemnly, proudly, at chest level, as though he was a little acolyte, a backyard altar boy. I guess it told me everything I needed to know about my past life, that I'd lie in bed crying while those pictures passed before my mind's eye, feeling the ordinary soft sweetness of those summer days, and yet listening at the same time for the noise of someone coming into the apartment to get me, to push me around, to punch me out, to take me out. I was lonely for that other Bobby, the one who whispered in my ear in bed so he wouldn't wake the boy, who sometimes held his hand over my mouth so I wouldn't make too much noise when he was on top of me. "You'll scare the kid, Fran," he'd say close to my ear, and I could tell by the sound of his voice that he liked that, liked that he made me squirm and scream that way.

But he made me scream those other ways, too, or at least moan and cry: please, no. That was my marriage: please, yes, sometimes; please, no, the others. If only I could have stayed with one Bobby and left the other.

"You had no choice," I said over and over to myself. Sometimes I said it out loud in the little box of a bedroom.

After that day in the supermarket, Robert was scared, too. I could tell by the way he behaved in the daylight, truculent and distant, when he'd kick a book across the floor or sit alone in his room, staring at the yellow aluminum siding of the house next door. I could tell by the way he behaved at night, trembling and clingy. He said the bathroom plumbing was keeping him awake, gurgling and burping through the thin wall, and asked if he could sleep in my bed. I wanted to let him, so much, if only to have someone I loved next to me, to help me sleep. But I knew it wasn't good for him. It reminded me of when he was a baby, when I'd had to let him cry himself to sleep, to teach him not to keep getting up in the middle of the night, to keep him from being so cranky during the day. Bobby held me down, the first night, when Robert wailed for twenty minutes straight and I wanted to go to him. The next night it was ten minutes, and the next he fell asleep before I'd even gotten down the hall. I thought about that all the time now, how sometimes you have to do hard things to your kids to do the right thing for them in the long run. But I still felt the way I'd felt that night, ready to give up, give in, at a moment's notice.

We struck a bargain, Robert and I. We dragged his mattress into my room, next to my bed. I draped my arm over the side and held his hand. He slept there for four days, then dragged the mattress back. It's easier to heal, I guess, when you're ten. I still hear noises in the night, the plumbing, the wind, the cars, the past.

I hurry down the dusty streets of Lake Plata, my walk just this side of a run, and wait for Robert to come home from school every day. Sometimes I hear him out in the courtyard talking to Bennie, the two of them fooling around, whacking each other with their sweatshirts, pulling off each other's caps. Sometimes I just hear the slam of a car door when a mother has arranged to drop him off, or when Mr. Riordan has driven some of them home from soccer. "Thank you," I hear Robert call. He is never really late. He knows.

"Hi," I say as he drops his backpack just inside the door, but it is as though now my real life has begun, as though I've shopped and cleaned and tended to other people in a kind of trance. I never felt this way before, when I worked at the hospital and Robert went after school to his grandmother's for an hour or two. But my life was different then, larger. Now it has been whittled away to its essentials. I make certain kinds of foods because Robert likes them. I bake so that he will have nice desserts. The refrigerator is covered with his test papers. I even bought a baby monitor, the kind we once kept by our bed so we could hear the sounds from his crib, so that he would not even whimper without me knowing it. Now I have the receiver under Robert's bed, the monitor under my pillow. Sometimes I can hear him mumbling in his dreams. It puts me to sleep, like the sound of the ocean, knowing he is there. Knowing that if someone opens his bedroom window, I will hear it.

Often I go in and watch as he sleeps the sleep of a ten-year-old, as close to unconsciousness as a healthy human being can be. I know my greatest fear is his fondest wish. Daddy. Daddy. Daddy. He loved Bobby as I once had, viscerally, from the gut, with no regard to events. Bobby was just the sort of father that a small boy would be likely to love. "Does your dad have a gun?" his friends could ask, and he could nod, safe and secure. Once in second grade he wrote a story about what we did, Bobby and I. The first sentence was "My daddy makes sure bad things never happen."

The copy of *One Fish, Two Fish* we'd brought from home sat on Robert's bedside table, and sometimes he read it, although once or twice he said he was going to give it to Chad Roerbacker.

The fish looked so friendly and familiar, smiling up from the page, their cowlicks splayed, their fins akimbo. One night Robert was paging through it and said, "Remember when I was five and you used to lie down next to me on the bed while I fell asleep?" I was sorry, later, standing by his bed, looking down at him, that I hadn't said or done more. Next night I slid out of my rubber flip-flops and lay down next to Robert, smiling, my arm over his chest.

"Mom, no offense, okay?" he said, "but I'm a little too big for this."

But before he went to sleep he would always suffer me to sit by the side of his bed, and he would ask me questions about my childhood, about whether I liked sharing a room with Aunt Grace, about whether it was scary to be home alone while my mother worked, about my father's job as a fireman and the big fires in which he'd been involved, as though he was constructing from the ground up a life he'd loved and lost, a life I'd seemingly obliterated in one trip. He particularly liked the one about the time a man with a gun had robbed the bakery on a Sunday morning when I was sixteen, in the desultory fallow period between the 9:00 and 10:30 masses, when I usually rearranged the doughnut trays and wiped down the glass cases. "You're kidding, right?" I'd said when he asked for the cash. And after I'd filled a brown bag with bills he'd demanded doughnuts, cream-filled, chocolate-frosted. "I'm not giving anybody pastry who just robbed the place," I'd said, and then Mr. Orlofsky from down the block had come in for his Sunday morning seedless rye, and the man had turned and run from the counter, clutching the bag and the gun, knocking Mr. Orlofsky down.

"Tell the doughnut story," Robert said, and then, after, "That was cool. That was brave."

"Jesus God, what a stupid thing to do," Bobby had said on our second date, when I'd told him the story.

"Tell the doughnut story," Robert said. "I told it to Bennie. He thought I made it up."

"I would have given him kaiser rolls," I said, "but not pastry."

"Tell it from the beginning." He played with my hands, with my fingers, as I told it again—the register, the bills falling into the bag like play money, the sound of the bell on the door as Mr. Orlofsky came inside. Each night, as I stood to go downstairs, he would ask one question:

Does Grandmom know where we are?

Does Aunt Grace know where we are?

Does Mrs. Selick, the third-grade teacher, or Father Charles, who gave him First Communion, or Mrs. Pinto?

And over and over I would say no. No, honey, no, Ba, until finally one night he told me he didn't want to be called Ba anymore, if I didn't mind, if it didn't hurt my feelings, no offense, but he was too old now.

He never asked "Does Daddy know where we are?" He knew that was the point. I'd sent Grace that note with the photographs because I hadn't wanted her to file a missing persons report. But I was as sure as I was sure of anything that Bobby would never do that, would know that the guys in the missing persons section almost always found a missing spouse healthier, happier, somewhere else. He would never countenance the whispers around the force: "You know Benedetto, the guy in narcotics? His wife took off on him, man. Took his kid, too."

Why had I been frightened of that young flat-faced cop at the door of the elementary school that first morning? There would be no outside interference. If Bobby came it would be on his own, slithering over the roof like a big palm frond in a high wind. But I'd be ready for him. Mr. Castro had a tangle of tools in the closet just inside the door of the Castro apartment, and one day I'd asked to borrow his crowbar, and hadn't given it back. It was under my bed. No matter when I touched it it was always cold, like a dead thing beneath me.

Robert allowed himself to be looked after now, to be babied, in his father's words. It was as though the supermarket had given him a taste of something, an inkling of terror and of loss. Our nighttime conversations were the ones he'd had when he was a smaller boy, with less scar tissue: "What if," I said at breakfast, and he said, softly, sweetly, "we went to the beach . . ."

". . . and you had a really big boogie board . . ."

". . . and got good enough at riding the waves that I could stand up like a surfer . . ."

". . . and dolphins swam up to shore and swam around you . . ."

". . . and I could understand what they were saying . . ."

"Yo, Robert," Bennie yelled from outside in the dusty quadrangle. "The bus is coming."

"We'll go to the beach soon," I said as I kissed Robert goodbye. "I promise."

It wasn't really good-bye at all, only see you soon, for every morning I followed the bus route on foot, met up with Cindy just as I had that first day. She usually brought me something: a jar of collagen cream, a crock of genuine Vermont maple syrup, tomatoes from her parents' farm. "Oh, please," she'd say dismissively when I tried to thank her. It was easier to thank her obliquely. "I love that perfume," I'd say, or "That's a good color on you," and she'd smile. Her teeth overlapped in the front, and she always smiled with her mouth closed, unless she was having a really good time, and then she forgot.

"What's in the bag?" she said the Monday morning after the supermarket, and I pulled out a jar of my red sauce, what Bobby's family always called gravy. "Bless you," she said. "I'll just dump it over some ziti tonight."

"If my mother-in-law could hear the way you say zee-tee, she'd have a stroke," I said.

"She's your ex-mother-in-law, hon, so who cares?" said Cindy. "She Italian?"

"She's a witch," I said.

"That's nice. What else you got in there?"

"Running shoes," I said.

"Oh, please," Cindy said.

That's really how I got to know Mike Riordan, by running three mornings a week, the mornings, after the library, that I didn't have coffee and muffins at Cindy's house. It had come to me suddenly, as I was trying to make things normal, ordinary, better, as I was laying shelf paper in the slightly sticky kitchen cabinets. It had come to me again as I rose from bed after those nights awake, listening, when my body would feel stiff and old. It had come to me finally in Kmart, buying white crepe-soled shoes to wear to work, stopping in front of cheap running shoes and remembering the expensive pair Grace had given me for my twenty-seventh birthday, white nylon mesh with turquoise and purple stripes and a bubble of some gold gel in the heel. "Running makes you feel young again," Grace had said.

"To hell with you," I'd said. "I still *am* young."

I couldn't think of Gracie too much now. It made it too hard, harder than it was any other time. But when I was running those first few months in 'Brooklyn, when I was twenty-seven and trying to get pregnant and she was twenty-one and trying to get into grad school, I thought of her every time I ran. I always imagined her making a loop around Riverside Park as I made an arc around the bayfront in Brooklyn. "I'm running with you in my mind," I said, when we talked about our best times and our injuries, our knees and our hamstrings. I worked the eight-to-four shift at South Bay and I'd get up at six and run in the morning, when the air felt as though someone had just blown it out into the Brooklyn streets, like it had been delivered fresh each morning the way they used to deliver our milk in those smooth glass bottles when I was little. The lights were on in some houses when I went out, the cars steaming in the driveways in wintertime, a few people already on their way to the bus stop. But the streets were quiet except for the thud of my running shoes on the pavement in a perfect rhythm that made me feel that living through any day was possible. Two, sometimes three miles, the sun coming up over the bay, painting a streak of silver across the undulating water, making me squint and stagger until I'd turn away from dead east into the narrow streets running north. I'd watch them run the marathon on television and at the start it looked more like rush hour on the IRT than running, all of them jockeying for a square foot of pavement across the Verrazano-Narrows Bridge. I never ran like that. I liked being alone. Bobby had worked evenings and nights a lot. "It's when the bad guys work, so it's when I have to work, too," he told Robert later on, when the boy was old enough to understand. So I'd do my day shift, go to bed early, run just after or just before daybreak, depending on the seasons, and come in and take a shower as quietly as I could manage, carrying my shoes out into the hallway so the sound of them on the floor would not disturb him. On the kitchen counter would be the dirty plate from Bobby's dinner the night before, that I always left on a warm setting in the oven. Ann Benedetto hadn't raised her son to get his own meals or wash his own dishes.

I stopped running when I was six months pregnant with Robert and started again when he was a year old and I went back to work. Bobby didn't want me to do either one, said we didn't need the money and I didn't need the exercise. But I worked part-time on a night shift for a couple of years, so that I was mostly at the hospital when Robert was asleep, and once he started school I was gone only when he was. But that one hour in the morning was for me. In the dark, in the dining room, I laced on my shoes, pulled on my sweatshirt, pounded the pavement until my throat burned with the effort of breathing. I even ran once with two broken ribs, just to show Bobby what I was made of. "Frannie, Frannie, Fran," he mumbled that morning as I stripped off my shorts, the bed smelling of sweat and scotch and semen, because he never wanted me more than when I was broken and bruised. "You are one fucking piece of work."

I ran in Lake Plata after I got home from school in the morning, making a circuit of the blocks around the apartment complex: Poinsettia, Hibiscus, Royalton, Largo, Miramar, the musical words that danced attendance on the flat frame houses with the attached garages. The heat was like a sock stuffed in your throat, and sweat ran from me like tears, tickling and taunting my legs and chest and arms. I left my wire-rimmed glasses on the battered chest in the bedroom and the sun made fluorescent spots in front of me and waves of black at the periphery of my vision. Sometimes, despite myself, I'd see Brooklyn in my mind, and it was as though if I ran hard and fast enough, I'd come around the corner and I'd be home, really home, up the street from the bay in Brooklyn. The towels would be soft on my body and the carpeting soft under my feet and Robert would be wandering around half-asleep, dogged by little-boy problems, lost shoes, misplaced homework. And Bobby would be—where? Somewhere else. We'd have the idea of Bobby in the house, as though any moment he might walk in. It would be like a perfume, like the smell of gravy cooking on Sunday, or the turkey on Thanksgiving. So sweet, the smell of safety. I could almost smell it over the smell of gasoline and petunias on the back streets of Lake Plata. Sometimes I cried as I ran, but it was so hot and I looked so raddled that you couldn't even tell. There was no one to see, anyhow. Everyone was inside or at work.

One morning there was a man standing at the corner of Largo and Miramar, leaning against the corner of a chain-link fence behind which a dog reared, snapped, snarled, filled with frustration at my flashing legs just out of his reach. By the front gate was a sign: BEWARE OF THE DOG it said. It seemed so completely superfluous that I almost laughed. The man nodded at me. His arms were folded across his chest, red as summer roses from the heat.

For a week I ran around the streets, different routes on different days, with certain landmarks to guide me: a trailer painted turquoise as bright as a postcard of the Caribbean, a white house with a black cat always unflappably sitting in one window, a lawn with a bumper crop of yellow plastic sunflowers with whirligig petals, occasionally stirred to a desultory turn in the still, mid-morning air. Once again I saw the man. This time he was reading a paper, standing at the same corner, and he didn't look up as I passed on the other side of the street. The third time I came upon him I was coming from the opposite direction, thumped around the corner and he was sitting in a parked car, a battered white sedan. It was near the end of my run and I was tired, had gone a good distance, four, maybe five miles. The sidewalk was cracked and heaved up just at the curb line, a nosegay of dried and dying dandelions growing where the earth beneath the concrete showed pebbly and brown. I stumbled, nearly went down, righted myself and felt a pain in my ankle, tried to continue quickly past him, saw him looking at me, noticed all at once his thick arms and chest, his odd disconnected half-smile, the way he seemed glad to see me as he leaned toward the open window. The dog was hurling itself at us both from behind the fence, and I wondered how I could have been foolish enough to assume them connected, man and animal. I was hemmed in by the car and the fence and I moved past him and yet waited, in my mind, to feel his hands. Maybe he muttered something; I don't know. But as I edged past him I ran faster, faster than I'd ever run before, all the way home. Locked the doors, checked the windows for the thousandth time, changed without showering because I was afraid that the sound of the water would mute the sound of someone coming in the window or the door, though they were locked, locked tight, what did they matter, locks? Once, in the emergency room, the cops brought in a woman who'd had to be carried, naked, from a building the city was demolishing. Wrapped in a blanket, her head tucked between her shoulders like a dying bird, she'd huddled in the corner of an examining room, and I'd asked her what she was afraid of. Her whisper was so soft that at first I didn't hear her. "Everything," she finally said a little louder. It shamed me now, to remember that I'd gone out to the nurses' station and said, under my breath, "What a head case this one is." It shamed me, now that I was afraid of everything myself. I'd never found out, after they took her up to psych, whether that woman had good reason to be afraid.

The next week I didn't run. I told myself it was the ankle. "It's a filthy habit, anyhow," Cindy said. "Get yourself one of those

Jane Fonda tapes." But one day I wore shorts, a T-shirt, and my shoes to school in the morning, and after Cindy had driven to pick up Chad from her mother and take him to tumbling class, I'd made a slow circuit of the track that sat, gray-brown and sun-burned, between the elementary school and the big sprawling middle school a block away. It was boring, that sort of running, no store windows to offer color and light, no "Good morning" from mailmen with their breath running in a stream of steam from between chapped lips. But from the track I could see the front and back entrances to the school, and the drive leading up to both. From the track I could see Robert and Bennie and the other boys who had begun to gather in a group around them shoot hoops on the blacktop during morning recess. If I could have run all day instead of working, I would have.

Mike Riordan fell into step beside me the third morning I was out there. He was wearing an Orlando Magic T-shirt and baggy running shorts. You can tell a lot by someone's running clothes. If the colors are bright, the fit fine, the logos designer, it almost always means fraud, someone who likes the idea of running better than the act itself. Mike Riordan's shorts and shirt looked ancient, one step removed from the rummage sale. The real deal.

"Okay if I join you?" he said, and I nodded, no words, because I was already breathing hard, the way I liked to, so that I felt really alive. For the next thirty minutes we said nothing at all, until as we were pulling up, panting, cramping, he added, "I have a free pe-riod now, and this beats evenings all to hell." Neither of us were chatty runners; both of us could go for almost an hour without giving up. Or maybe he slowed down for me. Or maybe I picked up for him. My fears cooled as my flushed face did, walking home to shower and change into my blue polyester uniform shift, to make my rounds. But at night I still set a folding chair beneath

Robert's window piled with boy stuff, video games and books and little bits of leftover Lego things he and Bennie worked on, things that would fall to the floor with a clatter if anyone came through the window.

I used Mike Riordan, those early days. I felt safer with him around, and I was unapologetic, unashamed about using him for protection, even though he had no idea I needed protecting, no idea that he was any more than my running partner. I'd never run with someone else before, and I was startled by the spurious and instantaneous intimacy it produced, the sound of the two of us breathing hard, ragged, in tandem, half-dressed, single-minded, perspiring and without the usual scrim of carefully arranged hair, polite smiles, makeup, and sunglasses. When I left school after my run, knowing that no stranger had entered the front office or peered through the chain-link of the playground fence, I left also knowing that no one could easily have contact with or news of Robert with Mr. Riordan standing guard. I remembered how he'd bellowed at the manager of the supermarket, and I felt less afraid for my son.

"He's sweet on you," Cindy said. "That's all I'm saying. That's it. He is."

"Oh, please," I said. "He's a friend. A male friend. Women have male friends."

"Well, now, dear heart, that's fine, except that if the good Lord had wanted women to have male friends he would have arranged for men and women to have something in common."

"You don't have men friends?"

"I have a husband. He sort of has friends. They're sort of my friends. You know the name of that tune."

I'd had a man friend once, or thought I had. Sometimes Ben Samuels and I ate lunch in the pale green cafeteria at the hospital, where everyone looked ill in the watery light from the glass-block windows. Once we went to a conference on trauma treatment in Manhattan, in the auditorium of the medical center where he'd gone to med school, and afterward he took me to a Japanese restaurant for dinner, where we sat on tatami mats, our shoes side by side at the sliding paper door, a pair of brown suede lace-ups, a pair of navy pumps. There was something about those empty shoes that suggested an indiscretion, but all we'd done was eat teriyaki and talk, of nothing, really, although both of us spoke a little more effusively than need be of our family lives.

Over tea he was surprised that I'd missed the piece in the Sunday *Times* about head injuries, more surprised when I said I didn't read the paper. "I can't believe a woman as smart as you can get through the day without *The New York Times*," he said, and I'd blushed, and been embarrassed, and replied in a flippant voice, "Cops hate the *Times*. They think it always takes the side of the bad guys. Cops spit on *The New York Times*. The *News* is the cop paper."

"But you're not a cop," he said. I've never forgotten the way he said that. It came back to me, even after he'd moved out West. "That's a good move for him," Winnie said when she heard about it, giving me a look.

I know Winnie thought I used Ben Samuels to get some of what I didn't get at home, someone to talk to, someone who took me seriously. I'd been happy in his friendship.

But happiness wasn't what I got from Mike Riordan's company. He made me feel safe, safer than I'd felt in a long time. And it made me feel safer having Robert at school with Mike there. Sometimes I think Mike sensed all that, without understanding exactly why, as he ran alongside me, stood on the sidelines in front of me at soccer games.

The first time I watched Robert zigzagging across the flat expanse of the school soccer field all I could think of, all I could watch was the stand of trees at one end. All I could think of was a familiar figure emerging from behind one of the tree trunks as everyone was staring the other way, downfield at the visitor's goal, of someone reaching out for the Lake Plata school forward with the floppy bangs and skinny legs, the quick kid who called instructions to his teammates in a surprisingly low voice as his feet churned up the turf. Bobby, motioning to Robert: come on, come here. Blink and he'd be gone, my son, floating off like a piece of ashy paper lifted from the fire by a wind up the chimney on a cold night. It was all I could do not to pull him off the sidelines when another boy went in in his place, and I think, turning and seeing me, knowing just what I looked like when I was terrified, Mike Riordan knew some of what I was feeling.

"I need a parent to go with us on the bus to Lakota, Tuesday," he said one day after we'd lost a home game 3 to 1.

"I'll be there," I said.

I'd never known a teacher to talk to, except for Grace, if an associate professor of American studies could be called a teacher. All those years of school with the nuns, grade school, high school, even nursing school, and the cool remove of their habits an instant bar to intimacy that remained when the black veils and white wimples gave way to street clothes and nurses' uniforms. Even the teachers at St. Stannie's had intimidated me, standing at the heavy school door and shutting it with a *thunk* when the last of the identically dressed children had hurried inside. I gave them my son, and twice a year they gave me a progress report—mediocre penmanship, decent spelling, an affinity for math and history. A good boy.

So for weeks I did what the kids did, called him Mr. Riordan, silly as it was, he five years younger than I, with that pink baby face and straw-colored baby hair. But it seemed to suit the circumstances. Mr. Riordan dropping Robert off after soccer practice and accepting a Pepsi at the kitchen table while he and Robert complained about the ref they'd had for the last game. Mr. Riordan taking Robert, Bennie, and two other boys to McDonald's to reward them for perfect attendance at the end of the first month of intramural practice and play. Mr. Riordan taking Robert and me to the International House of Pancakes after a Saturday morning game at which Robert had scored two goals.

"Let me say this," he'd said, bent over blueberry pancakes and bacon, wearing his yellow polo shirt with "Mike" embroidered over the heart. "You came to play today." He pointed his fork at Robert. "You came to play. And did. That second goal was a miracle."

"You looked good out there," I said, smiling.

"You looked great," Mr. Riordan said.

Mr. Riordan, the two of us sitting on the leatherette seats at the front of the bus, our conversation interrupted by the throwing of paper and the occasional muttered "asshole" from the seats behind. "Keep it clean, guys," Mr. Riordan yelled, "keep it clean." It's hard to call a teacher by his first name. Maybe that was when I started to call him Mike, on the bus. One day he had a lottery ticket in his top pocket, and when I mentioned it he blushed.

"I buy one every once in a while," he said, turning it over in his hands. "You know, you pick up the paper, some gum. Then you give the man a couple of numbers." He read them off the ticket: 19, 9, 44, 10, 21. "I don't even know how I picked these," he said.

"What would you do if you won? Would you quit your job?"

He shook his head. "Nah. Look at me. I play soccer with ten-year-olds for pay. Why would I quit?"

I laughed. "Mr. Riordan, Sean called me a Tampax," a boy named Andrew shouted from the back.

"Hold on," Mr. Riordan said, and walked to the back of the bus. I looked back, pretending I was watching the mediation, when what I was really looking for was Robert, the sheer pleasure of seeing him sitting quiet, maybe even content, near the back of the bus. He was staring out the window while Bennie talked to him about something. His profile looked hard, adult. He glanced up, saw me, waved. Mr. Riordan stopped by to talk to the two of them for a moment and they looked up at him, tipping their heads back on the slender straws of their necks, tipping them far back as though Mr. Riordan was a giant, or God. "He's doing it again," Andrew called. There was silence, then more bickering, then the rumble of a deeper voice, then silence again.

"You Tampax," I said, when he dropped back into his seat.

"I know," he said. "I do all the disciplinary stuff and one of my biggest problems is not laughing. One of the third-grade girls came in crying the other day. I sit her down, I give her a Kleenex. She's sniffing and blowing her nose and finally she says, "Joshua keeps telling me he loves me and I just want him to stop!"

"That is a great job," I said.

"I guess most people would quit. If they won the lottery, I mean."

"I wouldn't. I love to work. My mother always worked. When I was a kid, it was my father who didn't work. It was like a life sentence—guilty of emphysema. Sentenced to the big chair in front of the TV for the rest of his life. The poor guy was like a piece of furniture. I never wanted to be like that. I had my first job when I was sixteen."

"My mother never worked."

"How many kids did she have?"

"Seven."

"She worked," I said.

Out the windows of the bus the sun was sinking behind a grove of trees and a row of shacks the migrants used when they came to Florida to pick fruit. A stray dog chased after our tires, and the noise of the boys began to evaporate with the daylight, their conversation to go gray with fatigue. They'd lost, 4–2, in a tough game. Robert had played poorly.

"How's your hamstring?" Mr. Riordan said.

"Still sore."

"You should stay off it."

"Ha," I said. "I'll be out there tomorrow morning."

"I had Robert in my office the other day," Mr. Riordan said quietly. "I kept meaning to tell you."

"Why?"

"He got into some sort of argument with two of the boys. Apparently they were teasing him about the way he looks, how dark he is or something. You know how they are at this age. And he held one of them against the wall and said, 'I'm going to get you.' Mrs. Bernsen was just a little knocked out by the way he said it. Like he really meant it, if you know what I mean?"

I knew exactly what he meant. I closed my eyes and leaned against the window. Robert the Hobbit, Robert the Hobbit, making sure that no one got over on him, just as Daddy said. It was Bobby Benedetto's song, the one he sang as he paced his kitchen. I'm going to get that sucker who sells crack in the quad at the Lincoln projects. I'm going to get that asshole who laughed at us when we stopped him the other day. I'm going to get the jerk-off who threw the tennis ball at the patrol car, opened the hydrant, put his little brother out to work as a drug runner. Getting them all—that was Bobby Benedetto's vocation.

"Hey," Mike Riordan said, "it's no big deal. We talked. Or I talked and he listened. You know he's basically a good kid. He has some problems dealing with anger. And other stuff. I think he keeps things bottled up inside."

I know, I said. The divorce, I said, the move, the new school, the new friends. He would be fine. Fine. Fine. Fine. Sometimes you say a word so many times that it loses its meaning and shape in your mouth, until it's like a piece of gristly meat and you want to spit it out, or swallow and get it over with. Fine. First Robert said it, now I did. If we said everything was fine often enough maybe it would be true.

Even Mr. Riordan did it. One day as we were running, trickles of sweat outlining the curve of both our jaws, our breath coming hard and jagged, he suddenly said, softly, then more insistently, "Don't worry about him too much. Don't worry. He's fine." But of course he had no idea.

"He's fine," I said again.

"I know that," he said. "I do think it would do him some good to talk to somebody. Dr. Stern, maybe."

What could I say? There was no kid in the world who needed to talk to someone, as people always delicately said when they wanted you to see a shrink—I knew, I'd done it in the ER dozens of times myself—there was no kid who needed it more than Robert. There was no one who needed more to speak the words he couldn't say, to look at the things he couldn't see. Someday, I swore, I'd do that for him, so that he could give up the secret, once and for all, so that he could say that his father had lied to him, and his mother, too, all those mornings when they acted as though everything was all right. Fine. Fine. But not now. That was Robert Benedetto's story. And for now, no matter how bad it was for us both, Robert had to be Robert Crenshaw.

"I'll think about it," I finally said. "I really will. I know he needs to get things out of his system more."

"He might do better if a professional could help him with that. It might give him some ways to deal that would make him feel better."

"I know. I'm just not sure it's the right time."

"Well, think about it."

"I will. And promise you'll tell me if anything else happens. Or if you notice any kind of problem. I need to know. Please."

What could I tell him, this nice man with his nice open face, to explain away what seemed to be my stubborn refusal to help my child? That if Robert talked to the school psychologist about what was bothering him the gig was up, that bottling-up was part of the plan. I knew that for Robert's sake it would be a good idea for him to take a stroll twice a week through the maze of his memories, to try to reconcile the beloved father who'd done terrible things, the trusted mother who'd lied about them, the happy home that had been rotten at the root, like one of those trees in full leaf that blows over in a storm to reveal the hollow trunk. To talk about what it felt like to be suddenly plucked, still half asleep, from one existence, and set down a day later in another strange new one. But he would have to do it on his own. It was too dangerous for anyone else to know our secret. It was too dangerous for Robert to talk about what had really happened, who he really was. If he told a psychologist, he might tell a teacher. If he told a teacher, he might tell Bennie. And pretty soon everyone would know. Everyone, and Bobby. That was how Bobby would find us, through one missing brick in the wall between that life and this.

"He'll be okay," Mike Riordan said.

"I think so, too," I said.

One of our goalies was snoring behind us, a bandanna covering his shaved head. "Shane's starting a new fashion," I said. "Head lice," Mike Riordan whispered. "We managed to keep it pretty much contained to the fourth grade."

"Nearly there, folks," the driver said. Crickets were sawing away out in the muggy Florida night. It was already almost Thanksgiving.

"Do you know Chelsea Roerbacker?" I said, to change the subject.

I could see Mike Riordan's teeth in the dim gray light as he smiled. "I sure do," he said. "Speaking of Dr. Stern."

"I don't know how Cindy does it. It would drive me crazy, to have a kid of mine that frightened of that many things."

"You know what?" Mike said. "Most kids are that frightened of that many things. They're just too scared to admit it. And so are most adults. I think the amazing thing about Chelsea is that she puts it all out on the table."

"Mr. Riordan," somebody yelled. "Zachary spilled a juice box all over my pants. In the crotch."

"Go for it," I said.

He held up his lottery ticket and kissed it. "Please, God," he said.

I don't know exactly when I started to call him Mike, but I know that was the moment I began to think of him that way.

"Mr. Riordan," one of the boys moaned, "do you think we'll win next time?"

"Absolutely," he said.

For my birthday Cindy took me to the mall south of Lakota and bought me a decent haircut at a place called The Clip Joint. My birthday was November 10, or at least Beth Crenshaw's birthday was. Frannie Flynn's birthday was October 30, a hateful time to have a birthday, Mischief Night, the nasty stepbrother to Halloween, a day of soaped windows, egged windshields, staying inside, safe at home. I'd never had a birthday party, unless you counted the cake with butter-cream icing and pink roses my mother brought home in a white cardboard box from the bakery on the bottom floor of the office building in Manhattan where she worked. For my Sweet Sixteen I brought the cake home myself, from the bakery where I worked; now I knew the butter-cream was made out of shortening and sugar. "It's chocolate," my mother had said, when I cut into it, and Gracie had said, "Fran doesn't really like vanilla cake. You should have known that." She grew up fast, Grace; she always said what she thought. In bed that night she'd whispered, "What if I threw you a big birthday party at the Waldorf-Astoria . . ." But I pretended to be asleep.

Birthdays—that's how they get you. You wouldn't imagine that, would you, but Patty Bancroft said the biggest mistake people made was changing their name but keeping the same initials, and claiming the same date of birth. Patty Bancroft's people had shaved two years off my age as well, so that Beth Crenshaw, wearing a rubber cape in the beautician's chair that squeaked when you moved in it, was thirty-six years old.

"Manicure, pedicure, styling, color," Cindy said in the car. "On me. And Craig'll take the kids out waterskiing on Lake Lakota, then maybe Chuck-E-Cheese for lunch. Mine are happier than pigs in shit, excuse my language. Chad thinks Robert and Bennie are grown-ups, only more fun, and Chelsea thinks they're cute boys. Which they are. When's Robert's birthday, anyway?"

Someone who thought they knew children but didn't had assigned Robert a date of birth to replace April 30. "Fourth of July," I said.

"That's a tough one," Cindy said. "No school, so no school party. And everybody doing their own barbecues, beach trips, family deal. On the other hand, you'd always have fireworks. I guess I could work with that. You want your nails wrapped?"

I laughed. "What is having your nails wrapped?" I said.

"Oh, it's great. You'll see. They put these little pieces of linen on your nails, spray them until they get hard as a rock, file them, shape them."

"I can't have them too long."

"Don't be so negative."

"No one's messing around with my feet."

"You'll see. This'll be great."

She was right. Cindy was always right about things like that. My hair fell in soft layers around my face, a more buttery, warmer color than my own home dye job. My nails were painted with white tips and my feet massaged by a Korean woman in a pink smock who smiled all the time. It was pretty clear she didn't understand a word either of us said. It was early on a Saturday morning and we were the only people in the place except for two handsome, hard-looking, dark-haired women, the elder a shadow of the younger, who came in just as we were finishing. Between them they carried a long white box, and, setting it down carefully on the receptionist's Formica desk, they lifted out a crown of pearls and beads with a long tail of tulle the color of light coffee.

"Oh, that's gorgeous," Cindy said, watching everything in the salon's wall of mirrors, the ends of her hair falling like dandelion fluff on the shoulders of her rubber cape.

"A hundred and eighty dollars for a veil. Just for the veil!" said the older woman.

"Don't start," said her daughter as one of the beauticians began to set her hair in rollers.

"It would look beautiful with her hair up. Look at this." She held the veil out to us all: me, Cindy, the woman who was cutting Cindy's hair, the Korean woman who was shaving dead skin from my heels and smiling and nodding. "A chignon inside the band of beading, so that you could really appreciate, you see what I mean? Which would also mean a better view of the back of the dress when she's at the altar. See, they all look at the front of the dress, these girls, but most of what you see during a wedding is the back. You don't want the whole back of the dress hidden by all this hair."

"So you want your hair up?" said the beautician to the bride. The embroidery on her smock said her name was Jenna, and her

small, pinched features had settled during the mother's monologue into the carefully neutral look I'd learned long ago to adopt
with difficult patients.

"I told you what I want when I came in for the consult. I want
ringlets. She wants my hair up, but she's not the one getting
married."

"You look one hundred percent better with your hair up," her
mother said.

"Ma, you want your hair up, you get your hair up. I'm not getting my hair up."

"It'll ruin the pictures."

"Chris doesn't like my hair up. I don't like my hair up. I'm not
wearing my fucking hair up."

"You kiss your mother with that mouth?"

"You're done," said the woman who was blowing Cindy's hair
dry. The Korean manicurist handed us our purses so we wouldn't
smear our polish. "Look at how nice her nails look," said the
mother, pointing to my hands. "I told you you should have gotten
a French manicure."

"Ma, don't start," the daughter said. Cindy and I waited until
we were at the escalator before we began laughing. "What do you
bet she winds up with her hair up?" Cindy said.

"You think?"

"Oh, honey, I know."

My head smelled of flowers, and my hands looked elegant,
smooth, like they belonged to someone with drawers full
of sachets and closets with padded hangers. "They were so
Brooklyn," I said.

"So what?"

"Never mind. It's just an old expression. You were right about
the pedicure."

"I know I was. Happy birthday, honey."

Those were the times I felt bad about what I was doing, the times when I spoke aimlessly of a life in Wilmington that seemed an empty invention to my own ears, the times when Cindy patted my hand while she was telling another story of another friend getting screwed in divorce court. Cindy thought I was having a wonderful birthday, when my real birthday had been a week before and I'd cried most of the evening, thinking about Gracie somewhere, crying too. Gracie always helped me blow out the candles on my cake, even when I was a grown-up. I hated lying to Cindy, hated that I did it more or less every day just by letting her call me Beth. It was all I could do, sometimes, not to tell her everything.

"I bet Mr. Riordan'll like your hair," Cindy said, pulling the minivan onto the highway.

"I bet you've been waiting half an hour to say that. Ever since I got out of the chair."

"Tell the truth, I wanted to say something in the shop, but that Jenna lives in Lake Plata so I decided to protect your privacy."

"Thanks so much."

"So what is the deal here?"

"Cindy, you watch too much TV."

"You may be right, hon, but I can tell you that on TV the soccer coach and the player's lovely single mother wind up together. After many misadventures. Plus, I don't see too many other stars on your horizon. Except for Jim. He's a real romantic guy. That last time you ran into him leaving our house, I heard him say to the other guy in the truck, 'Man, would I like a piece of that!' What a sweetheart."

Jim was one of the laborers who worked for Craig's pool service. He was tanned from all those hours in the sun, and he took his shirt off every chance he got to display muscle definition that made him look like a Saturday morning cartoon superhero. The ends of his Fu Manchu mustache were always a little wet, and I had thought about what it would be like to sleep with him the first moment I saw him, balancing a shovel across the tight shelf of his shoulders, looking enough like Bobby Benedetto to be a first cousin. He smelled like sweat and chlorine, and I tried not even to look at him, those few times I'd run into him at the Roerbackers. But once he'd smiled at me, real slow, and I knew he knew what I was thinking.

"Like I said, you watch too much TV," I said to Cindy. "Mike Riordan is a very nice man. That's all."

"Oh, no. A nice man. That tears it. Remember how in high school, your girlfriend would go, oh, him, he's such a nice guy. And what that always meant was that she was dying to go out with the guy's nasty friend."

"Well, thank God high school is over."

"Oh, please. Life is high school, except everybody's either ten pounds lighter, or fifty pounds heavier."

I started to sort everyone I knew into one group or another. "You're right," I said.

"I am right, and I'm right about Mr. Riordan. And please don't tell me you're holding out for Mr. Right, because he ain't coming. He never comes."

"And this from a happily married woman."

"I'm happily married because I'm real realistic. The statute of limitations on finding them irritating as hell is four, maybe five years. It doesn't matter how good-looking they are or how much money they make; that's when you start to notice how they can't ever manage to put on a fresh roll of toilet paper or put dirty clothes in the hamper. You've been married, you know the drill:

Honey, where's my shirt? In the damn closet, dear, where it always is. Couple years gritting your teeth, and then you just got to get on with it. Or not, I guess." She looked over at me. "What got me going on that?"

"Mr. Riordan."

"Oh, never mind Mr. Riordan. Let me do your makeup when we get home. I got these new neutrals that'll look great on you."

Usually I resisted Cindy's sample case, but for once I went along with her. She made bacon, lettuce, and tomato sandwiches for us both, and then went to work on me with pencils and foam pads, powders and creams. Except for a mouth that was too big for the rest of my face, I looked good when she was finished. "Not a day over thirty," she said. Instead of thirty-six. Or thirty-eight. Another secret to keep straight, my very age.

"God, I wish you had a hot date tonight," she said. "Can I buy your clothes, too? No offense, hon, but you tend to play down your best feature. Your bod cries out for short white shorts and a crop top."

"You're the first person I've heard use the word *bod* since junior year high school."

"Or one of those little T-shirt dresses would be nice, too. And they're cheap. Dress Barn has them for forty bucks. That's where I got this." Cindy was wearing royal blue shorts and a print blouse with a ruffle down the front, white sandals, and a matching white belt.

"Can I ask you something without pissing you off?" I said.

"Shoot."

"How come you do all this—the makeup, the clothes? Don't you get tired of having to look perfect every day?"

And Cindy sat down heavily in the chair across from me, all the makeup piled on the glass table between us; with her face sort of sad and serious she looked like exactly what she was, a former prom queen who'd grown up, gotten married, and fought the good fight against losing her looks. "God, I'm sorry," I said. "I can't believe I said such a shitty thing."

"Don't rub your eyes," she said, "or that mascara will be all over your face. It's okay, anyhow. You're the only friend I've ever had who would ask me a question like that. Plus I think you're the only one I've ever known who I'd know how to answer. You know, most people, I'd just say, well, a girl's got to look her best, doesn't she? or one of those dumb-ass things you learn to say." I'd never heard Cindy swear before. I wanted to reach across the table for her hand, but she kept it curled up in her lap.

"I think it was the farm, you know it? It was just so dusty all the time, and the dirt came in the windows, so that no matter how often you'd dust there'd be this little bit of dirt that was always on the sills. And my mother would go out to make her deliveries and she'd smell so good and look nice, even though she's a kind of plain woman, you'll see when you meet her at Christmas. Then next morning she'd be up in a pair of men's overalls helping my dad out in the barns, and she'd smell like manure. And after a while I think I got like Scarlett O'Hara in the movie, you know? 'As God is my witness, I'm never going to be dirty again.'

"I fell like a ton of bricks my sophomore year for a boy named Jackson Islington, can you believe it, from some little place past Lakota. He was a senior, light-headed boy, but dark eyes, you know how nice that looks sometimes? And you'll know how crazy I was about him when I tell you I was only fifteen and he was already putting his hand up my skirt in the car, and I was letting him. He dropped me off one day and he was talking to my dad for the longest time and then my dad came in for dinner. I can still remember we were having macaroni and cheese and stewed tomatoes, and my daddy says to me, 'That's a nice young man. You don't meet too many anymore who have their hearts set on farming.'

"Lord, you should of heard that boy when I asked him about it next day coming home from school. Talking about the earth and watching things grow and the air in the early morning, making it sound like planting ten acres of feed corn was like being a priest or something. And then he started kissing me and he kissed my neck and then lower, the way he always did, I think that was what got me going in the first place, and then he kissed me on the mouth, stuck his tongue in the way he had a million times before, except I could taste the dirt, just taste it, so that I almost gagged.

"Even now sometimes I think, Cynthia Lee, what was wrong with you? Because when you're fifteen you're supposed to be able to just overlook those kinds of things, get all carried away and loopy in love. But I felt his hands on me and all I could think of was me all scrawny and dark the way my mother was, and dirt on the dining-room tablecloth. And that was that. That was that." There were tears in her eyes, and Cindy dabbed at them with one carefully bent knuckle. Then she laughed, the sort of shaky gasping laugh you laugh when you're trying to shake tears away, a laugh I'd laughed myself sometimes, talking to Grace about things.

"First date with Craig, I say to him, 'What do you think you'd like to do for a living?' He was seventeen, must have thought I was crazy. He said, 'I'm going into business.' The pool business gave me pause, with all the digging around, but he put that shower in the basement, right by the outside door, and he's clean and smelling of Christian Dior before he ever comes up those stairs." And with that she lifted her chin and smiled at me, the kind of brilliant smile one woman gives another that might as well be a punch in the nose, so little is it to be messed with. I looked down, fiddling with the tubes and pots on the table, looking at their labels: Terra Copper, Autumn Leaves, Sweet Peach, Sable. Almost despite myself I started to talk.

"I had this nun in eighth grade who wanted me to apply to this really good private school. She kept saying that she thought I had potential. Potential. I got to love the sound of that word. It sounds like somebody shot you out of a cannon. And then I talked to my parents about it, and my mother looked at the brochure I brought home. It was on this great paper, I remember, soft and shiny and there were beautiful color pictures of the kids in their uniforms, in science labs and reading in this big library. And my mother looked at it, and then she just said, 'Why?' That's all. It was like my whole life in one word. And it just stayed like that—when I wanted to go on a trip to Spain with the language club, or go to college. The answer was always the same: why? What's the point? I knew it was because they didn't have any money, with my father on disability and my mother working as a secretary. But it didn't feel like it was about money. It felt defeated. I'd look at this picture of the two of them on their bedroom dresser, thin and nice-looking and all happy and smiling, and it was just like defeat had taken over the whole house, until I didn't see the point either. I went to the local parochial girls' school and then I went to the local nursing school and then I got married and I guess I was just grateful for anything I could get.

"I didn't even really think about it until my sister got older. Because they did the same thing to her, except that she didn't pay any attention to them. What's the point, Grace? Take shorthand and typing, Grace. Dr. Edgar the dentist is looking for a receptionist, Grace. She'd just laugh at them sometimes, when we were in our room, make fun of them, even. She got herself a scholarship to private school for high school, and she got jobs and grants to work her way through college, and she rented a U-Haul so she could drive cross-country. My mother asked her why she was going all the way to Chicago for school. And she said, 'Because I want to.' Like it was the most natural thing in the world, to do what you wanted.

"Sometimes I'd see her looking at me and I could tell she felt sorry for me. God, that just about killed me, that little Gracie, whose diapers I'd changed, who I sang to and read to, who would yell 'Where Frannie?' running around the house, her diaper all droopy around her fat knees, who I taught all the line dances and how to roll her uniform skirt after school, that she would wind up feeling sorry for me. But, you know, I had no one, and Grace had me. That gave her confidence. Or at least a lesson in how not to do things." I shrugged. "She just made herself a completely different life. Just made it up, from scratch."

"Well, that's what you did," Cindy said.

"What?"

"Here," she said. "You made yourself a whole new life here. Just like your sister did."

"It's different."

"Oh, hon, that's what we all say," she said. "Of course it's different. Everything's so out of a clear blue sky that everything's always different. Like if I'd taken French instead of Spanish I might not have known Craig and my whole life would be different. Or if I'd gone all the way with Jackson before I knew what was what, everything would have been different. Scares me to think about it, it would have been so different. And if you weren't as nutty about Robert as I am about Chelsea I wouldn't have run into you and that would make things different."

"I am not nutty about Robert. He was in a new school, he was——"

"I know, I know. It was different than with Chelsea. That's fine. Anyhow, now we know everything we need to know about one another. You know how come I wear foundation and powder every day, and I know how come you don't. I thought we were just going to get our nails and hair done, and the next thing you know we're sitting here ripping our guts out."

"It's the birthday. There's something about a birthday that makes you think about your life that way. About how you got to be who you are. About whether you're happy with your life."

"I guess this might not be the best birthday to ask if you're happy with your life," Cindy said.

"I guess you're right. What about you?"

Cindy stared up at the ceiling. It was almost as if I could watch the years roll by behind the scrim of her eyes, her thinking about everything that had been, the man, the kids. Herself.

"I'm pretty happy with my life," she said finally. "But it isn't exactly what I expected."

"Amen," I said.

She leaned over, gave me a hug, put all the makeup in a tote bag she was giving away free with every order during the holidays. "Who's Frannie?" she said.

It was such a shock, but I didn't show a thing in my face. Besides, she wasn't looking at me, was looking down at the tools of her trade.

"What?" I said.

"You said your little sister called you Frannie. That she said 'Where Frannie?' all the time."

"It's an old nickname," I said, my breathing still ragged from talking, and listening, and feeling.

Cindy held out the tote bag, red with black patent trim. My mother-in-law would have loved it. "Well, Frannie, honey," she said, and just the word, that one word, sounded so good in her mouth. "Here's your new face. Happy birthday again. You're a new woman, swear to God."

"What happened to Jackson Islington?" I said.

"I haven't a clue," said Cindy. "What happened to your eighth-grade nun?"

"She left the convent, got married, and became a social worker."

"How about that?" Cindy said.

The sweet potatoes in the casserole dish on the kitchen counter looked like a photograph from some recipe in a magazine, if I do say so myself. The secret's in the bourbon, boiled down with butter and brown sugar until the whole mess is as thick as maple syrup. It was one of my mother's recipes. One of my mother's only recipes, unless you count the ones she read off the back of the can of cream of mushroom soup. At my mother-in-law's, where we always had Thanksgiving dinner, the sweet potatoes were tolerated, not welcome. The turkey, too, was more center-piece than main course, filled with sausage and aniseed, sur-rounded by platters of lasagna and artichokes stuffed with cheese. At Ann Benedetto's I used to eat the sweet potatoes myself, so that my casserole would not sit untouched on the sideboard, even though the food she served was always better. In the battle be-tween turkey and lasagna, turkey doesn't stand a chance.

The bourbon, that's what my mother always said. And the pecans. They were expensive, the pecans, almost three dollars a bag. The bourbon I bought in one of those tiny bottles they serve on the airlines. I was afraid of having booze in the house. The second week we were in Lake Plata I bought a bottle of cheap chardonnay, rough and vinegary on the back of my tongue, yet somehow it only lasted two days. After that, no more. Every bit of the bourbon went into the saucepan.

"Sweet potatoes are weird," Robert said, poking them with his finger the night before as they sat steaming on top of the narrow stove. "But they smell good."

They were crusty, brown and orange, and still fragrant if you put your face close enough, even stone cold on Thursday morning as I listened to Cindy on the phone, my heart sinking. Her voice was ragged, the static on the car phone in Craig's van like pebbles rolling around in the receiver. It was Thanksgiving, but instead of putting the turkey in the oven the Roerbackers were rolling south, down the spine of the state to the retirement village where Craig's parents lived and where, the night before, his father had had a stroke. And the Thanksgiving plans of the Crenshaw family, such as they were, were rolling away with them.

"I am so sorry," she kept saying. "I am just so sorry."

"Cindy, stop," I said, poking the potatoes. "Things happen."

"I know," she said. "I know."

"We'll make other plans," I said. "The Castros, maybe."

"Oh, I forgot about the Castros," she said, and her voice sounded a little lighter, the static a little more raucous, until somewhere along the highway we lost one another with a rattle, a strange sonic shriek, and a still pool of dead and empty air.

But of course I knew that the Castros had gone away, too, to celebrate Thanksgiving with some cousins in Orlando who had been, Robert told me, billionaires before they found it necessary to come to America and be reincarnated, driving cabs, cleaning motel rooms, another brace of people who'd been somebody else once. That morning, when I had stepped into the quadrangle of the Poinsettia complex, just to see the sky, to sniff the air, it had had the atmosphere of a place that had been evacuated, as though someone had forgotten to tell us about the coming storm, the floods, the tornadoes. But the only natural disaster was the holiday; our shabby little horseshoe of low-ceilinged duplexes was the sort of place to leave for a family gathering, not a place in which to have one. And we were leaving, too, leaving for the Roerbackers, with Cindy's family, and Craig's. Until Cindy and Craig and Chelsea and Chad—it almost makes me smile to give all their names together like that, and I still mocked Cindy from time to time—had gotten on the road at daybreak to travel to a hospital intensive care unit 250 miles away.

"Sweetie, we have a problem," I called upstairs to Robert, trying to keep the sound of bad news out of my voice. There was no answer and I trudged up, looked in at him on the bed, reading a magazine that Bennie had given him, an expert's guide to video games.

"Remember the game I told you about, that you said was way too expensive?" he said. "If I could get a used one for half-price, could I buy it?"

"I don't know," I said, sitting on the edge of the bed and dancing my fingers up his leg. "That was Cindy on the phone. She and the kids had to go to Mr. Roerbacker's daddy's house. He had a stroke last night and they had to go right away to see him. So we can't go to their house today."

"So where are we going to go?"

"I don't know," I said.

"I have to write a composition about Thanksgiving," Robert said.

"You don't have to write it today."

"I know. But what will I say if we don't have Thanksgiving?"

How had I forgotten what it would be like, to go to a cheap restaurant on that day of all days? I knew, knew in the way a person with scars can remember the pain of surgery. The first Thanksgiving after I met Bobby he'd invited me to his mother's for Thanksgiving. Grace and my mother and father had gone off to my aunt's house in the Catskills, carrying a cheesecake and a bottle of rosé wine, and I had set my hair, shaved my legs, ironed a dress that didn't need ironing.

I didn't know that Bobby hadn't told his mother until that morning, and I suppose he didn't know that she would fall entirely apart at the suggestion that there was a strange girl who expected to sit at her table, that white phony French-provincial table with the centerpiece of wax grapes in a silver basket, the table where only family sat. He sprung it on her; that's the way Bobby put it, as though I was a small animal with sharp teeth waiting to leap at the crepey white skin around Ann Benedetto's neck. I can imagine now what she must have been like that day: cold, affronted, then tremulous, a shaking hand to her only child's cheek, begging, begging, not today, not today. And so Bobby had changed my plans. I should have had some vision of the future then, as I listened to him talk on the phone. "It's no big thing," Bobby said. "I shouldn't've sprung it on her like that. She'll get used to the idea. You know, only child, all that. It's no big thing. She'll meet you at Christmas. I'll see you tomorrow. Don't eat too much turkey."

I could have stayed at home, heated up a can of soup, read a mystery novel. Instead I'd gone up to the Boulevard, to a Greek luncheonette, and had turkey with all the trimmings at a stool at the counter, two stools down from an old man with emphysema who smoked all through his meal.

"How was it?" Gracie said when they got home, carrying left-over turkey wrapped in tinfoil.

"Nice," I said.

"They put out a good spread, those people," my father had said, wheezing, falling into his chair and breathing into his oxygen mask as though it was the Fountain of Youth.

And still, remembering that, I took Robert to The Chirping Chicken, the two of us trudging along the shoulder of the highway because there were no sidewalks, there was no need for any, everybody rode in cars except for us. The linoleum and the fake leather on the booths was the color of the sun, so that you felt blinded when you walked inside. The gravy was the color of the sun, too, bright yellow with flecks of black pepper swimming on its oily sheen. At least it was not gray. That was what I remembered about the food in the luncheonette in Brooklyn, that the gravy was the color of cardboard, and I cried in the bathroom and blew my nose on a square of gray toilet paper, rubbing off the foundation and the powder I'd put on to go to Bobby's. I told Robert that story at The Chirping Chicken, and somehow I made it sound innocuous, even amusing, like something from one of the sitcoms, something that would have a laugh track. That's how I always tried to make life sound for Robert. I couldn't bear for him to feel pathetic, to see me as pathetic, too.

"These are really good mashed potatoes," he said. "They don't have one single lump."

"Did you not really want to go to the Roerbackers?" I said.

"No, it was okay. But it's like Grandmom didn't want you

to come when you weren't her family. I think Thanksgiving shouldn't be with someone else's family. I think it should just be with your family."

"What about Christmas?"

"Christmas is different."

I always did Christmas, at our house. I cooked standing rib roast and Murphy potatoes and caramelized onions and Ann Benedetto went to her brother's house on Long Island. Grace came to our house for Christmas, and Mrs. Pinto, whose children all lived in Florida. That was one of my biggest fears when I was out with Cindy at the mall, the possibility of running into one of Mrs. Pinto's daughters, with their big hair and their sharp eyes, fringed with lacquered lashes like anemones.

"Nana told me once Daddy hurt his finger on Thanksgiving and she carried him to the hospital because the cab didn't come. She said he was yelling and screaming and she was running down Ocean Avenue with him getting blood on her."

"I know that story," I said. "He needed eleven stitches in his hand. He fell on a bottle out in the backyard. He still has the scar."

"It's a big scar. When I got that cut on my head when I was five I got stitches but you can't even see." Robert raised his bangs to show his smooth, high, golden-brown forehead. There was the suggestion of a straight line across its center, as though someone had drawn faintly with a ruler. "Jesus, Frannie," Bobby had said, cradling the boy in his big arms on the sofa in the living room, running his lips softly over the bandage. "You should have called me at work. They could have raised me on the radio."

"It was only five stitches. And I got the plastic surgeon to do it."

"You know what, champ?" Bobby had said to Robert. "When you're grown-up, girls will say, oh, Robert, how'd you get that scar? And you can make up a story. You can tell them it was a racing-car accident. Or you were in a sword fight. You don't have to say you were bouncing on the bed and you hit the headboard. Which you're never going to do again as long as you live, so help me, God; keep him off the bed, Frances, do you hear me? Hear me, buddy?"

Robert had nodded, burying his face in his father's chest. Bobby had smiled at me over the brown head, so small, so fragile somehow. I'd felt Robert's head with my fingers for years after infancy to make sure that the bones had joined over the exposed fontanelle, the soft spot.

Why at that moment, pushing stuffing around the thick white plate with the side of my fork, did I suddenly remember what Patty Bancroft had said at the hospital? Winnie was discussing a case, a case of children brought in and then scattered to foster homes after their mother had been beaten into a coma in the middle of the night by an old boyfriend. "The children were asleep," Winnie had said, and Patty Bancroft had answered, spitting out the words, "The children are never asleep. They only pretend to be."

"Daddy broke his leg when he was in high school, in a car," Robert added, eating a roll. It was as though he had permission to talk about Bobby because I had done it first, but maybe only a distant Bobby, the Bobby he'd heard about in stories, not the man he knew, the man who did things while he was sleeping. Or pretending to be.

"He almost got shot, too, when you were a baby," I said, pushing him into the present. "Some man pulled a gun on him in the park but his partner got the guy to put it down."

"Daddy said it wasn't even loaded," Robert said. "He told me once."

"But he didn't know that until it was over. They were chasing the guy because he'd grabbed somebody's bag on Fifth Avenue."

"He told me."

"Your daddy is a good cop," I said. I didn't know if even that was true anymore. There was that teenager in the projects who said Bobby banged his face against the back divider in the patrol car. There was the minister who said Bobby had used a "racial pejorative" to a member of the congregation who'd complained when the cops tried to move along some teenagers from in front of a sub shop. I was like most cop wives; he told me just enough to make it a story but not so much that it'd make it real, feel what he felt, know what he knew. After a while I couldn't tell if he was a good cop. But at least he'd never come home with money in his pocket I couldn't explain, hadn't been like some of his friends, who suddenly came into A-frames in the Adirondacks or cheesy cruises to the Caribbean. "He's working a lot of overtime," the wives always said as though they were just passing the time of day, that breezy way they lied.

I looked down into my coffee cup. "I was really proud of your daddy then, Ba. I was proud of him lots of times. And I really loved him."

"But he hit you," Robert said. It was the first time he'd ever acknowledged it. Somehow it was like a benediction.

"Yeah," I said.

"Because you did stuff he didn't like."

I sighed. "Not exactly. Not really. You know how you know the things that will make me mad, like not doing your homework or being mean to someone or getting in a fight? The thing about Daddy was, it was really hard for me to tell what he didn't like. You couldn't really tell what would make him mad. And that made it hard. And even if you don't like what someone does, you can't hit them. When you're mad at someone, you have to talk to them, not beat them up. Beating them up is wrong. It's always wrong."

"You don't hit me," he said.

"No."

"You would never hit me."

"I would never hit you," I said.

"Daddy never hit me either."

"I know, Ba. What happened with Daddy and me, it had nothing to do with you," I said. It's what we're supposed to say, isn't it, whenever a marriage is ripped apart and the kids come tumbling out, tumbling down? And I don't know why, because it's such a big, bald-faced lie that any kid with half a brain could figure it out. Robert just nodded, played with the surface of his pumpkin pie. "That was kind of a dumb thing to say," I added. "What I meant was that it's possible for me and your daddy to be angry at each other without either of us being angry at you."

"I bet Daddy's mad at me."

"Why?"

"For going with you."

I leaned forward, took hold of his hand. It just lay there, a small warm thing half-asleep. "Ba, he'd know that you didn't have any choice in that. He'd know that I made you go."

"I bet he's mad at you."

"I'll bet he is, too," I said.

We walked home then, along the highway, and somehow it was better. Somehow it was good. The wind blew trash across our path, bits of wrappers, foil and plastic, and we must have looked a sight to anyone passing by. But it felt somehow festive, our isolation, as though we were having an adventure. "I'm full," Robert said, patting his belly, smiling up at me, kicking at a soda can along the gravel verge. I felt the ghost of Bobby at my shoulder, but it was the good Bobby, the Bobby who I'd found sitting quietly in the dark by the side of Robert's bed that night so many years ago, when our little boy woke up crying, reliving the fall on the bed, the doctor's hands, the needle with the lidocaine, the operating-theater light in his eyes. "I got him, Fran," Bobby had whispered to me, and I'd gone back to bed.

We walked over to the Lakeview with a Styrofoam container of food from The Chirping Chicken for Mrs. Levitt. Her hair was every which way when she opened the door, and there was a football game on the television. The living room was dark but when she saw Robert she moved around turning on the lights. "This is a beautiful boy," she said. "He should have some soda." Robert was frightened, I could tell, his eyes ricocheting around the room, lighting on the hospital bed then bouncing away. "It's all right," Mrs. Levitt said. "That's Mr. Levitt. He likes the Green Bay Packers, don't you, Irving?"

"That's college football," Robert said, looking at the TV.

"Aah," said Mrs. Levitt, "what do I know? Besides, you don't complain, right, Irving?" Her food was on the kitchen counter, and I put it on a plate and brought it to the card table. The two of us sat on either side of her as she ate, patting her mouth with a paper napkin. She held forkfuls out to Robert, but he shook his head.

"You make house calls on holidays, Mrs. Nurse?" she said, and I smiled. We didn't stay long, just long enough for her to feel as if she'd had company on the holiday. As we left she handed Robert an old, old copy of *The Adventures of Tom Sawyer* with a dark-green cover and a gilt fleur-de-lis on its spine. Inside in faded ink was a big, round, florid signature: Irving S. Levitt. Robert clutched the book as we walked home.

There were almost no cars on the highway, and the breeze was a little cold, as though even the tropics had to pay homage to the Pilgrims' chilly feast. It's as if life stops in America on holidays. Or maybe it's that way everywhere, all over the world, all the places I've never gone, countries I've never seen. It used to be that way on Sundays, when Gracie and I were young. The newsstands and the variety stores were quiet and dark, the OPEN signs in the windows flipped over to CLOSED. The little knots of people at the corners where the buses stopped on weekdays, workdays, were gone, and the streets had a sleepiness like the sleepiness indoors, where working people dozed in their chairs and children chafed at the torpor, bored with checkers and Old Maid and the bickering of their elders. Now only the holidays—the real holidays, not Presidents' Day, or Labor Day—have that bittersweet air of stop time I remember from Sunday, the sabbath. It was the way life had seemed to me when we'd first arrived in Lake Plata, like falling through nothing. It didn't seem that way as we walked home, the turkey I'd asked the waitress to give us for sandwiches in a plastic shopping bag in my hand. It seemed as though we were taking it easy, having a real holiday, nothing to do, no stories to tell. Or to make up as we went along.

"I love you, sweetie," I said.

"I love you, too. If I can get that video game for, like, half price, can we buy it?"

"Don't push your luck."

"Please?"

We had a good time, the rest of that desultory day. I know, because I read about it later in Robert's composition, which made it seem real to me, so real that I put the composition in my bedside drawer after it came home from school. We took out the pot of wallpaper paste I'd bought to paper the bathroom and used it instead to paste pictures from old *Sports Illustrated*s to Robert's closet door. Mattingly, Dr. J., Boomer Esiason, even the women from the Olympic basketball team. We sat cross-legged on the floor of his room, which was dingy and had a line of dirty rubber sole marks around the wall a foot above the molding, as though some kid had kicked and kicked and kicked and kicked. We made a mess, Robert and I. We'd never made much of a mess before. The closet door was covered with biceps, long legs, faces. It was almost like company. We crammed the leavings from the magazines into a garbage bag, and Robert stood back, his fists on his hips, and narrowed his eyes.

"This is the coolest thing we've ever done," he said. "Bennie's not gonna believe this."

"It looks really good," I said.

"How will we get it off?"

"Don't worry about that now," I said.

Then we watched an old movie on television, wound around one another on the scratchy old couch, and ate turkey sandwiches, and toasted each other with ginger ale. There was an old jar of maraschino cherries in the refrigerator door, just like in an ordinary house, like my real house, on the bay in Brooklyn, the jar of cherries you bought for one guest who drank Manhattans—Bobby's aunt Mae, his uncle Thomas's wife—and that ever after sat and sat on that shelf inside the door. I put a cherry in each of our sodas.

"I used to do that for Aunt Grace when we were little girls," I said. "I'd put the cherry juice in, too, and make it a Shirley Temple for her."

Maybe that was what did it. Or maybe it was just curling up on the couch with Robert, feeling him warm and pliant beside me, smelling his hair the way I used to smell Gracie's as I pulled it into an unruly ponytail. Or maybe it was just that it was, after all, Thanksgiving.

My sister's Thanksgivings were like those horrible short stories in *The New Yorker*, that seemed to have no beginning, no ending, no point. A visiting professor from Oxford who wanted to know all about the Pilgrims. A research assistant whose husband had just left her for another man and who wept in the kitchen and drank too much wine. The couple who lived down the hall from Grace, artists who brought couscous with cranberries in it. Oh, it was funny to hear all about it afterward, and I always did, because the last thing Grace did on Thanksgiving night was to call and tell me all about it.

"And, naturally, she's sitting at one end of the table telling me how satisfying it is to work with her husband, how close it's made them, and he's sitting at my end with his hand on my thigh," she'd say, and "Have you ever made stuffing with chestnuts? If not, don't, because it sucks!" and "Tell Robert this Brit brought me little plastic Pilgrims and I'm foisting them on him when he comes to see me next week." She always called me, just shy of eleven o'clock, Grace did. And so, after Robert stumbled from the couch to his room, his breath smelling of mayonnaise as I kissed him good night, I picked up the old rotary phone on the wall in the kitchen, poured myself more ginger ale, and sat on the linoleum cross-legged, my heart going like a mouse in a cage. She knew, when she picked up; I could tell she knew by the way her voice was, soft and whispery, not like Grace's insistent alto at all. She had to say it twice—"hello . . . hello?"—because the shock of hearing her overcame me suddenly, knocked the wind out of me.

"Happy Thanksgiving, baby girl," I finally said, and my voice wasn't my own either.

"Oh, my God," she said, and she started to cry, "oh, my God. Oh, Frannie. Oh, Frannie." For a minute or two all we did was cry.

"Where are you?" she finally wailed, and then immediately, in a more ordinary adult Grace voice, "Don't tell me. Don't tell me anything that matters. Don't tell me anything that I can give away."

"To Bobby."

"To Bobby. That son of a bitch." Her voice thickened again. "He sat in my living room and he cried. He cried. I almost felt sorry for him. I would have, if I hadn't seen your face. Even then, he got to me. I wound up telling him that if I heard from you I'd make you call him."

Her words caught in her throat, part grief, part fury. "A week later he comes back and wants to know, have you called, where are you, what's your address. And I said I had no idea, I hadn't heard anything from you. And he accused me of being an accessory to a kidnapping! I couldn't figure out what he was talking about at first. I said, Bob, don't forget that I saw her face. And he says to me, that's exactly why you don't want to fuck with me, Grace."

"Did he hurt you?"

You could hear the hum of the telephone static in the silence, in the moment when Grace tried to decide which would be better for me, the truth or a lie. She went for the lie. Don't we all?

"No," she said.

"Don't let him in again, Gracie. You can't take the chance. He just goes out of control."

"I know. I know. My God, Fran, what you've been living with all this time."

"We're fine," I said. "Robert's fine. He's getting settled. I'm working. I've got a place, and a little money."

"Let me send you more."

"I can't. I can't give you the address. Or the phone number. It's not that I don't trust you. It's just safer."

"The bastard could break my leg and I wouldn't tell him anything. That son of a bitch. My God, Frannie, I feel like such a fool. All those years you taking care of me, such good care, and you were in so much trouble and I didn't even figure it out, or do anything. Nothing. I did nothing." She started to cry again, my little sister, the way she had when she was a child, when I'd hold her head to my chest, hold it still to stop the sobs. "I didn't do anything to help you."

"You didn't know."

"How could none of us have known? I called Winnie at the hospital. She said the same thing. She suspected, but she said they all told themselves that you wouldn't put up with it."

"It's amazing how much you'll put up with," I said.

"I lie in bed at night and think about having him killed and dumped some place where no one will find him. Sometimes I can't believe it's me. I want him dead. If he were dead, then everything would be fine. You'd come back. You'd be safe. I pray that a car will run him down, or that some scumbag on the streets will shoot him."

"I'm safe now, sweetie," I said, matching Grace lie for lie. "Don't talk about killing anybody."

"Twice my mailbox has been broken into and the super thinks it's druggies, but I think it's him. I had my phone checked for bugs."

"Jesus, Grace, he wouldn't bug your phone."

"Oh yeah? You sit there and tell me you're sure he wouldn't do that."

"He might," I finally said. We were both silent again, the silence of two people who have long lived with and loved the sound of each other's breathing. That's what I wanted Robert to do, when he was grown-up, living a life away from me. I could hardly stand to think of it, but when I did I thought of telephone calls when I would just listen to him breathe over the line.

"How's Mom?" I finally said.

"The same. She told Aunt Faye you'd decided you needed a change of scene. She told me that Bobby was rude to her when he came to her house. Rude. Jesus God, what an understatement. 'He was really rude to me, Grace Ann,' she says."

"Oh, I bet he was," I said. "Never mind. Tell me the dinner story."

"What?"

"You know."

She thought I was crazy, wanting the old familiar story of her Thanksgiving dinner, the story of the strange food, the urban strays. But she did it. There'd been a defrocked priest who'd been prominent in the antiwar movement a quarter century before, who brought a bottle of good wine and then drank the whole thing himself. "It's the first time I've heard anyone actually use the word *imperialist* in conversation," Grace said. There was Grace's lesbian friend Trudi, who taught Virginia Woolf and Gertrude Stein and got into an argument with everyone else at the table about whether the Virgin Birth meant Mary was gay. There were two old women from the building who sounded like second cousins to Mrs. Levitt, who brought rutabagas that had turned out to be surprisingly good, and a graduate student from American Samoa who felt compelled to tell Grace in the kitchen just as she was whipping the cream for the pie that he loved her. "Oh, for God's sake, Ramon, cut that pie and put it on plates, I told him, and that was the end of that," Grace said in her old, wry, dismissive, strong Grace voice.

"We went out to dinner at a pretty bad restaurant," I said softly. "It was nice. We went to see one of my patients. We watched *Miracle on 34th Street* after. I think that's why I called."

"We watched it, too," Grace said. "Trudi cried and said she'd always been in love with Natalie Wood."

"We were watching the same movie at the same time. That's pretty good."

"I miss you so much," Grace said.

"I know."

"Give Robert a hug and tell him I miss him, too."

"I can't, Grace. I can't tell him I talked to you. I can't confuse him too much, about now and then, here and there. I can't stay on too much longer, either. I'm afraid. I'm afraid for you, mostly."

There was silence again. "*Breakfast at Tiffany's* is on the Movie Channel at midnight," Grace said. "You want to watch it together?"

"We don't get cable here."

"Will you call again?" Grace said.

"If it's safe," I said. "I'm with you every day in my mind. I'm running."

"I'm running with you in my mind," Grace said. I put down the phone in Florida and she hung up in New York.

I bought Robert the game he wanted for Christmas and hid it in the crawl space above the second floor. I bought Cindy a small sweet landscape I saw in a poster shop at the mall, and Mike Riordan a nylon jacket for running on rainy days. I bought presents for all my patients, although we weren't supposed to: a computer game for Jennifer, full of dragons and demons and a female superhero in a breastplate; a book for Melvin on smart investing and a romance novel for his wife; and, for Mrs. Levitt, a three-year subscription to *People* magazine. Christmas was coming, and I had enough money to buy presents. No one asked for the rent; I didn't get a phone bill. There were calluses on my heels from my running shoes. When the phone rang now I just answered it, listened to the home-care agency ask about taking on a short-term assignment, Cindy to ask whether I wanted her to drive me to school for soccer practice, the school to ask if Robert could take Tylenol for a headache. Twice it rang and no one was there. That happens to everyone, I told myself. To everyone.

"You all right?" Cindy said one morning in the library.

"I'm not sleeping real well," I said.

"Ladies," Mrs. Patrinian said, "not too loud please."

"You tried taking melatonin?" Cindy said. "One of the moms at Gymboree swears by it, says she can't even manage to stay up for the news now."

When we went back to her house that morning she made me muffins and searched her medicine cabinet for sleeping pills. "Nothing but under-eye concealer, hon, but to tell the truth you could use it," she said.

"Do I look that bad?"

"You look tired. Sort of frail. I don't know, some men like that look."

"Some men like single women in their twenties with no kids."

"You just stay away from those men, and keep on running around that track."

"You got a one-track mind," I said.

"Ha, ha," Cindy said.

I told Cindy about Grace, and a little about our parents, although I placed them all in Wilmington, Delaware, along with two older brothers and the accountant from whom I was divorced. I changed the subject Gracie taught from American studies to English literature, and I never mentioned Hunter College. I told her that my father had died of cancer, not of the emphysema he'd picked up as a New York City firefighter, all those buildings with asbestos insulation and two packs of Camels a day. I told her my mother was a secretary, even told her that she was the secretary to the head of a labor union. Soon I knew all about Craig and his pool business, about how Chelsea was afraid of thunderstorms, dogs, and insects, and how Chad was afraid of nothing, about Cindy's mom, Helen, and how she was one of the

people who discovered that the Avon bath oil repelled mosquitoes, since the farm had more mosquitoes than crops. She was a
second-generation Avon lady, Cindy was; she showed me the
story in the Avon annual report about her and her mother. Her
parents' farm was somewhere between Lake Plata and Jocasta,
and her mother had logged sometimes a hundred miles a day
dropping off eyebrow pencil and bath-oil beads to the wives of
other farmers, before the area was all built up, chock-full of retired Northerners and people who confused sunshine with gold.
Cindy went along when she got older, swiping those little sample
lipsticks that the Avon lady left at our apartment for me and
Gracie, even though our mother wouldn't buy a thing. A sea of
moisturizer managed to keep Cindy's parents' place afloat, the
thirsty faces of all those women baked leathery by the harsh
Florida sun.

Cindy and Craig had lived on the farm right after they were
married, then built their own place in a subdivision two miles
from the center of Lake Plata, in a redwood house with a lot of
windows and an aboveground pool with some kind of automatic
alarm on the surface so Chad wouldn't fall in and drown. Chelsea
was afraid they'd all drown, in the pool, at the beach, in the tub.
They lived at the end of a cul-de-sac, in an area of cul-de-sacs, as
though by eliminating through roads the people who lived there
could keep the rest of the world away. Every time I came for
coffee I took the measure of Cindy's kitchen, envying her her no-
wax linoleum and the double-door refrigerator with the automatic ice maker. But as my eyes roved around the white Formica
and the oak cabinets I was really walking through my own house
in my mind, up the four steps with the white iron railing, through
the storm door and into the foyer with the half-round table and
the gilded mirror over it, the one Bobby's mother gave us for a

housewarming present. It's funny how you get about a house when you've never had one, never ever thought you'd have one. The day we signed all those papers, with thirty-years this and thirty-years that, passing around the checks like in some grown-up board game, we'd gone over to the house and wandered about like a couple of kids, our words echoing in the emptiness. Buying the house made it seem as though it was us that was so solid, made of brick and plaster so that nothing could blow us over. I remember looking up the stairs and it was like they were reaching up, not to three bedrooms and a bath with a glassed-in stall shower, but to heaven. He'd shoved me a few times by then, even hit me in the stomach once. But I never looked up those stairs and imagined myself falling down them with a fist in the small of my back.

"This is it, baby," he said, and he pulled me down to the wall-to-wall, his words echoing in the empty, stripped-down rooms. And it was. I got carpet burns on my butt that day, and I was the happiest woman in the world. People can talk about self-respect all they want, and people do plenty, usually when they're talking about somebody else's business. But whenever I thought about leaving, sometimes as much as leaving Bobby I thought about leaving my house. Balloon shades and miniblinds and the way I felt at night sleeping on my extra-firm mattress under my own roof that we'd had hot-tarred the year after Robert was born—all of it helped keep me there. And if that sounds foolish, just think about that solid settled feeling you get when you open your cabinets and there are the mugs for the coffee that have held the coffee day after day, year after year, hanging in a row from cup hooks, all the same color, the same size. Small things: routine, order. That's what kept me there for the longest time. That, and love. That, and fear. Not fear of

Bobby, fear of winding up in some low-rent apartment subdivision with a window that looked out on a wall. Fear of winding up where I'd come from, where I was right now. It took me a dozen years of house pride and seventeen years of marriage before I realized there were worse things than a cramped kitchen and grubby carpeting.

I wondered how much damage Bobby had done to our house when he'd found us gone, with no one around to bruise or break. I wondered what he'd told his mother, whether he'd told his friends, or whether he'd just quietly set about the business of finding me. He had a half-dozen friends who were on full pension and working as investigators; maybe he'd called one of them. One hundred and thirty days I'd been gone. August. September. October. November. Someone would have thought of Patty Bancroft by now. When a car pulled to the curb in front of the apartment complex at two in the morning it rocked my world. Cindy gave me a bottle of melatonin, but I was afraid to take it, afraid to sleep deep. I dozed on and off each night, lulled by the sound of Robert's breathing over the baby monitor.

It's funny; with all the elaborate preparations that Patty Bancroft's people had made, I never doubted that some day he would find us. I always felt like I was just buying time, the time it takes to raise one boy from child to adult. I never figured out how hard it was going to be to do that until I started, and then the bitch of it was that it was too late to turn back, though I wouldn't have turned back anyhow. The bitch of it was that it takes so much time and effort to make things good for them, and so little to make them bad. The bitch of it is that we're never sure whether what we're doing is right or wrong.

Some of the damage is done. Robert watches too much, is too quiet. It's better when he's with other kids, but with adults he's always waiting for something to happen, like a psychic looking down at someone's palm. When he got thrown out of the super-market, he was angry and upset, but he wasn't surprised. It was as though he knew that grown-ups, at any moment, might go off like car alarms, loud, scary, for no reason at all. The truth is, that's the way Bobby made him. And me, too, by taking it. Robert has a look on his face too much of the time that people have when they think they've heard something moving around in the basement, heard the rumble of thunder so far away it just might be a truck in the next block. He had that look on his face that last time in Grace's apartment. That's how I think of the weeks before I left: the last time. The last time Bobby hit me. The last time I saw my sister. The last time I left my house, locking the door behind me.

The last time in Grace's apartment I saw Robert's face change, saw it go still and watchful, realized in a minute or two that he'd heard the elevator and the footsteps before we had, had been lis-tening for them. His eyes were huge but his shoulders hunched, as though he was trying to make himself small, smaller, tiny, in-visible. *Bang*, at the door. *Bang*, and Robert shrinking into him-self like a little old man. It's amazing, how furious the sound of knuckles meeting wood can sound.

"How the hell did he get upstairs?" Grace had said, and she made herself big, threw her bony shoulders back, marched in her clogs—*bang, bang*—to answer the banging at the door.

"Go away, Bob. Just go away."

"I want my wife and my son." I had been able to hear in Bobby's voice that he had been drinking, but not too much. "Now."

"Go away, Bob. You've done enough damage."

"This is none of your goddamn business, Grace. Frannie? Fran? You come out here and talk to me or I'll break the goddamn door down." I could feel Robert's shoulders vibrating beneath my fingertips, or maybe the vibrations were coming from inside me.

"How the hell did he get up here?" Gracie said, all her freckles standing out against the white of her face, and from the other side of the thick oak door of her apartment came what sounded like a chuckle. "I showed the doorman my badge, Grace." That voice again, that deep bass line, music to someone's ears, if not mine. You could just see him talking to the Russian émigré who minded the door of Grace's building, an old man in a faded blue-black uniform and ill-fitting hat. You could see Bobby flipping open the little leather case I'd given him when he made detective and the doorman falling back before him, perhaps even touching his hand to the corner of his hat. Sometimes I thought how hard it was to be a cop, to put on the clothes and be a force of law and then take them off and be no more than a man with a cheap sport shirt and a stack of bills. But sometimes it made things easier.

"Let him in," I said.

"No."

"Let him in, Grace. Or take Robert into the other room and I'll let him in."

"Aw, hell, Frances," Bobby had said when I unlocked the deadbolt and the other two Yale locks, but whether it was because of my betrayal in leaving him and going to Grace or because of the look of my face, which was mottled purple and black where it wasn't covered with adhesive tape, I don't know. Maybe he didn't know how bad he'd hurt me. He'd come in after midnight the night before and banged around the kitchen and the living room looking for something, muttering furiously to himself, waking me from a sound sleep, so that I couldn't go off again. I don't know why I went downstairs. I've asked myself that so many times, no matter what Patty Bancroft likes to say on television about placing blame where blame belongs. All I know is that if I'd done what I'd done so many times before, pretended to be asleep, ignored the staccato sounds of rage from below, I'd still be sleeping in my own bed now, and my son in his. Or maybe not. If it hadn't been my nose on a Wednesday in late July, it would have been my jaw on a Saturday in September. I suppose that's true. Like a cloud to a storm to a hurricane the thing between us had gotten bigger and blacker every day, until maybe it was bound to pick us up, smash us down, leave us all in ruins. In Lake Plata.

There wasn't even an argument. Or maybe Bobby had been having an argument with me in his head all day long—on the job, in the car, while he was banging around the kitchen. Maybe it was an argument made of saved string, a big, brightly colored ball of an argument, the synthesis of all the arguments we'd ever had before. Why the fuck do you baby the boy go to your sister's ignore my mother wear that skirt work so many hours look at me like that fuck my friends your friends strangers doctors everyone anyone the man in the moon? I'd stumbled down the stairs and into the hall in my long white nightgown and the light hurt my eyes and I couldn't see his, could only see half a dozen drawers and cabinets gaping open, as though he was looking for something. He probably was. Bobby was always looking for something, and neither of us knew what it was.

"Bobby, what is your problem?" I'd said, squinting in the light, and it happened, just like that, three good punches that I remember and then I came to maybe an hour later, covered in blood, my nose and tongue numb. I'd broken one and bitten right through the edge of the other. I'd fixed myself up with Bacitracin and bandages and gone to bed right beside him. I know people will find it hard to understand that, but it was my bed, I belonged there, I wasn't going to be thrown out of my own bed no matter what. I woke once to hear Bobby sending Robert off to school, pretended to be asleep when I heard our bedroom door open. I called in to work sick when Bobby was gone, waited for Robert to come home, spent $25 on a cab and took him to Grace's and let myself in and waited there in the shadows, no lights on, her apartment cheaper because it was at the back of the building. Robert fell asleep in her bedroom.

"I broke my nose," I said when Grace came in with her briefcase and her tote bag full of books.

She stood there, my baby sister, still that even if she is thirty-two, and her own face crumpled, and she sat on the arm of the sofa and took my head in her hands. She's little, Grace, but strong in her bones and muscles somehow; she lifts weights, too, just like Bobby, and when she raises those skinny arms over her head to stretch you can see all the connections in her body, everything, biceps, triceps, shoulder muscles like rubber bands.

"No, you didn't," she said. "You didn't break your nose. Don't you ever say you broke your nose. Someone else broke your nose. That son of a bitch. That bastard. I told Mom he was doing this. I told Mom about all these things that happen to you. That big bruise you had the last time we had lunch. The time you had the marks all over your one arm. And you know what she said? She said you always were a clumsy kid. Jesus God, if she could see you now."

We sat at Grace's round oak dining table, Bobby and I, while Grace took Robert into her bedroom. It was a small apartment and the table was really at one end of the living room, by casement windows that looked out over a sliver of 104th Street. "Where are you gonna sleep here, on the couch?" he said.

"Where's Robert gonna sleep?"

"Look at my face," I said.

"My son should be in my house. Not in some shit hole on the Upper West Side. You don't know this area like I do. He could get hurt here."

"Look at my face," I said.

"I'm taking you home," he said.

"No."

"Then I'm taking Robert home."

"I won't let you."

Then Bobby looked at my face, looked at it good, looked at it with a cold, cold look that he, for all the things he'd done to me, had never given me before. And like he'd been rehearsing it he said, real quiet, "What are you gonna do, Fran? Call the cops?".

That's when I knew. That's when I knew that this was the last time, that I was leaving. If there was a moment when I decided that Bobby Benedetto would never touch me again, it was at that moment. He was gloating, really, although for once you couldn't read his mood in his voice. He was telling me that I was trapped, that I was chained in some basement he'd created, a basement with flowered ironstone dishes all laid out neatly in the cupboards, with silk flowers in a vase on the dining-room table. He was telling me that I'd never get away, that he could do what he wanted and I couldn't do a thing about it.

As we were leaving, Gracie pulled me back into the little foyer for just a moment. "Please don't do this, Frannie," she said. "I'll help you. I'll do anything to help you."

"How?" I said. I was asleep on my feet and my face hurt so much that the pain was all I could think of.

"I'll think of something," she said.

"He's going to take my kid, Gracie," I said.

"We can stop him," she said. I laughed then, even though it hurt, a bitter choking chuckle halfway to a sob. "What are we going to do, Grace, call a cop?" I said.

That night I gave up and slept on the floor in Robert's room. Bobby saw the puddle of pillow and blanket on the floor and tried to put his hand out to me. I cringed, pulled away, then looked him full in the face. Once I saw a man in the psych ward reading the notebooks he'd written before he'd been given antihallucino-gens, reading the gibberish he'd written frantically, fanatically, as though it was the secret of the universe. Bobby looked a little like that when I pulled back from his big hand.

I'd taken two Percocets I had left over from having my wisdom teeth out, and when I woke up, my one cheek beating with every beat of my heart, the sun was making shards of daylight across the blue carpeting and the house was empty. I ran from room to room calling Robert's name, and finally I called the principal of his school, who called the counselor at the school day camp, who said that he was in gym, playing pillow polo. There were only ten days left of day camp. We were renting a house at the beach for the first two weeks of August, a cottage on Long Island Sound. But I wasn't going.

I'd called a family planning clinic in lower Manhattan to make an appointment for the next day. Then I'd called Patty Bancroft. And I bet Bobby thought it was because he'd broken my nose and bloodied my face. He'd never touched my face before; it was as though, as never before, he'd touched my insides, who I was, who I am. And it was his threat, too, that made me understand that I had to run to hide, to get away. What was I going to do, call a cop?

But maybe it was Robert who made me run, really. It was the look on his face on the way home from Grace's apartment that last time, the look on his face as we passed under the streetlight on our corner. The look on his face was nothing, nothing at all, the look he might have if he were watching a boring movie on television or playing with his food at the dinner table. The part of a little boy that would be frightened if his father threatened his mother and his aunt, the part of him that would be scared and screaming if his mother's face was all bruised and bloodied: that part of Robert was dead. Or been driven so deep inside that you couldn't see it and he couldn't feel it. I saw it for a moment when he came home that next day from day camp and saw me in the kitchen, in the sunlight; I saw the kind of horror and fear that a normal kid would feel. But then it was gone again, his face flat and closed, as he asked me whether I'd had an accident. So many accidents during his childhood, and all of them lies.

That's why I left when I did, how I did. During the long nights of a Florida winter, alive with wind sounds and whispers, as I imagined that Bobby was on the roof, at the door, jimmying a window open, I had a lot of time to think. And that's the truth. That's why I left. I'm a nurse, you know, a Catholic girl, a mother, and the wife of a man who wanted to suck the soul out of me and put it in his pocket. I'm not real good at doing things for myself. But for Robert? That was a different story.

O h, goodness gracious, you must be Beth. And Robert." Cindy was right, her mother was thin and dark, as though she'd been dried by the sun, a raisin of a woman with her daughter's big blue eyes and electric smile. She stood aside to let us into the house, her arm extended as though we were being welcomed to something magical.

"Merry Christmas," Craig said, getting up from the couch, a mug of eggnog with snowflakes painted on it in his hand.

"Merry Christmas," said Mike Riordan, who was sitting next to him.

"Hi, Mr. Riordan," said Robert. "What are you doing here?"

"You come in here, Beth," Cindy shouted from inside the kitchen.

When I'd been younger I'd worked at the hospital sometimes on Christmas Eve and Christmas Day, ceding the holiday to the older women with children and in-laws to cook for. But even in the lounge of the medical-surgical floor, or the emergency room, we managed to construct our own traditions, the fancy trays of meats and cheeses studded with radish roses, the plates of cannoli and cream puffs, the tiny tree with felt ornaments that one of the aides made, with each of our names spelled out on a bell or a star in glue and glitter. And later we'd made our own Christmases, Bobby and Robert and I. Christmas Eve dinner at Ann Benedetto's, scungilli and calamari and baccalà, the walk home through a cold Brooklyn night along streets bright as day with lit-up lawn reindeer and sleighs and Mr. Costanza's house, that got in the *Daily News* every year because it took $500 worth of Con Ed juice to light it for a week. Morning mass at St. Stannie's, the kids clutching whichever toy was the favorite that year, Ninja Turtles, Power Rangers, Battle Beasts, dinner in the early evening. And after the guests were gone and the dishwasher was humming and Robert was in bed, his new toys ranged around him like a bulwark, the smell of fresh plastic and evergreen in the air, Bobby would put on his Nat King Cole album and at the words "Chestnuts roasting on an open fire" he would take me in his arms and dance me slowly, seriously, around our small and narrow living room, singing along in a baritone grown a little uncertain with age. I can feel him, smell him, if I close my eyes and hum that song to myself.

It was the Florida weather that had saved me, as I'd climbed out of bed that morning to dress. It was as warm as April in New York, so that it made it hard to believe in reindeer in the snow or sleigh rides. Even Robert felt it: "It's weird to wear a short-sleeved shirt to Christmas," he'd said as he loaded new batteries into his video game. That was the new word, *weird*. "It's weird to be going to somebody else's house for Christmas," he said later, eating his cereal. "It's weird not to have a bigger tree," he mumbled, putting his bowl in the sink.

"That was the biggest tree I could afford," I said, my voice quavering. "Those were the presents I could afford. This is the kind of Christmas I could afford."

"It just feels weird," Robert said, his own voice unsteady, and I'd hugged him hard then.

"It's weird not to be with your father," I said. "And Aunt Grace, and Grandmom. It's the hardest thing in the world not to be with the people you love on Christmas Day."

"But I'm with you," he said. So sweet, sometimes, the way he would say things like that, as though just like his father he was two people, the one who hated where he was, and the one who'd made his peace with it. As I'd begun to do. I wondered, just for a moment, whether Bobby had done the same thing, whether even now he was sitting with a glass of red wine, saying "Ah, good riddance" to one of his cop friends while the wife checked on whether the ham was ready to glaze and the kids bickered over their new toys. But I looked down at Robert's shining hair and knew that that couldn't be true, no matter how much I wanted it. "My son," Bobby used to call him. "My boy." That possessive pronoun. My wife. My girl. He'd never give us up. Somewhere, somehow, I knew that he was listening to that Christmas song and seething. Robert went up the stairs of the Roerbacker house to help Chad with his new Duplo blocks and I went into the kitchen to arrange Cindy's baking-powder biscuits on a cookie sheet.

"Mama, honey, go sit back down," Cindy said, when Helen Manford followed me, pulling idly at the cord on a little Santa pin that made his eyes light up red and faintly demonic.

"I had a pin like that when I was a kid," I said. "I had a red Christmas coat one year and I wore that pin on the lapel."

Mrs. Manford smiled. Farm or no farm, dirt or no dirt, she still had a kind of beauty, with a grace of bone and posture that would forever survive sun and long hours and hard work. Next to her, her daughter, with her bright lips and hair in a curly twist, looked like a jumped-up imitation of the real thing.

"Go ahead and tell her," Cindy said, sipping some white wine, pouring me a glass. I could hear the men from the living room, like the rumble of thunder.

"I got this one when I was a girl, too. Fourteen, I think. I loved it so dearly that I managed to hold onto it. I even got the jeweler up on the highway to find some kind of new battery for it when it wouldn't light up anymore."

"Once when I was seven or eight," Cindy said, "there was a hurricane and they evacuated us all to the high school. Mama's running around, getting the picture albums and the records from the farm, bills and invoices and all that. All of a sudden she lets out this little yelp, runs back into her bedroom and comes out with her hand in a fist. 'Oh, for pity's sake, Helen,' my dad says, and sure enough it's Santa."

"You'd better take good care of him when he's yours."

"Oh, for pity's sake, Mama, you'll live forever." Cindy turned down a fruit sauce bubbling on the back of the stove. "I'm gonna kill us all with this meal."

"I don't want to hear one word about cholesterol on Christmas Day," Mrs. Manford said. "There's too much of that as there is. Cynthia Lee, it's not a good idea for you to be drinking and cooking at the same time. You'll burn yourself on that stove."

"It's a glass of wine, Mama. Want one?"

"No, ma'am," said Mrs. Manford.

"Take these spiced pecans out to the table for those guys to munch on," Cindy said, handing her mother a bowl.

"Well, they smell good," Mrs. Manford said doubtfully, carrying the food into the next room.

"There's a guest in that living room that you didn't tell me about," I said to Cindy.

"Well, since you two are such friends, I figured I didn't need to," Cindy said. "Hold this chafing dish." She poured creamed onions into it, then waved me over to the table and handed me a silver lid.

"That's all you're going to say?"

"Oh, for pity's sake. The poor man has his mama and two of his sisters coming with their kids tomorrow. He told Mrs. Patranian he was going to stay home today and straighten up his place. She was going to take him home and feed him lamb and some terrible bean stuff she was telling me about. You should have invited him yourself."

"We were coming here!"

"So, see—I saved you the trouble."

"You should have said."

"Good thing you dressed nice. You look good in green. Not like most blondes, who just look washed out." She squinted at me. "Wait a minute, wait a minute. I'm not so drunk that I don't notice you're not wearing your glasses. You finally get contacts?"

"Leave me in peace and give me something to do," I said.

"You knew he was coming after all," Cindy crowed, and I hit her with a dishtowel.

Cindy's Christmas was ham with raisin sauce and mashed sweet potatoes with marshmallows browning on top, creamed onions and baby peas, papier-mâché angels on the mantel in the living room, and a silvery white artificial tree with red lights and ornaments. "I know, I know, it's tacky," she said when I caught her buying evergreen fragrance in a can. "But I can't stand picking pine needles out of my carpet."

Craig was tending a fire in the fireplace, although it was almost seventy degrees outside and the air-conditioning was on. He and Mike and his father-in-law were talking about the football standings, pro, college, and local high school, and whether the mayor of Lakota was a crook, a smart politician, or both. Cindy's father, Ed, leaned forward and did most of the talking. He was a short fireplug of a man, while Craig was tall and quiet, a big bony man with a thatch of gray-brown hair, whose smile seemed to be a kind of muscle spasm he neither controlled nor invited. When he and Cindy were in the same room it felt as though they'd divvied up the parts of their marriage, and Cindy, along with kids and home decor, had gotten the part that controlled laughter and sociability. "He's my rock," she liked to say of Craig, and there was something stony, fossilized about him, a man prematurely old at forty. But I was inclined to like him because of the way he let Cindy clean up around him and chide him for his bottle caps and missing buttons as though nothing could be more welcome or more sensible than being chided. I liked him even more that night, when he rose beneath a brass chandelier that was bound and gagged in an endless rope of fake greenery and red ribbon, a dishtowel tucked in the waistband of his pants, raised a glass of white wine, and said, "Merry Christmas to all. Thank you for joining us, Mike and Beth and Robert."

"Thank *you*," I said.

"Don't speak too soon, Miss," said Ed Manford, bent over his plate. "You haven't tasted any of this yet. Maybe you don't know that our girl has a reputation as a chef." He laughed, one of those short barking laughs that seem to be the specialty of small men, and that are never really mirthful. "And I'm not talking Julia Child, that's for sure."

"Here we go," Cindy said under her breath.

"You're a nurse or a nurse's aide or something, aren't you?

You ever dealt with a case of ptomaine?" *Bark, bark.* "There's Pepto in that bathroom, isn't there, Craig?"

"Ed, don't start," said Helen Manford, turning her sweet potatoes over with her fork as though she expected to find something buried inside them.

"Did she tell you about her first try at home cooking?" Ed Manford added, leaning toward me until his beefy upper arm was against the side of my breast and I was back as far as I could go in my chair. "Barbecued chicken, done to a turn. Brown and crispy, like out of a picture in a cookbook. Just one little thing." The bark again, this time with more of an edge. "She didn't defrost it. Red and raw and all bloody inside. Good thing we had some bologna in the icebox."

"That was twenty years ago, Dad," Cindy said.

"She made a picnic last year for the soccer tournament," Mike said. "That was the best fried chicken I ever had. And that chocolate cake you brought. That was great, too."

"Remember that barbecue they had for the girl's third birthday, El?" Mr. Manford said, as though Mike had said nothing at all. "I was in the bathroom for the rest of the evening. I never figured whether it was the potato salad or the spareribs."

"No one else had a problem," Cindy said, but he didn't pay any attention. "How's your ham, Helen?" he asked. "Done enough?"

"It's perfect," said Craig Roerbacker. "Everything's perfect. As usual."

"Really. Great meal, Cindy. Great meal," said Mike.

"Not a whole lot of money in teaching, is there?" Mr. Manford said.

"Nope," Mike said. "You have to love it." He smiled at me. "And have a sense of humor."

"Spoon. Spoon. Spoon. Spoon," shouted Chad from the children's table set at one end of the room.

"Pipe down, little boy," said Ed Manford, shoveling in his food.

"Spoon!" Chad yelled again, happily.

"You be a good boy, now," said Helen.

"Leave him alone, Mama," said Cindy. "It's Christmas." Over at the children's table Robert was whispering to Chad and feeding him sweet potatoes, teaching him his favorite party trick, being good, being quiet. Teaching him to make himself disappear when the grown-ups started to raise their voices.

We all had coffee afterward in the living room, the fire burning blue in the stone fireplace, Mr. Manford asleep in the recliner chair. Both Cindy and her mother took aspirin after dinner. Chelsea hit Chad with Holiday Barbie because he'd disarranged the doll's hair; she'd been sent to her room, where she'd fallen asleep sprawled across her bed in a red lace party dress. "You're not supposed to be mean at Christmas, Mommy," she sobbed as she went up the stairs, Barbie's head going *bump-bump-bump* on the treads. Robert read *One Fish, Two Fish* to Chad—I could tell because from time to time I could hear Chad shout "Fish!" from upstairs.

"I told him if he went to sleep I'd kick the soccer ball with him tomorrow," Robert said when he finally came downstairs.

"Bless you, sweetie," Cindy said, her head tilted back in the circle of her husband's arm. From upstairs we all heard the word faintly: "Ball! Ball!" All of us laughed except for Mr. Manford, who was snoring, and Mrs. Manford, who was cleaning the kitchen, though Cindy had tried three or four times to persuade her not to.

Mike drove us home, of course. Cindy'd asked him before

we'd even arrived. The lights of the strip were glowing like deco-rations in the mist, but for the first time since we'd come to Lake Plata, maybe the only time all year, all the parking lots were empty, as though of one accord we had all decided to take one day off from cheap hamburgers and labor-saving appliances and in-stead come together in our living rooms. We passed house trailers set back behind the Price Club warehouse and tiny cinder-block houses that couldn't possibly have more than two rooms, and I was certain that each had some Christmas tradition, and perhaps as much of a divide between what we felt and what we wanted to feel as there'd been at Cindy's that night. I couldn't help thinking of how Cindy had once been in love with Jackson Islington, who wanted to settle down on a farm; I couldn't help thinking of Ed Manford's stubby hands, a faint tracery of black soil etched in so deep that it would never come out, no matter how much he scrubbed. He'd eaten everything on his plate, then taken seconds.

"How in the world did that hateful man ever produce someone as sweet as Cindy?" I said in a low voice after looking in back to make sure Robert was occupied with his new video game.

"That's a good question," Mike said. "You see it all the time. Some really good kids with terrible parents. And some great par-ents with tough kids."

"And then you've got Cindy and Craig, who seem so grounded, with Chelsea, who is scared to death of everything. Cindy couldn't use the electric knife for the ham because it freaks Chelsea out. I've never seen the point of an electric knife. It's just as easy to carve with the old-fashioned kind. Cindy said that as soon as Chelsea hears it humming, she starts to think someone's going to cut a hand off."

"I think the fear thing has to have something to do with Cindy's sister. I imagine that's why Cindy's parents are so strange with her, too. They probably look at Cindy and see Cathy. Although you'd think they'd be grateful to have Cindy and be a little nicer to her."

"Cindy doesn't have a sister."

"She did. She didn't tell you?" He shook his head. "That's weird. It's one of those famous stories that every town has. Sooner or later she must have known someone would tell you. Cindy was an identical twin. From what I've heard Mrs. Manford really used to do it up the way people used to with twins, twin girls mostly, curls and Mary Janes and matching dresses and all that. The story I heard was that one day their mother sent Cathy out to their cornfield to call Mr. Manford in for dinner. He was on one of those big tractors, those John Deeres with the huge wheels they use around here, where you sit up high off the ground. Apparently he never even saw her. Someone told me he thought he hit a rock."

"Jesus Christ," I said.

"Yeah. If I'd been the father it would have killed me. But I'd also like to think it would make me treasure the one I had left."

"I can't believe Cindy never told me."

"Maybe it's too hard for her to talk about it," he said as he pulled up in front of the house. "Here we are."

Robert had fallen asleep in the back, his game still buzzing in his hand. Mike Riordan carried him inside, laid him on the couch and turned to go. Our living room had a small tree stuck in a bucket of wet sand, decorated with glass balls and paper apples I'd found at the discount drugstore, and beneath it were a few packages. I handed him one. "Merry Christmas," I said. "I didn't bring it tonight because I didn't know you were going to be there."

"I didn't know you were coming, either."

He lifted the green jacket from its box, held it up in front of him as though he'd never seen a jacket before, had no idea what it was used for or what it might be. Robert stirred on the couch, then sat up. "That's a good jacket," Robert said faintly.

"If you've already got one—" I said.

"No," Mike said. "Thank you. I really needed this." He laughed. "I'll drop your presents by tomorrow. I didn't bring them because I didn't know—you know."

"Merry Christmas, Mr. Riordan," said Robert.

"Mr. Riordan was weird about his present," Robert said later as I tucked him in.

"I think he didn't like it but he was trying to be polite," I said.

"I liked everything I got," Robert said.

"Me too," I said. "I love you, Ba." I held him for a moment and realized that he was beginning to feel different in my arms, more geometric, less soft. The tears slid down my cheeks and onto his face.

"I love you, too, Mom," he said. "I had a really good Christmas. Don't be sad."

"I'm not, hon. I'm not." In the kitchen I picked up the phone, put it down, picked it up again. I wasn't even sure who I wanted to call. Or who I could afford to call. Patty Bancroft had called me, three days before, when the phone bills came, to ask icily about the twenty-three-minute call to New York on the evening of November 24. It hadn't felt like twenty-three minutes, those precious minutes on the phone to Grace. It had felt like no time at all. "You have no idea what can be done with phone records," Patty Bancroft had said coldly.

"How could anyone see my phone records? I haven't even seen them. I don't even know where they're delivered."

"Holidays are a difficult time, Elizabeth," she'd said. "People call home during the holidays, and people who are looking for them know that. And getting a copy of a phone record, for someone who knows how, is nothing. Nothing at all."

I'd hated the tone of her voice, as though she were talking to a child, a teenage girl who talked too long to her friends, a stupid adolescent with no idea of the results of her actions. But she'd scared me. I picked up the receiver in the kitchen, then put it down, then picked it up again. The dial tone turned into the manic high-pitched beeping of a phone off the hook, and I could hear the sing-song murmur of the recorded message: "If you wish to place a call . . ." Finally I hung up, then picked the phone up once more and dialed the number on an index card tacked to the kitchen doorjamb.

"Hello," she said, her voice a little hoarse, as though she had not had cause to use it that day.

"Hi, Mrs. Levitt. It's Beth Crenshaw. I know it's late, but is it all right if I say Merry Christmas?"

In the background I heard the sound of conversation, even music. "Is this a bad time?" I added.

"Ach, no," she said. "Irving and I are watching *White Christmas*, aren't we, Irving. A Christmas movie, what can it hurt? Not like having a tree, right? That Rosemary Clooney, it's a shame, how heavy she got. She was a nice-looking girl when she was young."

"She was, wasn't she?"

"But you can tell, the ones that have to watch it when they get a little older, or next thing you know, a backside out to here. Now she wears nothing but muumuus."

"But a beautiful voice."

"Beautiful. Merry Christmas, Mrs. Nurse. I'll tell you something—Irving likes you. I can tell. This one you like, Irving, I said."

"I'm glad. Tell him I said thank you."

"We'll see you Tuesday, won't we, Irving? I have a little something for the little boy."

And then I called Cindy, even though I'd just left her. "I just wanted to say thanks again," I said. "You saved my life with that dinner, and the presents and everything." I thought of Cindy's twin, of the early years, when she'd been able to look at a mirror image without even looking in the mirror, of sitting in the kitchen, or their room, or wherever she was when Cathy went out to call Ed Manford for dinner, of her hearing the shouting, the screams. Or maybe not. Maybe just hearing a silence where a moment before ordinary life had been. It had been a good story, that story about Jackson Islington. But it hadn't been the real story. Although I couldn't complain; it had been a good story I'd told her, the story of the nuns. But it hadn't been the real story, either.

"I love you, kid," I said.

"Love you, honey," she said. "I got to go to bed. I had too much wine." And in the kitchen I poured myself a glass of water and drank it by the living-room window, looked out over the dark quadrangle hung with motley lights from a gap I made with my two fingers in the blinds. Finally I went to bed, with Nat King Cole playing over and over in my head, with my stomach roiling with wine. I thought of Ed Manford leaning so close to me, of Cindy's sister disappearing beneath the big ridged wheels of a farm tractor. And I thought of Bobby. The Christmas before he'd given me a half-heart, cut down the center with a jagged line, hanging on a heavy gold chain. The other half he'd hung around his own neck, on the chain where he wore his miraculous medal, the image of the Virgin Mary his father had been given by his own parents when he became a cop, that Ann Benedetto had refused to have buried with her husband, had given to her son instead. I'd left the half-heart in my jewelry box, below the costume things. But I knew Bobby had found it, his heart, jettisoned, left. Maybe that had been enough. Maybe he had let me go. Maybe he was singing Nat King Cole into some other woman's ear, some woman he'd found to take my place, a woman who didn't make him angry or mean, who got all the good stuff and none of the bad. As Christmas Day darkened and deepened into the morning of the day after, I fell asleep, wondering.

The next morning Mike Riordan came by with two packages, beautifully, extravagantly wrapped, the work of a department store gift-wrapping department, all foil stars and glittery ribbon. "I thought you had company today," I said.

"They're coming at three," he said. "I cleaned up by stuffing everything in the closets."

For Robert he had gotten a Yankees baseball shirt, blue and white pinstripes. For me there was a runner's rain jacket, lightweight, deep green. It was more or less the same jacket I'd given him, except that his was size large, mine size small. The look on my face must have been funny.

"Don't tell Cindy," Mike said, "or she'll talk about it till next Christmas."

There was something called a Safe-Home party with kids, balloons, hot-dog wagons, and clowns at the school on New Year's Eve, Mike so busy that I only got to wave at him across a very crowded cafeteria, and then the holidays were over. Soccer ebbed, basketball flowed; Robert had practice three times a week after school, games every weekend, enough homework that he moved straight from his desk to the sink to brush his teeth and wash his face for bed. Jennifer got a new wheelchair and taught me to play a computer game called "Knockout"; she always won, the high score table a list of variations on her name and initials. Cindy and I ran a sale of books the library no longer needed, our hands and faces gray with the dust of years. And one day at the end of January, walking home from the Levitts, seeing familiar lights in now-familiar windows, it occurred to me that the tedium of this life had become comforting, that it felt real and lasting in its sheer ordinary drudgery, that in the same way I found it restful to run a route I'd run dozens of times before, so it had become restful to do these small tasks that I knew by heart, that asked no more of me than a kind of rote recitation of the body.

I was less fearful, but not foolhardy. I still scanned every crowd—at the mall, at the ball games—as careful as a snitch looking for a hit man. Not just for Bobby, for his dark head, his hawkish profile, but for his uncle Gerald, or some cop now retired who'd once shared a squad car with him, or a woman who knew us both from St. Stannie's. America turns out to be a very small country if you're trying to get lost in it. Mention you're from Omaha and it's a cinch: any stranger you meet will say he has a cousin there. It's why I had been able to come to Lake Plata and be absorbed by the town as completely as a stone falling into deep water: because there was no town, really, just a collection of strangers ranged around a commercial strip. No families who had lived on one block for three generations, or even the remnants of that sort of life, a son or a daughter living in a house a block or two away from where their parents had raised them.

One Saturday we went to a carnival outside town to celebrate the first win of the peewee basketball team. Every carnival is the same carnival. Literally. If you read the name on the tickets they make you buy in vast quantities for the rides, or look at the gaudy logos painted on trucks parked around the outskirts of the glittering circle, you might see the same name in an empty field in Florida as you see in a high-school parking area in Westchester or outside a mall in Oak Park, Illinois. Westhammer Amusements, Jensen Amusements, Richter Amusements. They just hook it all up to trailers or throw it all on flatbeds, the haunted house, the midway games with their bad odds and cheap toy prizes, the Tilt-a-Whirl and Cyclone. Three days later they pack it all up and haul it to the next town. Bobby would never let Robert go on any rides at a carnival. "Look at these dirtbags," he'd whisper if

Buddy or Jimmy or one of the other guys managed to drag us to one instead of just barbecuing in their backyards. "How tight do you think they made the screws on those things? Those look to you like the kinds of guys that take a lot of trouble with a wrench?" Not even the little boats that traveled in a tiny circle in a track of fetid water two feet deep, or the cars that were lower to the ground than Robert's tricycle. Someone else's children would be screaming from the Dragon Wagon, waving at us as the cars thundered up and down the track, and Robert would be standing, big-eyed, next to Bobby, a hand in his, as though my failure to recognize the clear and undeniable danger of this place removed me from them both. Crackerjack he could have, and cotton candy. But no hot dogs, or sausage and peppers cooked on a big griddle by women with tattoos. "What are you, nuts, Frances?" Bobby would say.

"You want a hot dog?" I said to Robert while I was taking food orders and we were trying to settle the boys on some splintered picnic benches. He nodded, then smiled. It felt like something to me, maybe a moving on, a moving over to some other place, where we made new rules and traditions. Hot dogs were no longer dangerous. We were living a different life. Every once in a while, at moments like this, it felt like mine. "Mrs. Bernsen asked us in school to talk about an adventure," Robert had said one night over leftover lasagna. "I talked about it being an adventure to move to a new place where you've never been before and where you don't know anyone." I'm not sure what showed in my face, but he'd added quickly, "I didn't talk about it before. Just now. Like meeting Bennie and everything."

"You are the best boy in the world," I'd said.

Mr. Castro was working nights as a janitor at the paper products plant and had agreed to come along to the carnival to help Mike and me keep the boys in order. He brought Bennie's little sister Sandy, who had just turned five, as a special treat for her birthday; he held tight to her hand as she danced and smiled and cried, "Popcorn, Papa! Popcorn, please?" Jason Illing's father was there, with his video camera, just as he was at every game, filming Jason slumped on the bench, the boy's shoulders bowing to his belly like an old man, filming the two minutes or so that Mike, who played everyone, cut no one, gave Jason to play. "Hold up your burger," Mr. Illing called, but Jason ignored him and hunched over his Dutch Fries and his root beer. Cindy came with us, too, after one of the other boys' mothers backed out. She had Chad in the stroller, and I'd managed to coax Chelsea from the little niche between Cindy's torso and the stroller handle onto a picnic bench, where she ate a hot dog slowly and thoughtfully.

"I don't like rides," Chelsea said.

"Can I tell you a secret?" I said. "Neither do I. They always make me feel like I'm going to throw up."

Chelsea nodded.

"Eleven, twelve," I heard Mike muttering to himself, and I laughed. "They're all here," I said.

"It's hard to keep track of sixteen of them in a place like this," he said.

"I know. But you don't really need to keep track of sixteen. Jason is under constant electronic surveillance, I never let Robert out of my sight, and Robert never makes a move without Bennie. Mr. Castro is keeping an eye on Jonathan, who always gives Bennie a hard time. That leaves twelve. And Cindy and I divided the twelve up on the bus. So all you really have to do is hand out tickets."

Of course, it wasn't as simple as that once the leavings of their lunch were bundled into waxed paper and tinfoil and chucked— underhand, overhand, to Jonathan Green from behind his brawny back, and why was I so happy when he missed by a foot?—into the metal drums used for trash. "Tilt-a-Whirl!" Mike yelled, and as of one accord most of the group would move toward the ride and some would scatter, to knock down weighted milk bottles with a hardball, to buy junky jewelry or sugar-coated nuts, to look at the Army Reserve tank.

"Can I put you in charge of stragglers?" I asked Cindy, who was trying to get mustard out of her shirt with a paper napkin and a cup of water she'd wangled out of the homemade lemonade stand.

"Not with herself hanging on to my midsection," she said, looking down at Chelsea. "I'm straggling myself."

"Chelse," I said, bending down, "will you come with me and we'll make sure the guys are okay on the rides?"

"I don't want to go on."

"Me neither. That's why I need your help."

Her hand in mine was sweaty, but sweetly curved. Cindy had put her hair into a French braid and she was wearing pink shorts and a matching shirt with ruffles of lace around the legs and sleeves. "You look so pretty today," I said.

"So do you," Chelsea said. "You look nice in a dress."

"It's a T-shirt dress, not a real dress. Your mom bought this for me for Christmas."

"I know. She likes to buy people clothes."

"They're making me go on," Mike shouted from a car on the Tilt-a-Whirl, wedged in between two of the smaller boys, his arms around each one.

When he came off he was rolling his eyes. "The only way you

keep from throwing up is by fixing on one stationary point and staring at it," he said.

"Really?"

"That's my theory."

"Did it work?"

"So far," he said. "I just stared straight at you."

I could feel the color come up in my face, see it in his. "What next?" I said.

"How about dinner and a movie?" We both looked down. "Never mind. I can't believe I said that. Jesus, Riordan."

"Beth, I have to go to the bathroom really bad," Chelsea said.

"We'll be at the House of Horrors," Mike said.

When we got back they were all still in line. Jason's father was panning the row of boys, calling "And your name is . . ." to each. A group of retarded children and their teachers were ahead of them. The children were wearing name tags and smiling, dancing in the sunshine, rolling their eyes at the demons and ghouls painted on the outside of the House of Horrors. "Are you sure?" one of the teachers kept asking, and they all nodded. But once inside we could hear shrieks and wails, and the ticket-taker flicked his cigarette into the grass and swore. "Keep your people back," he barked at Mike, who threw out his arms as though to restrain a regiment of unruly soldiers.

"Bring them back out," he yelled into the House of Horrors, and a moment later the teachers and the children hurried through the black door and down the up ramp, the adults rosy with embarrassment, the children drenched in sweat as though in an instant every bad thing they had ever imagined had come at them by the light of the cheap strobe, ready to rip their hearts out.

"Wow," said Chelsea.

"Go ahead," the ticket-taker yelled at Mike.

"Are you guys still up for this," Mike said, turning around.

"Oh, for Christ's sake," said the ticket-taker.

After that there was the Viper, and then the bumper cars. Chelsea thought about the bumper cars, but then she saw sparks fly from the tether to the ceiling when one of them hit the wall. "Are you gonna go on anything at all?" said Cindy. "Anything? They have pony rides."

"Maybe in a little while," she said.

"Pretty girl," said Mr. Castro.

"Thank you. Say thank you, hon," Cindy said, a little too loudly. Then Christopher Menendez threw up, and Mr. Castro took him to the men's room.

"Oh, my Lord, please don't put him in my car on the way home," Cindy said.

"This was a bad idea," Mike said.

"No it wasn't," I said. "This is just one of those things that sounds a lot better before and after than when you're actually doing it."

"That's what I like about her," he said, turning to Cindy. "Most women would say, yeah, it was a bad idea, let's get out of here. Or they'd say, no, it was a great idea, we're having a great time, and you'd know it was bull. Instead she said what she just said, which happens to be true and accurate."

"That's what I like about her, too," Cindy said, in a voice that sounded as though she was playing the ingénue in the school play.

"Ferris wheel and then call it a day?" Mike said.

"Sure," I replied.

Cindy looked at her manicure and then at Mike's back as he plowed through the crowds to the place by the bumper cars where he'd told the boys to assemble after their fifth go-round. She rubbed the nail on her index finger with a frown as though she'd found a flaw in the finish. Chad was splayed in the stroller fast asleep. "I'm not going to say anything," she finally said.

"Good," I said.

Both of us lapsed into the tired silence of adults who have been with children from morning to night. It seemed to me heroic that someone like Mike Riordan or Mrs. Bernsen did this every day, and with good humor. Even now, as he stood at the back of the group waiting for the Ferris wheel to empty, I could see that he was bantering with the boys, keeping them in line without hectoring them as I would have done. The Ferris wheel filled with children just before our group made it to the head of the line, and it began to spin slowly, a blur of smiles and antic waves to the parents and friends below. It was only late afternoon but the lights were already on around each rim, two circles of blue lights in the lengthening, darkening day, heavy clouds settling over the fields so flat around us.

I looked down. Chelsea's face was tipped back, her mouth a little open, watching the other children go up and around, and I thought I saw in her eyes the kind of sadness you sometimes see, as a nurse, when a child in a wheelchair watches other children run. And then there was something else, wonder and shock, too, and a tearing noise I thought at first was the sound of one of the rides, until I looked up and saw that one of the cars of the Ferris wheel was half hanging in the air, and dangling from it was a child, making a high-pitched noise, something like a cry, something like heavy breathing, *ah-ah-ah-ah-ah*.

I ran forward, dragging Chelsea with me, and saw that another child had already fallen to the packed dirt at the side of the Ferris wheel, a boy in blue shorts and one of those buzz cuts Robert kept begging for. "He's dead," Chelsea whispered as I knelt next to him, adults and children surging around to see. There was a terrible scream, and I heard the noise as the second child's body hit something and then she fell, remarkably, only a few yards from the other.

"All right," I cried, half turning, and in that instant I was myself again, Frances F. Benedetto, RN, taking no shit in the emergency room. "Here's the deal. This child can go under, big time, or I can help him. But to help him I need all of you to move back."

"Oh my God," a woman started to shriek, in a familiar timbre. "Oh my God!" Mike came up behind me, and I said, "Tell Cindy to get ahold of Mom or Grandma or whoever the hell that is and take her someplace and calm her down. Tell Cindy to lie to her. Tell her I'm a doctor. Tell her the kids are fine. Do you know CPR?"

"Yeah."

"No, I mean really know CPR. Not one class at the Y."

"I really know CPR."

"Then come right back." I looked up and raised my voice. "I need a tie or a scarf," I called. Then, looking around at the women in T-shirts and frayed shorts, the men in jeans and singlets, I added, "Or a belt. A belt would do it."

CPR, done by someone who knows how to do it, is like a calisthenic, like push-ups or leg lifts, a series of quick, synchronized, monotonous movements. Mike did it just right. The boy, who was probably concussed, began to wheeze and moan. The little girl had a compound fracture of the left leg, the bone poking jagged and white from just above her knobby, scabby little knee. But the tourniquet kept down the bleeding. She was in shock, staring straight up at the sky, whispering to herself, "Mommy, Mommy."

"You're okay, sweetie," I whispered back. "You broke your leg."

"I tried to hold on," she said.

"I know." Two ambulance attendants wheeled a gurney over in a cloud of dust. "I'd figure on a couple of busted ribs," I said. "Luckily the car they were in wasn't that far up. If they'd been at the top—" I shrugged.

"Nice work," one of them said. There was blood on my dress and my hands.

In the hospital I'd learned that there are really two kinds of people in the world, people who go hard and efficient in times of terrible trouble, and the ones like, it turned out, Grandma, who scream, shriek, go limp, sink to the floor, become patients themselves. PITAs, we called them in the ER, short for Pain In The Ass. All of the adults with me had fallen into the take-charge group. Cindy had managed to convince the grandmother that the children would be fine and to get her to breathe into a bag and drink an orange soda. Mr. Castro had rounded up all the boys and taken them to a tent filled with video games at the back of the fairgrounds.

And Jason Illing's father had taped the whole thing. While we were dropping off the boys, explaining to parents what had happened and assuring them that all of us were fine, he went to the local news station and sold a copy to them. Six months of being careful, dying my roots, talking about goddamned Delaware, feeling my breathing quicken at the sight of a patrol car and feeling it slow as my son slept silently in the next room. Six months, and that idiot, that moron, that fool maybe ruined it with his sorry little Sony, that he loved to hoist on the palm of his hand. "Weighs less than a sack of sugar," he liked to say.

We went to Cindy's house, where she brought out tortilla chips and salsa, perhaps in a salute to Mr. Castro, and beer in deference to the aftershock of the day's events. When we turned on the television, we were the lead story on the evening news, and there I was in the center of the film clip, a red flag to Bobby's bull.

The fear I felt as I watched was worse than it had been while I worked over those children. There was the little girl, her leg bent at a horrid acute angle, and there was Beth Crenshaw, using a brown leather belt as a tourniquet. You could scarcely see my face, except for once when I turned to look back, straight into the big eye of the camera. I was glowering the way I always did when I concentrated, so that a nursing professor had had to take me aside once and tell me that it was important not to look as though I was going to throttle the patient while I was threading an IV line. I could imagine someone watching the television news, someone channel-surfing in a motel room at Disney World or in the living room of a time-share in Delray, some cop's wife, some friend of Ann's from Sodality at St. Stannie's, seeing me in that instant and saying, "My God, that woman looks a lot like Bobby Benedetto's wife, doesn't she?" I closed my eyes and let my face fall forward into my cupped hands.

Bobby, I could hear them saying, I saw Fran on the news in Florida. Some little town up north, what was the name? At a carnival ride, taking care of some kids, a terrible accident. What's Fran doing in Florida? Lakota, that was the name of the place.

"You didn't look so bad," Cindy said, patting my arm. "Considering."

What a ghoul Illing was. He'd panned the crowd and come to rest on Chelsea, her eyes dilated, her mouth ajar. But the terror I'd seen there for a moment was gone, and in its place was a great overwhelming calm. Probably anyone else watching would have thought the child was in shock, but I had no doubt that she was at peace, having seen that she was not crazy or strange but in fact prescient, correct, that the world was indeed as frightening as she had always believed and that it was possible for children to eat funnel cake, stand in line, wave to their friends, and then simply fall out of the sky. And the look on Robert's face, when the ambulance finally wailed off down a dirt track and into the distance with a dust cloud behind it, was just as easy for me to read. He might as well have said it aloud: Daddy was right. Daddy was right.

"Are you okay?" I'd asked him in the car on the way to Cindy's house, and he'd nodded. Of course. Of course. He'd seen worse without ever admitting to fear, giving way to nightmares. The blank eyes again, the blank stare. My heart sank. It was like he'd traveled back in time, to a place where he wouldn't let himself feel a thing. "Those kids who fell will be fine," I'd said.

"I know," he'd said.

When I went upstairs to use the bathroom I found him in Chelsea's bedroom, Cindy bent over him, her arm around his shoulders. Sobs shook him and made it hard for him to talk, so that the words came out in the funny little burbles he'd babbled as a baby. There were tears and dirt mingled into a streaky mess on his face, and a wad of tissues in his hand. Cindy patted his back twice and then slipped past me and out of the room. She patted me, too, on her way out, and I took her place next to Robert and held him as he sobbed some more. Finally he managed to say, "It was just so scary. It was so scary." I held him and rocked him and my heart was so light, laughing almost inside me, because my boy knew to be afraid, to be frightened, to cry at blood and guts and pain. It was like he was normal. It was like something was alive inside him, something that could see terrible things and know them for what they were. It had been a real accident, this one, but he hadn't even used the word. He could tell a bad thing when he saw it, and I admitted to myself that I thought he'd lost that simple gift forever, until that moment.

Later, when Mike took us home, the telephone was ringing. "Let it go," I said, "let it go." But Robert picked it up, then handed it to me. "Irving and I saw you on the news," Mrs. Levitt said. "Next time you are being a hero, don't wear a dress so everyone can see your tushie. Your fanny. Ah, you know, your rear end."

"I know what a tush is, Mrs. Levitt." Mike Riordan was standing in the doorway, laughing.

Robert had gone upstairs. I could hear the water running. "He's fine," I said to Mike. "He's upset."

"It's good for him to get it out now. Better than bottling it up, you know?"

"I know," I said. "I know." He stood up and moved to the door. "You were good today," I added.

"So were you," he said. "You were great. Unbelievable. Plus I'm happy to hear you know what a tush is."

"I'm sorry I was so snotty about the CPR thing. There are just a lot of people who think they know how to do it from watching TV."

"I was a community ambulance volunteer for five years."

"I didn't know that, see."

He took a step toward me, with a funny little embarrassed smile, and took my face in his hands. Then he kissed me, very softly, the way a boy I'd liked in eighth grade who had braces top and bottom had once kissed me, as though he was afraid something harder would hurt me, or him. There were footsteps from upstairs, and he dropped his hands and moved away, toward the door.

"Boy," he said.

The phone didn't ring for three days, and when it finally did my hand lingered over it as though I was afraid the receiver would give off an electric shock. My heart pounded as I listened to the electronic tympani: *clink, bang, rattle, buzz, buzz, clink.* I was surprised that it had taken so long for Patty Bancroft to come looking for me. I had become her bad child, her prodigal daughter, the kind of person, like Maeve Banning at Queen of Peace, who always wound up in the principal's office, in the hot seat.

"Maeve Banning," Sister Eucharista would say over the intercom after morning prayers and the Pledge of Allegiance, "please come to the office." And we'd scarcely look up. Maeve Banning, the mothers would whisper, would wind up—well, you know. She hadn't. Of course she hadn't. Grace told me she was a lawyer now, a partner in a big law firm, helping corporations stay out of trouble.

I was Patty Bancroft's Maeve Banning. I made unauthorized phone calls. I wound up on the evening news.

"Elizabeth?" she said.

"Beth," I said again. She could never remember that that was the name I went by, and suddenly it occurred to me that it might be because they made us all Elizabeths, that huddled in apartments and small houses and trailer parks around the United States there was a great community of Elizabeths, like one of the medieval religious communities, committed to poverty and obedience. And silence, of course. Patty Bancroft was our public face, our voice, our leader. You could tell that she enjoyed that, that it made her feel good, to have gone from being powerless in her own home to being powerful in the world. I realized that that was what had always bothered me about her, that she enjoyed her work so much.

"We're working on relocating you to another part of the country," she said. "Perhaps next week, if we can set the arrangements in motion."

"What?"

"I gather that you were on television. That was a very, very foolish thing to do. And that your picture was in the newspaper. The impulse to be a Good Samaritan must be deeply ingrained in someone from your professional background, but I beg of you, not just for your own sake but for the sake of your own child and many others, don't yield to it in a public place ever again."

"Next time I see a kid bleeding to death I'll remember that."

"There's no point in sarcasm. You've only made things difficult for you and your son. Someone will let you know next week about the relocation."

"My name wasn't on TV. My name wasn't with my picture in the newspaper."

"That's not the point."

"We're not leaving. I'm not uprooting my boy again."

"I'm afraid that's the price you will have to pay. It is not unusual for us to move one family three or four times during as
many years. Particularly if they call attention to themselves or are
not assiduous about breaking off their ties with the past."

"Let me tell you something about myself, Mrs. Bancroft," I
said. "I like to take care of my own business. I'm someone who's
made her own way all her life." And the moment I said it, I knew
it wasn't true. I knew that my feeble minimum-wage jobs had
only been a pathetic hedge against the unpredictable life my parents made for Grace and me, a life of settling but not settling
down, of moving around but not up. And my life outside of the
home we shared, Bobby and I, had been a stage set, a sham. The
real Fran Flynn hadn't been the woman everyone saw in the hospital, in charge, in control. She'd been a punching bag, a mario-
nette. And now I was one of Patty Bancroft's puppets, a woman
scared to run around the block, scared to let her son go alone to
soccer games, a woman who'd take what she could get.

"Let me ask you this," Patty Bancroft said, "Do you want to
stay alive?" It was her trump card; I could tell by the way she said
it. The fact that Patty Bancroft and Bobby Benedetto so often said
the same things, so often made me feel the same about myself,
made me hate Patty Bancroft at that moment, no matter how
much good she'd done me and Robert. But she was playing out
of her league when she conjured up the worst that could happen.
I'd heard it all before. I'd heard it from the master. I'd heard it
when he found the card of a matrimonial lawyer in my pocket two
years before I left. He'd driven across the Verrazano-Narrows
Bridge from a wedding reception at 2:00 AM. dead drunk, snaking
the car in and out of the lanes while I held onto the edge of the
seat, the sullen gray of the water framed by the slender silver
cables that held the roadway miraculously aloft. "You want to get

home alive, Fran?" Bobby had said over and over, like there was a right answer and I hadn't gotten it yet. The next morning he made me waffles for breakfast. Waffles and pancakes, that was all he could cook. But he made good waffles, even hungover and pissed off. Death threats and Belgian waffles with bacon. What a life.

"What I'd like," I said to Patty Bancroft, "is to start paying rent on this apartment. I don't like being a charity case. I'd like to pay my own phone bills. I'm putting some money away. I don't need handouts anymore. I need the name and address of the landlord."

She was quiet for a long time, and for some reason I thought she was on an airplane, flying over her empire, the hidden world of women who had ceded the right to speak for themselves, even fend for themselves, to a woman who took the podium and the microphone to speak for them, fingering her pearls. Patty Bancroft talked about herself wherever she went, of how she had been married to a prosperous banker in a town in Indiana, of how he mostly beat her about the body, not on the face, so that no one ever saw when she was wearing a suit to a country-club lunch or a cocktail dress to the club for dinner. I'd realized, hearing her tell it at that hospital, that it sounded less like a life than a story. If Patty Bancroft had ever been a victim, it was long, long in the past. She enjoyed being on top. The way I was enjoying, at that moment, demanding custody of my own life for the first time since I started living it.

"I appreciate everything you've done," I added, "but we like it here. My son is settled in, I have a little bit of money put away. Just tell the landlord to come see me and I'll pay for this place."

"You make me very nervous, Beth," she said quietly.

"I'm sorry to hear that," I said. But I'd heard that before, too. I'd heard that from Bobby. "I don't know if you understand this," I finally said to Patty Bancroft, "but I can't worry anymore about how I make other people feel about me. I have to worry about how I feel about myself."

"You have to worry about staying safe. And keeping your child safe."

"That, too," I said.

Chastity is the other vow nuns take. Maybe that was why I was scheduled to go to another town, another house, another school, another identity, because Patty Bancroft, who said over and over again that she had finally been beaten senseless by her banker husband until her face had had to be rebuilt by one of the plastic surgeons who worked for her now pro bono, had never remarried. Maybe she knew about Mike Riordan. Maybe I'd known about Mike Riordan all along. Maybe I'd tried not to notice how awkward it was for him to look at me, even in the school library or on the sidelines of a game. Maybe I'd convinced myself that I wouldn't be seduced by how comforting it was, just to know that someone bigger than me was looking out for my son. That's what had first gotten to me about Bobby, the idea that someone would keep me safe and sound, look out for Frannie better than Frannie could look out for herself. The feel of his arm around me. The way he held my coat. Jesus Christ, the illusions you manage to sell yourself, better than any car salesman. I'd done it again with Mike Riordan, except that instead of convincing myself that he was everything, the way I had with Bobby twenty years ago, I'd convinced myself that he was nothing at all.

There was no lake in Lake Plata, just a sluggish reservoir and a community pool, but Mike took us to the ocean the Saturday after the trip to the carnival. He came with a cooler full of soda in the back of his Toyota, and an armful of old blankets; I made fried chicken and potato salad.

"Can Bennie come?" Robert asked.

"I think it would be better this time if it was just us," I said.

"Just us, like me and you?"

"And Mike," I said.

"I can't call him that," Robert said. "I have to call him Mr. Riordan."

"I think when we do things like this with him you can call him Mike."

"What do you mean, when we do things like this?"

"When we all go out together."

"Are we going to go someplace together after this?"

"I don't know," I said.

"I'm calling him Mr. Riordan," Robert said.

He compromised. He called him nothing at all. When we arrived at the beach, Robert ran toward the water, kicked his shoes aside at the tide line, and went in up to his knees while we struggled with the blanket. When Mike joined him in the surf, he moved away, as though the two were magnets, naturally, inevitably repelling one another. When I went into the water, he positioned himself between Mike and me almost unthinkingly. To anyone watching from the long crowded stretch of white beach, flat and glittering slightly in the midday sun, our movements must have looked like choreography of a strange sort. Our conversation was like that strange, dissonant modern music I picked up from time to time on classical stations, fit and starts with no melody. Mainly Mike talked to Robert, and Robert ignored him:

"I hear that that team from Lake Oijda is going to be good."

"Your mother makes good fried chicken."

"I brought a Frisbee if you want to play."

"Robert, you're being rude," I finally said.

"I just don't feel like talking," he mumbled, and ran back into the sea.

I stood to watch him pushing out into the deeper water. The swell of the waves, the air making a floating bolster of the seat of his striped trunks, the working of the wings of his shoulder blades as he fought the current—he looked as though he was trying to fly, to rise up, to take off. He was a good strong swimmer, my boy, although he'd been afraid of the water at first. But he did it to please his dad, when he was three, went to the Y in downtown Brooklyn, dipped his little pointed face below the surface of the water as though he was going into a cave.

I shouldn't have come to the beach. The beach was Bobby to me. The smell, the sharp sun, the sand. I could see his shoulders, the muscles working as he pulled his shirt over his head and swam out so that he was only a dark divot on the horizon. The life-guards would blow their whistles and demand he come back, and slowly, arrogantly, he would. He would walk over to the lifeguard stand and speak to them and then go back out, and this time they would leave him alone, as though he had some special dispensation from the everyday rules of safety and common sense. When Robert was smaller he would stand at the water's edge and watch, the whole line of his back rigid, and when he was older he would swim up and down in shallower water, parallel to the shore. And I knew he was just waiting for the day when he was brave enough to strike out after Bobby, shoulder to shoulder into water so deep that there was no imagining what was underneath your feet.

I can't swim. Never could. My skin burns and I keep my clothes on over my suit for all but a few minutes on the beach. My parents took us to Coney Island, when we were children, my mother carrying the rented umbrella and the bag of towels. It was a lot of trouble for nothing. Grace and I huddled in the shade, running in our T-shirts to and from the water like nocturnal animals woken up in the middle of the day. My insteps, peeking out from the broad shadow of the umbrella, burned so badly they had to be covered in salve as white as their natural color.

Bobby and Robert never even wore sunscreen.

"I think we've ruined a beautiful friendship here," I said.

"No we haven't. We're still friends."

"Not you and me. I don't know, maybe you and me. But definitely you and Robert."

Mike Riordan squinted through his sunglasses and shrugged. He was like me, already a bright, feverish-looking pink. An Irish tan, we'd called a sunburn when we were kids. "What would you have felt like if someone took your mother out?" he said.

I laughed. "It's not imaginable to me that anyone would take my mother out," I said.

"There you go," said Mike Riordan. "Sometimes I think it's the strangest thing—we grow up in our families seeing our parents as completely sexless beings, and then we're supposed to know how to have relationships."

"My parents were completely sexless beings."

"In your mind, maybe. That's what we all think. My parents used to send all of us to nine o'clock mass on Sundays and then they'd go to the eleven o'clock together. I was twenty-three years old before I finally figured out why they fought us so hard when one of us wanted to sleep in and go to later mass."

"I bet your mother just needed the sleep."

"Nope. I asked her one day. She said, oh, grow up, Michael, you have six brothers and sisters."

That was our first date, I suppose. At least that was what Robert seemed to assume. He appeared to know instantly, almost chemically, that Mr. Riordan had gone from being a friend to being a threat. I suppose I'd had a chemical reaction, too, the first time we went running together after the carnival. The sound of us breathing sounded different to me, and when we brushed up against one another accidentally, bare arm to bare arm, as we had dozens of times, we now both lurched back to our own side of the dusty track. No matter what Cindy said, and said, and said again, I wasn't attracted to Mike Riordan, didn't have a jones for him, as Clarice Blessing, the pretty, smart-mouthed black nurse in the ER on my shift, used to say about any good-looking man who came in with a broken bone or even a bullet wound. Once, I remember, Bobby came in when he'd had to get my signature on some bank papers and Clarice had been behind the front desk. "Tasty," she said, before someone told her who the dark guy in the pressed jeans and the white shirt was. "Tasty but dangerous." That's how I thought of my taste in men: tasty but dangerous. Mike Riordan was the least dangerous guy I'd ever known, and every time I thought to myself, well, Fran, he's just not your type, I had to remind myself that my type was the type who left marks.

"Bennie asked me if Mr. Riordan was your boyfriend," Robert said one day after school.

"Oh yeah? What'd you say?"

"I said you didn't have a boyfriend."

The next week Mike took us out for pizza and a PG movie. One Saturday we went bowling and then ate Chinese at a cinder-block place back behind the supermarket that turned out to be pretty good. Robert pointedly asked for chopsticks, while Mike used a fork. "You will have a great dinner with two people you really like," Mike read off his fortune cookie. "Let me see that," said Robert. He squinted in the dim light of the restaurant, hung with red-and-gold paper lanterns and signs for Chinese beer with a dragon curled around the bottle. "The journey of a thousand miles begins with a single step," Robert read accusingly. "Yeah, that too," Mike said. "I think that's what we're looking at right here, a single step."

"I hate fried rice," said Robert. "Fried rice isn't real Chinese food."

"Eat the dumplings," I said.

"Or whatever," said Mike, shoveling in fried rice with his fork. You had to admire his patience.

The beginning of March, the air softening, turning warmer, Mr. Castro took Bennie and Robert to a jai alai game at an arena an hour and a half south of Lake Plata, and Mike took me to a restaurant in Lakota named La Caravelle, where they set everything on fire at the table except the wine. I was starting to look at him differently, the way you do, seeing the pale hairs on the back of his hands, the places at the corners of his brow where his hairline was beginning to inch back along the crown, the V of his shirt where his throat met his chest. The fourth time we were out—Robert away for the night, me in a dress and heels—I was afraid of him. I kept my knees from nudging his beneath the table.

"Can I ask about your divorce?" Mike said when they had put the cherries flambé in front of us.

"Do you have to?"

"Robert seems like he thinks that you and his father will get back together."

"Did he say that?"

"Not exactly. He does seem to think that you won't be around here for long, like you're going back to where you come from. Which I guess means he believes you're going to get back together."

"Don't all kids say that?"

"Lots of them. Sometimes it's true."

"In this case it's not. I stayed with him a lot longer than I should have because eventually I thought I'd get perfect enough to make things better. I figured just by being nice, or being quiet, or being pretty, or sweet, or stupid, I could make things all right. I was wrong."

"For the record, I already think you're pretty perfect."

"Don't say that. That's what screws everything up, that *perfect* crap. Because the people who don't stay, they leave because its not perfect, because they think it's supposed to be. Or my sister. She gets involved with one shitty married guy after another and she's managed to convince herself that it's because she's working out this, that, or the other thing. But really it's because if she met some nice available man who loved her she'd have to settle. He'd be nice but not smart enough, or smart but not handsome enough, or something. No one likes to settle, even though we all do."

Mike looked down at his hands. "Sorry," he finally said.

"Jesus," I said. "What set me off that time?"

"I said you were perfect."

"Well, there you go," I said, and we both smiled and then looked down at the table again. The check lay there like a message, as though if I picked it up instead of a scrawl of abbreviated entrées and numbers there would be some words, some warning: Fran Benedetto, Fran Flynn, Beth Crenshaw, whoever you are, whatever you call yourself, why the hell are you doing what you're doing, out of the frying pan into the fire, you're not single, you're not ready, you're not interested, you're not who this man thinks you are, you're not who you think you are, you're not.

I looked at his hands. I couldn't help myself. They were big, the line of the knuckles knobby and square, and I wondered what he would say if I asked him if he'd ever hit a woman, and knew that I didn't need to ask. Whatever it was that had made me soft and wet and warm whenever Bobby Benedetto whispered in my ear was part of whatever it was that made him twist my arm and slap my face. I'd been seduced by the danger I only faintly divined when I was twenty years old and the danger was being caught by the cops with my jeans around my ankles on a bench along the beach in Far Rockaway. I looked at Mike Riordan across the table as he took his credit card from a brown leather wallet and knew that he was maybe the safest man I'd ever met, and that that was his bad luck, and mine, too. Patty Bancroft used to talk about how her husband had been two men, really, one mild and avuncular, the other a purple-faced monster. But Bobby was all of a piece, and if anyone had asked me, when we both were young, if I thought he could ever do what he did, I would have said, no, my God, are you crazy? and deep inside a part of me would have known, not that it was possible, but that it was inevitable.

"You look a little tired," Mike said.

"I am."

Cindy likes to lecture me about how different dating is today than it was twenty years ago when we did it last, but she gets most of her information from daytime talk shows and the dark hints she picks up from single mothers to whom she sells Avon on her evening calls. She keeps telling me that men now expect you to put out—she still says put out, Cindy, as though sex is transactional—on the first date. But that isn't the problem. The problem is that there is less to do on a date when you are a grownup. Dancing at bars seems silly, and there are no more of the kind of Saturday-night parties where you can French kiss in the corners. As we left La Caravelle, the owner in his rusty tuxedo bobbing and grinning and urging us to return, I realized that Mike Riordan and I were running out of restaurants.

"Love is lovelier the second time around," Cindy liked to say.

"How the hell would you know?"

"Oh, don't be so touchy," she said. "You know how few single men out there are really interested in a relationship?"

"I'm not interested in a relationship," I said.

"Oh, please," Cindy said.

"Please come inside," Mike said when we got to his place, in a condo complex out by the city limits. And when we were inside, in the living room with a couch and matching love seat that looked as though they'd been arranged in exactly the same way they'd been arranged in the furniture store, he said, "Please stay." I wasn't used to a man who asked, a man who said please, and, later, thank you, bashfully, boyishly, and something about it irritated me. But still I went along, maybe to prove to myself that I could love a nice man, a good man, a man who would look at his hands when I gave him a hard time and not use them against me. I went into the bedroom, listened to the sound of zippers coming down and shoes hitting the floor as though they were sounds from some dumb show on the radio, sound without pictures. I tried to be there, I really did, but it was as though the wine and the dark numbed me, sent me into a trance. I was watching myself doing what I was doing, envisioning the curve of my back above the slight swell of my hips, looking at the cesarean scar that his fingers found hidden beneath the hair. I kept my eyes shut, but it was as though my eyes were in his hands. He kept whispering my name, and the sound of it was soothing, almost hypnotic. Beth Beth Beth Beth, and "yes" I finally said, and perhaps it was that that made me open my eyes, and remember all in a rush suddenly

the last time I had had sex with another man, so vividly, so detailed that it might as well be happening again, in this strange bed
with the plaid sheets and the dark wood headboard. It was like
having a ghost there, hanging over me, pushing his knee between
my own, holding me down with the weight of his chest, his chest
hard and furred with black hair, his harsh guttural whisper, like
a knife at my throat: "Come on. Come on." Using himself as
though his whole body was a knife, cutting into me, breathing fire
and Canadian Club into the side of my face, his jaw set so hard
that I could feel the stone of the joint digging into my cheek.

"Beth," Mike Riordan whispered again, and I had to look up at
him, had to keep my eyes open, to remind myself that it was not
Bobby, that Bobby's hair was not light, his shoulders not sloped
that way, his face not soft like this. Mike looked back at me and he
must have seen something in my face. Maybe I was wearing the
look I'd had that last night with Bobby, as he raped me. There
ought to be a different word to describe what it is when it's your
husband who does it, when it's a man you've invited, longed for,
loved, hated, feared, known, desired. But there's only that one. I
remember sitting with a college student one night who'd been
pulled into an abandoned building near the subway and sodom-
ized by a teenager with a gun. "It's like he stole my soul," she
sobbed, eloquent in defeat. Maybe Mike looked down and saw the
face of a woman who'd had her soul stolen, who was broken and
empty, sere as a seed pod in autumn. Whatever was in my face, he
couldn't go on.

"Are you all right?" he said.

"Yeah," I said.

"I was hurting you."

"No. It's okay."

He fell back against the pillows, his forearms crossed over his face. He smelled like lemon cologne and his voice cracked like a boy's. "Oh, God," he said, "please don't say that. Don't say it's okay. For four years I lived with a woman who forced me to pry everything out of her with a crowbar. I'd say, Laurie, what's going on? What's the matter? It's okay. That's all she ever said."

"I'm fine," I said. "I'm tired." I could not look at him, nor he at me. I could still feel Bobby on me, like a weight on my chest.

"Beth," Mike said as I got out of the car at my own place.

"It's okay," I said over my shoulder, and went inside and took a shower.

I love to look at Robert when he is pushed and sleepy, his face a little crumpled, his eyes half-closed. Sometimes, after Bobby hit me, I'd go in and look at Robert and make myself feel better. Make myself settle down and shut up. When he's headed toward or away from sleep, Robert's face looks innocent, unmarked, as though nothing bad has ever happened to him. Will ever happen to him. He looked that way standing by my bed, holding an old earthenware bowl with a few greasy kernels at the bottom. "Could you make us some more peanut-butter popcorn?" he said, so nicely, even though he knew the answer was yes.

Only Robert and I knew that it was his eleventh birthday. He'd always liked the story, of how the pains came but the baby didn't, of how they'd taken us into an operating theater and put up a screen at my breastbone to shield Bobby and me from what was happening below, of how Bobby stood up to straighten out the crease in his pants legs and caught a glimpse of the incision like a big red mouth and the blood around the edges of the drape, of how he sat down hard on the metal stool at my head. "Are you okay?" I asked. "Bobby? Are you going to be all right?" The OB nurse, who'd been a class ahead of me at nursing school, gave him a big clean whiff of oxygen. Robert laughed, to think of his father so helpless. He liked that story. Loved it. I'd told it a hundred times. Bobby couldn't handle the sight of blood. What a laugh.

Robert's birthday was July 4 now, or at least Robert Crenshaw's was. But on April 9 we invited Bennie and three other boys from the basketball team for a sleepover in the living room. They came carrying sleeping bags and video games. Chelsea was on a sleepover that same night, her first, with a little girl named Melissa Erickson whose room, Cindy said, was entirely pink. She had been an in vitro baby, and her parents acted as though anything, from a playground spill to a B plus to a mosquito rattling around the stall shower in her pink bathroom was what my mother used to call "a federal case." It was a good beginning for Chelsea, who seemed less fearful now since the carnival, since she'd seen the worst with her own eyes. Melissa Erickson's parents were as fearful of life as Chelsea was. Maybe more.

It was Robert's first sleepover, too, unless you counted the nights he'd spent with Grace and his grandmother, Ann Benedetto bringing him back to the house with new sneakers, a new shirt, a toy, a book, a pocketful of candy and change. He'd spent the night at the Castros' a couple of times, but he'd never had a friend to his house overnight. Bobby had thought that that was fine. He didn't like strangers in the house. "I don't get all of this sleepover stuff," he'd said. "I never had anybody sleeping over at my house when I was a kid." And I'd never had anyone except Gracie, breathing in the next bed, her freckled legs tangled in the brown blanket. Robert always said that he didn't want any kids to stay over at his house anyway. Maybe he was afraid of what they would hear, of what they would say: Robert, what's the matter with your dad? Why's he yelling like that? What's that noise? Maybe he was afraid to let them into his nighttime life, those kids who hadn't learned when you needed to be deaf and blind. Maybe it was the dim memory of that night, when he was three, when he came downstairs, his face soft and pink, his eyes squinted shut against the light, and said, "Why you crabby, Daddy?" It was the first time he'd ever come downstairs when we were fighting. It was the last time he ever had. "Get back in bed, Robert," Bobby had said, his supple voice hard, not loud but mean, mean. "Don't you ever get out of your bed or come out of your room unless I say so."

"How come?" Robert had said.

"Get . . . up . . . stairs."

I stayed upstairs reading during the sleepover, listened to the murmur of the boys' voices from the living room, read and dozed and read some more. When I came down to make more popcorn they were halfway through the second *Star Wars* movie. "The guy who is Luke in the movie had a car accident and they had to, like, put his face back together," said a boy named Andrew Kovacs as the five of them lay on the floor, comic books and video cartridges around them.

"You can tell," Bennie said. "His face looks different after a while. Like his eyes are different sizes."

"I never had peanut-butter popcorn," said An Li Thong, a Vietnamese kid who was the goalie and whose school name had, naturally, become Goalie.

"His mom is a really good cook," said Bennie, as though I wasn't even there.

So normal, the long black velvet evening, the stars bright over central Florida, a moon almost full rising outside the bedroom window. It was hot during the days already, but at night it was only warm, a soft warm that felt good when I stepped outside before bed to look at the sky.

"Gentlemen," I said as I handed them a second bowl of popcorn, "here's the deal. I don't care how late you stay up"—Goalie cheered softly—"but if you wake me up, you're all going home. Hear me?" "Yes, Mrs. Crenshaw." "Thanks, Mrs. Crenshaw." "We'll be quiet." "We understand." The heavenly host, boy voices hovering between soprano and tenor, their words slurred by the popcorn in their mouths. Upstairs in the dark I could still hear them talking, hear the sound from the television, but it was muted, as though someone had thrown a blanket over them all, the way sound came through the walls when the couple who lived next door to my parents' apartment—the fourth one, I think, or maybe the fifth—would play the stereo late in the evening and fight with each other next to the bedroom where Grace and I slept. Gracie held a glass to the wall the first couple of times, to hear what they were saying, but it was dull. "She says who does he think she is, his mother?" Grace whispered to me. After a week or two we learned to sleep right through it.

In the pale blue light from the window I could make out the furniture in my room, the big scarred bureau, the landscape over it that I'd gotten from Cindy's basement, the rocking chair, the darker shadow of the closet door. And I realized, as one of the boys belched loudly downstairs and the others laughed, then chastised one another in loud whispers, that it had become my room. I knew its contours in the dark. To know the streets nearby, where Royalton met Poinsettia, where Miramar met the highway—that was one thing. To know a bedroom in the dark was something else, something final, something fine.

Even when I heard the sound of someone below, at the living-room window, I knew enough to feel only tired, tired and happy. I could tell by the whispers, a little louder than the whispers of the occasional tropical winds around the building, that the group of girls who were staying at the Castros', Bennie's sisters and their friends, had come to hassle the boys. One giggled, another squealed. The boys heard them, too. The movie was shut off, there were mutters from below, and the sound of the door opening. The crowbar beneath my bed seemed ridiculous, like a prop left over from another movie on this same set.

I opened the window and looked down on the five girls gathered in a little knot. I remembered doing this with Dee Stemple and some other girls once, when a group of the boys from Holy Cross were camping out in Mr. Dolan's chop shop, sleeping on the linoleum floors in the office. Two of the girls below were carefully holding something in their hands, like gifts. I coughed, and one of them dropped hers, and water arced up, little sparkles in the air.

"If anyone throws a water balloon into this house, you are in big trouble," I whispered, and they screamed and scattered.

Just after three I went downstairs to turn off the lights. All five boys were sleeping with their mouths open, their hair askew. Andrew had his thumb in his mouth. Goalie's little video game was still on; football players running at one another constantly, falling down, getting up, sending the ball in a spiral across the screen. I had met his parents at soccer games; they alternated, one staying at the restaurant while the other stood, silent, on the sidelines. I turned off the little game, turned off the lights, pulled the cool sheets over myself. This is the life I always wanted to have: five boys asleep on the floor, with nothing to wake them except the giggles of little girls. It felt so ordinary.

"God, you look chipper, considering," Andrew's mother said as the boys spilled out of the kitchen and toward the front door, climbing into her van to head out to a day-long basketball clinic at the middle school.

"In this case, looks are deceiving. I'm going back to bed."

But I never made it. I was stacking the cereal bowls in the sink when the phone rang. Again there was no answer, only breathing on the other end of the phone. All the ordinariness of the night before, the sense of being settled and secure, of my boy being an ordinary boy—all of it just slipped away.

"Bobby," I whispered, defeated, and then there was a cough, a gasp, a sob. "Mrs. Nurse?" came a small voice, and I leaned back against the counter.

On my way to the Levitts', I stopped and bought an extra-value meal from McDonald's, large fries and a Big Mac. Mrs. Levitt was sitting in the dark of an apartment in which the blinds had been neither raised nor opened. She smelled of perspiration and sleep and dirty clothes, and she did not speak as I opened the door with the key she'd given me and moved past her to the bed, stopping only to lay a hand lightly on her shoulder. It was the first time I had ever been in the apartment when there had been no sound, the television still, Irving's stertorous breathing silenced. Even the big Seth Thomas clock had wound down. Irving's body was a little cool and beginning to stiffen. Mrs. Levitt had pulled the sheet down to his ankles, as though one last time she wanted to look at what, for so long, had been the scarcely noticed landscape of her life, even more than her own body, which required a mirror to see.

"You waited for me," I said, taking her hand. She nodded. "That's good," I said. "Can I call now for someone to take care of things, or do you want to wait awhile?"

"A minute or two," she said, and shuffled into the kitchen in her house slippers. I could hear her open the bag I'd brought, then the sandwich wrapper.

"What time was it?" I called.

She carried her lunch to the card table on a cookie sheet. "Nothing for yourself?" she said.

I shook my head. There was a box of matzo on the card table, and I remembered that it was Passover. "I hope I didn't bring the wrong lunch," I said, looking at the box.

Mrs. Levitt saw me looking, and shrugged. "You think God's gonna be upset that I ate a hamburger?" she said, handing me the ketchup package to open.

She was silent, eating, and finally she patted her lips with a napkin. "I was watching the cable news around midnight, maybe," she said, "and I fell asleep on the couch, and then I woke up around six. Some kind of report on geese, they had, and the sound they made woke me right up, and I said to Irving, they'd wake the dead, those birds." Her shoulders rose high and fell, just one dry, strangled sob. "I was changing the channel to the one on NBC with that young girl I like, the one that just had the baby. Then I couldn't hear nothing from the bed." She said something else, one more sentence, but it was in German, Yiddish, or Hebrew. I couldn't tell the difference.

"I got to go to the bathroom, sweetheart," she said vaguely, and shuffled out of the room.

She looked better when she came back, more alive. She crossed to the hospital bed. "Take that thing out, sweetheart," she said, and I went over and removed the catheter tube. Then Mrs. Levitt pulled the sheet up over Irving, up to his bony chin, that stuck up now like the prow of his body, proud and hard. Then she leaned close to his ear and whispered something, then patted his shoulder.

"I was hungry," she said, sitting down and looking at the debris of her lunch.

We called the Jewish funeral home in Middle Lake, and an hour later two men came, black suits, soft voices, a collapsible gurney that came up and went down on the freight elevator. The hospital bed stood empty by the window, and as I opened the blinds, finally, the sun fell full upon the white sheets that Mrs. Levitt and I had changed only two days before.

"I can have this stripped and out of here in an hour or two," I said. "Or I can leave it just as it is. Whichever will make you feel a little bit better."

She sighed. "Leave it, sweetheart," she said.

"Is there someone I should call?"

She shook her head. "Irving had two older sisters," she said. "They treated him like a prince. His mother, too, like a king. They're all gone now."

"For you, I meant."

"I had two brothers and a sister. They're all gone a long time ago." She sipped at her soda, going warm and watery. "Almost fifty years we were married. It's a long time."

"It is a long time."

"Forty-eight years last month."

"How'd you meet him?"

"Ach, everyone wants to hear the story. He liberated me," she said, and I smiled and rubbed the thin skin of her hands, crosshatched, age-spotted.

"The fifth of May, they told us after. We didn't keep track of time. One girl who slept on the shelf above me, she made marks with a piece of stone on the wall. She died of something, coughing, coughing, you know, and then sometimes we didn't know what month it was, not even what year after a while.

"You could smell from a long way those little white flowers, so sweet. There were none of them so you could see, but you could smell. When we woke up all the guards were gone, and one lady who helped them, she was going down the road, looking back like she was afraid we would come after her. There was nothing to eat. There wasn't anything to eat for maybe a week or two. Two of the girls were dead, but we waited for someone to take them. They died all the time. You'd wake up in the morning and see that someone wasn't moving from their bunk and then you'd know, so that after a while it was nothing, like seeing a rat or the sun or anything else. Just someone dead again. A lot of them died with their eyes open. That's not so nice." She looked over at the hospital bed. "Otherwise it looks more like you're sleeping.

"We went outside because of the smell. You'd think after all that time we wouldn't notice. They soil themselves, see. Well, you know that, with the nursing and all. So we went outside. Sada, the girl I sat with, she was from a farm somewhere. She talked and talked always, at night, in the morning. She was a big fat girl when she came but she was skinny then like the rest of us, with no hair on her lower place, no bubbies either, either of us. We were modest when we came, like young girls, you know, but not after a while.

"We saw dust coming and she said it was the guards coming back. I thought maybe she was right because I saw the trucks and the uniforms. But then they got close and we could see that they were different from the guards. Then we saw the flags on one of the trucks, and we knew. One of them, young, with brown eyes and a little mustache, he came and stood by me, and he said something in English. But I didn't know it was English, I didn't know English. I said in German that I couldn't understand, that I couldn't speak English. Then in German he said, it will be all right now. He looked like he was crying a little bit. I said to him, we are Jewish, sir. You should know that I am Jewish. And he said, 'Yes, miss, so am I.' "

She waited a moment, as though always here in the story the audience had had something to say. But I was speechless.

"Sergeant Levitt. I never heard of such a thing, a Jewish soldier. And they had food. Sada stuffed herself and then was sick, right on the ground, like a dog. They took us to a special tent and gave us something for the bugs. The clothes were not so good." Her eyes shone suddenly, and she smiled. "But I was a pretty girl, even in ugly clothes."

"I learned the word later. Liberated. He liberated me. Everybody liked the story. One soldier, he put it in a special soldier's newspaper they had. Sergeant Levitt liberated me, and he brought me home and married me. His mother and sisters, they weren't so happy. There was a girl around the corner they liked better for him. Sophie, her name was. But he married me."

She pushed back the sleeve of one of her cardigans and there was the identification number. "You see?" she said.

"I see," I said, and nodded. I was crying, and Mrs. Levitt smiled and shrugged and patted my hand.

"Everybody likes that story," she said. "But, you know, after that, then we were married. Everybody thinks because of the story, it's like a fairy story. That's what one of Irving's nieces said once. Like a fairy story. I don't know. You got to live in the time you're living in. The past is the past, right, Irving?"

"It's an amazing story," I said.

"It's just a story," she said. "It's a long time ago, now."

"Are you going to bury him in the veterans' cemetery? Or Arlington, in Washington?"

Mrs. Levitt shook her head. "I already talked to the people at Perlman's. They'll cremate him. Then I can take him wherever I go." She looked over at the hospital bed. "You know what would have been the best thing for Irving? If he'd just gone home and married Sophie. She never married, that girl. She taught fourth grade in the public schools until they made her retire. Irving would have married her and thought about me, and I would have married somebody else, or maybe not, and thought about Irving, how he saved me." She sighed. "Ach, well. I don't know what I'll do with myself now. Maybe I'll move down to Miami. Two of my friends from home live in Miami. Both widows. Ruth and Esther, if you can believe it. I used to feel sorry for myself, tell people all my family was dead, they took them all away, my mama, my papa, my sister Rachel, my brothers. Now everyone I knew is dead. They got old. They got sick. Whatever." She lifted her hands to the sky. "Ah, what are you going to do?"

At the door I hugged her. "You look tired," she said.

"My son had four of his buddies spend the night last night. They stayed up, you know? They were good, but you still don't sleep. You could have called me earlier."

Mrs. Levitt smiled. "My sister and I, we did that. Rachel. She was the pretty one. I was smarter. Both of us in one big bed, the sheet over our heads, talking about the boys. You know, this and that. Our mama would yell at us, go to sleep. Go to sleep." She was smiling, Mrs. Levitt, but her eyes were full of tears. "Maybe your boy will want to take up golf," she finally said.

"Maybe," I said.

J ust so you'll be ready, I need to warn you that Mrs. Bernsen makes them all do family trees in fifth grade."

Cindy handed me a cup of coffee. "Is she out of her tiny mind?" she said.

It's exactly what I had told Mike Riordan when I picked Robert up after he'd been held in after school because of what Mike called "a verbal altercation" with the despised Jonathan Green, who had said that the New York Yankees were a bunch of losers. "We've done some talking about keeping your temper and agreeing to disagree," Mike had said, handing over Robert's backpack, trying not to look at me, or me at him, the horrible see-and-slide we'd both done with our eyes ever since we'd slept together. And Mike and I had had to agree to disagree about the genealogy lesson with which Mrs. Bernsen proposed to galvanize the fifth grade during the waning weeks of the school year, a lesson that might have made sense when she'd started teaching thirty years before but today was as perilous as walking down the center of Route 18. What would little Hillary Thompson, who stuttered like a jackhammer, do with her two stepfathers and their five collective children? What about Brittany McLeod, who had been adopted from Paraguay and was as small and dark as her parents, now divorced, each remarried, were big and fair?

"She says that this always gives the class a lift," Mike said, shrugging. "All I can tell you is every year I get complaints, and every year I hear afterward that it worked out fine."

"She's out of her mind," I said.

There was no spring in central Florida, just as there had been no real winter, no hiding the ungainly edges of its strip malls and ranch houses beneath the white hillocks of snow that lent charm to even the most charmless Northeastern town in the months that seemed to stretch endlessly between Christmas and Easter (or, as Mrs. Levitt informed me when I complained about the lack of seasons, between Hanukkah and Pesach). The change of seasons might touch the tired foliage in the farm fields and the shades of green on the development lawns, but on the narrow streets with their yards of yellow-white gravel and their struggling shrubs where I lived and worked, the seasons were visible only in the displays in the store windows, the green of Christmas giving way to the red of Valentine's Day and the purple of Easter and now the pink of Mother's Day. Robert walked to the strip and bought me a box of candy and a stuffed bear holding a balloon that said I Love You. Cindy made lasagna, but Mrs. Manford couldn't come, had stomach flu or some such. "Thank God it didn't happen the day after, or my dad would have sworn it was my cooking," Cindy said.

The next day Robert had no school, some teacher's conference or another, and he went with me to visit Mrs. Levitt. The television was on, as it always was, and the noon news featured a story about a police shootout in the Bronx, four officers dead and two wounded, the greatest carnage in twenty years for the New York City Police Department. As though still corded together my boy and I sank down side by side on the sofa and leaned toward the television, as though, face-to-face, it could tell us more than the sketchy story a woman in a bright red suit and matching lipstick was reading from a TelePrompTer. We didn't have cable in our apartment, couldn't afford it, but the Castros did, and Robert knew to flip to other news channels. For an hour we waited, watched, as though we were those people I'd seen so often in the public areas of the hospital, mouths agape, half-asleep in molded chairs, waiting for the doctor to bring them news. Finally there were names, and we sank back, exhausted. I put my arm around his shoulder.

"You know people who are police officers in New York?" Mrs. Levitt said softly, placing another cup of tea in front of me. "Family maybe?" And Robert looked into my face with fear and yearning, too, and I squeezed his shoulder.

"We have friends in the department," I said. "None of them were hurt."

"I'm glad Daddy's not dead," Robert said as we began walking home.

"Me, too," I said. "Really. I'm really happy that he's okay."

"Is he okay?" Robert said. "Do you know he's okay?"

"You heard the news."

"But I mean really okay, like every day."

"I hope so," I said.

How many times had I wished Bobby would die? I lost count years ago. It was my biggest fear when he was first a street cop that the phone would ring, that the chaplain would come to the door, that I would have to hear those bagpipes again that I'd heard wailing at his father's funeral, that all I'd have left was a piss-poor pension and his badge in the bottom of my jewelry box. Even on those days when he'd first twisted my arm, or shoved me into the wall, I still woke and peered at the digital clock and then lay back to wait if he was even a half hour behind his usual time. I'd be awake when he dropped his clothes in the corner, the belt buckle making a *ka-chunk* in the quiet house, when he slipped between the sheets, smelling of scotch and beer, tasting of it too as he put his arms around me and eased my nightgown up, hand over hand, like he was climbing a rope up into me.

And then there were the nights when I began to dread the sound of the door opening softly downstairs, two or three hours past the time he got off, the sound of his stumble on the stairs or the loud bangings of cabinet and refrigerator door from the kitchen, semaphore for discontent, an investigation going nowhere, a witness who'd been arrogant or uncooperative, even a car nosed a little too far toward the entrance to our driveway. The nights when he would pick a fight, throw open the bedroom door to say "Where the hell is the bread?" or ignore the regular breathing I learned to fake and come over me, into me, no matter what.

God forgive me, but there were so many times he went out to work and I would think the best thing that could happen to me was the call, the chaplain, the casket with the handsome cop I'd married inside it, who would never ever be able to lay a hand on me again, a fist in my face or rough fingers that opened me up as though I was a tunnel through which he was entitled, as a matter of right, to pass. When I was thinking about it rationally I knew it was no solution, that for my son his father would become a martyr, a man he would idolize and about whom he could never be told, never stand to hear the truth, the whole truth, nothing but. But often I was not thinking rationally, and I wished with all my heart that some lowlife's bullet would find a soft spot on Bobby's body, one of the soft spots I had lost the ability to find myself, with my hands or my tears or my words.

"Why did you say Daddy was a friend?" Robert said a week later, out of nowhere, as he was working on his family tree. "That day when you were talking to Mrs. Levitt? When the other police got hurt."

"Well, he sort of is," I said. But that was never true. Every time I saw a woman describe her husband as her best friend in some magazine or another, I always wondered what in the world she was talking about. Bobby and I had never been friends, ever, or I could never have loved him so completely and let him treat me so badly.

Hunched over a sheet of gleaming poster paper, Robert began to sketch out his family tree for Mrs. Bernsen, and as he did I thought of how little he asked about the past and the future. Any other child would have been at me constantly with questions, about when and whether we were going back. Any other child would have slipped up at school, told his friends where he was really from, boasted that his father was a policeman, pointed to the map of Italy during social studies and made a lie of the nondescript middle-American last name that he carried. But as I watched Robert spread his left arm wide around his work as though to hide or shelter it, I realized that he had been in training for this subterfuge almost his whole life, learning to ignore what was in the next room, to hide what he knew from others, to refrain from asking the wrong questions. His parents had always been in disguise; it was just a different disguise now, a different sort of false mustache, funny hat.

"Do you want help?" I asked nervously from the kitchen.

"Not yet," he said.

I made some macaroni and read a magazine and the new Avon catalogue and there was still no sound from the room. Then he appeared in the doorway, smiling, nodding his head, taking my hand and pulling me to the card table.

"I figured out how to do this," he said. "Like, once I don't mind what I call people, then it can be just like it really is. Here's Daddy, only I called him Robert Crenshaw. And here's Daddy's Daddy, and I called him the same thing. It's just the same, only with different names."

And so it was. As I filled him in on the generations that had gone before, I made amendments, but few were necessary. There was one telltale Giuseppe, Robert's paternal great-grandfather, but I named him Joe. My mother-in-law's maiden name was Stanowicz; I let her keep it. And mine? Pick one, I told Robert, making a game of it. Give me a name before I was married. He made it Wynn. Elizabeth Wynn. It sounded sort of grand.

"What about Grandmom?" he asked, and my mother went in true to life, O'Donnell as she'd been born and raised, too far out on a limb to shatter the disguise of our new existence.

"See, I know who they are," Robert said. "That's enough, right? That I know. Like everybody in the class will be looking and it will say Robert Crenshaw and I'll know what it's supposed to really be."

"That's right," I said.

"I know. Like, remember how Daddy took me that one time to the place where he was working in Central Park? There was this big policeman there, I can't remember his name, but he was really really big."

"McMichael. Captain McMichael. He was the station commander there."

"That was him, I think. And he kept looking at me and saying you're not a Benedetto. I know you're not. I knew your grandfather and I know your father. Nah, I can tell, you're not a Benedetto. And I think he was saying it like a joke, because I looked like Daddy, but I was only a little kid, like five, and I didn't really understand that it was a joke. I thought maybe he was right, that I was adopted or something, like that Korean kid in my old school who was always telling everybody he was Italian just because his name was Russo, and everybody thought he was really stupid. And Daddy could kind of tell that I was upset and when we went out to get ice cream from the Good Humor truck in the park we were sitting on this bench and he said to me, see this. And he pointed to that really big vein in my arm." He held it out, thin and bony, and pointed to the blue artery that ran behind the elbow, his grubby finger outlining it for me. "And then Daddy showed me the one he had. It was really big, and it kind of bulged out. And he said there's a part of me in you. And there's a part of you in me. And there's a part of me in all the kids you'll have, and their kids."

"That's true," I said.

"I know," he said, picking up his pencil again and coloring in some leaves. Then he asked casually, as though he was only wondering whether he should use a forest-green or a medium-green pencil, "Remember that time that Daddy busted Nana's mirror in the hall and then he said he was really, really sorry and got her another one? If he did that to you, would you say it was all right?"

"I don't know," I said.

"I don't mean like go back," he said, not looking up from the paper. "I mean like accept his apology."

"I don't know, sweetie," I said. "A lot of bad things happened with Daddy and me. He did a lot of things to me that he shouldn't have. He shouldn't have hit me. Ever. No one should ever hit another person. And he did, a lot. I know it's a hard thing to understand, why he did what he did. *I* don't even understand it. Maybe someday I will."

"I need to finish this," Robert said, his pencil point coming down hard on the poster paper.

Sometimes I felt as if I'd spent my life sitting on the closed lid of the toilet seat with the water running while I cried, and I wondered whether Robert, sitting downstairs working away on his project, heard the sound of the cold-water tap at full throttle as somehow soothing, the background noise of his childhood nights, as familiar as the rumble of the furnace coming on. It took me a long time to finish this time, to throw cold water on my wan face, to blow my nose and then use a little concealer to veil the flush of emotion. Then I folded laundry and changed sheets. Cotton had always helped me get over the humps.

By the time I went back downstairs the names were all neatly printed and Robert was working on his tree, a mighty oak by the look of it, many branched, thick-trunked, sketched in with colored pencils. And as I admired it, exclaiming over his neatness and the careful attention to the leaves, I realized I would have to tell Mike that Mrs. Bernsen was wiser than I, at least in this case. For there was Robert—just ROBERT, I noticed, with no surname at all—at the bottom of the trunk, at the roots, the base, the center of it all. He had not colored the leaves in yet, and the trunk and its branches looked for the moment less like a tree and more like a great brown river, the Nile, the Amazon, the Benedetto and Flynn river of blood, and there at its isthmus was this one child, so that it seemed that all of these people, from Poland, from Italy, from Ireland and the Bronx and Brooklyn, had come together for no other reason than to someday produce Robert Benedetto, in an event as meant, as important as that one in Bethlehem that he had learned about in catechism class at St. Stannie's. There was Robert, the reason for the collision of these incongruous constellations, the savior of us all.

"Is it all right?" he said.

"It's beautiful. It's perfect. I'm really, really proud of you."

He'd been proud of himself, too, I could tell. He'd rolled the poster paper carefully, tying it at each end with a bit of twine, and he'd carried it out to the bus in both hands. The way he stood with it reminded me of when he was four, in blue satin shorts and a white satin tuxedo shirt, the ring-bearer at the wedding of one of Ann Benedetto's godchildren. It reminded me of the way, his face solemn, he'd carried the blue satin pillow, held close to his narrow chest, down the long aisle of the church. Bennie was the same, the way he carried his. It was as though they had their lives in their hands, these beautiful dark-faced displaced boys. The look of them, so serious, so proud somehow, stayed with me all day, while I scolded the dialysis patient for eating too much junk and shopped for the woman with cerebral palsy.

"Hi," I said casually when Robert came back home that afternoon, letting a great cloud of warm air into the dim air-conditioned cool of the apartment. There was a laundry basket on the couch, and I was folding more sheets, matching corners, my arms spread in a kind of benediction, so I did not immediately see his face, and when I did I couldn't at first believe it, couldn't take it in. I stood holding the sheet across myself, like a curtain, my eyes and mouth wide above it, a cartoon woman.

"My God," I said, and pulled him into the light from the window.

It looked worse than it was. His upper lip was swollen on one side, purple and misshapen, and the area just below his left eye was beginning to color. There was a ribbon of blood beneath his mouth, but I discovered as I used my own spit to remove it, not taking the time for towel or water, that there was no wound beneath it. Maybe the gum had bled and had stopped bleeding.

"What happened?" I said.

"Jonathan Green is a jerk-off," he said, and his voice quavered deep in his throat like a birdcall.

"Sit down," I said. Ice, aspirin, tissues. I put them on the flimsy coffee table and put my arm around him. A shudder ran through him, and then he looked up, his fingers going to his lip. The colored pencils were still spread out on the kitchen table, a rainbow lying awry.

"Wait," he said, and went upstairs into the bathroom. I knew he was looking at himself in the mirror.

"This wasn't my fault," he said. "I pushed him first but he deserved it. He's had it coming all year. He's a jerk. The biggest jerk in the school. I hope I broke his nose. He called Bennie a spic. You know what a spic is?"

I nodded.

"We were talking in class about where we were from, and he started it then, he was starting to talk about how you shouldn't be allowed to live here unless you could speak English. He was saying that America was too small for Americans and all these other people were coming here and taking stuff away. He goes, like, oh, they can't even speak English. And Goalie was really embarrassed, I could tell, and this girl named Christie, you don't know her but her parents are Greek or something, and they can't speak English that good, I don't think. And I said that there were lots of people who couldn't speak that good English but were nice people."

"Didn't Mrs. Bernsen say anything?"

"She said I was right. She said her parents were German and it took them a long time to learn English and now look at her, she taught English. But then we got dismissed for the day, and we got outside, and Jonathan comes up, with Bennie right there, and he says I only said what I said because of my spic friend. That's what he said, 'Your spic friend.' I just shoved into him as hard as I could. He called Bennie a spic. Then he hit me. Then I hit him." Blood was beading up on his lower lip again, and I handed him a tissue. He pressed it to his mouth, hard.

"I sat on him and made him take it back," he finally said. His words were muffled by his lip, which was getting bigger. "Put some ice on that," I said.

He slumped down in the sofa, his back bent, his elbows on his knees, avoiding my eyes. There were lemon Popsicles in the freezer and I gave him one, two birds with one stone, the ice and the unexpected before-dinner treat.

"Jonathan is a jerk," I said. "He's been goading you from day one. And he's got a mean mouth on him. So now you know that he's mean down to the ground. Now you know that the only way to deal with Jonathan is to stay away from him. You're going to meet people like him your whole life. They're ignorant and spiteful and they call names because they figure it makes them big if they can make someone else small. Makes them high if they can make someone else low. Bennie is such a star, everyone likes him, and he's so good at sports and school that Jonathan had to pull him down. So he calls him a spic. So it tells you more about Jonathan than it does about Bennie."

"I said that," Robert said. "I said he didn't know what he was talking about. He didn't even know what a spic was. I knew from Daddy. Daddy talked about spics with Mr. Hogan and Mr. Carter. He said the spics live like animals and that they killed that policeman in Washington Heights. The one that Daddy helped train, when you went to the funeral. The spics killed him."

I winced. "Don't use that word, Ba," I said. "Spic is a word that people use to talk about people who are Spanish. Puerto Ricans, Cubans like Bennie. They're Latino, but people who don't like them call them spics."

"That's not what Daddy said. Daddy said the spics messed up the city."

"Maybe you didn't hear him right," I said, hearing the whole rant in my head, the way I'd heard it a dozen times. They breed like rabbits, they won't learn the language, they put their women to work filling nickel bags, the girls dress like whores, the boys can't keep their pants on, why the hell don't they stay where they belong? They were like the words to a song that I'd heard so many times I scarcely noticed it anymore, the words all blurred together.

"I thought spics were bad guys. Like robbers. Or guys who sold drugs."

"No," I said.

"So what are they?"

"Spic is a word that some people use to describe people who come from Spanish-speaking countries. The way people who don't like black people call them niggers."

"So when Daddy was talking about spics he was talking about Puerto Rican people? And Cuban people?"

"Ba," I said, and then, when I saw his face twist, "Robert. Sometimes police officers get very frustrated with all the bad stuff they see around them. They want to say bad things about bad guys and sometimes they use words they shouldn't use. Your daddy would tell you that if he was here."

Robert sucked on his Popsicle and stared into the middle distance, one eye beginning to close up into a shining slit, his other focused on nothing. For a long time we sat there, side by side, not touching. Finally he stood wearily, like an old man, sore and tired.

"I'm going up to do my homework," he said.

"Ba," I said. "It's all right."

"I don't really like to be called that anymore," he said.

Fifteen minutes later the bell rang, and Bennie was at the door. I could see tear streaks on his face. He was carrying a comic book. "Don't punish him," he said when I told him Robert was up in his room. I fried chicken, boiled rice, wondered how we would talk to each other at dinner. But when I went upstairs to call Robert he was asleep on his bed, his face turned to the window, soft and bruised like overripe fruit, a sweet peach, a golden plum. I left everything on the stove to keep warm.

I had to say this for Bobby: just like the other horrid things he did, he never did that one in front of the child, at least knowingly. He'd kept nigger out of the conversation, and whore, and all the rest, or at least he thought he had. But so much had taken place just within the range of Robert's peripheral vision, things I might never really know, things he might never admit to himself, things that made him what he was today, sleeping upstairs in his clothes, twitching slightly.

He slept through his favorite television program and Bennie stopping by, again, with a video game and another comic. There was a glossy moon, cut from the silver paper of early summer, outside the bathroom window as I got ready for bed, and its light shone across Robert's bed and spilled onto the floor of his room, where his schoolbooks, covered in brown paper, covered with doodles, lay in a motley pile. I stacked them on the floor next to his bed, but he never stirred. My own sleep was like clouds scudding across the sky, the white numbers on the digital clock looming out of the dark as I raised my head, 12:27, 1:12, 2:14. There was the sound of a siren someplace outside, wailing and then waning, and then I heard the sound of voices from downstairs. Underneath my bed was the crowbar I'd taken so long ago from Mr. Castro, and I closed my fingers around it and slid out of my room, down the hall and down the stairs.

"I know," I heard a voice say, and realized it was Robert's. He was in the kitchen, and when I reached the bottom of the stairs I could see through the door that he was on the telephone. He was sitting cross-legged in the clothes he'd slept in, his back against the refrigerator. In the moonlight I could see a stack of Oreo cookies on the floor, like pieces to a game, checkers maybe, or gambling chips.

"I know," he said again. "I want to, too." The silence seemed to vibrate. The crowbar felt heavy in my hand, and I wanted to put it down.

"Then why did you?" Robert said. And then, "I am. I'm playing soccer and basketball and baseball. I play third base. I'm getting pretty good." He rubbed his eyes, winced when he touched the bruises by mistake, pulled an Oreo apart and licked the cream. "I watched it, too," he said. "I knew you were watching it."

I should have moved sooner, but it was only then that I was sure. I stepped out of the blackness in my white nightgown and Robert dropped the receiver, staring at my face and then at the crowbar in my hand. The receiver bounced on its long cord three times gently against the wall, and then I picked it up with two fingers and dropped it into the cradle, but not before I heard his voice on the other end, deep and sleepy: "Robert? Hey? Robert?"

"Put the cookies back," I said.

"You lied to me," he said, rising to his feet, his eyes only a little lower than my own.

"About what?" I said.

"About a bunch of things."

"I didn't lie about anything, Robert. You did something really really foolish tonight. And if you ever do it again we'll have to move and start over someplace else. No Bennie. No Cindy. New school, new friends."

"I want to see my dad," Robert said. "You lied to me about him."

"About what?"

"About a lot of things. He said you lied about a lot of things."

"Tell me what he said."

"No. You'll just say bad things about him. He loves me. He misses me."

"I know that. I never denied that."

"He loves you, too, he said."

"Did you tell him where we were?"

"No," Robert said, his voice cracking.

"Did he ask you?"

He nodded.

"And what did you say?"

"I told him I wasn't allowed. He said he never meant that about the spics, that he had a friend in narcotics who's Puerto Rican. He said it was good that I stood up for my friend. He said sometimes you have to do that."

He said, he said, he said. It was like having him there in the room all over again as the words came at me, the old familiar justifications and accusations, all in Robert's voice, still high and light.

"Ba," I said, then stopped. "I didn't lie to you about anything."

I touched his face. "Do you remember when my face looked like this? Only worse. My nose broke. I'm lucky my jaw was okay."

His tears shook him, so that he bounced in my arms almost the way I had bounced him as a baby, trying to lull him to sleep. The front of my nightgown was wet. There was a little blood mixed with the tears.

"I didn't tell," he finally said.

"I know, honey."

"I wanted to ask about the spic thing," he said.

"I know."

I left the crowbar by the hall closet and together we climbed the stairs. An hour later, when I was certain he was asleep again, I went downstairs and pulled a business card from behind his baby picture in my wallet. It was an answering machine, I knew, and after the beep I said, "This is Elizabeth Crenshaw. I need to speak to Patty Bancroft immediately. She has my number."

After he'd left on the bus in the morning, more than a little proud of his raddled face, Bennie's arm around his shoulder, I walked over to the school. Mike Riordan was at his desk when I tapped at the door. When he saw me he looked the way I must look when Robert opens the door at the end of the day. It made me hate myself, that look—such happiness, such shamefaced yearning. To cover up he lobbed a wad of looseleaf into the toy basketball hoop stuck to the wall next to his desk with suction cups. There was a poster next to it of a cat trying to hold onto a high bar. "Hang in There, Baby!" it said underneath. We'd had it in the nurses' lounge at South Bay, too.

"I need help," I said, and I sat in the straight chair on the other side of his desk.

"Okay," he said.

"To begin with," I said, "my name is Frances Benedetto, and I'm from New York City." It was ten minutes to nine when I started, and nine-thirty by the time I was done. How short a time it took to tell him everything, to feel the secret fall from my shoulders like a yoke.

He drove me to Cindy's house the first Saturday after school let out, half a dozen foil containers filled with food slithering from side to side on the backseat. "Don't take those corners so wide," I said, "or you're going to have barbecued riblets and chicken wings all over the car." He frowned slightly into the sunlight and took his foot off the gas, until his little car was going maybe ten miles an hour and an elderly woman had edged around him and then pulled in front. "Ha ha ha," I said.

I'd been cooking for two days, and I'd had to smack the boys with a dishtowel on their shinny dark brown legs as they filched potato pancakes and mahogany-colored riblets. "You're a good cook, Mrs. Crenshaw," Bennie said politely. "Don't try to get around me with sweet talk," I said. Robert only smiled. The marks on his face were gone, and maybe it was only my imagination that he seemed quieter. He'd always been so quiet, anyhow.

"I understand him so much better now," Mike Riordan said

to me after I'd told him our story. "Thanks. It makes it easier for me."

It had made it easier for me, too. The notion that the man had seen me naked, had put his tongue into my mouth, had unbuttoned my dress—none of it meant anything compared to the fact that he knew where I really came from, what my name was, what I really did for a living, what my son had had to live through. Even his smile seemed to have knowledge in it, and understanding, and it had made me feel more myself and less afraid with him than with anyone else, even Cindy. That day when I came to talk to him he had leaned forward, asking no questions, looking me straight in the eye, and when I was finished he had come around the desk and sat in the chair the dads usually sat in, when Mike was having parent conferences. He had taken my hand and he had rubbed my fingers hard, as though they were cold and he was trying to bring back the blood into them. "You're amazing," was all he said.

He looked over at me in the car, speeding up and smiling now. "Robert's fine," he said, reading my mind.

"I know."

"No, you don't. But I do. He's a smart kid. He'll work all this out."

But I do know. I know it's not true. Children are resilient, some of the shrinks like to say, and everything marks them, say some of the others, and both things are true. Sometimes it seems as if Robert never called Bobby on the phone that night, never took his side over mine. Sometimes it seems as if Mike Riordan and I are no more than a boy's coach and a boy's mother, as though I never chose him over Robert. But Robert has scars as surely as I do, and his are more dangerous, because he cannot see them and so can believe they are not there.

"You think too much, Fran," Bobby told me once, when I was analyzing this or that. And he was right. I guess I do. What I'm thinking is that I can hardly hear his voice anymore, Bobby's voice, that ruled my life, that made me jerk like I was at the end of a leash. Even on the phone, it had sounded like the voice of someone I'd once known, a while ago. You think too much, Fran. I can't quite hear him say it.

He was right about that: I do think too much. If you're a good nurse you always do think too much, see too much, know too much. You look at the cleaned-up junkie with pneumonia who's telling you it's just a cold, a cold, man, a little vitamin C and some sleep and I'll be good as new, and you know, practically without double-gloving and drawing the blood, that he's slipped over the border from being HIV positive to having AIDS and is skidding toward the finish line of death. You see a little kid come into the waiting room with her mother, see the child do a slow and subtle lean back when the mother turns toward her, and you know, you just know, that the mother hits her. The X rays will only tell you how hard. Winnie used to say that she knew what some of them would tell her before they even opened their mouths from the set of their shoulders, the slant of their gaze. She used to say that it was like being a priest, sometimes. I felt the same way.

I call Grace now and I know that something is wrong. Suddenly there is an answering machine on her home phone. The message is curt, anonymous: "Please leave a message after the beep." Three times I've said, "Gracie, it's me." But I am afraid to give her the number here, afraid of who else might hear it, see it written by the phone on a scrap of paper. Twice I called her office, but it is the same thing there, the recorded voice, the honk at the end. "We're good," I said the last time. "We're fine." She's not. I can hear it in the cold timbre of her recorded voice. The cold in her makes cold in me. That, and Robert's phone call. And the television news program after the carnival. And what I know about Bobby, how good he is at finding out what he wants to know.

I look at the hump growing larger between Mrs. Levitt's perpetually slumped shoulders and I pretty much know that if she takes the slightest tumble two or three years from now, it'll be a broken hip and a nursing home, a walker if not a wheelchair. "Take your calcium pills," I say, banging the plastic bottle on the tiny kitchen counter. "Ach, they bind me up," she says, eating Chips Ahoy. I bring another kind of calcium, one that doesn't cause constipation. "You need to build up your bones," I remind her, and she looks at me pityingly, as though to say, Mrs. Nurse, what do you think happened to my bones those four years they fed me mealy grain and dirty water and did whatever it was to my insides that meant I would never have a child. I see Mrs. Levitt now always in terms of her great secret, the numbers on her arm, the story of her marriage, and I realize that everyone has, her whole life, ever since that May day half a century ago. I hid my wounds because I was ashamed, ashamed of Bobby and ashamed of myself for staying with him, but now I know that I was also afraid of being reduced, of becoming in the minds of all who knew me that poor woman whose husband beats her. Or used to. I have begun to think of myself as someone who used to get beat up by her husband. I am a recovering battered woman. God, I hate that term, all those classifications that seem to reduce our wounds to the same status as eye or hair color, that make us a type, a cover line in a magazine.

"The Holocaust survivors," Mrs. Levitt said savagely one day when she saw a story on the news. "Like a club. People have no shame."

I see and I know. I know by the dandelion yellow of my patient Melvin's skin that if he does not get a kidney transplant in the next ninety days I will be attending his funeral instead of taking his temperature. I know that my cerebral palsy patient is lonely for love and romance because of the name she uses when she goes into chat rooms on the computer: Sexyjen. I wonder how she describes herself when she is no more than a line of black letters on someone else's screen, wonder if she makes herself tall and lithe, with muscles that run smooth beneath the surface of tanned skin instead of arms and legs that shiver and shake in an uncontrollable dance. She wants to be someone else, somewhere else, and I can't blame her.

I know that Mike Riordan has decided to try to make things right by making them lighter. Robert plays baseball now, just like he told his dad, and Mike takes us out from time to time afterward. Bennie usually comes along and Robert measures the distance between his coach and his mother with his eyes. It is considerable. The week after we'd gone to bed together I had bought myself some contraceptive sponges, but I'd done it the way you buy aspirin in case some Saturday night you have a headache. Things are back to where they were. No more flaming steak or tuxedoed headwaiters. Still, whenever Mike brings us home, if it happens that Robert goes down the pavement to Bennie's or upstairs to start his homework, Mike steps inside the apartment, puts his arms around me and kisses me, less gently than he had that first time. Once, when we met in the Roerbackers' basement during a school swim party, he coming out of the concrete shower stall in his shorts, his hair wet and raked back with the marks of Craig's comb still in it, me in the blue tank suit Cindy lent me, smelling of coconut from the sunscreen, he had reached for me, held me for a long time, finally pushed back, groaning. "I'm a patient person," he said.

"You're being cruel to that poor man," Cindy had said next day as we watched the kids swim.

"I don't mean to be. He'd be better off if I stayed out of his way, but that's hard, under the circumstances."

"I like him," Cindy said.

"I like him, too."

"Then what's your problem?"

"I like you, too."

"And, honey, I'd have you in a minute if we were so inclined. But we're not. How come all of us are attracted to girlfriends who are nice and smart and helpful and love us and we're all attracted to guys who are mean and give us a hard time?"

"Craig's not mean."

"Craig's different. So's Mike Riordan. Which is the point I'm trying to make. You want to try this new scented insect repellent we're coming out with?"

"What's it smell like?"

Cindy sniffed. "Musk."

"No, thanks."

"Plus he loves kids," Cindy had said.

I knew when Cindy got pregnant almost before she did. Her hair went limp and one day, in the library, as we sent out overdue cards, she snapped at Mrs. Patrinian, "We know what we're doing here." Mrs. Patrinian turned red, and so, I think, did I. In April she started drinking herb tea in the morning instead of coffee, and when we all had burgers and beer out back she drank soda water. The buttons on her white blouse, the sleeveless one, bulged a bit, showing a patch of skin between her breasts. For some reason she didn't tell me right away. There were long pauses in our conversation, and she was dying to fill them with this, the most exciting news that any woman ever has. Or sometimes, the worst.

"My son misses his father," I had said to Mrs. Levitt, taking her blood pressure as she ate a frozen yogurt with her free hand. After Mr. Levitt died her doctor had given her a physical and pronounced her hypertense, overweight. The diagnosis had enabled him to continue sending me to the Levitt apartment. Nothing has changed there, except that the hospital bed is gone and Mrs. Levitt keeps the door to the terrace open, although the freshening warm breezes of a Florida spring will soon blow hot. "The air should come in," she had said the first time I noticed the sliding glass doors ajar. "You smell a little cold in the morning, you know it'll be a nice day. Too cold, with that hard feeling, snow. At least in Chicago. You need the fresh air." Irving is in a stainless-steel jar on an occasional table. It rattles if you shake it. Robert once asked what it was. "Ah, a knickknack thing," Mrs. Levitt had said, rolling her eyes at me.

"It is hard, for the children," she added quietly, licking a vanilla mustache from her upper lip. "Life is not easy."

"I feel foolish complaining, to you of all people."

"Why?"

"Your life."

Mrs. Levitt shrugged. "You shouldn't have told me it was yogurt," she said, looking at her cone. "I would have thought it was ice cream." She licked, then said, "The big things, eh. It's all the other things. Like now, whether to keep the cable, to move, what to do between breakfast and lunch."

"You're lonely," I said.

"No, no," Mrs. Levitt said. "Filling the hours when you're an old lady—it's not a feeling, just a job. Sometimes now I still talk to Irving. I'm entitled."

"I still shouldn't complain."

"You call that complaining? You don't know complaining. Anyway, other people's troubles don't take away yours. But don't be foolish and think somebody else is having everything fine."

Of course that was exactly what I had always thought, as a child walking home in my school uniform past the homes where it seemed reading lights shone yellow from the window to illuminate the evening hours of handsome and lively fathers, warm and sympathetic mothers, children who were tucked in tight beneath their blankets each night in rooms bright with wallpaper. There were even times, as an adult, when I had thought it of myself, of Bobby and Robert and me, eating beneath the brass chandelier in the small dining room, the dishes and glasses shining as though they'd been given to us as prizes, the flowered plates plaques to commemorate our love for one another. If it would all stay like this moment, I would think to myself. And then, as we cleared the table, stacked the dishes, darkened the house for the night, the feeling would be gone, as bright and ephemeral as the lamplight.

"Things will happen to a boy that you cannot help," Mrs. Levitt added.

"You sound like a fortune-teller."

"Just so. They always say these things that you can say about anyone. Life will be good and bad. You will meet people who can help you. Someone you love will die. Big deal."

"Did you take your calcium?"

She held out her cone. "Better than pills," she said. "Even better if it was chocolate. They make chocolate yogurt?"

Cindy eats frozen yogurt now, drinks milk, stops at the farm stand every day for fresh vegetables. I remember doing the same not long ago. A year ago. Only a year. A year ago I had a secret inside me, and, just like Cindy, I kept it a secret. Even Bobby didn't know I was pregnant. Even Grace. A good nurse would have known. Winnie had cocked her head on the side one afternoon when we were slow in the emergency room, put her hands on her big hips, screwed up a corner of her mouth. "How are you feeling?" she said. The way a woman walks, flat-footed, her toes turned out a little, her pelvis thrust forward as though her body's proud of itself—a good nurse knows.

I knew everything when I went to the clinic two days after Bobby broke my nose that last time. I lay on the table with the sheet over my knees and saw the bottle and the hose in the corner, and knew exactly how they would use it.

They were kind at the clinic.

"Let me tell you about the procedure," said the counselor, who kept looking at my battered face, at the bandages and the telltale perimeter of black and blue and red.

"I'm a nurse," I said. "I know."

When I'd assisted at abortions myself I'd told the patient there would be some cramping. Now I know that wasn't exactly true. It hurt. I was glad it hurt. The more it hurt the more I knew I had the guts to get up from the table and leave Bobby Benedetto. I wanted to know whether it was a boy or a girl, but I didn't ask, and it wouldn't really have made a difference. A boy to learn that a man can keep a woman in line with the flat of his hand; a girl to learn that men love you and hurt you in equal measure. None of the above, I kept thinking, none of the above, one of those pieces of nonsense that gets stuck somewhere between your mind and your mouth when you're having a hard time. The machine made a noise like the window air conditioner in our bedroom. I stared at the ceiling, my eyes dry and gritty. They gave us Lorna Doones and apple juice in the recovery room. "You'll get your girl," Bobby had said after my miscarriages. But he was wrong.

"We're done here," the doctor said.

Maybe that's what I felt when Mike Riordan came inside me, not Bobby, but the doctor, the speculum. I'd lain on the table and fiddled with the adhesive tape that pulled when I moved my mouth.

"What happened to your face?" the doctor said.

"I was in a car accident," I said.

I don't think about it very much anymore, what it felt like on the subway as I went from the clinic on the east side of Manhattan home to Brooklyn to make Robert a snack after school. That night I fell asleep planning my escape, and had a dream. I was running on the Coney Island boardwalk and I saw a little girl in a lime-green, ruffled bathing suit struggling in the waves. I ran to the edge of the ocean but two police officers were already there. "We'll handle this, ma'am," one of them said, and smiled at me. I turned around and started running again without looking back. It was quiet in my dream; there was no sound of the child, or the policemen splashing through the water.

She'd be six months old now. She'd be sitting up and babbling and laughing at her big brother's funny faces. I can't think about that too much. It's the worst thing that Bobby did to me, or that I did to myself because of him. But I can think about it more now than I could before, when I just let my mind drop a curtain over it. And I couldn't stop thinking about it in the car on the way to Cindy's baby shower. I couldn't stop thinking about it all day long. I thought about it as Mike and I brought the food in through the cellar door, Craig meeting us, Chelsea behind him hauling Chad around like a sack of grain, limp and pale. "Let me down!" he shouted, but Chelsea paid him no mind.

"I put so much soda on ice I had to use a second tub for it," Craig said. "The cake came and I put it in the fridge but it takes up all the room in there."

"It has a sugar umbrella on it," Chelsea said. "Can I have it after?"

"Absolutely," I said.

"Where's Robert?"

"He went on a camping trip with Mr. Castro and Bennie. Down to the Hidden Forest Game Preserve. Bennie's dad said they might see alligators."

"I don't like alligators," said Chelsea.

"Me neither."

"Hi, Mr. Riordan," Chelsea added.

I let Chelsea have what she wanted that day. The umbrella made her sick, what with the ribs and three cans of Coke, but I let her have it anyhow, even though it was pure spun sugar. We ate nearly all the food I'd made, the PTA mothers, two high school friends from Lakota, Mrs. Manford and two of her sisters, Cindy's aunts. Cindy had been out shopping with her mother and when she came in and saw the pile of boxes and the white lace umbrella hanging over the recliner in her den—I knew she'd kill me if we used the living room and spilled anything on the taupe carpet—she'd screamed and covered her face.

"I'm going to kill you for this, Beth, I swear I am," she said. But I just smiled, and smiled some more seeing her round and flushed, with the big hard swell of her belly beneath her flared white blouse, the maternity clothes a big improvement from the time when I was pregnant with Robert almost thirteen years before, when everything had had lace and ribbons and flowers, as though to have a baby you had to look like one. Five months gone she was, but she looked more, because she was carrying twins.

The sonogram said it was a boy and a girl, and she'd kept her pregnancy a secret for almost three months because the doctor wasn't sure if they were going to make it.

"I could have lost them both," she told me finally, and I thought of my lost child and then put the thought aside in the face of her happiness. She loved things to be special, Cindy, and twins are special. The boxes spilled forth duplicate treasures, two pairs of tiny denim overalls, two receiving blankets in soft flannel, two embroidered samplers, one pink, one blue. Two teddy bears, one in a bow tie and top hat, the other in a dress. "Oh, I love these," Chelsea moaned, as Chad wadded up the wrapping paper and applauded every new gift.

I went into Cindy's kitchen to refill the serving dishes she'd gotten as wedding presents, probably at a shower much like this one. I remembered going to Bermuda for a week with Buddy and Marie not long after I was married, and standing in the airport looking at the cities on the departure board, and thinking that I could take the traveler's checks and just go anywhere, Seattle, Cincinnati, Paris, Grand Rapids, Montego Bay, and start a whole new life. I don't know why I thought it at that moment; Bobby and I were still in love then. Maybe everybody thinks it at some time or another, just thinks about becoming another person, giving up the law for a life as a golf pro, trading teaching for waitressing and life in the scorching Caribbean sun. I remember Bobby telling me about two cops he knew in missing persons, and how they'd gone looking for an English teacher from Queens, happy family man with a new car and a nice lawn, who just went missing one day. Two years later they found him in Australia, teaching English: he had a nice lawn and a new car and a wife named Shelley, which had been the name of the wife he'd had before.

It had seemed just a funny story then, but now I knew it was the essential truth about human nature. We'd traveled across the country, Robert and I, and in some way wound up where we'd been before. I looked at Robin Pearson, who was the secretary of the PTA, talking to Meghan Dickson's mother, whose name I couldn't ever remember. They might as well have been Marie and Terri. The thing you took into a new life with you was yourself, and so you made it so much like it had been before, used and, yes, even comfortable. When I looked across at Cindy, pulling silver wrapping from a big box, I felt a spasm of pain and grief for Grace.

"Oh, look," Cindy said, unfolding a crib quilt, a pattern of hearts done in cross-stitch. She rummaged through the tissue for a card, and finally Mrs. Manford, in a tight light voice, said, "That one's from me, honey."

It made me remember Ann Benedetto then, too, remember how she had once proposed a toast at Christmas to "her boys," how she would give Bobby a cashmere sweater and a pair of outdoor boots, a book on baseball and a duffel bag, and hand me a bottle of perfume from the drugstore, even once a single pair of pantyhose in a size too big for me. I couldn't help it; my face would flush at the baldness of the insult, just as Cindy's face was flushing now, looking from the quilt to her mother and back again.

"It's beautiful, Mom," she said, but you could tell she was thinking what all the rest of us were thinking, that one blanket was an odd sort of gift for a woman expecting two babies. Especially for a woman who had once had two babies of her own. I looked at the aunts, Mrs. Manford's sisters, but they were talking about the high school bond issue.

"Charlie and Cathy," Cindy told me she was going to name

them. She'd never told me the story about her sister, the one that had surely given an entire dusty farming town a way of describing her: "Cindy Manford, poor thing, you remember, the child whose twin sister—yes, identicals too—their poor mother . . ." Mrs. Manford was reapplying her lipstick. "I find the quilting really takes my mind off things," she said.

There was a familiarity to it all, sharper, keener than anything that could be called déjà vu. It was just the way life is. Chad dirtied his diaper. Mrs. Manford asked Cindy why he wasn't potty-trained. Robin Pearson said she hadn't been able to potty-train her son until he was four. One of Cindy's high school friends said the preschool in Lakota, the good one at the Methodist Church, wouldn't take them if they weren't potty-trained. Chelsea said she was going to give the babies their baths. Mrs. Manford said she was too young. I said I'd help her. Cindy said she had to pee so often she might as well just stay in the bathroom. Her mother said she couldn't sell Avon if she had to keep using the bathroom. It had been nine days since Robert had called his father, dialing the number we had made him memorize when he was six, in case of kidnappers. It was not that the fear I'd felt that night, as I heard that voice come out of the receiver, so smooth, so shocking, had gone away exactly. It just seemed so much less real than what was going on around me, the way Mrs. Levitt's years in the camps seemed so much less real than the cans of Chef Boyardee ravioli on her shelves. Patty Bancroft had called me back, offered again to move us somewhere else, somewhere where we would be safe. But I'd realized, finally, that there was no safe place. "I'll take my chances," I'd said. I was on my own. This was my life.

"Look at all this loot," said Craig slowly, hands on hips, as he helped stack the pile of boxes after all the guests were gone.

"Bless you, hon," Cindy said, patting my shoulder. "I love you to pieces. Where's Robert?"

"Camping with the Castros."

"You got plans for tonight?"

"I'm going to bed early. This whole thing wore me out."

"I got a better idea, but I better not tell you," she said, looking into the kitchen, where Mike was eating leftover potato salad with his fingers.

"I appreciate your restraint."

"Yeah, whatever. I got to pee." She rubbed the small of her back, hunched over the pale-pink tablecloth I'd used for the dining-room table. "I'm going to need to get some stain remover on this right away," she said. "Chad, baby, are these your barbecue fingerprints here? There better not be any on the back of my couch."

"Happy birthday!" Chad shouted, spinning and falling onto his hands and knees, chortling.

"Did he drink Janice Dickson's wine?" Cindy said.

"That's her name!"

"Doesn't she have diarrhea of the mouth? Goodness, that's a terrible expression. I picked it up from Daddy."

Mike drove me home. In the late afternoon's faded light, he looked older somehow. "I'm going to have to get out to the course more if I want to get any good at golfing," he said.

"Craig's a nice man, isn't he?"

"Really a good guy. He likes you, too."

"That was fun," I said.

"You made enough noise up there."

"I think the mimosas really loosened things up. I wish Cindy could have had one."

We were driving right into the sun, the car threading its way in and out of the cars coming from the strip malls onto the strip, corrugated boxes and brown bags in the backseats, everyone cool and dry with the air-conditioning up all the way. High summer was coming on fast, and high summer was much the same here as anywhere else, punishing heat, sweat wet on the seat of your pants. Mike's hand was damp as he reached across and squeezed mine. No jones for him. Still no jones. But, Jesus God, it was good to have at least one person in the world who knew who I really was.

"You haven't asked me the $64,000 question," I finally said.

"What's that?"

"The question everyone's supposed to ask. The question we always asked at work about some woman who came into the ER all cut up. Why didn't you leave? How could you stay?"

"You did leave. I know why you stayed. You stayed because of Robert."

"Why did I leave?"

"Because of Robert, too. You must think I'm stupid."

"I think you're amazing," I said. A truck roared past us, shook the car as though there was a summer storm. "I had an abortion just before I left." The truck was so loud I didn't know if he had heard me. I could barely hear myself.

He was quiet for a long time, looking out at the road. Finally he said, "Did you say that so that I'll know, or because you think that if you tell me enough bad things I'll go away?"

"I don't know," I said.

"Why don't you come over for dinner?"

I shook my head. The sun glinted off his glasses and I couldn't see his eyes. "Not tonight," I said.

"Is there some point when you'll tell me either to take a hike or—whatever?"

"Whatever," I said, as we pulled up to the apartment complex. His eyes were dark, hurt the way Robert's eyes were sometimes, with no attempt to hide it. "Frances," he said.

"Beth, I'm still Beth."

"Frances. Beth. I'll call you whatever you want. I don't care. I don't care about anything. You want to tell me you're a serial killer? Go ahead. I don't care."

"Don't take a hike," I said.

"That's a good sign, right?"

"Yeah," I said, and went inside.

In the middle of the night I woke to the smell of smoke and moved out of bed and into Robert's room as fast as I could until I remembered that he was camping with Bennie, that he was not there, that his room was empty, his bed made, his school books scattered across the spread. I sniffed the air, my head up like a wild animal, followed the smell down the stairs, toward the kitchen, wondering whether I'd left the stove on, whether an electric line was smoldering somewhere in the cheap Sheetrock walls. The crowbar was still downstairs, in a corner by the door, and I picked it up, heavy and cold in my hand, as I saw the tip of a cigarette glowing in the living room. Marlboros. How in the world had I missed the familiar smell?

The way he looked at the crowbar in my hand made me flush. "Oh, what, Fran?" Bobby said, looking up from the frayed green tweedy armchair that I'd moved from one end of the living room to the other at least a half dozen times, trying to find a place where it wouldn't look so bad. "What, you're going to hit me over the head with a piece of pipe?" He shook his head. "Jesus Christ, sometimes I think you're brain damaged. Sit down."

After the first momentary taste of adrenaline, metallic and bitter in my mouth, I didn't feel much. Certainly not surprise. It seemed perfectly natural, Bobby sitting there. Made for each other, together forever: me and Bobby, Bobby and me. He was in front of me and the kitchen was to one side, and I could feel the phone on the wall where I couldn't reach it. Like always, he read my mind. "The phone's not working," he said, flicking ashes onto an old magazine on the coffee table. "Besides, what the hell are you going to tell the cops? There's a strange man who's in my place, who happens to be my husband. Yeah, what's he doing, lady? Oh, officer, he's smoking a cigarette? Hell, we'll be right over." He dragged in, deeply. "The response time here is about twelve minutes, anyhow. Sit down."

"I'm staying right where I am."

He shrugged. "Suit yourself," he said.

He looked good, Bobby. He always had. His jeans were pressed, and I wondered who was pressing them now. His polo shirt was tight and his pectoral muscles and his abs looked like an anatomical drawing. His arms were big, the muscles thick and rounded. He'd been working out hard, and suddenly I could picture him perfectly, in the basement of the house, my house, doing his concentration curls and his crunches, getting bigger and bigger, angrier and angrier, picking up my panties and my bottles of perfume, waiting, waiting. Around his neck I saw a glint of metal, and nestled in the V of the polo shirt, glowing from amid the fur on his chest, the old medal his father had worn. It looked different, somehow, and then I realized that it was flanked by two halves of a jagged heart, the half he'd kept himself and the one I'd worn and left in the jewelry box on our dresser in Brooklyn.

He looked handsome, Bobby, tasty and dangerous, just like Clarice Blessing had said that day in the ER. Tasty and dangerous. I figured he'd come to kill me.

"How you been, Frances Ann? You got yourself a real dump here. The whole place is maybe a third the size of our house. I was gonna sell it, but your name is on the deed and the lawyer said I couldn't sell it without your permission. Jesus Christ. I needed your permission to sell my own house.

"I had to tell him a story, about how you were in Florida. That's a laugh, right? Even before I knew you were in Florida I said you were in Florida. I had to make up more fucking stories to cover your ass, Fran. First you were real busy, then your mother was sick, then you were in Florida because my twenty years were almost up and we were gonna move down here." He lit one cigarette from the end of another. He'd smoked when we first started going out, but he'd quit after Robert was born. He put the dead butt out on the floor and ground it out with the front of his foot. He was wearing the soft black leather loafers he always got at the Italian leather-goods place on Avenue X. They were so shiny, in the dark. Bobby always shined his own shoes. "I don't know why the hell anybody comes down here," he added. "I wouldn't retire here on a bet." Two hearts that beat as one: Fran and Bobby, Bobby and Fran. Our wedding song had been "I've Got You Under My Skin." That was one way of putting it.

I was shivering in my thin nightgown and I wondered if he could see through it in the light from the streetlamps that oozed through the half-open blinds. He said something but his voice was so low that I couldn't make it out, his head down, the cigarette in his mouth. Then he looked up and his eyes were shining, black, like the shoes, and I could tell he was repeating what he'd just said.

"You took my son. My son. My child. You took my son away from me. What, were you nuts? Were you crazy, you didn't think I'd come after you? With my boy with you, filling him full of garbage? And for what? Because I made a mistake and came at you a little bit. Jesus, I should have broken both your legs, you bitch, so you couldn't've run.

"You had every fucking thing you could want. 'Why are you letting her work, Bob?' the other guys would say, but I let it go, figured if it made you happy, so be it. You had your house. My mother took care of your kid when you were at work, when you were late. All you had to do was pick up the phone. She'd say, how come she doesn't invite me over, Bob? I'd say, Ma, you got to give her a little space. Always standing up for you. Being the nice guy. Taking the kid to the park. Telling my friends to mind their own business. She's not too friendly, Bob, they'd say, and I'd tell them, well, she's just quiet. Knowing it was a lie, because you could be plenty nice when you wanted to. But you didn't want to be.

"You think it was such a goddamn picnic living with you, Fran, you always out of the house bandaging people up or whatever, give me your tired, your poor, but God forbid my husband needs a break. Sitting at the kitchen table pretending to listen to me, your skinny little Irish lips getting tighter and tighter when I talk, like you got something sour in your mouth. My mother's a bitch, my friends are crude. You tell my boy I'm a bigot, Fran? You're telling my son things when you don't know shit.

"You want to hear something fucking sad? I loved you. I really fucking loved you, Frances. But nothing was ever right, nothing was ever good enough. You wanted to do what you wanted to do, go off with your sister, go off to the hospital, go off with your dyke girlfriends, just go off, go off, instead of being home, where you belonged. And even when you stayed home you looked at me and you looked scared all the time, like something bad's gonna happen. What the hell do you think that's like, to look at your wife and see that she's always looking back at you, sideways, sneaky, like you're a grenade that's gonna go off in her hand. Half the time I only came at you to wipe that goddamned look off your face."

It was the first time in a long time it had been like this, the two of us really alone, without Robert a wall or a floor or a room away, so that I didn't have to think about protecting him, about keeping my voice down. I don't know why I didn't scream then. Maybe I was making the same mistake I'd always made, that sooner or later he'd see sense, that I'd see behind his eyes the Bobby who used to kiss my knuckles, one at a time, when my hands were chapped from washing them with Lubriderm at the hospital. "You had no right to hurt me, Bobby," I said.

"Hurt you? Hurt you? What the hell do you think you did to me? I used to come home, the house is all dark, I'm beating off in bed right next to my wife because she's sound asleep. My boy won't look me in the eye because she's been telling him shit—"

"I never said anything—"

"DON'T YOU FUCKING INTERRUPT ME!" My back was against the wall at the foot of the stairs, and I kept hoping that the walls were thin enough that somebody would hear. But they always did hear, other people, always had heard and did nothing, left us alone.

"I come home one night and my wife and my son are gone, but everything's still there so they couldn't have gone too far, and I go to see your sister, and your mother, and that big dyke you worked with at the hospital. And she has the nerve to say to me, you been beating on her all this time, haven't you? And I say, you been diddling her all this time, too. She shut the fucking door in my face and called the cops. The cops!" Bobby threw back his head and laughed. I could see that his hair was going silver at the temples. He looked good. Handsome. I couldn't stop shivering.

"It took me a while, I gotta give you that. Your sister, now, she is one tough bitch. No matter what I tried on her she wouldn't give you up. I had her so she wouldn't even pick up the phone, but she wouldn't give you up no matter what I did. That woman, what's-her-name, the one who's always on television with the snotty voice, you can't get near her, but some of her people are pussies, pure and simple. Jesus, talk about folding. The one who drove you down here, with the dogs, she was easy to shake up. And the guy in New York, when I threatened to have the New York City Police Department all over him like a cheap suit. That scared them, you could tell. They would have given you up sooner or later."

He took a drag on his cigarette and smiled. What a smile Bobby had always had. It changed his whole face. This one made him look so scary I almost looked away. "I didn't even need to wait," he said. "I got this little box on the phone, caller ID. All these scared little cunts in the city buy 'em, like it's somehow gonna help them when the bad man calls. You can scramble the numbers up so they don't come through, but my good luck is, I know a guy in the department, he can unscramble them. That little box sat there for a long time, Frannie, but I didn't take the damn thing off, and look what happened. Here I am. Because my son is loyal. A loyal boy. He calls his father and I write down the number and"—he waved his cigarette around the dark living room—"here I am. In Shitsville. Home of a woman who had everything a woman could want and left it all in a mess. In a big fucking mess for me to clean up."

"Bobby—"

"Ah, shit, Frances, don't bother. I don't want to hear your bull-shit. Even when I was good you looked at me like I was gonna be bad any minute. You looked at me like you were just waiting." He laughed again. "I didn't want to keep you waiting, Fran. Not like you kept me waiting, a whole year, to see my boy."

"He's not here," I said.

"You don't think I know that? You don't think I know exactly where he is, and where he goes to school? That's why I waited, Fran. I could have been here two days after he called me. But I waited another week, and you know why? Because I'm a good father. I'm a goddamned good father. I waited so I wouldn't fuck up the school year. So he could finish at that piece-of-shit public school where you put him. Don't they all hate you, Fran, that you're getting special treatment for your kid because you're fucking the teacher?"

"I—"

"Never mind the lying. I'm so fucking tired of your lying. Lie, lie, lie." He sighed heavily. "Frannie, Frannie, Fran. I know where you been working, Fran, and for who. I even know how much money you make. I know your phone number here. You got a loose window in the back. The screen flips right out, and the pane is so flimsy it takes maybe a minute to get it out with a glass cutter. If I told you once, I told you a hundred times you're bad with security, Fran. Any animal could get in here. Anyone. My boy isn't safe here."

"We're not going back, Bobby."

"I wouldn't have you back on a bet, you bitch." He stubbed out his cigarette. "You know what the worst part about this whole thing is? I loved you so much, Frances Ann. Sometimes I used to fall asleep, after I had a couple of drinks, and I'd have dreams, but they weren't made-up dreams, crazy shit. They were like movies of real stuff, like home movies. Like that time we went to the beach when Robert was a baby and we put up that big umbrella so he wouldn't get burned, and I took all those pictures with the Instamatic, you sitting there next to that little box you kept him in. I was holding him, jumping the waves, and I looked back at you and you had that little smile you had sometimes, real sweet, real nice. I woke up and the burning in my gut was so bad I thought I was dying.

"I loved the shit out of you, and look what you did to me."

"I loved you, too, Bobby."

How come I had so lost the ability to read him, to understand what went on beneath the black holes of his eyes? Or maybe I'd never had it at all. A dozen times, as he'd talked and talked, I'd felt myself pressing into the wall behind me, so that my heels ached where the molding hit them. Maybe it was the words, or the sudden wash of feeling, the sadness that came over me like a kind of faintness, that made me lean forward as I said those last words, and meant them with all my heart even as I felt the metal of that crowbar in my hand: I loved you, too, Bobby. They were barely out of my mouth when he came out of the chair, like a cat, so quick I scarcely knew it until he was holding me against the wall, pressing against me with his body, his forearm against my throat, the way the older cops had taught him when he was a rookie. He'd showed me once as a joke, so many years ago, my head buzzing, the floor coming up to meet my face. This time was no joke. He brought his knee hard against my wrist, and the crowbar fell to the carpet with a thump and rolled onto my foot, mocking me.

In the past it had always been like I'd been waiting for it, almost grateful, like he'd said, that the waiting was over. Maybe he was right, that I'd spent years with a look in my eyes that told him a scream was always hiding in my throat. But somehow it had always been Bobby, so that even when he was pushing me around, yelling right in my face, I could smell the smell of him, feel the feel of him that I knew so well. This time it was like a stranger coming at me. The hard hands no longer felt familiar, the breath tarred with cigarettes and some kind of booze was noxious; the feel of him through his pants, up against my groin, felt like something strange and criminal. Even the voice was no longer as hypnotic as it had once been, somehow different, diminished, tinny. Or maybe it was that I was somebody different, that Beth Crenshaw wasn't going to let this man bloody and beat her. I used all of me to fight back against it, my hands, my knees, my feet, everything but my voice, held captive in my throat by the iron of his arm. I let my eyes close, went limp, and started to slide down the wall, and I felt him relax, a noise in his throat like crooning, like purring, and as he let down his guard for just a moment I came up hard against him, surprised him, almost knocked him over.

"That's it," he said, reaching for me, grabbing me around the throat. And then I saw points of color against black, like the fireworks we watched every year on the Fourth from the Coney Island boardwalk. That's it. That's the last thing I remember.

My daughter has red hair and the sort of disposition associated with it, willful, a little wild. Since she learned to speak she has appended a question mark to almost every sentence she has spoken: Mommy, what this thing? Mommy, water hot? Mommy, have that? How come? Why not? Probably most people cannot understand her. Her words are like soup, the smooth broth of the vowels, the chunky consonants, and she swirls them around in her little mouth until they sound more like mush than anything else. Sometimes I even have to translate for her father, the beloved, the adored Daddy. But I know everything she says. Everything.

Sometimes people see us all together in the supermarket and they remark on the tangle of orange curls, like a flag above the wire cart. The two of us so blond, they cannot quite figure out where this rogue gene comes from. Loving Care No. 27, California Blonde, makes me look a little less like my daughter's mother, but I have a sentimental attachment to it. Besides, it makes me look a little more like Mike's wife, an attachment much more tenuous than the attachment between me and Grace Ann. "Gwacen," she calls herself, all one word. "Let's say grace," we say before holiday dinners, and she screams with laughter, two years old and full, as my father might have said, of piss and vinegar.

My name is Beth Crenshaw. I did not change it to Riordan, nor back to Flynn. I left Frances behind. Beth Crenshaw is the name of the me I am today, Grace Ann's mother. And Robert's mother, too. No matter what.

It was Mike who found me, half a day after I'd found Bobby smoking in my living room. There was a pile of dead butts on the floor and my nightgown was up around my sternum, as though he'd looked me over one more time. He didn't rape me; I checked. He'd contemptuously left the front door unlocked, Bobby, as though there was nothing worth safeguarding in the apartment anymore. I had an onyx and lapis lazuli necklace of bruises from ear to ear. I don't know whether that was what Bobby wanted, or whether he meant to kill me and miscalculated. Or perhaps at the last minute he saw in me what I'd always seen in him, someone hated, feared, and yet beloved, and could not give that final squeeze. Perhaps at the last minute the death grip was a hug instead, or his twisted version of one.

Or maybe this is exactly what he intended. "Frannie, Frannie, Fran," I can hear him say in his rich deep voice. "Killing's too good for you. I want you to suffer." And I do, every day.

"He went home," Mrs. Castro said when Mike and I ran to the apartment at the end of the row, Bennie's puzzled, troubled face peering from the kitchen doorway as he read our expressions. "He is home a long time."

I like to think his father met Robert outside, at the front door, and not in the living room. I like to think that if Robert had seen me on the floor, he would have made so much noise that someone would have heard him. That he would have flown to the Castros, screaming, crying. That he would have taken my side over Bobby's. I like to think that Bobby told him some story, some irresistible fairy tale about redemption, forgiveness, the happy family come back to life like Snow White awakened from her long sleep in the glass casket by her handsome prince. I like to think he did not know that he was leaving me until he was already going sixty miles an hour down some highway somewhere.

All I know is that my boy is gone, and I don't know where to find him. Mike made me go to the police, and they took pictures of my throat, and took down the address and telephone number of my husband, and duly noted the fact that he was a New York City police detective, and that I had no legal papers granting me custody of my own child. They listened carefully, and they took a few notes, and nodded their heads, but I could see in their eyes that the budget of a small-town police force, four men strong, didn't extend to flying to Brooklyn to look for a man who'd done to his wife what so many men had done. And I knew that even if it had, Bobby would not be there, just as I had not been there that day a year before when he'd come home from work. After all, what could I say Bobby had done that I had not done myself?

Mike found a private investigator, and together we went and I told him my story. He seemed like a nice man, a former Texas sheriff with a big stuffed sailfish over his desk and a hunk of Red Man tobacco puffing out his upper lip. He pushed the check back across the desk. "You seem like good people," he said, "so I'm not gonna bullshit you. Your boy is gone, and he's gonna be hard to find. Your ex is a cop, which means he knows things about making himself scarce. Look how easy it was for you. But let's say you go looking for him and maybe you find him. What then? You got no case, is what. You took this guy's kid and absconded with him. He took him back. It's maybe you who could get in trouble for this. Assault charges, you might try against him, but it won't necessarily help you get the child. He goes to court and says you disappeared with his boy for a year, you are gonna get your head handed to you."

"We won't give up on this boy," Mike said.

"I appreciate your sentiments, mister. I got two boys of my own. But what I'm saying to you is, you may not have a choice. You could grab him back, if you could find him. And then maybe your husband could grab him again. And so on, and so forth. You get the idea. Ping-Pong, only the kid's the ball." He turned to me, shaking his head. "If you were divorced and you had custody, I might be able to find him and you could get him back. You don't even have a custodial snatch here. I don't even know what to call the situation you got."

I knew what to call it. It was like death, except I had to go on living with it. I couldn't look at Mike Riordan when he stopped by with cardboard bakery boxes of cookies and stacks of magazines because I knew he had spent his day with kids at the local day camp, breathing in the sweet fragrance of their skin and hair, listening to the staccato sound of their light feet, hearing their high voices calling to one another across the ball field, teaching them how to kick a soccer ball into the goal the way my own boy had once done and, maybe, a thousand miles away, was doing again. I slept in my clothes and canceled out on Cindy whenever she asked me to dinner. And then one July day, three weeks after Bobby found me, almost a year to the day from the day Robert and I had disappeared, the bell rang in the still apartment, the air so thick with dust motes that it looked like a blizzard when I moved, and I lunged for the door like a crazy woman.

"Frannie," she said, in a voice so thick with sorrow I almost didn't hear the word. And Grace was in my arms and I in hers. She cleaned and cooked as though I was an invalid. She cried with me and read to me. Once I heard her on the phone. "She's not ready to talk yet," she said. Once she handed me an envelope. It was full of documents: my birth certificate. My nursing license. Robert's baptismal certificate. I ran my fingers over the notary's seals.

I hadn't even thought about that, right away, that I was free now, that I didn't have to hide because what I'd had worth hiding was already gone. But Mike had thought of it, and he'd found Grace through the college, and told her everything, and picked her up at the airport. And when Mrs. Levitt called and told me that she needed me to come, she was having fainting spells and heart palpitations, it was Mike who had put her up to it, though she didn't admit it until months later, when she was demanding I be nicer to him.

"You must make a life for your son to come back to, Mrs. Nurse," she said to me one day, eating a Happy Meal, handing me the toy, Donald Duck on a motorcycle. "Don't waste your time crying. Crying is nothing. It does nothing."

Cindy came by one night in August with a bottle of wine, and I drank most of it and finally cried, slurring my words, mucus dripping onto her shoulder as I told her all of it, all the blood and all the beatings, everything, both of Bobby's babies, the one he'd taken from me and the one I'd taken from myself. She put me in the bathtub with some sort of sweet-smelling oil, trimmed my hair and gave me a manicure, big as she was with child, with children. The day that Grace flew in and the day that Cindy pushed her way past me into the stale air of the apartment: those were the days when I started to come back to life.

I bought an answering machine so that if Robert called when I was out I would get his message; I bought one of those caller ID machines Bobby had boasted about so that if Robert called when I was home I would know where the call was coming from. I kept Robert's enrollment current at school. "Tell them he'll be back soon," I told Mike on the phone, though I told him not to stop by, no, there was nothing he could bring over, nothing I needed. Except the one thing I did not have.

No one came for the rent, and the home-care agency got me a new patient, whose wife had Alzheimer's. I relieved Mr. Dean while he went out bowling or to the movies with friends; I sat with his wife while she picked at her skirt and said, "I don't know. I don't know anymore." We were two crazy ladies, sitting in the living room of a little brick ranch house watching tabloid shows on television. We sat with tray tables in front of us; Mrs. Dean played some sort of solitaire that seemed to have no real rules, and I sent out flyers to schools and police departments. "Have you seen this boy?" the flyer said. Grace printed them on her computer. The photograph of Robert came out grainy, flat, anyboy in black and white.

Two schools called, and one police department, but the boys were too young, too old, too small, too light, too not mine. One night, after Mrs. Dean and I watched a miniseries about a beautiful woman who owned the best boutique in Beverly Hills, I came home to see a red light glowing in the darkness of the kitchen. For just a moment I thought it was the glowing tip of a cigarette, and thought that Bobby had come back to finish me off. But my heart leapt, too, because if Bobby was there, Robert would be with him. I was happy at the thought of Bobby's hands on my throat, as long as I could put my arms around Robert one last time.

It was only the light on the answering machine. There was no voice on the message for a few moments, only noise: traffic, big trucks, horns, a faint shouted conversation between two men in the background. Then a deep breath. "Mom," he said, and I bent over the machine and hugged it to my chest so that the sound was muffled for a moment.

"I'm all right. Daddy is all right, too. He's being really nice. He really missed me when I was gone." There's a silence there, on the tape, a long one. A car honks. The background noise sounds like highway traffic, a gas station, maybe, or a pay phone on a shopping strip. "Are you all right? Mom?" More silence. "We had lunch at McDonald's. Tell Bennie I said 'hi.' Tell him I saw *Batman* on TV." Another silence, another breath. "I miss you a lot. I have to go. I love you. Don't worry, I'm good. We move around a lot." Tears then. "I hope you're not hurt. I hope you're all right. I'm sorry. I have to go."

I listened to that tape all night, that first night. I felt as if I was there, could see the trucks whizz by, feel the breeze around the booth, see the boy feeding the phone with spare change, culled from the top of strange bureaus and the slots of vending machines. By morning I knew every word, every nuance, every shift in timbre and tone. He was afraid, my little boy. Maybe afraid Bobby was going to find him talking on the phone, the way I had that night in the kitchen. Maybe afraid of something more. I wasn't imagining it, the way his voice broke when he said he hoped I was all right. Mike heard it, too. "That son of a bitch told him you were dead," he said. "I just know it. I feel it."

A week later on the machine there was the recording of an operator. "You have a collect call. Caller, at the tone state your name." The operator cut it off there, while I sat and cried and played over and over again the snippet of dead air where the name should be. I changed the message on my machine, changed it to begin: This machine accepts collect calls. There were none, not after that one attempt.

In October, after school began again, I took $300 and flew to New York City. Grace thought I was coming in on Tuesday evening, but my flight landed just after dawn, and instead of taking a cab to her apartment I went to Brooklyn, to the narrow house Bobby and I had bought thirteen years before, where our words and our actions lived on in the walls, which we haunted. I rang the bell and a pretty girl, twenty-five, maybe thirty, opened it with a dishtowel in her hands. Her hair and eyes were dark; if she was not Italian, she could pass. She was the sort of woman Bobby Benedetto should have married, who would never have complained, soft and yielding as a feather pillow.

"He's not here," she said. "My husband and me, we rent the house from his mother. She lives over on Ocean Avenue. Maybe she can tell you where he's living now. I think maybe Florida someplace." My mirror still hung in the foyer, the one that Ann Benedetto had given us, and in it I could see my reflection, my hair brushing my shoulders now, brushing the collar of a dress I'd gotten on sale with Cindy, too flimsy, really, for an autumn day in the Northeast. I'd have to borrow a sweater from Grace. No, I said, I didn't need directions. I knew the way to Mrs. Benedetto's house. The other Mrs. Benedetto. The only Mrs. Benedetto.

I could hear the bell ringing inside, the gold chimes in the white hallway; I could tell by the faint sound of her footsteps from inside that she'd come from the kitchen to the front door. I remembered the day, maybe seven or eight years before, when we had stood there together looking out the window that gave onto the yard, both of us staring at Bobby out back with a beer, watching Robert weave in and out of the rows of tomato plants. I felt that day like loneliness was more than a feeling, that it was a state of being, like zero gravity or the bends, and we were in the place where you learned to feel it in your marrow, the bathysphere in which you felt it all around you, pressing in on you, on the dishwasher, the pot holders, the spice rack, the forks and spoons, the emptiness inside.

"I want to ask you something," I had said that day to Ann Benedetto. "What was your husband like?"

"What kind of question is that?"

I didn't know what kind of question it was. It was maybe the first direct one I'd asked Bobby's mother, but I was emboldened by the tenderness in my elbow where I'd hit one of the dining-room chairs after he shoved me, after I said I wanted to stay home Sundays, not go to Ocean Avenue.

"Was he good to you?"

"He was my husband."

"Did he ever hit you?"

She'd narrowed her eyes to look at me, and her dislike was an atmosphere, too, as thick as the isolation of the two of us in that clean, clean room, our distance from each other and from the man outside, calling to his son.

"My son is a good man," she said. "Nobody can tell me different."

Her face was hard then, and it was hard when she opened the door to find me standing on her concrete steps, clean the way steps are when someone sweeps them every day. Her hair had just been done, the sculptured waves of iridescent black, the sheen of hair dye and hair spray. She gave me a long look, and I her, and then she began to close the door again. I held it open with the flat of my hand. "I want my son back home," I said.

"So do I," she said. "And we're both out of luck."

Grace told Mike about that, the two of them doing their dance around me, and he traveled to New York on his own, and hired a detective there. Mike made friends with some people who ran a group for missing children, and he mailed more flyers to more schools with Robert's picture, the one he had taken in Lake Plata during fifth grade, his smile big, his face thin, his eyes bright, a false tableau of trees and clouds and endless fields behind him. He's never given up, Mike, and neither have I. Four years it's been, and still I have the tape in my drawer, that I listen to from time to time when Grace Ann is napping. And that photograph, on my bedside table. "That's your brother," I tell my little girl. "You'll see him soon. When he comes home."

"Bruvver," Grace Ann says.

I imagine him, my Robert, his voice just beginning to break when he gets excited, the down on the curve of his jaw thickening until he can't help but see it when he looks in the mirror, turns his head on an angle, and feel it with the flat of his hand as though he's caressing and measuring himself. Maybe his father is with another woman now, just as I am with another man, and maybe when he's had too much to drink he smacks her, hard, knocks her down, even, and Robert tries to shut his eyes and his ears and maybe sometimes he has a few drinks himself, sneaks a can from the refrigerator, so that the hard sounds are softer, the cotton padding of beer wrapped around the sharp edges.

I see Robert in my mind's eye, and he's tall now, and he's handsome, and he feels things as deeply as he always did, but doesn't speak of them much. And maybe he has found a girl of his own and she tests him, taunts him, innocently, because sometimes it's fun to test and taunt, at least for most of us, and he grabs her, hard, and scares her a little bit. But it feels like love to her, the grip on her forearms, and she thinks it's because he loves her so much, and maybe in the beginning that is it. And by the time it turns to something else—well, it's too late.

I think of my Robert and I think of that maybe girl, and you know what? I don't give a damn about her, about her bruises and even her broken bones. I should. But I don't. I love my boy. I always have. I always will. Somewhere between my head, where I know so much, and my gut, where I can almost feel her pain, is my Robert. My heart.

In six months Robert will be sixteen, old enough to get on a plane, to pick up the phone, to make his own way. It's been four years since I lost him, but he knows where to find me. My phone number has never changed. When I left the apartment to move in with Mike, and later, when we bought this house, with its three bedrooms and its trellis of clematis by the garage, I gave our new address to the woman who had taken my place there. And maybe he'll knock at the apartment door and the woman will say, oh, your mother wanted you to know exactly where to find her. And he'll drive to the house and I'll open the door and he'll say, Mommy, it's all right. I've taken the best of both of you and left the rest behind. The part of the river that runs with blood stops with you. It does not flow on through me. I pray every day that that is true. I wonder sometimes why Captain McMichael said that day in the precinct house that Robert was no Benedetto. Was he teasing him? Or wishing him a happy life?

I would have a happy life now, if only he were here. Mike was telling the truth, when he said he was a patient man. He wasn't a fool; twice I told him to go away, and he went. For a while he dated a student teacher at the middle school, a little girl with a squeaky voice and long, long brown hair. I saw them once, going into a diner hand in hand, when I was on my way to the Deans' house. She made him look so big, in the way I made Bobby look so dark, so many years ago. Mike told me she broke up with him because she said he wasn't ready to make a commitment. But he was. Just not to her.

He took care of me, sometimes near, sometimes at a distance, for a long time before I bothered to take any care of him. I suppose I love him now, although it's not what I once thought of as love. I know that I love what he is, and what he has given me, a life that feels ordinary, uneventful, and full. It's hard to make ends meet, what with the retainers for the detectives and the trips Mike makes from time to time, when we get a lead that seems promising. He was promoted to principal; I work part-time and Cindy takes care of Grace Ann along with the twins. Chad bosses all three of them around. We run together every morning, Mike and I, with the baby in a special running stroller Cindy gave us for a gift when she threw me a shower. There's a bedroom in our house done in green and yellow where Mike's mother and my sister Grace sleep when they come to visit. But there's a bulletin board over the desk with a picture of the soccer team and a Yankees game schedule pinned to it. In the drawer of the desk there's a letter from Bennie, that I promised him I'd send to Robert if I ever had an address to send it to. It's Robert's room, that room. It's waiting for him, just as I am.

I think of myself as Beth Crenshaw most of the time now, because if I think of myself as Fran Benedetto there is a piece of me missing so big that the pain doubles me over, clawing at my gut, and Bobby gets me again, and I can't let that happen. Because I am Grace Ann Riordan's mother, too, a little girl who has nothing to fear except that she will be denied a second helping of crackers at snack time. She hears nothing through the walls except, perhaps, the occasional sound of her father saying her mother's name in a kind of groan: Beth, Beth. Her father loves her pure, and loves her mother the same. And her mother loves her father a little more each day. I trust him, deep down, which is more important than I once understood. "The luckiest day of my life was the day I met you," Mike said the day we were married at the municipal building. I don't know if it's legal, don't know if I'm divorced, don't even care. I don't give a damn for the law. What did the law ever do for me? Mike wanted to be my husband; that was good enough. The rest is all Frannie's life. That's not me. This is the me I made. The past? Like Mrs. Levitt said, "It's only a story."

Three or four times a year I let myself go back. The men take the children somewhere, bowling or to the movies, and Cindy and I have the night alone, just the two of us, and I drink a couple of glasses of wine, and I sob and I scream and she holds me and cries into my hair. "He loves you, honey," she says. "I know he does. He'll be back. He'll be back." The last time she said to me, "I want you to know that if I ever meet that man, I'm going to slip a serrated knife between his ribs." Then she put cucumber slices over my eyes to bring the swelling down. I don't know what made me say it, lying there, seeing a wash of green light through my lids. But I reached out my hand for her, and said, so low she had to lean toward me to hear, "When are you going to tell me about your sister?"

I don't know what her face looked like while she talked. I kept those cucumber slices where they were, so that she didn't have to face me if she didn't want to. She didn't cry; it was almost like she was talking about somebody else, talking about a little girl curled up in a chair in a dark corner of the living room, reading a book, reading *Mother West Wind's Children*. Listening to her mother call for her: Cindy. Cindy, come here. Cynthia Lee, I need you. Smiling to herself when her mother gave up, opened the screen door, went around to the side of the house, paused right beneath the living-room window, at the edge of the flower beds. "Cathy," she said, "go call your father for supper."

What could I say, as I held her close? That it wasn't her fault? That she should let the guilt go? Words, words. They mean nothing, less than nothing. I know.

Cindy thinks it's arbitrary, the nights I invite her over, something that happens now and then for no particular reason. That's not true. What happens, every once in a while, is that the phone rings. And on the other end I hear nothing but breathing. This happens to everyone, I tell myself, but I don't believe it. I stay on and listen to the sound of what I think of as love, until whoever is at the other end hangs up. I don't know whether I'm hearing Robert or Bobby, or some stranger. Maybe I'll never know. But I believe it's Robert, and I believe he knows I know, and I hang on. Six months ago the phone rang again, and I heard the breathing, and as I listened, Grace Ann looked up at me from her high chair and cried, in her demanding fashion, "Mama!" Whoever was on the phone hung up suddenly, a sound like a book banging shut. "Robert," I cried, but there was only the echoing emptiness of the severed connection. "Ober!" Grace Ann replied happily.

Those are the nights, after the phone calls, when Cindy and I sit together, alone, and I grieve with the sound of sweet breathing still in my ears.

Cindy stood up for Mike and me at the municipal building, holding Charlie. So did Craig, holding Cathy. And Grace. Chelsea has decided that Aunt Grace is Wonder Woman, with her easy polysyllabic vocabulary and her knotty biceps. Afterward we had a party by the Roerbackers' pool. "To our new daughter," said Mike's mother, and she gave me a cameo her husband had given her for her birthday years before, and hugged me tight.

That was the only time I cried, that and afterward, when Mike said, "Can we have a baby right away?" I had a second glass of champagne, and when I went to the bathroom I looked at myself in the mirror for a long time, looked at myself in the silk suit, my hair curling around my face, Shhhhhell pink on my lips, I looked to make sure I knew who I was, that I was really real. I put my fingers to my mouth and shaped the word but did not say it, held it inside in deference to the day. Robert. Robert. I got pregnant that very night, in the four-poster in the bedroom of a guest house in Key West.

Robert, Robert. Where is he now? What does he feel or think? Maybe he's in Italy or Brazil, Canada or Mexico. I don't think he believes I'm dead, and I know he knows I love him. I know how persuasive Bobby can be, how he can hold you in thrall, make you wonder about things you're sure about, tolerate things you never thought you'd allow. I was only twenty-one when he started in on me. Maybe Bobby told Robert that I knew exactly where they'd gone, that I'd given him away to his father. Could Robert have believed that for even a moment? Did he wonder about it now, if he'd been the person at the other end of the phone when another child called my name, the name that once only he was entitled to? Perhaps none of the lies Bobby had to tell him, to woo him, to win him, had the simple power of that sound, the sound of someone else calling me *Mama*.

Cindy said, when I told her the truth, or most of it, "Just tell me one thing. Is Beth Crenshaw more or less the same person as—what's the other, now? I don't know why I have such a mental block about that name."

"Frances Benedetto."

"Is Beth more or less the same as Frances?"

"Only the names were changed," I said.

And I suppose in a way that's true. When I was Fran, Frannie, Frannie, Fran, I felt like two people at once, the woman who seemed so in control and content, and the one with the black eyes and broken bones, the one who loved her husband and feared and hated him, all at the same time. Beth Crenshaw is two people, too. There's the one who pulls weeds in the yard with her daughter's head glowing in the sunshine beside her, who smiles across the supper table at Mike and stacks his shirts neatly in the second drawer, who comes down the street in her little compact car and, for just a moment, forgetting, loves her lovely little life. And there's the one with the hole inside her, bigger than anything. There's not a day when I haven't wondered whether I did the right thing, leaving Bobby. But of course if I hadn't, there would have been no Mike. And therefore no Grace Ann. Your children make it impossible to regret your past. They're its finest fruits. Sometimes its only ones.

"Oh, honey," Cindy likes to say, "you had no choice."

Everyone says that, that I did the right thing, that I shouldn't look back, that I had no choice. Maybe they're right. I still don't know.